Great Supernatural Stories

101 HORRIFYING TALES

Great SUPERNATURAL STORIES

COMPILED BY STEFAN DZIEMIANOWICZ

FALL RIVER PRESS
New York

FALL RIVER PRESS
New York
An Imprint of Sterling Publishing Co., Inc.
1166 Avenue of the Americas
New York, NY 10036

ISBN 978-1-4351-6620-2

Manufactured in the United States of America

6 8 10 9 7

sterlingpublishing.com

Contents

Introduction

In the concluding paragraphs of his landmark essay "Supernatural Horror in Literature," first published in its entirety in 1939, horror master H. P. Lovecraft offered the following observations regarding the tale of supernatural horror:

> For those who relish speculation regarding the future, the tale of supernatural horror provides an interesting field. Combated by a mounting wave of plodding realism, cynical flippancy, and sophisticated disillusionment, it is yet encouraged by a parallel tide of growing mysticism, as developed both through the fatigued reaction of "occultists" and religious fundamentalists against materialistic discovery and through the stimulation of wonder and fancy by such enlarged vistas and broken barriers as modern science has given us with its intra-atomic chemistry, advancing astrophysics, doctrines of relativity, and probings into biology and human thought. At the present moment the favoring forces would appear to have somewhat of an advantage; since there is unquestionably more cordiality shewn toward weird writing than when, thirty years ago, the best of Arthur Machen's work fell on the stony ground of the smart and cocksure 'nineties. Ambrose Bierce, almost unknown in his own time, has now reached something like general recognition.

At the time Lovecraft wrote these words, supernatural horror fiction was establishing itself as a popular fiction genre in the pulp fiction magazines that flourished in the first half of the twentieth century. The authors whom he mentions by name, Arthur Machen and Ambrose Bierce—both of whom are represented in *Great Supernatural Stories*, along with Lovecraft himself—wrote in the late nineteenth and early twentieth centuries, at a time when the idea of supernatural fiction as a fiction genre was only beginning to gain traction. Consequently, these authors' tales of the supernatural were looked on in their day as no different from their non-supernatural stories.

Lovecraft, who died in 1937, clearly anticipated the burgeoning popularity of the tale of the supernatural, but he surely could not have imagined that by the end of the twentieth century supernatural horror fiction would be a robust and thriving literary genre, and that several of its best writers would be charting regularly on the best-seller lists with books that appealed to readers beyond the genre's traditional niche audience. *Great Supernatural Stories* represents a selection of tales published in the watershed period just prior to the tide of tales that Lovecraft saw flood and eventually alter the topography of the popular fiction landscape. It contents span nearly a century and include the work of well-known literary writers—Edgar Allan Poe, Robert Louis Stevenson, Rudyard Kipling, Robert S. Hichens, and H. G. Wells, to name but a few—and writers such as Lovecraft himself, for whom the tale of the supernatural was a specialty. This volume also includes stories by relatively unknown writers whose contribution represents one of a handful of stories they published in their lifetime.

The selections for *Great Supernatural Stories* feature all of the most common figures in the pantheon of supernatural beings: ghosts, vampires, witches, shapeshifters, and zombies. By definition, though, the supernatural has a much broader scope than these entities alone embody, and that is virtually limitless in its expression. This is evident in the book's oldest story, Edgar Allan Poe's "The Masque of the Red Death," whose palace setting is haunted by a phantom—not a ghost, but a being who incarnates an inescapable pestilence ravaging the surrounding countryside. William Hope Hodgson's "Demons of the Sea," written nearly three-quarters of a century later, takes the tale of the supernatural in a direction opposite to that of Poe's story. Do its sea-spawned monsters represent a natural species hitherto overlooked by science or an expression of "the stimulation of wonder and fancy by such enlarged vistas and broken barriers as modern science has given us"?

It's safe to say that all of the stories in this volume fall somewhere between the extremes of the familiar and the previously unimagined possibilities in supernatural literature. You, the reader, may feel that some of the selections range even farther afield. To that extent, *Great Supernatural Stories* features some of the most imaginatively conceived representations of the tale of supernatural horror. These stories have helped to shape a literary tradition that still exerts its influence today.

—Stefan Dziemianowicz
New York, 2017

Accessory Before the Fact

Algernon Blackwood

At the moorland cross-roads Martin stood examining the sign-post for several minutes in some bewilderment. The names on the four arms were not what he expected, distances were not given, and his map, he concluded with impatience, must be hopelessly out of date. Spreading it against the post, he stooped to study it more closely. The wind blew the corners flapping against his face. The small print was almost indecipherable in the fading light. It appeared, however—as well as he could make out—that two miles back he must have taken the wrong turning.

He remembered that turning. The path had looked inviting; he had hesitated a moment, then followed it, caught by the usual lure of walkers that it "might prove a short cut."

The short-cut snare is old as human nature. For some minutes he studied the sign-post and the map alternately. Dusk was falling, and his knapsack had grown heavy. He could not make the two guides tally, however, and a feeling of uncertainty crept over his mind. He felt oddly baffled, frustrated. His thought grew thick. Decision was most difficult. "I'm muddled," he thought; "I must be tired," as at length he chose the most likely arm. "Sooner or later it will bring me to an inn, though not the one I intended." He accepted his walker's luck, and started briskly. The arm read, "Over Litacy Hill" in small, fine letters that danced and shifted every time he looked at them; but the name was not discoverable on the map. It was, however, inviting like the short cut. A similar impulse again directed his choice. Only this time it seemed more insistent, almost urgent.

And he became aware, then, of the exceeding loneliness of the country about him. The road for a hundred yards went straight, then curved like a white river running into space; the deep blue-green of heather lined the banks, spreading upwards through the twilight; and occasional small pines stood solitary here and there, all unexplained. The curious adjective, having made its appearance, haunted him. So many things that afternoon were similarly unexplained: the short cut, the darkened map, the names on the sign-post, his own erratic impulses, and the growing strange confusion that crept upon his spirit. The entire country-side needed explanation, though perhaps "interpretation" was the truer word. Those little lonely trees had made him see it. Why had he lost his way so easily? Why did he suffer vague impressions to influence his direction? Why was he here—exactly *here?* And why did he go now "over Litacy Hill"?

Then, by a green field that shone like a thought of daylight amid the darkness of the moor, he saw a figure lying in the grass. It was a blot upon the landscape, a mere huddled patch of dirty rags, yet with a certain horrid picturesqueness too; and his mind—though his German was of the schoolroom order—at once picked out the German equivalents as against the English. *Lump* and *Lumpen* flashed across his brain most oddly. They seemed in that moment right, and so expressive, almost like onomatopoeic words, if that were possible of sight. Neither "rags" nor "rascal" would have fitted what he saw. The adequate description was in German.

Here was a clue tossed up by the part of him that did not reason. But it seems he missed it. And the next minute the tramp rose to a sitting posture and asked the time of evening. In German he asked it. And Martin, answering without a second's hesitation, gave it, also in German, "*halb sieben*"—half-past six. The instinctive guess was accurate. A glance at his watch when he looked a moment later proved it. He heard the man say, with the covert insolence of tramps, "T'ank you; much opliged." For Martin had not shown his watch—another intuition subconsciously obeyed.

He quickened his pace along that lonely road, a curious jumble of thoughts and feelings surging through him. He had somehow known the question would come, and come in German. Yet it flustered and dismayed him. Another thing had also flustered and dismayed him. He had expected it in the same queer fashion: it was right. For when the ragged brown thing rose to ask the question, a part of it remained lying on the grass—another brown, dirty thing. There were two tramps. And he saw both faces clearly. Behind the untidy beards, and below the old slouch hats, he caught the look of unpleasant, clever faces that watched him closely while he passed. The eyes followed him. For a second he looked straight into those eyes, so that he could not fail to know them. And he understood, quite horridly, that both faces were too sleek, refined, and cunning for those of ordinary tramps. The men were not really tramps at all. They were disguised.

"How covertly they watched me!" was his thought, as he hurried along the darkening road, aware in dead earnestness now of the loneliness and desolation of the moorland all about him.

Uneasy and distressed, he increased his pace. Midway in thinking what an unnecessarily clanking noise his nailed boots made upon the hard white road, there came upon him with a rush together the company of these things that haunted him as "unexplained." They brought a single definite message: That all this business was not really meant for him at all, and hence his confusion and bewilderment; that he had intruded into someone else's scenery, and was trespassing upon another's map of life. By some wrong *inner* turning he had interpolated his person into a group of foreign forces which operated in the little world of someone else. Unwittingly, somewhere, he had crossed the threshold, and now was fairly in—a trespasser, an eavesdropper, a Peeping Tom. He was listening, peeping; overbearing things he had no right to know, because they were intended for another. Like a ship at sea he was intercepting wireless messages he could not properly interpret, because his Receiver was not accurately tuned to their reception. And more—these messages were warnings!

Then fear dropped upon him like the night. He was caught in a net of delicate, deep forces he could not manage, knowing neither their origin nor purpose. He had walked into some huge psychic trap elaborately planned and baited, yet calculated for another than himself. Something had lured him in, something in the landscape, the time of day, his mood. Owing to some undiscovered weakness in himself he had been easily caught. His fear slipped easily into terror.

What happened next happened with such speed and concentration that it all seemed crammed into a moment. At once and in a heap it happened. It was quite inevitable. Down the white road to meet him a man came swaying from side to side in drunkenness quite obviously feigned—a tramp; and while Martin made room for him to pass, the lurch changed in a second to attack, and the fellow was upon him. The blow was sudden and terrific, yet even while it fell Martin was aware that behind him rushed a second man, who caught his legs from under him and bore him with a thud and crash to the ground. Blows rained then; he saw a gleam of something shining; a sudden deadly nausea plunged him into utter weakness where resistance was impossible. Something of fire entered his throat, and from his mouth poured a thick sweet thing that choked him. The world sank far away into darkness. . . . Yet through all the horror and confusion ran the trail of two clear thoughts: he realised that the first tramp had sneaked at a fast double through the heather and so come down to meet him; and that something heavy was torn from fastenings that clipped it tight and close beneath his clothes against his body. . .

Abruptly then the darkness lifted, passed utterly away. He found himself peering into the map against the sign-post. The wind was flapping the corners against his cheek, and he was poring over names that now he saw quite clear. Upon the arms of the sign-post above were those he had expected to find, and the map recorded them quite faithfully. All was accurate again and as it should be. He read the name of the village he had meant to make—it was plainly visible in the dusk, two miles the distance given. Bewildered, shaken, unable to think of anything, he studied the map into his pocket unfolded, and hurried forward like a man who has just wakened from an awful dream that had compressed into a single second all the detailed misery of some prolonged, oppressive nightmare.

He broke into a steady trot that soon became a run; the perspiration poured from him; his legs felt weak, and his breath was difficult to manage. He was only conscious of the overpowering desire to get away as fast as possible from the sign-post at the cross-roads where the dreadful vision had flashed upon him. For Martin, accountant on a holiday, had never dreamed of any world of psychic possibilities. The entire thing was torture. It was worse than a "cooked" balance of the books that some conspiracy of clerks and directors proved at his innocent door. He raced as though the country-side ran crying at his heels. And always still ran with him the incredible conviction that none of this was really meant for himself at all. He had overheard the secrets of another. He had taken the warning for another into himself, and so altered its direction. He had thereby prevented its right delivery. It all shocked him beyond words. It dislocated the machinery of his just and accurate soul. The warning was intended for another, who could not—would not—now receive it.

The physical exertion, however, brought at length a more comfortable reaction and some measure of composure. With the lights in sight, he slowed down and entered the village at a reasonable pace. The inn was reached, a bedroom inspected and engaged, and supper ordered with the solid comfort of a large Bass to satisfy an unholy thirst and complete the restoration of balance. The unusual sensations largely passed away, and the odd feeling that anything in his simple, wholesome world required explanation was no longer present. Still with a vague uneasiness about him, though actual fear quite gone, he went into the bar to smoke an after-supper pipe and chat with the natives, as his pleasure was upon a holiday, and so saw two men leaning upon the counter at the far end with their backs towards him. He saw their faces instantly in the glass, and the pipe nearly slipped from between his teeth.

Clean-shaven, sleek, clever faces—and he caught a word or two as they talked over their drinks—German words. Well dressed they were, both men, with nothing about them calling for particular attention; they might have been two tourists holiday-making like himself in tweeds and walking-boots. And they presently paid for their drinks and went out. He never saw them face to face at all; but the sweat broke out afresh all over him, a feverish rush of heat and ice together ran about his body; beyond question he recognised the two tramps, this time not disguised—*not yet* disguised.

He remained in his corner without moving, puffing violently at an extinguished pipe, gripped helplessly by the return of that first vile terror. It came again to him with an absolute clarity of certainty that it was not with himself they had to do, these men, and, further, that he had no right in the world to interfere. He had no *locus standi* at all; it would be immoral . . . even if the opportunity came. And the opportunity, he felt, would come. He had been an eavesdropper, and had come upon private in—formation of a secret kind that he had no right to make use of, even that good might come—even to save life. He sat on in his corner, terrified and silent, waiting for the thing that should happen next.

But night came without explanation. Nothing happened. He slept soundly. There was no other guest at the inn but an elderly man, apparently a tourist like himself. He wore gold-rimmed glasses, and in the morning Martin overheard him asking the landlord what direction he should take for Litacy Hill. His teeth began then to chatter and a weakness came into his knees. "You turn to the left at the cross-roads," Martin broke in before the landlord could reply; "you'll see the sign-post about two miles from here, and after that it's a matter of four miles more." How in the world did he know, flashed horribly through him. "I'm going that way myself," he was saying next; "I'll go with you for a bit—if you don't mind!" The words came out impulsively and ill-considered; of their own accord they came. For his own direction was exactly opposite. *He did not want the man to go alone.* The stranger, however, easily evaded his offer of companionship. He thanked him with the remark that he was starting later in the day. . . . They were standing, all three, beside the horse-trough in front of the inn, when at that very moment a tramp, slouching along the road, looked up and asked the time of day. And it was the man with the gold-rimmed glasses who told him.

"T'ank you; much opliged," the tramp replied, passing on with his slow, slouching gait, while the landlord, a talkative fellow, proceeded to remark upon the number of Germans that lived in England and were ready to swell the Teutonic invasion which *he*, for his part, deemed imminent.

But Martin heard it not. Before he had gone a mile upon his way he went into the woods to fight his conscience all alone. His feebleness, his cowardice, were surely criminal. Real anguish tortured him. A dozen times he decided to go back upon his steps, and a dozen times the singular authority that whispered he had no right to interfere prevented him. How could he act upon knowledge gained by eavesdropping? How interfere in the private business of another's hidden life merely because he had overheard, as at the telephone, its secret dangers? Some inner confusion prevented straight thinking altogether. The stranger would merely think him mad. He had no "fact" to go upon. . . . He smothered a hundred impulses . . . and finally went on his way with a shaking, troubled heart.

The last two days of his holiday were ruined by doubts and questions and alarms—all justified later when he read of the murder of a tourist upon Litacy Hill. The man wore gold-rimmed glasses, and carried in a belt about his person a large sum of money. His throat was cut. And the police were hard upon the trail of a mysterious pair of tramps, said to be—Germans.

Aidu

Hero Despard

In the early fall of 1880 I was in Dahbol, India, having run down from Bombay, upon a sister who had set up a little bungalow there.

Dahbol is charmingly situated between the sea and the wooded heights of the Western Ghauts, and as nothing pressed me at the time, I remained there, spending my time rambling about the place and sometimes running into a chance adventure. Thus it happened that the following strange experience befell me.

One evening, in the cool of the late twilight, I was strolling about through the sea-end of the town, and, stopping before a small temple which was a little removed from the houses around, stood studying out the lines of the usual grotesque figures cut upon its face. Dense shadows cast by the rising moon threw the entrance into such obscurity that nothing could be seen within. In fact, I thought the place deserted for the time, and was about to obey an impulse to step up into the shadows banked in the doorway, when, suddenly, a human figure hurled itself upon me from out the darkness with such force that I staggered back and almost lost my footing. I had instinctively thrown out my arms and clasped the figure for support, and now, as I recovered my balance and looked down, it was into the face of the fairest woman I have ever seen in any land.

The marvelousness of her beauty served to steady my faculties where ordinarily I should have felt bewildered, and, still holding her close, for she trembled as if she would fall from my arms, I said in such Hindustani as I was capable of:

"Something has frightened you. You are fleeing from danger?"

"Sir," she answered, in a voice soft and rich, though broken by low gasps, "I must hasten"; and she pulled against my arms for release.

From my knowledge of the country, I felt sure no woman like the one who stood before me could safely venture into the streets at this hour, and, having an Anglo-Saxon's feelings for all womankind, I acted on a quickly formed resolve.

"I do not know what sends you out into the night, nor what pursuit you fear, but I am ready to take you where you wish to go," I said.

"I must go far from this place,—and alone," she answered, speaking agitatedly.

"We will go," I said reassuringly. "I will take you to your own people."

Upon this her slender body trembled anew, and replying, "I have no people. I cannot stay here," she turned from me and began to walk quickly away.

I as quickly followed, walking behind her through street after street, she choosing the deserted by-ways, until we came out through some suburban orchards, and finally reached the edge of a stretch of thick forest which belts the eastern side of the town. Here she stopped suddenly, and, turning to me, said entreatingly:

"Leave me! You cannot help."

I looked at the town behind, at the forest in front, and felt it a moral impossibility to obey.

"I think I can," I ventured, "if you will confide in me. I have a sister here in whose care I can place you, and if anything is threatening you I can hide you with her. She is an English doctor, and is devoting her life to work among your countrywomen."

It would be impossible to describe the changes of expression which flashed over her face at this. Relief, questioning, consent, and doubt arose from the depths of her dark eyes and looked out at me. For some time she stood thus, inwardly debating, and at last answered:

"Yes, if I may come out alone once in seven days."

"You shall have perfect liberty, of course," I eagerly assured her.

This promise seemed so completely to allay any lurking feeling of fear or doubt that at once she laid her hand upon mine, saying, "I will go with you."

Now, I had no hesitation whatever in taking this girl to my sister, who, as I had said, lived in India for the purpose of dealing with the conditions of life surrounding the Oriental women. Indeed, no sooner had she seen Aidu and heard her story than she insisted upon taking this beautiful waif into our household as one of ourselves; and as time passed and the lovableness of her nature was fully revealed to us, we found that we had rescued one of the rarest of pearls from the depths of the human sea around us.

She was pathetically gentle, and when the first constraint of the situation wore off showed herself possessed of a brilliant though unformed mind.

My sister built many hopes upon Aidu—for that was the name of our waif—as a future coadjutor in her chosen work; though I may as well confess at once that I had other intentions about her.

After only a few weeks spent in her society, I found myself deeply in love, and but for one singular, inexplicable circumstance would have begged her then and there to become my wife.

The mystery was this:

While she looked the perfection of sweet and elastic health and possessed an unusually pure vitality, no one ever saw Aidu partake of food. At first we thought that perhaps she shrank from burdening us, and believed that in some way she secretly procured cheap food outside. To all questions on the subject she returned a jesting reply, or else remained pleadingly silent. Once only, during each week, was she seen to leave the house, when she went upon those twilight walks for which she had stipulated. And the mystery of her sustenance, puzzling at first, grew darker and denser every day, the more so as Aidu steadily became more radiant in health and tinted like a ripe pomegranate from a fountain of rich vitality. Indeed, she seemed the incarnation of some flawless vital force consciously masking itself in human form.

But there came a day when I could restrain my love no longer.

My jealousy of those walks, during which she went I knew not where nor whom to see, became at last unbearable, and I determined to push my misgivings to a conclusion by questioning her outright.

Late in the afternoon of one of these seventh days of the week, on which she never failed of her twilight walk, I sought her where she sat in the shade of a trellised veranda, and, seating myself beside her, took her hands in my own.

"Aidu, you must know how I love you!" I said impetuously. I could wipe out the fact of my own soul sooner than I could forget the measureless depth and meaning of the look she gave me, straight from her lifted eyes! Oh, cold and reasonable Westerner! Never, even through eternity, will you know the infinity of meaning hidden in the lotus-heart of love, never having looked into the eyes of Aidu raised in a pure and perfect confession!

"I love you!" she murmured. Echo of my own words only, but enough.

"You will not go out alone again, now, Aidu?" I questioned pleadingly.

"I would *try* to do what you ask, even that which I cannot," she said wistfully.

Having gained so much, I was in a measure satisfied; but I determined, in virtue of my now undoubted right, to follow her should she again go on her secret errand. This I hoped she would not do; but later I saw her steal out from the house and walk away, not briskly, as was usual, but with a certain languor, as if pulling against her will. It was an easy matter to follow her at a little distance, for she went straight forward, as to a well-known goal, never once looking back. On she went, past the houses of the town, out into a stretch of the suburban orchards, until we stood again upon the edge of the same tangled forest where we had stopped on the evening I first found her. Surely, it could not be that Aidu would venture within those dense shadows!

Yes, even here she did not hesitate, but forced her way through the gloomy thicket, deftly stepping over obstructions and pushing away the drooping vines as if the path were a clear and familiar one. And all the while I followed, possessed by an intensity of curiosity and feeling which must have given me the eyes of a night animal, for I never for a moment lost sight of her; but, while she walked easily and swiftly, I rushed on, panting through excitement, until when, at hut, she halted and leaned back against a tree in an attitude of expectation, I stopped, trembling and weak from agitation.

And now that happened which is burnt into my memory forever.

As she stood there, motionless, her slight figure in its snowy garments dully outlined against the dark tree trunk, I noted that Aidu's eyes were fixed upon a certain spot in the ground before her, whither mine followed. At first I saw only a faint glow in the grass at her feet, like the light of two phosphorescent insects side by side, but as this rapidly grew and widened, the shape of a dark head was outlined within the rays. Brighter and brighter the light grew until—yes, a cobra's hooded head appeared! and from the glowing eyes streamed the rapidly increasing light in a coruscating flood.

Horror-stricken, I looked at Aidu! She was gazing down into those burning, venomous eyes, whose radiance was momentarily intensified until her rapt face and figure, the coiled length of the serpent, and even the grass and trees around were illuminated as by the shining of two small suns.

Under this compelling gaze Aidu's languor melted. Her form dilated and changed in my sight as if the very crucible of vital life were there, purging away the particles of mortality and building her form anew out of imperishable materials. Her glowing beauty was indescribable; it was a revelation.

And now the monster slowly raised himself, stretching up out of his coils, until his scintillating, fiery orbs were on a level with the smiling, dewy eyes of the woman whom I loved. She leaned gently forward and softly stroked the mottled neck. A tremor shook my whole body. In that moment I was overwhelmed by the horrible certainty that here I beheld the rites of the ancient mystic serpent worship still practised in certain parts of India; and that Aidu, my Aidu, served as the unwilling instrument of the priests of the temple, from whose fearful power she had vainly attempted to escape on the night of our first meeting.

Crazed by a fury of conflicting emotions, I seized a stone that lay near and hurled it upon the erect serpent. It struck his neck just below the level of Aidu's matchless chin, and as the ugly head dropped suddenly down upon the coils of his body, slowly settling to the ground, the wonderful light faded, and a heartrending shriek from Aidu rang through the woods. I sprang to her side, and lifted her in my arms!

"Aidu! my love!" I cried, "speak to me."

But the exquisite form hung relaxed in my embrace, and the white lids slowly shut down over the eyes of my love. The fearful spell had been broken, but at what cost! By arresting too suddenly that strange, magnetic current, I had checked the fountain from which her life was fed.

Aidu was dead!

The Armless Man

W. G. Litt

I first met Bob Masters in the hotel at a place called Fourteen Streams, not very far from Kimberley.

I had for some months been trying to find gold or diamonds by digging holes in the veldt. But since this has little or nothing to do with the story, I pass by my mining adventures and come back to the hotel. I came to it very readily that afternoon, for I was very thirsty.

A tall man standing at the bar turned his head as I entered and said "Good-day" to me. I returned the compliment, but took no particular notice of him at first.

Suddenly I heard the man say to the barman:

"I'm ready for another drink."

That surprised me, because his glass was still three-quarters full. But I was still more startled by the action of the barman who lifted up the glass and held it whilst the man drank.

Then I saw the reason. The man had no arms.

You know the easy way in which Englishmen chum together anywhere out of England, whilst in their native country nothing save a formal introduction will make them acquainted? I made some remark to Masters which led to another from him, and in five minutes' time we were chatting on all sorts of topics.

I learnt that Masters, bound for England, had come in to Fourteen Streams to catch the train from Kimberley, and, having a few hours to wait, had strolled up to the collection of tin huts calling itself a town.

I was going down to Kimberley too, so of course we went together, and were quite old friends by the time we reached that city.

We had a wash and something to eat, and then we walked round to the post-office. I used to have my letters addressed there, *poste restante*, and call in for them when I happened to be in Kimberley.

I found several letters, one of which altered the whole course of my life. This was from Messrs. Harvey, Filson, and Harvey, solicitors, Lincoln's Inn Fields. It informed me that the sudden death of my cousin had so affected my uncle's health that he had followed his only son within the month. The senior branch of the family being thus extinct the whole of the entailed estate had devolved on me.

The first thing I did was to send off two cablegrams to say that I was coming home by the first available boat, one to the solicitors, the other to Nancy Milward.

Masters and I arranged to come home together and eventually reached Cape Town. There we had considerable trouble at the shipping office. It was just about the time of year when people who live in Africa to make money, come over to England to spend it, and in consequence the boats were very crowded. Masters demanded a cabin to himself, a luxury which was not to be had, though there was one that he and I could share. He made a tremendous fuss about doing this, and I thought it very strange, because I had assisted him in many ways which his mutilation rendered necessary. However, he had to give way in the end, and we embarked on the Castle liner.

On the voyage he told me how he had lost his arms. It seemed that he had been sent up country on some Government job or other, and had had the ill-fortune to be captured by the natives. They treated him quite well at first, but gave him to understand that he must not try to escape. I suppose that to most men such a warning would be a direct incitement to make the attempt. Masters made it and failed. They cut off his right arm as a punishment. He waited until the wound was healed and tried again. Again he failed. This time they cut off his other arm.

"Good Lord," I cried. "What devils!"

"Weren't they!" he said. "And yet, you know, they were quite good-tempered chaps when you didn't cross them. I wasn't going to be beaten by a lot of naked natives though, and I made a third attempt.

"I succeeded all right that time, though, of course, it was much more difficult. I really don't know at all how I managed to worry through. You see, I could only eat plants and leaves and such fruit as I came across; but I'd learnt as much as I could of the local botany in the intervals."

"Was it worth while?" I asked. "I think the first failure and its result would have satisfied me."

"Yes," he said slowly, "it was worth while. You see, my wife was waiting for me at home, and I wanted to see her again very badly—you don't know how badly."

"I think I can imagine," I said. "Because there is a girl waiting for me too at home."

"I saw her before she died," he continued.

"Died?" I said.

"Yes," he answered. "She was dying when I reached home at last, but I was with her at the end. That was something, wasn't it?"

I do hate people to tell me this sort of thing. Not because I do not feel sorry for them; on the contrary, I feel so sorry that I absolutely fail to find words to express my sympathy. I tried, however, to show it in other ways, by the attentions I paid him and by anticipating his every wish.

Yet there were many things that were astonishing about his actions, things that I wonder now I did not realise must have been impossible for him to do for himself, and that yet were done. But he was so surprisingly dexterous with his lips, and feet too, when he was in his cabin that I suppose I put them down to that.

I remember waking up one night and looking out of my bunk to see him standing on the floor. The cabin was only faintly lit by a moonbeam which found its way through the porthole. I could not see clearly, but I fancied that he walked to the door and opened it, and closed it behind him. He did it all very quickly, as quickly as I could have done it. As I say, I was very sleepy, but the sight of the door opening and shutting like that woke me thoroughly. Sitting up I shouted at him.

He heard me and opened the door again, easily, too, much more easily than he seemed to be able to shut it when he saw me looking at him.

"Hullo! Awake, old chap?" he said. "What is it?"

"Er—nothing," I said. "Or rather I suppose I was only half awake; but you seemed to open that door so easily that it quite startled me."

"One does not always like to let others see the shifts to which one has to resort," was all the answer he gave me.

But I worried over it. The thing bothered me, because he had made no attempt to explain.

That was not the only thing I noticed.

Two or three days later we were sitting together on deck. I had offered to read to him. I noticed that he got up out of his chair. Suddenly I saw the chair move. It gave me a great shock, for the chair twisted apparently of its own volition, so that when he sat down again the sunlight was at his back and not in his eyes, as I knew it had been previously. But I reasoned with myself and managed to satisfy myself that he must have turned the chair round with his foot. It was just possible that he could have done so, for it had one of those light wicker-work seats.

We had a lovely voyage for three-quarters of the way, and the sea was as calm as any duckpond. But that was all altered when we passed Cape Finisterre. I have done a lot of knocking about on the ocean one way and another, but I never saw the Bay of Biscay deserve its reputation better.

I'd much rather see what is going on than be cooped up below, and after lunch I told Bob I was going up on deck.

"I'll only stay there for a bit," I said. "You make yourself comfortable down here."

I filled his pipe, put it in his mouth, and gave him a match; then I left him.

I made my way up and down the deck for a time, clutching hold of everything handy, and rather enjoyed it, though the waves drenched me to the skin.

Presently I saw Masters come out of the companion-way and make his way very skilfully towards me. Of course it was fearfully dangerous for him.

I staggered towards him, and, putting my lips to his ear, shouted to him to go below at once.

"Oh, I shall be all right!" he said, and laughed.

"You'll be drowned—drowned," I screamed. "There was a wave just now that well, if I hadn't been able to cling on with both hands like grim death, I should have gone overboard. Go below."

He laughed again and shook his head.

And then what I dreaded happened. A vast mountain of green water lifted up its bulk and fell upon us in a ravening cataract. I clutched at Masters, but trying to save him and myself handicapped me badly. The strength of that mass of water was terrible. It seemed to snatch at everything with giant hands, and drag all with it. It tossed a hen-coop high, and carried it through the rails.

I felt the grip of my right hand loosen, and the next instant was carried, still clutching Masters with my left, towards that gap in the bulwark.

I managed to seize the end of the broken rail.

It held us for a moment, then gave, and for a moment I hung sheer over the vessel's side.

In that instant I felt fingers tighten on my arm, tighten till they bit into the flesh, and I was pulled back into safety.

Together we staggered back, and got below somehow. I was trembling like a leaf, and the sweat dripped from me. I almost screamed aloud.

It was not that I was frightened of death. I've seen too much of that in many parts of the earth to dread it greatly. It was the thought of those fingers tightening on me where no fingers were.

Masters did not speak a word, nor did I, until we found ourselves in the cabin.

I tore the wet clothes off me and turned my arm to the mirror. I knew I could not have been mistaken when I felt them.

There on the upper arm, above the line of sunburn that one gets from working with sleeves rolled up, there on the white skin showed *the red marks of four slender fingers and a thumb*! I sat down suddenly at sight of them, and pulling open a drawer, found a flask of neat brandy, and gulped it down, emptied it in one gulp.

Then I turned to him and pointed to the marks.

"In God's name, how came these here?" I said. "What—what happened up there on deck?"

He looked at me very gravely.

"I saved you," he said, "or rather I didn't, for I could not. But *she* did."

"What do you mean?" I stammered.

"Let me get these clothes off," he said, "and some dry ones on; and I'll tell you."

Words fail to describe my feelings as I watched the clothes come off him and dry ones go on just as if hands were arranging them.

I sat and shuddered. I tried to close my eyes, but the weird, unnatural sight drew them as a lodestone.

"I'm sorry that you should have had this shock," he said. "I know what it must have been like, though it was not so bad for me when they seemed to come, for they came gradually as time went on."

"What came gradually?" I asked.

"Why, these arms! They're what I'm telling you about. You asked me to tell you, I thought?"

"Did I?" I said. "I don't know what I'm saying or asking. I think I'm going mad, quite mad."

"No," he said, "you're as sane as I am, only when you come across something strange, unique for that matter, you are naturally terrified. Well, it was like this. I told you about my adventures with the natives up country. That was quite true. They cut off both my arms—you can see the stumps for that matter. And I told you that I came home to find my wife dying. Her heart had always been weak, I'd known that, and it had gradually grown more feeble. There must have been, indeed there was, a strange sort of telepathy between us. She had had fearful attacks of heart failure on both occasions when the natives had mutilated me, I learnt on comparing notes.

"But I had known too, somehow, that I must escape at all costs. It was the knowledge that made me try again after each failure. I should have gone on trying to escape as long as I had lived, or rather as long as she had lived. I knelt beside her bed and she put out her arms and laid them round my neck.

" 'So you have come back to me before I go,' she said. 'I knew you must, because I called you so. But you have been long in coming, almost too long. But I knew I had to see you again before I died.'

"I broke down then. I was sorely tried. No arms even to put round her!

" 'Darling, stay with me for a little, only for a little while!' I sobbed.

"She shook her head feebly. 'It is no use, my dear,' she said, 'I must go.'

" 'I'll come with you,' I said, 'I'll not live without you.'

"She shook her head again.

" 'You must be brave, Bob. I shall be watching you afterwards just as much as if I still lived on earth. If only I could give you my arms! A poor, weak woman's arms, but better than none, dear.'

"She died some weeks later. I spent all the time at her bedside, I hardly left her. Her arms were round me when she died. Shall I ever feel them round me again? I wonder! You see, they are mine now.

"They came to me gradually. It was very strange at first to have arms and hands which one couldn't see. I used to keep my eyes shut as much as possible, and try to fancy that I had never lost my arms.

"I got used to them in time. But I have always been careful not to let people see me do things that they would know to be impossible for an armless man. That was what took me to Africa again, because I could get lost there and do things for myself with these hands."

" 'And they twain shall be one flesh,' " I muttered.

"Yes," he said, "I think the explanation must be something of that sort. There's more than that in it, though; these arms are other than flesh."

He sat silent for a time with his head bowed on his chest. Then he spoke again:

"I got sick of being alone at last, and was coming back when I met you at Fourteen Streams. I don't know what I shall do when I do get home. I can never rest. I have—what do they call it—*Wanderlust*?"

"Does she ever speak to you from that other world?" I asked him.

He shook his head sadly.

"No, never. But I know she lives some where beyond this world of ours. She must, because these arms live. So I try always to act as if she watches everything. I always try to do the right thing, but, anyway, these arms and hands would do good of their own accord. Just now up on the deck I was very frightened. I'd have saved myself at any cost almost, and let you go. But I could not do that. The hands clutched you. It is her will, so much stronger and purer than mine, that still persists. It is only when she does not exert it that I control these arms."

That was how I learnt the strangest tale that ever a man was told, and knew the miracle to which I owed my life.

It may be that Bob Masters was a coward. He always said that he was. Personally I do not believe it, for he had the sweetest nature I ever met.

He had nowhere to go to in England and seemed to have no friends. So I made him come down with me to Englehart, that dear old country seat of my family in the Western shires which was now mine.

Nancy lived in that country, too.

There was no reason why we should not get married at once. We had waited long enough.

I can see again the old, ivy-grown church where Nancy and I were wed, and Bob Masters standing by my side as best man.

I remember feeling in his pocket for the ring, and as I did so, I felt a hand grasp mine for a moment.

Then there was the reception afterwards, and speech-making—the usual sort of thing.

Later Nancy and I drove off to the station.

We had not said good-bye to Bob, for he'd insisted on driving to the station with the luggage; said he was going to see the last of us there.

He was waiting for us in the yard when we reached it, and walked with us on to the platform.

We stood there chatting about one thing and another, when I noticed that Nancy was not talking much and seemed rather pale. I was just going to remark on it when we heard the whistle of the train. There is a sharp curve in the permanent way outside the station, so that a train is on you all of a sudden.

Suddenly to my horror I saw Nancy sway backwards towards the edge of the platform. I tried vainly to catch her as she reeled and fell—right in front of the oncoming train. I sprang forward to leap after her, but hands grasped me and flung me back so violently that I fell down on the platform.

It was Bob Masters who took the place that should have been mine, and leapt upon the metals.

I could not see what happened then. The station-master says he saw Nancy lifted from before the engine when it was right upon her. He says it was as if she was lifted by the wind. She was quite close to Masters. "Near enough for him to have lifted her, sir, if he'd had arms." The two of them staggered for a moment, and together fell clear of the train.

Nancy was little the worse for the awful accident, bruised, of course, but poor Masters was unconscious.

We carried him into the waiting-room, laid him on the cushions there, and sent hot-foot for the doctor.

He was a good country practitioner, and, I suppose, knew the ordinary routine of his work quite well. He fussed about, hummed and hawed a lot.

"Yes, yes," he said, as if he were trying to persuade himself. "Shock, you know. He'll be better presently. Lucky, though, that he had no arms."

I noticed then, for the first time, that the sleeves of the coat had been shorn away.

"Doctor," I said, "how is he? Surely, if he isn't hurt he would not look like that. What exactly do you mean by shock?"

"Hum—er," he hesitated, and applied his stethoscope to Master's heart again.

"The heart is very weak," he said at length.

"Very weak. He's always very anæmic, I suppose?"

"No," I answered. "He's anything but that. He's—Good Lord, he's bleeding to death! Put ligatures on his arms. Put ligatures on his arms."

"Please keep quiet, Mr. Riverston," the doctor said. "It must have been a dreadful experience for you, and you are naturally very upset."

I raved and cursed at him. I think I should have struck him, but the others held me. They said they would take me away if I did not keep quiet.

Bob Masters opened his eyes presently, and saw them holding me.

"Please let him go," he said. "It's all right, old man. It's no use your arguing with them, they would not understand. I could never explain to them now, and they would never believe you. Besides, it's all for the best. Yes, the train went over them and I'm armless for the second time. But—not for long!"

I knelt by his side and sobbed. It all seemed so dreadful, and yet, I don't think that then I would have tried to stay his passing. I knew it was best for him.

He looked at me very affectionately.

"I'm so sorry that this should happen on your wedding-day," he said. "But it would have been so much worse for you if she had not helped."

His voice grew fainter and died away.

There was a pause for a time, and his breath came in great sighing sobs.

Then suddenly he raised himself on the cushions until he stood upright on his feet, and a smile broke over his face a smile so sweet that I think the angels in Paradise must look like that.

His voice came strong and loud from his lips.

"Darling!" he cried. "Darling, your arms are round me once again! I come! I come!"

"One of the most extraordinary cases I have ever met with," the doctor told the coroner at the inquest. "He seemed to have all the symptoms of excessive hæmorrhage."

As It Was Written

Ulric Daubeny

Millicent could never listen to the howling of a dog with equanimity. To use her own expression, it "poured cold water down her back," and never failed to move her to take instant action, partly from compassion for the author of the outcry, but primarily to remove the cause.

The lament on this particular occasion was so insistent that she halted in mid-pace, and turned her head enquiringly in the direction from whence it came. The only habitation visible from the lane was creeper grown, and apparently unoccupied, but a repetition of the uncanny call dispelled all doubts, so she hurried towards a break in the line of hedge, which marked the entrance drive. The gate, bearing in faded characters a name, The Hermitage, pushed open stiffly, creaking upon hinges long disused, its expostulation finding an immediate echo in a further long-drawn-howl. The sound was eerie when heard at fall of day, with the drive already plunged in half-light by a tangled, overhanging growth, and as the girl stepped forward, she felt increasingly uncomfortable.

A curious silence had now fallen, broken only by the patter of feminine heels upon the moss-grown gravel. Millicent began to think her errand was to be a fool's one, when a turn of path brought into view the house, and with it a half-bred collie, waiting at the foot of the front steps.

"What's the matter, boy?" she hailed in soothing tones, to be met with a response as strange as it was unexpected. The dog had moved towards her, tail commencing to wave to and fro, when suddenly he turned again, and with the utmost savagery, bounded up the steps, and hackles bristling, tore at the woodwork of the door with fangs a-drip, pausing ever and again to take deep-drawn sniffs, before giving vent to a paroxysm of frenzied scratching.

Millicent, though not a coward with strange dogs, felt rather frightened. She watched awhile in doubt, then moved to retrace her footsteps along the drive, but another melancholy howl arrested her. The dismal utterance, again so unexpected, caused her very flesh to creep.

"My dear dog, what is the matter?" she beseeched, advancing tentatively, with open hand. The collie had now left the immediate doorway, and came to meet her, with troubled eyes. "Want to be let in? Come on, then!" The animal gave an understanding whine, so lightly tripping up the steps, she seized the knocker, and gave it a resounding tap.

The sound echoed cavernously, surprising Millicent into questioning why she should be knocking at an obviously empty house, for a heap of withered leaves had accumulated against the door, which itself was scaled and dusty. Then, glancing at the dog, whose beseeching eyes asked plainly to enter, she recalled the probability of a caretaker, and knocked again.

A mass of leaden clouds began to engulf the setting sun, and a sudden perceptible tremor in the still air spoke of distant thunder; the collie's tail was drooping, his whole attitude suggestive that a further howl was imminent. Meanwhile, all within kept silent.

The atmosphere of heavy omen, together with the deserted aspect of the house and grounds so acted upon her nerves, that the girl felt she should scream, if she remained there any longer. Still hesitating, she made as if to descend the steps, when once again the behaviour of the dog restrained her. He was staring, as if fascinated, towards the door, hackles slowly raising, and eyes ablaze. Millicent likewise turned, and in obedience to an impulse, bent to the level of the letter-box, and peered within. In this position she remained for several seconds, every muscle tense, until a sudden relaxation left her staggering backwards, and next moment she was tearing down the drive, face blanched, and eyes luminous with horror. Fortunately, the entrance gate had remained ajar, and through this she projected, her wild stampede meeting with no interruption until she voluntarily slackened pace, after the first, straggling houses of the village had been passed.

Once dropped to a walk, she soon recovered self-possession, though her breath came in long, unsteady gasps, and her heart throbbed painfully. She forged ahead until the Police Station was at hand, then, with an excited gesture, hailed the shirt-sleeved sergeant, who was working in his garden. In a miraculously short space of time he presented himself clad in faultless uniform and startled her as she leant with outstretched arm against the doorpost.

"Anything the matter, Miss?" he queried sharply, apprizing her with searching look. She stared stupidly for a time; then the reply was uttered in a dry, hard whisper—

"Yes. Murder at The Hermitage!"

The sergeant goggled at her in astonishment. He made as if to speak, but failing, swallowed awkwardly, and without comment, led the way into the office.

A steaming cup of tea, proffered by the sergeant's kindly wife, did much to restore Millicent's equilibrium, and after a short interval, she found herself commencing to recount the adventure with unanticipated calm. But as the story advanced she became increasingly flustered by the peculiar attitude of the sergeant. He seemed obviously distrait, and more than once she surprised in him a look of introspective wonder suggesting an incredulity of what she aid. The position grew more and more intolerable until finally she hesitated, and broke off.

"Well, Miss?" the sergeant prompted, after a short pause. His tone was almost what one would use in speaking to a child—or idiot. "Well, Miss, what was it you saw inside the letter-box?"

Making an effort she pulled herself together, and the words continued breathlessly.

"As I was about to tell, something prompted me to bend until my eyes were level with the opening, when I found myself looking into an entrance hall with staircase ascending slightly to one side. At the bottom, crumpled in a horrible position lay the body of an old lady—dead. But it was not that which held me terror-stricken. Feet were approaching into view, stockinged feet creeping softly down the carpeted stairs. Step by step they advanced, tip-toeing cautiously, then trousered legs appeared, then a man's body. Ah, the memory of that cruel face, and those dreadful, gloating eyes!"

The girl paused for a moment to regain her breath. Her voice was hoarse, when once again she took up the narrative.

"The murderer's gaze was shifting, shifting towards the door, towards the letter-box. . . . I noticed that his hand was wet with blood; blood trickled onto the linoleum in the hall. . . . . Then I ran—"

She broke off finally, and with an unsteady hand, reached for the remainder of the cup of tea. The sergeant continued motionless, idly fingering a pencil, and without making any attempt to move. His listless attitude astonished Millicent. To her excited fancy, the interview was assuming all the unreal horror of a nightmare.

"Why do you stare like that?" she flashed impatiently. "Are you not going to-to do something?"

"Certainly, Miss, I'll go up and see about it, if you wish," he replied civilly. "But it's like this. There can have been no murder at The Hermitage, because the house is empty!"

"But I tell you, I saw the people! They may be caretakers. I saw the blood upon the carpet—"

"That' s another thing, Miss. There is no carpet or linoleum. The place has been untenanted for the past five years. We keep the key here, at the Station, and go up regular, to see that everything's all right. I was up there day before yesterday, and—"

"You don't believe a word I say!" Millicent interposed excitedly. "No, don't apologise. You think I am either mad or dreaming, but you are wrong. I saw everything exactly as I have described it. Besides, the dog knew that something was the matter or he would never have attracted my attention. . . . Of course, Sergeant, if you choose to neglect your duty—"

The man rose quickly, reaching for his helmet, and a bunch of keys.

"I am going up to The Hermitage at once," he announced stiffly. "If you care to remain here, or in the parlour, you may do so, Miss. I'd like you to wait for my report."

"Indeed, no! I am not now afraid. I am coming with you!" Expostulations would be unavailing, decided the sergeant, as without further parley the two set off at a brisk pace.

Darkness was falling swiftly as they passed together up the desolate drive, and approached the front door of The Hermitage. A sudden shadow emerging from the bushes tattled both but it was only the collie who trotted towards Millicent with deep grunts of welcome.

"Farmer Burrows' dog," the sergeant volunteered shortly. "He is always wandering around this house."

They had now come to the front steps, where the girl hung back, breath catching painfully in her throat. The collie stood close by gazing silently towards the door, to which the sergeant advanced without the slightest hesitation. Next moment it was standing open. The policeman flashed his lantern on the interior the dog fled yelping down the drive, tail tightly wedged between his legs—and Millicent swayed from side to side, as if she were about to fall.

Yet there appeared not the remotest reason for alarm. There were no indications of humanity, either living or dead—merely an empty house, the bare boards of hall and ascending staircase thickly dust-covered. With a slight shrug, the sergeant set about making a formal examination of the house, and then, quietly closing the door behind him, presented his negative report.

"Are you quite satisfied, Miss?" he added, good-naturedly. The girl just nodded. She felt too dazed to speak.

Millicent despatched a warning telegram that night, and returned home next morning, looking little better for her holiday. The extraordinary experience—vision—she knew not how to describe it—absorbed every waking thought for many days. Though scarcely a believer in the supernatural, she was not a sceptic and came in time to form the definite conclusion that what she had seen could be nothing other than a very elaborate form of a "ghost." This idea took such possession of her, that in order to regain her peace of mind, she wrote a private letter to the sergeant, enquiring if in the past any deed of violence had been perpetrated at The Hermitage.

The reply came by return of post, conclusive, and to the point.

Madam,

In answer to your enquiry, I can testify from personal knowledge, that no such occurrence as you suggest has taken place at The Hermitage, since it was built.

Respectfully yours,
P. Smith, Sergeant

Two years had passed, and now the memory of that dread experience seldom, if ever recurred to Millicent. Indeed, it is doubtful whether it had crossed her mind for many weeks, prior to that day on which the chance sight of an illustrated paper recalled the vision in all its pristine horror.

She had been travelling in an omnibus, and gazing half consciously at the pictures in a newspaper, which the passenger opposite was reading. Suddenly the reproduction of a portrait seemed to stand out in relief upon the printed page. Millicent gave vent to a suppressed cry, and for a moment felt like swooning. The reader opposite dropped his paper, glancing above it with round eyes of surprise, but the girl had already staggered to her feet, motioning for the vehicle to stop.

Outside, in the fresher air, she soon recovered, feeling furiously mortified that her nerves should play her false, but presently a paper shop proved irresistible, so blaming her stupidity, she went inside, and bought the offending sheet.

With admirable strength of mind, she kept the journal until she had reached home, and was safe within the privacy of her bedroom. Then, biting her lip until the blood commenced to trickle, she turned to the pictorial back page. There was no denying the likeness to her visionary murderer. It was strikingly exact, and with growing perturbation, she read the short description—*VILLAGE MYSTERY Mr. Talc, stepson of the murdered lady, who in company with a friend, discovered the crime.*

Over the page were printed full particulars, headed by three lines of heavy type—

THE HERMITAGE MYSTERY
Fingerprint Clue.
Police Still Baffled.

Millicent held herself in leash for three whole days, and then, as no sign came of a solution to the mystery, she took her courage in both hands, and set off for the country. Arriving at her destination, she found a pony trap at the station, which carried her along the peaceful lane towards the village.

Her breathing became uneven as The Hermitage drew near. With some surprise, she found difficulty in recognising the situation: trees had been cut down, the house re-painted, also the entrance gate, and she noticed that the carriage drive no longer tunnelled beneath a too luxuriant growth. Then, as a bend in the lane was about to shut the ill-omened house from view, the sun could be seen shining upon drawn blinds. The Hermitage was now a dwelling of the dead.

Arrived at the rustic Constabulary Branch, she stated her business to a young policeman, who admitted her to the parlour, with a request that she should wait. Some time elapsed before voices sounded in the passage, and a man, heavily bandaged about the neck, stepped rapidly past the parlour window. That fleeting glimpse sufficed. Millicent was left, pressing both hands against her bosom, and desperately fighting for her breath. Next moment the door opened, and a man stood on the threshold; she turned to meet the sergeant, whom she had first seen on that never-to-beforgotten afternoon.

"The—the murderer! Why don't you arrest him?" she choked, nodding her head towards the roadway.

"Beg pardon, Miss, but that is Mr. Talc, the gentleman who found his murdered step-mother. He has just called to complain of Farmer Burrows' dog, who has bitten him badly about the throat!"

"Ah! do you not remember that evening, two years ago, when I came to tell you what I had seen inside The Hermitage? You, of course, did not believe me, but I understand all now. It was a vision—You must admit that I described the unfortunate woman exactly as now reported in the papers?"

The sergeant nodded.

"Well, he, that man, was the man who murdered her. I say it, for I should know the face among a million."

"Impossible, Miss. Not the least suspicion is attached to Mr. Talc. He had been away from home, and was met by a chance acquaintance in the village, who accompanied him to the house. It was those two who discovered the poor lady."

"But the finger prints? Have his been compared?"

"The public know the evidence a well as I do, Miss. Bloodstained prints were found upon the dress and elsewhere but having no grounds to suspect the gentleman, we naturally cannot ask for an impression of his fingers."

"But you must! He is the murderer, I tell you! In the vision, I saw that his hand was wet—"

An authoritative tap at the door cut short the sentence. The sergeant moved towards it with alacrity, and next moment ushered in the detective from Scotland Yard.

A few days later, the gutter-press journals were black with smudgy photographs and vulgar headlines. "HERMITAGE MYSTERY SOLVED," the latter variously ran. "Murderer Stepson. Fingerprints Obtained by Ruse. Prisoner Pleads Guilty. Latest Details!"

The Astrologer

Dick Donovan

The Black Forest is rich in story and tradition of a weird and thrilling kind, but nothing can excel in ghastly horror that which is told of the sole heir of the once illustrious family of Di Venoni. For generations this family had held tyrannical sway over the district. Their power was tremendous; their word was law; they ruled with a hand of iron, and the peasants were their slaves. They were exceedingly wealthy. Their men were said to be brave, their women beautiful. But, as seems to be the fate of all powerful families sooner or later, they began to decay. The fatuous habit of intermarrying produced the usual result, and the curse of insanity fell upon them. Many were the tragedies that this led to; and the time came at last when there was but one sole remaining male representative. This was a youth, handsome and well proportioned, but of eccentric habits, and occasionally displaying those fatal signs which were only too well known. Nevertheless, it was believed that Reginald Di Venoni might escape the curse. The best medical advice was sought, and the opinion was that the chances were strongly in his favour, and he would escape.

Reginald was brought up under the care of his mother, who had been left a widow for some years. She was a haughty, austere, proud, and disdainful lady, who guarded her son with peculiar jealousy; for on him, as she knew, depended the existence of her house. If he failed, then indeed the power of the Di Venonis would be gone, and the family would crumble to decay.

The lady and her son lived in a large castle, which for generations had been the Di Venoni's stronghold, and had withstood and repelled many a determined attack. It was a gloomy pile, distinguished for its strength rather than its beauty, although internally much had been done for the comfort of the occupants. The castle was situated in Suabia, just on the borders of the forest. It stood on elevated ground, and anyone standing on the turrets commanded an immense panorama of great beauty.

At some little distance rose the ruins of the once powerful castle of Rudstein. This had originally been the home of the Di Venoni; but an evil genius seemed to enter into it, and for two or three generations such ill-luck attended the family that they decided to desert their ancestral home. It was unroofed, and left to wind and weather and the evil things that haunt the great forest. One tower was left standing only, as a sort of landmark. In the meantime the new castle had risen, and here the family installed themselves. Here many of them paid the debt of nature, and here the last male representative was born. Here in lonely grandeur the widowed mother lived, surrounded by a retinue of servants and retainers, and having for companion her one sister—a much younger woman, of great beauty and lively disposition. She was known as the Lady Hilda, and it was said that she and her sister were by no means always in accord. She protested against the gloomy surroundings in which the scion of the noble house was being brought up, and she urged Madame Di Venoni to keep more company, and relieve the castle, if possible, of the air of brooding melancholy which seemed to envelope it. But madame had her own notions. She wanted to mould her son after her own fashion. She was afraid of exposing him to evil influences. She would not depart from the traditions of her race.

One day, when Reginald was about six years of age, a traveller came to the castle and begged for hospitality. It had been a terrible day—wild, stormy, and wet. The traveller was a mysterious looking man, who seemed to have travelled far on foot, and was weary, wet, and hungry. He was a foreigner, and spoke but little German. He was invited into the servants' great hall, where food and drink were set before him, and as night approached he was conducted to a chamber situated on the top of a tower. That night a very violent storm, which had been threatening all day, burst over the country and did enormous damage. The thunder was terrific; the lightning incessant; the rain descended in a deluge. During the time that the storm was at its height a female servant, happening to glance from her window, which commanded a full view of the tower where the traveller was lodged, averred that she saw him walking about on the flat roof of the tower, and exposed to the full fury of the storm. She declared that he had more the appearance of a fiend than a man; that occasionally he broke into wild eldritch laughter, and ever and anon raised his hands aloft, as if daring the heavens and defying the lightning.

Frightened almost into a fit, and yet fascinated, the woman watched him for some time, and at last saw him conversing with the arch enemy of man himself. The following morning the servant hurried to her mistress, and told her this silly story, the outcome of ignorance, superstition, and fear; and she insisted that the traveller who had been entertained and lodged in the castle was an evil being, who held converse with the devil, and that unless he were put to death some terrible calamity would result from his visit.

The lady, who was only a degree or two less superstitious than the menial, was much impressed, for she lived in a district where superstition was very rife. People travelled very little in those days, and credence was given to the wildest and most outrageous stories; while a belief in the power of certain persons to hold communication with Satan was very common, especially in the Black Forest district. Indeed, even at the present day, when railways and telegraphs encircle the globe, natives of some of the remote districts in the forest still cling to this belief, and have all sorts of charms to protect themselves against the malignant influences of witches, warlocks, and forest demons.

Madame Di Venoni, having listened to the wild and weird story of the servant, summoned her major domo, and bade him bring the stranger to her. This was done, and when the stranger was ushered into her presence he bowed low and reverentially to the mistress of the castle, who, however, regarded him with something like awe, for truly enough he was a striking and remarkable man, and calculated to unfavourably impress anyone who was superstitious. He had a dark, swarthy face. His eyes were intensely black and piercing, his hair like jet.

"Whence come you?" demanded the lady, imperiously.

"From Rhenish Prussia," answered the man proudly, and drawing himself up as if by gesture he would resent the manner in which she addressed him.

"And whither go you?"

"To Russia."

"With what object?"

"In search of knowledge."

Madame was incensed by his proud air, and eyeing him suspiciously, said:

"Unless I am mistaken, you are a man of evil nature, and in communication with the enemies of the human race."

The man laughed.

"No, madame," he answered, "unless the stars that shine so gloriously in the heavens above are enemies of the human race, for it is from the stars I derive my knowledge."

This apparently mysterious answer appalled the lady, for she felt no doubt now that the man was a fiend, and she was about to summon her attendants and have him expelled when her little son burst into the room, followed by his aunt. The child was laughing merrily, and had come to show his mother some grotesque heads he had been drawing on a sheet of paper. But, catching sight of the stranger, he was instantly silenced and clung to his aunt's skirts, while the Lady Hilda regarded the man with intense interest.

"Is that your son?" he asked.

"No," answered Lady Hilda, "I am a single woman. He is the son of my sister there, the Lady Di Venoni."

The man turned to madame, and speaking in a strange, far-away voice, and as if inspired by some strange prophetic instinct, he said:

"That boy is the hope and prop of your race. But have a care, have a care, for a curse is upon him. Take him from this gloomy dwelling. Show him the bright and fair scenes of the earth. Teach him charity and tolerance. Strengthen his body and broaden his mind, and watch his footsteps lest he stray. His life hangs by a thread only."

Madame was horrified. She no longer doubted that this audacious stranger was an evil thing whose death would be a benefit to all men. As she caught her son up in her arms she screamed, and when her attendants rushed in she ordered them to beat the stranger and set the dogs upon him. Folding his arms he stood like a rock, and gazed at her with scorn and defiance. But he was dragged from the apartment and roughly hurried down the great stairs to the courtyard, where a call was made to let the dogs loose, but at that instant the Lady Hilda appeared upon the scene, and interposed to save the stranger from the fury and violence of the menials. She peremptorily ordered them to release him, and when that was done she bade him depart at once, saying:

"Your safety, your life, depends upon the speed with which you leave this castle behind you. You have spoken well and truly, and your advice is the advice of a wise man; but ignorance and tradition are powerful factors; they are difficult to counteract."

The man bent his knee, and taking Lady Hilda's hand, kissed it gracefully, saying:

"I thank you, lady, and do not doubt that this generous act of yours will go unrewarded; but, I pray you let me have a word with you out of earshot of these human wolves, who seem panting to rend me to pieces."

Unmindful of the angry looks darted at her, and the menacing attitude of the menials, she retired for a moment or two to a corner of the courtyard with the stranger, who, availing himself of the opportunity, said:

"Have you the courage to meet me alone in the forest, in order that I may give you some information?"

"Yes."

"Good. Meet me, then, to-night at the tower of the ruins of Rudstein, as the moon rises. No harm shall befall you, but good will come out of it."

She pledged herself to meet him. Then she ordered the gates to be thrown open, and the man departed, followed by the jeers and taunts of the people. Lady Hilda turned furiously upon them and upbraided them for their cowardice in attacking a defenceless man. She was not a favourite with them, but she had power, and they were silenced.

That night, as the moon was rising, Lady Hilda slipped out of the castle by a secret door, and hastily made her way to the ruins of Rudstein, where the stranger was waiting for her. For two hours they talked together, and, loving her nephew as she did, she anxiously inquired about his future.

"His hope lies in separating him from his mother," said the stranger. "It may seem unnatural and cruel, but she is too strongly influenced in the traditions of her race to see that the boy's welfare depends on every means being taken to save him from the curse of his ancestors."

"But how know you all this?" she answered, somewhat awed, and yet recognising the soundness of his advice.

"I read it in the stars," he answered mysteriously. "They are wondrous books in which the past and the future of men can be read for those who have eyes to see."

Many more questions were asked and answered, and Lady Hilda returned to the castle deeply impressed by the strange man's manner. Again and again she visited him, and his influence over her became all-powerful. Of course, these visits were secret ones, and she kept her own counsel. The stranger took up his abode in the tower, where there was no fear of his being disturbed, for people had a dread of the ruins, as they said they were haunted. Lady Hilda procured him books and other things that he said he wanted, and she kept him supplied with food and money. During the time that this was taking place she was urging her sister to quit the castle, retire to the capital, and there bring up her son in the shadow of the court. But this the mother strenuously refused to do, while the ill-feeling between her and her sister increased. At last Lady Hilda disappeared, and with her her nephew. She was ultimately traced to Cologne after some months' absence, and she and the boy were brought back. Within a week of her return she was found dead in her bed. She had been poisoned.

The burial of a dead Di Venoni was invariably an imposing sight, and there was no exception in Lady Hilda's case. None of the mummery and pomp and ceremony were omitted, and for three days the body lay in state in the great entrance hall, and those who were entrusted with watching the corpse at night averred that one night as the great bell of the castle was tolling the solemn midnight hours peculiar dark-eyed man suddenly appeared. There was something so weird and strange in his appearance that they were dumbfounded with horror, and their horror was increased when they saw him lift the shrouded corpse from its coffin, press it to his breast, fondle it and kiss it, and lavish upon it all the manifestations of extreme love and affection. At last he replaced the body and disappeared as mysteriously as he came. This wonderful story soon spread from lip to lip, with additions and exaggerations, and great was the consternation when, as the unhappy lady was being borne to the burial vault of the Di Venoni in the neighbouring church, the remarkable stranger was recognised amongst the crowd. He seemed bowed in sorrow, but when an attempt was made to seize him be avoided it, and, as everyone declared, made himself invisible.

Years passed away. Reginald Di Venoni grew into manhood. He had become a self-willed, passionate, gloomy man, who avoided his mother—now an old and decrepit woman—and made no secret of the fact that he disliked her. For a long time he had abandoned himself to the pleasures of the chase, and he tried to give some color and tone to his gloomy and monotonous life by riotous living.

One evening he had been out hunting, and having got separated from his followers, he was returning alone when, on reaching the ruins of Rudstein, his horse shied, and Reginald beheld a weird looking old man standing amidst the ruins. His hair was white, and he had a long, grey beard.

"Who are you?" demanded Reginald boldly, for he was courageous and daring to recklessness at times.

"One who has watched you from childhood, and who would now speak into your ear words of wisdom. Make your horse fast to that tree and follow me."

Curiosity, no less than some spell which he seemed incapable of resisting, prompted him to do the bidding of the stranger, who led the way up the mouldering stairs of the tower. On arriving at the top he threw open a door and revealed an apartment, the floor of which was strewn with books written in strange characters. In one corner stood a large vase engraved with the signs of the Zodiac, and encircled by mysterious letters. A huge telescope was placed in the centre of the room, and pointed through a small aperture in the ceiling. As the old man entered he took up an ebony wand from a table near and with it drew circles in the air, then, turning to Reginald, said in a solemn and warning voice:

"Man of ill-starred fortune, you were born under an unlucky planet, and your future is involved in darkness. But for the sake of her whom I loved, your aunt, the Lady Hilda, I would save you from your doom."

Reginald laughed somewhat scornfully. Although he was not without superstition he placed little faith in the wild stories which he had heard from his childhood, and he was in the habit of saying that there was little that was called supernatural that could not be explained by natural laws.

"Ah, now I remember you," he exclaimed. "Years ago, when I was a child, you came to my mother's castle. You frightened me then, and strangely impressed me."

"And yet why should that have been?" asked the stranger. "I was a simple student of the occult, and was travelling the world in quest of knowledge. I had heard something of your family. I knew the curse that rested upon your house, and even then I would have tried to avert it; but your mother would have set her dogs upon me as she set her menials. To your aunt I owed my life, and my love for her grew. By my advice she took you away to the capital, but that act cost her her life. For her sake I would now save you. Since her death I have made long journeys into different countries, but have always been drawn back here by some influence I could not resist. My days, nay, my hours are numbered now; but before I join the sweet Lady Hilda I would render you a service."

Reginald was far from impressed, and laughed again, saying:

"It is kind of you, but suppose I decline your good offices. Indeed, I am capable of taking care of myself and my fortunes; and, frankly, do not desire any service at the hands of a half-witted imposter, as I believe you to be. For myself, I have no belief either in God or Devil, therefore am not likely to be frightened by anything you can tell me or anything you can do."

The old man's face assumed a look of sorrow and distress, and, speaking in a voice that betrayed his emotion, he said:

"Sad indeed it is that you should lack reverence. But have a care, have a care! I warn you against infidelity, and against those sins which, if indulged in, will bring you to ruin. Listen, I say, and take heed. The star of your destiny already wanes in the heavens, and the fortunes of the proud family of Venoni must decline with it. When the stars shine to-night look to the west, and you will see your planet, distinguishable by its unusual brilliancy. Look to it, I say, and let your thoughts wander from it to the God who rules the universe, and to Him put up a prayer of repentance and a cry for light and guidance. But should you see a dull red meteor shoot across the face of your star of nativity, it will be a sign that a deed of blood will be done, and you will perpetrate it."

For a moment or two Reginald was really impressed by the awe-inspiring tone and manner of the old man. But once more he broke into a scornful laugh, and said:

"If this is all you have brought me here for, you do but waste my time, and I will depart."

"Go!" answered the old man. "You pronounce your doom. But let me exact a promise from you. On the night of the third day from now return to this apartment, and, if you find me dead, give my body Christian burial."

"Yes; you shall have burial, as one of my dogs should," Reginald replied. "But since you are an unwelcome tenant in this ruined tower, which is part of my property, I shall give instructions to have you driven away. However, as you confess to having liked my aunt, whom I loved better than I loved my mother, I will see that you do not want. You shall be furnished with means sufficiently ample to enable you to live where your inclinations prompt, only you must quit the tower."

"This is my living place, as it is to be my death place," exclaimed the old man. "And again I charge you, return here in three days, or fail at your peril."

Reginald was exasperated. His temper was aroused now, as he thought the old man was defying him, and he strode hastily from the room, hurried down the stairs, and, flinging himself on his horse, galloped to the castle, with the intention of giving orders to eject the strange old man from the tower at once. But by the time he reached the courtyard he had changed his mind, and he could not help confessing to himself that some indefinable sense of fear restrained him. At any rate, he would let the old fellow remain where he was for a few days longer.

Three days passed away, and the night came. Then Reginald remembered the man's request; at first he had no intention of returning to the ruins. As the evening wore on, however, he felt impelled by a feeling of overmastering curiosity to pay another visit to the wizard, if wizard he was. So, without making known his intention to anyone, he armed himself with a formidable spear used in boar hunting, and, calling his faithful boarhound "Wanga" to his side, he set off for the tower.

The night was beautifully fine. The air was still, the sky was cloudless, the stars shone with extraordinary brilliancy. As Reginald pursued his way he looked to the west, and saw an unusually bright star, and knew, according to what the old man had told him, that it was the star of his nativity. He reached the ruins in about half an hour's rapid walking. A weird silence seemed to pervade the place. No light was visible. There wasn't a sign of the old man's existence. Reginald told "Wanga" to precede him up the mouldering stairs, but the great hound whined and drew back and crouched at his master's feet, and remained unmoved even by the vigorous kick which his master gave him. So, with a muttered oath, Reginald mounted the stairs alone. He pushed open the door and peered in. The window of the chamber was screened by a curtain, on a shelf burned a small lamp, at the table sat the old man. He was dressed in a suit of black velvet embroidered with gold, while round his waist was a massive belt of silver. He wore a skull-cap on his head, in his thin white hand he grasped the ebony rod, while the index finger of the right hand was fixed on a passage in an open book that lay on the table before him.

Reginald spoke to him. There was no answer, no movement. For the first time he felt a sense of fear. He spoke again, but still no answer came. He advanced a few steps into the room.

"Do you not see I am here?" he exclaimed.

The old man rose up, not as a living being, but like a mechanical figure. The face was the face of a corpse. The eyes were dull and glazed, but for an instant they lighted up as they turned upon the speaker, though the light faded immediately, and without a sound the old man sank to the floor, dead.

The situation was so weird, so ghastly, so dramatic, that Reginald's fears were now fully aroused, and with a suppressed moan of horror he turned and fled. The dog was still crouching at the foot of the stairs, but rose with a cry of joy as his master appeared. As Reginald left the ruins he glanced at the west. His star of nativity was burning brilliantly, but suddenly a dull red meteor shot across it, and remembering then the old man's prophecy, he was so overcome that he dropped senseless to the ground in a faint. In a few minutes, finding that something was wrong, the faithful hound rushed back to the castle, and by his howling and barking attracted attention. When the servants hurried to the great gateway he indicated that something was wrong; so torches were procured and the dog was followed to where his master still lay insensible on the ground. He was raised up and carried back, but when he came to his senses he was in a raging fever. He frequently became delirious, and in the hour of his lunacy was accustomed to talk of an evil spirit that had visited him in his slumbers. His mother was shocked at such evident symptoms of derangement. She remembered the fate of her husband, and implored Reginald, as the last descendant of a great house, to recruit his health and raise his spirits by travel. Only with great difficulty was he induced to quit the home of his infancy. The expostulations of his mother, however, at last prevailed, and he left the Castle di Venoni for the sunny land of Italy.

Months passed, and a constant succession of novelty had produced so beneficial an effect, that scarcely any traces remained of the mysterious malady which had so suddenly overtaken him. Occasionally, however, his mind was disturbed and gloomy, but a perpetual recurrence of amusement diverted the influence of past recollection, and rendered him at least as tranquil as it was in the power of his nature to permit.

He continued for years abroad, during which time he wrote frequently to his mother, who still continued at the Castle di Venoni, and at last announced his intention of settling at Venice. He had remained but a few months in the city, when, at the gay period of the Carnival, he was introduced, as a foreign nobleman, to the beautiful daughter of the Doge. She was amiable, accomplished, and endowed with every requisite to ensure permanent felicity. Reginald was charmed with her beauty, and infatuated with the excelling qualities of her mind. After a time he confessed his attachment, and was informed with a blush that the affection was mutual. Nothing, therefore, remained but application to the Doge, who was instantly addressed on the subject, and implored to consummate the felicity of the young couple. The request was attended with success, and the happiness of the lovers was complete.

On the day fixed for the wedding, a brilliant assemblage of beauty thronged the ducal palace of St. Mark. All Venice crowded to the festival, and, in the presence of the gayest noblemen of Italy, Reginald Count di Venoni received the hand of Marcelia, the envied daughter of the Doge. In the evening, a masqued festival was given at the palace; but the young couple, anxious to be alone, escaped from the scene of revelry, and hurried in a gondola to the old palace that had been prepared for their reception on the grand canal.

It was a fine moonlight night. The stars were reflected in the silver bosom of the Adriatic. The sounds of music and sweet voices singing, mellowed and softened by distance, were wafted to them on the gentle breeze. Venice seemed to glitter with tens of thousands of lamps, and the gondoliers, as they passed and repassed, uttered their peculiar cries.

The young couple felt supremely happy, and they directed their boatman to propel the boat leisurely along, that they might enjoy the enrapturing beauty of the scene; for Venice—the sea set jewel—had never looked more beautiful, and the languid air of the summer night begot a delicious sense of dreaminess and a forgetfulness of the pain and misery of the world.

As Reginald lay back with his head pillowed in the lap of his bride he happened to turn his eyes to the west, and there beheld his star of nativity as brilliant as ever. Instantly his mind reverted to that awful night when the old wizard died, and he remembered the dull red meteor, and the weird prophecy. Ile became so agitated that his wife was alarmed, and inquired the reason of it; but he only laughed, said it was merely a passing memory that disturbed him, and soon her kisses and caresses restored him to serenity.

The succeeding six months were uninterrupted by a single untoward incident. He passionately loved Marcelia, and was beloved in return. His rough, uncouth nature had been smoothed down and refined by his wife and the society in which he moved. He felt supremely happy, and though at times a remembrance of the awful night in the ruins of Rudstein disturbed him, he managed to shake off the influence, and find a soothing balm in the caresses of his young bride.

One day, however, there came to him an urgent message to repair to his birthplace without delay, as his mother lay at the point of death. Although he had never borne her any very strong affection, he felt it was his duty to obey the summons, and so in company with his wife he journeyed with all speed to the Black Forest.

On reaching the castle he found that his mother was already in the throes of death, and delirious; as soon as he entered her presence she rose up in her bed, without seeming to recognise him, and cursed him for being an unnatural and unfilial son. It was an awful scene, and affected Reginald in an appalling manner. Without recanting a word, or, indeed, noticing him in any way, she fell back on her pillow and expired.

For some days Reginald was prostrated, and when his gentle and loving wife tried to soothe and comfort him he repulsed her furiously, until she was broken-hearted. But when he recovered his senses he lavished caresses upon her, and gave every manifestation that he loved her devotedly. A few days later, however, he was wandering with Marcelia through a very picturesque and beautiful part of the forest, when they seated themselves on a bank overlooking a stream. For some little time Reginald remained absorbed in thought, then he began to pick up handfuls of earth and scatter them in the water, and, with a wild glare in his eyes, he mumbled:

"This is a hateful world. All is dust and vanity. Nothing brings joy, or contentment, or peace. I am the last of my race. Why seek longer to support a rotten fabric. My kindred have squandered their substance, and destroyed the vitality of the family. Let us follow my mother through the gates of death. Come, give me your hand, Marcelia, and we will die together."

His wife was horribly alarmed, and used every endeavour to soothe him; presently he grew calmer, and rose and allowed her to lead him away. They continued to wander further afield, at his request, until night closed, and the stars were burning. Brilliant above all the rest shone the fatal western planet, the star of Reginald's nativity. He gazed at it for some time with horror, and pointed it out to the notice of Marcelia.

"The hand of heaven is in it!" he mentally exclaimed, "and the proud fortunes of Venoni hasten to a close." At this instant the ruined tower of Rudstein appeared in sight, with the moon shining fully upon it. "It is the place," resumed the maniac, "where a deed of blood must be done, and I am fated to perpetrate it! But fear not, my poor girl," he added, in a milder tone, while the tears sprang to his eyes, "your husband cannot harm you; he may be wretched, but he never shall be guilty!" Although Marcelia was dreadfully alarmed she concealed her feelings as much as possible, and induced him to hurry back. When he reached the castle he looked ghastly ill, and, going to bed, sank into a sort of coma.

Night waned, morning dawned on the upland hills of the scenery, and with it came a renewal of Reginald's disorder. The day was stormy, and in unison with the troubled feeling of his mind. He rose with the dawn, and, without a word to anyone, went off into the forest, nor did he return until the evening. Distressed beyond measure at his absence, she waited in dread suspense for his return, and sat at her casement gazing across the vast expanse of forest, which the westering sun was now flooding with a crimson light. Suddenly her door flew open, and Reginald made his appearance. His eyes were red and seemed to blaze with the light of madness, while his whole frame was convulsed as if he suffered from agonising spasms of pain.

"It was not a dream," he exclaimed, "I have seen her, and she has beckoned us to follow."

"Seen her, seen who?" asked Marcelia, alarmed at his frenzy.

"My mother," replied the maniac. "Listen while I tell you the strange story. I thought, as I was wandering in the forest, a sylph of heaven approached, and revealed the countenance of my mother. I flew to join her, but was withheld by a wizard, who pointed to the western star. On a sudden loud shrieks were heard, and the sylph assumed the guise of a demon. Her figure towered to an awful height, and she pointed in scornful derision to you; yes, to you, my wife. With rage she drew you towards me. I seized—I murdered you, and strange cries and groans filled the air. I heard the voice of the fiendish astrologer shouting as from a charnel house, 'Your destiny is accomplished, and the victim may retire with honour.' Then, I thought, the fair front of heaven was obscured, and thick gouts of clotted clammy blood showered down in torrents from the blackened clouds of the west. The star shot through the air, and—the phantom of my mother again beckoned me to follow."

The maniac ceased, and rushed in agony from the apartment. Marcelia followed, and discovered him leaning in a trance against the wainscot of the library. With gentlest motion she drew his hand in hers, and led him into the open air. They rambled on, heedless of the gathering storm, until they discovered themselves at the base of the tower of Rudstein. Suddenly the maniac paused. A horrid thought seemed flashing across his brain, as with giant grasp he seized Marcelia in his arms, and bore her to the fatal apartment. In vain she shrieked for help, for pity. "Dear Reginald, it is Marcelia who speaks, you cannot surely harm her." He heard—he heeded not, nor once staid his steps till he reached the room of death. On a sudden his countenance lost its wildness, and assumed a more fearful, but composed look of determined madness. He advanced to the window, dragged away the rotting curtain, and gazed on the stormy face of heaven. Dark clouds flitted across the horizon, and thunder echoed in the distance. To the west the fatal star was still visible, but shone with sickly lustre. At this instant a flash of lightning illumined the whole apartment, and threw a broad red glare upon a skeleton that mouldered upon the floor. Reginald observed it with affright, and remembered the unburied astrologer. He advanced to Marcelia, and, pointing to the rising moon, "A dark cloud is sailing by," he shudderingly exclaimed, "but ere the full orb again shines forth you shall die; I will accompany you in death, and hand in hand will we pass into the presence of our people."

The poor girl shrieked for pity, but her voice was lost in the angry ravings of the storm.

The cloud in the meantime sailed on—it approached—the moon was dimmed, darkened, and finally buried in its gloom. The maniac marked the hour, and rushed with a fearful cry towards his victim. With murderous resolution he grasped her throat, while the helpless hand and half-strangled articulation implored his compassion. After one final struggle the hollow death rattle announced that life was extinct, and that the murderer held a corpse in his arms. An interval of reason now occurred, and on the partial restoration of his mind Reginald discovered himself the unconscious murderer of Marcelia. Madness—deepest madness again took possession of his faculties. He laughed—he shouted aloud with the unearthly yellings of a fiend, and in the raging violence of his delirium he rushed out, climbed to the summit of the tower, and hurled himself headlong from it.

In the morning the bodies of the young couple were discovered, and buried in the same tomb. The fatal ruin of Rudstein still exists, but is now commonly avoided as the residence of the spirits of the departed. Day by day it slowly crumbles to earth, and affords a shelter for the night raven or the wild things of the forests. Superstition has consecrated it to herself, and the tradition of the country has invested it with all the awful appendages of a charnel house. The wanderer who passes at nightfall shudders while he surveys its utter desolation, and exclaims as he travels on:

"Surely this is a spot where guilt may thrive in safety, or bigotry weave a spell to enthral her misguided votaries."

The Basilisk

R. Murray Gilchrist

Marina gave no sign that she heard my protestation. The embroidery of Venus's hands in her silk picture of The Judgment of Paris was seemingly of greater import to her than the love which almost tore my soul and body asunder. In absolute despair I sat until she had replenished her needle seven times. Then impassioned nature cried aloud:—"You do not love me!"

She looked up somewhat wearily, as one debarred from rest. "Listen," she said. "There is a creature called a Basilisk, which turns men and women into stone. In my girlhood I saw the Basilisk—I am stone!"

And, rising from her chair, she departed the room, leaving me in amazed doubt as to whether I had heard aright. I had always known of some curious secret in her life: a secret which permitted her to speak of and to understand things to which no other woman had dared to lift her thoughts. But alas! it was a secret whose influence ever thrust her back from the attaining of happiness. She would warm, then freeze instantly; discuss the purest wisdom, then cease with contemptuous lips and eyes. Doubtless this strangeness had been the first thing to awaken my passion. Her beauty was not of the kind that smites men with sudden craving: it was pale and reposeful, the loveliness of a marble image. Yet, as time went on, so wondrous became her fascination that even the murmur of her swaying garments sickened me with longing. Not more than a year had passed since our first meeting, when I had found her laden with flaming tendrils in the thinned woods of my heritage. A very Dryad, robed in grass color, she was chanting to the sylvan deities. The invisible web took me, and I became her slave.

Her house lay two leagues from mine. It was a low-built mansion lying in a concave park. The thatch was gaudy with stonecrop and lichen. Amongst the central chimneys a foreign bird sat on a nest of twigs. The long windows blazed with heraldic devices; and paintings of kings and queens and nobles hung in the dim chambers. Here she dwelt with a retinue of aged servants, fantastic women and men half imbecile, who salaamed before her with eastern humility and yet addressed her in such terms as gossips use. Had she given them life they could not have obeyed with more reverence. Quaint things the women wrought for her—pomanders and cushions of thistledown; and the men were never happier than when they could tell her of the first thrush's egg in the thornbush or the sege of bitterns that haunted the marsh. She was their goddess and their daughter. Each day had its own routine. In the morning she rode and sang and played; at noon she read in the dusty library, drinking to the full of the dramatists and the platonists. Her own life was such a tragedy as an Elizabethan would have adored. None save her people knew her history, but there were wonderful stories of how she had bowed to tradition, and concentrated in herself the characteristics of a thousand wizard fathers. In the blossom of her youth she had sought strange knowledge, and had tasted thereof, and rued.

The morning after my declaration she rode across her park to the meditating walk I always paced till noon. She was alone, dressed in a habit of white lutestring with a loose girdle of blue. As her mare reached the yew hedge, she dismounted, and came to me with more lightness than I had ever beheld in her. At her waist hung a black glass mirror, and her half-bare arms were adorned with cabalistic jewels.

When I knelt to kiss her hand, she sighed heavily. "Ask me nothing," she said. "Life itself is too joyless to be more embittered by explanations. Let all rest between us as now. I will love coldly, you warmly, with no nearer approaching." Her voice rang full of a wistful expectancy: as if she knew that I should combat her half-explained decision. She read me well, for almost ere she had done I cried out loudly against it:—"It can never be so—I cannot breathe—I shall die?"

She sank to the low moss-covered wall. "Must the sacrifice be made?" she asked, half to herself. "Must I tell him all?" Silence prevailed a while, then turning away her face she said: "From the first I loved you, but last night in the darkness, when I could not sleep for thinking of your words, love sprang into desire."

I was forbidden to speak.

"And desire seemed to burst the cords that bound me. In that moment's strength I felt that I could give all for the joy of being once utterly yours."

I longed to clasp her to my heart. But her eyes were stern, and a frown crossed her brow.

"At morning light," she said, "desire died, but in my ecstasy I had sworn to give what must be given for that short bliss, and to lie in your arms and pant against you before another midnight. So I have come to bid you fare with me to the place where the spell may be loosed, and happiness bought."

She called the mare: it came whinnying, and pawed the ground until she had stroked its neck. She mounted, setting in my hand a tiny, satin-shod foot that seemed rather child's than woman's. "Let us go together to my house," she said. "I have orders to give and duties to fulfil. I will not keep you there long, for we must start soon on our errand." I walked exultantly at her side, but, the grange in view, I entreated her to speak explicitly of our mysterious journey. She stooped and patted my head. "'Tis but a matter of buying and selling," she answered.

When she had arranged her household affairs, she came to the library and bade me follow her. Then, with the mirror still swinging against her knees, she led me through the garden and the wilderness down to a misty wood. It being autumn, the trees were tinted gloriously in dusky bars of coloring. The rowan, with his amber leaves and scarlet berries, stood before the brown black-spotted sycamore; the silver beech flaunted his golden coins against my poverty; firs, green and fawn-hued, slumbered in hazy gossamer. No bird carolled, although the sun was hot. Marina noted the absence of sound, and without prelude of any kind began to sing from the ballad of the Witch Mother: about the nine enchanted knots, and the trouble-comb in the lady's knotted hair, and the master-kid that ran beneath her couch. Every drop of my blood froze in dread, for whilst she sang her face took on the majesty of one who traffics with infernal powers. As the shade of the trees fell over her, and we passed intermittently out of the light, I saw that her eyes glittered like rings of sapphires. Believing now that the ordeal she must undergo would be too frightful, I begged her to return. Supplicating on my knees—"Let me face the evil alone!" I said, "I will entreat the loosening of the bonds. I will compel and accept any penalty." She grew calm. "Nay," she said, very gently, "if aught can conquer, it is my love alone. In the fervour of my last wish I can dare everything."

By now, at the end of a sloping alley, we had reached the shores of a vast marsh. Some unknown quality in the sparkling water had stained its whole bed a bright yellow. Green leaves, of such a sour brightness as almost poisoned to behold, floated on the surface of the rush-girdled pools. Weeds like tempting veils of mossy velvet grew beneath in vivid contrast with the soil. Alders and willows hung over the margin. From where we stood a half-submerged path of rough stones, threaded by deep swift channels, crossed to the very centre. Marina put her foot upon the first step. "I must go first," she said. "Only once before have I gone this way, yet I know its pitfalls better than any living creature."

Before I could hinder her she was leaping from stone to stone like a hunted animal. I followed hastily, seeking, but vainly, to lessen the space between us. She was gasping for breath, and her heart-beats sounded like the ticking of a clock. When we reached a great pool, itself almost a lake, that was covered with lavender scum, the path turned abruptly to the right, where stood an isolated grove of wasted elms. As Marina beheld this, her pace slackened, and she paused in momentary indecision; but, at my first word of pleading that she should go no further, she went on, dragging her silken mud-bespattered skirts. We climbed the slippery shores of the island (for island it was, being raised much above the level of the marsh), and Marina led the way over lush grass to an open glade. A great marble tank lay there, supported on two thick pillars. Decayed boughs rested on the crust of stagnancy within, and divers frogs, bloated and almost blue, rolled off at our approach. To the left stood the columns of a temple, a round, domed building, with a closed door of bronze. Wild vines had grown athwart the portal; rank, clinging herbs had sprung from the overteeming soil; astrological figures were enchiselled on the broad stairs.

Here Marina stopped. "I shall blindfold you," she said, taking off her loose sash, "and you must vow obedience to all I tell you. The least error will betray us." I promised, and submitted to the bandage. With a pressure of the hand, and bidding me neither move nor speak, she left me and went to the door of the temple. Thrice her hand struck the dull metal. At the last stroke a hissing shriek came from within, and the massive hinges creaked loudly. A breath like an icy tongue leaped out and touched me, and in the terror my hand sprang to the kerchief. Marina's voice, filled with agony, gave me instant pause. "*Oh, why am I thus torn between the man and the fiend? The mesh that holds life in will be ripped from end to end! Is there no mercy?*"

My hand fell impotent. Every muscle shrank. I felt myself turn to stone. After a while came a sweet scent of smouldering wood: such an Oriental fragrance as is offered to Indian gods. Then the door swung to, and I heard Marian's voice, dim and wordless, but raised in wild deprecation. Hour after hour passed so, and still I waited. Not until the sash grew crimson with the rays of the sinking sun did the door open.

"Come to me!" Marina whispered. "Do not unblindfold. Quick—we must not stay here long. He is glutted with my sacrifice."

Newborn joy rang in her tones. I stumbled across and was caught in her arms. Shafts of delight pierced my heart at the first contact with her warm breasts. She turned me round, and bidding me look straight in front, with one swift touch untied the knot. The first thing my dazed eyes fell upon was the mirror of black glass which had hung from her waist. She held it so that I might gaze into its depths. And there, with a cry of amazement and fear, *I saw the shadow of the Basilisk*.

The Thing was lying prone on the floor, the presentment of a sleeping horror. Vivid scarlet and sable feathers covered its gold-crowned cock's-head, and its leathern dragon-wings were folded. Its sinuous tail, capped with a snake's eyes and mouth, was curved in luxurious and delighted satiety. A prodigious evil leaped in its atmosphere. But even as I looked a mist crowded over the surface of the mirror: the shadow faded, leaving only an indistinct and wavering shape. Marina breathed upon it, and, as I peered and pored, the gloom went off the plate and left, where the Chimera had lain, the prostrate figure of a man. He was young and stalwart, a dark outline with a white face, and short black curls that fell in tangles over a shapely forehead, and eyelids languorous and red. His aspect was that of a wearied demon-god.

When Marina looked sideways and saw my wonderment, she laughed delightedly in one rippling running tune that should have quickened the dead entrails of the marsh. "I have conquered!" she cried. "I have purchased the fulness of joy!" And with one outstretched arm she closed the door before I could turn to look; with the other she encircled my neck, and, bringing down my head, pressed my mouth to hers. The mirror fell from her hand, and with her foot she crushed its shards into the dank mould.

The sun had sunk behind the trees now, and glittered through the intricate leafage like a charcoal-burner's fire. All the nymphs of the pools arose and danced, grey and cold, exulting at the absence of the divine light. So thickly gathered the vapours that the path grew perilous. "Stay, love," I said. "Let me take you in my arms and carry you. It is no longer safe for you to walk alone." She made no reply, but, a flush arising to her pale cheeks, she stood and let me lift her to my bosom. She rested a hand on either shoulder, and gave no sign of fear as I bounded from stone to stone. The way lengthened deliriously, and by the time we reached the plantation the moon was rising over the further hills. Hope and fear fought in my heart: soon both were set at rest. When I set her on the dry ground she stood a-tiptoe, and murmured with exquisite shame: "To-night, then, dearest. My home is yours now."

So, in a rapture too subtle for words, we walked together, arm-enfolded, to her house. Preparations for a banquet were going on within: the windows were ablaze, and figures passed behind them bowed with heavy dishes. At the threshold of the hall we were met by a triumphant crash of melody. In the musician's gallery bald-pated veterans stood to it with flute and harp and viol-de-gamba. In two long rows the antic retainers stood, and bowed, and cried merrily: "Joy and health to the bride and groom!" And they kissed Marina's hands and mine, and, with the players sending forth that half-forgotten tenderness which threads through ancient song-books, we passed to the feast, seating ourselves on the dais, whilst the servants filled the tables below. But we made little feint of appetite. As the last dish of confections was removing, a weird pageant swept across the further end of the banqueting-room: Oberon and Titania with Robin Goodfellow and the rest, attired in silks and satins gorgeous of hue, and bedizened with such late flowers as were still with us. I leaned forward to commend, and saw that each face was brown and wizened and thin-haired: so that their motions and their epithalamy felt goblin and discomforting; nor could I smile till they departed by the further door. Then the tables were cleared away, and Marina, taking my finger-tips in hers, opened a stately dance. The servants followed, and in the second maze a shrill and joyful laughter proclaimed that the bride had sought her chamber. . . .

Ere the dawn I wakened from a troubled sleep. My dream had been of despair: I had been persecuted by a host of devils, thieves of a priceless jewel. So I leaned over the pillow for Marina's consolation; my lips sought hers, my hand crept beneath her head. My heart gave one mad bound—then stopped.

Basilissa

John Buchan

I

When Vernon was a very little boy he was the sleepiest of mortals, but in the spring he had seasons of bad dreams, and breakfast became an idle meal. Mrs. Ganthony, greatly concerned, sent for Dr Moreton from Axby, and homely remedies were prescribed.

"It is the spring fever," said the old man. "It gives the gout to me and nightmares to this baby; it brings lads and lasses together, and scatters young men about the world. An antique complaint, Mrs. Ganthony. But it will right itself, never fear. *Ver non semper viret.*" Chuckling at his ancient joke, the doctor mounted his horse, leaving the nurse only half comforted. "What fidgets me," she told the housekeeper, "is the way his lordship holds his tongue. For usual he'll shout as lusty as a whelp. But now I finds him in the morning with his eyes like moons and his skin white and shiny, and never a cheep has he given the whole blessed night, with me laying next door, and it open, and a light sleeper at all times, Mrs. Wace, ma'am."

Every year the dreams came, generally—for his springs were spent at Severns—in the big new night-nursery at the top of the west wing, which his parents had built not long before their death. It had three windows looking over the moorish flats which run up to the Lancashire fells, and from one window, by craning your neck, you could catch a glimpse of the sea. It was all hung, too, with a Chinese paper whereon pink and green parrots squatted in wonderful blue trees, and there seemed generally to be a wood fire burning. Vernon's recollections of his childish nightmare are hazy. He always found himself in a room different from the nursery and bigger, but with the same smell of wood smoke. People came and went, such as his nurse, the butler, Simon the head-keeper, Uncle Appleby his guardian, Cousin Jennifer, the old woman who sold oranges in Axby, and a host of others. Nobody hindered them from going away, and they seemed to be pleading with him to come too. There was danger in the place; something was going to happen in that big room, and if by that time he was not gone there would be mischief. But it was quite clear to him that he could not go.

He must stop there, with the wood smoke in his nostrils, and await the advent of a terrible Something. But he was never quite sure of the nature of the compulsion. He had a notion that if he made a rush for the door at Uncle Appleby's heels he would be allowed to escape, but that somehow he would be behaving badly. Anyhow, the place put him into a sweat of fright, and Mrs. Ganthony looked darkly at him in the morning.

Vernon was nine before this odd spring dream began to take definite shape—at least he thinks he must have been about that age. The dream-stage was emptying. There was nobody in the room now but himself, and he saw its details a little more clearly. It was not any apartment in the modern magnificence of Severns. Rather it looked like one of the big old panelled chambers which the boy remembered from visits to Midland country houses, where he had arrived after dark and had been put to sleep in a great bed in a place lit with dancing firelight. In the morning it had looked only an ordinary big room, but at that hour of the evening it had seemed an enchanted citadel. The dreamroom was not unlike these, for there was the scent of a wood fire and there were dancing shadows, but he could not see clearly the walls or the ceiling, and there was no bed. In one corner was a door which led to the outer world, and through this he knew that he might on no account pass. Another door faced him, and he knew that he had only to turn the handle and enter it. But he did not want to, for he understood quite clearly what was beyond. There was another room like the first one, but he knew nothing about it, except that opposite the entrance another door led out of it. Beyond was a third chamber, and so on interminably. There seemed to the boy no end to this fantastic suite. He thought of it as a great snake of masonry, winding up hill and down dale away to the fells or the sea. Yes, but there was an end. Somewhere far away in one of the rooms was a terror waiting on him, or, as he feared, coming towards him. Even now it might be flitting from room to room, every minute bringing its soft tread nearer to the chamber of the wood fire.

About this time of life the dream was an unmitigated horror. Once it came while he was ill with a childish fever, and it sent his temperature up to a point which brought Dr Moreton galloping from Axby. In his waking hours he did not, as a rule, remember it clearly; but during the fever, asleep and awake, that sinuous building, one room thick, with each room opening from the other, was never away from his thoughts. It fretted him to think that outside were the cheerful moors where he hunted for plovers' eggs, and that only a thin wall of stone kept him from pleasant homely things. The thought used to comfort him for a moment when he was awake, but in the dream it never came near him. Asleep, the whole world seemed one suite of rooms, and he, a forlorn little prisoner, doomed to wait grimly on the slow coming through the many doors of a Fear which transcended word and thought.

He was a silent, self-absorbed boy, and though the fact of his nightmares was patent to the little household, the details remained locked in his heart. Not even to Uncle Appleby would he tell them when that gentleman, hurriedly kind, came down to visit his convalescent ward. His illness made Vernon grow, and he shot up into a lanky, leggy boy—weakly, too, till the hills tautened his sinews again. His Greek blood—his grandmother had been a Karolides—had given him a face curiously like the young Byron, with a finely-cut brow and nostrils, and hauteur in the full lips. But Vernon had no Byronic pallor, for his upland home kept him sunburnt and weather-beaten, and below his straight Greek brows shone a pair of grey and steadfast and very English eyes.

He was about fifteen—so he thinks—when he made the great discovery. The dream had become almost a custom now. It came in April at Severns during the Easter holidays—a night's discomfort (it was now scarcely more) in the rush and glory of the spring fishing. There was a moment of the old wild heart-fluttering; but a boy's fancy is quickly dulled, and the endless corridors were now more of a prison than a witch's ante-chamber. By this time, with the help of his diary, he had fixed the date of the dream: it came regularly on the night of the first Monday of April. Now the year I speak of he had been on a long expedition into the hills, and had stridden homewards at a steady four miles an hour among the gleams and shadows of an April twilight. He was alone at Severns, so he had his supper in the big library, where afterwards he sat watching the leaping flames in the open stone hearth. He was very weary, and sleep fell upon him in his chair. He found himself in the wood-smoke chamber, and before him the door leading to the unknown. But it was no indefinite fear that lay beyond. He knew clearly—though how he knew he could not tell—that each year the Something came one room nearer, and was even now but ten rooms off. In ten years his own door would open, and then—

He woke in the small hours, chilled and amazed, but with a curious new assurance in his heart. Hitherto the nightmare had left him in gross terror, unable to endure the prospect of its recurrence, till the kindly forgetfulness of youth had soothed him. But now, though his nerves were tense with fright, he perceived that there was a limit to the mystery. Some day it must declare itself, and fight on equal terms. As he thought over the matter in the next few days he had the sense of being forewarned and prepared for some great test of courage. The notion exhilarated as much as it frightened him. Late at night, or on soft dripping days, or at any moment of lessened vitality, he would bitterly wish that he had been born an ordinary mortal. But on a keen morning of frost, when he rubbed himself warm after a cold tub, or at high noon of summer, the adventure of the dream almost pleased him. Unconsciously he braced himself to a harder discipline. His fitness, moral and physical, became his chief interest, for reasons which would have been unintelligible to his friends and more so to his masters. He passed through school an aloof and splendid figure, magnificently athletic, with a brain as well as a perfect body—a good fellow in everybody's opinion, but a grave one. He had no intimates, and never shared the secret of the spring dream. For some reason which he could not tell, he would have burned his hand off rather than breathe a hint of it. Pure terror absolves from all conventions and demands a confidant, so terror, I think, must have largely departed from the nightmare as he grew older. Fear, indeed, remained, and awe and disquiet, but these are human things, whereas terror is of hell.

Had he told any one, he would no doubt have become self-conscious and felt acutely his difference from other people. As it was, he was an ordinary schoolboy, much beloved, and, except at odd moments, unaware of any brooding destiny. As he grew up and his ambition awoke, the moments when he remembered the dream were apt to be disagreeable, for a boy's ambitions are strictly conventional and his soul revolts at the abnormal. By the time he was ready for the University he wanted above all things to run the mile a second faster than any one else, and had vague hopes of exploring wild countries. For most of the year he lived with these hopes and was happy; then came April, and for a short season he was groping in dark places. Before and after each dream he was in a mood of exasperation; but when it came he plunged into a different atmosphere, and felt the quiver of fear and the quick thrill of expectation. One year, in the unsettled moods of nineteen, he made an attempt to avoid it. He and three others were on a walking tour in Brittany in gusty spring weather, and came late one evening to an inn by an estuary where seagulls clattered about the windows. Youth-like they ordered a great and foolish feast, and sat all night round a bowl of punch, while school songs and "John Peel" contended with the dirling of the gale. At daylight they took the road again, without having closed an eye, and Vernon told himself that he was rid of his incubus. He wondered at the time why he was not more cheerful. Next April he was at Severns, reading hard, and on the first Monday of the month he went to bed with scarcely a thought of what that night used to mean. The dream did not fail him. Once more he was in the chamber with the wood fire; once again he was peering at the door and wondering with tremulous heart what lay beyond. For the Something had come nearer by two rooms, and was now only five doors away. He wrote in his diary at that time some lines from Keats' "Indian Maid's Song":—

> I would deceive her,
> And so leave her,
> But ah! she is so constant and so kind.

And there is a mark of exclamation against the "she," as if he found some irony in it.

From that day the boy in him died. The dream would not suffer itself to be forgotten. It moulded his character and determined his plans like the vow of the young Hannibal at the altar. He had forgotten now either to fear or to hope; the thing was part of him, like his vigorous young body, his slow kindliness, his patient courage. He left Oxford at twenty-two with a prodigious reputation which his remarkable athletic record by no means explained. All men liked him, but no one knew him; he had a thousand acquaintances and a hundred friends, but no comrade. There was a sense of brooding power about him which attracted and repelled his little world. No one forecast any special career for him; indeed, it seemed almost disrespectful to condescend upon such details. It was not what Vernon would do that fired the imagination of his fellows, but what they dimly conceived that he already was. I remember my first sight of him about that time, a tall young man in the corner of a club smoking-room, with a head like Apollo's and eyes which received much but gave nothing. I guessed at once that he had foreign blood in him, not from any oddness of coloring or feature but from his silken reserve. We of the North are angular in our silences; we have not learned the art of gracious reticence.

His twenty-third April was spent in a hut on the Line, somewhere between the sources of the Congo and the Nile, in the trans-African expedition when Waldemar found the new variety of okapi. The following April I was in his company in a tent far up on the shoulder of a Kashmir mountain. On the first Monday of the month we had had a heavy day after ovis, and that night I was asleep almost before my weary limbs were tucked into my kaross. I knew nothing of Vernon's dream, but next morning I remember that I remarked a certain heaviness of eye, and wondered idly if the frame of this Greek divinity was as tough as it was shapely.

II

Next year Vernon left England early in March. He had resolved to visit again his grandmother's country and to indulge his passion for cruising in new waters.

His 20-ton yawl was sent as deck cargo to Patras, while he followed by way of Venice. He brought one man with him from Wyvenhoe, a lean gipsy lad called Martell, and for his other hand he found an Epirote at Corfu, who bore a string of names that began with Constantine. From Patras with a west wind they made good sailing up the Gulf of Corinth, and, passing through the Canal, came in the last days of March to the Piraeus. In that place of polyglot speech, whistling engines, and the odour of gasworks, they delayed only for water and supplies, and presently had rounded Sunium, and were beating up the Euripus with the Attic hills rising sharp and clear in the spring sunlight. Vernon had no plans. It was a joy to him to be alone with the racing seas and the dancing winds, to scud past little headlands, pink and white with blossom, or to lie of a night in some hidden bay beneath the thymy crags. It was his habit on his journeys to discard the clothes of civilisation. In a blue jersey and old corduroy trousers, bareheaded and barefooted, he steered his craft and waited on the passing of the hours. Like an acolyte before the temple gate, he believed himself to be on the threshold of a new life.

Trouble began under the snows of Pelion as they turned the north end of Euboea. On the morning of the first Monday in April the light west winds died away, and sirocco blew harshly from the south. By midday it was half a gale, and in those yeasty shallow seas with an iron coast on the port the prospect looked doubtful. The nearest harbour was twenty miles distant, and as no one of the crew had been there before it was a question if they could make it by nightfall. With the evening the gale increased, and Constantine advised a retreat from the maze of rocky islands to the safer deeps of the Aegean. It was a hard night for the three, and there was no chance of sleep. More by luck than skill they escaped the butt of Skiathos, and the first light found them far to the east among the long seas of the North Aegean, well on the way to Lemnos. By eight o'clock the gale had blown itself out, and three soaked and chilly mortals relaxed their vigil. Soon bacon was frizzling on the cuddy-stove, and hot coffee and dry clothes restored them to comfort.

The sky cleared, and in bright sunlight, with the dregs of the gale behind him, Vernon stood in for the mainland, where the white crest of Olympus hung in the northern heavens. In the late afternoon they came into a little bay carved from the side of a high mountain. The slopes were gay with flowers, yellow and white and scarlet, and the young green of crops showed in the clearings. Among the thyme a flock of goats was browsing, shepherded by a little girl in a saffron skirt, who sang shrilly in snatches. Midway in the bay and just above the anchorage rose a great white building, which showed to seaward a blank white wall pierced with a few narrow windows. At first sight Vernon took it for a monastery, but a look through the glasses convinced him that its purpose was not religious. Once it had been fortified, and even now a broad causeway ran between it and the sea, which looked as if it had once held guns. The architecture was a jumble, showing here the enriched Gothic of Venice and there the straight lines and round arches of the East. It had once, he conjectured, been the hold of some Venetian sea-king, then the palace of a Turkish conqueror, and now was, perhaps, the homely manor-house of this pleasant domain.

A fishing-boat was putting out from the shore. He hailed its occupant and asked who owned the castle.

The man crossed himself and spat overboard. "Basilissa," he said, and turned his eyes seaward.

Vernon called Constantine from the bows and asked him what the word might mean. The Epirote crossed himself also before he spoke. "It is the Lady of the Land," he said, in a hushed voice. "It is the great witch who is the Devil's bride. In old days in spring they made sacrifice to her, but they say her power is dying now. In my country we do not speak her name, but elsewhere they call her 'Queen.'" The man's bluff sailorly assurance had disappeared, and as Vernon stared at him in bewilderment he stammered and averted his eyes.

By supper-time he had recovered himself, and the weather-beaten three made such a meal as befits those who have faced danger together. Afterwards Vernon, as was his custom, sat alone in the stern, smoking and thinking his thoughts. He wrote up his diary with a ship's lantern beside him, while overhead the starless velvet sky seemed to hang low and soft like an awning. Little fires burned on the shore at which folk were cooking food—he could hear their voices, and from the keep one single lit window made an eye in the night.

He had leisure now for the thought which had all day been at the back of his mind. The night had passed and there had been no dream. The adventure for which he had prepared himself had vanished into the Ægean tides. He told himself that it was a relief, that an old folly was over, but he knew in his heart that he was bitterly disappointed. The fates had prepared the stage and rung up the curtain without providing the play. He had been fooled, and somehow the zest and savour of life had gone from him. No man can be strung high and then find his preparation idle without suffering a cruel recoil.

As he scribbled idly in his diary he found some trouble about dates. Down in his bunk was a sheaf of Greek papers bought at the Piraeus and still unlooked at. He fetched them up and turned them over with a growing mystification. There was something very odd about the business. One gets hazy about dates at sea, but he could have sworn that he had made no mistake. Yet here it was down in black and white, for there was no question about the number of days since he left the Piraeus. The day was not Tuesday, as he had believed, but Monday, the first Monday of April.

He stood up with a beating heart and that sense of unseen hands which comes to all men once or twice in their lives. The night was yet to come, and with it the end of the dream. Suddenly he was glad, absurdly glad; he could almost have wept with the joy of it. And then he was conscious for the first time of the strangeness of the place in which he had anchored. The night was dark over him like a shell, enclosing the half-moon of bay and its one lit dwelling. The great hills, unseen but felt, ran up to snows, warding it off from a profane world. His nerves tingled with a joyful anticipation. Something, some wonderful thing, was coming to him out of the darkness.

Under an impulse for which he could give no reason, he called Constantine and gave his orders. Let him be ready to sail at any moment—a possible thing, for there was a light breeze off shore. Also let the yacht's dinghy be ready in case he wanted it. Then Vernon sat himself down again in the stern beside the lantern, and waited. . . .

He was dreaming, and did not hear the sound of oars or the grating of a boat alongside. Suddenly he found a face looking at him in the ring of lamplight—an old bearded face curiously wrinkled. The eyes, which were grave and penetrating, scanned him for a second or two, and then a voice spoke,—

"Will the Signor come with me? There is work for him to do this night."

Vernon rose obediently. He had waited for this call these many years, and he was there to answer it. He went below and put a loaded revolver in his trouser-pocket, and then dropped over the yacht's side into a cockleshell of a boat. The messenger took the oars and rowed for the point of light on shore.

A middle-aged woman stood on a rock above the tide, holding a small lantern. In its thin flicker he made out a person with the air and dress of a French maid. She cast one glance at Vernon, and then turned wearily to the other. "Fool, Mitri!" she said. "You have brought a peasant."

"Nay," said the old man, "he is no peasant. He is a Signor, and as I judge, a man of his hands."

The woman passed the light of her lantern over Vernon's form and face. "His dress is a peasant's, but such clothes may be a nobleman's whim. I have heard it of the English."

"I am English," said Vernon in French.

She turned on him with a quick movement of relief.

"You are English and a gentleman? But I know nothing of you, only that you have come out of the sea. Up in the House we women are alone, and my mistress has death to face, or a worse than death. We have no claim on you, and if you give us your service it means danger—oh, what danger! The boat is waiting. You have time to go back and go away and forget that you have seen this accursed place. But, O Monsieur, if you hope for Heaven and have pity on a defenceless angel, you will not leave us."

"I am ready," said Vernon.

"God's mercy," she sighed, and, seizing his arm, drew him up the steep causeway, while the old man went ahead with the lantern. Now and then she cast anxious glances to the right where the little fires of the fishers twinkled along the shore. Then came a point when the three entered a narrow uphill road, where rocky steps had been cut in a tamarisk thicket. She spoke low in French to Vernon's ear,—

"My mistress is the last of her line, you figure; a girl with a wild estate and a father long dead. She is good and gracious, as I who have tended her can witness, but she is young and cannot govern the wolves who are the men of these parts. They have a long hatred of her house, and now they have it rumoured that she is a witch and blights the crops and slays the children. No one will look at her; the priest—for they are all in the plot—signs himself and crosses the road; the little ones run screaming to their mothers. Once, twice, they have cursed our threshold and made the blood mark on the door. For two years we have been prisoners in the House, and only Mitri is true. They name her Basilissa, meaning the Queen of Hell, whom the ancients called Proserpine. There is no babe but will faint with fright if it casts eyes on her, and she as mild and innocent as Mother Mary. . . ."

The woman stopped at a little door in a high wall of masonry. "Nay, wait and hear me out. It is better that you hear the tale from me than from her. Mitri has the gossip of the place through his daughter's husband, and the word has gone round to burn the witch out. The winter in the hills has been cruel, and they blame their sorrow on her. The dark of the moon in April is the time fixed, for they say that a witch has power only in moonlight. This is the night, and down on the shore the fishers are gathered. The men from the hills are in the higher woods."

"Have they a leader?" Vernon asked.

"A leader?" her voice echoed shrilly. "But that is the worst of our terrors. There is one Vlastos, a lord in the mountains, who saw my mistress a year ago as she looked from the balcony at the Swallow-singing, and was filled with a passion for her. He has persecuted her since with his desires. He is a king among these savages, being himself a very wolf in man's flesh. We have denied him, but he persists, and this night he announces that he comes for an answer. He offers to save her if she will trust him, but what is the honour of his kind? He is like a brute out of a cave. It were better for my lady to go to God in the fire than to meet all Hell in his arms. But this night we must choose, unless you prove a saviour."

"Did you see my boat anchor in the bay?" Vernon asked, though he already knew the answer.

"But no," she said. "We live only on the landward side of the House. My lady told me that God would send a man to our aid. And I bade Mitri fetch him."

The door was unlocked and the three climbed a staircase which seemed to follow the wall of a round tower. Presently they came into a stone hall with curious hangings like the old banners in a church. From the open flame of the lantern another was kindled, and the light showed a desolate place with crumbling mosaics on the floor and plaster dropping from the cornices. Through another corridor they went, where the air blew warmer and there was that indefinable scent which comes from human habitation. Then came a door which the woman held open for Vernon to enter. "Wait there, Monsieur," she said. "My mistress will come to you."

It was his own room, where annually he had waited with a fluttering heart since he was a child at Severns. A fire of wood—some resinous thing like juniper—burned on the hearth, and spirals of blue smoke escaped the stone chimney and filled the air with their pungent fragrance. On a Spanish cabinet stood an antique silver lamp, and there was a great blue Chinese vase filled with spring flowers. Soft Turcoman rugs covered the wooden floor—Vernon noted every detail, for never before had he been able to see his room clearly. A woman had lived here, for an embroidery frame lay on a table and there were silken cushions on the low divans. And facing him in the other wall there was a door.

In the old days he had regarded it with vague terror in his soul. Now he looked at it with the hungry gladness with which a traveller sees again the familiar objects of home. The hour of his destiny had struck. The thing for which he had trained himself in body and spirit was about to reveal itself in that doorway. . . .

It opened, and a girl entered. She was tall and very slim, and moved with the free grace of a boy. She trod the floor like one walking in spring meadows. Her little head on the flowerlike neck was bent sideways as if she were listening, and her eyes had the strange disquieting innocence of a child's. Yet she was a grown woman, nobly made, and lithe and supple as Artemis herself when she ranged with her maidens through the moonlit glades. Her face had the delicate pallor of pure health, and above it the masses of dark hair were bound with a thin gold circlet. She wore a gown of some soft white stuff, and had thrown over it a cloak of russet furs.

For a second—or so it seemed to Vernon—she looked at him as he stood tense and expectant like a runner at the start. Then the hesitation fled from her face. She ran to him with the confidence of a child who has waited long for the coming of a friend and has grown lonely and fearful. She gave him both her hands and in her tall pride looked him full in the eyes. "You have come," she sighed happily. "I did not doubt it. They told me there was no help, but, you see, they did not know about you. That was my own secret. The Monster had nearly gobbled me, Perseus, but of course you could not come quicker. And now you will take me away with you? See, I am ready. And Elise will come too, and old Mitri, for they could not live without me. We must hurry, for the Monster is very near."

In that high moment of romance, when young love had burst upon him like spring, Vernon retained his odd discipline of soul. The adventure of the dream could not be satisfied by flight, even though his companion was a goddess.

"We will go, Andromeda, but not yet. I have something to say to the Monster."

She broke into a ripple of laughter. "Yes, that is the better way. Mitri will admit him alone, and he will think to find us women. But you will be here and you will speak to him." Then her eyes grew solemn. "He is very cruel, Perseus, and he is full of evil. He may devour us both. Let us be gone before he comes."

It was Vernon's turn to laugh. At the moment no enterprise seemed too formidable, and a price must be paid for this far-away princess. And even as he laughed the noise of a great bell clanged throughout the house.

Mitri stole in with a scared face, and it was from Vernon that he took his orders. "Speak them fair, but let one man enter and no more. Bring him here, and see that the gate is barred behind him. After that make ready for the road." Then to the girl: "Take off your cloak and wait here as if you were expecting him. I will stand behind the screen. Have no fear, for I will have him covered, and I will shoot him like a dog if he lays a finger on you."

From the shelter of the screen Vernon saw the door open and a man enter. He was a big fellow of the common mountain type, gorgeously dressed in a uniform of white and crimson, with boots of yellow untanned leather, and a beltful of weapons. He was handsome in a coarse way, but his slanting eyes and the heavy lips scarcely hidden by the curling moustaches were ugly and sinister. He smiled, showing his white teeth, and spoke hurriedly in the guttural Greek of the north. The girl shivered at the sound of his voice, and to the watcher it seemed like Pan pursuing one of Dian's nymphs.

"You have no choice, my Queen," he was saying. "I have a hundred men at the gate who will do my bidding, and protect you against those fools of villagers till you are safe with me at Louko. But if you refuse me I cannot hold the people. They will burn the place over your head, and by to-morrow's morn these walls will be smouldering ashes with your fair body in the midst of them."

Then his wooing became rougher. The satyr awoke in his passionate eyes. "Nay, you are mine, whether you will it or not. I and my folk will carry you off when the trouble begins. Take your choice, my girl, whether you will go with a good grace, or trussed up behind a servant. We have rough ways in the hills with ungracious wenches."

"I am going away," she whispered, "but not with you!"

The man laughed. "Have you fetched down friend Michael and his angels to help you? By Saint John the Hunter, I would I had a rival. I would carve him prettily for the sake of your sweet flesh."

Vernon kicked aside the screen. "You will have your chance," he said. "I am ready."

Vlastos stepped back with his hand at his belt. "Who in the devil's name are you?" he asked.

"One who would dispute the lady with you," said Vernon.

The man had recovered his confidence. "I know nothing of you or whence you come, but to-night I am merciful. I give you ten seconds to disappear. If not, I will spit you, my fine cock, and you will roast in this oven."

"Nevertheless the lady goes with me," said Vernon, smiling.

Vlastos plucked a whistle from his belt, but before it reached his mouth he was looking into the barrel of Vernon's revolver. "Pitch that thing on the floor," came the command. "Not there! Behind me! Off with that belt and give it to the lady. Quick, my friend."

The dancing grey eyes dominated the sombre black ones. Vlastos flung down the whistle, and slowly removed the belt with its silver-mounted pistols and its brace of knives.

"Put up your weapon," he muttered, "and fight me for her, as a man should."

"I ask nothing better," said Vernon, and he laid his revolver in the girl's lap.

He had expected a fight with fists, and was not prepared for what followed. Vlastos sprang at him like a wild beast and clasped him round the waist. He was swung off his feet in a grip that seemed more than human. For a second or two he swayed to and fro, recovered himself, and by a back-heel stroke forced his assailant to relax a little. Then, locked together in the middle of the room, the struggle began. Dimly out of a corner of his eye he saw the girl pick up the silver lamp and stand by the door holding it high.

Vernon had learned the rudiments of wrestling among the dalesmen of the North, but now he was dealing with one who followed no ordinary methods. It was a contest of sheer physical power. Vlastos was a stone or two heavier, and had an uncommon length of arm; but he was clumsily made, and flabby from gross living. Vernon was spare and hard and clean, but he lacked one advantage—he had never striven with a man save in friendly games, and the other was bred to kill. For a minute or two they swayed and stumbled, while Vernon strove for the old Westmorland "inside click." Every second brought him nearer to it, while the other's face was pressed close to his shoulder.

Suddenly he felt a sharp pain. Teeth met in his flesh, and there was the jar and shiver of a torn muscle. The thing sickened him, and his grip slackened. In a moment Vlastos had swung him over in a strangle-hold, and had his neck bent almost to breaking.

On the sickness followed a revulsion of fierce anger. He was contending not with a man, but with some shaggy beast from the thicket. The passion brought out the extra power which is dormant in us all against the last extremity. Two years before he had been mauled by a leopard on the Congo, and had clutched its throat with his hand and torn the life out. Such and no other was his antagonist. He was fighting with one who knew no code, and would gouge his eyes if he got the chance. The fear which had sickened him was driven out by fury. This wolf should go the way of other wolves who dared to strive with man.

By a mighty effort he got his right arm free, and though his own neck was in torture, he forced Vlastos' chin upward. It was a struggle of sheer endurance, till with a snarl the other slackened his pressure. Vernon slipped from his grasp, gave back a step, and then leaped for the under-grip. He seemed possessed with unholy strength, for the barrel of the man gave in his embrace. A rib cracked, and as they swayed to the breast-stroke, he felt the breath of his opponent coming in harsh gasps. It was the end, for with a twist which unlocked his arms he swung him high, and hurled him towards the fireplace. The head crashed on the stone hearth, and the man lay stunned among the blue jets of wood-smoke.

Vernon turned dizzily to the girl. She stood, statue-like, with the lamp in her hand, and beside her huddled Mitri and Elise.

"Bring ropes," he cried to the servants. "We will truss up this beast. The other wolves will find him and learn a lesson." He bound his legs and arms and laid him on a divan.

The fire of battle was still in his eyes, but it faded when they fell upon the pale girl. A great pity and tenderness filled him. She swayed to his arms, and her head dropped on his shoulder. He picked her up like a child, and followed the servants to the sea-stair.

But first he found Vlastos' whistle, and blew it shrilly. The answer was a furious hammering at the castle door.

Far out at sea, in the small hours, the yacht sped eastward with a favouring wind. Behind in the vault of night at a great distance shone a point of brightness, which flickered and fell as if from some mighty fire.

The two sat in the stern in that first rapture of comradeship which has no words to fit it. Her head lay in the crook of his arm, and she sighed happily, like one awakened to a summer's dawn from a night of ill dreams. At last he spoke.

"Do you know that I have been looking for you for twenty years?"

She nestled closer to him.

"And I," she said, "have been waiting on you from the beginning of the world."

The Bell of St. Sépulcre

M. P. Shiel

It was during my tramp through Provence three summers ago that I came one evening to Leburn-les-Bruyères, a hamlet near the bottom of the Bezons valley. Here I found the inn so poor, that I resolved to tramp on to Cargnac, four miles off.

"But," said an old vigneron, whom I asked to put me on the path through the forest, "you should go round about by the road."

"Why?" I asked him—"that means another kilomètre?"

"We of these parts hardly use the path now," was his answer: "don't you go that way"—with a certain earnestness and admonition . . .

"What, wolves about here?" I asked him.

He lowered his voice to say: "You may see someone named La Mère Gouvion"—as if to say "you may see Beelzebub."

I supposed that he meant a ghost, and, as I knew something of Southern superstitiousness, and was in a hurry, I handed him a franc, and went on by the forest-path.

I found it in some parts choked with bush—myrtle, kermes-oak—which I had to part before me; and by the moonshine above the bush I saw in that short distance two of those mounds named barrows, placed there by "the fairies"; then, when I had tramped three kilomètres through a rather intolerable solitude, the shock came: three metres to my left within a sort of clearing I saw the woman . . .

She was seated on a fragment of one of those rocks that they call "menhirs."

I had the impression in the hazy moonshine that she was moving her shoulders slowly from side to side, her hand supporting her jaw, some grace in the fall of her rags suggesting a statue set on a pedestal. Her stature, I could see, was gigantic—her great arms like clubs, her great bosom and spread of shoulder, her mouth open in a cavern of darkness that looked oblong, her hair black-and-grey, a tangle of snakes; and, as I walked past, her eyes followed me with that kind of gaze with which an ox stops cropping to gaze after a passer.

The image of this woman filled my mind until I got to Cargnac, near nine; and that same night, while sitting in an inn-garden with swings, nine-pins, arbours, I was told by my host the story of "La Mère Gouvion."

"She came," he told me, "of a well-to-do family who owned land on the far side of Lebrun-les-Bruyères, her father being a mighty big man, known as a hard bargainer as far as Avignon and Orange, and in Lebrun everybody feared him, even the cure, for it was said that he did not believe in the good God, he drank half a litre of cognac every night, so that one could hear him marching up and down his verandah to a late hour, quarrelling with nobody, and carrying on; terrible he was when the drink had him, like a man mad with sun-stroke.

"And one summer, when the phylloxera had rotted his vine-leaves, and things were looking bad for harvest, on an awful night long remembered he raised his hand, defied the heavens to do their worst, and challenged the bell of St. Sépulcre to ring in his hearing—for the bell was said to be a little audible from his yard.

"His wife ran to hide under a bed, dreading the bell-toll, his daughter Maude herself trembled. Some had it to say that the bell did ring in his hearing; however that was, he perished shortly afterwards in convulsions, and was buried without the blessing of the Church.

"Soon after him his good woman also passed away: and Maude Gouvion was left mistress of all.

"And now things began to look alive indeed. If the patch of yellowish moss appeared on all the vine leaves of the parish, Maude Gouvion's trellises were still green."

Maude's spray and pruning-scissors should, no doubt, have accounted for this prosperity, but there were those who thought of black magic when the mulberry-disease and the failure of the madder-crop, which were the cry all round, seemed to keep clear of her fields.

"The truth was that her man roiled for her with the consciousness of her hard eyes behind them, for she was more masterful than any man; and, moreover, she covered her land with a new-fangled sort of sandy stuff from Marseilles, so that, the next vintage, sixty barrels of light wine rolled off in her cart to Avignon, as against le père Gouvion's maximum of fifty-three.

"Meanwhile, no one could stand the sight of her passions, if anything went wrong, as when she threw big Huguénin, the blacksmith, down some stairs for laming a mule in shoeing. In Lebrun-les-Bruyères the cure called 'Silence!' at anyone who mentioned her name. She had not once been inside the church door since her father's death."

But one Sunday morning, she being then thirty-five, Maude, to everyone's astonishment, turned up in the little church in the valley. "Never," said my landlord, "was seen such finery, rings and ribbons, though Maude was ordinarily slatternly in dress;

and she carried her head high, as though the church was not good enough for her feet, while the cure stammered and changed color.

"And why do you think she did this? It was as a preliminary to coming out as a married woman, for she was about to marry the little Tombarel, the shoemaker, as was soon known. And there was a great whispering and excitement then, for everyone knew that no one would have wished to marry Maude, rich as she was, a woman whose own father, as report said, had heard the bell: so that Maude must have fixed upon the little Tombarel for her own reasons, and done her own wooing."

"But which bell is it," I asked, "that you keep speaking of?"

He looked astonished. "Well, I should have thought that even a stranger . . . I mean—do I not?—the bell of St. Sépulcre."

"What does this bell do?" I asked him.

"It is a sound which one should not hear," he answered, with a frown. "It is believed to bring—well, I could not tell you—evil upon chose who hear it."

He was silent. Then: "But talking of this poor little Tombarel, everyone pitied him. It is said that, on his taking a pair of sabots to the presbytère, the priest admonished him to trust to the saints for protection from the Evil One; and, in saying this, he was supposed to throw a scone at Maude Gouvion. A week before the civil marriage Tombarel ran away to Cazalès, but Maude followed him, and, it was said, knocked him down with a box; so they came back together, and were married.

"Soon afterwards Maude gave birth to her son Pierre. As for the poor Tombarel, he did not survive his marriage three months.

"This Pierre grew up a sickly, pale lad; but the uglier everybody thought him, the prouder his mother was of him. He was everything to her—she went foolish with love only to look at him.

"He was a cripple, with disease of the hip-joint, and three times a week for years his mother took him over to La Risolette to be seen to. When the doctor told her that the child could not possibly live, she only laughed, and said the man was a fool who did not know his business. And live it did.

"But Pierre had a mental disease as well—his crazy craving for blood: for to sling a pebble from a catapult into the eye of a pig was his delight. At thirteen he was the death of a little girl, and later on was discovered with a cut that he had made in his own neck. His mother slung him to her shoulder that day, with that square opening of the mouth which was her way in her agitations, and ran to La Risolette with the dead weight, not waiting for a cart. It was the feat of a horse."

Such, then, was Pierre. The children shrank from contact with him, and it got to be a prophecy in the village that the day would come when the bell of St. Sépulcre would sound upon the ears of Maude Gouvion's son.

"But," said mine host, in a *patois* whose quaintness I despair of quite conveying, "whatever he did, if he stuck a calf, or half killed a child, or lay down all day fuddled by the roadside, his mother still laughed and petted him: this only made her love him the more proudly and the more loudly. She was foolish with her love."

"Pierre," he went on, "was sweet on Rosalie Tissot, granddaughter of Tissot, the schoolmaster, the prettiest goldenhaired fairy that ever was, engaged to be married to Martin Dejoie, who was a carpenter at La Risolette. Pierre lay in wait for her everywhere, with a patience which was strange for him; but she laughed at his shrunken form, with a derision in which there was ever more terror than laughter, knowing how cruelly he loved her, hardly knowing perhaps what a peril lay in her laughter.

"When the date of her marriage with Martin Dejoie came near, Pierre went and threw himself at his mother's knees in a room where she sat shelling peas, saying to her: 'Mother, I hall go and kill myself, for I am the laughing-stock of the place because I am not like others, and, if I do not have Rosalie, they will laugh at me the more.' Now, his mother's heart was like a harp to him, he knew that to tell her of the folks' laughing was to lash her into a scratching cat, and, 'Wait, Pierre,' says she now over her pease, quite quietly: 'wait, my son; you shall marry this girl.'

"That same night when the village was asleep Mother Gouvion wrapped her head up, and came down upon Tissot's cottage near the church, Tissot nearly dropping dead with fright when he hobbled from bed in his red-wool nightcap and saw her standing there, so big that she had to bend her body to get in. Well, she offered everything for Rosalie—eight thousand francs in the Crédit at Avignon, the olives, the two presses, the stock and plant—all should be Pierre's and Rosalie's: and meantime the old Tissot sat shivering, hands on knees, not knowing what to say.

"At last he stammers that Rosalie would not consent, since her marriage with Martin Dejoie was a marriage of love. 'Rosalie is only a child,' says la Mère Gouvion; 'leave her to me.' 'Well, well,' says Tissot.

"So Mother Gouvion returned home satisfied. If only matters had rested there! But she had hardly gone when Tissot woke up his grandson, and sent him with a note to tell Martin Dejoie to be sure to come over to Lebrun the next morning. So Martin Dejoie came; but, on coming, he put his head in at the school-door, the children saw him, and two hours later Mother Gouvion knew all about that meeting. The two men had a confabulation together, Tissot declaring that the only way was for Martin to carry off Rosalie secretly to Avignon the night before the ten days' notice was up, and marry her there. But it was no secret in the village that three of the days were already gone, and the silly old man did not stop to consider that Mother Gouvion would surely know when the ten days would expire. As a matter of fact, she had no sooner heard of that interview between Tissot and Dejoie than she knew perfectly well what bad been settled. It is said in Lebrun-les-Bruyères that she sent a message that same evening to Dejoie, asking him to come and talk the matter over with her, but that Dejoie would not even receive the message. If this is true, it was the last attempt made by la Mère Gouvion to change Dejoie's mind in his scheme to outwit her."

At eleven, then, in the night preceding that tenth day of notice, Martin Dejoie, a tall active chap, was crossing the moor between La Risolette and Lebrun-les-Bruyères, the moor on which stands St. Sépulcre. He was coming to meet Rosalie, who, with Tissot's old *gouvernante*, was waiting for him in a cart behind the presbytère-wood, to be off with him to Avignon; and he was taking the shortest road to her, though people coming from La Risolette to Lebrun usually make a détour to avoid the moor, so desolate is its barren expanse, on which grows only vine-stumps and some lavender-shrubs, with here or there a miasmatic "clair" (pool), or a cypress standing out blighted against the sky, or a gang of those black rocks, having hollows, that the Provencals call "cagnards." Over all north-west winds draw along volumes of a white dust, wide-winged, there being often mistral over the moor when the valleys lie tranquil.

At one part of this Dead Sea Border of Provence stands, where it has stood since the time of the Franks, the ruins of St. Sépulcre, choked now with brambles, hiding behind a strange rankness of vegetation. But the belfry remains broken, and, they say, the bell-rope, and the bell.

I will not delay to tell you the ancient tale of bale which gave to this bell its awesomeness among all those glens: but for the poor wretch who hears its tone life is practically over heart fails and brain—this throughout a district of skeptical France extending from beyond Lebrun-les-Bruyères quite on I believe, to Hudin: the hearer of the bell is accursed; what he sets about shall fail, and shall rebound with tribulation upon his head; if he be not instantly struck down, his life will still be poisoned; the air will hurt him; water will burn him; his blessedness will be in death.

On the night when Martin Dejoie started out for Rosalie from La Risolette the mist on the moor was luminous with moonlight, and only a little wind moved: so that Mother Gouvion could see some distance from the church-step, where she stood hidden within the mass of sarsaparilla and kermesoaks that choked the church-portal. "For many years no foot had ventured so near St. Sépulcre as hers this night, and she drank brandy from a vial to keep her defiance bright in her brain—all that I am telling you now being only what la Mère Gouvion herself revealed long afterwards, and every word's true. She had groped to see if the bell-rope was still there, intending, if not, to drag herself up like a cat to get at the bell; but the rope was there, still pretty strong, though rotted—she could see a little by the rays of moonlight that came through the ruins; and now she stood peering between the bushes at the footpath over the moor, waiting for Martin Dejoie to appear: for she understood that, with such a business in hand, he would not make a detour round St. Pierre, but would come over the moor.

"At last, near eleven, a sound of someone whistling reached her, for Martin did not like to be passing so near the bell, so was whistling to himself for company; and at once Mother Gouvion set to work, first plugging up her ears with cotton-wool, and over this a bandage, her plan being to make the bell clang, yet not hear it herself. Her only trouble was the doubt whether the man coming was Martin. Suppose it was Pierre himself? Pierre sometimes crossed the moor at night; Pierre whistled. But it was all right—it was Martin—she saw that, when he had got opposite. He stopped his whistling then, bent his head, crossed his breast—in the vigour of his life—a young man just going to be married—suddenly dang, dang, clang for him . . .

"On her face she lay watching him where he had dropped against one of the cagnards; then she stole away home, elated, thinking in herself, 'I didn't hear the bell-sound! I didn't hear it!'

"Well, Rosalie and Tissot waited in vain for Martin Dejoie that night; it was not till five days later that his body was found at the bottom of that ravine north of the moor that is called 'Le Dé du Diablo.' Whether he rumbled down there in his distraction, or dashed himself down in his despair, is not known, but he was believed to have heard the bell; and it was years before anyone supposed that his death was not owing to an act of God.

"And so la Mère Gouvion kept her word; and Rosalie in a few months was married to Pierre.

"But," said my host, in his Doric patois, "it was never a good thing for la Mère Gouvion that she did what she had done. Rosalie was the worst wife that Pierre could have had, for she was so winning and sweet, and he loved her so much, that for months at a time he was a changed lad: and the result was this, that there would ensue reactions, during which the white face of that little lame man became a fright in the valley, he going about like a dog with the hydrophobia his eyes alight. Once he stabbed his mother in the arm, and sometimes had to be watched lest he should stab himself. And so it went on near five years.

"And they had misfortunes in the vineyard, too. There came three bad years, when even L'Hermitage and La Nerte and the big vintages of Provence came to nothing; and the fourth year la Mère Gouvion's madder-yield was a gone hope before May; and she had to sign a paper with the agent at Cargnac which almost compromised the shelter over her head. So she was not very happy in her mischief-doing, after all.

"But she adored her 'petit,' her 'little one,' never less, gloried in secret over the deed she had done for him; and when he made himself a terror she hugged herself, preferring terror to laughing-stock. 'They won't grin with their ugly gums at my petit, my little one, now,' she'd say.

"And one bitter winter's night all came to an end . . .

"Pierre had broken loose again; screams reached even to the village from the Gouvion vineyard; and presently a girl came running down to the presbytère, saying that Rosalie would be killed. Heaven knows what really happened, for Rosalie was never seen again, so it is supposed that Pierre must have killed her, and that la Mère Gouvion did away with her body somehow; but no body was ever discovered, so that all that part of the business remains a mystery. Mother Gouvion, who raved out a great deal of what I am saying now during her brief imprisonment afterwards, never said anything about this matter.

"However, when the curé hears this, he begins to pray, than saddles his mule, and gallops off through the gale for Avignon. Before midnight a body of *sergents* arrive at the vineyard; they search for Pierre; Pierre cannot be found. La Mère Gouvion, sewing, with her mouth opened square, tells them that she does not know where he has gone to."

A wild night—I have seen three such in Provence—lightnings that terrify, a very deluge of water, tempest from the north calling to whirlwind from the west: a Southern storm . . . Mother Gouvion dashed out into it the moment she found herself free of the *sergents*—forgot her uncovered head, but remembered to take every sou she possessed. She had arranged to meet Pierre out on the moor, the only safe meeting-place, intending, it seems, to take, or send, him to the coast, to get him aboard a ship—nothing would be impossible to her. The officers, it was true, were scouring the valley on horseback with lanterns; but they were nothing; she would outwit them . . .

But when, on reaching the moor, she ran to the agreed *cagnard*, Pierre was not in it; to the next—Pierre not there; and with distracted runs she dashed from *cagnard* to *cagnard*. Her heart misgave her now, her glance questioned the heavens—they were black enough; and, stumbling about within a tempest of hair, a pillar of seaweed that stumbles, she lifted her voice: "*Pierre*!"—wayward boy of her heart: where, then, was he?

And another terror struck her—the bell . . . it was believed to bleat some midnights when storms were abroad on the moor . . . "But not to-night!"—and, as she said this, a vaster tantrum of the tempest terrorized her. She stumbled and was down in the mud; a prayer broke from her.

A night of climaxes of wind: and in the midst of each the woman beseeching, coaxing: "Any other night, not to-night; it would not be right; would be hard on a poor mother's heart"—for hours, till the gale began to abate, and the danger ended.

It was only toward morning, when, though the darkness was as black as ever, the storm had lulled and her dreads of the bell were at rest, it was then that, all at once—she heard it. Not a clamorous clang, clang, this time, as when she had rung it for Martin Dejoie, but one toll only, floating out doleful on the breast of the trembling air.

It was over, then? No hope? Suddenly the woman threw up her head, gnashed, shook her fist, as her father before her had done, at the bell, at the heavens. "Blast away bell . . . !" Bells were nothing: she would discover her little one as soon as there was a little light—would tear him from the clutch of the *sergents*: it would be all right yet . . .

"On setting out once more to search, she found herself just in front of the church, and, as some sheet-lightning was playing then, she chanced to observe the mark of a man's foot before the church-portal. At this she started, chilled to the marrow by a sense of the supernatural: for it was not to be believed that any living being would have come so near the bell on a night so wild. Under her breath she uttered 'Martin Dejoie?' . . . for what power had rung the bell in her hearing? it had not been the wind!

"Just then a tramp of horses' hoofs reached her ears—the *sergents* still ransacking the countryside for Pierre; and she ran into the bush at the church-door, lest they might spy her in the play of the lightning. Five years before she had stood just there—and done a thing. And now her flesh shivered to see the sarsaparilla freshly trampled, the branches parted: someone had entered St. Sépulcre that night! and at the thought of the vengeance of the murdered dead her heart turned faint."

But some fascination led her steps over the threshold, and she stood in the still thicker gloom within, hearing the rasping of her own throat, hearing the gallop of a heart thumping out the whole gamut of fright, pride, desperation; till, all at once, a blaze of lightning searched the church, and by it was revealed to her the reason why the bell had rung: it was because someone had tied the bell-rope round his throat, kicked away a stone, and hanged himself there. He hung still now: and eye to eye they looked—mother and son.

They found her the next morning wandering on the moor, harmless and listless, with a slanting smile; and they took her to the asylum at Avignon where, after many weeks, something resembling reason returned to her. When they had gathered her story from her mutterings, they let her out again; but she would not go home, took up her abode in woods, etc., sleeping in *cagnards*, living on olives, nuts, fruits. Her favourite haunt (if she still lives) is the "menhir" by the abandoned path between Lebrun-les-Bruyères and Cargnac.

The Black Cat

William J. Wintle

If there was one animal that Sydney disliked more than another it was a cat. Not that he was not fond of animals in a general way—for he had a distinct affection for an aged retriever that had formerly been his—but somehow a cat seemed to arouse all that was worst in him. It always appeared to him that if he had passed through some previous stage of existence, he must have been a mouse or a bird and thus have inherited—so to speak—an instinctive dread and hatred for the enemy of his earlier days.

The presence of a cat affected him in a very curious fashion. There was first of all a kind of repulsion. The idea of the eyes of the animal being fixed on him; the thought of listening for a soundless tread; and the imagined touch of the smooth fur: all this made him shudder and shrink back. But this feeling quickly gave place to a still stranger fascination. He felt drawn to the creature that he feared—much as a bird is supposed, but quite erroneously, to be charmed by a snake. He wanted to stroke the animal and to feel its head rubbing against his hand: and yet at the same time the idea of the animal doing so filled him with a dread passing description. It was something like that morbid state in which a person finds actual physical pleasure in inflicting pain on himself. And then there was sheer undisguised fear. Pretend as he might Sydney was in deadly fear when a cat was in the room. He had tried and tried, time and again, to overcome it; but without success. He had argued from the well-known friendliness of the domestic cat; from its notorious timidity; and from its actual inability to do any very serious harm to a strong and active man. But it was all of no use. He was afraid of cats and it was useless to deny it.

At the same time, Sydney was no enemy to cats. He was the last man in the world to hurt one. No matter how much his slumber might be disturbed by the vocal efforts of a love-sick marauder on the roof in the small hours of the morning, he would never think of hurling a missile at the offender. The sight of a half-starved cat left behind when its owner was away in the holiday season filled him with a pity near akin to pain. He was a generous subscriber to the Home for Lost Cats. In fact, his whole attitude was inconsistent and contradictory. But there was no escape from the truth—he disliked and feared cats.

Probably this obsession was to some extent fostered by the fact that Sydney was a man of leisure. With more urgent matters to occupy his thoughts, he might have outgrown these fancies with the advance of middle age. But the possession of ample means, an inherited dislike for any kind of work calling for energy, and two or three interesting hobbies which filled up his time in an easy and soothing fashion, left him free to indulge his fancies. And fancies, when indulged, are apt to become one's masters in the end; and so it proved with Sydney.

He was engaged in writing a book on some phase of Egyptian life in the olden days, which involved considerable study of the collections in the British Museum and elsewhere, as well as much search for rare books among the antiquarian bookshops. When not out on these pursuits, he occupied an old house which like most old and rambling places of its kind was the subject of various queer stories among the gossips of the neighbourhood. Some tragedy was supposed to have happened there at some date not defined, and in consequence something was supposed to haunt the place and to do something from time to time. Among local gossips there was much value in that nebulous term "Something," for it covered a multitude of inaccurate recollections and of foggy traditions. Probably Sydney had never heard the reputation of his house, for he led a retired life and had little to do with the neighbours. But if the tales had reached his ears, he gave no sign; nor was he likely to do so. Apart from the cat obsession, he was a man of eminently balanced mind. He was about the last person to imagine things or to be influenced by any but proved facts.

The mystery which surrounded his untimely end came therefore as a great surprise to his friends: and the horror that hung over his later days was only brought to partial light by the discovery of a diary and other papers which have provided the material for this history. Much still remains obscure, and cannot now be cleared up; for the only man who could perhaps throw further light on it is no longer with us. So we have to be content with such fragmentary records as are available.

It appears that some months before the end, Sydney was at home reading in the garden, when his eye happened to rest upon a small heap of earth that the gardener had left beside the path. There was nothing remarkable about this; but somehow the heap seemed to fascinate him. He resumed his reading; but the heap of earth was insistent in demanding his attention. He could not keep his thoughts off it, and it was hard to keep his eyes off it as well. Sydney was not the man to give way to mental dissipation of this kind, and he resolutely kept his eyes fixed on his book. But it was a struggle; and in the end he gave in. Be looked again at the heap; and this time with some curiosity as to the cause of so absurd an attraction.

Apparently there was no cause; and he smiled at the absurdity of the thing. Then he started up suddenly, for he saw the reason of it. The heap of earth was exactly like a black cat! And the cat was crouching as if to spring at him. The resemblance was really absurd, for there were a couple of yellow pebbles just where the eyes should have been. For the moment, Sydney felt all the repulsion and fear that the presence of an actual cat would have caused him. Then he rose from his chair, and kicked the heap out of any resemblance to his feline aversion. He sat down again and laughed at the absurdity of the affair—and yet it somehow left a sense of disquiet and of vague fear behind. He did not altogether like it.

It must have been about a fortnight later when he was inspecting some Egyptian antiquities that had recently reached the hands of a London dealer. Most of them were of the usual types and did not interest him. But a few were better worth attention; and he sat down to examine them carefully. He was specially attracted by some ivory tablets, on which he thought he could faintly trace the remains of handwriting. If so, this was a distinct find, for private memoranda of this sort are very rare and should throw light on some of the more intimate details of private life of the period, which are not usually recorded on the monuments. Absorbed in this study, a sense of undefined horror slowly grew upon him and he found himself in a kind of day dream presenting many of the uncanny qualities of nightmare. He thought himself stroking an immense black cat which grew and grew until it assumed gigantic proportions. Its soft fur thickened around his hands and entwined itself around his fingers like a mass of silky, living snakes; and his skin tingled with multitudinous tiny bites from fangs which were venomous; while the purring of the creature grew until it became a very roar like that of a cataract and overwhelmed all his senses. He was mentally drowning in a sea of impending catastrophe, when, by an expiring effort, he wrenched himself free from the obsession and sprang up. Then he discovered that his hand had been mechanically stroking a small unopened animal mummy, which proved on closer examination to be that of a cat.

The next incident that he seems to have thought worth recording happened a few nights later. He had retired to rest in his usual health and slept soundly. But towards morning his slumbers were disturbed by a dream that recalled the kind of nocturnal fear that is common in childhood. Two distant stars began to grow in size and brilliancy until he saw that they were advancing through space towards him with incredible speed. In a few moments they must overwhelm him in a sea of fire and flame. Onwards they came, bulging and unfolding like great flaming flowers, growing more dazzling and blinding at every moment; and then, just as they were upon him, they suddenly turned into two enormous cat's eyes, flaming green and yellow. He sprang up in bed with a cry, and found himself at once wide awake. And there on the window-sill lay a great black cat, glowering at him with lambent yellow eyes. A moment later the cat disappeared.

But the mysterious thing of it was that the window-sill was not accessible to anything that had not wings. There was no means by which a cat could have climbed to it. Nor was there any sign of a cat in the garden below.

The date of the next thing that happened is not clear, for it does not appear to have been recorded at the time. But it would seem to have been within a few days of the curious dream. Sydney had occasion to go to a cupboard which was kept locked. It contained manuscripts and other papers of value; and the key never left his possession. To his knowledge the cupboard had not been opened for at least a month past. He now had occasion to refer to a collection of notes in connection with his favorite study. On opening the cupboard, he was at once struck by a curious odour. It was not exactly musky, but could only be described as an animal odour, slightly suggestive of that of a cat. But what at once arrested Sydney's notice and caused him extreme annoyance was the fact that the papers had been disturbed. The loose papers contained in some pigeon-holes at the back had been drawn forwards into a loose heap on the shelf. They looked for all the world like a nest, for they had been loosely arranged in a round heap with a depression in the middle. It looked as if some animal had coiled itself up to sleep there; and the size of the depression was just such as would be made by a cat.

Sydney was too much annoyed by the disturbance of his papers to be greatly impressed at the moment by their curious arrangement; but it came home to him as a shock when he began to gather the papers together and set them in order. Some of them seemed to be slightly soiled, and on closer examination he found that they were besprinkled with short black hairs like those of a cat.

About a week afterwards he returned later in the evening than usual, after attending a meeting of a scientific society to which he belonged. He was taking his latch key from his pocket to open the door when he thought that something rubbed against his leg. Looking down, he saw nothing; but immediately afterwards he felt it again, and this time he thought he saw a black shadow beside his right foot. On looking more closely, nothing was to be seen; but as he went into the house he distinctly felt something soft brush against his leg. As he paused in the hall to remove his overcoat, he saw a faint shadow which seemed to go up the stairs. It was certainly only a shadow and nothing solid, for the light was good and he saw it clearly. But there was nothing in motion to account for the passing shadow. And the way the shadow moved was curiously suggestive of a cat.

The next notes in the book that Sydney seems to have devoted to this curious subject appear to be a series of mere coincidences: and the fact that he thought them worth recording shows only too clearly to what an extent his mind was now obsessed. He had taken the numerical value of the letters C, A, T, in the alphabet, 3, 1, and 20 respectively, and by adding them together had arrived at the total 24. He then proceeded to note the many ways in which this number had played its part in the events of his life. He was born on the 24th of the month, at a house whose number was 24; and his mother was 24 years old at the time. He was 24 years old when his father died and left him the master of a considerable fortune. That was just 24 years ago. The last time he had balanced his affairs, he found that he was worth in invested funds—apart from land and houses—just about 24 thousand pounds. At three different periods, and in different towns, he had chanced to live at houses numbered 24; and that was also the number of his present abode. Moreover the number of his ticket for the British Museum Reading Room ended with 24, and both his doctor and his solicitor were housed under that same persistent number. Several more of these coincidences had been noted by him; but they were rather far-fetched and are not worth recording here. But the memoranda concluded with the ominous question, "Will it all end on the 24th?"

Soon after these notes were written, a much more serious affair had to be placed on record. Sydney was coming downstairs one evening, when he noticed in a badly lighted comer of the staircase something that he took to be a cat. He shrank back with his natural dislike for the animal; but on looking more closely he saw that it was nothing more than a shadow cast by some carving on the stair-head. He turned away with a laugh; but, as he turned, it certainly seemed that the shadow moved! As he went down the stairs he twice stumbled in having to save himself from what he thought was a cat in danger of being trodden upon; and a moment later he seemed to tread on something soft that gave way and threw him down. He fell heavily and shook himself badly.

On picking himself up with the aid of his servant he limped into his library, and there found that his trousers were torn from a little above the ankle. But the curious thing was that there were three parallel vertical tears—just such as might be caused by the claws of a cat. A sharp smarting led to further investigation; and he then found that there were three deep scratches on the side of his leg, exactly corresponding with the tears in the trousers.

In the margin of the page on which he recorded this accident, he has added the words, "This cat means mischief." And the whole tone of the remaining entries and of the few letters that date from this time shows only too clearly that his mental outlook was more or less tinged and obscured by gloomy forebodings.

It would seem to have been on the following day that another disturbing trifle occurred. Sydney's leg still pained him, and he spent the day on a couch with one or two favourite books. Soon after two o'clock in the afternoon, he heard a soft thud, such as might be caused by a cat leaping down from a moderate height. He looked up, and there on the window-sill crouched a black cat with gleaming eyes; and a moment later it sprang into the room. But it never reached the floor—or, if it did, it must have passed through it! He saw it spring; he saw it for the moment in mid-air; he saw it about to alight on the floor; and then—it was not there!

He would have liked to believe that It was a mere optical delusion; but against that theory stood the awkward fact that the cat in springing down from the window knocked over a flower-pot; and there lay the broken pieces in evidence of the fact.

He was now seriously scared. It was bad enough to find himself seeing things that had no objective reality; but it was far worse to be faced by happenings that were certainly real, but not to be accounted for by the ordinary laws of nature. In this case the broken flower-pot showed that if the black cat was merely what we call a ghost for lack of any more convenient term, it was a ghost that was capable of producing physical effects. If it could knock a flower-pot over, it could presumably scratch and bite—and the prospect of being attacked by a cat from some other plane of existence will hardly bear being thought of.

Certainly it seemed that Sydney had now real ground for alarm. The spectre cat—or whatever one likes to call it—was in some way gaining power and was now able to manifest its presence and hostility in more open and practical fashion. That same night saw a proof of this. Sydney dreamed that he was visiting the Zoological Gardens when a black leopard of ferocious aspect escaped from its cage and sprang upon him. He was thrown backwards to the ground and pinned down by the heavy animal. He was half crushed by its weight; its claws were at his throat; its fierce yellow eyes were staring into his face—when the horror of the thing brought the dream to a sudden end and he awoke. As consciousness returned he was aware of an actual weight on his chest; and on opening his eyes be looked straight into the depths of two lambent yellow flames set in a face of velvet black. The cat sprang off the bed and leaped through the window. But the window was closed and there was no sound of breaking glass.

Sydney did not sleep much more that night. But a further shock awaited him on rising. He found some small bloodstains on his pillow; and an inspection before the looking-glass showed the presence of two groups of tiny wounds on his neck. They were little more than pin-pricks; but they were arranged in two semi-circular groups, one on either side of the neck and just such as might be caused by a cat trying to grasp the neck between its two forepaws.

This was the last incident recorded in Sydney's diary; and the serious view that he took of the situation is shown by certain letters that he wrote during the day, giving full instructions to his executors and settling various details of business—evidently in view of his approaching end.

What happened in the course of the final scene of the tragedy we can only guess from the traces left behind: but there is sufficient evidence to show that the horror was an appalling one.

The housekeeper seems to have been awakened once during the night by a strange noise which she could only describe as being like an angry cat snarling; while the parlour maid, whose room was immediately above that occupied by Sydney, says that she dreamt that she heard her master scream horribly once or twice.

In the morning, Sydney did not answer when called at his usual hour; and, as the door was found to be locked, the housekeeper presently procured assistance and had it broken open. He was found crouching on the floor and leaning against the wall opposite the window. The carpet was saturated with blood; and the cause was quickly evident. The unfortunate man's throat had been torn open on either side, both jugular veins being severed. So far as could be made out, be had retired to bed and had been attacked during sleep, for the sheets were bespattered with blood. He had apparently got out of bed in his struggles to overcome the Thing that had him fast in its fearful grip. The look of horror on his distorted face was said by the witnesses to be past description.

Both window and door were fastened, and there was nothing to show how the assailant entered. But there was something to show how it left. The bloodstains on the floor recorded the footprints of a gigantic cat. They led across the floor from the corpse to the opposite wall—and there they ceased. The cat never came back; but whether it passed through the solid wall or melted into thin air, no one knows. In some mysterious way it came and went; and in passing it did this deed of horror.

It was a curious coincidence that the tragedy took place on Christmas Eve—the 24th day of the month!

The Bold Dragoon, or, The Adventure of My Grandfather

Washington Irving

My grandfather was a bold dragoon, for it's a profession, d'ye see, that has run in the family. All my forefathers have been dragoons and died upon the field of honor except myself, and I hope my posterity may be able to say the same; however, I don't mean to be vainglorious. Well, my grandfather, as I said, was a bold dragoon, and had served in the Low Countries. In fact, he was one of that very army, which, according to my uncle Toby, "swore so terribly in Flanders." He could swear a good stick himself; and, moreover, was the very man that introduced the doctrine Corporal Trim mentions, of radical heat and radical moisture; or, in other words, the mode of keeping out the damps of ditch water by burnt brandy. Be that as it may, it's nothing to the purport of my story. I only tell it to show you that my grandfather was a man not easily to be humbugged. He had seen service; or, according to his own phrase, "he had seen the devil"—and that's saying every thing.

Well, gentlemen, my grandfather was on his way to England, for which he intended to embark at Ostend;—bad luck to the place for one where I was kept by storms and head winds for three long days, and the divil of a jolly companion or pretty face to comfort me. Well, as I was saying, my grandfather was on his way to England, or rather to Ostend—no matter which, it's all the same. So one evening, towards nightfall, he rode jollily into Bruges. Very like you all know Bruges, gentlemen, a queer, old-fashioned Flemish town, once they say a great place for trade and money-making, in old times, when the Mynheers were in their glory; but almost as large and as empty as an Irishman's pocket at the present day. Well, gentlemen, it was the time of the annual fair. All Bruges was crowded; and the canals swarmed with Dutch boats, and the streets swarmed with Dutch merchants; and there was hardly any getting along for goods, wares, and merchandises, and peasants in big breeches, and women in half a score of petticoats.

My grandfather rode jollily along in his easy, slashing way, for he was a saucy, sunshiny fellow—staring about him at the motley crowd, and the old houses with gable ends to the street and storks' nests on the chimneys; winking at the ya vrouws who showed their faces at the windows, and joking the women right and left in the street; all of whom laughed and took it in amazing good part; for though he did not know a word of their language, yet he always had a knack of making himself understood among the women.

Well, gentlemen, it being the time of the annual fair, all the town was crowded; every inn and tavern full, and my grandfather applied in vain from one to the other for admittance. At length he rode up to an old rackety inn that looked ready to fall to pieces, and which all the rats would have run away from, if they could have found room in any other house to put their heads. It was just such a queer building as you see in Dutch pictures, with a tall roof that reached up into the clouds; and as many garrets, one over the other, as the seven heavens of Mahomet. Nothing had saved it from tumbling down but a stork's nest on the chimney, which always brings good luck to a house in the Low Countries; and at the very time of my grandfather's arrival, there were two of these long-legged birds of grace, standing like ghosts on the chimney top. Faith, but they've kept the house on its legs to this very day; for you may see it any time you pass through Bruges, as it stands there yet; only it is turned into a brewery—a brewery of strong Flemish beer; at least it was so when I came that way after the battle of Waterloo.

My grandfather eyed the house curiously as he approached. It might not altogether have struck his fancy, had he not seen in large letters over the door,

HEER VERKOOPT MAN GOEDEN DRANK

My grandfather had learnt enough of the language to know that the sign promised good liquor. "This is the house for me," said he, stopping short before the door.

The sudden appearance of a dashing dragoon was an event in an old inn, frequented only by the peaceful sons of traffic. A rich burgher of Antwerp, a stately ample man, in a broad Flemish hat, and who was the great man and great patron of the establishment, sat smoking a clean long pipe on one side of the door; a fat little distiller of Geneva from Schiedam, sat smoking on the other, and the bottle-nosed host stood in the door, and the comely hostess, in crimped cap, beside him; and the hostess' daughter, a plump Flanders lass, with long gold pendants in her ears, was at a side window.

"Humph!" said the rich burgher of Antwerp, with a sulky glance at the stranger.

"Der duyvel!" said the fat little distiller of Schiedam.

The landlord saw with the quick glance of a publican that the new guest was not at all, at all, to the taste of the old ones; and to tell the truth, he did not himself like my grandfather's saucy eye.

He shook his head—"Not a garret in the house but was full."

"Not a garret!" echoed the landlady.

"Not a garret!" echoed the daughter.

The burgher of Antwerp and the little distiller of Schiedam continued to smoke their pipes sullenly, eyed the enemy askance from under their broad hats, but said nothing.

My grandfather was not a man to be browbeaten. He threw the reins on his horse's neck, cocked his hat on one side, stuck one arm akimbo—

"Faith and troth!" said he, "but I'll sleep in this house this very night!"

As he said this he gave a slap on his thigh, by way of emphasis—the slap went to the landlady's heart.

He followed up the vow by jumping off his horse, and making his way past the staring Mynheers into the public room. May be you've been in the barroom of an old Flemish inn—faith, but a handsome chamber it was as you'd wish to see; with a brick floor, a great fire-place, with the whole Bible history in glazed tiles; and then the mantel-piece, pitching itself head foremost out of the wall, with a whole regiment of cracked tea-pots and earthen jugs paraded on it; not to mention half a dozen great Delft platters hung about the room by way of pictures; and the little bar in one corner, and the bouncing bar-maid inside of it with a red calico cap and yellow ear-drops.

My grandfather snapped his fingers over his head, as he cast an eye round the room: "Faith, this is the very house I've been looking after," said he.

There was some farther show of resistance on the part of the garrison, but my grandfather was an old soldier, and an Irishman to boot, and not easily repulsed, especially after he had got into the fortress. So he blarney'd the landlord, kissed the landlord's wife, tickled the landlord's daughter, chucked the bar-maid under the chin; and it was agreed on all hands that it would be a thousand pities, and a burning shame into the bargain, to turn such a bold dragoon into the streets. So they laid their heads together, that is to say, my grandfather and the landlady, and it was at length agreed to accommodate him with an old chamber that had for some time been shut up.

"Some say it's haunted!" whispered the landlord's daughter, "but you're a bold dragoon, and I dare say you don't fear ghosts."

"The divil a bit!" said my grandfather, pinching her plump cheek; "but if I should be troubled by ghosts, I've been to the Red Sea in my time, and have a pleasant way of laying them, my darling!"

And then he whispered something to the girl which made her laugh, and give him a good-humored box on the ear. In short, there was nobody knew better how to make his way among the petticoats than my grandfather.

In a little while, as was his usual way, he took complete possession of the house: swaggering all over it;—into the stable to look after his horse; into the kitchen to look after his supper. He had something to say or do with every one; smoked with the Dutchmen; drank with the Germans; slapped the men on the shoulders, tickled the women under the ribs:—never since the days of Ally Croaker had such a rattling blade been seen. The landlord stared at him with astonishment; the landlord's daughter hung her head and giggled whenever he came near; and as he turned his back and swaggered along, his tight jacket setting off his broad shoulders and plump buckskins, and his long sword trailing by his side, the maids whispered to one another—"What a proper man!"

At supper my grandfather took command of the table d'hôte as though he had been at home; helped everybody, not forgetting himself; talked with every one, whether he understood their language or not; and made his way into the intimacy of the rich burgher of Antwerp, who had never been known to be sociable with any one during his life. In fact, he revolutionized the whole establishment, and gave it such a rouse, that the very house reeled with it. He outsat every one at table excepting the little fat distiller of Schiedam, who had sat soaking for a long time before he broke forth; but when he did, he was a very devil incarnate. He took a violent affection for my grandfather; so they sat drinking, and smoking, and telling stories, and singing Dutch and Irish songs, without understanding a word each other said, until the little Hollander was fairly swampt with his own gin and water, and carried off to bed, whooping and hiccuping, and trolling the burthen of a Low Dutch love song.

Well, gentlemen, my grandfather was shown to his quarters, up a huge Staircase composed of loads of hewn timber; and through long rigmarole passages, hung with blackened paintings of fruit, and fish, and game, and country frollics, and huge kitchens, and portly burgomasters, such as you see about old-fashioned Flemish inns, till at length he arrived at his room.

An old-times chamber it was, sure enough, and crowded with all kinds of trumpery. It looked like an infirmary for decayed and superannuated furniture; where everything diseased and disabled was sent to nurse, or to be forgotten. Or rather, it might have been taken for a general congress of old legitimate moveables, where every kind and country had a representative. No two chairs were alike: such high backs and low backs, and leather bottoms and worsted bottoms, and straw bottoms, and no bottoms; and cracked marble tables with curiously carved legs, holding balls in their claws, as though they were going to play at nine pins.

My grandfather made a bow to the motley assemblage as he entered, and having undressed himself, placed his light in the fire-place, asking pardon of the tongs, which seemed to be making love to the shovel in the chimney corner, and whispering soft nonsense in its ear.

The rest of the guests were by this time sound asleep; for your Mynheers are huge sleepers. The house maids, one by one, crept up yawning to their attics, and not a female head in the inn was laid on a pillow that night without dreaming of the Bold Dragoon.

My grandfather, for his part, got into bed, and drew over him one of those great bags of down, under which they smother a man in the Low Countries; and there he lay, melting between, two feather beds, like an anchovy sandwich between two slices of toast and butter. He was a warm-complexioned man, and this smothering played the very deuce with him. So, sure enough, in a little while it seemed as if a legion of imps were twitching at him and all the blood in his veins was in fever heat.

He lay still, however, until all the house was quiet, excepting the snoring of the Mynheers from the different chambers; who answered one another in all kinds of tones and cadences, like so many bull-frogs in a swamp. The quieter the house became, the more unquiet became my grandfather. He waxed warmer and warmer, until at length the bed became too hot to hold him.

"May be the maid had warmed it too much?" said the curious gentleman, inquiringly.

"I rather think the contrary," replied the Irishman. "But be that as it may, it grew too hot for my grandfather."

"Faith there's no standing this any longer," says he; so he jumped out of bed and went strolling about the house.

"What for?" said the inquisitive gentleman.

"Why, to cool himself to be sure," replied the other, "or perhaps to find a more comfortable bed—or perhaps—but no matter what he went for—he never mentioned; and there's no use in taking up our time in conjecturing."

Well, my grandfather had been for some time absent from his room, and was returning, perfectly cool, when just as he reached the door he heard a strange noise within. He paused and listened. It seemed as if some one was trying to hum a tune in defiance of the asthma. He recollected the report of the room's being haunted; but he was no believer in ghosts. So he pushed the door gently ajar, and peeped in.

Egad, gentlemen, there was a gambol carrying on within enough to have astonished St. Anthony.

By the light of the fire he saw a pale weazen-faced fellow in a long flannel gown and a tall white night-cap with a tassel to it, who sat by the fire, with a bellows under his arm by way of bagpipe, from which he forced the asthmatical music that had bothered my grandfather. As he played, too, he kept twitching about with a thousand queer contortions; nodding his head and bobbing about his tasselled night-cap.

My grandfather thought this very odd, and mighty presumptuous, and was about to demand what business he had to play his wind instruments in another gentleman's quarters, when a new cause of astonishment met his eye. From the opposite side of the room a long-backed, bandy-legged chair, covered with leather, and studded all over in a coxcomical fashion with little brass nails, got suddenly into motion; thrust out first a claw foot, then a crooked arm, and at length, making a leg, slided gracefully up to an easy chair, of tarnished brocade, with a hole in its bottom, and led it gallantly out in a ghostly minuet about the floor.

The musician now played fiercer and fiercer, and bobbed his head and his night-cap about like mad. By degrees the dancing mania seemed to seize upon all the other pieces of furniture. The antique, long-bodied chairs paired off in couples and led down a country dance; a three-legged stool danced a hornpipe, though horribly puzzled by its supernumerary leg; while the amorous tongs seized the shovel round the waist, and whirled it about the room in a German waltz. In short, all the moveables got in motion, capering about; pirouetting, hands across, right and left, like so many devils, all except a great clothes-press, which kept curtseying and curtseying, like a dowager, in one corner, in exquisite time to the music;—being either too corpulent to dance, or perhaps at a loss for a partner.

My grandfather concluded the latter to be the reason; so, being, like a true Irishman, devoted to the sex, and at all times ready for a frolick, he bounced into the room, calling to the musician to strike up "Paddy O'Rafferty," capered up to the clothes-press and seized upon two handles to lead her out:—When, whirr!—the whole revel was at an end. The chairs, tables, tongs, and shovel slunk in an instant as quietly into their places as if nothing had happened; and the musician vanished up the chimney, leaving the bellows behind him in his hurry. My grandfather found himself seated in the middle of the floor, with the clothes-press sprawling before him, and the two handles jerked off and in his hands.

"Then after all, this was a mere dream!" said the inquisitive gentleman.

"The divil a bit of a dream!" replied the Irishman: "there never was a truer fact in this world. Faith, I should have liked to see any man tell my grandfather it was a dream."

Well, gentlemen, as the clothes-press was a mighty heavy body, and my grandfather likewise, particularly in rear, you may easily suppose two such heavy bodies coming to the ground would make a bit of a noise. Faith, the old mansion shook as though it had mistaken it for an earthquake. The whole garrison was alarmed. The landlord, who slept just below, hurried up with a candle to inquire the cause, but with all his haste his daughter had hurried to the scene of uproar before him. The landlord was followed by the landlady, who was followed by the bouncing bar-maid, who was followed by the simpering chambermaids all holding together, as well as they could, such garments as they had first lain hands on; but all in a terrible hurry to see what the devil was to pay in the chamber of the bold dragoon.

My grandfather related the marvellous scene he had witnessed, and the prostrate clothes-press, and the broken handles, bore testimony to the fact. There was no contesting such evidence; particularly with a lad of my grandfather's complexion, who seemed able to make good every word either with sword or shillelah. So the landlord scratched his head and looked silly, as he was apt to do when puzzled. The landlady scratched—no, she did not scratch her head,—but she knit her brow, and did not seem half pleased with the explanation. But the landlady's daughter corroborated it by recollecting that the last person who had dwelt in that chamber was a famous juggler who had died of St. Vitus's dance, and no doubt had infected all the furniture.

This set all things to rights, particularly when the chambermaids declared that they had all witnessed strange carryings on in that room;—and as they declared this "upon their honors," there could not remain a doubt upon the subject.

The Brazen Cross

H. B. Marriott-Watson

I laughed at her vivacious display of fear, and went a space further into the wood. I called to her, but she stood irresponsive on the white road. I retraced my way to the verge of the open, and took hold of her hand.

"Come," I said, "this superstition is ridiculous. You have gone this path many a time; it is the shortest track to the village."

"It is Christmas Eve," she returned with a nervous shiver.

"What of that?" I answered lightly. "A wood is all one at Christmas or midsummer."

She shook her head, but I could see she was plainly yielding to my persuasion.

"It was an ancient place of burial," she said, "where are still the disfigured bones of those that lived before Christ."

"Every foot of green earth covers some decay," I said. "Come; the white road takes a tedious circuit into the valley."

"They say," she went on, and a thin tremble ran in her voice—"they say that evil spirits take possession of this place on this night. They must vanish with the midnight bells for a twelvemonth; on Christmas Eve alone are they abroad."

"I see," I answered, laughing; "it is their protest against a Saviour. But come; for the wind is rising, and a gale is growing on the moor."

Her eyes shifted fearfully as she regarded me, and her skirts were fluttering in the fern. As she stood thus silent, there entered into my heart that fierce desire of her which had so long been beating about my soul. I snatched her hand, and, bending to her, held that wondering gaze with mine. A still peace stole into her face; the warm blood trembled in her fingers; I knew her for my captive, as she knew me for hers. We were thus for some short seconds, and then a sigh, as it were the distant voice of some encaged spirit, escaped her lips; and my own mind followed the course of her thoughts. I loosened my grasp of her hand, but ere it fell from me a thrill started through her body, and the fingers closed upon mine with a little convulsive catch. In an instant an ecstasy had taken me, and she was swaying in my arms, passive and unafraid. The supreme delight of that moment touches me even now to the very quick of my being. I strained her to me, my voice murmuring words of endearment. She withdrew herself from me, watching my eyes with a troubled gaze.

"You will marry in this New Year," she said earnestly. "It is laid upon you. What would she think? You have your honour. You have been mad, and you have infected me with madness. It is the evil spirits of this field"; and she shuddered.

"I will be no slave to a preposterous notion of honour," I cried. "Is a man bound from his childhood? What our fathers have declared to us—shall we take that upon the mere statement? I have lived as a fool—"

"But you shall die as a man of honour," she broke in upon my fervour.

"Rather," said I, "as a man of taste." I took her into my arms again, and her reluctant body yielded to my strenuous passion.

"Remember," she murmured. "Ah, remember."

"There is nothing irreparable," I answered. "All will wear a gay face in a week. She cares nothing for me; and I, even at this hour, have seen the folly of obedience. Your love has turned the stream of my life from a smooth and narrow channel. That is all. Better the contentment of two hearts than of a very giddy vanity."

She made no sign, but it seemed to me that she surrendered herself to my pleading.

"We will take the track through the wood?" I said, caressing her.

"Yes," she whispered faintly.

The grey clouds were flying in troops over the moon, and the wind clapped boisterously about our ears as we passed into the shelter of the pines. Over the moor, which stretched solitary to the black hills, it scudded and romped towards the back parts of the valley; and as I turned upon the very threshold of the wood it seemed as though the plain was in the possession of many roystering tenants—so much of stir and motion was visible among the bracken and the gorse. On the outset of the forest the straight columns of the firs were creaking, but the inner recesses lay hushed and dark, secluded in a shelving bottom. I think that the noises of the fierce wind, which blew with an icy breath, had restored to her a sense of security; for though we might not now be heard without shouting, she clung restfully to my arm, and the short snatches of light that blinked through the flying clouds revealed a soft and happy smile moving on her face. As for myself, I had now my world, and was become its veritable captain. The wood roared in our ears; we slipped from the embrace of the gale, and dropped down into the silent close which had been the ancient sepulchre of ancient peoples. And here a great change befell. In the quiet of that place I could hear the wind howling on the moor, and the sound of our footsteps struck harshly on the stillness. I had scant room but for the one burning thought; yet for a moment the strangeness of this unspeakable stillness flashed through my mind, and I perceived with an ignoble joy that her old fears were recurring to her. She will press closer to me, I thought; and was filled with an extravagant delight of her touch. Suddenly, and when we were about the heart of the thicket, little noises got up among the dead leaves, and a thin whistling in the skeleton branches. She clutched me in a quick terror, and I soothed her gently.

"It is nothing, my love," I said; "the wind has broken into the valley."

"It is the graves," she gasped. "The spirits are come out."

She turned her face aslant towards the growing noises, which appeared to creep along the ground; the dead leaves hissed and slithered. Her body bent across me, and her arms went round my neck; but she held her eyes towards that crawling noise.

"Sweetheart," I said, "be brave."

But on that instant a rushing fury filled the air, and a great wind tore through the trees; vacancy shrieked and moaned at us; and the gabble of a thousand voices mocked us in the branches. In my sight was nothing save the stirless wood and the empty sky; in my ears were outrageous sounds innumerable. At the first outset of these strange presences she gave a low cry and tightened upon me; and then a flash swept over my eyes, and in that second her arms were ript from my neck, and with a long wail of fear she fled down the deep paths and vanished with the noises into the wood.

When I returned to the full possession of my wits I drew myself together and sped after her. The way she had taken led over a heavy slope, down which I was plunged into an infernal blackness where the underwood rose thick and sheer upon all sides. Informed with a pricking dread I called to her at the top of my voice, and clamours awoke in the gully; but I could see no sign of her, and the copse was now as empty and as silent as a churchyard under the moon. In this desperate mood I ran along the track, crying to the night without response, and presently burst out upon the meadows that lay at the back of the village. Here, too, all was silent, though the wrack was racing in the sky, and the frosty lights twinkled in the distant cottages. I had stood irresolute and fearful for some minutes, the subject of a rising horror, when there was a sudden crackle of branches, and I saw her fleeting upon me out of the dense brushwood. The apparition was so abrupt that I momentarily started aback, but, as quickly recovering, rushed to meet her with a thrill of gladness. She made a weird figure in her flight; her hair streaming at her back, her dress disordered on her bosom, her hands clenching in the air. She would have swung by me in her panic, had

I not arrested her with my arm. She stayed, panting and wide-orbed, gazing at me with a distraught look, as it were of exultation.

"Sweetheart," I said, "you have been very foolish to allow this terror," and made to take her in my arms.

She broke into laughter, murmurous and sweet, staring at me still from between her unblinking lids. The thought that came to me then was fraught with unspeakable horror, and I watched her in awe. The eyes shone spectrally on mine; the lips parted, as it seemed, in a mocking smile; and the dishevelled hair was curving and heaving in ragged waves on her head. Her face was the face of a maenad aflame. "My heart," I said, all agitation, "be mine, be mine again. In the name of God," I cried, "close those eyes and come to me! Remember, we have been in love's land this night."

"I remember," she answered, and her voice rang shrilly in the air, "that this night we have been with the dead."

She threw herself back, and laughed, and I saw the tresses jigging on her head, screwing and whirling like the snakes in the head of a Medusa. Her laughter shook her, and, breaking from me she danced over the meadows into the night. And then I knew that the vulgar superstition of this place was true, and that the devils of the immemorial graveyard had crept into her hair and were gnawing at her brain.

That Christmas Day was a time of doubt and agony to me. I had no word of her whom I loved, and from her who was to be my wife came many weary messages. Impatiently between the thought of both I stood in the balance, unable to resolve my mind. My course had seemed plain before—plain and troublesome; to disengage myself from an arduous contract was clearer wisdom than to go shuffling through an unlovely marriage.

But now I could be sure of nothing, for she that had divorced me from my duty was in the possession of an Evil so gross as to withhold her humanity from her. And as the week wore on towards the New Year I was in no better case. Everywhere I heard of the visitation that had fallen upon her family, and all the countryside had pity on her. All day, I heard, she would keep the house, singing (they whispered) profane and hideous catches, the anxious care of her parents; but at nights, when the stars were full, she was abroad, riotous and mad, in the copses. The thought was too grievous for me, and I haunted the park at moonrise to get some more certain knowledge of her. On these excursions I saw her once, and the sight was pitiful and abhorrent. It was not that her awful tenants had robbed her of her beauty; that was unchanged—nay, rather raised to an unnatural glory by her madness. But to see her flying wildly through the trees, her large and mocking eyes sparkling under the stars, and the devils jigging in her hair, took me with such a sense of horror that I fled, ashamed and sick. She dangled an arm to me as she flashed past, tossing up her face and screaming at the sky. Thereafter I had no hope of her, but, schooling myself to the straight lines of duty, began with a poor heart to prepare against my wedding.

It was on the first day of the New Year that I was finally to resign from my dearest hope and open a fresh and uninspiring life with my cold bride. The thing had got thus far, and must reach the end. It was a bright, white morning (for the snow had fallen betimes) when I entered the little church, dumb to the fate arranged for me. As the service proceeded, the pitiable pretence, both of her and of myself, grew well-nigh intolerable, and I think never marriage has been imposed upon such indifferent auditors. But within a little of the end, and while we were yet upon the precincts of the altar, there came a sharp sound from the lower part of the church, and turning swiftly I perceived *her* coming up the aisle. She moved slowly, as though each step were made against an invisible resistance; her hair was twisting and coiling on her bare head; her wintry eyes were fastened upon me. I gave a short cry, but she took no notice, merely gazing from her wild and struggling eyes as she dragged herself towards the chancel. The church rose in a mutter of fear. I made a step to her. But at the chancel rails, and where the great Brazen Cross uplifts itself below the oriel windows, she fell suddenly to her knees. I watched her face. The devils jigged in her hair; it stirred gently, and then flowed soft and rich about her neck; a shudder rushed through her; she hid her face in her hands. And when she raised it again, and her eyes sought mine, they were filled with a quiet smile of love, dewy with tears, and desolate with a sad and hopeless pain.

Brent's Folly

Marjorie Bowen

They said each Brent had his folly, a horse, a woman, a building, an idea, but the present Brent outshone his ancestors by the blatant coarseness of his particular caprice.

When his father had seriously encumbered the estates to build on another wing with a massive ballroom that accorded ill with the Tudor Manor house, the county had remarked that the historic folly of the Brents had passed the limits of the picturesque and romantic and become very like stupidity.

The next Brent, however, excelled the foolish action of his father, for his folly took the form of flesh and blood; to make a mistake about a woman, said the county, was worse than to make a mistake about a building, though there were some cynics who declared that the latter error was worse because the woman passed with her generation and was easily forgotten, whereas the stone and brick remained a lasting annoyance till someone had the courage, time, and money to remove it.

But while she was there, certainly the woman was the greater cause for marvel, the greater shame to the good taste and intelligence of the Brents.

If she had been outrageous, impossible, an actress, a foreigner, a milkmaid, it might have been a folly forgiven and even admired.

If she had been ugly and very rich, or beautiful and very poor, it would have been a thing condoned—an action with at least a motive, some reason to explain the extravagance, the departure from the usual which was more or less expected of the Brents.

But here there was nothing of wonderful, nothing of romantic—nothing to make people startle and stare.

She was the younger daughter of a dull, middle-class family of correct education and morals, neither plain nor pretty, with bad health and a lethargic temperament, and most dismal dull in company.

She excelled in nothing, her taste was of the worst, she could not manage her servants nor her acquaintances, she was jealous and sullen and entirely indifferent to all that makes the fire and color of life.

And she was five years older than her husband, and after many years of marriage was still childless.

And this was the folly of the last Brent, Sir Roger, handsome, accomplished, brilliant, wealthy.

People asked each other what hidden motive had induced him to offer all to this woman who could not even appreciate what he gave.

Of all the follies of the Brents this was the most inexplicable.

If she had been only wicked, the thing might have been understood, if she had shown the least sign of any of the arts and graces of an enchantress he would have stood excused.

But she was neutral, she was nothing, she had not a single charm that would have induced an ordinary man to choose her for the love of a season, and instead Roger Brent had chosen her for his wife—this was what was neither understood nor forgiven.

The county disapproved and showed its disapproval; Sir Roger lost many friends; he became a gloomy self-absorbed man, withdrawn slightly from his fellows.

He rarely left Brent Manor; he was a good landlord, a good neighbour, a fine figure among the country gentry—if it had not been for his marriage.

But that had ruined all; Sir Roger at forty was considered as a man with no longer any possibilities before him; he would live and die the squire of Brent Manor, nothing more.

For, like damp ashes on fire, his wife seemed to have choked and stifled all that was eager, ambitious and ardent in Sir Roger; he had sacrificed to this nullity all that a man could sacrifice to beauty and worth.

When Charles Denton, who had known and envied Sir Roger in the days of their common youth, returned to England from Spain, where he had been fulfilling honourable and profitable duties for His Majesty's Government, he heard from several the story of the folly of the last of the Brents.

The last of the Brents and the last of the follies it appeared, since there was no one of the name to carry on the family and the family traditions.

Denton was sorry; he had almost loved Sir Roger, they had been constantly together until Denton's foreign appointment had separated them.

He wrote to Sir Roger and asked if he might spend some of his leave at Brent Manor; Sir Roger responded cordially, and Denton went down to Brent with a little ache of regret at his heart for the fate of his friend.

He found him as much changed as the reports in London had led him to believe he would be, and despite his preparation he was shocked, almost startled.

Sir Roger, for whom "brilliant" had always seemed the most fitting epithet, had become almost dull; he was silent, almost shy, even with the old friend whom he had seemed so glad to welcome.

His clothes were of an ancient pattern, he was listless in his manner, the unpowdered hair was plentifully sprinkled with grey, the handsome face hard and lined.

The Manor house, too, seemed ill-kept and gloomy.

Denton had an impression of gloom from all his surroundings.

At supper he saw the lady of the house. She was neatly dressed in a gay sacque; her manner was dull and civil.

Denton eyed her in vain for a single merit; her figure was ill-shaped and slightly stooping, her hands and feet were large, her complexion was of an ugly pallor, her features soft and heavy, eyes and hair of a colorless brown, her movements without meaning, her words without grace.

Denton inwardly sighed and the supper hour passed heavily.

She left them early and Denton, spurred by a deep impulse, turned swiftly to his host and asked:

"Why did you marry her?"

Sir Roger was sitting in a dejected attitude with his head a little lowered.

As his friend spoke he looked up, and a smile touched his sombre features.

"You are the first who has had the courage to demand that question," he responded.

"Or the bad taste," apologized Denton.

Sir Roger shrugged his shoulders.

"The others were silent and stayed away, you speak and come," he said.

Denton was indignant for his friend.

"Why should they stay away? The lady is well enough."

"She blights," said Sir Roger decisively.

Denton wondered that such a mediocrity should have that power—but it was what he had heard in London.

"A woman," he replied, "can keep in a woman's place—why should she interfere with your friends?"

Sir Roger smiled again.

"She is so dull, she deadens, so stupid she frightens, so unlovely she depresses."

"And yet you married her!"

"Yes, I married her."

"Why, Roger, why?"

"You wonder?"

"Who would not wonder, you who had everything, might have married a Princess, you might have had the best of life—instead—"

"This!" finished Sir Roger.

"There must be a reason."

"You think so?"

"Assuredly."

"Would you like to hear it?"

"Certainly—I came here to hear it," smiled Denton.

Sir Roger for a while was silent; he was turning over the incidents of his past as one turns the leaves of a long closed book, with wonder and a little sadness at ancient things that once meant so much and now mean so little.

"Is it worth while?" he asked at length.

He rested his elbows on the table and looked rather drearily at his friend.

"What?"

"To tell you—to tell anyone how it happened," replied Sir Roger.

Denton looked with profound compassion at his lined face, his bowed figure, his gray sprinkled hair, his careless dress.

And Brent looked with a dull envy at the neat elegance of his friend, who, powdered, fashionable, alert, seemed indeed to come from another world than that duty circle which comprised the life of Brent Manor.

"Tell me," said Denton quietly.

Sir Roger laughed.

"Tell you why I married Lily Walters?" he asked.

"Yes."

Sir Roger shrugged his shoulders.

"Why not?" he answered.

He turned his eyes, still handsome but lustreless, towards the log fire which flickered in the sculptured chimney place, and his fine hands dropped and clasped slackly on the dark surface of the sombre oak table, where stood the glasses and the fruit and the bottles of old wine.

Then, like one who reads aloud slowly, and with a certain difficulty, he began his strange relation.

"I greatly loved my life. I had everything to make existence pleasant. Health, name, money—wits—you know what I had, my friend."

"Everything."

"Everything. But I wished for more. I had a lust for knowledge, for power, for experience—I wished to reach the limits of every sensation.

"For me there was no wine powerful enough, no woman beautiful enough, no gold bright enough—

"I wished to prove everything—to see everything—to know everything.

"For five years I travelled from one country to another; I had enough money to obtain all my desires.

"I had friends, lovers, horses, houses, ships, I travelled sometimes in a coach and six, sometimes on foot, sometimes I lodged in palaces, sometimes I slept in a ditch. I kissed princesses by the light of a hundred candles, and peasant girls by the dewy light of dawn, I stayed at the most dissolute courts in Italy, and I shut myself for months in the austerity of a Spanish convent.

"I experienced poverty, luxury, every day I gained knowledge.

"I practised in music, poetry, botany, medicine, painting, sculpture, astronomy—I sat at the feet of wise men and drew crude knowledge from the unlettered of all countries.

"Still I was not satisfied.

"My health remained vigorous and my mind restless.

"So far I had not found one woman whom I could not replace, one friend whose company was a necessity, one art or science to which I wished to devote my life.

"Then at The Hague I met a certain Doctor Strass, and under his guidance I began to seriously study alchemy and occultism.

"In this I found at last something that absorbed my whole being.

"Here was the love, the passion that should absorb my life.

"For three years I lived for nothing else. I resolved to find the elixir of life."

Denton moved back out of the candlelight, so that he might more clearly see his friend's face, but Sir Roger was absolutely grave.

He spoke as a man who, with quiet deliberation, relates sober sense.

"The elixir of life," he repeated. "The magic powder that should confer on me eternal youth and eternal enjoyment."

"A strange whim," said Denton quietly. "You who had everything."

"I wished to keep everything," responded Sir Roger, "but more than that even, I wished for power."

"The last temptation of the Devil!" smiled his friend.

"I wished for power," repeated Brent, "but I cannot explain. Enough that the thing took hold of me.

"I lived for that alone. Occult studies absorbed my time and largely my fortune and my health.

"I seemed ever on the verge of a discovery; but I attained nothing."

He paused, and a bitter sadness darkened his sensitive face.

"Nothing," he repeated. "I but underlined the failures of others, but repeated once more the tale of delusion and disappointment.

"But in this I had more strength than some, in that I resolved to cease the fruitless and perilous study that had fascinated my entire soul.

"I determined to free myself from what was becoming an incubus.

"I was frightened by the fate of others whom I saw as half mad, half idiotic old men fumbling with their philtres and muttering over their furnaces; in short, I vowed to free myself from what I at last saw as but a net or device of the devil to draw me away from a useful and enjoyable life.

"With this resolve strong within me I returned to England, and my desire for the normal desires of my former life was increased by the sight of familiar faces and sights.

"I made up my mind to enter politics, and was on the point of taking steps in this direction, when an event occurred which again altered everything."

He paused and pressed the palms of his hands to his brows. Denton was regarding him curiously.

"One day a sober-looking person came to see me. He seemed a doctor or a lawyer of the better sort.

"He was not English; I took him to be a Dutchman or of the Low German nationality—he was habited very neatly and very precise in his speech.

"'I hear,' said he without preamble, 'that you have studied alchemy.'

"'For a while,' said I, 'but I have left that business.'

"Whereat he smiled quietly and drew from his pocket a little box of tortoiseshell like a gentleman's box for snuff, and opening it, he drew out, wrapped in two foldings of scarlet silk, a piece of stone the size of a walnut and the color of amber. 'This is what you have been looking for,' he said calmly; 'this is what the vulgar called the Philosopher's Stone.'

"At these words all the blood went back on my heart, and I begged for a portion with tears in my eyes.

"Whereupon he very comfortably took off a paring with his nail, for the stone was soft like soap, and laid it in the palm of my hand.

"And while I was yet too amazed to speak he left me.

"I had yet with me my retorts and crucibles, and that night I very eagerly tested the portion of the stone on a piece of lead, and when in the morning I poured it forth it was pure rich gold. When this was set I took it round to the jeweller who worked for the court, and asked him what it was, and he told me that it was indeed gold of a finer quality than he had ever handled before.

"I was like a madman, for I had no means of finding my stranger, but that day he came again, and without preamble asked me if I was satisfied, and what I would do to possess the secret which, he declared, had become indifferent to him, as he had passed on to higher studies.

"And he told me about the wonders of this stone, how a few drops of it dissolved in water, if allowed to stand, would leave great rubies and pearls at the bottom, and if taken would confer youth and beauty on him who drank.

"And presently he showed me this experiment, and we sat up all night talking, and in the morning there were the jewels hard and glistening in our hands.

"And then he propounded to me what he would have me do—take some poor mean creature to wife, and with the elixir make her into a goddess."

Brent paused thoughtfully; Denton was still looking at him with intent eyes.

Sir Roger continued:

"I was to marry her first, to show my trust. I was to present her to the town, and afterwards transform her. The idea pleased me beyond words; it was what no man had ever done before.

"I agreed.

"My stranger presented me to Lily Walters. I easily obtained the consent of her family—in brief, I made a match that confounded all my friends.

"My Dutchman was at the church, and afterwards presented me with a packet, which he said contained the recipe for the famous stone.

"Such was my impatience that I opened it in the coach ere we had reached home.

"It was blank paper.

"I left my bride to run to the stranger's lodging, but he had left.

"I never saw him again."

Sir Roger ended abruptly and turned his straight gaze on his friend's serious face.

"And that is why I married Lily Walters," he concluded.

"And the rubies?" asked Denton, quietly.

"She wears them now and then, set in the gold I made with the paring of stone."

Denton was silent.

"I have searched Europe for that man," continued Sir Roger sullenly. "I hope yet to kill him before I die."

"You would be justified," said Denton, easily. He rose and crossed to the fire, still looking covertly and intently at his friend.

Sir Roger muttered to himself a little, and presently fell asleep with his head bowed on his heart.

Denton softly left the room.

He was startled to see Lady Brent waiting in the shadows of the great hall.

"I don't think Sir Roger is very well," said Denton, quietly.

Her plain face quivered and her short-sighted eyes narrowed.

"I always wait up when there is anyone here," she said simply. "I never know what he will do."

They looked at each other.

"He had a strange life before I married him," continued Lady Brent. "He brought me a ruby necklace, and told me it had been made by the Philosopher's Stone."

"Those studies turn a man's brain," said Denton.

"Oh!" answered Lady Brent in her thin ugly voice. "Roger has been mad a long time; no one knows the life I lead with him."

THE BRIDE

ANNA MCCLURE SHOLL

CARLTON HAD NOT SEEN ROBERT ARNOLD SINCE THEIR COLLEGE DAYS, BUT THEY HAD kept up a desultory correspondence, less the result of present sympathy than a tribute to the memory of the youthful enthusiasms they had shared. From Arnold's letters Carlton judged that these enthusiasms had either departed altogether or were in abeyance since he had become part of the fashionable world to which his inherited wealth and gentle birth gave him access. This merging of the poet in the modern man of society seemed to Carlton scarcely a matter of regret, since Arnold in his college days had been over-sensitive, high-strung, and inclined to walk by the light of his dreams. Having adapted himself to this new conception of his old friend, formed partly from his letters and partly from a clever book he had written, Carlton was wholly unprepared for the strange appeal which broke the silence of a year. The letter, the handwriting of which betrayed mental agitation, began abruptly:

"I should like to see you, Carlton, if you can possibly spare me a week out of your busy life. I say a week, since no less time would suffice for the need I have of you at this crisis to explain itself. I have always thought myself a well-balanced man, not given to fancies, but something so astounding has come into my life that I am forced to conclude its reality in the face of reason and judgment. I cannot write you in detail about it. On paper it would seem madness. Wire me that you will come at once. You do not know how much I need you!"

The day after Carlton received this letter he was on his way to Arnold's home, which he had not visited since they were sophomores. It was in a lonely part of the country, six miles from the station of a branch road. Arnold met his guest in the fading dusk, his face, through all its pallor, alight with welcome. The years had added a becoming firmness, verging on severity, to the well-modelled mouth and chin, but the deep blue eyes held their old dreamy look, not unmingled now with some vague suggestion of terror or apprehension.

As they drove through the twilight they talked of college days, of old associations, of things said and done long ago. But Carlton discerned a certain restlessness in Arnold's manner, particularly after they had entered the two-mile driveway which led through the grounds of the estate to the house. He glanced from side to side as if he expected to see some one or something emerge from the park-like shrubbery.

"You are all alone, Arnold?"

"Yes, but I've always been more or less alone. My mother died, you may know, when I was a little chap—my father a year and a half ago. Then I came back to the estate. I never fancied living here in my father's time. He was austere, and there was little sympathy between us. Besides, he liked his solitude—shut up with his books."

"And you have few neighbors?"

"The Whartons to the west, the McDonalds to the east. I am engaged to Miss Isabel Wharton. We—we are to be married—in a fortnight."

He said the words with so much hesitation and restraint that his friend was immediately puzzled. Surely, this engagement could have no connection with his strange letter? Yet—why should a man on the verge of a presumably happy marriage write such a letter? Could there be business difficulties? No, a man would not write mystically of these. Arnold's letter had suggested an overwrought condition, due to grappling with something intangible.

"Then congratulations are in order," Carlton said, with something of Arnold's own hesitation reflected in his voice.

"Save them, Carlton, until I am safely married."

"You see obstacles?"

"A great obstacle—yes. That is why—I sent for you." He paused; then placed his hand impulsively on his old chum's arm. "Could you—would you, stay here till after the wedding?"

"My dear fellow, yes, if it will be of any service to you!"

"Ah, you are still the old Carlton! I'll tell you all after dinner over our cigars."

They dined in state in the fine old-fashioned room, sacred to polished mahogany and ancient silver urns. Across the branched candlesticks and the mass of hot-house roses in the centre of the table, Arnold faced his guest with a look of almost pitiful gladness and temporary content. They talked again of their college days, but the conversation was lacking in logical issues. They were both preoccupied.

"Is it light enough for you?" Arnold said once. "I have a kind of passion for candles, but the electric light could be turned on if you wish."

"I should like for a moment to see clearly that portrait which hangs on the wall just back of your chair. Through the dimness it bears a remarkable likeness to you."

As Carlton said the words, Arnold turned pale, and a look of trouble deepened in his face, but he motioned to the butler, who pressed a button. The portrait flashed from the wall with the vigor and reality of life. It was of a man of about thirty, clad in the fashion of half a century ago. He had the same gallant bearing, and his mouth and chin were very like Arnold's. The eyes were of the same deep blue, but they had an expression which Carlton had never seen in Robert's—a coldness and cruelty that put the spectator at once out of sympathy with the portrait.

"Surely, an ancestor?" was the comment of the guest. He saw the wine-glass tremble in Arnold's hand.

"My grandfather, Robert Arnold. He died before I was born."

"The resemblance between you and the portrait is very striking. It might almost *be* you—except for the eyes."

Arnold's wine-glass went over with a crash. The butler hurried to his side. In the slight confusion which followed, the subject was dropped.

When they went to the library after dinner, a wood fire was burning on the hearth, and the heavy red curtains were drawn before the windows, although it was scarcely past the middle of October. Carlton then remembered that in the long drawing room across the great square hall the curtains were also unlooped and hanging straight.

Arnold did not seem inclined to talk. He smoked in silence, but his visitor discerned in him the same restless apprehension he had exhibited on the drive from the station, and did not attempt commonplaces, his interest in the coming revelation being too keen.

The silence of the house was almost oppressive. Not even the ticking of a clock broke it. Carlton was all the more startled, then, when suddenly against the window-pane behind the curtains of the nearest window there came a sharp tapping, as if some one knocked with bony knuckles on the glass. So imperative was the summons that he instinctively rose to his feet and reached for the curtain, but in the same instant Arnold caught his arm. Carlton turned. Arnold's face was ashen.

"For God's sake, don't look! don't look!" he whispered hoarsely.

"But there is some one there!"

"That is just it—there's some one there!"

Carlton felt himself grow cold. This, then, was why all the curtains were unlooped. Then common-sense asserted itself.

"What does this mean, Arnold?" he said almost sharply. "If there's some one there, we ought to—" He paused, puzzled. Again the rapping came, sharp and clear.

"Thank God, you hear it too," exclaimed the host.

"Of course I hear it."

Carlton stepped to the curtain, but he was again held back by a cry from Arnold, who was sitting in his arm-chair, grasping the arms rigidly.

"Carlton! lock the door!" he said in a strained, intense voice. "Lock the door and keep me in here."

"And keep you in here!"

"She'll conquer. Her will is stronger than mine."

Carlton's brain whirled.

"For God's sake, Arnold, of whom are you talking?"

He looked up piteously.

"Of the woman who knocks."

"Who is she? Where does she live? What is she doing here?"

"She doesn't live. She is dead."

"Are you mad?"

"No, but I soon shall be if this keeps on. Come close to the fire. I am cold. No, wait." He rose and rang a bell. A young man-servant answered.

"James, there have been sounds on the porch as if some one were prowling about the place. Will you go out and search the grounds near the house?"

The man bowed, but cast a puzzled look upon his master.

When they were alone again, Carlton said eagerly:

"Arnold, tell me what this means!"

He drew a long breath, looked from side to side, listened, then began:

"It was last December that I first saw her, when I began regularly to live here. Up to that time I had found the place too lonely, and I had spent my winters in town. Then I met Isabel Wharton, young, beautiful, good," he spoke the words softly as one speaks of the dead. "From that time this place seemed paradise, because she lived here. Our intimacy grew. By the middle of March—last March—our engagement was announced. Carlton, all my dreams came back to me.

"But before the engagement I had seen this—this—woman twice. Twice in the grounds among the trees, a white figure with a long braid of black hair. I wondered what woman was straying through my grounds, and why she was in white in the dead of winter. But she was too far off for me to see her features distinctly. I concluded she must be one of the maids from the house.

"The third time I saw her was the day after my engagement to Miss Wharton. I was coming through the grounds by a by-path. It was a bitter March day, and the snow had an ice-crust. I slipped and slid along over the frozen ground, thinking of Isabel, when she stood before me—this creature—in the middle of the path. I stood quite still myself with a queer horror suddenly icing my veins, for her dark eyes were full of such utter misery and such a baleful appeal. It was all over in a few seconds, but I had time to see a long scar across her deathly white face on the left cheek, and that her eyebrows met. She was in white, and her hair was in a braid over her shoulder.

"I remember stammering out something—asking her if she were lost or ill—then suddenly found myself talking to the air. I looked about. I was alone in the woods. An awful oppression seized me which I wouldn't let deepen into terror; but I felt as I did when a little boy, left alone in the dark, with my father away off in the great library and all the servants gone. I hurried on to the house, trying to believe I had imagined it; but I knew I had not. That night I was sitting alone in the library, making out an itinerary for our wedding-trip. Some one knocked sharply on the window-pane. I drew the curtain. The woman I had seen in the woods was staring at me through the window with that same awful look. I rushed out of doors and around to the porch. There was no one there. The moon was full and it was very light, but not a trace of the creature could I see. In the hall I met the old housekeeper, a woman who was lady's maid in the household when my grandfather was young. When she saw my face she asked me if I were ill. I called her into the library.

"'Hannah,' I said, 'there's a strange woman lingering about the grounds and the house, and I want the servants to find her.' Then I told her what had happened, and I described the woman.

"She grew as white as the snow outside.

"'Heaven have mercy, Master Robert!' she cried.

"'You know the woman?' I asked.

"'You say she has a long scar running from ear to chin across the left cheek?' was Hannah's reply.

"'Yes; do you know her?'

"'And meeting eyebrows, very black?'

"'Yes.'

"'And all in white.'

"'Yes, yes,' I said, impatiently. 'Do you know her?'

"She began to tremble.

"'Do you know this woman? Speak out, Hannah!'

"'God spare us. It's Jane Adams!'

"'Jane Adams?'

"'The woman who was in love with your grandfather. The woman who thought she was married to him. You never knew the story, Master Robert.'

"'But this woman is young.'

"'So was Jane Adams when she died.'

"Then she broke down, and between her frightened sobs she told me the story. She herself was born in the same village with this unfortunate woman, who would have been beautiful had it not been for this scar on the left cheek, the result of an accident in childhood. Despite the disfigurement she was much sought after, for she was of a magnetic and emotional temperament. Not that Hannah described her in these words, but I recognized the type in her homely phrases—and—I myself had seen her. When she was about twenty she attracted the notice of my grandfather, who was then twenty-five years old. He had no intention of marrying her, but she was a good girl, so he went through a mock ceremony with her which she believed was legal; later he deserted her and her child to make a real marriage with an Englishwoman of position.

"The poor girl's people would not believe her story of the marriage, and they turned her out, but there were many who did believe it. After the death of her child she went mad from grief and shame and would wander about this place clothed in white, for she thought she was a bride, and would knock on the windows and peer in looking for my grandfather, but he never came back in her life-time. She died young; and Hannah tells me she is buried not far from here."

Carlton looked at his host in utter astonishment. That he might have been the victim of an hallucination he could believe, but that this hallucination should exactly answer the description of a woman dead before Arnold was born was more than Carlton could accept. Some one, he thought, was lying, or was self deceived. Yet it was plainly evident that Arnold believed in his story; that he was haunted by a horror of some kind.

"Arnold," he said, "supposing this to be true, and not the result of an overwrought state, what did you mean by saying, 'She will conquer!'"

"I mean that I feel the grip of a will stronger than mine—a will which I am resisting with all the force of my nature."

"Still supposing it, wild as it seems, to be true; at least true to you. Why should she want you—you, and not some one else?"

"Can't you see? It is horribly obvious to me, since I learned her story. You, yourself, said at dinner that the likeness between me and the portrait of my grandfather when a young man is almost perfect. People who remember my grandfather say I am his very image. Carlton"—his voice sank to a hoarse whisper—"she thinks I am he!"

Carlton arose and paced the room. "Had they both gone mad together?" he thought.

"Does Miss Wharton know?" he finally asked.

"Yes; and old Hannah is faithful. Isabel hopes that after the marriage all will be well. We shall travel for a year."

"Arnold, could it be imagination?"

"How could I conjure up a woman I'd never heard of—a woman who has been in her grave these fifty years?"

"Has—does the apparition appear often?"

"I won't look."

"You mean—?"

"I mean that I am conscious of some one being near me."

"Have you ever seen her—inside the house?"

"Thank God, no! That would be fatal! You'll not leave me, Carlton, will you, until after the day," he added in a beseeching tone, as if he could not believe his friend's word.

The days went by swiftly, and in their prosaic light the experience of Arnold seemed to Carlton a strange delusion and nothing more. The knocking he did not attempt to explain. He met Isabel Wharton, and found her all that Arnold had said—a woman to bring back to one the dreams and hopes of one's youth. But her brightness was dimmed by an ever-haunting fear. The visitor saw it in her eyes.

"Stay close to him," she said to Carlton one day. "He has told you I have—a rival."

Carlton watched over Arnold as one watches over a sick man. He had shaken off all belief in his friend's fancy, except the belief that it was real to him, when something occurred which sent him, too, for an hour into the place of torment where Arnold dwelt. On the afternoon before the wedding Carlton was sitting alone in the library, reading Erdmann's "History of Philosophy," when he experienced a curious sensation of being watched. He looked up. There, outside the window, almost at his elbow, she stood, the woman of Arnold's horror. If death should masquerade as grief and desperate longing, it would wear her shape. He saw the scar, the meeting brows. Then he struggled to his feet as one oppressed with awful nightmare, and through that nightmare he experienced the dread consciousness that the turning of the woman's head from side to side meant that she was looking for some one else.

Carlton said nothing to Arnold, but to himself he said, "Am I too stricken with the same disease?" The bridegroom, for his part, was boyishly, radiantly happy. He seemed on this, the eve of his wedding day, to have passed already into the sunshine of its release. Carlton breathed at last, freely. No apparition of terror, he thought, could cross the boundary of that happy consciousness.

The friends retired early, and Carlton fell into an uneasy sleep, due less to anxiety for Arnold than to the memory of what he had seen that afternoon. Was it real, or was it a mental projection, the outcome of intense sympathy with his poor friend in his delusion? Carlton was feverish with perplexity. Long after midnight he awoke and tossed about for the space of an hour, then fell into a deep slumber. He was awakened in the broad daylight by a rapping at the door, and when he answered it was opened, and a little old woman, very feeble with extreme age, stood on the threshold. He recognized Hannah, the housekeeper. There was a look of fear and apprehension on her face.

"Is there anything wrong?" he said at once.

"I hope not, sir," she quavered. "But Master Robert's bed has not been slept in, and the night-light was burning yet, when his man went to call him at eight. I've sent the gardeners over the grounds, but they can't find him. If you would help us, sir!"

When Carlton had dressed he went first to Robert's room. They had left the shutters closed, and the night-light burning. He saw that the bed had not been slept in. An arm-chair was drawn up to the table on which the lamp stood. Lying by the lamp was an opened volume, its leaves crushed, as if it had been thrown down in great haste. He saw that it was Spenser's poems, and that it was open at the "Epithalamium." The housekeeper had followed him.

"Have you sent yet to Miss Wharton's?"

"No, sir. We didn't want to alarm her."

"He may be there. I'll drive over."

Carlton knew the moment he saw Isabel Wharton's face that Arnold was not there, and she knew in the same instant why Carlton had come. She stood in the doorway, her face very white against the gloom, very white and still, as if she had known for a long time what the dawn of her wedding day would bring. There was presage of coming horror in the calmness.

"He may have gone for a walk," Carlton said, the words sounding foolish as he spoke them.

"No," she answered quietly. "I think I know where we will find him."

"You know?"

"I fear."

She stood for a moment irresolute; then she said, "Let the groom stay here with the dog-cart. It's a long way around, but across fields it is short. We can walk."

She threw a golf cape over her shoulders and joined Carlton. She had no hat on, and the damp east wind blew stray locks of hair about her face. She went straight across the fields with a seeming certainty of her goal that filled her companion with a nameless horror. They went through a wood, and the air was full of flying leaves. The gray, ragged clouds seemed just beyond the rocking tree-tops. She did not break the silence, and Carlton's own apprehension had passed the bounds of speech.

They had walked about a mile and a half when in the distance Carlton saw a graveyard. Then he knew her goal.

She went directly to a certain deserted quarter of it, where the poorer graves were, but before they came to the one she was seeking, Carlton saw what the end of the quest was to be.

The dead form of Robert Arnold was lying face downward on the damp leaves, with one arm convulsively clasped about a rough, grass-grown mound. The small, rude stone at the head had something carved on it. Bending over, Carlton read the initials "J. A.," and the date, "1850."

The Bus-Conductor

E. F. Benson

My friend, Hugh Grainger, and I had just returned from a two days' visit in the country, where we had been staying in a house of sinister repute which was supposed to be haunted by ghosts of a peculiarly fearsome and truculent sort. The house itself was all that such a house should be, Jacobean and oak-panelled, with long dark passages and high vaulted rooms. It stood, also, very remote, and was encompassed by a wood of sombre pines that muttered and whispered in the dark, and all the time that we were there a south-westerly gale with torrents of scolding rain had prevailed, so that by day and night weird voices moaned and fluted in the chimneys, a company of uneasy spirits held colloquy among the trees, and sudden tattoes and tappings beckoned from the window-panes. But in spite of these surroundings, which were sufficient in themselves, one would almost say, to spontaneously generate occult phenomena, nothing of any description had occurred. I am bound to add, also, that my own state of mind was peculiarly well adapted to receive or even to invent the sights and sounds we had gone to seek, for I was, I confess, during the whole time that we were there, in a state of abject apprehension, and lay awake both nights through hours of terrified unrest, afraid of the dark, yet more afraid of what a lighted candle might show me.

Hugh Grainger, on the evening after our return to town, had dined with me, and after dinner our conversation, as was natural, soon came back to these entrancing topics.

"But why you go ghost-seeking I cannot imagine," he said, "because your teeth were chattering and your eyes starting out of your head all the time you were there, from sheer fright. Or do you like being frightened?"

Hugh, though generally intelligent, is dense in certain ways; this is one of them.

"Why, of course, I like being frightened," I said. "I want to be made to creep and creep and creep. Fear is the most absorbing and luxurious of emotions. One forgets all else if one is afraid."

"Well, the fact that neither of us saw anything," he said, "confirms what I have always believed."

"And what have you always believed?"

"That these phenomena are purely objective, not subjective, and that one's state of mind has nothing to do with the perception that perceives them, nor have circumstances or surroundings anything to do with them either. Look at Osburton. It has had the reputation of being a haunted house for years, and it certainly has all the accessories of one. Look at yourself, too, with all your nerves on edge, afraid to look round or light a candle for fear of seeing something! Surely there was the right man in the right place then, if ghosts are subjective."

He got up and lit a cigarette, and looking at him—Hugh is about six feet high, and as broad as he is long—I felt a retort on my lips, for I could not help my mind going back to a certain period in his life, when, from some cause which, as far as I knew, he had never told anybody, he had become a mere quivering mass of disordered nerves. Oddly enough, at the same moment and for the first time, he began, to speak of it himself.

"You may reply that it was not worth my while to go either," he said, "because I was so clearly the wrong man in the wrong place. But I wasn't. You for all your apprehensions and expectancy have never seen a ghost. But I have, though I am the last person in the world you would have thought likely to do so, and, though my nerves are steady enough again now, it knocked me all to bits."

He sat down again in his chair.

"No doubt you remember my going to bits," he said, "and since I believe that I am sound again now, I should rather like to tell you about it. But before I couldn't; I couldn't speak of it at all to anybody. Yet there ought to have been nothing frightening about it; what I saw was certainly a most useful and friendly ghost. But it came from the shaded side of things; it looked suddenly out of the night and the mystery with which life is surrounded."

"I want first to tell you quite shortly my theory about ghost-seeing," he continued, "and I can explain it best by a simile, an image. Imagine then that you and I and everybody in the world are like people whose eye is directly opposite a little tiny hole in a sheet of cardboard which is continually shifting and revolving and moving about. Back to back with that sheet of cardboard is another, which also, by laws of its own, is in perpetual but independent motion. In it too there is another hole, and when, fortuitously it would seem, these two holes, the one through which we are always looking, and the other in the spiritual plane, come opposite one another, we see through, and then only do the sights and sounds of the spiritual world become visible or audible to us. With most people these holes never come opposite each other during their life. But at the hour of death they do, and then they remain stationary. That, I fancy, is how we 'pass over.'

"Now, in some natures, these holes are comparatively large, and are constantly coming into opposition. Clairvoyants, mediums are like that. But, as far as I knew, I had no clairvoyant or mediumistic powers at all. I therefore am the sort of person who long ago made up his mind that he never would see a ghost. It was, so to speak, an incalculable chance that my minute spy-hole should come into opposition with the other. But it did: and it knocked me out of time."

I had heard some such theory before, and though Hugh put it rather picturesquely, there was nothing in the least convincing or practical about it. It might be so, or again it might not.

"I hope your ghost was more original than your theory," said I, in order to bring him to the point.

"Yes, I think it was. You shall judge." I put on more coal and poked up the fire. Hugh has got, so I have always considered, a great talent for telling stories, and that sense of drama which is so necessary for the narrator. Indeed before now, I have suggested to him that he should take this up as a profession, sit by the fountain in Piccadilly Circus, when times are, as usual, bad, and tell stories to the passers-by in the street, Arabian fashion, for reward. The most part of mankind, I am aware, do not like long stories, but to the few, among whom I number myself, who really like to listen to lengthy accounts of experiences, Hugh is an ideal narrator. I do not care for his theories, or for his similes, but when it comes to facts, to things that happened, I like him to be lengthy.

"Go on, please, and slowly," I said. "Brevity may be the soul of wit, but it is the ruin of storytelling. I want to hear when and where and how it all was, and what you had for lunch and where you had dined and what—"

Hugh began:

"It was the 24th of June, just eighteen months ago," he said. "I had let my flat, you may remember, and came up from the country to stay with you for a week. We had dined alone here—"

I could not help interrupting.

"Did you see the ghost here?" I asked. "In this square little box of a house in a modern street!"

"I was in the house when I saw it."

I hugged myself in silence.

"We had dined alone here in Graeme Street," he said, "and after dinner I went out to some party, and you stopped at home. At dinner your man did not wait, and when I asked where he was, you told me he was ill, and, I thought, changed the subject rather abruptly. You gave me your latch-key when I went out, and on coming back, I found you had gone to bed. There were, however, several letters for me, which required answers. I wrote them there and then, and posted them at the pillar-box opposite. So I suppose it was rather late when I went upstairs.

"You had put me in the front room, on the third floor, overlooking the street, a room which I thought you generally occupied yourself. It was a very hot night, and though there had been a moon when I started to my party, on my return the whole sky was cloud-covered, and it both looked and felt as if we might have a thunderstorm before morning. I was feeling very sleepy and heavy, and it was not till after I had got into bed that I noticed by the shadows of the window-frames on the blind that only one of the windows was open. But it did not seem worth while to get out of bed in order to open it, though I felt rather airless and uncomfortable, and I went to sleep.

"What time it was when I awoke I do not know, but it was certainly not yet dawn, and I never remember being conscious of such an extraordinary stillness as prevailed. There was no sound either of foot-passengers or wheeled traffic; the music of life appeared to be absolutely mute. But now instead of being sleepy and heavy, I felt, though I must have slept an hour or two at most, since it was not yet dawn, perfectly fresh and wide-awake, and the effort which had seemed not worth making before, that of getting out of bed and opening the other window, was quite easy now, and I pulled up the blind, threw it wide open, and leaned out, for somehow I parched and pined for air. Even outside the oppression was very noticeable, and though, as you know, I am not easily given to feel the mental effects of climate, I was aware of an awful creepiness coming over me. I tried to analyse it away, but without success; the past day had been pleasant, I looked forward to another pleasant day to-morrow, and yet I was full of some nameless apprehension. I felt, too, dreadfully lonely in this stillness before the dawn.

"Then I heard suddenly and not very far away the sound of some approaching vehicle; I could distinguish the tread of two horses walking at a slow foot's pace. They were, though yet invisible, coming up the street, and yet this indication of life did not abate that dreadful sense of loneliness which I have spoken of. Also in some dim unformulated way that which was coming seemed to me to have something to do with the cause of my oppression.

"Then the vehicle came into sight. At first I could not distinguish what it was. Then I saw that the horses were black and had long tails, and that what they dragged was made of glass, but had a black frame. It was a hearse. Empty.

"It was moving up this side of the street. It stopped at your door.

"Then the obvious solution struck me. You had said at dinner that your man was ill, and you were, I thought, unwilling to speak more about his illness. No doubt, so I imagined now, he was dead, and for some reason, perhaps because you did not want me to know anything about it, you were having the body removed at night. This, I must tell you, passed through my mind quite instantaneously, and it did not occur to me how unlikely it really was, before the next thing happened.

"I was still leaning out of the window, and I remember also wondering, yet only momentarily, how odd it was that I saw things—or rather the one thing I was looking at—so very distinctly. Of course, there was a moon behind the clouds, but it was curious how every detail of the hearse and the horses was visible. There was only one man, the driver, with it, and the street was otherwise absolutely empty. It was at him I was looking now. I could see every detail of his clothes, but from where I was, so high above him, I could not see his face. He had on grey trousers, brown boots, a black coat buttoned all the way up, and a straw hat. Over his shoulder there was a strap, which seemed to support some sort of little bag. He looked exactly like—well, from my description what did he look exactly like?"

"Why—a bus-conductor," I said instantly.

"So I thought, and even while I was thinking this, he looked up at me. He had a rather long thin face, and on his left cheek there was a mole with a growth of dark hair on it. All this was as distinct as if it had been noonday, and as if I was within a yard of him. But—so instantaneous was all that takes so long in the telling—I had not time to think it strange that the driver of a hearse should be so unfunereally dressed.

"Then he touched his hat to me, and jerked his thumb over his shoulder."

"'Just room for one inside, sir,' he said.

"There was something so odious, so coarse, so unfeeling about this that I instantly drew my head in, pulled the blind down again, and then, for what reason I do not know, turned on the electric light in order to see what time it was. The hands of my watch pointed to half-past eleven.

"It was then for the first time, I think, that a doubt crossed my mind as to the nature of what I had just seen. But I put out the light again, got into bed, and began to think. We had dined; I had gone to a party, I had come back and written letters, had gone to bed and had slept. So how could it be half-past eleven? . . . Or—*what* half-past eleven was it?

"Then another easy solution struck me; my watch must have stopped. But it had not; I could hear it ticking.

"There was stillness and silence again. I expected every moment to hear muffled footsteps on the stairs, footsteps moving slowly and smally under the weight of a heavy burden, but from inside the house there was no sound whatever. Outside, too, there was the same dead silence, while the hearse waited at the door. And the minutes ticked on and ticked on, and at length I began to see a difference in the light in the room, and knew that the dawn was beginning to break outside. But how had it happened then that if the corpse was to be removed at night it had not gone, and that the hearse still waited, when morning was already coming?

"Presently I got out of bed again, and with the sense of strong physical shrinking I went to the window and pulled back the blind. The dawn was coming fast; the whole street was lit by that silver hueless light of morning. But there was no hearse there.

"Once again I looked at my watch. It was just a quarter-past four. But I would swear that not half an hour had passed since it had told me that it was half-past eleven.

"Then a curious double sense, as if I was living in the present and at the same moment had been living in some other time, came over me. It was dawn on June 25th, and the street, as natural, was empty. But a little while ago the driver of a hearse had spoken to me, and it was half-past eleven. What was that driver, to what plane did he belong? And again *what* half-past eleven was it that I had seen recorded on the dial of my watch?

"And then I told myself that the whole thing had been a dream. But if you ask me whether I believed what I told myself, I must confess that I did not.

"Your man did not appear at breakfast next morning, nor did I see him again before I left that afternoon. I think if I had, I should have told you about all this, but it was still possible, you see, that what I had seen was a real hearse, driven by a real driver, for all the ghastly gaiety of the face that had looked up to mine, and the levity of his pointing hand. I might possibly have fallen asleep soon after seeing him, and slumbered through the removal of the body and the departure of the hearse. So I did not speak of it to you."

There was something wonderfully straightforward and prosaic in all this; here were no Jacobean houses oak-panelled and surrounded by weeping pine-trees, and somehow the very absence of suitable surroundings made the story more impressive. But for a moment a doubt assailed me.

"Don't tell me it was all a dream," I said. "I don't know whether it was or not. I can only say that I believe myself to have been wide awake. In any case the rest of the story is—odd."

"I went out of town again that afternoon," he continued, "and I may say that I don't think that even for a moment did I get the haunting sense of what I had seen or dreamed that night out of my mind. It was present to me always as some vision unfulfilled. It was as if some clock had struck the four quarters, and I was still waiting to hear what the hour would be.

"Exactly a month afterwards I was in London again, but only for the day. I arrived at Victoria about eleven, and took the underground to Sloane Square in order to see if you were in town and would give me lunch. It was a baking hot morning, and I intended to take a bus from the King's Road as far as Graeme Street. There was one standing at the corner just as I came out of the station, but I saw that the top was full, and the inside appeared to be full also. Just as I came up to it the conductor who, I suppose, had been inside, collecting fares or what not, came out on to the step within a few feet of me. He wore grey trousers, brown boots, a black coat buttoned, a straw hat, and over his shoulder was a strap on which hung his little machine for punching tickets. I saw his face, too; it was the face of the driver of the hearse, with a mole on the left cheek. Then he spoke to me, jerking his thumb over his shoulder.

" 'Just room for one inside, sir,' he said.

"At that a sort of panic-terror took possession of me, and I knew I gesticulated wildly with my arms, and cried, 'No, no!' But at that moment I was living not in the hour that was then passing, but in that hour which had passed a month ago, when I leaned from the window of your bedroom here just before the dawn broke. At this moment too I knew that my spy-hole had been opposite the spy-hole into the spiritual world. What I had seen there had some significance, now being fulfilled, beyond the significance of the trivial happenings of to-day and to-morrow. The Powers of which we know so little were visibly working before me. And I stood there on the pavement shaking and trembling.

"I was opposite the post-office at the corner, and just as the bus started my eye fell on the clock in the window there. I need not tell you what the time was.

"Perhaps I need not tell you the rest, for you probably conjecture it, since you will not have forgotten what happened at the corner of Sloane Square at the end of

July, the summer before last. The bus pulled out from the pavement into the street in order to get round a van that was standing in front of it. At the moment there came down the King's Road a big motor going at a hideously dangerous pace. It crashed full into the bus, burrowing into it as a gimlet burrows into a board."

He paused.

"And that's my story," he said.

By Word of Mouth

Rudyard Kipling

Not though you die to-night, O Sweet, and wail,
A spectre at my door,
Shall mortal Fear make Love immortal fail—
I shall but love you more,
Who, from Death's house returning, give me still
One moment's comfort in my matchless ill.

Shadow Houses

This tale may be explained by those who know how souls are made, and where the bounds of the Possible are put down, I have lived long enough in this country to know that it is best to know nothing, and can only write the story as it happened.

Dumoise was our Civil Surgeon at Meridki, and we called him "Dormouse," because he was a round little, sleepy little man. He was a good Doctor and never quarrelled with any one, not even with our Deputy Commissioner, who had the manners of a bargee and the tact of a horse. He married a girl as round and as sleepylooking as himself. She was a Miss Hillardyce, daughter of "Squash" Hillardyce of the Berars, who married his Chiefs daughter by mistake. But that is another story.

A honeymoon in India is seldom more than a week long; but there is nothing to hinder a couple from extending it over two or three years. This is a delightful country for married folk who are wrapped up in one another. They can live absolutely alone and without interruption—just as the Dormice did. These two little people retired from the world after their marriage, and were very happy. They were forced, of course, to give occasional dinners, but they made no friends hereby, and the Station went its own way and forgot them; only saying, occasionally, that Dormouse was the best of good fellows, though dull. A Civil Surgeon who never quarrels is a rarety, appreciated as such.

Few people can afford to play Robinson Crusoe anywhere—least of all in India, where we are few in the land, and very much dependent on each others' kind offices. Dumoise was wrong in shutting himself from the world for a year, and he discovered his mistake when an epidemic of typhoid broke out in the Station in the heart of the cold weather, and his wife went down. He was a shy little man, and five days were wasted before he realized that Mrs. Dumoise was burning with something worse than simple fever, and three days more passed before he ventured to call on Mrs. Shute, the engineer's wife, and timidly speak about his trouble. Nearly every household in India knows that Doctors are very helpless in typhoid. The battle must be fought out between Death and the Nurses, minute by minute and degree by degree. Mrs. Shute almost boxed Dumoise's ears for what she called his "criminal delay," and went off at once to look after the poor girl. We had seven cases of typhoid in the Station that winter and, as the average of death is about one in every five cases, we felt certain that we should have to lose somebody. But all did their best. The women sat up nursing the women, and the men turned to and tended the bachelors who were down, and we wrestled with those typhoid cases for fifty-six days, and brought them through the Valley of the Shadow in triumph. But, just when we thought all was over, and were going to give a dance to celebrate the victory, little Mrs. Dumoise got a relapse and died in a week and the Station went to the funeral. Dumoise broke down utterly at the brink of the grave, and had to be taken away.

After the death, Dumoise crept into his own house and refused to be comforted. He did his duties perfectly, but we all felt that he should go on leave, and the other men of his own Service told him so. Dumoise was very thankful for the suggestion—he was thankful for anything in those days—and went to Chini on a walking-tour. Chini is some twenty marches from Simla, in the heart of the Hills, and the scenery is good if you are in trouble. You pass through big, still deodar-forests, and under big, still cliffs, and over big, still grass-downs swelling like a woman's breasts; and the wind across the grass, and the rain among the deodars says:—"Hush—hush—hush." So little Dumoise was packed off to Chini, to wear down his grief with a full-plate camera, and a rifle. He took also a useless bearer, because the man had been his wife's favorite servant. He was idle and a thief, but Dumoise trusted everything to him.

On his way back from Chini, Dumoise turned aside to Bagi, through the Forest Reserve which is on the spur of Mount Hutton. Some men who have travelled more than a little say that the march from Kotegarh to Bagi is one of the finest in creation. It runs through dark wet forest, and ends suddenly in bleak, nipped hill-side and black rocks. Bagi dâk-bungalow is open to all the winds and is bitterly cold. Few people go to Bagi. Perhaps that was the reason why Dumoise went there. He halted at seven in the evening, and his bearer went down the hillside to the village to engage coolies for the next day's march. The sun had set, and the night-winds were beginning to croon among the rocks. Dumoise leaned on the railing of the verandah, waiting for his bearer to return. The man came back almost immediately after he had disappeared, and at such a rate that Dumoise fancied he must have crossed a bear. He was running as hard as he could up the face of the hill.

But there was no bear to account for his terror. He raced to the verandah and fell down, the blood spurting from his nose and his face iron-gray. Then he gurgled:—"I have seen *the Memsahib*! I have seen the *Memsahib*!"

"Where?" said Dumoise.

"Down there, walking on the road to the village. She was in a blue dress, and she lifted the veil of her bonnet and said:—'Ram Dass, give my *salaams* to the *Sahib*, and tell him that I shall meet him next month at Nuddea.' Then I ran away, because I was afraid."

What Dumoise said or did I do not know. Ram Dass declares that he said nothing, but walked up and down the verandah all the cold night, waiting for the *Memsahib* to come up the hill and stretching out his arms into the dark like a madman. But no *Memsahib* came, and, next day, he went on to Simla cross-questioning the bearer every hour.

Ram Dass could only say that he had met Mrs. Dumoise and that she had lifted up her veil and given him the message which he had faithfully repeated to Dumoise. To this statement Ram Dass adhered. He did not know where Nuddea was, had no friends at Nuddea, and would most certainly never go to Nuddea; even though his pay were doubled.

Nuddea is in Bengal, and has nothing whatever to do with a Doctor serving in the Punjab. It must be more than twelve hundred miles from Meridki.

Dumoise went through Simla without halting, and returned to Meridki there to take over charge from the man who had been officiating for him during his tour. There were some Dispensary accounts to be explained, and some recent orders of the Surgeon-General to be noted, and, altogether, the taking-over was a full day's work. In the evening, Dumoise told his *locum tenens*, who was an old friend of his bachelor days, what had happened at Bagi; and the man said that Ram Dass might as well have chosen Tuticorin while he was about it.

At that moment, a telegraph-peon came in with a telegram from Simla, ordering Dumoise not to take over charge at Meridki, but to go at once to Nuddea on special duty. There was a nasty outbreak of cholera at Nuddea, and the Bengal Government, being shorthanded, as usual, had borrowed a Surgeon from the Punjab.

Dumoise threw the telegram across the table and said:—"Well?"

The other Doctor said nothing. It was all that he could say.

Then he remembered that Dumoise had passed through Simla on his way from Bagi; and thus might, possibly, have heard first news of the impending transfer.

He tried to put the question, and he implied suspicion into words, but Dumoise stopped him with :—"If I had desired *that*, I should never have come back from Chini. I was shooting there. I wish to live, for I have things to do. . . . but I shall not be sorry."

The other man bowed his head, and helped, in the twilight, to pack up Dumoise's just opened trunks. Ram Dass entered with the lamps.

"Where is the *Sahib* going?" he asked,

"To Nuddea," said Dumoise softly.

Ram Dass clawed Dumoise's knees and boots and begged him not to go. Ram Dass wept and howled till he was turned out of the room. Then he wrapped up all his belongings and came back to ask for a character. He was not going to Nuddea to see his *Sahib* die, and, perhaps to die himself.

So Dumoise gave the man his wages and went down to Nuddea alone; the other Doctor bidding him good-bye as one under sentence of death.

Eleven days later, he had joined his *Memsahib*; and the Bengal Government had to borrow a fresh Doctor to cope with that epidemic at Nuddea. The first importation lay dead in Chooadanga Dâk-Bungalow.

The Case of Sir Alister Moeran

Margaret Strickland

"Ethne?" My aunt looked at me with raised brows and smiled. "My dear Maurice, hadn't you heard? Ethne went abroad directly after Christmas, with the Wilmotts, for a trip to Egypt. She's having a glorious time!"

I am afraid I looked as blank as I felt. I had only landed in England three days ago, after two years' service in India, and the one thing I had been looking forward to was seeing my cousin Ethne again.

"Then, since you did not know she was away, you, of course, have not heard the other news?" went on my aunt.

"No," I answered in a wooden voice. "I've heard nothing."

She beamed. "The dear child is engaged to a Sir Alister Moeran, whom she met in Luxor. Everyone is delighted, as it is a splendid match for her. Lady Wilmott speaks most highly of him, a man of excellent family and position, and perfectly charming to boot."

I believe I murmured something suitable, but it was absurd to pretend to be overjoyed at the news. The galling part of it was that Aunt Linda knew, and was chuckling, so to speak, over my discomfiture.

"If you are going up to Wimberley Park," she went on sweetly, "you will probably meet them both, as your Uncle Bob has asked us all there for the February house-party. He cabled an invitation to Sir Alister as soon as he heard of the engagement. Wasn't it good of him?"

I replied that it was; then, having heard quite enough for one day of the charms of Ethne's fiancé, I took my leave.

That night, after cursing myself for a churl, I wrote and wished her good luck. The next morning I received a letter from Uncle Bob asking me to go to Wimberley; and early in the following week I travelled up to Cumberland. I received a warm welcome from the old General. As a boy I used to spend the greater part of my holidays with him, and being childless himself, he regarded me more or less as a son.

On February 16th Ethne, her mother, and Sir Alister Moeran arrived. I motored to the station to meet them. The evening was cold and raw and so dark that it was almost impossible to distinguish people on the badly lighted little platform. However, as I groped my way along, I recognised Ethne's voice, and thus directed, hurried towards the group. As I did so two gleaming, golden eyes flashed out at me through the darkness.

"Hullo!" I thought. "So she's carted along the faithful Pincher!" But the next moment I found I was mistaken, for Ethne was holding out both hands to me in greeting. There was no dog with her, and in the bustle that followed, I forgot to seek further for the solution of those two fiery lights.

"It was good of you to come, Maurice," Ethne said with unmistakable pleasure, then, turning to the man at her side, "Alister, this is my cousin, Captain Kilvert, of whom you have heard me speak."

We murmured the usual formalities in the usual manner, but as my fingers touched his, I experienced the most curious sensation down the region of my spine. It took me back to Burma and a certain very uncomfortable night that I once passed in the jungle. But the impression was so fleeting as to be indefinable, and soon I was busy getting everyone settled in the car.

So far, except that he possessed an exceptionally charming voice, I had no chance of forming an opinion of my cousin's *fiancé*. It was half-past seven when we got back to the house, so we all went straight up to our rooms to dress for dinner.

Everyone was assembled in the drawing-room when Sir Alister Moeran came in, and I shall never forget the effect his appearance made. Conversation ceased entirely for an instant. There was a kind of breathless pause, which was almost audible as my uncle rose to greet him. In all my life I had never seen a handsomer man, and I don't suppose anyone else there had either. It was the most startling, arresting style of beauty one could possible imagine, and yet, even as I stared at him in admiration, the word "Black!" flashed into my mind.

Black! I pulled myself up sharply. We English, who have lived out in the East, are far too prone to stigmatise thus anyone who shows the smallest trace of being a "half breed"; but in Sir Alister's case there was not even a suspicion of this. He was no darker than scores of men of my own nationality, and besides, he belonged, I knew, to a very old Scottish family. Yet, try as I would to strangle the idea, all through the evening the same horrible, unaccountable notion clung to me.

That he was the personality of the gathering there was not the slightest doubt. Men and women alike seemed attracted by him, for his individuality was on a par with his looks.

Several times during dinner I glanced at Ethne, but it was easy to see that all her attention was taken up by her lover. Yet, oddly enough, I was not jealous in the ordinary way. I saw the folly of imagining that I could stand a chance against a man like Moeran, and, more over, he interested me too deeply. His knowledge of the East was extraordinary, and later, when the ladies had retired, he related many curious experiences.

"Might I ask," said my uncle's friend, Major Faucett, suddenly, "whether you were in the Service, or had you a Government appointment out there?"

Sir Alister smiled, and under his moustache I caught the gleam of strong, white teeth.

"As a matter of fact, neither. I am almost ashamed to say I have no profession, unless I may call myself an explorer."

"And why not?" put in Uncle Bob. "Provided your explorations were to some purpose and of benefit to the community in general, I consider you are doing something worth while."

"Exactly," Sir Alister replied. "From my earliest boyhood I have always had the strangest hankering for the East. I say strange, because to my parents it was inexplicable, neither of them having the slightest leaning in that direction, though to me it seemed the most natural desire in the world. I was like an alien in a foreign land, longing to get home. I recollect, as a child, my nurse thought me a beastly uncanny kid because I loved to lie in bed and listen to the cats howling and fighting outside. I used to put my head half under the blankets and imagine I was in my lair in the jungle, and those were the jackals and panthers prowling around outside."

"I suppose you'd been reading adventure books," Uncle Bob said, with a laugh. "I played at much the same game when I was a youngster, only in my case it was Redskins."

"Possibly," Sir Alister answered with a slight shrug, "only mine wasn't a game that I played with any other boys, it was a gnawing desire, which simply had to be satisfied; and the opportunity came. When I was fourteen, the father of a school friend of mine, who was going out to India, asked me to go out with him and the boy for the trip. Of course, I went."

"I wonder," the Major remarked, "that you ever came back once you got there, since you were so frightfully keen."

"I was certain I should return," he replied grimly.

A pause followed his last words, then Uncle Bob rose and led the way to the drawing-room, where for the remainder of the evening Sir Alister was chiefly monopolised by the ladies.

* * * * *

"Well, Maurice," Uncle Bob said, when on the following evening I was sitting in his study having my usual before-dinner chat with him, "and how do you like Ethne's future husband?"

I hesitated. "I—I really don't know," I replied.

"Come, boy," he said, with his whimsical smile, "why not be frank and own to a very natural jealousy?"

"Because," I answered simply, "the feeling Sir Alister Moeran inspires in me is not jealousy, curiously enough. It's something else, some thing indefinable that comes over me now and again. Dogs don't like him, and that's always a bad sign, to my thinking."

My uncle's bushy eyebrows went up slightly.

"When did you make this discovery?"

"This morning," I replied. "You know I took him and Ethne round the place. Well, the first thing I noticed was that Mike refused to come with us, although both Ethne and I called him. As we passed through the hall, he slunk away into the library. I thought it a bit strange, as he's usually so frantic to go out with me. Still, I didn't attach any significance to the matter until later, when we visited the kennels. I don't know why, but one takes it for granted that a man is keen on dogs somehow and—"

"Isn't Sir Alister?"

"They are not keen on him, anyhow," I answered grimly. "They had heard my voice as we approached and were all barking with delight, but directly we entered the place there was a dead silence, save for a few ominous growls from Argo. It was a most extraordinary sight. They all bristled up, so to speak, sniffing the air as though on the scent of something. I let Bess and Fritz loose, but instead of jumping up, as they usually do, they hung back and showed the whites of their eyes in a way I've never seen before. I actually had to whistle to them sharply several times before they came, and then it was in a slinking manner, taking good care to put Ethne and me between themselves and Moeran, and looking askance at him the whole while."

"H'm!" murmured the General with puckered brows. "That was certainly odd, very odd!"

"It was," I agreed, warming to the subject, "but there's odder still to come. I dare say you'll think it all my fancy, but the minute those animals put their heads up and sniffed in that peculiar way, I distinctly smelt the musky, savage odour of wild beasts. You know it well, anyone who has been through a jungle does."

Uncle Bob nodded. "I know it, too; 'Musky' is the very word the smell of sun-warmed fur. Jove, how it carries me back! I remember once, years ago, coming upon a litter of lion cubs, in a cave, when I was out in Africa—"

"Yes! Yes!" I cried eagerly. "And that is what I smelt this morning. Those dogs smelt it, too. They felt that there was some thing alien, abnormal in their midst."

"That something being—Sir Alister Moeran?"

I felt myself flush up under his gaze. I got up and walked about the room.

"I don't understand it," I said doggedly. "I tell you plainly, Uncle Bob, I don't under stand. My impression of the man last night was 'black,' but he's not black, I know that perfectly well, no more than you or I are, and yet I can't get over the behaviour of those hounds. It wasn't only one of 'em, it was the whole lot. They seemed to regard him as their natural enemy! And that smell! I'm sure Ethne detected it too, for she kept glancing about her in a startled, mystified way."

"And Sir Alister?" queried the General. "Do you mean to say he did not notice any thing amiss?"

I shrugged my shoulders. "He didn't appear to. I called attention myself to the singular attitude of the hounds, and he said quite casually: 'Dogs never do take to me much.' "

Uncle Bob gave a short laugh. "Our friend is evidently not sensitive." He paused and rubbed his chin thoughtfully, then added: "It certainly is rather curious, but, for Heaven's sake, boy, don't get imagining all sorts of things!"

This nettled me and made me wish I had held my tongue. I was quite aware that my story might have sounded somewhat fantastic from a stranger; still, he ought to have known me better than to accuse me of imagination. I abruptly changed the subject, and shortly after left the room.

But I could not banish from my mind the incident of the morning. I could not forget the appealing faces of those dogs. Ethne and Sir Alister had left me there and returned to the house together, and, after their departure, those poor, dumb beasts had gathered round me in a way that was absolutely pathetic, licking and fondling my hands, as though apologising for their previous misconduct. Still, I understood. That bristling up their spines was precisely the same sensation I had experienced when I first met Sir Alister Moeran.

As I was slowly mounting the stairs on my way up to dress, I heard someone running up after me, and turned round to find Ethne beside me.

"Maurice," she said, rather breathlessly, "tell me, you did not punish Fritz and Boss for not coming at once when you called them this morning?"

"No," I answered.

She gave a nervous little laugh. "I'm glad of that. I thought perhaps—" She stopped short, then rushed on, "You know how queer mother is about cats—can't bear one in the room, and how they always fly out directly she comes in? Well, dogs are the same with Alister. He—he told me so himself. It seems funny to me, and I suppose to you, because we're so fond of all kinds of animals; but I don't really see why it should be any more extraordinary to have an antipathy for dogs than for cats, and no one thinks anything of it if you dislike cats."

"That is so," I said thoughtfully.

"Anyway," she went on, "it is not our own fault if a certain animal does not instinctively take to us."

"Of course not," I replied stoutly. "You're surely not worrying about it, are you?"

She hastened to assure me that she was not, but I could see that my indorsing her opinion was a great relief to her. She had been afraid that I should think it unnatural. I did for that matter, but I could not, of course, tell her so.

That night Sir Alister and I sat up late talking after the other men had retired. We had got on the subject of India and had been comparing notes as to our different adventures. From this we went on to discussing perilous situations and escapes, and it was then that he narrated to me a very curious incident.

"It happened when I was only twenty-one," he said, "the year after my father died. I think I told you that as soon as ever I became my own master, I packed up and was off to the East. I had a friend with me, a boy who had been my best pal at school. They used to call us 'Black and White.' He was fair and girlish-looking, and his name was Buchanan. He was just as keen on India as I was, and purposed writing a book afterwards on our experiences.

"Our intention was to explore the wildest, most savage districts, and as a start we selected the province of Orissa. The forests there are wonderful, and it is there, if anywhere, that the almost extinct Indian lion is still to be found. We engaged two sturdy hillmen to accompany us and pushed our way downwards from Calcutta over mountains, rivers and through some of the densest jungles I've ever traversed. It was on the outskirts of one of the latter that the tragedy took place. We had pitched our tents one evening after a long, tiring day, and turned in early to sleep, Buchanan and I in one, and the two Bhils in the other."

Sir Alister paused for a few moments, toying with his cigar in an abstracted manner, then continued in the same clear, even voice:

"When I awoke next morning, I found my friend lying beside me dead, and blood all round us! His throat was torn open by the teeth of some wild beast, his breast was horribly mauled and lacerated, and his eyes were wide, staring open, and their expression was awful. He must have died a hideous death and known it!"

Again he stopped, but I made no comment, only waited with breathless interest till he went on.

"I called the two men. They came and looked, and for the first time I saw terror written on their faces. Their nostrils quivered as though scenting something; then 'Tiger!' they gasped simultaneously.

"One of them said he had heard a stifled scream in the night, but had thought it merely some animal in the jungle. The whole thing was a mystery. How I came to sleep undisturbed through it all, how I escaped the same fate, and why the tiger did not carry off his prey—"

"You are sure it was a tiger?" I put in.

"I think there was no doubt of it," Sir Alister replied. "The Bhils swore the teeth-marks were unmistakable, and not only that, but I saw another case seven years later. The body of a young woman was found in the compound outside my bungalow, done to death in precisely the same way. And several of the natives testified as to there being a tiger in that vicinity, for they had found three or four young goats destroyed in similar fashion."

"Who was the girl? "I asked.

Moeran slowly turned his lucent, amber eyes upon me as he answered. "She was a German, a sort of nursery governess at the English doctor's. He was naturally frightfully upset about it, and a regular panic sprang up in the neighbourhood. The natives got a superstitious scare—thought one of their gods was wroth about something and demanded sacrifice; but the white people were simply out to kill the tiger."

"And did they?" I queried eagerly.

Sir Alister shook his head. "That I can't say, as I left the place very soon afterwards and went up to the mountains."

A long silence followed, during which I stared at him in mute fascination. Then an unaccountable impulse made me say abruptly: "Moeran, how old are you?"

His finely-marked eyebrows went up in surprise at the irrelevance of my question, but he smiled.

"Funny you should ask! It so happens that it's my birthday to-morrow. I shall be thirty-five."

"Thirty-five!" I repeated. Then with a shiver I rose from my seat. The room seemed to have turned suddenly cold.

"Come," I said, "let's go to bed."

Next night at dinner I proposed Sir Alister's health, and we all drank to him and his "bride-to-be." They had that day definitely settled the date of their marriage for two months ahead; Ethne was looking radiant and everyone seemed in the best of spirits.

We danced and romped and played rowdy games like a pack of children. Nothing was too silly for us to attempt. While a one-step was in full swing some would-be wag suddenly turned off all the lights. It was then that for a moment I caught sight of a pair of glowing, fiery eyes shining through the darkness. Instantly my thoughts flew back to that meeting at the station, when I had fancied that Ethne had her dog in her arms. A chill, sinister feeling crept over me, but I kept my gaze fixed steadily in the same direction. The next minute the lights went up, and I found myself staring straight at Sir Alister Moeran. His arm was round Ethne's waist and she was smiling up into his face. Almost immediately they took up the dance again, and I and my partner followed suit. But all my gaiety had departed. An indefinable oppression seized me and clung to me for the rest of the evening.

As I emerged from my room next morning I saw old Giles, the butler, hurrying down the corridor towards me.

"Oh, Mr. Maurice—Captain Kilvert, sir!" he burst out, consternation in every line of his usually stolid countenance. "A dreadful thing has happened! How it's come about I can't for the life of me say, and how we're going to tell the General, the Lord only knows!"

"What?" I asked, seizing him by the arm. "What is it?"

"The dawg, sir," he answered in a hoarse whisper, "Mike—in the study—"

I waited to hear no more, but strode off down the stairs, Giles hobbling beside me as fast as he could, and together we entered the study.

In the middle of the floor lay the body of Mike. A horrible foreboding gripped me, and I quickly knelt down and raised the dog's head. His neck was torn open, bitten right through to the windpipe, the blood still dripping from it into a dark pool on the carpet.

A cold, numbing sensation stole down my spine and made my legs grow suddenly weak. Beads of perspiration gathered on my forehead as I slowly rose to my feet and faced Giles.

"What's the meaning of it, sir?" he asked, passing his hand across his brow in utter bewilderment. "That dawg was as right as possible when I shut up last night, and he couldn't have got out."

"No," I answered mechanically, "he couldn't have got out."

"Looks like some wild beast had attacked him," muttered the old man, in awed tones, as he bent over the lifeless body. "D'ye see the teeth marks, sir? But it's not possible—not possible."

"No," I said again, in the same wooden fashion. "It's not possible."

"But how're we going to account for it to the General?" he cried brokenly. "Oh, Mr. Maurice, sir, it's dreadful!"

I nodded. "You're right, Giles! Still, it isn't your fault, nor mine. Leave the matter to me. I'll break it to my uncle."

It was a most unenviable task, but I did it. Poor Uncle Bob! I shall never forget his face when he saw the mutilated body of the dog that for years had been his faithful companion. He almost wept, only rage and resentment against the murderer were so strong in him that they thrust grief for the time into the background. The mysterious, incomprehensible manner of the dog's death only added to his anger, for there was apparently no one on whom to wreak his vengeance.

The news caused general concern throughout the house, and Ethne was frightfully upset.

"Oh, Alister, isn't it awful?" she exclaimed, tears standing in her pretty blue eyes. "Poor, darling Mike!"

"Yes," he answered rather absently. "It's most unfortunate. Valuable dog, too, wasn't it?"

I walked away. The man's calm, handsome face filled me suddenly with unspeakable revulsion. The atmosphere of the room seemed to become heavy and noisome. I felt compelled to get out into the open to breathe.

I found the General tramping up and down the drive in the rain, his chin sunk deep into the collar of his overcoat, his hat pulled low down over his eyes. I joined him without speaking, and in silence we paced side by side for another quarter of an hour.

"Uncle Bob," I said abruptly at last, "take my advice. Have one of the hounds indoors to-night—Princep, he's a good watch-dog."

The General stopped short in his walk and looked at me.

"You've something on your mind, boy. What is it?"

"This," I answered grimly. "Whoever, or whatever killed Mike was in the house last night, or got in, after Giles shut up. It may still be there for all we know. In the dark, dark deeds are done, and—well, I think it's wise to take precautions."

"Good God, Maurice, if there is any creature in hiding, we'll soon have it out! I'll have the place searched now. But the thing's impossible, absurd!"

I shrugged my shoulders. "Then Mike died a natural death?"

"Natural?" he echoed fiercely. "Don't talk rubbish!"

"In that case," I said quietly, "you'll agree to let one of the dogs sleep in."

He gave me a long, troubled, searching look, then said gruffly: "Very well, but don't make any fuss about it. Women are such nervous beings and we don't want to upset anyone."

"You needn't be afraid of that," I replied, "I'll manage it all right."

There was no further talk of Mike that day. The visitors, seeing how distressed the General was, by tacit consent avoided the subject, but everyone felt the dampening effect.

That night, before I retired to my room, I took a lantern, went out to the kennels and brought in Princep, a pure-bred Irish setter. He was a dog of exceptional intelligence, and when I spoke to him, explaining the reason of his presence indoors, he seemed to know instinctively what was required of him.

As I passed the study I noticed a light coming from under the door. Somewhat surprised, I turned the handle and looked in. My uncle was seated before his desk in the act of loading a revolver. He glanced up sharply as I entered.

"Oh, it's you, is it? Got the dog in?"

"Yes," I replied, "I've left him in the library with the door open."

He regarded the revolver pensively for a few moments, then laid it down in front of him.

"You've no theory as to this—this business?"

I shook my head, I could offer no explanation. Yet all the while there lurked, deep down in my heart, a hideous suspicion, a suspicion so monstrous that had I voiced it, I should probably have been considered mad. And so I held my peace on the subject and merely wished my uncle good-night.

It was about one o'clock when I got into bed, but my brain was far too agitated for sleep. Something I had heard years ago, some old wives' tales about a man's life changing every seven years, kept dinning in my head. I was striving to remember how the story went, when a slight sound outside caught my ear. In a second I was out of bed and had silently opened the door. As I did so, someone passed close by me down the corridor.

Cautiously, with beating heart, I crept out and followed. However, I almost exclaimed aloud in my amazement, for the light from a window fell full on the figure ahead of me, and I recognised my cousin Ethne. She was sleep-walking, a habit she had had from her childhood, and which apparently she had never outgrown.

For some minutes I stood there, undecided how to act, while she passed on down the stairs, out of sight. To wake her I knew would be wrong. I knew, also, that she had walked thus a score of times without coming to any harm. There was, therefore, no reason why I should not return to my room and leave her to her wandering, yet still I remained rooted to the spot, all my senses strained, alert. And then suddenly I heard Princep whine. A series of low, stertorous growls followed, growls that made my blood run cold! With swift, noiseless steps, I stole along to the minstrel's gallery which overlooked that portion of the hall that communicated with the library. As I did so, there arose from immediately below me a succession of sharp snarls, such as a dog gives when he is in deadly fear or pain.

A shaft of moonlight fell across the polished floor, and by its aid I was just able to distinguish the form of Princep crouched against the wainscoting. He was breathing heavily, his head turned all the while towards the opposite side of the room. I looked in the same direction. Out of the darkness gleamed two fiery, golden orbs, two eyes that moved slowly to and fro, backwards and forwards, as though the Thing were prowling round and round. Now it seemed to crouch as though ready to spring, and I could hear the savage growling as of some beast of prey.

As I watched, horrified, fascinated, a *portiére* close by was lifted, and the white-robed figure of Ethne appeared. All heedless of danger she came on across the hall, and the Thing, with soft, stealthy tread, came after her. I knew then that there was not an instant to be lost, and like a flash I darted along the gallery and down the stairs. But ere I gained the hall a piercing scream rent the air, and I was just in time to see Ethne borne to the ground by a great, dark form, which had sprung at her like a tiger.

Half frantic, I dashed forward, snatching as I did so a rapier from the wall, the only weapon handy. But before I reached the spot, a voice from the study doorway called: "Stop!" and the next moment the report of a pistol rang out.

"Good God!" I cried. "Who have you shot?"

"Not the girl," answered the grim voice of my uncle, "you may trust my aim for that! I fired at the eyes of the Thing. Here, quick, get lights and let's see what has happened."

But my one and only thought was for Ethne. Moving across to the dark mass on the floor, I stretched out my hand. My fingers touched a smooth, fabric-like cloth, but the smell was the smell of fur, the musky, sun-warmed fur of the jungle! With sickening repugnance, I seized the Thing by its two broad shoulders and rolled it over. Then I carefully raised Ethne from the ground. At that moment Giles and a footman appeared with candles. In silence my uncle took one and came towards me, the servants with scared, blanched countenances following.

The light fell full upon the dead, upturned face of Sir Alister Moeran. His upper lip was drawn back, showing the strong, white teeth. The two front ones were tipped with blood. Instantly my eyes turned to Ethne's throat, and there I saw deep, horrible marks, like the marks of a tiger's fangs; but, thank God, they had not penetrated far enough to do any serious injury! My uncle's shot had come just in time to save her.

"Merely fainted, hasn't she?" he asked anxiously.

I nodded. My relief at finding this was so, was too great for words.

"Heaven be praised!" I heard him mutter. Then lifting my beautiful, unconscious burden in my arms, I carried her upstairs to her room.

Can I explain, can anyone explain, the mysterious vagaries of atavism? I only know that there are amongst us, rare instances fortunately, but existent nevertheless men with the souls of beasts. They may be cognisant of the fact or otherwise. In the case of Sir Alister I feel sure it was the latter. He had probably no more idea than I what far-reaching, evil strain it was that came out in his blood and turned him, every seven years, practically into a vampire.

The Case of the Witch-Woman

Hilda Morris

I am a nurse in St. Margaret's Hospital, and my name is Ellen Graves. I am thirty-five years old, and I am,—or at least, I was, before the events which I am about to narrate took place,—a person of cheerful disposition, sound common sense, and few illusions. That I am so still, is doubtful. Few persons could witness the things which I have seen, without a resulting shock to the sense called "common," and a sharpening of those intuitions which perceive danger in commonplace surroundings.

The doctors generally gave me woman patients, and frequently of the neurasthenic type, as my personality is—or was—supposed to be calm and restful.

Early last fall, I was assigned to the case of a young woman, a schoolteacher, who was suffering from a nervous breakdown. She was a pretty young thing, with great mournful brown eyes, and appealing ways, like a child. She was ill for a long time, and I became very fond of her. When she grew better, and her eyes could smile a little, we had happy chats together. We talked of books, and fancy-work, comparing our likes and dislikes. We were particularly fond, as breadwinning women often are, of describing the kind of home we should like to have for our very own.

"I like a fireplace—a big one—a tea-table and the very newest magazines, piled up beside a deep chair," she pictured, like a little girl playing house.

"Yes, and a cat," I added. "I like a fireplace and a big, purry cat beside it."

Her eyes had been happy, but at the word "cat," they clouded over; a worried nervous frown drove the smile from her face.

"I had an awful dream last night," she confided. "That's what woke me up, you know. It was about a cat."

I did not want her to tell the dream if it had been unpleasant, and I moved hastily to put up the shade and speak of the sunshine, but she went on:

"I thought it was here, in this room, glaring at me, from the corner. It was a very big cat, a black one. It was just going to spring at me, when I woke up, all shivery, and you came in."

"Well, there isn't a cat within three blocks of this building, so you needn't worry. And how do you know that the cat was not going to rub against you and purr? Do you want milktoast or custard for supper?"

I thought I had driven the ugly dream successfully away. We talked on for a while longer, and I told her some of the funny incidents that happen daily in a big hospital. When I left her for the night, she was cheerful again, yawning sleepily, and declaring that she intended making up whole weeks of sleep.

I spent the hour between eleven and twelve at the desk in the hospital corridor. I was on duty, and being very tired, I endeavored to keep myself awake by writing letters and forcing my mind to attention. In spite of this, I think I must have dropped off for a few minutes, pen in hand, for I have a recollection of being roused out of unconsciousness by the sound of a piercing shriek. It was not the cry of mere physical suffering, such as nurses become hardened to, but a shriek of fear—wild, unreasoning fear. I realized, after a breathless instant, that it came from the direction of the room occupied by the little school-teacher. As I sped down the long corridor, the sound was repeated once, and then there was silence.

I entered, and snapping on the light, found my patient rigid with terror, her wide gaze fixed on her hands, which she held stiffly before her face. It was some moments before I could rouse her, and a period of hysteria ensued, during which she cried repeatedly: "The cat. The black cat! It bit my wrists! Look, they are bleeding!"

I examined her wrists, and found not so much as a scratch on them. Yet she declared that they were bitten and bleeding, and seemed unable to take her eyes from them. To quiet her, I bound them up, and giving her a sedative, sat with her until she slept.

The doctor believed the hallucination to be due to a slight relapse in her nervous condition, and I reproached myself for having allowed her to recall the ugly dream of the night previous.

Strangely enough, the patient declared that she had not been asleep when the apparition appeared. She said than an enormous black cat had appeared suddenly at her bedside, dim in the half-light, with glaring yellow eyes. She had cowered away into the far corner of her bed, when it sprang at her and attacked her wrists. She insisted that I search the premises and be sure that there was no cat about.

This I knew to be an absurd precaution. There never had been such an animal in the hospital, which was a large building set in a park that occupied a whole square. Vacant lots extended for two squares on two sides of it, the river bounded the third side, and a large public school building stood in the middle of the square on the fourth. To humor my patient, how ever, I made a search and inquiries, finding, as I had expected, that no cat had ever been seen in the hospital.

The young woman became quite cheerful by the afternoon of the next day, and the doctor decided that the frightful fancy had done no serious harm to her condition. I left her light burning low, and sat in the corridor near her door, occupying myself, as I had the night before, with writing letters.

The hours passed and all was quiet, save for the muffled night sounds of a great hospital. Another nurse was to take my place at twelve, and when she arrived, I arose sleepily, intending to hurry off to bed for my brief hours of rest.

But before I reached the door, there was a cry, a heart-rending shriek of terror, such as had sounded from my patient's room on the night previous.

The other nurse stood rooted to the spot with fear. She was a brave, strong girl, fearless every day before death, but the scream filled her, as it did me, with unspeakable horror.

I dashed into the room to find my patient white and still, one wrist locked tightly about the other, as though to stanch a flow of blood. We revived her with difficulty. Her pulse was so low that I was frightened and sent for an interne.

He was much puzzled. Her condition, he said, had taken a decided turn for the worse. She appeared to be suffering from a sudden and most unaccountable anaemia, as if she had suffered a loss of blood. She insisted on keeping her hand locked about her wrist, declaring that it bled.

I bound it up tightly, to humor her, and she murmured something unintelligible about "the cat." We decided that it would be best to move her to another room, where the strange hallucination might not pursue. This was done, but she still felt afraid in the hospital, and after a few days, was taken away to the home of friends. Her recovery there was slow, I have heard, and the physicians were never able to exactly explain her condition.

The room which she had occupied, remained vacant for several days. When next it was assigned to a patient, I was again given the case. This time it was a woman of about my own age, a rather stout woman, who had always been in robust health, until a sudden attack of appendicitis laid her low. Her physical condition was splendid, her blood perfectly pure, and she had made rapid strides toward recovery from her operation. She was impatient to return home to her husband and children, and worried occasionally over the way things might be going on at home. Her two little girls came daily, with their nurse, and regaled her with stories of their school and play.

"The kitty's had a fit," the six-year-old announced one day in pleased interest. "She's better now, but she had a awful fit."

Mrs. Sturtevant showed the first sign of nervousness I had ever seen in her. She shivered slightly. "Don't speak of cats," she said, "I had a horrible dream of a cat last night. I want you to get rid of that kitten before I come home."

The conversation veered away from the subject, but I felt a distinct sense of apprehension. To make it worse, I did not know exactly of what I was afraid. I asked the nurse who was on hall duty to look in on my patient once or twice during the night, and I went off to bed.

But I could not sleep, which was unusual for me. As the hour neared twelve, I decided to get up and sit by the window, thinking that the moonlit view of the broad placid river nearby might quiet my nerves.

I had barely taken my place at the window when I heard it—Mrs. Sturtevant's scream. I suppose I had been waiting for it, without daring to acknowledge that fact to myself. I sped down the hall in dressing-gown and slippers, regardless of regulations. I found the other nurse, herself terrified, endeavouring to quiet Mrs. Sturtevant, who kept repeating, hysterically, "The cat! The cat!" Like the little school-teacher, she declared that her wrists had been attacked and were bleeding. She appeared to feel very weak. I bound up her wrists and stayed with her until morning.

The other nurse was in a very nervous condition. She declared that she had hurried to the room immediately upon hearing the scream, and that she had distinctly seen a large dark body disappearing through the window which led to the roof. She had leaned out to look after it, and was sure that it had re-entered the building through one of the windows of a charity ward, some distance away.

Nearly every one in the hospital had heard the shriek, and there were numerous inquiries as to its cause. It was decided to make a thorough search for the cat, and see whether a stop could not be put to these unfortunate occurrences. The fact that Mrs. Sturtevant had been lying awake when it appeared to her, made it seem probable that the animal really existed. A thorough search, however, failed to reveal any trace of the cat, nor could any person in the institution affirm that he had ever seen a cat there. The hospital authorities were satisfied by noon of the day following, to let the matter drop. But Miss Banning, the other nurse, and I, decided to watch.

We said nothing more of the matter to Mrs. Sturtevant, but I assured her that I would be near her that night, and leaving the light burning, I succeeded in getting her to sleep. She slept, but neither Miss Banning nor I could do so. As midnight drew near and nothing occurred, we felt a trifle more easy, and I urged her off to bed.

"Wait until after twelve," she insisted. Even as she spoke, the clock chimed, and with it came Mrs. Sturtevant's shriek of terror. I have never heard anyone else scream as did the occupant of that room. We were standing near the door and entered in a second.

There on the bed, stood an enormous black cat, larger than any that I have ever seen. It had an indescribably evil appearance, its mouth hungry and snarling, eyes glowing like green coals, back arched and rigid, with stiff upright fur. For a half second we gazed, fascinated. Then, before we could stop it, the thing dashed through the window, and as I leaned out, I saw it clearly in the moonlight enter one of the windows of the charity ward.

Needless to say, another search was made. But nothing came of it. I think the hospital authorities came to regard us as slightly mad, though no one could deny that the fright of my patients had been real enough.

Mrs. Sturtevant, though terribly shaken up, was unhurt. She declared that the creature had sprung at her wrists, and would have attacked them, had it not been frightened away. She refused to pass another night in the room, however, and as her condition was favorable, she was taken to her home.

I was decidedly averse to receiving another patient in that room. It was in a new section of the hospital, and there was a room next to it which had not yet been furnished. When I was assigned to another case in the first room, I begged leave to move the furniture into the room next door, which was of the same size and shape.

This case was that of a little girl who had broken her leg and collarbone in a tom-boy attempt at tree-climbing. Her name was Susan, and she was the delightful, tanned, healthy kind of little girl that tom-boys usually are. She was very impatient and restless, and I had a hard time keeping her quiet. I read her story after story, and answered countless questions.

One day, after she had been there about a week, I sat reading to her from "Alice in Wonderland," and came to the part about the "Cheshire Cat."

"Ugh!" said Susan, "don't read that, please! I hate cats, and I dreamed about a horrid one last night."

I almost dropped the book in my perturbation at this remark. Then, not wishing her mind to dwell on the dream, I turned to another part of the book and we were soon laughing gaily over the "Royal Croquet." But as I read, a sudden suspicion entered my mind. Going to the window and leaning out under the pretense of wanting air, I discovered two things which disturbed me very much. The room in which Susan lay, and the room which my former patients had occupied, were the only two rooms opening on to the roof which led to the charity ward. In one of the gray snow-patches which lingered on the roof, I saw distinctly the footprints of a cat.

I determined to make my own investigations before complaining to the hospital authorities again, as I had already got myself laughed at for my persistence in believing that a cat lurked about the hospital. It was not yet noon, and I had plenty of time to make a search before night, when, I felt sure, the thing was bound to appear again.

Going to the charity ward, I asked one of the nurses whether she had seen a cat, and told her what had occurred. She had laughed at us before, and was not inclined to take this seriously.

"I've not seen the cat," she assured me, "and I've got worries enough of my own. One of my patients has taken to sleep-walking, and has frightened the others half to death. They spoke of it some nights ago, but I never caught her at it until last night. And then, would you believe it, she was just climbing in the window. Goodness knows how long she'd been out on that roof, and if she had fallen off and killed herself, the blame would be mine."

This was exciting enough to make me forget, for a minute, my anxiety over the cat apparition.

"Who is the patient?" I asked with some curiosity.

"That old crone in the bed near the window. She's Italian. Lived in a hovel by the railroad tracks, and was injured by a train. She nearly bled to death. She really needed a blood infusion, but charity patients can't have that, unless they have devoted friends, and she has none, apparently. But she's been getting better lately. The doctors say it's quite wonderful. She'll probably leave before long."

The story was commonplace enough, surely. Yet something in it interested me. I walked over and looked at the old woman. Her black beady eyes stared at me without winking, her skin was like yellow parchment, her nose hooked as an eagle's beak, over a toothless mouth. She was a decidedly ugly old woman.

"She looks like a witch," I remarked, going back to the other nurse.

"Yes, with the evil eye," she agreed, and we both laughed.

I returned to the subject of the cat, and after securing a promise from the nurse that she would be doubly watchful that night, I went in search of Miss Banning.

We decided to watch together, by Susan's door. This time, however, we were determined that the animal should not escape us. Miss Banning had secured a promise from one of the internes that he would come up about twelve o'clock with his revolver. If the thing appeared, he was to shoot it.

I cannot begin to tell how long the hours seemed until twelve; though I had expected and dreaded the nocturnal visitor before, never had I experienced such a wild feeling of apprehension as I did that night. Miss Banning, too, was affected. We started at every sound. When Susan called for a drink, I shook as though she had screamed. When the rubber-soled internes came down the hall, their noiseless tread seemed to my excited fancy like the padding of gigantic feline feet.

It drew near to twelve, and our ears were strained to catch the slightest sound from Susan's room. I tiptoed in and found her asleep, and coming out softly, I left the door ajar. It was only a minute later that I heard a soft sound, softer even than Miss Banning's whispered question. Creeping cautiously to the door, I saw it move. Even as I reached it, the latch clicked and I heard the key turn in the lock. Susan was alone with the thing.

Miss Banning fainted at Susan's scream. I think I should have done so too, had not the interne arrived just then, revolver in hand. Somehow, I managed to gasp out what had happened. We dashed into the empty room next door to Susan's, and through its window to the roof. All the time, we heard the child's cries, wild at first, then low and gasping. By the time that we reached her sill, they had ceased altogether.

There stood the cat. I could swear that its snarl was human. Its frightful mouth dripped blood, its eyes flashed fire. For one instant, it stood so, its devilish forepaws resting on Susan's white wrist. Then, as the doctor fired, it sprang. I felt it brush past me heavily. I can feel it yet. The bullet went home, for it gave a hoarse cry of anguish as it thudded heavily from the roof. I fainted then, for the first time in my life.

The interne must have unlocked the doer and called for aid, for when I became conscious, one of the nurses was bending over Susan, who lay moaning pitifully.

"Did he kill it?" I asked.

"Hush!" said the nurse. "Do get me some water."

I pulled myself together, as a nurse must, and went into the corridor for water. I had gone but a step, when the nurse from the charity ward came bounding down the hall with a frenzied look.

"She's gone!" she cried. "My old woman's gone! They saw her come out on the roof, but she isn't there. Did she come in your window?"

Who had turned the key in that lock?

It must have been my sixth sense that revealed the answer. I could only stare at her dumbly.

Dr. Andrews came back from the park below, and reported that the cat had not been killed, but had apparently made off for the river. It must have been badly injured, however, for a trail of blood lay on the snow for some little distance. Dr. Andrews had seen nothing of the old woman.

A thorough search revealed no trace of her. The river was dragged, but with no results. It was as if the earth had swallowed the old woman.

Susan, recovered from her fright, and apparently suffering from the same strange weakness which had affected the little school-teacher, could tell us nothing. She had been awakened, she said, by the touch of the cat at her wrists. We told the child that the cat had been driven away and would trouble her no more, and indeed it did not. She soon forgot her horrible experience, and before long, recovered her perfect health.

Doctor Andrews was deputed the day after the occurrence, to go with others on a search in the neighborhood of the Italian woman's hovel. He told me the result of those inquiries, and I set them down here, with no word of comment. Who, in this modern world, could comment on a maze of facts that leads to only one horrible and preposterous conclusion?

The woman's hovel was unoccupied. Italian neighbors testified to that. They had never seen her since she was taken to the hospital. They knew nothing of her, except that she had been a witch and they had feared her.

One Guiseppe Romano volunteered to search the cabin with the gentlemen. The door, strangely enough, was ajar. There was but one room—a dark, filthy place, full of vile odors.

Guiseppe shivered and crossed himself.

"Dios!" he exclaimed, pointing.

In the center of the floor, stretched a huge black cat, dead.

It had been shot.

CHUNIA, AYAH

ALICE PERRIN

"I HOPE YOU CLEARLY UNDERSTAND THAT I DO NOT BELIEVE IN GHOSTS?"

The little grey-haired spinster paused and regarded me with suspicion, and, alarmed lest I should, after all, lose the story I had been so carefully stalking, l vehemently reassured her on the point, whereupon, to my relief she continued—

"It certainly was a most extraordinary thing, and even now I hardly know what to make of it, though it happened a long time ago. One chilly day, when I was in India keeping house for my brother, I received a letter from a friend begging me to pay her a long-promised visit. She wrote that her husband was going into camp for a month to a part of his district where she could not accompany him, so that she and her little girl would be all alone, and I should be doing her a great kindness by coming. So the end of it was I accepted the invitation, though I greatly disliked leaving my brother to the tender mercies of the servants, and after a long, hot journey arrived at my destination at five o'clock one evening.

"My friend, Mrs. Pollok, was on the platform to meet me, and outside the station a bamboo cart was waiting, into which we climbed, and were soon bowling along the bard, white road at a brisk pace. Mary at once began to relate anecdotes of her little girl, whose name was Dot—how tall she was for her age (twenty months!), how much she ate, what she tried to say, what the ayah said about her, and so on.

"Now I must confess that I am not very fond of children; I like them well enough in their proper place (if that is not too near me), but I do not know how to behave towards them and am always nervous as to what they will do or say next. Therefore, fond as I was of Mary herself, the subject of her conversation did not particularly interest me. When we arrived at the house, she actually inquired which I would do first—see Dot or have some tea! I boldly elected for tea, as I was exceedingly tired and thirsty, and I also reflected that if I did not at once make a determined stand, I should be Dot-ridden for the remainder of my visit.

"After tea I was taken to my room, and Mary brought her treasure to me for exhibition. She was the most lovely child I had ever beheld, with a grave, sweet face that quite won my unmotherly heart and for once my prejudices completely melted away. Mary put her into my arms and stood by in an ecstasy of pride and delight as I proceeded to tap the pin-cushion, rattle my keys, and perform various idiotic antics in my efforts to amuse Dot, who, I felt sure, would set up a howl in a few moments. But she watched my foolish attempts to be entertaining with an attentive gravity that was quite embarrassing, and charmed though I was with the little creature, I felt relieved when she held out her arms to go back to her mother.

"Mary called for the ayah to come and take the child to her nursery, and a woman with a sullen, handsome face entered and took her charge away. I remarked that the ayah looked bad-tempered, upon which Mary assured me that she could trust the child anywhere with her, and that she was a perfect treasure.

"The next morning I was awakened by a soft little pat on my face, and, opening my eyes, I found Dot holding herself upright by the corner of my pillow.

"'Why, little one, are you all alone?' I said, lifting her on to the bed, and then I discovered that her feet were dripping with water.

"She held up one wet little foot and examined it carefully, and then pointed to the bathroom door, which was open, and from where I lay I could see an over-turned jug and streams of water on the floor—evidently Dot's handiwork. I put on my dressing-gown and took the child to her mother, explaining what had happened, and Mary hastily pulled off the soaking little shoes and socks and called for the ayah, who presently entered, and stood silently watching her mistress.

"'What do you mean by leaving the child in this way?' exclaimed Mary, angrily, and gathering up Dot's shoes and socks, she threw them to the ayah, bidding her bring others that were dry. One of the little shoes struck the woman on the cheek, for Mary was annoyed and had flung them with unnecessary force, and never shall forget the look on the ayah's face as she left the room to carry out the order. It was the face of a devil, but Mary did not see it, for she was busy rubbing the cold little feet in her hands.

"'Mary,' I said impulsively, 'I am sure that ayah is a brute. Do get rid of her. I never saw anything so dreadful as the look she gave you just now.'

"'My dear,' answered Mary, with good-humoured impatience, 'you have taken an unreasonable dislike to Chunia. She knew she was in the wrong and felt ashamed of herself.'

"So the matter dropped but I could not get over my dislike to Chunia, and as my visit wore on, and I became more and more attached to dear little Dot, I could hardly endure to see the child in her presence.

"My month with Mary passed quickly away, and I was really sorry when it was over, more especially as, on my return home, my brother was called away unexpectedly on business, and I was left alone. I missed Dot more than could have believed possible, for I had become ridiculously devoted to the small, round bundle of humanity, with the great dark eyes and short yellow curls, and my feelings are not to be described when the letter came from Mr. Pollok giving me the awful news of the child's death.

"I read the letter over and over again, hardly able to believe it. The whole thing was so hideously sudden! I had only left Mary and Dot such a short time ago, and when last I had seen the child she was in her mother's arms on the platform of the railway station, kissing her little fat hands laboriously to me in farewell, and looking the picture of life and health.

"Poor Mr. Pollok wrote in a heart-broken strain. It appeared that the child had strayed away one afternoon and must have fallen into the river, which ran past the bottom of the garden, for the little sun-hat was found floating in the stream, and close to the water's edge lay a toy that she had been playing with all day. Every search had been made, but no further trace could be found. The poor mother was distracted with sorrow, and Mr. Pollok had telegraphed for leave, as he meant to take her to England at once. He added that the ayah, Chunia, had been absent on three days' leave when the dreadful accident happened, or, they both felt convinced, it would never have occurred at all. Mary, he wrote, sent me a message to beg me to take the woman into my service, as she could not endure the idea of one who had been so much with their darling going to strangers, for the poor woman had been a faithful servant, and was stricken and dumb with grief.

I telegraphed at once that would take Chunia willingly. I forgot my old antipathy to her, and only remembered that I should have someone about me who had known and loved the child so well. When the woman arrived I was quite shocked at her altered appearance. Her face seemed to have shrunk to half its former size, and her eyes looked enormous, and shone with a strange brilliancy. She was very quiet at first, but burst into a flood of tears when I tried to speak to her of poor little Dot, so I gave it up, as I saw she could hardly bear the subject mentioned.

"She helped me to undress the first night, and then, instead of leaving the room, she stood looking at me without speaking.

"'What is it?' I inquired.

"'Mem-sahib,' she said in a whisper, glancing over her shoulder, 'may I sleep in your dressing-room tonight?'

"I willingly gave her permission, for I saw that the woman's nerves were unstrung and that she needed companionship. Then I got into bed, and must have been asleep for some hours when I awoke thinking I had heard a shrill voice crying in the compound. I listened, and again it came, a high, beseeching wail. It was certainly the voice of a child, and the awful pleading and despair expressed in the sound was heart-rending. I felt sure some native baby had wandered into the grounds and was calling hopelessly for its mother.

"I lit a candle and went into my dressing-room, where, to my astonishment, I saw Chunia crouching against the outer door that led into the verandah, holding it fast with both hands as though she were shutting someone out.

"I asked what she was doing, and whether she knew whose child was crying outside. She sprang to her feet and answered sullenly that she had heard no child crying. I opened the door and went out into the verandah, but nothing was to be seen or heard, and I had no reply to my shouts of inquiry; so, concluding that it must have been my fancy, or perhaps some prowling animal, I returned to bed, and slept soundly for the rest of the night.

"The next evening I dined out, and on my return was surprised to hear someone talking in my dressing-room. I hurried in, and again found Chunia kneeling in front of the outer door imploring somebody to 'go away' at the top of her voice. Directly she saw me she came towards me excitedly.

"'Oh! mem-sahib!' she shrieked, 'tell her to go away!'

"'Tell who?' I demanded.

"'Dottie-babba,' she wailed, wringing her hands. 'She cries to come to me—listen to her—listen!'

"She held her breath and waited, and I solemnly declare that as I stood and listened with her, I heard a child crying and moaning on the other side of the door. I was mute with horror and bewilderment, while the plaintive cry rose and fell, and then, flinging the door open, I held the candle high above my head. There was no need of a light, for the moon was full, but no child could I see, and the verandah was quite empty. I determined to sift the matter to the bottom, so I went to the servants' quarters and called them all up. But no one could account for the crying of a child, and though the compound was thoroughly searched nothing was discovered. So the servants returned to their houses and I to my verandah, where I found Chunia in a most excited state.

"'Mem-sahib,' she said, with her fists clenched and her eyes starting out of her head, 'will she go away if I tell you all about it?'

"'Yes, yes,' I cried soothingly, 'tell me what you like.'

"She silently took my wrist and dragged me into the dressing-room, shutting the door with the utmost caution.

"'Stand with your back against it,' she whispered, 'so that she cannot enter.'

"I feared I was in the presence of a mad woman, so I did as she bade me, and waited quietly for her story. She walked up and down the room and began to speak in a kind of chant.

"'I did it,' she sang. 'I killed the child, little Dottie-babba, and she has followed me always. You heard her cry tonight and last night. The mem-sahib angered me the day she struck me with the shoe, and then a devil entered into my heart. I asked for leave, and went away, but it was too strong, it drew me back, and it said kill! kill! I fought and struggled against the voice, but it was useless. So on the second day of my leave I crept back and hid among the bushes till I saw the child alone, and then I took her away and killed her. She was so glad to see me, and laughed and talked, but when she saw the devil in my eyes she grew frightened, and cried just as you heard her cry tonight. I took her little white neck in my hands—see, mem-sahib, how large and strong my hands are—and I pressed and pressed until the child was dead, and then the devil left me. I looked and saw what I had done. I could not unclasp her fingers from my skirt, they clung so tightly, so I took it off and wrapped her in it—'

"The woman stopped suddenly. I had listened in silence, repressing the exclamations of horror that rose to my lips.

"'What did you do then?' I asked.

"Chunia looked wildly round.

"'I forget,' she murmured; 'the river, I ran quickly to the river—'

"Then there came a shriek from the dry, parched lips, and flinging her arms above her head she fell at my feet unconscious and foaming at the mouth.

"Afterwards Chunia was found to be raving mad, and the doctor expressed his opinion that she must have been in a more or less dangerous state for some months past I told him of her horrible confession to me, but he said that possibly the whole thing was a delusion on her part.

"I went to see her once after she had been placed under restraint, but the sight was so saddening that I never went again. She was seated on the floor of her prison patting an imaginary baby to sleep, spoke to her she only gazed at me with dull, vacant eyes, and continued the monotonous chant as though she had not seen me at all."

"And the child you heard crying?" I ventured to ask.

"Oh! How can I tell what it was? I don't know," she answered with impatient perplexity. "I can't believe that it was the spirit of little Dot, and yet—and yet—*what was it?*"

The Conjurer

Richard Middleton

Certainly the audience was restive. In the first place it felt that it had been defrauded, seeing that Cissie Bradford, whose smiling face adorned the bills outside, had failed to appear, and secondly, it considered that the deputy for that famous lady was more than inadequate. To the little man who sweated in the glare of the limelight and juggled desperately with glass balls in a vain effort to steady his nerve it was apparent that his turn was a failure. And as he worked he could have cried with disappointment, for his was a trial performance, and a year's engagement in the Hennings' group of music-halls would have rewarded success. Yet his tricks, things that he had done with the utmost ease a thousand times, had been a succession of blunders, rather mirth-provoking than mystifying to the audience. Presently one of the glass balls fell crashing on the stage, and amidst the jeers of the gallery he turned to his wife, who served as his assistant.

"I've lost my chance," he said, with a sob; "I can't do it!"

"Never mind, dear," she whispered. "There's a nice steak and onions at home for supper."

"It's no use," he said despairingly. "I'll try the disappearing trick and then get off. I'm done here." He turned back to the audience.

"Ladies and gentlemen," he said to the mockers in a wavering voice, "I will now present to you the concluding item of my entertainment. I will cause this lady to disappear under your very eyes, without the aid of any mechanical contrivance or artificial device." This was the merest showman's patter, for, as a matter of fact, it was not a very wonderful illusion. But as he led his wife forward to present her to the audience the conjurer was wondering whether the mishaps that had ruined his chance would meet him even here. If something should go wrong—he felt his wife's hand tremble in his, and he pressed it tightly to reassure her. He must make an effort, an effort of will, and then no mistakes would happen. For a second the lights danced before his eyes, then he pulled himself together. If an earthquake should disturb the curtains and show Molly creeping ignominiously away behind he would still meet his fate like a man. He turned round to conduct his wife to the little alcove from which she should vanish. She was not on the stage!

For a minute he did not guess the greatness of the disaster. Then he realised that the theatre was intensely quiet, and that he would have to explain that the last item of his programme was even more of a fiasco than the rest. Owing to a sudden indisposition—his skin tingled at the thought of the hooting. His tongue rasped upon cracking lips as he braced himself and bowed to the audience.

Then came the applause. Again and again it broke out from all over the house, while the curtain rose and fell, and the conjurer stood on the stage, mute, uncomprehending. What had happened? At first he had thought they were mocking him, but it was impossible to misjudge the nature of the applause. Besides, the stage-manager was allowing him call after call, as if he were a star. When at length the curtain remained down, and the orchestra struck up the opening bars of the next song, he staggered off into the wings as if he were drunk. There he met Mr. James Hennings himself.

"You'll do," said the great man; "that last trick was neat. You ought to polish up the others though. I suppose you don't want to tell me how you did it? Well, well, come in the morning and we'll fix up a contract." And so, without having said a word, the conjurer found himself hustled off by the Vaudeville Napoleon. Mr. Hennings had something more to say to his manager.

"Bit rum," he said. "Did you see it?"

"Queerest thing we've struck."

"How was it done do you think?"

"Can't imagine. There one minute on his arm, gone the next, no trap, or curtain, or anything."

"Money in it, eh?"

"Biggest hit of the century, I should think."

"I'll go and fix up a contract and get him to sign it to-night. Get on with it." And Mr. James Hennings fled to his office.

Meanwhile the conjurer was wandering in the wings with the drooping heart of a lost child. What had happened? Why was he a success, and why did people stare so oddly, and what had become of his wife? When he asked them the stage hands laughed, and said they had not seen her. Why should they laugh? He wanted her to explain things, and hear their good luck. But she was not in her dressing-room, she was not anywhere. For a moment he felt like crying.

Then, for the second time that night, he pulled himself together. After all, there was no reason to be upset. He ought to feel very pleased about the contract, however it had happened. It seemed that his wife had left the stage in some queer way without being seen. Probably to increase the mystery she had gone straight home in her stage dress, and had succeeded in dodging the stage-door keeper. It was all very strange; but, of course, there must be some simple explanation like that. He would take a cab home and find her there already. There was a steak and onions for supper.

As he drove along in the cab he became convinced that this theory was right. Molly had always been clever, and this time she had certainly succeeded in surprising everybody. At the door of his house he gave the cabman a shilling for himself with a light heart. He could afford it now. He ran up the steps cheerfully and opened the door. The passage was quite dark, and he wondered why his wife hadn't lit the gas.

"Molly!" he cried, "Molly!"

The small, weary-eyed servant came out of the kitchen on a savoury wind of onions.

"Hasn't missus come home with you, sir?" she said.

The conjurer thrust his hand against the wall to steady himself, and the pattern of the wall-paper seemed to burn his finger-tips.

"Not here!" he gasped at the frightened girl. "Then where is she? Where is she?"

"I don't know, sir," she began stuttering; but the conjurer turned quickly and ran out of the house. Of course, his wife must be at the theatre. It was absurd ever to have supposed that she could leave the theatre in her stage dress unnoticed; and now she was probably worrying because he had not waited for her. How foolish he had been.

It was a quarter of an hour before he found a cab, and the theatre was dark and empty when he got back to it. He knocked at the stage door, and the night watchman opened it.

"My wife?" he cried.

"There's no one here now, sir," the man answered respectfully, for he knew that a new star had risen that night.

The conjurer leant against the doorpost faintly.

"Take me up to the dressing-rooms," he said. "I want to see whether she has been there while I was away."

The watchman led the way along the dark passages. "I shouldn't worry if I were you, sir," he said. "She can't have gone far." He did not know anything about it, but he wanted to be sympathetic.

"God knows," the conjurer muttered, "I can't understand this at all."

In the dressing-room Molly's clothes still lay neatly folded as she had left them when they went on the stage that night, and when he saw them his last hope left the conjurer, and a strange thought came into his mind.

"I should like to go down on the stage," he said, "and see if there is anything to tell me of her."

The night watchman looked at the conjurer as if he thought he was mad, but he followed him down to the stage in silence. When he was there the conjurer leaned forward suddenly, and his face was filled with a wistful eagerness.

"Molly!" he called, "Molly!"

But the empty theatre gave him nothing but echoes in reply.

Dalton's Inspiration

Stella B. McDonald

Maurice Dalton was discouraged. It seemed to him he had spent all his life painting pictures of rural scenes, in which there were forever the same clump of trees spreading their branches over artistic little streams, the same always-blue sky, and the same familiar cows disporting themselves in the background. "Sweet things," the women called them, while the men shrugged their shoulders and bought them for their wives. And Dalton had always remained indifferent to the shrugs so long as his pictures had a certain demand and brought him fair prices.

But yesterday the demon of discontent had entered his brain. "Hang the luck," thought Dalton to himself, "I ought to have been a girl and painted on velvet with a pen. I'm not sure that I didn't work worsted butterflies when I was a kid." By which it will be seen that Giles Dalton, artist, possessed no exalted opinion of himself, or of women's accomplishments.

The change had occurred the night before, at a musicale, when his friend Mott had introduced him to a stunning girl, and she, with a charmingly rude smile, had said, "I hope you are no relative of Dalton, the artist."

Dalton unblushingly disclaimed any kinship with himself, and Miss Forsythe had gone on to say, "That man has honestly made me despise the country as he sees it. Ugh! I loathe his green fields, and his cows haunt my very dreams. It is incomprehensible to me how a man can plod on and on with such characterless, inane daubs as his."

Dalton smiled feebly and said, "Don't you think maybe you are a bit rough on the fellow? Maybe he would have soared higher but found his talent unequal to his aspirations."

"No," replied Miss Forsythe, "I was talking to Carl Brooks, an intimate friend of his, and he said this Dalton was perfectly contented and would die painting daisy-studded meadows. Bah! I can just picture such a man—slender, blond, effeminate, with white hands and a Van Dyke, and of all detestable things, I think a beard is the climax."

Dalton reared his dark head on his broad shoulders and passed his hand over his smooth, square-jawed face with a sense of peculiar satisfaction. Then he asked, "Do you paint, Miss Forsythe?"

Her eyes danced as she replied, "Only once in a great while, Mr. Dalton, when I am unusually pale. But seriously, there is nothing on earth appeals to me like a splendid canvas. I can sing and play, but am not fond of music; I write and read, but books bore me. I do not sketch, model or paint, but it is the regret of my life. Nothing moves me like art, and I have inspiration enough for any number of masterpieces, but I cannot execute a thing."

"Why don't you become acquainted with Dalton, the artist, and give him some of your ideas? He may not have the making of a genius in him, but, anyway, his evolution under your personal supervision would be most interesting."

"Here comes Auntie," interrupted Miss Forsythe, as a stately woman advanced toward them; "were you looking for me? Well," she said over her shoulder to Dalton as she turned away, "I have an idea that would place any artist who learns it among the ranks of the old masters and that would build up a new school in art. Come, Auntie."

Dalton noticed her profile as she stood a moment in the crowd. It was not remarkable for beauty or for youth, but there was a sense of dignified purpose in every feature—a certain knowledge of something self-contained that appealed more than mere good looks. She wore a pale yellow gown of some loosely flowing material that reflected its warmth into her ivory skin and pale gold hair. But it was her eyes with which Dalton was most impressed, eyes of a peculiar hazel, with golden glints in them that reached into one's memory and lodged there. Dalton thought of Le Gallienne's "Golden Girl": he still felt strangely excited over the conversation when he made his adieus and went for his coat and hat.

As he went down the steps under the awning, he was conscious of a tall, graceful figure in a gorgeous cloth-of-gold cloak beside him for an instant as Miss Forsythe and her aunt moved toward their carriage. Leaning toward her he whispered, "Of course you knew I am Dalton, the artist."

"Yes," she replied, with a direct, golden gaze into his eyes, "and I knew that you knew I knew."

And thus had come Dalton's awakening to something more ambitious, and the dawn of the next day found him sitting in his evening clothes, with the fire long gone out, but with an unwonted fever in his veins that made him insensible to cold or fatigue.

The next morning, blue and discouraged, Dalton went to his studio with lagging steps, which finally halted before an easel bearing the canvas he had left unfinished the day before—"Sunset on the Farm."

Yesterday it had seemed good to him, but now it jarred upon his newly developed taste so roughly that he struck out at it with his fist and demolished a bunch of sheep that were gamboling with incompleted anatomy on a hillside. Around the studio were others of the same style—inane, without character—the kind that are never remembered after the first exclamation of "How pretty!"

Dalton placed one on the fire-dogs in the huge fireplace and watched its painted corners curl up with a feeling of peculiar satisfaction. Picture followed picture until the studio was stripped, and when the last one was gone with a final burst of little sparks that reached out viciously for him, he turned his feet wearily from the studio and went down into the street like an old man tired of life.

At luncheon at the Club, he sat next to his old chum, Carl Brooks. After a little talk, Dalton was wondering how he could lead the conversation to the subject that filled his mind, when Brooks introduced it himself, by saying, "I saw you doing the society act at the Belmont's last night."

"Yes," replied Dalton, with a carefully careless manner, "I heard that you had been saying a good word for me behind my back."

Brooks grinned. "Oh, thunder, old man! I did give you a blast, but you know you are confoundedly apathetic in your art, and I hope Miss Forsythe brought it home to you."

"She did that all right. But I'll forgive you if you'll tell me something about her. Who is she?"

"She is the last of the Philip Forsythes, about thirty years old, spends most of her time abroad and can afford the luxury of unlimited letters of credit. She hasn't a rep. as a beauty, but her cleverness and those weird yellow eyes render her interesting, and a certain elusiveness and mystery about her make some people declare her fascinating. That rather grand lady who always accompanies her is her aunt, and I fancy the fair Forina leads her a dance."

"What an absurd name," interposed Dalton, "it's a sort of a cross between a breakfast-food and Raphael's lady-love—neither of them very desirable articles. But tell me, she talked to me in a rather unusual way for a first meeting—is eccentricity her pose?"

"Not in the least," replied Brooks, "her father was a decidedly queer duck and tried to bear out the Martian theory and similar fairy-tales. In fact some went so far as to say he was not strictly *compos mentis*. The daughter is as genuine as they make 'em, but a bit too progressive for the average mind. Hence, she is dubbed eccentric."

Dalton frowned in a preoccupied manner, and then remarked, "Well, she's decidedly interesting, and she's played havoc in my studio."

"How do you mean?"

"Simply that I've destroyed every canvas in it."

"For Heaven's sake! Aren't you going to paint any more?"

"I don't know what I'm going to do. I know that I never want to go into the country again—I'd be ashamed to look a cow in the face." He slouched up out of his chair, reached for his hat, and added, "You don't happen to know where she's stopping, do you?"

"No," replied Brooks, "but I can find out and let you know, for my mother and her aunt are warm friends. Shall I find you at the studio?"

"Yes. Many thanks. Ta-ta, old man," and Dalton's broad back vanished through the door.

Dalton returned to his studio in a listless, disinterested way, and a pang of self-pity swept over him as he beheld the bare walls, and skeleton-like easels. First pulling a cord that let fall a soft yellow drapery over the skylight, thus flooding the room with a mellowness that veiled somewhat its desolation, he lighted his meerschaum, and sat ruminating over his life until it seemed to him his future stretched out in a waste too dreary to be contemplated. He was a failure, and he had not even recognized the fact until the frank scorn of a woman had opened his eyes. Now, what was left to him? If he were starving to death, he could never produce anything rural again, and he had absolutely no talent for painting any other subject. How long he had sat there he did not know—he was conscious only that the Sleepy Hollow chair was alluringly adaptable to the curves of one's body, and the mellow light most restful to one's tired brain.

Suddenly before his eyes appeared a thin, vapory mist, which rapidly grew in density until he seemed to be enveloped in a yellowish fog, except that instead of being chill and depressing, it gave out a subtle warmth that vaguely exhilarated him. He sat up in his chair, tossing his head to shake off any possible trick of the imagination, but in every direction his gaze met the peculiar yellow haze. He sank back again, trying to calm his bewitched mind, then sprang up quickly and stood trembling, facing one corner of the room. There the fog had dissolved so as to leave clear a picture, the composition of which burned into Dalton's brain as a branding-iron marks the flesh of a steer. A woman stood on his model-platform—Forina Forsythe, clad in a gold gown of some exquisite fabric that fell in shimmering folds around her lithe body. In her hands she held a crystal, into which she was gazing with such horror as could only be the expression of utmost fear, and as Dalton looked closer, he also saw, in the glass ball, the scene that caused such terror in her eyes. In miniature what appeared like a piece of stone was shown, across which was lying a woman's arm in the relaxation of death. The rest of the woman's body was lost in the reflection of the glass, but Dalton could easily detect upon the arm the same antique scarab bracelet that he had noticed on Miss Forsythe's. One other detail added to the grewsomeness of the whole—a fat loathsome worm was undulating slowly but steadily toward the woman's upturned palm.

Dalton shuddered and recalled with repulsion that he was one of the most enthusiastic followers of the new fad of crystal-gazing. How horrible it all was, and how the woman was suffering! If only he could catch an expression like that on canvas it would be a masterpiece! Still, ought not he to destroy the illusion and end such agony even though it be imaginary?

He started toward the platform, when, almost as though Forina spoke to him, a voice seemed to say, "Paint! Paint! Work!"

Dalton threw back his shoulders, laughed aloud and dashed through the fog to the opposite corner where he kept fresh canvasses. Selecting the largest, snatching up charcoal, and dragging an easel, he made his way back to the point from which every detail of the picture was clear to him. Then throwing himself into a chair, he began to sketch with an unwonted boldness.

The seconds rushed into minutes, and the minutes into hours, and Dalton replaced charcoal with paint and worked with feverish concentration. He was dimly conscious that some one rapped on the studio door and then departed, and somewhere in the mist-filled room a telephone rang several times. But Dalton was beyond being disturbed, and his brushes flew from palette to canvas as though guided by the shade of a Guido. Once he realized that night had descended, but though the room was full of dark, cloudy shadows, the light about the model-platform and easel was as softly strong as summer sunshine. Not once did Forina's slender figure falter from the trying position; not once did her horror-stricken gaze wander from the crystal, and still Dalton painted on, though the heat of fever crept over his brow, his head throbbed, and he felt a faintness that almost conquered him.

Somewhere out of the night a clock struck three, but the silence was unbroken save for the strokes of the brush as it flew over the canvas. Then followed such sounds as mark the progress of day in the city—the rumbling of the milk-carts, the cries of the newsboys, children's laughter and shouts on their way to school, a street-piano grinding out the complaint that "Everybody works but father." The bells and whistles proclaimed the respite of noon after the morning's labor, and then came the children returning at four, and the whistles again at six announcing that day's work over.

Dalton was painting in the last reflection in the crystal when he felt a peculiar numbness steal over him, the hand holding the brush fell powerless to his side, and the woman on the model-platform seemed melting away. He tried to pull himself together and to put out a detaining hand, but it was no use; he felt much the same sensation he had once experienced while taking chloroform—the struggle to remain cognizant of surroundings and the gradual slipping away into unreal space.

Several hours later they broke in the door and found him lying there, unconscious, before a canvas which startled them into awe and admiration as they gazed. Could this be the work of Dalton, the gay, self-satisfied dilettante? And if he had produced this work of art, who had been his model? What miracle had taken place?

The next day the doctor's fussy little back had scarcely disappeared, when Dalton pulled himself weakly out of bed and into bath-robe and slippers, and climbed the stairs to his studio. At the door he paused, hesitating to destroy what he knew must have been a chimera of his tired brain when he had sat down with his meerschaum in the Sleepy Hollow chair. Then he went inside, closed the door after him and walked straight to the spot where he recalled that his canvas had been placed. Again he paused and brushed his hand in bewilderment over his eyes, scarcely able to grasp the miracle of the painting before him—such beauty of coloring, such dignity, such intelligent understanding of his subject he saw in the work. Even as he wondered he gave a shout of exultation as he realized that ambition and inspiration had claimed him, and that he was young and full of strength and energy to carry out his new ideals. He had felt that there was more than an ordinary interest attached to his meeting with Miss Forsythe, he must see her and tell her what this marvellous dream of her had accomplished for him.

He went hurriedly to the telephone and called up Brooks, who had promised to obtain her address for him.

Mr. Brooks was not there, so the maid answered. He and his mother had gone to Mrs. Forsythe's to see if they could be of any assistance.

"Assistance?" asked Dalton.

"Yes, Mr. Dalton; did you not see it in the papers?"

"Papers?" he repeated stupidly.

"Yes, sir; they are full of it."

"Full of what?"

"Miss Forsythe, sir. She was gone all day yesterday and the night before, and last night the police found her right near your studio, and she was dead, sir. The doctors say she must have fainted and struck her head on the stone curbing as she fell, for there is a terrible gash in her left temple. Anyway, she's dead, Mr. Dalton, and they say Mrs. Forsythe is almost crazy. Yes, sir, what did you say, sir? Mr. Dalton?—Well, he's polite to ring off like that."

Dalton dropped the receiver and stumbled over to a chair into which he literally fell, trying to grasp what he had heard. His gaze fixed on the glorious canvas from which the golden girl stood out mysteriously, and then wandered to the bare model-platform, and the empty years stretched out wearily before him as he pondered the never-solved problem—the miracle of his inspiration.

The Damned Thing

Ambrose Bierce

I. One Does Not Always Eat What Is on the Table

By the light of a tallow candle, which had been placed on one end of a rough table, a man was reading something written in a book. It was an old account book, greatly worn; and the writing was not, apparently, very legible, for the man sometimes held the page close to the flame of the candle to get a stronger light upon it. The shadow of the book would then throw into obscurity a half of the room, darkening a number of faces and figures; for besides the reader, eight other men were present. Seven of them sat against the rough log walls, silent and motionless, and, the room being small, not very far from the table. By extending an arm any one of them could have touched the eighth man, who lay on the table, face upward, partly covered by a sheet, his arms at his sides. He was dead.

The man with the book was not reading aloud, and no one spoke; all seemed to be waiting for something to occur; the dead man only was without expectation. From the blank darkness outside came in, through the aperture that served for a window, all the ever unfamiliar noises of night in the wilderness—the long, nameless note of a distant coyote; the stilly pulsing thrill of tireless insects in trees; strange cries of night birds, so different from those of the birds of day; the drone of great blundering beetles, and all that mysterious chorus of small sounds that seem always to have been but half heard when they have suddenly ceased, as if conscious of an indiscretion. But nothing of all this was noted in that company; its members were not overmuch addicted to idle interest in matters of no practical importance; that was obvious in every line of their rugged faces—obvious even in the dim light of the single candle. They were evidently men of the vicinity—farmers and woodmen.

The person reading was a trifle different; one would have said of him that he was of the world, worldly, albeit there was that in his attire which attested a certain fellowship with the organisms of his environment. His coat would hardly have passed muster in San Francisco: his footgear was not of urban origin, and the hat that lay by him on the floor (he was the only one uncovered) was such that if one had considered it as an article of mere personal adornment he would have missed its meaning. In countenance the man was rather prepossessing, with just a hint of sternness; though that he may have assumed or cultivated, as appropriate to one in authority. For he was a coroner. It was by virtue of his office that he had possession of the book in which he was reading; it had been found among the dead man's effects—in his cabin, where the inquest was now taking place.

When the coroner had finished reading he put the book into his breast pocket. At that moment the door was pushed open and a young man entered. He, clearly, was not of mountain birth and breeding: he was clad as those who dwell in cities. His clothing was dusty, however, as from travel. He had, in fact, been riding hard to attend the inquest.

The coroner nodded; no one else greeted him.

"We have waited for you," said the coroner. "It is necessary to have done with this business to-night."

The young man smiled. "I am sorry to have kept you," he said. "I went away, not to evade your summons, but to post to my newspaper an account of what I suppose I am called back to relate."

The coroner smiled.

"The account that you posted to your newspaper," he said, "differs probably from that which you will give here under oath."

"That," replied the other, rather hotly and with a visible flush, "is as you choose. I used manifold paper and have a copy of what I sent. It was not written as news, for it is incredible, but as fiction. It may go as a part of my testimony under oath."

"But you say it is incredible."

"That is nothing to you, sir, if I also swear that it is true."

The coroner was apparently not greatly affected by the young man's manifest resentment. He was silent for some moments, his eyes upon the floor. The men about the sides of the cabin talked in whispers, but seldom withdrew their gaze from the face of the corpse. Presently the coroner lifted his eyes and said: "We will resume the inquest."

The men removed their hats. The witness was sworn.

"What is your name?" the coroner asked.

"William Harker."

"Age?"

"Twenty-seven."

"You knew the deceased, Hugh Morgan?"

"Yes."

"You were with him when he died?"

"Near him."

"How did that happen—your presence, I mean?"

"I was visiting him at this place to shoot and fish. A part of my purpose, however, was to study him, and his odd, solitary way of life. He seemed a good model for a character in fiction. I sometimes write stories."

"I sometimes read them."

"Thank you."

"Stories in general—not yours."

Some of the jurors laughed. Against a sombre background humor shows high lights. Soldiers in the intervals of battle laugh easily, and a jest in the death chamber conquers by surprise.

"Relate the circumstances of this man's death," said the coroner. "You may use any notes or memoranda that you please."

The witness understood. Pulling a manuscript from his breast pocket he held it near the candle, and turning the leaves until he found the passage that he wanted, began to read.

II. WHAT MAY HAPPEN IN A FIELD OF WILD OATS

". . . The sun had hardly risen when we left the house. We were looking for quail, each with a shotgun, but we had only one dog. Morgan said that our best ground was beyond a certain ridge that he pointed out, and we crossed it by a trail through the *chaparral*. On the other side was comparatively level ground, thickly covered with wild oats. As we emerged from the *chaparral*, Morgan was but a few yards in advance. Suddenly, we heard, at a little distance to our right, and partly in front, a noise as of some animal thrashing about in the bushes, which we could see were violently agitated.

"'We've started a deer,' said. 'I wish we had brought a rifle.'

"Morgan, who had stopped and was intently watching the agitated chaparral, said nothing, but had cocked both barrels of his gun, and was holding it in readiness to aim. I thought him a trifle excited, which surprised me, for he had a reputation for exceptional coolness, even in moments of sudden and imminent peril.

"'O, come!' I said. 'You are not going to fill up a deer with quail-shot, are you?'

"Still he did not reply; but, catching a sight of his face as he turned it slightly toward me, I was struck by the pallor of it. Then I understood that we had serious business on hand, and my first conjecture was that we had 'jumped' a grizzly. I advanced to Morgan's side, cocking my piece as I moved.

"The bushes were now quiet, and the sounds had ceased, but Morgan was as attentive to the place as before.

" 'What is it? What the devil is it?' I asked.

" 'That Damned Thing!' he replied, without turning his head. His voice was husky and unnatural. He trembled visibly.

"I was about to speak further, when I observed the wild oats near the place of the disturbance moving in the most inexplicable way. I can hardly describe it. It seemed as if stirred by a streak of wind, which not only bent it, but pressed it down—crushed it so that it did not rise, and this movement was slowly prolonging itself directly toward us.

"Nothing that I had ever seen had affected me so strangely as this unfamiliar and unaccountable phenomenon, yet I am unable to recall any sense of fear. I remember—and tell it here because, singularly enough, I recollected it then—that once, in looking carelessly out of an open window, I momentarily mistook a small tree close at hand for one of a group of larger trees at a little distance away. It looked the same size as the others, but, being more distinctly and sharply defined in mass and detail, seemed out of harmony with them. It was a mere falsification of the law of aerial perspective, but it startled, almost terrified me. We so rely upon the orderly operation of familiar natural laws that any seeming suspension of them is noted as a menace to our safety, a warning of unthinkable calamity. So now the apparently causeless movement of the herbage, and the slow, undeviating approach of the line of disturbance were distinctly disquieting. My companion appeared actually frightened, and I could hardly credit my senses when I saw him suddenly throw his gun to his shoulders and fire both barrels at the agitated grass! Before the smoke of the discharge had cleared away I heard a loud savage cry—a scream like that of a wild animal—and, flinging his gun upon the ground, Morgan sprang away and ran swiftly from the spot. At the same instant I was thrown violently to the ground by the impact of something unseen in the smoke—some soft, heavy substance that seemed thrown against me with great force.

"Before I could get upon my feet and recover my gun, which seemed to have been struck from my hands, I heard Morgan crying out as if in mortal agony, and mingling with his cries were such hoarse savage sounds as one hears from fighting dogs. Inexpressibly terrified, I struggled to my feet and looked in the direction of Morgan's retreat; and may heaven in mercy spare me from another sight like that! At a distance of less than thirty yards was my friend, down upon one knee, his head thrown back at a frightful angle, hatless, his long hair in disorder and his whole body in violent movement from side to side, backward and forward. His right arm was lifted and seemed to lack the hand—at least, I could see none. The other arm was invisible. At times, as my memory now reports this extraordinary scene, I could discern but a part of his body; it was as if he had been partly blotted out—I can not otherwise express it—then a shifting of his position would bring it all into view again.

"All this must have occurred within a few seconds, yet in that time Morgan assumed all the postures of a determined wrestler vanquished by superior weight and strength. I saw nothing but him, and him not always distinctly. During the entire incident his shouts and curses were heard, as if through an enveloping uproar of such sounds of rage and fury as I had never heard from the throat of man or brute!

"For a moment only I stood irresolute, then, throwing down my gun, I ran forward to my friend's assistance. I had a vague belief that he was suffering from a fit or some form of convulsion. Before I could reach his side he was down and quiet. All sounds had ceased, but, with a feeling of such terror as even these awful events had not inspired, I now saw the same mysterious movement of the wild oats prolonging itself from the trampled area about the prostrate man toward the edge of a wood. It was only when it had reached the wood that I was able to withdraw my eyes and look at my companion. He was dead."

III. A MAN THOUGH NAKED MAY BE IN RAGS

The coroner rose from his seat and stood beside the dead man. Lifting an edge of the sheet he pulled it away, exposing the entire body, altogether naked and showing in the candle-light a clay-like yellow. It had, however, broad maculations of bluish-black, obviously caused by extravasated blood from contusions. The chest and sides looked as if they had been beaten with a bludgeon. There were dreadful lacerations; the skin was torn in strips and shreds.

The coroner moved round to the end of the table and undid a silk handkerchief, which had been passed under the chin and knotted on the top of the head. When the handkerchief was drawn away it exposed what had been the throat. Some of the jurors who had risen to get a better view repented their curiosity, and turned away their faces. Witness Harker went to the open window and leaned out across the sill, faint and sick. Dropping the handkerchief upon the dead man's neck, the coroner stepped to an angle of the room, and from a pile of clothing produced one garment after another, each of which he held up a moment for inspection. All were torn, and stiff with blood. The jurors did not make a closer inspection. They seemed rather uninterested. They had, in truth, seen all this before; the only thing that was new to them being Harker's testimony.

"Gentlemen," the coroner said, "we have no more evidence, I think. Your duty has been already explained to you; if there is nothing you wish to ask you may go outside and consider your verdict."

The foreman rose—a tall, bearded man of sixty, coarsely clad.

"I should like to ask one question, Mr. Coroner," he said. "What asylum did this yer last witness escape from?"

"Mr. Harker," said the coroner, gravely and tranquilly, "from what asylum did you last escape?"

Harker flushed crimson again, but said nothing, and the seven jurors rose and solemnly filed out of the cabin.

"If you have done insulting me, sir," said Harker, as soon as he and the officer were left alone with the dead man, "I suppose I am at liberty to go?"

"Yes."

Harker started to leave, but paused, with his hand on the door latch. The habit of his profession was strong in him—stronger than his sense of personal dignity. He turned about and said:

"The book that you have there—I recognize it as Morgan's diary. You seemed greatly interested in it; you read in it while I was testifying. May I see it? The public would like—"

"The book will cut no figure in this matter," replied the official, slipping it into his coat pocket; "all the entries in it were made before the writer's death."

As Harker passed out of the house the jury reentered and stood about the table on which the now covered corpse showed under the sheet with sharp definition. The foreman seated himself near the candle, produced from his breast pocket a pencil and scrap of paper, and wrote rather laboriously the following verdict, which with various degrees of effort all signed:

"We, the jury, do find that the remains come to their death at the hands of a mountain lion, but some of us thinks, all the same, they had fits."

IV. AN EXPLANATION FROM THE TOMB

In the diary of the late Hugh Morgan are certain interesting entries having, possibly, a scientific value as suggestions. At the inquest upon his body the book was not put in evidence; possibly the coroner thought it not worth while to confuse the jury. The date of the first of the entries mentioned can not be ascertained; the upper part of the leaf is torn away; the part of the entry remaining is as follows:

". . . would run in a half circle, keeping his head turned always toward the centre and again he would stand still, barking furiously. At last he ran away into the brush as fast as he could go. I thought at first that he had gone mad, but on returning to the house found no other alteration in his manner than what was obviously due to fear of punishment.

"Can a dog see with his nose? Do odors impress some olfactory centre with images of the thing emitting them? . . .

"Sept 2.—Looking at the stars last night as they rose above the crest of the ridge east of the house, I observed them successively disappear—from left to right. Each was eclipsed but an instant, and only a few at the same time, but along the entire length of the ridge all that were within a degree or two of the crest were blotted out. It was as if something had passed along between me and them; but I could not see it, and the stars were not thick enough to define its outline. Ugh! I don't like this. . . ."

Several weeks' entries are missing, three leaves being torn from the book.

"Sept. 27.—It has been about here again—I find evidences of its presence every day. I watched again all of last night in the same cover, gun in hand, double-charged with buckshot. In the morning the fresh footprints were there, as before. Yet I would have sworn that I did not sleep—indeed, I hardly sleep at all. It is terrible, insupportable! If these amazing experiences are real I shall go mad; if they are fanciful I am mad already.

"Oct. 3.—I shall not go—it shall not drive me away. No, this is *my* house, my land. God hates a coward. . . .

"Oct. 5.—I can stand it no longer; I have invited Harker to pass a few weeks with me—he has a level head. I can judge from his manner if he thinks me mad.

"Oct. 7.—I have the solution of the problem; it came to me last night—suddenly, as by revelation. How simple—how terribly simple!

"There are sounds that we can not hear. At either end of the scale are notes that stir no chord of that imperfect instrument, the human ear. They are too high or too grave. I have observed a flock of blackbirds occupying an entire treetop—the tops of several trees—and all in full song. Suddenly—in a moment—at absolutely the same instant—all spring into the air and fly away. How? They could not all see one another—whole treetops intervened. At no point could a leader have been visible to all. There must have been a signal of warning or command, high and shrill above the din, but by me unheard. I have observed, too, the same simultaneous flight when all were silent, among not only blackbirds, but other birds—quail, for example, widely separated by bushes—even on opposite sides of a hill.

"It is known to seamen that a school of whales basking or sporting on the surface of the ocean, miles apart, with the convexity of the earth between them, will sometimes dive at the same instant—all gone out of sight in a moment. The signal has been sounded—too grave for the ear of the sailor at the masthead and his comrades on the deck—who nevertheless feel its vibrations in the ship as the stones of a cathedral are stirred by the bass of the organ.

"As with sounds, so with colors. At each end of the solar spectrum the chemist can detect the presence of what are known as 'actinic' rays. They represent colors—integral colors in the composition of light—which we are unable to discern. The human eye is an imperfect instrument; its range is but a few octaves of the real 'chromatic scale.' I am not mad; there are colors that we cannot see.

"And, God help me! the Damned Thing is of such a color!"

A Dead Man's Bargain

Clive Pemberton

The conversation in the smoke-room had flowed unflaggingly, as conversation will when a cosmopolitan gathering comes together, and the pipes are drawing well and none is a laggard with the glass. There were a dozen grouped around the blazing log fire—men from all parts and in diverse walks of life. Topic after topic was broached, descanted upon at length or dismissed with a word, and at last the subject of supernatural agency was started.

"I can't and don't believe in what some people call supernatural agencies," said a stout, jovial faced man, drawing briskly at a mammoth briar. "I remember a man telling me once of a visitation he had from his mother-in-law—deceased ten years—and it nearly killed him—the shock of seeing her again, I suppose," and he laughed ponderously into his glass.

"I don't believe in spirits or such things either," chimed in a matter-of-fact commercial. "You see, I'm one to only believe in what my eyes show me, and spirits that come to worry folk and frighten them out of their wits always—"

"Yet supernatural happenings are on record whether you believe in them or not."

All turned simultaneously to learn from whom the interruption had come. It proceeded from a man who was sitting somewhat apart from the group round the fireplace. At the first glance, all noticed the same strange thing about him. The face was that of a young man, but the hair, which grew somewhat long and disheveled, was snow-white, and in the eyes there lurked an expression such as is only seen in those having once undergone some shock or neverto-be-forgotten ordeal. There was a moment of silence, then the first speaker addressed the stranger, who, after his quietly-spoken words, had retired into the background again as though embarrassed at having spoken.

"I don't think any of us here but are open to conviction," said the commercial, looking invitingly round. He turned to the stranger. "If you have a story to tell, sir, you will not have to complain of inattention. What do you say, gentlemen?"

The affirmative was unanimous, and the stranger slowly drew his chair forward into the circle. Amid a flattering silence he commenced his story.

You ask yourselves why I, young in years, should have the face of a worn old man and hair whiter than Time could ever bleach it? Listen to the true story of my awful and inexplicable experience—an experience that in one short hour changed the color of my hair from brown to white, and carved lines on my face that nothing will ever erase while memory lasts to haunt me with the recollection of the most fearful ordeal mortal man ever went through and emerged alive to speak of.

At the time of which I speak—some five years ago—I was living in a remote little town in the Midlands which I will call L——. From my earliest years, the passion of my life had been music, and an annuity of two hundred a year allowed me to follow my natural inclinations without fear of being harassed by financial difficulties. Insignificant and even unimportant though L—— was, it yet possessed one object of interest and antiquity—the Parish Church. This was a fine old building erected in the reign of Elizabeth—rich in stained glass and well preserved stone frescoes. But its greatest attraction—to me, at any rate—was the organ—a superb instrument combining the immortal work of Father Smith with the modern improvements in mechanism by the latter-day builders. The whole instrument had been reconstructed and made perfect by the generosity of a rich patron some two years before, and on the completion of the work a new organist was appointed—a stranger to L—named Reuben Chelston. I suppose it was our equal enthusiasm in the one pursuit that drew us together, for, in a very short time, Reuben Chelston and I were firm and inseparable companions. As an executant on the organ I have never heard his equal; but as time went on and I got to know him better, I found that he was a man possessed of some very extraordinary theories regarding the supernatural, and in the creed of spiritualism he thoroughly believed. At first his extraordinary doctrines—delivered at lightning speed and with a kind of hysterical excitement that invariably seized him when on the subject—astonished me not a little, and would have led many to incline towards the belief that he was mad; but constant and close contact with the man had given me a deeper insight into his temperament than others possessed, and as I never attempted to argue the matter with him or try to convince him to the contrary, no harm was done. There was seldom an evening that I did not spend with him in the empty church, listening while he played as only he *could* play. In my mind's eye I can see him now, his great shaggy head thrown back, eyes closed in a sort of ecstatic trance, and the most wonderful melodies ravishing the air as his hands swept over the keys.

Strange melodies they were sometimes that his fancy would conceive, and if some of those extemporaneous pieces he played to me could be reproduced, they would, I am convinced, rank with some of the finest compositions the world has ever heard. It was about a year after the beginning of our somewhat curious intimacy that I first noticed the beginning of a strange change in my friend. He had repeatedly told me that he had confided in me as in no other living person, for, indeed, I was his only companion and he seemed to possess no other friends or acquaintances. He was always a man of moods, now grave, now gay, and subject to curious lapses of sullenness when he appeared to be thinking deeply over something known only to himself. It was the summer time, and after the usual practice in the Church one evening, he returned with me to my rooms. Once or twice I was on the point of asking him what was amiss, for he seemed to be laboring under some excitement that he found difficult to suppress. For a long time after we had finished the meal he sat silent, his eyes fixed vacantly on the wall and his lips moving rapidly as though he were repeating some set formula to himself over and over again. Suddenly he turned to me—his voice wonderfully quiet and well under control.

"Harold," he said; "I am going away for a while."

"Going away?" I repeated. "Where to? what for?"

"I am going away from here," he went on, not appearing to notice my questions, "because I cannot do what I have to do here."

"What have you to do which cannot be done here?" I asked, curiously. He was silent for a moment, then he seemed to rouse himself, and his voice sounded clear and distinct.

"As you know," he said, fixing his eyes—the most wonderful eyes ever set in a man's head—on mine, "I have confided things to you that nobody save myself knows of. Have you noticed that I have been away every Wednesday night for the past six weeks?"

"Why, yes," I replied, quickly, "but I did not like to—"

"Quite so," he said, lifting his thin white hand; "but I want you to know why I have been away and what took me away. I have been attending seances—spiritualistic seances!"

I was silent as I heard this, and he went on again quickly after a short pause.

"Harold, why cannot you think as I do?" he cried, a note of pettish irritation in his voice. "I tell you that great marvels can be unfolded by those who return for a fleeting space from the other side. Something will be revealed to me tomorrow night, and then—and then—"

My thoughts had been wandering a little when he commenced speaking, but as he said this my attention was arrested in an instant.

"How can anything be revealed to you tomorrow night?" I said, looking closely at him. "You don't mean that you—that you—?"

I broke off as he leaned swiftly towards me.

"This I do tell you," he said, in a kind of awed whisper. "Tomorrow night, myself and one medium will await that which I have been told will be given to me. Such a melody as the world has never yet heard the equal of will be given to me, note by note, by—"

"By whom?" I said sharply, as he suddenly checked himself. He sat silent and thoughtful for a moment.

"That I cannot tell you," he replied, at last. "But this I do promise you, Harold. You shall be the first to hear the wonderful melody, be it what it is." He dropped his voice to a thrilling whisper. "What if it should be so stupendously unearthly as to be unfit for mortal ears?"

The suddenly conceived idea seemed to move him to ungovernable excitement. He rose and paced the floor with eager, nervous strides. For my part I sat silent and thoughtful. The idea was preposterous, even fraught with a vague suggestion of evil that struck a warning note within my prosaic being.

"Chelston," I said suddenly, looking up at him; "I am going to ask you to do—or rather *not* to do—something."

He paused and looked at me with dilated eyes.

"Well?" he said, quickly.

"I want you not to do what you—you have just told me you are going to do!"

He made a quick movement with his hands.

"Why do you ask me such an impossible thing?" he said, half angrily.

"Because I instinctively feel that some evil will come of it," I rejoined, boldly. "If we were meant to—to—"

"Enough!" he interposed, peremptorily. "What I have told you I *shall* do! Remember, I promise you that you shall be the first to hear it. Nothing shall prevent you hearing first! Think of me tomorrow night! . . ."

The following day he left L—— before anybody was up and about. It was a blistering hot day—the hottest of that summer—and, situated in a cup-like valley as the town was, it was almost insufferable. All that never-to-be-forgotten day, I felt strangely depressed and restless. I could not settle to anything, and though I tried hard to interest myself in a composition I was at work on, I could not shake off the vague foreboding of a nameless disaster that seemed hanging over me. During the afternoon, the barometer fell with that sudden and ominous rush that heralds an approaching thunder-storm. Tired with doing nothing all day and still overshadowed by that same feeling of depression, I determined to walk to the church in the cool of the evening and spend an hour at the organ. The air was still humid and oppressive when I started, although the great heat had gone with the hazing of the sun by a bank of black, uprising clouds. I noticed them as I waited outside the verger's cottage while he fetched the keys.

"It looks as if a storm was brewing, Trench," I said, pointing to the sullen bank of clouds.

"Ay!" he replied, shading his eyes with his hand—"It dew that to be sure, an' it'll be on us afore we expects it, I reckon. I wouldn't be too long if I were you, sir. It will be rain when it does come down!"

I agreed with him, and having taken the keys, went on to the church. Having let myself in, I locked the door behind me and mounted the gallery steps to the organ loft. The church—even in bright daylight—was always dim and somewhat gloomy, owing to every window being composed of richly colored stained glass. Now, with the gathering murky gloom without, the interior was almost completely dark, only the white stone pillars and alabaster statues gleaming white and indistinct at the far end below should here explain that when the instrument had been renovated and enlarged, a waterdriven engine had been installed, thereby rendering the services of a bellows man unnecessary. Afterwards, I would have given the world if another had been with me . . . But I am anticipating. Having lighted the desk lamps and uncovered the keyboards, I pulled down the lever that controlled the engine, and from the vault far below, I heard the dull thud! thud! of the pistons as they drove the air into the bellows. In a few moments I was lost in a world of melody, and as I put fancy after fancy into execution, the minutes slipped on into long after the hour I had intended to stop. Suddenly I lifted my hands from the keys, and closed my eyes as the gilt music support on the desk before me glinted like an electric spark. It was a gleaming flash of lightning that had stealthily darted from the window on my left and had been reflected in the brass rest. With my hands grasping the stops I listened intently. The rain was pattering down on the roof above with harsh force, and yes! faint but unmistakable was the distant mutter and roll of thunder. Quite suddenly—more suddenly than I can describe—I was seized with that strange sensation which everybody has felt at some time when in an empty building—the sensation that I was not *alone* and was being *watched*! I sat perfectly rigid, straining my ears to hear—what? I do not know, but while I would have given anything to have looked behind me, I found myself powerless to move my head or even glance in the slanting mirror that commanded a view of the gallery and well behind and below me. How long I sat thus I do not know, but a second gleaming of lightning—far more vivid than the first—recalled me to action. Seizing the handle that controlled the engine, I turned it off, then pulled the knob of the ledge that covered the key boards. It would not *move*! Something seemed to be holding it back! I tugged and pulled at it but to no purpose, and as my strange nervousness—it was positive *fear* by this time!—kept that was descending on the roof above me. The last breath of wind ebbed out of the empty bellows with a curious momentarily increasing, I at last desisted, for my one desire was to get outside despite the avalanche of rain ticking sound; then, amid a strange, deathly still lull both within and without, I turned out one of the gas jets. As I did so, a peculiar thing happened. A draught—faint, yet perfectly distinct—swept behind me; but, with an describable feeling of terror, I noticed that the flame beside me did not flicker or become actuated by it in the slightest degree. A kind of frantic desire seized me to tear madly down the steps and out into the raging storm, for fragments of Reuben Chelston's strange conversations recurred to me, and, try as I would, I could not shut them out. With a sudden· effort I turned out the remaining gas-jet, and in black darkness groped my way to the door. I had just reached it when I again distinctly felt a slight stirring of the air—just what a draught would be if caused by somebody passing! Down the steps I crept, one by one, the lightning blazing in at the windows with blinding brilliancy and alarming rapidity. To get to the door, I had to walk the whole length of the aisle, and, with my heart wildly beating, I sped up it, twisting my head round mechanically at every yard. I was about twothirds up, perhaps, when I suddenly stopped. What was that? I strained my ears, my heartbeats humming in my head. It came again, sending a thrill of horror through me, for clearly enough I heard the sudden throb of the engine far below and then the sound of the bellows filling. Like the crash of brazen cymbals in my ears it was borne in upon me that I was *not alone*! Somebody had started the engine—somebody was in the building with me. Summoning all my presence of mind, I called out—

"Who is there?"

The echo of my voice was drowned in an appalling crash of thunder; but as it died away, I fancied that a wild laugh came from the gallery! And then—and then—How can I describe what followed? I cannot—simply cannot, for my brain reels at the recollection of it. The storm seemed to suddenly subside—the rain ceased to clatter on the roof, and in an unbroken silence, the organ began to sound. If I could command the language and descriptive power of the greatest mind that ever lived, I could not convey the faintest conception of the weird music that flooded the empty building and poured into my shivering ears; but instinctively I knew that it was a death march—unearthly and of such somber grandeur as no living brain of man ever conceived. It seemed to tell of phrases that are faintly imagined and seen, shadow-like as in a dream, and awe-struck and bewildered I crouched down on the cold stone floor covering my ears, for I knew such melody was never meant for human ears to hear. How long it lasted I cannot say, but it gradually died away as gently and imperceptibly as a summer breeze, and as it did so, the clock in the tower slowly struck nine. Then action came to me, and springing to my feet, I flew to the door and fumbled with the key. The rain was falling heavily without as I tore open the door, and I felt that strange soft wind I had felt twice before pass me from *behind*! It passed me—passed me into the night and was gone! . . .

The man with the white hair ceased speaking, and lifting his hand to his forehead, brushed away a gleam that shone there. He lifted his glass and drank a little.

"A strange thing," said one, breaking the silence; "but—"

"How I got home I never knew," he continued, appearing not to notice the interruption; "but the sequel to that strange night's experience came two hours later. A telegram came for me with the news that Reuben Chelston had died suddenly at half past eight at the conclusion of a spiritualistic seance. And, as the last notes of that terrible dead march died away and I opened the door, the clock in the tower struck nine, and—and I felt that wind pass me! . . ."

There was silence in the room—a silence that remained unbroken.

Death and the Woman

Gertrude Atherton

Her husband was dying, and she was alone with him. Nothing could exceed the desolation of her surroundings. She and the man who was going from her were in the third-floor-back of a New York boarding-house. It was summer, and the other boarders were in the country; all the servants except the cook had been dismissed, and she, when not working, slept profoundly on the fifth floor. The landlady also was out of town on a brief holiday.

The window was open to admit the thick unstirring air; no sound rose from the row of long narrow yards, nor from the tall deep houses annexed. The latter deadened the rattle of the streets. At intervals the distant elevated lumbered protestingly along, its grunts and screams muffled by the hot suspended ocean.

She sat there plunged in the profoundest grief that can come to the human soul, for in all other agony hope flickers, however forlornly. She gazed dully at the unconscious breathing form of the man who had been friend, and companion, and lover, during five years of youth too vigorous and hopeful to be warped by uneven fortune. It was wasted by disease; the face was shrunken; the night garment hung loosely about a body which had never been disfigured by flesh, but had been muscular with exercise and full-blooded with health. She was glad that the body was changed; glad that its beauty, too, had gone some other-where than into the coffin. She had loved his hands as apart from himself; loved their strong warm magnetism. They lay limp and yellow on the quilt: she knew that they were already cold, and that moisture was gathering on them. For a moment something convulsed within her. *They* had gone too. She repeated the words twice, and, after them, "*forever.*" And the while the sweetness of their pressure came back to her.

She leaned suddenly over him. HE was in there still, somewhere. *Where?* If he had not ceased to breathe, the Ego, the Soul, the Personality, was still in the sodden clay which had shaped to give it speech. Why could it not manifest itself to her? Was it still conscious in there, unable to project itself through the disintegrating matter which was the only medium its Creator had vouchsafed it? Did it struggle there, seeing her agony, sharing it, longing for the complete disintegration which should put an end to its torment? She called his name, she even shook him slightly, mad to tear the body apart and find her mate, yet even in that tortured moment realising that violence would hasten his going.

The dying man took no notice of her, and she opened his gown and put her cheek to his heart, calling him again. There had never been more perfect union; how could the bond still be so strong if he were not at the other end of it? He was there, her other part; until dead he must be living. There was no intermediate state. Why should he be as entombed and unresponding as if the screws were in the lid? But the faintly beating heart did not quicken beneath her lips. She extended her arms suddenly, describing eccentric lines, above, about him, rapidly opening and closing her hands as if to clutch some escaping object; then sprang to her feet, and went to the window. She feared insanity. She had asked to be left alone with her dying husband, and she did not wish to lose her reason and shriek a crowd of people about her.

The green plots in the yards were not apparent, she noticed. Something heavy, like a pall, rested upon them. Then she understood that the day was over and that night was coming.

She returned swiftly to the bedside, wondering if she had remained away hours or seconds, and if he were dead. His face was still discernible, and Death had not relaxed it. She laid her own against it, then withdrew it with shuddering flesh, her teeth smiting each other as if an icy wind had passed.

She let herself fall back in the chair, clasping her hands against her heart, watching with expanding eyes the white sculptured face which, in the gathering dark, was becoming less defined of outline. Did she light the gas it would draw mosquitoes, and she could not shut from him the little air he must be mechanically grateful for. And she did not want to see the opening eye—the falling jaw.

Her vision became so fixed that at length she saw nothing, and closed her eyes and waited for the moisture to rise and relieve the strain. When she opened them his face had disappeared; the humid waves above the house-tops put out even the light of the stars, and night was come.

Fearfully, she approached her ear to his lips; he still breathed. She made a motion to kiss him, then threw herself back in a quiver of agony—they were not the lips she had known, and she would have nothing less.

His breathing was so faint that in her half-reclining position she could not hear it, could not be aware of the moment of his death. She extended her arm resolutely and laid her hand on his heart. Not only must she feel his going, but, so strong had been the comradeship between them, it was a matter of loving honour to stand by him to the last.

She sat there in the hot heavy night, pressing her hand hard against the ebbing heart of the unseen, and awaited Death. Suddenly an odd fancy possessed her. Where was Death? Why was he tarrying? Who was detaining him? From what quarter would he come? He was taking his leisure, drawing near with footsteps as measured as those of men keeping time to a funeral march. By a wayward deflection she thought of the slow music that was always turned on in the theatre when the heroine was about to appear, or something eventful to happen. She had always thought that sort of thing ridiculous and inartistic. So had He.

She drew her brows together angrily, wondering at her levity, and pressed her relaxed palm against the heart it kept guard over. For a moment the sweat stood on her face; then the pent-up breath burst from her lungs. He still lived.

Once more the fancy wantoned above the stunned heart. Death—*where* was he? What a curious experience: to be sitting alone in a big house—she knew that the cook had stolen out—waiting for Death to come and snatch her husband from her. No; he would not snatch, he would steal upon his prey as noiselessly as the approach of Sin to Innocence—an invisible, unfair, sneaking enemy, with whom no man's strength could grapple. If he would only come like a man, and take his chances like a man! Women had been known to reach the hearts of giants with the dagger's point. But he would creep upon her.

She gave an exclamation of horror. Something was creeping over the windowsill. Her limbs palsied, but she struggled to her feet and looked back, her eyes dragged about against her own volition. Two small green stars glared menacingly at her just above the sill; then the cat possessing them leaped downward, and the stars disappeared.

She realised that she was horribly frightened. "Is it possible?" she thought. "Am I afraid of Death, and of Death that has not yet come? I have always been rather a brave woman; *He* used to call me heroic; but then with him it was impossible to fear anything. And I begged them to leave me alone with him as the last of earthly boons. Oh, shame!"

But she was still quaking as she resumed her seat, and laid her hand again on his heart. She wished that she had asked Mary to sit outside the door; there was no bell in the room. To call would be worse than desecrating the house of God, and she would not leave him for one moment. To return and find him dead—gone alone!

Her knees smote each other. It was idle to deny it; she was in a state of unreasoning terror. Her eyes rolled apprehensively about; she wondered if she should see It when It came; wondered how far off It was now. Not very far; the heart was barely pulsing. She had heard of the power of the corpse to drive brave men to frenzy, and had wondered, having no morbid horror of the dead. But this! To wait—and wait—and wait—perhaps for hours—past the midnight—on to the small hours—while that awful, determined, leisurely Something stole nearer and nearer.

She bent to him who had been her protector, with a spasm of anger. Where was the indomitable spirit that had held her all these years with such strong and loving clasp? How could he leave her? How could he desert her? Her head fell back and moved restlessly against the cushion; moaning with the agony of loss, she recalled him as he had been. Then fear once more took possession of her, and she sat erect, rigid, breathless, awaiting the approach of Death.

Suddenly, far down in the house, on the first-floor, her strained hearing took note of a sound—a wary, muffled sound, as if some one were creeping up the stair, fearful of being heard. Slowly! It seemed to count a hundred between the laying down of each foot. She gave a hysterical gasp. Where was the slow music?

Her face, her body, were wet—as if a wave of death-sweat had broken over them. There was a stiff feeling at the roots of her hair; she wondered if it were really standing erect. But she could not raise her hand to ascertain. Possibly it was only the coloring matter freezing and bleaching. Her muscles were flabby, her nerves twitched helplessly.

She knew that it was Death who was coming to her through the silent deserted house; knew that it was the sensitive ear of her intelligence that heard him, not the dull coarse-grained ear of the body.

He toiled up the stair painfully, as if he were old and tired with much work. But *how* could he afford to loiter, with all the work he had to do? Every minute, every second, he must be in demand to hook his cold hard finger about a soul struggling to escape from its putrefying tenement. But probably he had his emissaries, his minions: for only those worthy of the honour did he come in person.

He reached the first landing and crept like a cat down the hall to the next stair, then crawled slowly up as before. Light as the footfalls were, they were squarely planted, unfaltering; slow, they never halted.

Mechanically she pressed her jerking hand closer against the heart; its beats were almost done. They would finish, she calculated, just as those footfalls paused beside the bed.

She was no longer a human being; she was an Intelligence and an EAR. Not a sound came from without, even the Elevated appeared to be temporarily off duty;

but inside the big quiet house that footfall was waxing louder, louder, until iron feet crashed on iron stairs and echo thundered.

She had counted the steps—one—two—three—irritated beyond endurance at the long deliberate pauses between. As they climbed and clanged with slow precision she continued to count, audibly and with equal precision, noting their hollow reverberation. How many steps had the stair? She wished she knew. No need! The colossal trampling announced the lessening distance in an increasing volume of sound not to be misunderstood. It turned the curve; it reached the landing; it advanced—slowly—down the hall; it paused before her door. Then knuckles of iron shook the frail panels. Her nerveless tongue gave no invitation. The knocking became more imperious; the very walls vibrated. The handle turned, swiftly and firmly. With a wild instinctive movement she flung herself into the arms of her husband.

When Mary opened the door and entered the room she found a dead woman lying across a dead man.

The Demons of the Sea

William Hope Hodgson

"Come out on deck and have a look, Darky!" Jepson cried, rushing into the half deck. "The Old Man says there's been a submarine earthquake, and the sea's all bubbling and muddy!"

Obeying the summons of Jepson's excited tone, I followed him out. It was as he had said; the everlasting blue of the ocean was mottled with splotches of a muddy hue, and at times a large bubble would appear, to burst with a loud "pop." Aft, the skipper and the three mates could be seen on the poop, peering at the sea through their glasses. As I gazed out over the gently heaving water, far off to windward something was hove up into the evening air. It appeared to be a mass of seaweed, but fell back into the water with a sullen plunge as though it were something more substantial. Immediately after this strange occurrence, the sun set with tropical swiftness, and in the brief afterglow things assumed a strange unreality.

The crew were all below, no one but the mate and the helmsman remaining on the poop. Away forward, on the topgallant forecastle head the dim figure of the man on look-out could be seen, leaning against the forestay. No sound was heard save the occasional jingle of a chain sheet, of the flog of the steering gear as a small swell passed under our counter. Presently the mate's voice broke the silence, and, looking up, I saw that the Old Man had come on deck, and was talking with him. From the few stray words that could be overheard, I knew they were talking of the strange happenings of the day.

Shortly after sunset, the wind, which had been fresh during the day, died down, and with its passing the air grew oppressively hot. Not long after two bells, the mate sung out for me, and ordered me to fill a bucket from overside and bring it to him. When I had carried out his instructions, he placed a thermometer in the bucket.

"Just as I thought," he muttered, removing the instrument and showing it to the skipper; "ninety-nine degrees. Why, the sea's hot enough to make tea with!"

"Hope it doesn't get any hotter," growled the latter; "if it does, we shall all be boiled alive."

At a sign from the mate, I emptied the bucket and replaced it in the rack, after which I resumed my former position by the rail. The Old Man and the mate walked the poop side by side. The air grew hotter as the hours passed and after a long period of silence broken only by the occasional "pop" of a bursting gas bubble, the moon arose. It shed but a feeble light, however, as a heavy mist had arisen from the sea, and through this, the moonbeams struggled weakly. The mist, we decided, was due to the excessive heat of the sea water; it was a very wet mist, and we were soon soaked to the skin. Slowly the interminable night wore on, and the sun arose, looking dim and ghostly through the mist that rolled and billowed about the ship. From time to time we took the temperature of the sea, although we found but a slight increase therein. No work was done, and a feeling as of something impending pervaded the ship.

The fog horn was kept going constantly, as the lookout peered through the wreathing mists. The captain walked the poop in company with the mates, and once the third mate spoke and pointed out into the clouds of fog. All eyes followed his gesture; we saw what was apparently a black line, which seemed to cut the whiteness of the billows. It reminded us of nothing so much as an enormous cobra standing on its tail. As we looked it vanished. The grouped mates were evidently puzzled; there seemed to be a difference of opinion among them. Presently as they argued, I heard the second mate's voice:

"That's all rot," he said. "I've seen things in fog before, but they've always turned out to be imaginary."

The third shook his head and made some reply I could not overhear, but no further comment was made. Going below that afternoon, I got a short sleep, and on coming on deck at eight bells, I found that the steam still held us; if anything, it seemed to be thicker than ever. Hansard, who had been taking the temperatures during my watch below, informed me that the sea was three degrees hotter, and that the Old Man was getting into a rare old state. At three bells I went forward to have a look over the bows, and a chin with Stevenson, whose lookout it was. On gaining the forecastle head, I went to the side and looked down into the water. Stevenson came over and stood beside me.

"Rum go, this," he grumbled.

He stood by my side for a time in silence; we seemed to be hypnotized by the gleaming surface of the sea. Suddenly out of the depths, right before us, there arose a monstrous black face. It was like a frightful caricature of a human countenance. For a moment we gazed petrified; my blood seemed to suddenly turn to ice water; I was unable to move. With a mighty effort of will, I regained my self-control and, grasping Stevenson's arm, I found I could do no more than croak, my powers of speech seemed gone. "Look!" I gasped. "Look!"

Stevenson continued to stare into the sea, like a man turned to stone. He seemed to stoop further over, as if to examine the thing more closely. "Lord," he exclaimed, "it must be the devil himself!"

As though the sound of his voice had broken a spell, the thing disappeared. My companion looked at me, while I rubbed my eyes, thinking that I had been asleep, and that the awful vision had been a frightful nightmare. One look at my friend, however, disabused me of any such thought. His face wore a puzzled expression.

"Better go aft and tell the Old Man," he faltered.

I nodded and left the forecastle head, making my way aft like one in a trance. The skipper and the mate were standing at the break of the poop, and running up the ladder I told them what we had seen.

"Bosh!" sneered the Old Man. "You've been looking at your own ugly reflection in the water."

Nevertheless, in spite of his ridicule, he questioned me closely. Finally he ordered the mate forward to see it he could see anything. The latter, however, returned in a few moments, to report that nothing unusual could be seen. Four bells were struck, and we were relieved for tea. Coming on deck afterward, I found the men clustered together forward. The sole topic of conversation with them was the thing that Stevenson and I had seen.

"I suppose, Darky, it couldn't have been a reflection by any chance, could it?" one of the older men asked.

"Ask Stevenson," I replied as I made my way aft.

At eight bells, my watch came on deck again, to find that nothing further had developed. But, about an hour before midnight, the mate, thinking to have a smoke, sent me to his room for a box of matches with which to light his pipe. It took me no time to clatter down the brass-treaded ladder, and back to the poop, where I handed him the desired article. Taking the box, he removed a match and struck it on the heel of his boot. As he did so, far out in the night a muffled screaming arose. Then came a clamor as of hoarse braying, like an ass but considerably deeper, and with a horribly suggestive human note running through it.

"Good God! Did you hear that, Darky?" asked the mate in awed tones.

"Yes, sir," I replied, listening—and scarcely noticing his question—for a repetition of the strange sounds. Suddenly the frightful bellowing broke out afresh. The mate's pipe fell to the deck with a clatter.

"Run for'ard!" he cried. "Quick, now, and see if you can see anything."

With my heart in my mouth, and pulses pounding madly I raced forward. The watch were all up on the forecastle head, clustered around the lookout. Each man was talking and gesticulating wildly. They became silent, and turned questioning glances toward me as I shouldered my way among them.

"Have you seen anything?" I cried.

Before I could receive an answer, a repetition of the horrid sounds broke out again, profaning the night with their horror. They seemed to have definite direction now, in spite of the fog that enveloped us. Undoubtedly, too, they were nearer. Pausing a moment to make sure of their bearing, I hastened aft and reported to the mate. I told him that nothing could be seen, but that the sounds apparently came from right ahead of us. On hearing this he ordered the man at the wheel to let the ship's head come off a couple of points. A moment later a shrill screaming tore its way through the night, followed by the hoarse braying sounds once more.

"It's close on the starboard bow!" exclaimed the mate, as he beckoned the helmsman to let her head come off a little more. Then, singing out for the watch, he ran forward, slacking the lee braces on the way. When he had the yards trimmed to his satisfaction on the new course, he returned to the poop and hung far out over the rail listening intently. Moments passed that seemed like hours, yet the silence remained unbroken. Suddenly the sounds began again, and so close that it seemed as though they must be right aboard of us. At this time I noticed a strange booming note mingled with the brays. And once or twice there came a sound that can only be described as a sort of "gug, gug." Then would come a wheezy whistling, for all the world like an asthmatic person breathing.

All this while the moon shone wanly through the steam, which seemed to me to be somewhat thinner. Once the mate gripped me by the shoulder as the noises rose and fell again. They now seemed to be coming from a point broad on our beam. Every eye on the ship was straining into the mist, but with no result. Suddenly one of the men cried out, as something long and black slid past us into the fog astern. From it there rose four indistinct and ghostly towers, which resolved themselves into spars and ropes, and sails.

"A ship! It's a ship!" we cried excitedly. I turned to Mr. Gray; he, too, had seen something, and was staring aft into the wake. So ghostlike, unreal, and fleeting had been our glimpse of the stranger, that we were not sure that we had seen an honest, material ship, but thought that we had been vouchsafed a vision of some phantom vessel like the *Flying Dutchman*. Our sails gave a sudden flap, the clew irons flogging the bulwarks with hollow thumps. The mate glanced aloft.

"Wind's dropping," he growled savagely. "We shall never get out of this infernal place at this gait!"

Gradually the wind fell until it was a flat calm. No sound broke the deathlike silence save the rapid patter of the reef points, as she gently rose and fell on the light swell. Hours passed, and the watch was relieved and I then went below. At seven bells we were called again, and as I went along the deck to the galley, I noticed that the fog seemed thinner, and the air cooler. When eight bells were struck I relieved Hansard at coiling down the ropes. From him I learned that the steam had begun to clear about four bells, and that the temperature of the sea had fallen ten degrees.

In spite of the thinning mist, it was not until about a half an hour later that we were able to get a glimpse of the surrounding sea. It was still mottled with dark patches, but the bubbling and popping had ceased. As much of the surface of the ocean as could be seen had a peculiarly desolate aspect. Occasionally a wisp of steam would float up from the nearer sea, and roll undulatingly across its silent surface, until lost in the vagueness that still held the hidden horizon. Here and there columns of steam rose up in pillars, which gave me the impression that the sea was hot in patches. Crossing to the starboard side and looking over, I found that conditions there were similar to those to port. The desolate aspect of the sea filled me with an idea of chilliness, although the air was quite warm and muggy. From the break of the poop the mate called to me to get his glasses.

When I had done this, he took them from me and walked to the taffrail. Here he stood for some moments polishing them with his handkerchief. After a moment he raised them to his eyes, and peered long and intently into the mist astern. I stood for some time staring at the point on which the mate had focused his glasses. Presently something shadowy grew upon my vision. Steadily watching it, I distinctly saw the outlines of a ship take form in the fog.

"See!" I cried, but even as I spoke, a lifting wraith of mist disclosed to view a great four-masted bark lying becalmed with all sails set, within a few hundred yards of our stern. As though a curtain had been raised, and then allowed to fall, the fog once more settled down, hiding the strange bark from our sight. The mate was all excitement, striding with quick, jerky steps, up and down the poop, stopping every few moments to peer through his glasses at the point where the four-master had disappeared in the fog. Gradually, as the mists dispersed again, the vessel could be seen more plainly, and it was then that we got an inkling of the cause of the dreadful noises during the night.

For some time the mate watched her silently, and as he watched the conviction grew upon me that in spite of the mist, I could detect some sort of movement on board of her. After some time had passed, the doubt became a certainty, and I could also see a sort of splashing in the water alongside of her. Suddenly the mate put his glasses on top of the wheel box and told me to bring him the speaking trumpet. Running to the companionway, I secured the trumpet and was back at his side.

The mate raised it to his lips, and taking a deep breath, sent a hail across the water that should have awakened the dead. We waited tensely for a reply. A moment later a deep, hollow mutter came from the bark; higher and louder it swelled, until we realized that we were listening to the same sounds we had heard the night before. The mate stood aghast at this answer to his hail; in a voice barely more than a hushed whisper, he bade me call the Old Man. Attracted by the mate's hail and its unearthly reply, the watch had all come aft and were clustered in the mizzen rigging in order to see better.

After calling the captain, I returned to the poop, where I found the second and third mates talking with the chief. All were engaged in trying to pierce the clouds of mist that half hid our strange consort and to arrive at some explanation of the strange phenomena of the past few hours. A moment later the captain appeared carrying his telescope. The mate gave him a brief account of the state of affairs and handed him the trumpet. Giving me the telescope to hold, the captain hailed the shadowy bark. Breathlessly we all listened, when again, in answer to the Old Man's hail, the frightful sounds rose on the still morning air. The skipper lowered the trumpet and stood with an expression of astonished horror on his face.

"Lord!" he exclaimed. "What an ungodly row!"

At this, the third, who had been gazing through his binoculars, broke the silence.

"Look," he ejaculated. "There's a breeze coming up astern." At his words the captain looked up quickly, and we all watched the ruffling water.

"That packet yonder is bringing the breeze with her," said the skipper. "She'll be alongside in half an hour!"

Some moments passed, and the bank of fog had come to within a hundred yards of our taffrail. The strange vessel could be distinctly seen just inside the fringe of the driving mist wreaths. After a short puff, the wind died completely, but as we stared with hypnotic fascination, the water astern of the stranger ruffled again with a fresh catspaw. Seemingly with the flapping of her sails, she drew slowly up to us. As the leaden seconds passed, the big four-master approached us steadily. The light air had now reached us, and with a lazy lift of our sails, we, too, began to forge slowly through that weird sea. The bark was now within fifty yards of our stern, and she was steadily drawing nearer, seeming to be able to outfoot us with ease. As she came on she luffed sharply, and came up into the wind with her weather leeches shaking.

I looked toward her poop, thinking to discern the figure of the man at the wheel, but the mist coiled around her quarter, and objects on the after end of her became indistinguishable. With a rattle of chain sheets on her iron yards, she filled away again. We meanwhile had gone ahead, but it was soon evident that she was the better sailor, for she came up to us hand over fist. The wind rapidly freshened and the mist began to drift away before it, so that each moment her spars and cordage became more plainly visible. The skipper and the mates were watching her intently when an almost simultaneous exclamation of fear broke from them.

"My God!"

And well they might show signs of fear, for crawling about the bark's deck were the most horrible creatures I had ever seen. In spite of their unearthly strangeness there was something vaguely familiar about them. Then it came to me that the face that Stevenson and I had seen during he night belonged to one of them. Their bodies had something of the shape of a seal's, but of a dead, unhealthy white. The lower part of the body ended in a sort of double-curved tail on which they appeared to be able to shuffle about. In place of arms, they had two long, snaky feelers, at the ends of which were two very humanlike hands, which were equipped with talons instead of nails. Fearsome indeed were these parodies of human beings!

Their faces, which, like their tentacles, were black, were the most grotesquely human things about them, and the upper jaw closed into the lower, after the manner of the jaws of an octopus. I have seen men among certain tribes of natives who had faces uncommonly like theirs, but yet no native I had ever seen could have given me the extraordinary feeling of horror and revulsion I experienced toward these brutal-looking creatures.

"What devilish beasts!" burst out the captain in disgust.

With this remark he turned to the mates, and as he did so, the expressions on their faces told me that they had all realized what the presence of these bestial-looking brutes meant. If, as was doubtless the case, these creatures had boarded the bark and destroyed her crew, what would prevent them from doing the same with us? We were a smaller ship and had a smaller crew, and the more I thought of it the less I liked it.

We could now see the name on the bark's bow with the naked eye. It read *Scottish Heath*, while on her boats we could see the name bracketed with Glasgow, showing that she hailed from that port. It was a remarkable coincidence that she should have a slant from just the quarter in which yards were trimmed, as before we saw her she must have been drifting around with everything "aback." But now in this light air she was able to run along beside us with no one at her helm. But steering herself she was, and although at times she yawed wildly, she never got herself aback. As we gazed at her we noticed a sudden movement on board of her, and several of the creatures slid into the water.

"See! See! They've spotted us. They're coming for us!" cried the mate wildly.

It was only too true, scores of them were sliding into the sea, letting themselves down by means of their long tentacles. On they came, slipping by scores and hundreds into the water, and swimming toward us in droves. The ship was making about three knots, otherwise they would have caught us in a very few minutes. But they persevered, gaining slowly but surely, and drawing nearer and nearer. The long, tentacle-like arms rose out of the sea in hundreds, and the foremost ones were already within a score of yards of the ship before the Old Man bethought himself to shout to the mates to fetch up the half dozen cutlasses that comprised the ship's armory. Then, turning to me, he ordered me to go down to his cabin and bring up the two revolvers out of the top drawer of the chart table, also a box of cartridges that was there.

When I returned with the weapons he loaded them and handed one to the mate. Meanwhile the pursuing creatures were coming steadily nearer, and soon half a dozen of the leaders were directly under our counter. Immediately the captain leaned over the rail and emptied his pistol into them, but without any apparent effect. He must have realized how puny and ineffectual his efforts were, for he did not reload his weapon.

Some dozens of the brutes had reached us, and as they did so, their tentacles rose into the air and caught our rail. I heard the third mate scream suddenly, and turning, I saw him dragged quickly to the rail, with a tentacle wrapped completely around him. Snatching a cutlass, the second mate hacked off the tentacle where it joined the body. A gout of blood splashed into the third mate's face, and he fell to the deck. A dozen more of those arms rose and wavered in the air, but they now seemed some yards astern of us. A rapidly widening patch of clear water appeared between us and the foremost of our pursuers, and we raised a wild shout of joy. The cause was soon apparent; the wind, now that it had come, was freshening rapidly and the ship was running some eight knots through the water.

Away in our wake, the barque was still yawing. Presently we hauled up the port tack and left the *Scottish Heath* running away to leeward, with her devilish crew of octopus-beasts aboard her.

The Third Mawas struggling to his feet with a dazed look. Something fell from him as rose and I stooped to pick it up. It was the severed portion of the talon-like hand that had gripped him.

Three weeks later we anchored in San Francisco. There the captain made a full report of the affair to the authorities, with the result that a gunboat was despatched to investigate. Six weeks later she returned to report that she had been unable to find any signs, either of the ship herself or of the fearful creatures that had attacked her. And since then nothing, as far as I know, has ever been heard of the four-masted barque *Scottish Heath*, last seen by us in the possession of creatures that may rightly be called demons of the sea.

Whether she still floats, occupied by her hellish crew, or whether some storm has sent her to her last resting place beneath the waves is surely a matter of conjecture. Perchance on some dark, fog-bound night, a ship in that wilderness of waters may hear cries and sounds beyond those of the wailing of the winds. Then let them look to it, for it may be that the demons of the sea are near them.

The Desert Drum

Robert S. Hichens

I

I am not naturally superstitious. The Saharaman is. He has many strange beliefs. When one is at close quarters with him, sees him day by day in his home, the great desert, listens to his dramatic tales of desert lights, visions, sounds, one's common-sense is apt to be shaken on its throne. Perhaps it is the influence of the solitude and the wide spaces, of those far horizons of the Sahara where the blue deepens along the edge of the world, that turns even a European mind to an Eastern credulity. Who can tell? The truth is that in the Sahara one can believe what one cannot believe in London. And sometimes circumstances chance if you like to call it so steps in, and seems to say, "Your belief is well founded."

Of all the desert superstitions the one which appealed most to my imagination was the superstition of the desert drum. The Saharaman declares that far away from the abodes of men and desert cities, among the everlasting sand dunes, the sharp beating, or dull, distant rolling of a drum sometimes breaks upon the ears of travellers voyaging through the desolation. They look around, they stare across the flats, they see nothing. But the mysterious music continues. Then, if they be Saharabred, they commend themselves to Allah, for they know that some terrible disaster is at hand, that one of them at least is doomed to die.

Often had I heard stories of the catastrophes which were immediately preceded by the beating of the desert drum. One night in the Sahara I was a witness to one which I have never been able to forget.

On an evening of spring, accompanied by a young Arab and a negro, I rode slowly down a low hill of the Sahara, and saw in the sandy cup at my feet the tiny collection of hovels called Sidi-Massarli. I had been in the saddle since dawn, riding over desolate tracks in the heart of the desert. I was hungry, tired, and felt almost like a man hypnotised. The strong air, the clear sky, the everlasting flats devoid of vegetation, empty of humanity, the monotonous motion of my slowly cantering horse all these things combined to dull my brain and to throw me into a peculiar condition akin to the condition of a man in a trance. At Sidi-Massarli I was to pass the night. I drew rein and looked down on it with lack-lustre eyes.

I saw a small group of palm-trees, guarded by a low wall of baked brown earth, in which were embedded many white bones of dead camels. Bleached, grinning heads of camels hung from more than one of the trees, with strings of red pepper and round stones. Beyond the wall of this palm garden, at whose foot was a furrow full of stagnant brownish-yellow water, lay a handful of wretched earthen hovels, with flat roofs of palmwood and low wooden doors. To be exact, I think there were five of them. The Bordj, or Travellers' House, at which I was to be accommodated for the night, stood alone near a tiny source at the edge of a large sand dune, and was a small, earth-colored building with a pink tiled roof, minute arched windows, and an open stable for the horses and mules. All round the desert rose in humps of sand, melting into stony ground where the saltpetre lay like snow on a wintry world. There were but few signs of life in this place; some stockings drying on the wall of a ruined Arab cafe, some kids frisking by a heap of sacks, a few pigeons circling about a low square watchtower, a black donkey brooding on a dust heap. There were some signs of death; carcasses of camels stretched here and there in frantic and fantastic postures, some bleached and smooth, others red and horribly odorous.

The wind blew round this hospitable township of the Sahara, and the yellow light of evening began to glow above it. It seemed to me at that moment the dreariest place in the dreariest dream man had ever had.

Suddenly my horse neighed loudly. Beyond the village, on the opposite hill, a white Arab charger caracoled, a red cloak gleamed. Another traveller was coming in to his night's rest, and he was a Spahi. I could almost fancy I heard the jingle of his spurs and accoutrements, the creaking of his tall red boots against his high peaked saddle. As he rode down towards the Bordj by this time, I, too, was on my way I saw that a long cord hung from his saddle-bow, and that at the end of this cord was a man, trotting heavily in the heavy sand like a creature dogged and weary. We came in to Sidi-Massarli simultaneously, and pulled up at the same moment before the arched door of the Bordj, from which glided a one-eyed swarthy Arab, staring fixedly at me. This was the official keeper of the house. In one hand he held the huge door key, and as I swung myself heavily on the ground I heard him, in Arabic, asking my Arab attendant, D'oud, who I was and where I hailed from.

But such attention as I had to bestow on anything just then was given to the Spahi and his companion. The Spahi was a magnificent man, tall, lithe, bronze-brown and muscular. He looked about thirty-four, and had the face of a desert eagle. His piercing black eyes stared me calmly out of countenance, and he sat on his spirited horse like a statue, waiting patiently till the guardian of the Bordj was ready to attend to him. My gaze travelled from him along the cord to the man at its end, and rested there with pity. He, too, was a fine specimen of humanity, a giant, nobly built, with a superbly handsome face, something like that of an undefaced Sphinx. Broad brows sheltered his enormous eyes. His rather thick lips were parted to allow his panting breath to escape, and his dark, almost black skin, was covered with sweat. Drops of sweat coursed down his bare arms and his mighty chest, from which his ragged burnous was drawn partially away. He was evidently of mixed Arab and negro parentage. As he stood by the Spahi's horse, gasping, his face expressed nothing but physical exhaustion. His eyes were bent on the sand, and his arms hung down loosely at his sides. While I looked at him the Spahi suddenly gave a tug at the cord to which he was attached. He moved in nearer to the horse, glanced up at me, held out his hand, and said in a low, musical voice, speaking Arabic:

"Give me a cigarette, Sidi."

I opened my case and gave him one, at the same time diplomatically handing another to the Spahi. Thus we opened our night's acquaintance, an acquaintance which I shall not easily forget.

In the desolation of the Sahara a travelling intimacy is quickly formed. The one-eyed Arab led our horses to the stable, and while my two attendants were inside unpacking the tinned food and the wine I carried with me on a mule, I entered into conversation with the Spahi, who spoke French fairly well. He told me that he was on the way to El Arba, a long journey through the desert from Sidi-Massarli, and that his business was to convey there the man at the end of the cord.

"But what is he? A prisoner?" I asked.

"A murderer, monsieur," the Spahi replied calmly.

I looked again at the man, who was wiping the sweat from his face with one huge hand. He smiled and made a gesture of assent.

"Does he understand French?"

"A little."

"And he committed murder?"

"At Tunis. He was a butcher there. He cut a man's throat."

"Why?"

"I don't know, monsieur. Perhaps he was jealous. It is hot in Tunis in the summer. That was five years ago, and ever since he has been in prison."

"And why are you taking him to El Arba?"

"He came from there. He is released, but he is not allowed to live any more in Tunis. Ah, monsieur, he is mad at going, for he loves a dancing-girl, Aïchouch, who dances with the Jewesses in the cafe by the lake. He wanted even to stay in prison, if only he might remain in Tunis. He never saw her, but he was in the same town, you understand. That was something. All the first day he ran behind my horse cursing me for taking him away. But now the sand has got into his throat. He is so tired that he can scarcely run. So he does not curse any more."

The captive giant smiled at me again. Despite his great stature, his powerful and impressive features, he looked, I thought, very gentle and submissive. The story of his passion for Aïchouch, his desire to be near her, even in a prison cell, had appealed to me. I pitied him sincerely.

"What is his name?" I asked.

"M'hammed Bouaziz. Mine is Said."

I was weary with riding and wanted to stretch my legs, and see what was to be seen of Sidi-Massarli ere evening quite closed in, so at this point I lit a cigar and prepared to stroll off.

"Monsieur is going for a walk?" asked the Spahi, fixing his eyes on my cigar.

"Yes."

"I will accompany monsieur,"

"Or monsieur's cigar-case," I thought.

"But that poor fellow," I said, pointing to the murderer. "He is tired out."

"That doesn't matter. He will come with us."

The Spahi jerked the cord and we set out, the murderer creeping over the sand behind us like some exhausted animal.

By this time twilight was falling over the Sahara, a grim twilight, cold and grey. The wind was rising. In the night it blew half a gale, but at this hour there was only a strong breeze in which minute sand-grains danced. The murderer's feet were shod with patched slippers, and the sound of these slippers shuffling close behind me made me feel faintly uneasy. The Spahi stared at my cigar so persistently that I was obliged to offer him one. When I had done so, and he had loftily accepted it, I half turned towards the murderer. The Spahi scowled ferociously. I put my cigar-case back into my pocket. It is unwise to offend the powerful if your sympathy lies with the powerless.

Sidi-Massarli was soon explored. It contained a Café Maure, into which I peered. In the coffee niche the embers glowed. One or two ragged Arabs sat hunched upon the earthen divans playing a game of cards. At least I should have my coffee after my tinned dinner. I was turning to go back to the Bordj when the extreme desolation of the desert around, now fading in the shadows of a moonless night, stirred me to a desire. Sidi-Massarli was dreary enough. Still it contained habitations, men. I wished to feel the blank, wild emptiness of this world, so far from the world of civilisation from which I had come, to feel it with intensity. I resolved to mount the low hill down which I had seen the Spahi ride, to descend into the fold of desert beyond it, to pause there a moment, out of sight of the hamlet, listen to the breeze, look at the darkening sky, feel the sand-grains stinging my cheeks, shake hands with the Sahara.

But I wanted to shake hands quite alone. I therefore suggested to the Spahi that he should remain in the Cafe Maure and drink a cup of coffee at my expense.

"And where is monsieur going?"

"Only over that hill for a moment."

"I will accompany monsieur."

"But you must be tired. A cup of—"

"I will accompany monsieur."

In Arab fashion he was establishing a claim upon me. On the morrow, when I was about to depart, he would point out that he had guided me round Sidi-Massarli, had guarded me in my dangerous expedition beyond its fascinations, despite his weariness and hunger. I knew how useless it is to contend with these polite and persistent rascals, so I said no more.

In a few minutes the Spahi, the murderer and I stood in the fold of the sand dunes, and Sidi-Massarli was blotted from our sight.

II

The desolation here was complete. All around us lay the dunes, monstrous as still leviathans. Here and there, between their strange, suggestive shapes, under the dark sky one could see the ghastly whiteness of the saltpetre in the arid plains beyond, where the low bushes bent in the chilly breeze. I thought of London—only a few days' journey from me—revelled for a moment in my situation, which, contrary to my expectation, was rather emphasised by the presence of my companions. The gorgeous Spahi, with his scarlet cloak and hood, his musket and sword, his high red leggings, the ragged, sweating captive in his patched burnous, ex-butcher looking, despite his cord emblem of bondage, like reigning Emperor they were appropriate figures in this desert place. I had just thought this, and was regarding my Sackville Street suit with disgust, when a low, distinct and near sound suddenly rose from behind a sand dune on my left. It was exactly like the dull beating of a tom-tom. The silence preceding it had been intense, for the breeze was as yet too light to make more than the faintest sighing music, and in the gathering darkness this abrupt and gloomy noise produced, I supposed, by some hidden nomad, made a very unpleasant, even sinister impression upon me. Instinctively I put my hand on the revolver which was slung at my side in a pouch of gazelle skin. As I did so, I saw the Spahi turn sharply and gaze in the direction of the sound, lifting one hand to his ear.

The low thunder of the instrument, beaten rhythmically and persistently, grew louder and was evidently drawing nearer. The musician must be climbing up the far side of the dune. I had swung round to face him, and expected every moment to see some wild figure appear upon the summit, defining itself against the cold and gloomy sky. But none came. Nevertheless, the noise increased till it was a roar, drew near till it was actually upon us. It seemed to me that I heard the sticks striking the hard, stretched skin furiously, as if some phantom drummer were stealthily encircling us, catching us in a net, a trap of horrible, vicious uproar. Instinctively I threw a questioning, perhaps an appealing, glance at my two companions. The Spahi had dropped his hand from his ear. He stood upright, as if at attention on the parade-ground of Biskra. His face was set—afterwards I told myself it was fatalistic. The murderer, on the other hand, was smiling. I remember the gleam of his big white teeth. Why was he smiling? While I asked myself the question the roar of the tom-tom grew gradually less, as if the man beating it were walking rapidly away from us in the direction of Sidi-Massarli. None of us said a word till only a faint, heavy throbbing, like the beating of a heart, I fancied, was audible in the darkness. Then I spoke, as silence fell.

"Who is it?"

"Monsieur, it is no one."

The Spahi's voice was dry and soft.

"What is it?"

"Monsieur, it is the desert drum. There will be death in Sidi-Massarli to-night."

I felt myself turn cold. He spoke with such conviction. The murderer was still smiling, and I noticed that the tired look had left him. He stood in an alert attitude, and the sweat had dried on his broad forehead.

"The desert drum?" I repeated.

"Monsieur has not heard of it?"

"Yes, I have heard but—it—can't be. There must have been someone."

I looked at the white teeth of the murderer, white as the saltpetre which makes winter in the desert.

"I must get back to the Bordj," I said abruptly.

"I will accompany monsieur."

The old formula, and this time the voice which spoke it sounded natural. We went forward together. I walked very fast. I wanted to catch up that music, to prove to myself that it was produced by human fists and sticks upon an instrument which, however barbarous, had been fashioned by human hands. But we entered Sidi-Massarli in a silence, only broken by the soughing of the wind and the heavy shuffle of the murderer's feet upon the sand.

Outside the Café Maure D'oud was standing with the white hood of his burnous drawn forward over his head; one or two ragged Arabs stood with him.

"They've been playing tom-toms in the village, D'oud?"

"Monsieur asks if—"

"Tom-toms. Can't you understand?"

"Ah! Monsieur is laughing. Tom-toms here! And dancers, too, perhaps! Monsieur thinks there are dancers? Fatma and Khadija a and Aïchouch—"

I glanced quickly at the murderer as D'oud mentioned the last name, a name common to many dancers of the East. I think I expected to see upon his face some tremendous expression, a revelation of the soul of the man who had run for one whole day through the sand behind the Spahi's horse, cursing at the end of the cord which dragged him onward from Tunis.

But I only met the gentle smile of eyes so tender, so submissive, that they were as the eyes of a woman who had always been a slave, while the ragged Arabs laughed at the idea of tom-toms in Sidi-Massarli.

When we reached the Bordj I found that it contained only one good-sized room, quite bare, with stone floor and white walls. Here, upon a deal table, was set forth my repast; the foods I had brought with me, and a red Arab soup served in a gigantic bowl of palm-wood. A candle guttered in the glass neck of a bottle, and upon the floor were already spread my gaudy striped quilt, my pillow, and my blanket. The Spahi surveyed these preparations with a deliberate greediness, lingering in the narrow doorway.

I sat down on a bench before the table. My attendants were to eat at the Café Maure.

"Where are you going to sleep?" I asked of D'oud.

"At the Café Maure, monsieur, if monsieur is not afraid to sleep alone. Here is the key. Monsieur can lock himself in. The door is strong."

I was helping myself to the soup. The rising wind blew up the skirts of the Spain's scarlet robe. In the wind—was it imagination?—I seemed to hear some thin, passing echoes of a tom-tom's beat.

"Come in," I said to the Spahi. "You shall sup with me to-night, and you shall sleep here with me."

D'oud's expressive face became sinister. Arabs are almost as jealous as they are vain.

"But, monsieur, he will sleep in the Café Maure. If monsieur wishes for a companion, I—"

"Come in," I repeated to the Spahi. "You can sleep here to-night."

The Spahi stepped over the lintel with a jingling of spurs, a rattling of accoutrements. The murderer stepped in softly after him, drawn by the cord. D'oud began to look as grim as death. He made a ferocious gesture towards the murderer.

"And that man? Monsieur wishes to sleep in the same room with him?"

I heard the sound of the tom-tom above the wail of the wind.

"Yes," I said.

Why did I wish it? I hardly know. I had no fear for, no desire to protect myself. But I remembered the smile I had seen, the Spahi's saying, "There will be death in Sidi-Massarli to-night," and I was resolved that the three men who had heard the desert drum together should not be parted till the morning. D'oud said no more. He waited upon me with his usual diligence, but I could see that he was furiously angry. The Spahi ate ravenously. So did the murderer, who more than once, however, seemed to be dropping to sleep over his food. He was apparently dead tired. As the wind was now become very violent I did not feel disposed to stir out again, and I ordered D'oud to bring us three cups of coffee to the Bordj. He cast a vicious look at the Spahi and went out into the darkness. I saw him no more that night. A boy from the Café Maure brought us coffee, cleared the remains of our supper from the table, and presently muttered some Arab salutation, departed, and was lost in the wind.

The murderer was now frankly asleep with his head upon the table, and the Spahi began to blink. I, too, felt very tired, but I had something still to say. Speaking softly, I said to the Spahi:

"That sound we heard to-night—"

"Monsieur?"

"Have you ever heard it before?"

"Never, monsieur. But my brother heard it just before he had a stroke of the sun. He fell dead before his captain beside the wall of Sada. He was a tirailleur."

"And you think this sound means that death is near?"

"I know it, monsieur. All desert people know it. I was born at Touggourt, and how should I not know?"

"But then one of us—"

I looked from him to the sleeping murderer.

"There will be death in Sidi-Massarli tonight, monsieur. It is the will of Allah. Blessed be Allah."

I got up, locked the heavy door of the Bordj, and put the key in the inner pocket of my coat. As I did so, I fancied I saw the heavy black lids of the murderer's closed eyes flutter for a moment. But I cannot be sure. My head was aching with fatigue. The Spahi, too, looked stupid with sleep. He jerked the cord, the murderer awoke with a start, glanced heavily round, stood up. Pulling him as one would an obstinate dog, the Spahi made him lie down on the bare floor in the corner of the Bordj, ere he himself curled up in the thick quilt which had been rolled up behind his high saddle. I made no protest, but when the Spahi was asleep, his lean brown hand laid upon his sword, his musket under his shaven head, I pushed one of my blankets over to the murderer, who lay looking like a heap of rags against the white wall. He smiled at me gently, as he had smiled when the desert drum was beating, and drew the blanket over his mighty limbs and face.

I did not mean to sleep that night. Tired though I was my brain was so excited that I felt I should not. I blew out the candle without even the thought that it would be necessary to struggle against sleep. And in the darkness I heard for an instant the roar of the wind outside, the heavy breathing of my two strange companions within. For an instant then it seemed as if a shutter was drawn suddenly over the light in my brain. Blackness filled the room where the thoughts develop, crowd, stir in endless activities. Slumber fell upon me like a great stone that strikes a man down to dumbness, to unconsciousness.

Far in the night I had a dream. I cannot recall it accurately now. I could not recall it even the next morning when I awoke. But in this dream, it seemed to me that fingers felt softly about my heart. I was conscious of their fluttering touch. It was as if I were dead, and as if the doctor laid for a moment his hand upon my heart to convince himself that the pulse of life no longer beat. And this action wove itself naturally into the dream I had. The fingers so soft, so surreptitious, were lifted from my breast, and I sank deeper into the gulf of sleep, below the place of dreams. For I was a tired man that night. At the first breath of dawn I stirred and woke. It was cold. I put out one hand and drew up my quilt. Then I lay still. The wind had sunk. I no longer heard it roaring over the desert. For a moment I hardly remembered where I was, then memory came back and I listened for the deep breathing of the Spahi and the murderer. Even when the wind blew I had heard it. I did not hear it now. I lay there under my quilt for some minutes listening. The silence was intense. Had they gone already, started on their way to El Arba? The Bordj was in darkness, for the windows were very small, and dawn had scarcely begun to break outside and had not yet filtered in through the wooden shutters which barred them. I disliked this complete silence, and felt about for the matches I had laid beside the candle before turning in. I could not find them. Someone had moved them, then. The heaviness of sleep had quite left me now, and I remembered clearly all the incidents of the previous evening. The roll of the desert drum sounded again in my ears. I threw off my quilt, got up, and moved softly over the stone floor towards the corner where the murderer had lain down to sleep. I bent down to touch him and touched the stone. They had gone, then! It was strange that I had not been waked by their departure. Besides, I had the key of the door. I thrust my hand into the breast-pocket of my coat which I had worn while I slept. The key was no longer there. Then I remembered my dream and the fingers fluttering round my heart. Stumbling in the blackness I came to the place where the Spahi had lain, stretched out my hands and felt naked flesh. My hands recoiled from it, for it was very cold.

Half-an-hour later the one-eyed Arab who kept the Bordj, roused by my beating upon the door with the butt end of my revolver, came with D'oud to ask what was the matter. The door had to be broken in. This took some time. Long before I could escape, the light of the sun, entering through the little arched windows, had illumined the nude corpse of the Spahi, the gaping red wound in his throat, the heap of murderer's rags that lay across his feet.

M'hammed Bouaziz, in the red cloak, the red boots, sword at his side, musket slung over his shoulder, was galloping over the desert on his way to freedom.

But six months later he was taken at night outside a cafe by the lake at Tunis. He was gazing through the doorway at a girl who was posturing to the sound of pipes between two rows of Arabs. The light from the café fell upon his face, the dancer uttered a cry.

"M'hammed Bouaziz!"

"Aïchouch!"

The law avenged the Spahi, and this time it was not to prison they led my friend of Sidi-Massarli, but to an open space before a squad of soldiers just when the dawn was breaking.

The Doll's Ghost

F. Marion Crawford

It was a terrible accident, and for one moment the splendid machinery of Cranston House got out of gear and stood still. The butler emerged from the retirement in which he spent his elegant leisure, two grooms of the chambers appeared simultaneously from opposite directions, there were actually housemaids on the grand staircase, and those who remember the facts most exactly assert that Mrs. Pringle herself positively stood upon the landing. Mrs. Pringle was the housekeeper. As for the head nurse, the under nurse, and the nursery maid, their feelings cannot be described. The head nurse laid one hand upon the polished marble balustrade and stared stupidly before her, the under nurse stood rigid and pale, leaning against the polished marble wall, and the nursery-maid collapsed and sat down upon the polished marble step, just beyond the limits of the velvet carpet, and frankly burst into tears.

The Lady Gwendolen Lancaster-Douglas-Scroop, youngest daughter of the ninth Duke of Cranston, and aged six years and three months, picked herself up quite alone, and sat down on the third step from the foot of the grand staircase in Cranston House.

"Oh!" ejaculated the butler, and he disappeared again.

"Ah!" responded the grooms of the chambers, as they also went away.

"It's only that doll," Mrs. Pringle was distinctly heard to say, in a tone of contempt.

The under nurse heard her say it. Then the three nurses gathered round Lady Gwendolen and patted her, and gave her unhealthy things out of their pockets, and hurried her out of Cranston House as fast as they could, lest it should be found out upstairs that they had allowed the Lady Gwendolen Lancaster-Douglas-Scroop to tumble down the grand staircase with her doll in her arms. And as the doll was badly broken, the nursery-maid carried it, with the pieces, wrapped up in Lady Gwendolen's little cloak. It was not far to Hyde Park, and when they had reached a quiet place they took means to find out that Lady Gwendolen had no bruises. For the carpet was very thick and soft, and there was thick stuff under it to make it softer.

Lady Gwendolen Douglas-Scroop sometimes yelled, but she never cried. It was because she had yelled that the nurse had allowed her to go downstairs alone with Nina, the doll, under one arm, while she steadied herself with her other hand on the balustrade, and trod upon the polished marble steps beyond the edge of the carpet. So she had fallen, and Nina had come to grief.

When the nurses were quite sure that she was not hurt, they unwrapped the doll and looked at her in her turn. She had been a very beautiful doll, very large, and fair, and healthy, with real yellow hair, and eyelids that would open and shut over very grown-up dark eyes. Moreover, when you moved her right arm up and down she said "Pa-pa," and when you moved the left she said "Ma-ma," very distinctly.

"I heard her say 'Pa' when she fell," said the under nurse, who heard everything. "But she ought to have said 'Pa-pa.'"

"That's because her arm went up when she hit the step," said the head nurse. "She'll say the other 'Pa' when I put it down again."

"Pa," said Nina, as her right arm was pushed down, and speaking through her broken face. It was cracked right across, from the upper corner of the forehead, with a hideous gash, through the nose and down to the little frilled collar of the pale green silk Mother Hubbard frock, and two little three-cornered pieces of porcelain had fallen out.

"I'm sure it's a wonder she can speak at all, being all smashed," said the under nurse.

"You'll have to take her to Mr. Puckler," said her superior. "It's not far, and you'd better go at once."

Lady Gwendolen was occupied in digging a hole in the ground with a little spade, and paid no attention to the nurses.

"What are you doing?" enquired the nursery-maid, looking on.

"Nina's dead, and I'm diggin' her a grave," replied her ladyship thoughtfully.

"Oh, she'll come to life again all right," said the nursery-maid.

The under nurse wrapped Nina up again and departed. Fortunately a kind soldier, with very long legs and a very small cap, happened to be there; and as he had nothing to do, he offered to see the under nurse safely to Mr. Puckler's and back.

Mr. Bernard Puckler and his little daughter lived in a little house in a little alley, which led out off a quiet little street not very far from Belgrave Square. He was the great doll doctor, and his extensive practice lay in the most aristocratic quarter. He mended dolls of all sizes and ages, boy dolls and girl dolls, baby dolls in long clothes, and grown-up dolls in fashionable gowns, talking dolls and dumb dolls, those that shut their eyes when they lay down, and those whose eyes had to be shut for them by means of a mysterious wire. His daughter Else was only just over twelve years old, but she was already very clever at mending dolls' clothes, and at doing their hair, which is harder than you might think, though the dolls sit quite still while it is being done.

Mr. Puckler had originally been a German, but he had dissolved his nationality in the ocean of London many years ago, like a great many foreigners. He still had one or two German friends, however, who came on Saturday evenings, and smoked with him and played picquet or "skat" with him for farthing points, and called him "Herr Doctor," which seemed to please Mr. Puckler very much.

He looked older than he was, for his beard was rather long and ragged, his hair was grizzled and thin, and he wore horn-rimmed spectacles. As for Else, she was a thin, pale child, very quiet and neat, with dark eyes and brown hair that was plaited down her back and tied with a bit of black ribbon. She mended the dolls' clothes and took the dolls back to their homes when they were quite strong again.

The house was a little one, but too big for the two people who lived in it. There was a small sitting-room on the street, and the workshop was at the back, and there were three rooms upstairs. But the father and daughter lived most of their time in the workshop, because they were generally at work, even in the evenings.

Mr. Puckler laid Nina on the table and looked at her a long time, till the tears began to fill his eyes behind the horn-rimmed spectacles. He was a very susceptible man, and he often fell in love with the dolls he mended, and found it hard to part with them when they had smiled at him for a few days. They were real little people to him, with characters and thoughts and feelings of their own, and he was very tender with them all. But some attracted him especially from the first, and when they were brought to him maimed and injured, their state seemed so pitiful to him that the tears came easily. You must remember that he had lived among dolls during a great part of his life, and understood them.

"How do you know that they feel nothing?" he went on to say to Else. "You must be gentle with them. It costs nothing to be kind to the little beings, and perhaps it makes a difference to them."

And Else understood him, because she was a child, and she knew that she was more to him than all the dolls.

He fell in love with Nina at first sight, perhaps because her beautiful brown glass eyes were something like Else's own, and he loved Else first and best, with all his heart. And, besides, it was a very sorrowful case. Nina had evidently not been long in the world, for her complexion was perfect, her hair was smooth where it should be smooth, and curly where it should be curly, and her silk clothes were perfectly new. But across her face was that frightful gash, like a sabre-cut, deep and shadowy within, but clean and sharp at the edges. When he tenderly pressed her head to close the gaping wound, the edges made a fine grating sound, that was painful to hear, and the lids of the dark eyes quivered and trembled as though Nina were suffering dreadfully.

"Poor Nina!" he exclaimed sorrowfully. "But I shall not hurt you much, though you will take a long time to get strong."

He always asked the names of the broken dolls when they were brought to him, and sometimes the people knew what the children called them, and told him. He liked "Nina" for a name. Altogether and in every way she pleased him more than any doll he had seen for many years, and he felt drawn to her, and made up his mind to make her perfectly strong and sound, no matter how much labor it might cost him.

Mr. Puckler worked patiently a little at a time, and Else watched him. She could do nothing for poor Nina, whose clothes needed no mending. The longer the doll doctor worked, the more fond he became of the yellow hair and the beautiful brown glass eyes. He sometimes forgot all the other dolls that were waiting to be mended, lying side by side on a shelf, and sat for an hour gazing at Nina's face, while he racked his ingenuity for some new invention by which to hide even the smallest trace of the terrible accident.

She was wonderfully mended. Even he was obliged to admit that; but the scar was still visible to his keen eyes, a very fine line right across the face, downwards from right to left. Yet all the conditions had been most favourable for a cure, since the cement had set quite hard at the first attempt and the weather had been fine and dry, which makes a great difference in a dolls' hospital.

At last he knew that he could do no more, and the under nurse had already come twice to see whether the job was finished, as she coarsely expressed it.

"Nina is not quite strong yet," Mr. Puckler had answered each time, for he could not make up his mind to face the parting.

And now he sat before the square deal table at which he worked, and Nina lay before him for the last time with a big brown paper box beside her. It stood there like her coffin, waiting for her, he thought. He must put her into it, and lay tissue paper over her dear face, and then put on the lid, and at the thought of tying the string his sight was dim with tears again. He was never to look into the glassy depths of the beautiful brown eyes any more, nor to hear the little wooden voice say "Pa-pa" and "Ma-ma." It was a very painful moment.

In the vain hope of gaining time before the separation, he took up the little sticky bottles of cement and glue and gum and color, looking at each one in turn, and then at Nina's face. And all his small tools lay there, neatly arranged in a row, but he knew that he could not use them again for Nina. She was quite strong at last, and in a country where there should be no cruel children to hurt her she might live a hundred years, with only that almost imperceptible line across her face to tell of the fearful thing that had befallen her on the marble steps of Cranston House.

Suddenly Mr. Puckler's heart was quite full, and he rose abruptly from his seat and turned away.

"Else," he said unsteadily, "you must do it for me. I cannot bear to see her go into the box."

So he went and stood at the window with his back turned, while Else did what he had not the heart to do.

"Is it done?" he asked, not turning round. "Then take her away, my dear. Put on your hat, and take her to Cranston House quickly, and when you are gone I will turn round."

Else was used to her father's queer ways with the dolls, and though she had never seen him so much moved by a parting, she was not much surprised.

"Come back quickly," he said, when he heard her hand on the latch. "It is growing late, and I should not send you at this hour. But I cannot bear to look forward to it any more."

When Else was gone, he left the window and sat down in his place before the table again, to wait for the child to come back. He touched the place where Nina had lain, very gently, and he recalled the softly tinted pink face, and the glass eyes, and the ringlets of yellow hair, till he could almost see them.

The evenings were long, for it was late in the spring. But it began to grow dark soon, and Mr. Puckler wondered why Else did not come back. She had been gone an hour and a half, and that was much longer than he had expected, for it was barely half a mile from Belgrave Square to Cranston House. He reflected that the child might have been kept waiting, but as the twilight deepened he grew anxious, and walked up and down in the dim workshop, no longer thinking of Nina, but of Else, his own living child, whom he loved.

An undefinable, disquieting sensation came upon him by fine degrees, a chilliness and a faint stirring of his thin hair, joined with a wish to be in any company rather than to be alone much longer. It was the beginning of fear.

He told himself in strong German-English that he was a foolish old man, and he began to feel about for the matches in the dusk. He knew just where they should be, for he always kept them in the same place, close to the little tin box that held bits of sealing-wax of various colors, for some kinds of mending. But somehow he could not find the matches in the gloom.

Something had happened to Else, he was sure, and as his fear increased, he felt as though it might be allayed if he could get a light and see what time it was. Then he called himself a foolish old man again, and the sound of his own voice startled him in the dark. He could not find the matches.

The window was grey still; he might see what time it was if he went close to it, and he could go and get matches out of the cupboard afterwards. He stood back from the table, to get out of the way of the chair, and began to cross the board floor.

Something was following him in the dark. There was a small pattering, as of tiny feet upon the boards. He stopped and listened, and the roots of his hair tingled. It was nothing, and he was a foolish old man. He made two steps more, and he was sure that he heard the little pattering again. He turned his back to the window, leaning against the sash so that the panes began to crack, and he faced the dark. Everything was quite still, and it smelt of paste and cement and wood-filings as usual.

"Is that you, Else?" he asked, and he was surprised by the fear in his voice.

There was no answer in the room, and he held up his watch and tried to make out what time it was by the grey dusk that was just not darkness. So far as he could see, it was within two or three minutes of ten o'clock. He had been a long time alone. He was shocked, and frightened for Else, out in London, so late, and he almost ran across the room to the door. As he fumbled for the latch, he distinctly heard the running of the little feet after him.

"Mice!" he exclaimed feebly, just as he got the door open.

He shut it quickly behind him, and felt as though some cold thing had settled on his back and were writhing upon him. The passage was quite dark, but he found his hat and was out in the alley in a moment, breathing more freely, and surprised to find how much light there still was in the open air. He could see the pavement clearly under his feet, and far off in the street to which the alley led he could hear the laughter and calls of children, playing some game out of doors. He wondered how he could have been so nervous, and for an instant he thought of going back into the house to wait quietly for Else. But instantly he felt that nervous fright of something stealing over him again. In any case it was better to walk up to Cranston House and ask the servants about the child. One of the women had perhaps taken a fancy to her, and was even now giving her tea and cake.

He walked quickly to Belgrave Square, and then up the broad streets, listening as he went, whenever there was no other sound, for the tiny footsteps. But he heard nothing, and was laughing at himself when he rang the servants' bell at the big house. Of course, the child must be there.

The person who opened the door was quite an inferior person, for it was a back door, but affected the manners of the front, and stared at Mr. Puckler superciliously under the strong light.

No little girl had been seen, and he knew "nothing about no dolls."

"She is my little girl," said Mr. Puckler tremulously, for all his anxiety was returning tenfold, "and I am afraid something has happened."

The inferior person said rudely that "nothing could have happened to her in that house, because she had not been there, which was a jolly good reason why"; and Mr. Puckler was obliged to admit that the man ought to know, as it was his business to keep the door and let people in. He wished to be allowed to speak to the under nurse, who knew him; but the man was ruder than ever, and finally shut the door in his face.

When the doll doctor was alone in the street, he steadied himself by the railing, for he felt as though he were breaking in two, just as some dolls break, in the middle of the backbone.

Presently he knew that he must be doing something to find Else, and that gave him strength. He began to walk as quickly as he could through the streets, following every highway and byway which his little girl might have taken on her errand. He also asked several policemen in vain if they had seen her, and most of them answered him kindly, for they saw that he was a sober man and in his right senses, and some of them had little girls of their own.

It was one o'clock in the morning when he went up to his own door again, worn out and hopeless and broken-hearted. As he turned the key in the lock, his heart stood still, for he knew that he was awake and not dreaming, and that he really heard those tiny footsteps pattering to meet him inside the house along the passage.

But he was too unhappy to be much frightened any more, and his heart went on again with a dull regular pain, that found its way all through him with every pulse. So he went in, and hung up his hat in the dark, and found the matches in the cupboard and the candlestick in its place in the corner.

Mr. Puckler was so much overcome and so completely worn out that he sat down in his chair before the work-table and almost fainted, as his face dropped forward upon his folded hands. Beside him the solitary candle burned steadily with a low flame in the still warm air.

"Else! Else!" he moaned against his yellow knuckles. And that was all he could say, and it was no relief to him. On the contrary, the very sound of the name was a new and sharp pain that pierced his ears and his head and his very soul. For every time he repeated the name it meant that little Else was dead, somewhere out in the streets of London in the dark.

He was so terribly hurt that he did not even feel something pulling gently at the skirt of his old coat, so gently that it was like the nibbling of a tiny mouse. He might have thought that it was really a mouse if he had noticed it.

"Else! Else!" he groaned right against his hands.

Then a cool breath stirred his thin hair, and the low flame of the one candle dropped down almost to a mere spark, not flickering as though a draught were going to blow it out, but just dropping down as if it were tired out. Mr. Puckler felt his hands stiffening with fright under his face; and there was a faint rustling sound, like some small silk thing blown in a gentle breeze. He sat up straight, stark and scared, and a small wooden voice spoke in the stillness.

"Pa-pa," it said, with a break between the syllables.

Mr. Puckler stood up in a single jump, and his chair fell over backwards with a smashing noise upon the wooden floor. The candle had almost gone out.

It was Nina's doll voice that had spoken, and he should have known it among the voices of a hundred other dolls. And yet there was something more in it, a little human ring, with a pitiful cry and a call for help, and the wail of a hurt child. Mr. Puckler stood up, stark and stiff, and tried to look round, but at first he could not, for he seemed to be frozen from head to foot.

Then he made a great effort, and he raised one hand to each of his temples, and pressed his own head round as he would have turned a doll's. The candle was burning so low that it might as well have been out altogether, for any light it gave, and the room seemed quite dark at first. Then he saw something. He would not have believed that he could be more frightened than he had been just before that. But he was, and his knees shook, for he saw the doll standing in the middle of the floor, shining with a faint and ghostly radiance, her beautiful glassy brown eyes fixed on his. And across her face the very thin line of the break he had mended shone as though it were drawn in light with a fine point of white flame.

Yet there was something more in the eyes, too; there was something human, like Else's own, but as if only the doll saw him through them, and not Else. And there was enough of Else to bring back all his pain and to make him forget his fear.

"Else! my little Else!" he cried aloud.

The small ghost moved, and its doll-arm slowly rose and fell with a stiff, mechanical motion.

"Pa-pa," it said.

It seemed this time that there was even more of Else's tone echoing somewhere between the wooden notes that reached his ears so distinctly, and yet so far away. Else was calling him, he was sure.

His face was perfectly white in the gloom, but his knees did not shake any more, and he felt that he was less frightened.

"Yes, child! But where? Where?" he asked. "Where are you, Else?"

"Pa-pa!"

The syllables died away in the quiet room. There was a low rustling of silk, the glassy brown eyes turned slowly away, and Mr. Puckler heard the pitter-patter of the small feet in the bronze kid slippers as the figure ran straight to the door. Then the candle burned high again, the room was full of light, and he was alone.

Mr. Puckler passed his hand over his eyes and looked about him. He could see everything quite clearly, and he felt that he must have been dreaming, though he was standing instead of sitting down, as he should have been if he had just waked up. The candle burned brightly now. There were the dolls to be mended, lying in a row with their toes up. The third one had lost her right shoe, and Else was making one. He knew that, and he was certainly not dreaming now. He had not been dreaming when he had come in from his fruitless search and had heard the doll's footsteps running to the door. He had not fallen asleep in his chair. How could he possibly have fallen asleep when his heart was breaking? He had been awake all the time.

He steadied himself, set the fallen chair upon its legs, and said to himself again very emphatically that he was a foolish old man. He ought to be out in the streets looking for his child, asking questions, and enquiring at the police stations, where all accidents were reported as soon as they were known, or at the hospitals.

"Pa-pa!"

The longing, wailing, pitiful little wooden cry rang from the passage, outside the door, and Mr. Puckler stood for an instant with white face, transfixed and rooted to the spot. A moment later his hand was on the latch. Then he was in the passage, with the light streaming from the open door behind him.

Quite at the other end he saw the little phantom shining clearly in the shadow, and the right hand seemed to beckon to him as the arm rose and fell once more. He knew all at once that it had not come to frighten him but to lead him, and when it disappeared, and he walked boldly towards the door, he knew that it was in the street outside, waiting for him. He forgot that he was tired and had eaten no supper, and had walked many miles, for a sudden hope ran through and through him, like a golden stream of life.

And sure enough, at the corner of the alley, and at the corner of the street, and out in Belgrave Square, he saw the small ghost flitting before him. Sometimes it was only a shadow, where there was other light, but then the glare of the lamps made a pale green sheen on its little Mother Hubbard frock of silk; and sometimes, where the streets were dark and silent, the whole figure shone out brightly, with its yellow curls and rosy neck. It seemed to trot along like a tiny child, and Mr. Puckler could almost hear the pattering of the bronze kid slippers on the pavement as it ran. But it went very fast, and he could only just keep up with it, tearing along with his hat on the back of his head and his thin hair blown by the night breeze, and his horn-rimmed spectacles firmly set upon his broad nose.

On and on he went, and he had no idea where he was. He did not even care, for he knew certainly that he was going the right way.

Then at last, in a wide, quiet street, he was standing before a big, sober-looking door that had two lamps on each side of it, and a polished brass bell-handle, which he pulled.

And just inside, when the door was opened, in the bright light, there was the little shadow, and the pale green sheen of the little silk dress, and once more the small cry came to his ears, less pitiful, more longing.

"Pa-pa!"

The shadow turned suddenly bright, and out of the brightness the beautiful brown glass eyes were turned up happily to his, while the rosy mouth smiled so divinely that the phantom doll looked almost like a little angel just then.

"A little girl was brought in soon after ten o'clock," said the quiet voice of the hospital doorkeeper. "I think they thought she was only stunned. She was holding a big brown-paper box against her, and they could not get it out of her arms. She had a long plait of brown hair that hung down as they carried her."

"She is my little girl," said Mr. Puckler, but he hardly heard his own voice.

He leaned over Else's face in the gentle light of the children's ward, and when he had stood there a minute the beautiful brown eyes opened and looked up to his.

"Pa-pa!" cried Else, softly, "I knew you would come!"

Then Mr. Puckler did not know what he did or said for a moment, and what he felt was worth all the fear and terror and despair that had almost killed him that night. But by and by Else was telling her story, and the nurse let her speak, for there were only two other children in the room, who were getting well and were sound asleep.

"They were big boys with bad faces," said Else, "and they tried to get Nina away from me, but I held on and fought as well as I could till one of them hit me with something, and I don't remember any more, for I tumbled down, and I suppose the boys ran away, and somebody found me there. But I'm afraid Nina is all smashed."

"Here is the box," said the nurse. "We could not take it out of her arms till she came to herself. Should you like to see if the doll is broken?"

And she undid the string cleverly, but Nina was all smashed to pieces. Only the gentle light of the children's ward made a pale green sheen in the folds of the little Mother Hubbard frock.

"Doubles" and Quits

Arthur Quiller-Couch

Here is a story from Troy, containing two ghosts and a moral I found it, only last week, in front of a hump-backed cottage that the masons are pulling down to make room for the new Bank. Simon Hancock, the outgoing tenant, had fetched an empty cider-cask, and set it down on the opposite side of the road; and from this Spartan seat watched the work of demolition for three days, without exhaustion and without emotion. In the interval between two avalanches of dusty masonry, he spoke to this effect:—

Once upon a time the cottage was inhabited by a man and his wife. The man was noticeable for the extreme length of his upper lip and gloom of his religious opinions. He had been a mate in the coasting trade, but settled down, soon after his marriage, and earned his living as one of the four pilots in the port. The woman was unlovely, with a hard eye and a temper as stubborn as one of St. Nicholas's horns. How she had picked up with a man was a mystery, until you looked at *him*.

After six years of wedlock they quarrelled one day, about nothing at all: at least, Simon Hancock, though unable to state the exact cause of strife, felt himself ready to swear it was nothing more serious than the cooking of the day's dinner. From that date, however, the pair lived in the house together and never spoke. The man happened to be of the home-keeping sort—possessed no friends and never put foot inside a public-house. Through the long evenings he would sit beside his own fender, with his wife facing him, and never a word flung across the space between them, only now and then a look of cold hate. The few that saw them thus said it was like looking on a pair of ugly statues. And this lasted for four years.

Of course the matter came to their minister's ears—he was a "Brianite"—and the minister spoke to them after prayer-meeting, one Wednesday night, and called at the cottage early next morning, to reconcile them. He stayed fifteen minutes and came away, down the street, with a look on his face such as Moses might have worn on his way down from Mount Sinai, if only Moses had seen the devil there, instead of God.

At the end of four years, the neighbours remarked that for two days no smoke had issued from the chimney of this cottage, nor had anyone seen the front door opened. There grew a surmise that the quarrel had flared out at last, and the wedded pair were lying within, in their blood. The anticipated excitement of finding the bodies was qualified, however, by a very present sense of the manner in which the bodies had resented intrusion during life. It was not until sunset on the second day that the constable took heart to break in the door.

There were no corpses. The kitchen was tidy, the hearth swept, and the house empty. On the table lay a folded note, addressed, in the man's handwriting, to the minister.

"Dear Friend in Grace," it began, "*we have been married ten years, and neither has broken the other; until which happens, it must be hell between us. We see no way out but to part for ten years more, going our paths without news of each other. When that time's up, we promise to meet here, by our door, on the morning of the first Monday in October month, and try again. And to this we set our names."*—here the two names followed.

They must have set out by night; for an extinguished candle stood by the letter, with inkpot and pen. Probably they had parted just outside the house, the one going inland up the hill, the other down the street towards the harbour. Nothing more was heard of them. Their furniture went to pay the quarter's rent due to the Squire, and the cottage, six months later, passed into the occupation of Simon Hancock, waterman.

At this point Simon shall take up the narrative:—

"I'd been tenant over there"—with a nod towards the ruin—"nine year an' goin' on for the tenth, when, on a Monday mornin', about this time o' year, I gets out o' bed at five o'clock an' down to the quay to have a look at my boat; for 'twas the fag-end of the Equinox, and ther'd been a 'nation gale blowin' all Sunday and all Sunday night, an' I thought she might have broke loose from her moorin's.

"The street was dark as your hat and the wind comin' up it like gas in a pipe, with a brave deal o' rain. But down 'pon the quay day was breakin'—a sort of blind man's holiday, but enough to see the boat by; and there she held all right. You know there's two postes 'pon the town-quay, and another slap opposite the door o' the 'Fifteen Balls'? Well, just as I turned back home-long, I see a man leanin' against thicky post like as if he was thinkin', wi' his back to me and his front to the 'Fifteen Balls' (that was shut, o' course, at that hour). I must ha' passed within a yard of en, an' couldn' figure it up how I'd a-missed seein' en. Hows'ever, 'Good-mornin'!' I calls out, in my well-known hearty manner. But he didn' speak nor turn. 'Mornin'!' I says again. 'Can 'ee tell me what time 'tis? for my watch is stopped'—which was a lie; but you must lie now and then, to be properly sociable.

"Well, he didn' answer; so I went on to say that the 'Fifteen Balls' wudn' be open for another dree hour; and then I walked slap up to en, and says what the Wicked Man said to the black pig. 'You'm a queer Christian,' I says, 'not to speak. What's your name at all? And let's see your ugly face.'

"With that he turned his face; an' by the man! I wished mysel' further. 'Twas a great white face, all parboiled, like a woman's hands on washin' day. An' there was bits o' sticks an' chips o' sea-weed stuck in his whiskers, and a crust o' salt i' the chinks of his mouth; an' his eyes, too, glarin' abroad from great rims o' salt.

"Off I sheered, not azackly runnin', but walkin' pretty much like a Torpointer; an' sure 'nough the fellow stood up straight and began to follow close behind me. I heard the water go squish-squash in his shoon, every step he took. By this, I was fairly leakin' wi' sweat. After a bit, hows'ever, at the corner o' Higman's store, he dropped off; an' lookin' back after twenty yards more, I saw him standin' there in the dismal grey light like a dog that can't make up his mind whether to follow or no. For 'twas near day now, an' his face plain at that distance. Fearin' he'd come on again, I pulled hot foot the few steps between me an' home. But when I came to the door, I went cold as a flounder.

"The fellow had got there afore me. There he was, standin' 'pon my door-step—wi' the same gashly stare on his face, and his lips a lead-color in the light.

"The sweat boiled out o' me now. I quavered like a leaf, and my hat rose 'pon my head. 'For the Lord's sake, stand o' one side,' I prayed en; 'do'ee now, that's a dear!' But he wudn' budge; no, not though I said several holy words out of the Mornin' Service.

"'Drabbet it!' says I, 'let's try the back door. Why didn' I think 'pon that afore?' And around I runs.

"There 'pon the back door-step was a woman!—an' pretty well as gashly as the man. She was just a 'natomy of a woman, wi' the lines of her ribs showin' under the gown, an' a hot red spot 'pon either cheek-bone, where the skin was stretched tight as a drum. She looked not to ha' fed for a year; an', if you please, she'd a needle and strip o' calico in her hands, sewin' away all the while her eyes were glarin' down into mine.

"But there was a trick I minded in the way she worked her mouth, an' says I, 'Missus Polwarne, your husband's a-waitin' for 'ee, round by the front door.'

"'Aw, is he indeed?' she answers, holdin' her needle for a moment—an' her voice was all hollow, like as if she pumped it up from a fathom or two. 'Then, if he knows what's due to his wife, I'll trouble en to come round,' she says; 'for this here's the door *I* mean to go in by.'

But at this point Simon asserts very plausibly that he swooned off; so it is not known how they settled it.

The Downs

Amyas Northcote

I am venturing to set down the following personal experience, inconclusive as it is, as I feel that it may interest those who have the patience to study the phenomena of the unseen world around us. It was my first experience of a psychical happening and its events are accordingly indelibly imprinted on my memory.

The date was, alas, a good many years ago, when I was still a young man and at the time was engaged in reading hard for a certain examination. My friend J. was in similar plight to myself and together we decided to abjure home and London life and seek a quiet country spot, where we might devote ourselves to our work amidst pleasant and congenial surroundings.

J. knew of such a place: a farm belonging to a Mr. Harkness, who was a distant connection of his own by marriage. Mr. Harkness was a childless widower and lived much to himself at Branksome Farm, attended to only by an elderly housekeeper and one or two servants. Although he called himself a farmer and did in fact farm fairly extensively, he was a man of cultivated and even learned tastes, widely read and deeply versed in the history and folklore of his neighbourhood. At the same time, although good-natured, he was the most reserved and tactiturn man I ever met, and appeared to have a positive horror of communicating his very considerable fund of local knowledge to outsiders like ourselves. However, he was glad to welcome us as paying guests for the sake of his relationship to J., and he and his housekeeper certainly took great care to make us comfortable and happy.

Branksome Farm is a large old-fashioned house, surrounded by the usual farm buildings and situated in a valley winding its way among the Downs. The situation is beautiful and remote, and it would astonish many of our City dwellers to know that within two or three hours' railway journey from London there still are vast stretches of open Downland on which one may walk for hours without sight of a human being, and traversed only by winding roads which run from one small town or hamlet to another, linking a few lonely cottages or farms to civilization on their route. Behind the house Branksome Down, the highest in the neighbourhood, rises steeply, and beyond it at a distance of about three miles is Willingbury, the nearest town, whence the railway runs to London.

It is necessary to describe the geography of the country between Willingbury and Branksome a little more closely. The two places lie, as is usually the case in the Down country, in valleys between the hills and by road are distant from each other about six to seven miles, being separated by the long ridge of Branksome Down. But actually the distance between them does not exceed three miles across the Down: the path from Branksome, a mere sheep-track, leading up to the top of Branksome Down whence the wanderer sees before him a wide shallow dip in the Down, nearly circular, about three-quarters of a mile across and at the other side sloping up to another gentle ridge. Arrived at the summit of this second elevation the traveller gazes down on the Willingbury-Overbury road and following another sheep-track down the hill-side he reaches the road about a mile outside Willingbury.

The whole Down is covered with sweet, short turf, unbroken by trees or shrubs and, at the time of my story, was unmarred by fencing of any form. Flocks of sheep tended by shepherds and their watchful dogs were almost its sole inhabitants, save for the shy, wild life that clings to all natural shelters. Of the beauty of this Down and, in fact, of the whole neighbourhood it is useless to speak. To anyone who has once felt the fascination of a walk in the fresh, pure air, over the springy and centuries-old turf, and who has allowed his eyes to wander over the miles and miles of open Down, studded here and there with rare belts of trees, and has watched the shifting lights play over the near and distant hills, it is needless to speak, and to anyone who has never yet been fortunate enough to find himself in Downland in fine weather one can hardly make its fascination clear in words, and one can only advise him to go and explore its beauties for himself.

Well, it was at Branksome Farm that J. and I took up our abode and commenced a course of steady reading, tempered and varied by long walks about the country. Our time passed pleasantly and profitably, and we discovered one day with regret that more than half of it had elapsed. Dismayed at this discovery we began to set our wits to work to find an excuse for prolonging our stay at Branksome, when suddenly an event happened which entirely altered our plans.

Returning one day from our accustomed walk, J. found a telegram waiting for him, which called him to London without delay and the contents of which appeared to indicate the probability of his being unable to return to Branksome. No time was to be lost in making a start if he was to catch the afternoon train at Willingbury and, as it was really quicker to walk across the Down than to drive round the roads behind Mr. Harkness' rather slow old mare, he threw a few clothes hastily into a bag and departed for the station. I accompanied him to see him off and we made the best possible speed to Willingbury. But we had miscalculated the time; the afternoon train had gone, and we found on inquiry that there would be no other until the night mail for London, which passed through Willingbury shortly before 11 P.M.

J. urged me not to wait for this but to leave him at the little inn and go back to Branksome before dark, but I was anxious to keep him company and cheer up his rather depressed spirits, so finally we agreed to dine together at the *Blue Lion* and spend the evening there until the train left. I was perfectly confident in my ability to find my way back over the Down to Branksome at night, as the path was very familiar to us, and I expected to be aided by the light of the moon which would rise about ten o'clock. In due course the train arrived, and having seen J. safely on his way to London I turned my steps towards the Willingbury–Overbury road and its junction with the Branksome sheep-track.

It was a little after 11 P.M. when I left Willingbury on my homeward way, and I was disappointed to find that the moon had failed me, being completely hidden behind a thick canopy of cloud. The night was profoundly still as well as being very dark, but I was confident in my powers of finding my way and I strode contentedly along the road till I reached the point where it was necessary I should diverge on to the Down. I found the commencement of the sheep-track without difficulty, as my eyes were now accustomed to the surrounding obscurity, and set myself to climbing the Down as quickly as possible.

I must make it clear that up to the present time I had been in my usual state of health and spirits, although the latter were somewhat depressed at J.'s sudden departure and the break up of our pleasant association together. Up to this night, also, I had never in the least suspected that I was possessed of any special psychic intelligence. It is true that I had known that I was in the habit of occasionally dreaming very vividly and consecutively, but I had never given this faculty a serious thought, nor, like most young men in their twenties, had I ever given any consideration to psychic matters. It must be remembered also that I am writing of nearly forty years ago, when an intelligent interest in the potentialities of unseen beings and kindred topics was far less common than it is today.

Well, I commenced my ascent of the hill, and I had not gone very far when I became aware of a certain peculiar change taking place in myself. I fear I shall find it very difficult to describe my sensations in a fashion intelligible to those who have never experienced anything similar, whilst to those who have undergone psychic ordeals my description will probably appear bald and inadequate. I seemed to be in some mysterious fashion divided into a dual personality. One, the familiar one, was myself, my body, which continued to walk up the sheep-track, keenly alive to the need to keep a sharp look out against losing my way or stumbling over some obstruction. This personality also felt loneliness and a certain degree of nervousness. The darkness, silence and immensity of the empty country round me were oppressive. I feared something, I was not quite sure what, and I anxiously wished I was at the end of my journey with the farm lights shining out to welcome me. My other personality was more vague and ill-defined; it seemed to be separated from my body and from my outer consciousness and to be floating in a region where there was neither space nor time. It seemed to be aware of another world, a world surrounding and intermingling with this one, in which all that is or was or will be was but one moment and in which all places near or far, the Down and the remotest of the invisible stars, were but one spot. All was instantaneous and all was eternal. I am not clear how long this mood lasted, but it was probably only a few minutes before my earthly self was brought or appeared to be brought into entire control of my personality by a sudden shock.

As I walked I became aware that I was not alone. There was a man moving parallel with me on my right at the distance of some four or five yards. So suddenly and so silently had he appeared that he seemed to have risen from the earth. He was walking quite quietly at my own pace abreast of me, but apparently taking no notice of me, and I observed that his footsteps made no sound on the soft turf. The dim light made it difficult to see him at all distinctly, but he was evidently a tall, powerfully built fellow, dressed in a long cloak, which, partly covering his face, fell nearly to his feet. On his head he wore a queer-shaped, three-cornered hat and in his hand he carried what appeared to be a short, heavy bludgeon.

I was greatly startled. I am a small and by no means robust man and the apparition of this odd-looking stranger on these lonely Downs was disquieting. What did he want? Had he followed me down the road from Willingbury, and, if so, for what purpose? However, I decided it was best not to appear alarmed and after taking another glance at the man, I wished him good evening.

He took not the faintest notice of my salutation, which he appeared not even to have heard, but continued to advance up the hill by my side in dead silence.

After a few moments I spoke again; and this time my voice sounded strange in my own ears, as if it did not come from my lips, but from somewhere far away.

"A dark night," I said.

And now he answered. In a slow, measured voice, but one in which there sounded a note of hopelessness and misery, he said: "It is dark to you. It is darker for me."

I scarcely knew what to reply, but I felt that my courage was at an ebb and that I must maintain it by endeavouring to keep up a conversation, difficult though this might prove. Accordingly I went on: "This is a strange place to walk in at night. Have you far to go?"

He did not turn his head or look at me.

"Your way is short and easy, but mine is long and hard. How long, O Lord, how long?" he cried. As he uttered the last words his voice rose to a cry and he tossed his arms above his head, letting them fall to his side with a gesture of despair.

We had now almost reached the top of the Down, and as we neared the summit I became aware that the wind was rising. At the moment we were sheltered from it by the brow of the hill, but I could hear its distant roaring, and as we reached the summit it broke upon us with a rush.

With it and mingled in its sounds came other sounds, the sounds of human voices, of many voices, in many keys. There were sounds of wailing, of shouting, of chanting, of sobbing, even at times of laughter. The great, shallow bowl of Branksome Down was alive with sounds. I could see nothing, save my strange companion, who continued to move steadily forward; and I, dreading his company and yet dreading even more to be left alone, accompanied him. The night was still profoundly dark and, though as I advanced the voices often sounded quite near, I saw nothing until after we had passed the centre of the depression and were mounting the opposite slope. At that moment the wind tore aside the clouds and the moon streamed down full upon the Downs. By her light I saw a marvellous and a terrifying sight. The whole of Branksome Down was alive with people hurrying hither and thither, some busy and absorbed in their occupations, whatever they might be, others roaming aimlessly and tossing their arms into the air with wild and tragic gesticulations. The crowd appeared to be of all sorts and conditions and to be dressed in the fashions of all the ages, though ancient costumes seemed to predominate. Here I saw a group of persons clothed apparently in the priestly robes of ancient Britain; there walked a soldier wearing the eagle-crested helmet of Rome. Other groups there were in dresses of later date, the steel-clad knight of the Middle Ages, the picturesque dress and flowing hair of a cavalier of the Seventeenth Century. But it was impossible to fix the shifting crowd. As I gazed, absorbed, at one figure, it melted and was gone and another took its place, to fade likewise as I watched.

My companion paid no heed to the throng. Steadily he passed on towards the crest of the hill, at intervals raising his arms and letting them fall with his old gesture of despair and uttering at the same time his mournful cry of "How long, how long?"

We passed onward and upward and reached the top of the Down, my companion now a few yards in front of me. As he reached the crest of the hill, he stopped and, lifting his arms above his head, stood motionless. Suddenly he wavered, his figure expanded, its lines became vague and blurred against the background, it faded and was gone. As it vanished the wind dropped suddenly, the sound of human voices ceased and gazing round me I saw the plain bare and still in the moonlight.

I was now at the top of the hill, and looking downwards I saw a light burning in a window of Branksome Farm. I stumbled down the hill in haste, and as I approached the house saw Mr. Harkness standing at the open door. He looked at me strangely as I entered.

"Have you come across Branksome Down tonight," he exclaimed, "tonight of all the nights in the year?"

"Yes," I replied.

"I should have warned you," he said, "but I expected you back before dark. Branksome Down is an ill place tonight and men have vanished upon it before now and never been heard of again. No shepherd will set foot upon it tonight, for this is the night in the year when, folk say, all those that ever died violent deaths upon the Downs come back to seek their lost rest."

The Eleventh of March

Amelia B. Edwards

Forty years ago!

An old pocket-book lies before me, bound in scarlet morocco, and fastened with a silver clasp. The leather is mildewed; the silver tarnished; the paper yellow; the ink faded. It has been hidden away at the back of an antique oaken bureau since the last day of the year during which I had it in use; and that was forty years ago. Ay, here is a page turned down—turned down at Wednesday, March the eleventh, eighteen hundred and twenty-six. The entry against that date is brief and obscure enough.

> Wednesday, March 11th.—Walked from Frascati to Palazzuola, the ancient site of Alba Longa, on the Alban lake. Lodged at Franciscan convent. Brother Geronimo. Dare one rely on the testimony of the senses? *Dieu sait tout.*

Brief as it is, however, that memorandum tires a train of long-dormant memories, and brings back with painful vividness all the circumstances to which it bears reference. I will endeavour to relate them as calmly and succinctly as possible.

I started on foot from Frascati immediately after breakfast, and rested midway in the shade of a wooded ravine between Marino and the heights of Alba Longa. I seem to remember every trivial incident of that morning walk. I remember how the last year's leaves crackled under my feet, and how the green lizards darted to and fro in the sunlight. I fancy I still hear the slow drip of the waters that trickled down the cavernous rocks on either hand. I fancy I still smell the heavy perfume of the violets among the ferns. It was not yet noon when I emerged upon the upper ridge, and took the path that leads to Monte Cavo. The woodcutters were busy among the chestnut slopes of Palazzuola. They paused in their work, and stared at me sullenly as I passed by. Presently a little turn in the footway brought the whole lake of Albano before my eyes. Blue, silent, solitary, set round with overhanging woods, it lay in the sunshine, four hundred feet below, like a sapphire at the bottom of a malachite vase. Now and then, a soft breath from the west ruffled the placid mirror, and blurred the pictured landscape on its surface. Now and then, a file of mules, passing unseen among the forest-paths, sent a faint sound of tinkling bells across the lake. I sat down in the shade of a clump of cork-trees, and contemplated the panorama. To my left, on a precipitous platform at the verge of the basin, with Monte Cavo towering up behind, stretched the long white façade of the Convent of Palazzuola; on the opposite height, standing clear against the sky, rose the domes and pines of Castel Gondolfo; to the far right, in the blinding sunshine of the Campagna, lay Rome and the Etruscan hills.

In this spot I established myself for the day's sketching. Of so vast a scene, I could, necessarily, only select a portion. I chose the Convent, with its background of mountain, and its foreground of precipice and lake; and proceeded patiently to work out, first the leading features, and next the minuter details of the subject. Thus occupied (with an occasional pause to watch the passing of a cloud-shadow, or listen to the chiming of a distant chapel-bell), I lingered on, hour after hour, till the sun hung low in the west, and the woodcutters were all gone to their homes. I was now at least three miles from either the town of Albano or the village of Castel Gondolfo, and was, moreover, a stranger to the neighbourhood. I looked at my watch. There remained but one half hour of good daylight, and it was important that I should find my way before the dusk closed in. I rose reluctantly, and, promising myself to return to the same spot on the morrow, packed away my sketch, and prepared for the road.

At this moment, I saw a monk standing in an attitude of meditation upon a little knoll of rising ground some fifty yards ahead. His back was turned towards me; his cowl was up, his arms were folded across his breast. Neither the splendour of the heavens, nor the tender beauty of the earth, was anything to him. He seemed unconscious even of the sunset.

I hurried forward, eager to inquire my nearest path along the woods that skirt the lake; and my shadow lengthened out fantastically before me as I ran. The monk turned abruptly. His cowl fell. He looked at me, face to face. There were not more than eighteen yards between us. I saw him as plainly as I now see the page on which I write. Our eyes met . . . My God! shall I ever forget those eyes?

He was still young, still handsome, but so lividly pale, so emaciated, so worn with passion, and penance, and remorse, that I stopped involuntarily, like one who finds himself on the brink of a chasm. We stood thus for a few seconds—both silent, both motionless. I could not have uttered a syllable, had my life depended on it. Then, as abruptly as he had turned towards me, he turned away, and disappeared among the trees. I remained for some minutes gazing after him. My heart throbbed painfully. I shuddered, I knew not why. The very air seemed to have grown thick and oppressive; the very sunset, so golden a moment since, had turned suddenly to blood.

I went on my way, disturbed and thoughtful. The livid face and lurid eyes of the monk haunted me. I dreaded every turn of the path, lest I should again encounter them. I started when a twig fell, or a dead leaf fluttered down beside me. I was almost ashamed of the sense of relief with which I heard the sound of voices some few yards in advance, and, emerging upon an open space close against the convent, saw some half dozen friars strolling to and fro in the sunset. I inquired my way to Albano, and learned that I was still more than two miles distant.

"It will be quite dark before the Signore arrives," said one, courteously. "The Signore would do well to accept a cell at Palazzuola for the night."

I remembered the monk, and hesitated.

"There is no moon now," suggested another; "and the paths are unsafe for those who do not know them."

While I was yet undecided, a bell rang, and three or four of the loiterers went in.

"It is our supper hour," said the first speaker. "The Signore will at least condescend to share our simple fare; and afterwards, if he still decides to sleep at Albano, one of our younger brethren shall accompany him as far as the Cappucini, at the entrance to the town."

I accepted this proposition gratefully, followed my entertainers through the convent gates, and was ushered into a stone hall, furnished with a long dining table, a pulpit, a clock, a double row of deal benches, and an indifferent copy of the Last Supper of Leonardo da Vinci. The Superior advanced to welcome me.

"You have come among us, Signore," he said, "on an evening when our table is but poorly provided. Although this is not one of the appointed fast-days of the Church, we have been abstaining at Palazzuola in memory of certain circumstances connected with our own brotherhood. I hope, however, that our larder may be found to contain something better suited to a traveller's appetite than the fare you now see before you."

Saying thus, he placed me at his right hand at the upper end of the board, and there stood till the monks were all in their places. He then repeated a Latin grace; after which each brother took his seat and began. They were twenty-three in number, twelve on one side, and eleven on the other; but I observed that a place was left vacant near the foot of the table, as if the twelfth man were yet to come. The twelfth, I felt sure, was he whom I had encountered on the way. Once possessed with this conviction, I could not keep from watching the door. Strange! I so dreaded and loathed his coming, that I almost felt as if his presence would be less intolerable than the suspense in which I awaited it!

In the meantime the monks ate in silence; and even the Superior, whose language and address were those of a well-informed man, seemed constrained and thoughtful. Their supper was of the most frugal description, and consisted of only bread, salad, grapes, and maccaroni. Mine was before long reinforced with a broiled pigeon and a flask of excellent Orvieto. I enjoyed my fare, however, as little as they seemed to enjoy theirs. Fasting as I was, I had no appetite. Weary as I was, I only longed to push my plate aside, and resume my journey.

"The Signore will not think of going farther to-night," said the Superior, after an interval of prolonged silence.

I muttered something about being expected at Albano.

"Nay, but it is already dusk, and the sky hath clouded over suddenly within the last fifteen minutes," urged he. "I fear much that we have a storm approaching. What sayest thou, Brother Antonio?"

"It will be a wild night," replied the brother with whom I had first spoken.

"Ay, a wild night," repeated an old monk, lower down the table; "like this night last year—like this night two years ago!"

The Superior struck the table angrily with his open hand.

"Silence!" he exclaimed authoritatively. "Silence there; and let Brother Anselmo bring lights."

It was now so dark that I could scarcely distinguish the features of the last speaker, or those of the monk who rose and left the room. Again the profoundest silence fell upon all present. I could hear the footsteps of Brother Anselmo echo down the passage, till they died away; and I remember listening vaguely to the ticking of the clock at the farther end the refectory, and comparing it in my own mind to the horrible beating of an iron heart. Just at that moment a sharp gust of wind moaned past the windows, bearing with it a prolonged reverberation of distant thunder.

"Our storms up here in the mountain are severe and sudden," said the Prior, resuming our conversation at the point where it had been interrupted; "and even the waters of yonder placid lake are sometimes so tempestuous that no boat dare venture across. I fear, Signore, that you will find it impossible to proceed to Albano."

"Should the tempest come up, reverend father," I replied, "I will undoubtedly accept your hospitality, and be grateful for it; but if. . . ."

I broke off abruptly. The words failed on my lips, and I pushed away the flask from which I was about to fill my glass.

Brother Anselmo had brought in the lamps, and there, in the twelfth seat at the opposite side of the table, sat the monk. I had not seen him take his place. I had not heard him enter. Yet there he sat, pale and deathlike, with his burning eyes fixed full upon me! No one noticed him. No one spoke to him. No one helped him to the dishes on the table. He neither ate, nor drank, nor held companionship with any of his fellows; but sat among them like an excommunicated wretch, whose penance was silence and fasting.

"You do not eat, Signore," said the prior.

"I—I thank you, reverend father," I faltered. "I have dined."

"I fear, indifferently. Would you like some other wine? Our cellar is not so ill-furnished as our larder."

I declined by a gesture.

"Then we will retire to my room, and take coffee."

And the Superior rose, repeated a brief Latin thanksgiving, and ushered me into a small well-lighted parlour, opening off a passage at the upper end of the hall, where there were some half-dozen shelves of books, a couple of easy chairs, a bright wood fire, and a little table laden with coffee and cakes. We had scarcely seated ourselves when a tremendous peal of thunder seemed to break immediately over the convent, and was followed by a cataract of rain.

"The Signore is safer here than on the paths between Palazzuola and Albano," said the Superior, sipping his coffee.

"I am, indeed," I replied. "Do I understand that you had a storm here on the same night last year, and the year before?"

The Prior's face darkened.

"I cannot deny the coincidence," he said, reluctantly; "but it is a mere coincidence, after all. The—the fact is that a very grievous and terrible catastrophe happened to our community on this day two years ago; and the brethren believe that heaven sends the tempest in memory of that event. Monks, Signore, are superstitious; and if we consider their isolated lives, it is not surprising that they should be so."

I bowed assent. The Prior was evidently a man of the world.

"Now, with regard to Palazzuola," continued he, disregarding the storm, and chatting on quite leisurely, "here are twenty-three brethren, most of them natives of the small towns among the mountains hereabout; and of that twenty-three, not ten have even been so far as Home in their lives."

"Twenty-three," I repeated. "Twenty-four, surely, *mio padre!*"

"I did not include myself," said the Prior, stiffly.

"Neither did I include you," I replied; "but I counted twenty-four of the order at table just now."

The Prior shook his head.

"No, no, Signore," said he. "Twenty-three only."

"But I am positive," said I.

"And so am I," rejoined he, politely but firmly.

I paused. I was certain. I could not be mistaken.

"Nay, *mio padre,*" I said; "they were twenty-three at first; but the brother who came in afterwards made the twenty-fourth."

"Afterwards!" echoed the Prior. "I am not aware that any brother came in afterwards."

"A sickly, haggard-looking monk," pursued I, "with singularly bright eyes—eyes which, I confess, produced on me a very unpleasant impression. He came in just before the lights were brought."

The Prior moved uneasily in his chair, and poured out another cup of coffee.

"Where did you say he sat, Signore?" said he.

"In the vacant seat at the lower end of the table, on the opposite side to myself."

The Prior set down his coffee untasted, and rose in great agitation.

"For God's sake, Signore," stammered he, "be careful what you say! Did you—did you see this? Is this true?"

"True?" I repeated, trembling I knew not why, and turning cold from head to foot. "As true as that I live and breathe! Why do you ask?"

"Sickly and haggard-looking, with singularly bright eyes," said the Prior, looking very pale himself. "Had it—had it the appearance of a young man?"

"Of a young man worn with suffering and remorse," I replied. "But—but it was not the first time, *mio padre!* I saw him before—this afternoon—down near the chestnut-woods, on a knoll of rising ground, overlooking the lake. He was standing with his back to the sunset."

The Prior fell on his knees before a little carved crucifix that hung beside the fireplace.

"Requiem æternam dona eis, Domine; et lux perpetua luceat eis," said he, brokenly.

The rest of his prayer was inaudible, and he remained for some minutes with his face buried in his hands.

"I implore you to tell me the meaning of this," I said, when he at length rose, and sank, still pale and agitated, into his chair.

"I will tell what I may, Signore," he replied; "but I must not tell you all. It is a secret that belongs to our community, and none of us are at liberty to repeat it. Two years ago, one of our brethren was detected in the commission of a great crime. He had suffered, struggled against it, and at last, urged by a terrible opportunity, committed it. His life paid for the offence. One who was deeply wronged by the deed, met him as he was flying from the spot, and slew him as he fled. Signore, the name of that monk was the Fra Geronimo. We buried him where he fell, on a knoll of rising ground close against the chestnut woods that border the path to Marino. We had no right to lay his remains in consecrated ground; but we fast, and say masses for his soul, on each anniversary of that fearful day."

The Prior paused and wiped his brow.

"But, *mio padre* . . ." I began.

"This day last year," interrupted he, "one of the woodcutters yonder took a solemn oath that he met the Fra Geronimo on that very knoll at sunset. Our brethren believed the man—but I, heaven forgive me! was incredulous. Now, however . . ."

"Then—then you believe," faltered I, "you believe that I have seen . . ."

"Brother Geronimo," said the Prior, solemnly.

And I believe it too. I am told, perhaps, that it was an illusion of the senses. Granted; but is not such an illusion, in itself, a phenomenon as appalling as the veriest legend that superstition evokes from the world beyond the grave? How shall we explain the nature of the impression? Whence comes it? By what material agency is it impressed upon the brain? These are questions leading to abysses of speculation before which the sceptic and the philosopher alike recoil—questions which I am unable to answer. I only know that these things came within the narrow radius of my own experience; that I saw them with my own eyes; and that they happened just forty years ago, on the eleventh of March, anno Domini eighteen hundred and twenty-six.

The Face in the Glass

Mary Elizabeth Braddon

I. The Warning

In far-distant Yorkshire, many years ago, stood an old manor-house—a grey, grim building surrounding an open courtyard, in the middle of which played a melancholy fountain. The house was close to the wide moors that stretch away to the city of York, and beside the village there was not another place within miles. Except for the housekeeper and the usual staff of servants the house had been uninhabited now for some time, for the late owner had been a great traveller, and had been drowned during his last voyage; close at home too, which made it all the sadder, and he was brought back to be buried in the dreary family vault one day in the spring before my story opens. Since that occurrence the housekeeper declared that, whenever there were storms out at sea, the wind used to howl and wail down the long passages like a soul in pain, and that a dreadful sound of dripping water always was to be heard in the room where the poor body was laid, in the interval before the funeral. There were also some mysterious chambers in the mansion where the doors disappeared periodically, and entrance to them was thereby prevented for months together; and when they were at last restored, the walls would be found adorned with diabolical sketches of fiends, and the furniture would be arranged in anything but an artistic manner.

However, this did not seem to weigh very heavily on the spirits of the new owners, Mr. and Mrs. Monroe, a high-spirited, courageous couple, who had not long been married, and were as happy as the day was long. Mrs. Monroe, indeed, professed herself most anxious to see one of these wonderful ghosts; but then she was strong-minded, and actually thought nothing of going to bed alone in the dark, and she would visit the haunted chambers and walk about the passages at night until the servants almost believed she must be a ghost herself, so extremely fearless was she on the subject. Nor was her husband in any way behindhand in assisting her in her ghost hunts, but he was out a great deal hunting and shooting just then, and often came home simply to dine and fall asleep, sometimes even over the dinner-table itself, with sheer fatigue.

Mrs. Monroe had been one of a large family who lived in a cheerful house in sunny Kent, and had had very little time there for the reading, writing, and walking, with which she now filled up her days in the most satisfactory manner and she had not yet found the time hang heavily on her hands; but still she was not very sorry when the first hard frosts of the rigorous Yorkshire winter bound up the ground into an iron mass, and put a stop to the outdoor amusements which took her husband so constantly away from her side. Occasional falls of snow too, rather spoiled his shooting, and he could only putter about the house, farm, and the little park, getting an occasional sea-bird that was driven in from the coast, and that gave him an evening's work looking it out in one of his numerous Bewick-illustrated books, for as he never could find it there, the occupation was as endless as it was enthralling. This was very well for the first fortnight or so, and Mrs. Monroe could go out with him to look for the birds, and could help him with his Bewick at night; but at last the snow began to fall in earnest; and after four days of it with scarcely a break in the chilly grey sky, when the post had never come in at all, and the one newspaper of the week had never been delivered, Mrs. Monroe was beginning to wonder if it would be wicked to pray for a thaw; for she foresaw that unless something new could be contrived in the way of amusement for her lord and master, she would discover what having too much of a good thing was like; for even her company had begun to pall, and he became first fidgety, next complaining, then fractious about his dinner, and then very, very cross.

At last a bright idea struck her. "Hugh," she said, "let us get Betty's keys from her this very moment, and go in for a regular ghost hunt. The evening has come on very rapidly, and the moon on the snow will make the rooms as bright as day. See," she added, drawing apart the heavy crimson curtains that hung over the deep, small-paned windows, "the clouds are all gone and tomorrow you may be able to shoot again, and we may never have such a glorious opportunity for months to come, so don't let us miss it. We're both tired of sitting over the fire, and a rush through all those mysterious rooms above our bedroom floor will give us an appetite for dinner; even if we are not rewarded by the sight of the much-to-be-desired bogie."

"It will be horribly cold," answered Hugh, shrugging up his shoulders and stretching out his hands to the big fire that blazed up the chimney; "and besides, if we did see a ghost, it would be the death of you; you know it's only because you didn't believe in Betty's stories that you are so courageous."

"My dear Hugh," said Ruth, impressively, "I don't for one moment believe we shall see anything worse than ourselves, as old nurse used to say; but if we did, what could possibly happen to us? I have been up and about all hours of the night, especially when Betty was so ill the week before last, and really if there were anything to be seen, I should have seen it then. However, I won't go now if you don't like it."

"Oh, we'll go," answered Hugh. "I was rather lazy, that's all." And so saying, he rang the bell and ordered the keys; and after a little delay a goodly assortment of all sizes and species of key was brought them, and off started Mr. and Mrs. Monroe on their ghost hunt.

Hugh's spirits rose with the search, and they went upstairs and downstairs, unlocking many a cupboard and room that had not been looked at for months, and maybe years, but not a ghost was to be seen. Every now and then a most suggestive rustle was to be heard among the dusty hangings of the oak four-posters, and Hugh and Ruth held each other's hands a little tighter than usual; but on investigation it turned out to be either the wind that was beginning to rise, or a shimmer from the lamp they carried showed them a little grey mouse scuttling away under the beds; now and then, too, a dreary groan seemed to pierce the darkness as they opened some heavy door; but this, too, generally turned out to be caused by the rustiness of the hinges.

They were getting gradually in extremely high spirits, and as the hunt proceeded, and nothing was found, they were laughing and talking loudly, when suddenly they come upon a door at the very end of the passage that led down to the inhabited portion of the house, which they had not noticed before. Of course it was locked, as they discovered at once, and after trying to unlock it with every key they had, they came to the conclusion that they would have to go downstairs after one that would fit the lock; when suddenly the wind seemed to rise yet higher, and a rather strong puff came through the keyhole (through which Mrs. Monroe was peeping to see if the key had been left there), extinguishing the lamp she held, and they were at once plunged in darkness. However, Mr. Monroe soon lighted it again. "The windows must all be open," said he, "in which case it was quite time we investigated our domain. I dare say old Betty has lost the key, and is afraid I shall scold her for her carelessness. However, if you aren't frightened, Ruth," he added, turning to his wife, "I'll run down and ask her about it. If she's lost it, I'll have the door broken open and those windows shut, for there's wind enough here for a ship in full sail."

"Yes, do," answered Mrs. Monroe brightly; "doubtless here's the sailor's ghost that makes our nights so extremely squally when the wind is high; and if we can· get rid of him, perhaps I shall not be driven to have a new maid every time the wind blows from the north-west; which is beginning to be rather a trouble, especially now when the snow is so deep. I should never get one out from York."

"Well, wait there, then," said Mr. Monroe, and he hurried off into the downstairs regions and asked the old housekeeper for the missing key. She rose from her seat by the fire, trembling, and in a hurried manner said, "Now doant'ee, Master Hugh."

"Doant'ee," repeated Hugh scornfully, "doant'ee what? if you've lost the key, what does it matter? We'll soon get a new one; but if you haven't, and it's any of your superstitious nonsense, you ought to know us better than to try on any of that with us. Be quick, too, for it's mighty cold up there. The windows are open, I think, and though the night is still, the wind seems to chill one through."

"Master Hugh," said Betty impressively, "in that room has lain dead many members of the Monroe family; somehow or other every member has either died there or been carried thither in his coffin to wait for his funeral day. And tonight, Master Hugh," she added waxing more eloquent as her dread of his taking the key increased—"tonight is the anniversary of the day Master Charles was brought there drowned and dead from Flamborough Bay; and you know that as sure as you go into that room, so sure will you see reflected in the glass the face of any member of the family who has to die before the year is out; and on the bed, Master Hugh, you'll see the coffin, with its dreadful drip, drip, drip from the shroud of the poor dead boy, just as it dripped ceaselessly with seawater until they buried him out of our sight."

"What on earth are you about, Hugh?" broke in a voice from the doorway. "I am nearly frozen to death, and I want to get into the room."

"Give me the key, Betty," said Hugh, "I'll run the risk of the ghosts, coffin and all, and besides, we are ghost hunting. So, my dear," he went on, turning to his wife, who, tired of waiting, had come down to see what he was doing, "according to Betty we may cry Eureka, for the ghost is found"; and, laughing very much, the two young people took the key from Betty's unwilling hand, and rushing up the wide oak staircase, they were soon at the door of the ghost-chamber.

The wind seemed to have risen in their short absence, and as they rested for a moment, after their hurried race up the stairs, there seemed to come to them the regular drip, drip, drip, that old Betty had prophesied. Even their stout hearts quailed somewhat, but with an impatient "Imagination of course," Hugh turned the key in the lock, and the door came open. Only a bare boarded chamber, and in the middle the bed that had held so many, many corpses: three tiny windows all close shuttered, but through the chinks came stray moonbeams, and a most tremendous rush of wind that agitated the light chintz hangings to the bed, until all sorts and shapes of figures seemed in the folds, peeping and glaring at the newcomers. Between each window was hung a looking-glass, and above the mantelpiece was another—other furniture was there none.

"A window must be broken," said Mrs. Monroe, and so saying she advanced to throw open the shutters, which she had no sooner done than she was alarmed by hearing her husband fall with a loud bang behind her, with the muttered exclamation "My God!"

Ruth tore to the bell, and rang a tremendous peal, and before the servants came rushing up she had dragged Hugh into her arms, and regardless of any ghosts that might be about, turned all her attention to her husband, wishing heartily that she could get at some of the water she heard so continually dripping near her. Just as the servants reached her she caught sight of a thin stream of water meandering towards them, making a line of light through the dust, and she stooped forward to dip her handkerchief into it, when Betty, who, notwithstanding her age, was the first to answer the summons she had been awaiting breathlessly ever since the key had left her hands—rushed forward, and with a "M—m—missus, that's corpse water," deluged Hugh and Ruth with the contents of a jug she had brought up with her, convinced that it would be required. Hugh was carried out of the room into his own, and just as Ruth turned to lock the door, she saw, or fancied she saw, in the moonlight that now flooded the room, the pale shadow of a coffin on the bed, from which proceeded the thin stream of water which she had so nearly used for her husband; and with a shudder of horror, but with a promise to herself to re-investigate the subject, she closed and locked the door, slipping the key into her pocket, and followed Hugh into his room.

By this time he had come to himself, and was beginning to wonder what on earth had been the matter; but the moment he saw his wife, the remembrance of the horror came back to him, and he nearly fainted again.

When he was all right once more, which was not until the next day, and they were seated at a late breakfast, Ruth implored him to tell her quietly and calmly all he had seen; but all she could draw from him was the assurance that no power on earth should induce him to tell her, and that he wished to forget all about it as soon as he could. "Ghosts? oh, ghosts were nonsense, of course, but still there was no need to talk of them."

"But Hugh," said Ruth mysteriously, "*I* saw it too, and I didn't mind a bit. After all," she added, alarmed at the expression on her husband's face, "it might have been only a leak in the roof that allowed the water to come in; and moonbeams do take such curious shapes, especially when reflected from the snow, that I believe the coffin only existed in our imagination; and I shall go up again tonight, and set the matter straight once and for all. If there really should be a ghost—well, we must use all our endeavours to lay the perturbed spirit; but if there isn't, we had surely better discover that it is so, for really you look white and ready to faint at the mere idea of it."

"You must do nothing of the kind," answered Hugh decidedly. "I saw neither coffin nor water, and what I did see was probably nothing of any consequence, but I cannot mention it to you of all people under the sun—at all events not until the first shock has worn off. And I must ask you to give up any idea you may have of going there again." Before Ruth had any time to either give him the desired promise, or argue him out of his absurd superstition, as she characterised his ideas in her own mind, Hugh had caught sight of the weekly postman laboring at last through the melting mud in the avenue; and doubtless wishing to forget all about the affair of the night before, he went out to meet him.

"Very sorry, sir," said the postman, "to be late, but still more sorry to be the bearer of bad news: your poor brother's heart-broke. He 've lost his missus, and wants to see you at once. The funeral's tomorrow, and he does hope the roads will be open enough to allow of you to come to him, for he 's terribly cut up about it."

Hugh took the letters and went in, and who shall say how thankful he was at the bad news? for he had fully believed he had seen his wife 's face in the glass in the ghost room last night, and now it had turned out—so he thinks—to be that of his younger brother's wife, who was his wife 's sister, and who resembled Ruth greatly. In his joy at the load lifted off his mind he almost forgot he had to tell his wife of her sister's death, and he was glad to find her absent on her household duties, where she remained until he had read his letters and felt in a more saddened frame of mind. Poor Ruth was in so much trouble, and at the same time in such a bustle to get her husband and his groom and garments off in time, that the ghost quite slipped both their minds, and it was only when he was halfway to York, and had got out on to the open moor, where the snow was rapidly melting under a warm north-west rain, that Hugh wished he had told Ruth all about it, and had asked her to give him the promise he wished for in the morning. But it was too late now, and so he jogged on until the forty-five miles of damp, cold riding were over, and he found himself entering the dark, narrow streets of York.

II. The Fulfilment

After the first sad questions and answers had passed between Mr. Monroe and his brother Edgar, Hugh proceeded to tell how alarmed he had been in the ghost-chamber the night before by the apparition in the glass. Edgar looked up from his seat by the fire, and said, "What time did you see it, Hugh?"

"I can't in the least tell," answered Hugh, "but I should say about six or a little after. But what does that matter? the warning was conveyed to me, if only I had not at once jumped to the conclusion that it must be Ruth."

"Mary died the day before yesterday," said Edgar; "she was sitting there, looking to me as well as you are, and all of a sudden she fell forward, and must have died instantly. Thank God," he added, in broken accents, "she never suffered at all. Doctor Bareham told me that her death was instantaneous; and it's just as her father died too. It must be in the family."

"God forbid," exclaimed Hugh, jumping up. "Don't for Heaven's sake talk like that; Mary and Ruth are sisters, remember. Think of what you are saying."

"I never could see why we pray against sudden death," said Edgar, still in the same quiet tone of voice. "Think how mercifully one glides out of all the turmoil and pain of this mortal life into perfect rest. Would I could lie down at once by Mary's side and sleep too!"

"Merciful for those who go," said Hugh, "but not for those that remain behind. Think of the shock! But it is getting late, and I have had a long ride. I must go to bed"; and bidding his brother goodnight, he went up the staircase into the room appointed for him.

Just across the narrow passage was that other quiet room, in which lay the body of his sister-in-law, under the doorway of which came a thin line of light and a subdued murmur of talk, that showed someone was still in the room with her. Hugh had not seen her since the day on which the two brothers and sisters had been married. He took up his candle again, and going across the passage, knocked at the door. It was opened about an inch by the old family nurse who had come to live with Mary on her marriage, and she, seeing who it was, came out, and shutting the door carefully behind her, drew Hugh back again into his own room, and shut that door too. "Now, Mr. Monroe," said she, "I know what you want; but listen to me, and don't ask to see poor Miss Mary again. You had far better remember her as she was the last time you saw her, a bonnie, happy bride, than take away in your mind how she looks now; and besides," she added, "she is so like dear Miss Ruth, that I am sure you should not look at her; it can do her no good now, poor lamb, and may give you a shock you will not easily get over—and you look white and tired enough now too."

"All right, Povis," answered Hugh; "perhaps you are right, but I thought Mr. Edgar might feel hurt. Anyhow, I'll leave it to you to explain matters, and as I really am almost done up, I'll take your advice. So goodnight"; and the old nurse having gone back to her melancholy task of watching by the coffin, Hugh proceeded to hurry into bed. As he was seated on the side of his bed, divesting himself of his garments, he happened to catch sight of himself in the looking-glass, and there, looking as if it were over his shoulder, was the dreadful face of the night before. This time the eyes were opened, and seemed to look in an imploring and appealing manner into his own, as if urging some action upon him. Only the face was to be seen, as if the head were cut off at the neck, or as if the head and body were enveloped in a grey fog, out of which loomed the fair appealing features of his wife—for that it was his wife Hugh never thought of doubting. He rose and hurried forward to the glass, but as he advanced the face gradually vanished; and although he stood for some time trembling and looking in all directions it did not come again. So putting it down in his own mind to imagination, he hastened to get into bed, and being dreadfully tired, soon fell fast asleep.

The morning found himself rested, and his intellect clear and alert. He rose and dressed, but when he was brushing his hair in the glass a cold wind seemed to pass over him. The brushes were poised in mid-air, and there looking again at him over his shoulders, the sad grey eyes meeting his, was the face of his wife. This time more of the figure became visible as he looked, and as he stared helplessly into the eyes before him, a hand was raised, and on one finger he saw their betrothal ring shine, the curious old ring by which all the eldest sons of the Monroe family had been betrothed since time immemorial.

"What do you wish?" asked Hugh, in a curious, hard voice that sounded weird and far off to his own ears. "What do you want?" The pale lips upturned as if to speak. No words came from them, but in the room echoed like the strain of distant music brought from afar on a soft breeze, the words, "Too late! Too late!" and then the vision vanished.

Utterly miserable, utterly unstrung, Hugh finished his dressing and hurried downstairs to his brother, who sat in almost the same attitude and place where he had left him last night, looking haggard and miserable in the pale light that struggled in at the closed blinds. He started up when he saw Hugh, and asked him what was the matter. Hugh told him the whole story, and ended by saying he must order his horse and go home at once.

"You cannot leave me like this," urged Edgar, "just for a vision or a dream, or what was most likely your own tired brain playing you a trick. You have not recovered the first shock, and then dear Mary's death harrowed you again; believe me, it is only your fancy. And what can have happened to Ruth since ten o'clock yesterday morning? I shall never get over this terrible day without you, and I do beg and implore of you to remain till tomorrow at least when I shall be thankful to ride back with you and remain for a little time."

Hugh still persisted in his desire to go home at once but Edgar used so many entreaties, and at last wept in the dreadful manner that men shed tears, and so he felt obliged to give in; and what with making all arrangements, and going to and from the churchyard, and consoling and comforting his brother during the trying ceremony, the day went quickly by, and evening found them sitting again over the dining-room fire. Hugh had gone into his room several times in the course of the day, and each time had gazed with a shuddering horror at the glass; but he had never seen the face again; and he was beginning to think that, the night once over, and his ride fairly begun towards home, he could then afford to laugh at superstition and all such follies, when a low, curious sort of moan caused both brothers to look up and listen intently. Just as Edgar was going to speak, the moan grew louder and louder, until it sounded like a tremendous wind wailing through the room. Hugh started to his feet, and just at that moment the door of the room blew open violently, and there glided in a thin grey figure, that passed on silently and awfully until it reached the fireplace. The door closed after it quietly, and as Hugh and Edgar, grasping each other's hands in a clasp that was agony, advanced with slow steps towards it, a misty veil that enveloped it faded gradually and slowly away, and with a mutual shudder of horror they recognised the figure of Ruth Monroe.

The wind and moaning had gradually died away, and a dreadful silence filled the room, which felt suddenly chill and damp, as if the veil of mist had faded into the atmosphere. Ruth never stirred, never took her eyes off those of her husband, into which she gazed with the same appealing glance as she had done before. Edgar's voice trembled as he spoke, but he addressed her by her name, and implored her to speak to them. At the sound of his voice the figure raised her hand, and then moving her lips just as the face in the glass had done, words unformed and soundless seemed to pervade the room, but in such an indistinct manner that neither brother could make them out in the least; and on Hugh's darting forward to take the outstretched hand the figure slowly vanished, leaving no trace of its extraordinary visit.

"It's no use," ejaculated Hugh; "I shall go mad if I don't get home. Something dreadful must have happened. I shall order George and the horses, and be off at once;

another night like last night or another apparition will be the death of me." And so saying he rang the bell, and ordered his man and the horses to be ready at once. So they started, through the quiet York streets, clattering over the stones, and out into the night through Micklegate Bar. The morning was beginning to struggle through the cold thick fog that hung over the village as they drew near to the Grange, and the tired horses and men paused as they got on the bridge, and gazed at the house that stood quietly among the trees. Hugh eagerly pushed his tired horse up the avenue, and hurrying up the steps, rang the bell as if to wake the dead as well as the living.

The door was opened at the same moment by old Betty, who was in the act of letting out the doctor, who, when he saw Mr. Monroe, paused in an undecided manner on the doorstep.

"For Heaven's sake," ejaculated Hugh, "my wife—" The doctor took him by the arm and led him into the dining-room. "My dear Mr. Monroe," he said, "you must prepare yourself for a terrible calamity; your dear wife has received a shock that will either kill her, or result in her being out of her mind for the rest of her life. I cannot tell how or what has caused this, but Betty tells me that she was found in the death-room last night in a state of insensibility, and since then she has been calling for you in a dreadful manner. Listen," he added; "you can hear her now," and opening the door Hugh heard his name called in the same weird accents as those used by the figure that had visited him in York. Shaking off the doctor's detaining hand he flew upstairs, and there, sitting up in bed, and watched by the horrified maids, was his wife, calling perpetually on his name. The moment she saw him she stopped, looked fondly at him in the same sorrowful manner that the ghost did, and then said, "I have waited for you to say goodbye. I went three times to see you, but I wanted you at home. There *is* a ghost upstairs. I saw myself laid out on that dreadful bed, and it killed me. The doctor always said any shock would. And it nearly killed you. I am only waiting to kiss you before I go."

Poor Hugh threw himself on his knees and clasped her in his arms. As he did so the eyes closed, the mouth fell into lines of infinite repose, the arms crossed themselves on Ruth's breast, and she lay back dead, and *as cold as marble* in her husband's embrace.

For days and nights Hugh lay between life and death, and it was months before he could bear to be told the whole story; months before he could hear how she was found in the old room upstairs, having gone up thither to see what had so alarmed Hugh, notwithstanding the tearful prayers of old Betty and her unspoken promise to her husband; but when he did, and when he had again visited the awful room, it was only to give orders for that part of the house to be demolished, and rebuilt in such a manner that no trace whatever should remain of the death-chamber of the Monroes; and it was not until another wife and half-a-dozen noisy children had been given to him that he was known to smile again; and if ever at Christmas-time the conversation turned on that most enthralling topic, he would abruptly change the subject, and he never could be got to tell the story of the face in the glass.

The glass itself was not destroyed, and the Monroes still keep it, and regard it with superstitious reverence, for as sure as there is to be a death in the family in the ensuing year, so sure on the night of All Souls is the face of the victim to be seen in the glass—at least so tells the housekeeper, adding, with a smile on her rubicund countenance, "No one tempts Providence by going to look in the glass there; for the ghost can only be seen by a Monroe, and it would be very dreadful, you know, sir, if they saw their own faces looking at them out of the glass."

Force Majeure

J. D. Beresford

As a midge before an elephant, so is man when opposed to Fate. The elephant breathes or lies down, and the high shrill of the midge is done. The midge believes passionately that the looming monster which shuts out his whole world has come across the earth with this one awful purpose of destroying his little life. But the elephant knows less of the midge than the midge knows of the elephant. . . .

George Coleman was not a figure that one would associate with the blunderings of outrageous destiny. He was of the type that seems born to move easily and contentedly through life; neither success nor failure; a tall, thin, fair man, reasonably intelligent, placidly thirty-five, and neither too diligent nor noticeably lazy. He was one of the many who had failed to find briefs; and one of the few who had, nevertheless, succeeded in earning a decent income. He had obtained, through special influence, a post as legal secretary and adviser to a great firm of financiers in the City. The post was almost a sinecure and the salary £800 a year. Added to that, he had another £300 of his own. He spent his holidays in Switzerland or Italy or Norway.

Any suburb would have made him a church-warden, but he preferred to go on living in his chambers, in Old Buildings, Lincoln's Inn. He was used to the inconveniences, and the place satisfied his feeble feeling for romance.

His friend Morley Price, the architect, told him that there was a sinister influence about those chambers. They were on the fifth floor, and boasted a dormer window that might have been done by Sime, in a mood of final recklessness. The dormer was in the sitting-room, and looked out on to the court. Price loved to lie back in his chair and stare at it, attempting vainly to account by archaeology and building construction for the twists and contortions of the jambs and soffit.

"It's a filthy freak, Coleman," was his usual conclusion; "not the work of a decent human mind, but a horrid, sinister growth that comes from within. One day it will put out another tentacle and crush you." After that he would fit his pipe into the gap in his front teeth and return to another attempt at formulating a theory of causation. He had always refused to consider any artificial substitute for those lost teeth. He said that the hole was the natural place for his pipe. Also, that the disfigurement was distinguished and brought him business.

If it had been Morley Price, now. . . . However, it was the absurdly commonplace George Coleman.

The beginning of it all was ordinary enough. He fell in love with a young woman who lived in Surbiton. She was pretty, dark, svelt, and looked perfectly fascinating with a pole at the stern of a punt, while her fox-terrier, Mickie, barked at swallows from the bow.

Coleman was quite acceptable. He punted even better than she did, and he was devoted to dogs, and more especially to Mickie. Nothing could have been more satisfactory and altogether delightful before the elephant came a vast, ubiquitous, imperturbable beast that the doctors called typhoid.

After Muriel died, Coleman took Mickie home to his chambers in Old Buildings, Lincoln's Inn. Mickie was more than a legacy; he was a sacred trust. Coleman had sworn to cherish him when his lovely mistress had been called away to join the headquarters of that angelic host to which she had hitherto belonged as a planetary member. She had appeared to be more concerned about Mickie than about George, at the last. She had not known George so long.

But it was George who cherished her memory. Mickie settled down at once. Within a week Muriel might never have existed, so far as he was concerned. If there was no longer a punt for him, there was a dormer window with a broad, flat seat that served equally well; and in place of migrant swallows there were perennial sparrows.

Coleman was not more sentimental than the average Englishman. At first he was "terribly cut up," as he might have phrased it; but six weeks after Muriel's death the cuts, in normal conditions, would doubtless have cicatrized.

Unhappily, the conditions were anything but normal. The vast bulk of the elephant was between him and any possible road of escape. In this second instance Fate assumed the form of certain mannerisms in Mickie.

He was quite an ordinary fox-terrier, with prick-ears that had spoiled him for show purposes, but he had lived with Muriel from puppyhood, and all his reactions showed her influence. He had, in fact, all the mannerisms of a spoilt lap-dog. He craved attention—he could not bark at the sparrows without turning every few seconds to Coleman for praise and encouragement; he was fussy and restless, on Coleman's lap one minute and up at the window the next; he was noisy and mischievous, and had no sense of shame; when he was reprimanded he jumped up joyfully and tried to lick Coleman's face.

And every one of his foolish tricks was inextricably associated in Coleman's mind with Muriel. . . .

At the end of six weeks Coleman was conscious that he had mourned long enough. He began to feel that it was not healthy for a man of thirty-five to continue in grief for one girl when there were so many others. He decided that the time had come when his awful gloom might melt into resigned sadness. Moreover, a sympathetic young woman he knew, who had a fine figure and tender eyes, had quite noticeably ceased to insist upon the fact that she was sorry for him. In other circumstances Coleman would have changed his unrelieved tie for one with a faint, white stripe.

But Mickie, cheerful beast as he was, stood between Coleman and half-mourning. Mickie was an awful reminder. Muriel had died, but her personality lived on. Every time Mickie barked Coleman could hear Muriel's clear, happy voice say: "Oh, Mickie, darling, shut up; you'll simply *deafen* mummy if you bark like that!"

Mickie began to get on Coleman's nerves. Sometimes when he was alone with him in the evening he regarded him with a heart full of evil desires; thoughts of losing him in the country, of selling him to a dog-fancier in Soho, of sending him to live with a married sister in Yorkshire. But that was just the breaking-point with Coleman. He was a shade too sentimental to shirk a sacred trust. Muriel, almost with her "dying breath," had confided Mickie to his keeping; bright, beautiful, happy Muriel who had loved and trusted him. Coleman would have regarded himself as a damned soul if he had been false to that trust.

Then he tried to train Mickie. He might as well have tried to train the dormer window. Mickie was four years old, and long past any possibility of alteration by the methods of Coleman. For he simply could not beat the dog; it would have been too sickeningly like beating Muriel.

His gloom deepened, and the young woman with the tender eyes lost sight of him for days at a time. She had no idea of the true state of the case; she merely thought that he was rather silly to go on making himself miserable about a little feather-brained thing like Muriel Hepworth.

The awful thing happened nearly ten weeks after Muriel's death. For many days Coleman had met no one outside his office routine. Most afternoons and every evening he had been shut up with the wraith of a happy voice which laughingly reproved the unchangeable Mickie. He had begun to imagine foolish things; to try experiments; he had kept away from any sight of those tender eyes for nearly a fortnight, hoping to lay the ghost of that insistent, inaudible voice.

It was a hot July evening, and Mickie was on and off the window-sill every moment, divided between furious contempt for the sparrows and the urgent desire for his master's co-operation and approval.

The voice of Muriel filled the room.

Coleman heaved himself out of his chair with a deep groan and went to the window. Below the sill a few feet of sloping tiles pitched steeply down to a narrow eaves-gutter; below the eaves-gutter was a sheer fall of fifty feet on to a paved court.

Mickie had his fore-feet on the sill; he was barking delightedly now that he had an audience.

The fantastic contortions of the dormer seemed to bend over man and dog; and the evil thing that had come to stay with Coleman crept into his brain and paralysed his will.

He stretched out his hand and gave Mickie a strong push.

Mickie slithered down the tiles, yelped, turned clean round, missed the gutter with his hind feet, but caught it at the last moment with both front paws, and so hung, shrieking desperately, struggling to lift himself back to safety while his whole body hung over the abyss.

For a moment man and dog stared into each other's eyes.

Then the virtue returned to Coleman. He was temporarily heroic. "Hold on, old man, hold on," he said tenderly, and began to work his shoulders down the short length of tiles, while he felt about inside the room with his feet trying to maintain some sort of hook on jamb or window board.

He was a long, thin man, and the feat was not a difficult one; the trouble was that he was too slow over it. For as he gingerly lifted one hand from the tiles to grasp Mickie's neck, the dog gave one last terrified yelp and let go.

Coleman heard the thud of his fall into the court.

He could not summon up courage to go down and gather up the mangled heap he so vividly pictured in his imagination.

That night he believed he was going mad, but he slept well and awoke with a strange sense of relief. He awoke much later than usual; a new and beautiful peace reigned that morning.

Strangely enough, neither his bedmaker nor the porter made any reference to Mickie; and while Coleman wondered at their failure to comment on so remarkable a tragedy, he could not bring himself to ask a question.

All through the day, as he worked at his office, a delicious sense of lightness and freedom exhilarated him. He dined at the Cock in Fleet Street, and when he returned to the exquisite stillness of his chambers he sat down to write to the girl with tender eyes. . . .

He thought he had closed the outer door.

He was enormously startled when he heard a strangely familiar patter of feet behind him.

He did not turn his head; he sat cold and rigid, and his ringers began to pick at the blotting-paper. He sat incredibly still and waited for the next sign.

It came with excruciating suddenness: a shrill, joyful, agonising bark, followed with a new distinctness by the echo of a voice that said: "Oh! Mickie, darling, you'll simply *deafen* mummy if you bark like that."

He did not move his body, but slowly and reluctantly first his eyes and then his head turned awfully to the window. . . .

The porter told Morley Price that he had not seen Mr. Coleman fall. He thought he heard a dog bark, he said, just like the little tarrier as Mr. Coleman'd been so fond of; and he was surprised because the pore little feller 'ad fallen out o' the self-same winder the night afore, and he 'adn't cared to speak of it to Mr. Coleman knowin' 'ow terrible cut-up 'e'd be about it. . . .

The chambers have remained unlet ever since.

Morley Price went up there once on a still July evening, and rushed out again with his hands to his ears.

The Garde Chasse

Catherine Crowe

We resided a great deal on the Continent before I was married, and my mother had a favourite maid, named Françoise, who lived with her many years—a most trustworthy, excellent creature, in whom she had the greatest confidence; insomuch, that when I married, being very young and inexperienced, as she was obliged to separate from me herself, she transferred Françoise to my service, considering her better able to take care of me than anybody else.

I was living in Paris then, where Françoise, who was a native of Metz, had some relations settled in business, whom she often used to visit. She was generally very chatty when she returned from these people; for I knew all her affairs, and, through her, all their affairs; and I took an interest in whatever concerned her or hers.

One Sunday evening, after she had been spending the afternoon with this family, observing that she was unusually silent, I said to her while she was undressing me, "Well, Françoise, haven't you anything to tell me? How are your friends? Has Madame Pelletier got rid of her grippe?"

Françoise started as if I had awakened her out of a reverie, and said, "Oh! Oui, Madame; oui, mercie; elle se porte bien aujourd'hui."

"And Monsieur Pelletier and the children, are they well?"

"Oui, Madame, mercie; ils se porte bien."

These curt answers were so unlike those she generally gave me, that I was sure her mind was pre-occupied, and that something had happened since we parted in the morning; so I turned round to look her in the face, saying, "Mais, qu'avez-vous done, Françoise? Qu'estce qu'il y a?"

Then I saw what I had not observed before, that she was very pale, and that her cheeks had a glazed look, which showed that she had been crying.

"Mais, ma bonne Françoise," I said; "vous avez quelque chose—est-il arrivé quelque malheur a Metz?"

"C'est cela, Madame," answered Françoise, who had a brother there whom she had not seen for several years, but to whom she still continued affectionately attached. His name was Benoît, and he was in a good service as garde fores tier to a nobleman, who possessed very extensive estates, "près de chez nous," as Françoise said. He had a wife and children; and some time before the period I am referring to, Françoise had told me with great satisfaction, that in order to make him more comfortable, the Prince de M—— had given Benoît the privilege of gathering up all the dead wood in the forest to sell for firewood, which, as the estate was very large, rendered his situation extremely profitable. When she said, "C'est cela, Madame," Françoise, who had just encased me in my dressing-gown, sunk into a chair, and having declared that she was "bête, très bête," she gave way to a hearty good cry, after which, being somewhat relieved, she told me the following strange story.

"You remember," she said, "that the Prince was so good as to give Benoît all the dead wood of the forest—and a great thing it was for him and his family, as you will think, when I tell you it was upwards of two thousand francs a year to him. In short, he was growing rich, and perhaps he was getting to think too much of his money and too little of the 'bon Dieu'—at all events, this privilege which the Prince gave him to make him comfortable, and which made him a great man among the foresters, has been the cause of a dreadful calamity."

"How?" said I.

"We never heard anything of what had happened," said she, "till yesterday, when Monsieur Pelletier received a letter from Benoît's wife, and another from a cousin of ours, relating what I am going to tell you, and saying that both he and his family had wished to keep it secret, but that it was no longer possible."

"Well, and what has happened?"

"La chose la plus incroyable! Eh, bien, Madame, it appears that one day last autumn, Benoît went out in the forest to gather the dead wood. He had his cart with him, and as he gathered it he bound it into faggots and threw it in the cart.

"He had extended his search this day to a remote part of the forest, and found himself in a spot he did not remember to have visited before; indeed, it was evident to him that he had not, or he could not have escaped seeing an old wooden cross which was lying on the ground, and had apparently fallen into that recumbent position from old age. It was such a cross as is usually set up where a life has been lost, whether by murder or by suicide; or sometimes when poor wanderers are frozen to death or lost in the deep winter snows. He looked about for the grave, but saw no indication of one; and he tried to remember if any catastrophe had happened there in his time, but could recall none. He took up the cross and examined it. He saw that the wood was decayed, and it bore such marks of antiquity, that he had no doubt the person whose grave it had marked had died before he was born—it looked as if it might be a hundred years old.

"Eh, bien," said Françoise, wiping her eyes, into which the tears kept starting, "of course you will think that Benoît, or anybody in the world who had the fear of God before his eyes, as he could not find the grave to replace it as it should be, would have laid it reverently down where he had found it, saying a prayer for the soul of the deceased; but alas! the demon of avarice tempted him, and he had not the heart to forego that poor cross, but bound it up into a faggot with the rest of the dead wood he found there, and threw it into his cart!"

"Well, Françoise," said I, "you know I am not a Catholic, but I respect the custom of erecting these crosses, and I do think your brother was very wrong; I suppose he has lost the Prince's favour by such impious greediness."

"Pire que ça! worse than that," she replied. "It appears that while he was committing this wicked action, he felt an extraordinary chill come over him, which made him think that, though it had been a mild day, the evening must have suddenly turned very cold, and hastily throwing the faggot into his cart, he directed his steps homeward. But, walk as he would, he still felt this chill down his back, so that he turned his head to look where the wind blew from, when he saw, with some dismay, a mysterious-looking figure following close upon his footsteps. It moved noiselessly on, and was covered with a sort of black mantle that prevented his discerning the features. Not liking its appearance, he jumped into the cart, and drove home as fast as he could, without looking behind him; and when he got into his own farmyard he felt quite relieved, particularly, as, when he alighted, he saw no more of this unpleasant-looking stranger. So he began unloading his cart, taking out the faggots, one by one, and throwing them upon the ground; but when he threw down the one that contained the cross, he received a blow upon his face, so sharp that it made him stagger, and involuntarily shout aloud. His wife and children were close by, but there was no one else to be seen; and they would have disbelieved him and fancied he had accidentally hit himself with the faggot, but that they saw the distinct mark on his cheek of a blow given with an open hand. However, he went into supper, perplexed and uncomfortable; but when he went to bed this fearful phantom stood by his side, silent and terrible, visible to him, but invisible to others. In short, Madame, this awful figure haunted him, till, in spite of his shame, he resolved to consult our cousin Jerome about it.

"But Jerome laughed, and said it was all fancy and superstition. 'You got frightened at having brought away this poor devil's cross, and then you fancy he's haunting you,' said he.

"But Benoît declared that he had thought nothing about the cross, except that it would make firewood, and that he had no more believed in ghosts than Jerome. 'But now,' said he, 'something must be done. I can get no sleep, and am losing my health; if you can't help me, I must go to the priest and consult him.'

" 'Why don't you take back the cross and put it where you found it?' said Jerome.

" 'Because I am afraid to touch it, and dare not go to that part of the forest.'

"So Jerome, who did not believe a word about the ghost, offered to go with him and replace the cross. Benoît gladly accepted, more especially as he said he saw the apparition standing even then beside him, apparently listening to the conversation. Jerome laughed at the idea; however, Benoît lifted the cross reverently into the cart and away they went into the forest. When they reached the spot, Benoît pointed out the tree under which he had found it; and as he was shaking and trembling, Jerome took up the cross and laid it on the ground; but as he did so, be received a violent blow from an invisible hand, and at the same moment saw Benoît fall to the ground. He thought he had been struck too, but it afterwards appeared that he had fainted from having seen the phantom with its upraised hand striking his cousin. However, they left the cross and came away; but there was an end to Jerome's laughter, and he was afraid the apparition would now haunt him. Nothing of the sort happened; but poor Benoît's health had been so shaken by this frightful occurrence that he cannot get the better of it; his friends have advised change of scene, and he is coming to Paris next week."

This was the story Françoise told me, and in a few days I heard that he had arrived, and was staying with Monsieur Pelletier; but the shock had been too great for his nerves, and he died shortly after. They assured me that, previous to that fatal expedition into the forest, he had been a bale, hearty man, totally exempt from superstitious fancies of any sort; and, in short, wholly devoted to advancing his worldly prosperity and getting money.

The Ghost and the Bone-Setter

J. Sheridan Le Fanu

In looking over the papers of my late valued and respected friend, Francis Purcell, who for nearly fifty years discharged the arduous duties of a parish priest in the south of Ireland, I met with the following document. It is one of many such; for he was a curious and industrious collector of old local traditions—a commodity in which the quarter where he resided mightily abounded. The collection and arrangement of such legends was, as long as I can remember him, his hobby; but I had never learned that his love of the marvellous and whimsical had carried him so far as to prompt him to commit the results of his inquiries to writing, until, in the character of residuary legatee, his will put me in possession of all his manuscript papers. To such as may think the composing of such productions as these inconsistent with the character and habits of a country priest, it is necessary to observe, that there did exist a race of priests—those of the old school, a race now nearly extinct—whose education abroad tended to produce in them tastes more literary than have yet been evinced by the *alumni* of Maynooth.

It is perhaps necessary to add that the superstition illustrated by the following story, namely, that the corpse last buried is obliged, during his juniority of interment, to supply his brother tenants of the churchyard in which he lies, with fresh water to allay the burning thirst of purgatory, is prevalent throughout the south of Ireland.

The writer can vouch for a case in which a respectable and wealthy farmer, on the borders of Tipperary, in tenderness to the corns of his departed helpmate, enclosed in her coffin two pair of brogues, a light and a heavy, the one for dry, the other for sloppy weather; seeking thus to mitigate the fatigues of her inevitable perambulations in procuring water and administering it to the thirsty souls of purgatory. Fierce and desperate conflicts have ensued in the case of two funeral parties approaching the same churchyard together, each endeavouring to secure to his own dead priority of sepulture, and a consequent immunity from the tax levied upon the pedestrian powers of the last-comer. An instance not long since occurred, in which one of two such parties, through fear of losing to their deceased friend this inestimable advantage, made their way to the churchyard by a short cut, and, in violation of one of their strongest prejudices, actually threw the coffin over the wall, lest time should be lost in making their entrance through the gate. Innumerable instances of the same kind might be quoted, all tending to show how strongly among the peasantry of the south this superstition is entertained. However, I shall not detain the reader further by any prefatory remarks, but shall proceed to lay before him the following:

Extract from the MS. Papers of the late Rev. Francis Purcell, of Drumcoolagh

I tell the following particulars, as nearly as I can recollect them, in the words of the narrator. It may be necessary to observe that he was what is termed a well-spoken man, having for a considerable time instructed the ingenious youth of his native parish in such of the liberal arts and sciences as he found it convenient to profess—a circumstance which may account for the occurrence of several big words in the course of this narrative, more distinguished for euphonious effect than for correctness of application. I proceed then, without further preface, to lay before you the wonderful adventures of Terry Neil.

"Why, thin, 'tis a quare story, an' as thrue as you're sittin' there; and I'd make bould to say there isn't a boy in the seven parishes could tell it better nor crickther than myself, for 'twas my father himself it happened to, an' many's the time I heerd it out iv his own mouth; an' I can say, an' I'm proud av that same, my father's word was as incredible as any squire's oath in the counthry; and so signs an' if a poor man got into any unlucky throuble, he was the boy id go into the court an' prove; but that doesn't signify—he was as honest and as sober a man, barrin' he was a little bit too partial to the glass, as you'd find in a day's walk; an' there wasn't the likes of him in the counthry round for nate laborin' an' baan diggin'; and he was mighty handy entirely for carpenther's work, and men din' ould spudethrees, an' the likes i' that. An' so he tuk up with bone-settin', as was most nathural, for none of them could come up to him in mendin' the leg iv a stool or a table; an' sure, there never was a bone-setter got so much custom-man an' child, young an' ould—there never was such breakin' and mendin' of bones known in the memory of man. Well, Terry Neil—for that was my father's name—began to feel his heart growin' light, and his purse heavy; an' he took a bit iv a farm in Squire Phelim's ground, just undher the ould castle, an' a pleasant little spot it was; an' day an' mornin' poor crathurs not able to put a foot to the ground, with broken arms and broken legs, id be comin' ramblin' in from all quarters to have their bones spliced up. Well, yer honour, all this was as well as well could be; but it was customary when Sir Phelim id go anywhere out iv the country, for some iv the tinants to sit up to watch in the ould castle, just for a kind of compliment to the ould family—an' a mighty unplisant compliment it was for the tinants, for there wasn't a man of them but knew there was something quare about the ould castle. The neighbours had it, that the squire's ould grandfather, as good a gintlenlan—God be with him—as I heer'd, as ever stood in shoe-leather, used to keep walkin' about in the middle iv the night, ever sinst he bursted a blood vessel pullin' out a cork out iv a bottle, as you or I might be doin', and will too, plase God—but that doesn't signify. So, as I was sayin', the ould squire used to come down out of the frame, where his picthur was hung up, and to break the bottles and glasses—God be marciful to us all—an' dthrink all he could come at—an' small blame to him for that same; and then if any of the family id be comin' in, he id be up again in his place, looking as quite an' as innocent as if he didn't know anything about it—the mischievous ould chap.

"Well, your honour, as I was sayin', one time the family up at the castle was stayin' in Dublin for a week or two; and so, as usual, some of the tinants had to sit up in the castle, and the third night it kem to my father's turn. 'Oh, tare an' ouns!' says he unto himself, 'an' must I sit up all night, and that ould vagabone of a sperit, glory be to God,' says he, 'serenadin' through the house, an' doin' all sorts iv mischief?' However, there was no gettin' aff, and so he put a bould face on it, an' he went up at nightfall with a bottle of pottieen, and another of holy wather.

"It was rainin' smart enough, an' the evenin' was darksome and gloomy, when my father got in; and what with the rain he got, and the holy wather he sprinkled on himself, it wasn't long till he had to swally a cup iv the pottieen, to keep the cowld out iv his heart. It was the ould steward, Lawrence Connor, that opened the door—and he an' my father wor always very great. So when he seen who it was, an' my father tould him how it was his turn to watch in the castle, he offered to sit up along with him; and you may be sure my father wasn't sorry for that same. So says Larry:

"'We'll have a bit iv fire in the parlour,' says he.

"'An' why not in the hall?' says my father, for he knew that the squire's picthur was hung in the parlour.

"'No fire can be lit in the hall,' says Lawrence, 'for there's an ould jackdaw's nest in the chimney.'

" 'Oh thin,' says my father, 'let us stop in the kitchen, for it's very unproper for the likes iv me to be sittin' in the parlour,' says he.

" 'Oh, Terry, that can't be,' says Lawrence; 'if we keep up the ould custom at all, we may as well keep it up properly,' says he.

" 'Divil sweep the ould custom!' says my father—to himself, do ye mind, for he didn't like to let Lawrence see that he was more afeard himself.

" 'Oh, very well,' says he. 'I'm agreeable, Lawrence,' says he; and so down they both wint to the kitchen, until the fire id be lit in the parlour—an' that same wasn't long doin'.

"Well, your honour, they soon wint up again, an' sat down mighty comfortable by the parlour fire, and they beginned to talk, an' to smoke, an' to dhrink a small taste iv the pottieen; and, moreover, they had a good rousin' fire o' bogwood and turf, to warm their shins over.

"Well, sir, as I was sayin' they kep' convarsin' and smokin' together most agreeable, until Lawrence beginn'd to get sleepy, as was but nathural for him, for he was an ould sarvint man, and was used to a great dale iv sleep.

" 'Sure it's impossible,' says my father, 'it's gettin' sleepy you are?'

" 'Oh, divil a taste,' says Larry; 'I'm only shuttin' my eyes,' says he, 'to keep out the parfume o' the tibacky smoke, that's makin' them wather,' says he. 'So don't you mind other people's business,' says he, stiff enough, for he had a mighty high stomach av his own (rest his sowl), 'and go on,' says he, 'with your story, for I'm listenin',' says he, shuttin' down his eyes.

"Well, when my father seen spakin' was no use, he went on with his story. By the same token, it was the story of Jim Soolivan and his ould goat he was tellin'—an' a plisant story it is—an' there was so much divarsion in it, that it was enough to waken a dormouse, let alone to pervint a Christian goin' asleep. But, faix, the way my father tould it, I believe there never was the likes heerd sinst nor before, for he bawled out every word av it, as if the life was fairly lavin' him, thrying to keep ould Larry awake; but, faix, it was no use, for the hoorsness came an him, an' before he kem to the end of his story Larry O'Connor beginned to snore like a bagpipes.

" 'Oh, blur an' agres,' says my father, 'isn't this a hard case,' says he, 'that ould villain, lettin' on to be my friend, and to go asleep this way, an' us both in the very room with a sperit,' says he. 'The crass o' Christ about us!' says he; and with that he was goin' to shake Lawrence to waken him, but he just remimbered if he roused him, that he'd surely go off to his bed, an' lave him complately alone, an' that id be by far worse.

"'Oh thin,' says my father, 'I'll not disturb the poor boy. It id be neither friendly nor good-nathured,' says he, 'to tormint him while he is asleep,' says he; 'only I wish I was the same way, myself,' says he.

"An' with that he beginned to walk up an' down, an' sayin' his prayers, until he worked himself into a sweat, savin' your presence. But it was all no good; so he dthrunk about a pint of sperits, to compose his mind.

"'Oh,' says he, 'I wish to the Lord I was as asy in my mind as Larry there. Maybe,' says he, 'if I thried I could go asleep'; an' with that he pulled a big arm-chair close beside Lawrence, an' settled himself in it as well as he could.

"But there was one quare thing I forgot to tell you. He couldn't help, in spite av himself, lookin' now an' thin at the picthur, an' he immediately obsarved that the eyes av it was follyin' him about, an' starin' at him, an' winkin' at him, wheriver he wint. 'Oh,' says he, when he seen that, 'it's a poor chance I have,' says he; 'an' bad luck was with me the day I kem into this unforthunate place,' says he. 'But any way there's no use in bein' freckened now,' says he; 'for if I am to die, I may as well parspire undaunted,' says he.

"Well, your honour, he thried to keep himself quite an' asy, an' he thought two or three times he might have wint asleep, but for the way the storm was groanin' and creakin' through the great heavy branches outside, an' whistlin' through the ould chimleys iv the castle. Well, afther one great roarin' blast iv the wind, you'd think the walls iv the castle was just goin' to fall, quite an' clane, with the shakin' iv it. All av a suddint the storm stopt, as silent an' as quite as if it was a July evenin'. Well, your honour, it wasn't stopped blowin' for three minnites, before he thought he hard a sort iv a noise over the chimley-piece; an' with that my father just opened his eyes the smallest taste in life, an' sure enough he seen the ould squire gettin' out iv the picthur, for all the world as if he was throwin' aff his ridin' coat, until he stept out clane an' complate, out av the chimley-piece, an' thrun himself down an the floor. Well, the slieveen ould chap—an' my father thought it was the dirtiest turn iv all—before he beginned to do anything out iv the way, he stopped for a while to listen wor they both asleep; an' as soon as he thought all was quite, he put out his hand and tuk hould iv the whisky bottle, an dhrank at laste a pint iv it. Well, your honour, when he tuk his turn out iv it, he settled it back mighty cute entirely, in the very same spot it was in before. An' he beginned to walk up an' down the room, lookin' as sober an' as solid as if he never done the likes at all. An' whinever he went apast my father, he thought he felt a great scent of brimstone, an' it was that that freckened him entirely; for he knew it was brimstone that was burned in hell, savin' your presence. At any rate, he often heerd it from Father Murphy, an' he had a right to know what belonged to it—he's dead since, God rest him. Well, your honour, my father was asy enough until the sperit kem past him; so close, God be marciful to us all, that the smell iv the sulphur tuk the breath clane out iv him; an' with that he tuk such a fit iv coughin', that it al-a-most shuk him out iv the chair he was sittin' in.

"'Ho, ho!' says the squire, stoppin' short about two steps aff, and turnin' round facin' my father, 'is it you that's in it?—an' how's all with you, Terry Neil?'

"'At your honour's sarvice,' says my father (as well as the fright id let him, for he was more dead than alive), 'an' it's proud I am to see your honour to-night,' says he.

"'Terence,' says the squire, 'you're a respectable man' (an' it was thrue for him), 'an industhrious, sober man, an' an example of inebriety to the whole parish,' says he.

"'Thank your honour,' says my father, gettin' courage, 'you were always a civil spoken gintleman, God rest your honour.'

"'*Rest* my honour?' says the sperit (fairly gettin' red in the face with the madness), 'Rest my honour?' says he. 'Why, you ignorant spalpeen,' says he, 'you mane, niggarly ignoramush,' says he, 'where did you lave your manners?' says he. 'If I *am* dead, it's no fault iv mine,' says he; 'an' it's not to be thrun in my teeth at every hand's turn, by the likes iv you,' says he, stampin' his foot an the flure, that you'd think the boords id smash undther him.

"'Oh,' says my father, 'I'm only a foolish, ignorant poor man,' says he.

"'You're nothing else,' says the squire: 'but any way,' says he, 'it's not to be listenin' to your gosther, nor convarsin' with the likes iv you, that I came *up*—down I mane,' says he—(an' as little as the mistake was, my father tuk notice iv it). 'Listen to me now, Terence Neil,' says he: 'I was always a good masther to Pathrick Neil, your grandfather,' says he.

"' 'Tis thrue for your honour,' says my father.

"'And, moreover, I think I was always a sober, riglar gintleman,' says the squire.

"'That's your name, sure enough,' says my father (though it was a big lie for him, but he could not help it).

"'Well,' says the sperit, 'although I was as sober as most men—at laste as most gintlemin,' says he; 'an' though I was at different pariods a most extempory Christian, and most charitable and inhuman to the poor,' says he; 'for all that I'm not as asy where I am now,' says he, 'as I had a right to expect,' says he.

"'An' more's the pity,' says my father. 'Maybe your honour id wish to have a word with Father Murphy?'

"'Hould your tongue, you misherable bliggard,' says the squire; 'it's not iv my sowl I'm thinkin'—an' I wondther you'd have the impitence to talk to a gintleman consarnin' his sowl; and when I want *that* fixed,' says he, slappin' his thigh, 'I'll go to them that knows what belongs to the likes,' says he. 'It's not my sowl,' says he, sittin' down opossite my father; 'it's not my sowl that's annoyin' me most—I'm unasy on my right leg,' says he, 'that I bruk at Glenvarloch cover the day I killed black Barney.'

"My father found out afther, it was a favourite horse that fell undher him, afther leapin' the big fence that runs along by the glin.

"'I hope,' says my father, 'your honour's not unasy about the killin' iv him?'

"'Hould your tongue, ye fool,' said the squire, 'an' I'll tell you why I'm unasy on my leg,' says he. 'In the place, where I spend most iv my time,' says he, 'except the little leisure I have for lookin' about me here,' says he, 'I have to walk a great dale more than I was ever used to,' says he, 'and by far more than is good for me either,' says he; 'for I must tell you,' says he, 'the people where I am is ancommonly fond iv cowld wather, for there is nothin' betther to be had; an', moreover, the weather is hotter than is altogether plisant,' says he; 'and I'm appinted,' says he, 'to assist in carryin' the wather, an' gets a mighty poor share iv it myself,' says he, 'an' a mighty throublesome, wearin' job it is, I can tell you,' says he; 'for they're all iv them surprisinly dthry, an' dthrinks it as fast as my legs can carry it,' says he; 'but what kills me intirely,' says he, 'is the wakeness in my leg,' says he, 'an' I want you to give it a pull or two to bring it to shape,' says he, 'and that's the long an' the short iv it,' says he.

"'Oh, plase your honour,' says my father (for he didn't like to handle the sperit at all), 'I wouldn't have the impidence to do the likes to your honour,' says he; 'it's only to poor crathurs like myself I'd do it to,' says he.

"'None iv your blarney,' says the squire. 'Here's my leg,' says he, cockin' it up to him—'pull it for the bare life,' says he; an' 'if you don't, by the immortial powers I'll not lave a bone in your carcish I'll not powdher,' says he.

"When my father heerd that, he seen there was no use in purtendin', so he tuk hould iv the leg, an' he kep' pullin' an' pullin', till the sweat, God bless us, beginned to pour down his face.

"'Pull, you divil!' says the squire.

"'At your sarvice, your honour,' says my father.

"'Pull harder,' says the squire.

"My father pulled like the divil.

" 'I'll take a little sup,' says the squire, rachin' over his hand to the bottle, 'to keep up my courage,' says he, lettin' an to be very wake in himself intirely. But, as cute as he was, he was out here, for he tuk the wrong one. 'Here's to your good health, Terence,' says he; 'an' now pull like the very divil.' An' with that he lifted the bottle of holy wather, but it was hardly to his mouth, whin he let a screech out, you'd think the room id fairly split with it, an' made one chuck that sent the leg clane aff his body in my father's hands. Down wint the squire over the table, an' bang wint my father half-way across the room on his back, upon the flure. Whin he kem to himself the cheerful mornin' sun was shinin' through the windy shutthers, an' he was lying flat an his back, with the leg iv one of the great ould chairs pulled clane out iv the socket an' tight in his hand, pintin' up to the ceilin', an' ould Larry fast asleep, an' snorin' as loud as ever. My father wint that mornin' to Father Murphy, an' from that to the day of his death, he never neglected confission nor mass, an' what he tould was betther believed that he spake av it but seldom. An', as for the squire, that is the sperit, whether it was that he did not like his liquor, or by rason iv the loss iv his leg, he was never known to walk agin."

THE GHOST OF MOHAMMED DIN

CLARK ASHTON SMITH

"I'LL WAGER A HUNDRED RUPEES THAT YOU WON'T STAY THERE OVER-NIGHT," said Nicholson.

It was late in the afternoon, and we were seated on the veranda of my friend's bungalow in the Begum suburb at Hyderabad. Our conversation had turned to ghosts, on which subject I was, at the time, rather skeptical, and Nicholson, after relating a number of blood-curdling stories, had finished by remarking that a nearby house, which was said to be haunted, would give me an excellent chance to put the matter to the test.

"Done!" I answered, laughing.

"It's no joking matter," said my friend, seriously. "However, if you really wish to encounter the ghost, I can easily secure you the necessary permission. The house, a six-roomed bungalow, owned by one Yussuf Au Borah, is tenanted only by the spirit who appears to regard it as his exclusive property.

"Two years ago it was occupied by a Moslem merchant named Mohammed Din, and his family and servants. One morning they found the merchant dead—stabbed through the heart, and no trace of his murderer, whose identity still remains unrevealed.

"Mohammed Din's people left, and the place was let to a Parsee up from Bombay on business. He vacated the premises abruptly about midnight, and told a wild tale the next morning of having encountered a number of disembodied spirits, describing the chief one as Mohammed Din.

"Several other people took the place in turn, but their occupancy was generally of short duration. All told tales similar to the Parsee's. Gradually it acquired a bad reputation, and the finding of tenants became impossible."

"Have you ever seen the ghost yourself?" I asked.

"Yes; I spent a night, or rather part of one, there, for I went out of the window about one o'clock. My nerves were not strong enough to stand it any longer. I wouldn't enter the place again for almost any sum of money."

Nicholson's story only confirmed my intention of occupying the haunted house. Armed with a firm disbelief in the supernatural, and a still firmer intention to prove it all rot, I felt myself equal to all the ghosts, native and otherwise, in India. Of my ability to solve the mystery, if there were any, I was quite assured.

"My friend," said Nicholson to Yussuf Ali Borah an hour later, "wishes to spend a night in your haunted bungalow."

The person addressed, a fat little Moslem gentleman, looked at me curiously.

"The house is at your service, Sahib," he said, "I presume that Nicholson Sahib has told you the experiences of the previous tenants?"

I replied that he had. "If the whole thing is not a trumped-up story, there is doubtless some trickery afoot," said I, "and I warn you that the trickster will not come off unharmed. I have a loaded revolver, and shall not hesitate to use it if I meet any disembodied spirits."

Yussuf 's only answer was to shrug his shoulders.

He gave us the keys, and we set out for the bungalow, which was only a few minutes' walk distant. Night had fallen when we reached it. Nicholson unlocked the door and we entered, and lighting a lamp I had brought with me, set out on a tour of inspection. The furniture consisted chiefly of two charpoys, three tabourets, an old divan quite innocent of cushions, a broken punkah, a three-legged chair and a dilapidated rug. Everything was covered with dust; the shutters rattled disconsolately, and all the doors creaked. The other rooms were meagrely furnished. I could hear rats running about in the dark. There was a compound adjoining, filled with rank reed and a solitary pipal tree. Nicholson said that the ghost generally appeared in one of the rooms opening upon it, and this I selected as the one in which to spend the night. It was a fitting place for ghosts to haunt. The ceiling sagged listlessly, and the one charpoy which it contained had a wobbly look.

"Sleep well," said Nicholson. "You will find the atmosphere of this spirit-ridden place most conducive to slumber."

"Rats!" said I.

"Yes, there are plenty of rats here," he answered as he went out.

Placing the lamp on a tabouret, I lay down, with some misgivings as to its stability, on the charpoy. Happily, these proved unfounded, and laying my revolver close at hand, I took out a newspaper and began to read.

Several hours passed and nothing unusual happened. The ghost failed to materialize, and about eleven, with my fine skepticism greatly strengthened, and feeling a trifle ashamed concerning the hundred rupees which my friend would have to hand over the next morning, I lay down and tried to go to sleep. I had no doubt that my threat about the revolver to Yussuf Ali Borah had checked any plans for scaring me that might have been entertained.

Scarcely were my eyes closed when all the doors and windows, which had been creaking and rattling all evening, took on renewed activity. A light breeze had sprung up, and one shutter, which hung only by a single hinge, began to drum a tune on the wall. The rats scuttled about with redoubled energy, and a particularly industrious fellow gnawed something in the further corner for about an hour. It was manifestly impossible to sleep. I seemed to hear whisperings in the air, and once thought that I detected faint footsteps going and coming through the empty rooms. A vague feeling of eeriness crept upon me, and it required a very strong mental effort to convince myself that these sounds were entirely due to imagination.

Finally the breeze died down, the loose shutter ceased to bang, the rat stopped gnawing, and comparative quiet being restored, I fell asleep. Two hours later I woke, and taking out my watch, saw, though the lamp had begun to burn dimly, that the hands pointed to two o'clock. I was about to turn over, when again I heard the mysterious footsteps, this time quite audibly. They seemed to approach my room, but when I judged them to be in the next apartment, ceased abruptly. I waited five minutes in a dead silence, with my nerves on edge and my scalp tingling.

Then I became aware that there was something between me and the opposite wall. At first it was a dim shadow, but as I watched, it darkened into a body. A sort of phosphorescent light emanated from it, surrounding it with pale radiance.

The lamp flared up and went out, but the figure was still visible. It was that of a tall native dressed in flowing white robes and a blue turban. He wore a bushy beard and had eyes like burning coals of fire. His gaze was directed intently upon me, and I felt cold shivers running up and down my spine. I wanted to shriek, but my tongue seemed glued to the roof of my mouth. The figure stepped forward and I noticed that the robe was red at the breast as though with blood.

This, then, was the ghost of Mohammed Din. Nicholson's story was true, and for a moment my conviction that the supernatural was all nonsense went completely to pieces. Only momentarily, however, for I remembered that I had a revolver, and the thought gave me courage. Perhaps it was a trick after all, and anger arose in me, and a resolve not to let the trickster escape unscathed.

I raised the weapon with a quick movement and fired. The figure being not over five paces distant, it was impossible to miss, but when the smoke had cleared it had not changed its position.

It began to advance, making no sound, and in a few moments was beside the charpoy. With one remaining vestige of courage I raised my revolver and pulled the trigger three times in succession, but without visible effect. I hurled the weapon at the figure's head, and heard it crash against the opposite wall an instant later. The apparition, though visible, was without tangibility.

Now it began to disappear. Very slowly at first it faded, then more rapidly until I could make out only the bare outlines. Another instant and all was gone but the outline of one hand, which hung motionless in the air. I got up and made a step towards it, then stopped abruptly, for the outlines again began to fill in, the hand to darken and solidify. Now I noticed something I had not before seen—a heavy gold ring set with some green gem, probably an emerald, appeared to be on the middle finger.

The hand began to move slowly past me towards the door opening into the next apartment. Lighting the lamp, I followed, all fear being thrown aside and desiring to find the explanation of the phenomenon. I could hear faint footfalls beneath the hand, as though the owner, though invisible, were still present. I followed it through the adjoining apartment and into the next, where it again stopped and hung motionless. One finger was pointed toward the further corner, where stood a tabouret, or stand.

Impelled, I think, by some force other than my own volition, I went over and lifting the tabouret, found a small wooden box, covered with dust, beneath.

Turning about I saw that the hand had disappeared.

Taking the box with me, I returned to my room. The thing was made of very hard wood and in size was perhaps ten inches in length by eight in width and four in height. It was light, and the contents rustled when I shook it. I guessed them to be letters or papers, but having nothing to pry the box open with, I concluded to wait until morning before trying to.

Strange as it may seem I soon fell asleep. You would naturally think that a man would not feel inclined to slumber immediately after encountering a disembodied spirit. I can give no explanation of it.

The sun was streaming through the window when I awoke, and so cheerful and matter-of-fact was the broad daylight that I wondered if the events of the night were not all a dream. The presence of the box, however, convinced me that they were not.

Nicholson came in and appeared much surprised and a trifle discomfited to find me still in possession.

"Well," he inquired, "what happened? What did you see?"

I told him what had occurred and produced the box as proof.

An hour afterwards, Nicholson, with a short native sword and considerable profanity, was trying to pry the thing open. He finally succeeded. Within were a number of closely-written sheets of paper and some letters, most of which were addressed to Mohammed Din.

The papers were mostly in the form of memoranda and business accounts such as would be made by a merchant. They were written in execrable Urdu, hopelessly jumbled together, and though all were dated, it was no small task to sort them out. The letters were mostly regarding business affairs, but several, which were written in a very fair hand, were from a cousin of Mohammed Din's, one Ali Bagh, an Agra horse-trader. These, too, with one exception, were commonplace enough. Nicholson knitted his brows as he read it, and then handed it to me. The greater part, being of little interest, has escaped my memory, but I recollect that the last paragraph ran thus:

"I do not understand how you came by the knowledge, nor why you wish to use it to ruin me. It is all true. If you have any love for me, forbear."

"What does that mean?" asked Nicholson. "What secret did Mohammed Din possess that he could have used to ruin his cousin?"

We went through the memoranda carefully, and near the bottom found the following, dated April 21, 1881, according to our notation:

> To-day I found the letters which I have long been seeking. They are ample proof of what I have long known, but have hitherto been unable to substantiate, that Ali Bagh is a counterfeiter, the chief of a large band. I have but to turn them over to the police, and he will be dragged away to jail, there to serve a term of many years. It will be good revenge—part compensation, at least, for the injuries he has done me.

"That explains Ali Bagh's letter," said Nicholson. "Mohammed Din was boastful enough to write to him, telling him that he knew of his guilt and intended to prove it."

Next were several sheets in a different hand and signed "Mallek Khan." Mallek Khan, it seemed, was a friend of Ali Bagh's, and the sheets were in the form of a letter. But being without fold, it was quite evident they had not been posted.

The communication related to certain counterfeiting schemes, and the names of a number of men implicated appeared. This, plainly, was the proof alluded to by Mohammed Din, and which he had threatened his cousin to turn over to the police.

There was nothing else of interest save the following in Mohammed Din's hand, dated April 17th, 1881:

To-morrow I shall give the papers to the authorities. I have delayed too long, and was very foolish to write to Ali Bagh.

I passed a man in the street today who bore a resemblance to my cousin. . . . I could not be sure . . . But if he is here, then may Allah help me, for he will hesitate at nothing. . . .

What followed was illegible.

"On the night of April 21st," said Nicholson, "Mohammed Din was killed by a person or persons unknown." He paused and then went on: "This Ali Bagh is a man with whom I have had some dealings in horses, and an especially vicious crook it was that he got three hundred rupees out of me for. He has a bad reputation as a horse-dealer, and the Agra police have long been patiently seeking evidence of his implication in several bold counterfeiting schemes. Mallek Khan, one of his accomplices, was arrested, tried and sentenced to fifteen years' imprisonment, but refused to turn State's evidence on Ali Bagh. The police are convinced that Ali Bagh was as much, if not more implicated, than Mallek Khan, but they can do nothing for lack of proof. The turning over of these papers, however, as poor Mohammed Din would have done had he lived, will lead to his arrest and conviction.

"It was Ali Bagh who killed Mohammed Din, I am morally convinced, his motive, of course, being to prevent the disclosure of his guilt. Your extraordinary experience last night and the murdered man's papers point to it. Yet we can prove nothing, and your tale would be laughed at in court."

Some blank sheets remained in the bottom of the box, and my friend tilted them out as he spoke. They fluttered to the veranda and something rolled out from amongst them and lay glittering in the sunshine. It was a heavy gold ring set with an emerald—the very same that I had seen upon the apparition's finger several hours before.

A week or so later, as the result of the papers that Nicholson sent to the Agra police, accompanied by an explanatory note, one Ali Bagh, horse-trader, found himself on trial, charged with counterfeiting. It was a very short trial, his character and reputation going badly against him, and it being proven that he was the leader of the gang of which Mallek Khan was thought to be a member, he was sentenced to a somewhat longer term in jail than his accomplice.

The Ghost Ship

C. A. Borden

It was early in the spring of 1907 that a most remarkable experience occurred to me, so remarkable indeed, that I lost no time in narrating it.

Wise men have looked askance at me while I recounted it, and fools have laughed, yet, not daunted, I offer this tale to the world, to ridicule or believe as it will.

Ever since a boy I have been fond of the sea. Its vastness, its strength and even its loneliness have always attracted and fascinated me.

Many were the days I spent on its great, heaving bosom, even before I reached my teens—fishing, sailing or rowing. When quite young I learned to sail, and by the time that I was eighteen I was an expert. I shipped before the mast on a lumber schooner for two years, studied navigation and at twenty-five was first mate on the schooner *Frances Howard* of San Francisco. I have since acted in the capacity of first officer on the passenger steamers plying between San Francisco and Japan, and it was on my return from one of these trips that my story begins.

For two years I had been running back and forth between here and the Orient without missing a voyage, and it was on the home bound run in February of this year that I decided, as I paced the bridge on my night watch, to take a vacation, something that I had not done for twelve years, since I had left my father's roof. So, as soon as we made port and I could leave, I went to the offices of the company and made arrangements to have them put another in my place for the next six months.

I then took a car out to my father's house on Devisidero Street.

The old people were delighted to learn that I was to be with them for a time, and immediately commenced making plans for my entertainment.

I had been in town for about a week when one day, while down on the water front, I met my old friend, Shirley Keith.

I had known Shirley for years and liked him. He was a genial sort of fellow, with blue eyes and a jovial laugh; a laugh which lie always used when greeting a friend, and which made one feel immediately at home with him.

"Well, Jack Kent," he said, as he put forth his hand, "what are you doing ashore? I haven't seen you for a month of Sundays."

"Just loafing," I replied. "I am taking a little vacation after twelve years of the strenuous life."

"Well, you no doubt need it, though you certainly don't appear to. But come on and go to lunch with me somewhere—I'm in a hurry."

I accepted, so he took me to Tait's, where we selected a table near the orchestra.

When we were seated and had given our orders, Keith said: "You know that I have purchased the schooner yacht, *Morpheus*?"

"What, not the 'Ghost Ship'?"

"The same," he said with a laugh, "though I have not been annoyed by any nocturnal visitors since my ownership."

"Of course this ghost business is all bosh," I said. "A ghost is the hallucination of a diseased mind. Still there are some very wise men who believe in the existence of the supernatural, though I for one am not bothered by any such fool superstition, not that I consider myself wise in any sense of the word."

"Well according to her previous owners, very unusual things have occurred aboard the *Morpheus,* but I'm not worried, and in fact only wish that something of the kind would occur to me for a little excitement," he said.

"I may have a chance to see something of the kind, as I am going to take her to Los Angeles the end of the week and spend the summer in southern waters."

"That sounds very nice," I said.

"You had better come with me."

"I should like to, but I have determined to take a vacation ashore, and, besides, I have no stomach for ghosts."

"Rats!" he said, "I can fancy your being afraid of ghosts, and as far as the vacation is concerned, we will be ashore half of the time."

I wanted to go from the very start, and only needed a little persuasion to decide me, so we had not yet finished our noonday repast when I consented.

"Good," said Keith, reaching for my hand, "I knew that you would come around all right, and now we will go down to the boat."

He told me on the way that he had a crew of five men, beside a cook and mate, the latter's name being Hanson.

Keith summoned the launch by whistling through his fingers, and soon a beautifully finished boat, propelled by a two-horse gasoline engine, lay snorting alongside the wharf.

As we approached the yacht I noticed her fine lines and tapering spars, with the sunlight shimmering on her mahogany rails and brass work.

We climbed the companionway and stood upon her white deck. There was a general bustle and stir among her crew, scraping and splicing were going on, and the odor of fresh paint filled the air. I stood in the cockpit, looking forward, and could find no fault nor flaw in her construction.

She measured one hundred and twelve feet over all, with a ninety-five-foot water line. Her twenty-foot beam and high freeboard marked her the weather boat, while her towering masts and graceful lines showed the racer.

Keith watched me as I looked her over and noted the pleased expression on my face.

"So you like her looks, do you, old man?" he asked.

"I should say I do, she is superb."

"Come below," he said, leading the way down the after-companionway.

Below, she was even more attractive than on deck. The main saloon was a beauty, finished in rosewood and magnificently appointed. Forward of the saloon were eight staterooms, bath and galley and opening off of the galley was the forecastle.

I was immensely pleased with her appearance and said so. Keith called up the scuttle to the mate, who instantly came below.

The mate was plainly a Norwegian, both by accent and appearance. He was a large man, with strong, kindly face and a decided blond.

"Mr. Hanson, let me introduce you to Mr. Kent, who is going to be with us this summer."

The mate extended his hand and expressed himself very gravely as being glad to know me.

"How are the men getting along?" asked Keith.

"Very well, sir," answered the mate, respectfully. "We will be ready to leave at any time after tonight."

"Good! but I will not want to leave before Saturday at noon. I have some business that I must attend to."

We spent the rest of the afternoon on a tour of inspection and about six o'clock were taken ashore.

It was Thursday when Keith took me aboard and I put in the following day in moving my effects out and laying in a supply of white ducks, etc., which I thought might come in handy in Southern latitudes.

We were to sail Saturday at noon, but Saturday morning Keith came aboard and said that his business would detain him for several days and asked me if I would mind taking the *Morpheus* down to San Pedro for him.

"But what is your reason for not keeping the yacht over until you are ready to go yourself?"

"I want her to be down there next week, as I have made some engagements that I must keep, so if you will sail her down, I will take the train when I have completed my transactions, and arrive as soon as you will."

I gladly consented, and he went ashore, promising to be down Thursday or Friday of the following week.

At twelve o'clock we slipped our moorings and with all lower sails set, tore out of the Golden Gate, propelled by a brisk northeasterly breeze.

It was a cold, dreary sort of day, and the heavy chop outside was being lashed into foam by the wind.

The *Morpheus* leapt over the waves, churning the water into milky whiteness under her bows, and leaving a seething ribbon of white in her wake.

Hanson and myself, who had become good friends by this time, stood chatting behind the man at the wheel until we were clear of the headlands, when I went below for a nap.

I was awakened at four bells for dinner.

After a hearty meal, I lit my pipe and went on deck to find that the wind had risen during the afternoon and that we were bowling along at a good fifteen knots.

Hanson went to get his dinner and I stood watch.

Before he came on deck again, the wind, which had been blowing so steadily, suddenly dropped to a fitful breeze, and at last ceased altogether, leaving the sails flapping idly and the water slopping under our after overhang.

We lay in the trough of the swell, rolling heavily for several hours, and we were still in this position when I turned in.

Everything loose was banging and rattling, the fore boom tore back and forth on the traveller directly over my cabin, the doors slammed and squeaked and the sea swashed alongside with a hollow sough.

But these things didn't bother me, and I quickly fell asleep.

I was soon awake, however, and standing up looking out of my port. The wind had come up again, but from the opposite direction and we were careening wildly to starboard and rushing through the water. I was soon on deck and saw that quite a wind was blowing and was growing steadily worse.

Hanson had called all hands and was giving orders, while the men were running here and there, tightening things down and getting in sail. The foresail and jib were quickly furled, and we rode more steadily under mainsail and staysail. I then went below to finish my sleep and didn't come on deck again until eight bells had struck and Hanson came down.

The wind was still blowing heavily and we were running South-South-West, but not making much time on account of the headseas which were continually piling up before us.

Toward morning the wind was blowing almost a hurricane and all the next day we stood hove to.

Sunday evening it abated somewhat and we again continued our course, out of which we had been blown many miles.

Monday morning the cook told me at breakfast that strange noises during the previous night had alarmed the crew, and that they had heard that the schooner was haunted. I laughed at this and told the mate, who shook his head and smiled.

That day one of the crew came to me himself and said that he had heard peculiar sounds issuing from below the ship. He couldn't explain the sounds except that they were most terrifying.

I asked him what he had been drinking and sent him forward.

That night during my watch below I was aroused by the cook, who came to tell me that the man on watch forward had strangely disappeared, and no trace of him could be found.

The man's name was Christensen.

I went on deck, where Hanson corroborated the statement.

We came to the conclusion that he had fallen overboard, though no one had seen him go, and there were two other men on deck at the time.

Tuesday night another member of the crew went in the same mysterious manner, but this time the mate was watching him. He saw him start violently, give a little cry and grope toward the rail like a blind man. He called to him, but the man gave no heed. He called again, but still the fellow paid no attention, and steadily approached the rail.

Hanson rushed forward, and the man, whose name was Bergstrom, looked over his shoulder at the sound of the mate's feet,—a fearful expression came over his face,—and, with a scream of terror which caused the mate to pause, leaped into the sea.

Hanson hurried to the rail, but the wind was blowing strongly and it was a pitch black night, so he saw no sign of the unfortunate seaman, and by the time that he had run aft, pushed the wheelsman aside and put the schooner into the wind, Bergstrom was several hundred yards astern.

He lowered a boat and sent men out with lanterns, but they came back without Bergstrom, after spending an hour or more rowing back and forth.

When I came on deck a little while later, to relieve the mate, two of the three remaining members of our crew and the cook stood against the foremast, while the third was at the wheel. I noticed the latter's face, thrown out in strong relief against the black sky by the binnacle light. It wore a strained, frightened expression, and every now and then he glanced over his shoulder at the dark, heaving sea, and seeing me behind him, started, and again fixed his eyes on the compass.

I ordered the men against the foremast to turn in, and stood the forward watch myself, but nothing unusual happened during the rest of the night and Hanson looked relieved when I reported all well at dawn.

I am not easily frightened, yet I must admit that the singular disappearance of two of our crew, in such an unaccountable manner, strangely moved me.

That night I determined to stand watch with the mate, to be on hand if anything out of the ordinary might occur.

Immediately after dinner I lit my pipe and went on deck, where I took up my position behind the forward skylight, a good vantage point from which to watch the man on the forecastle deck.

Everything ran smoothly for several hours, the watches were called and changed, and the wind, which had been blowing steadily all day, still blew us along at a rapid pace. I became sleepy after two hours of watching, with nothing to break the monotony, and at last dozed off.

I had been asleep for perhaps five minutes when I was awakened by a roar from the mate and the sound of running feet behind me. I instantly sprang to my feet and saw the forward lookout groping toward the rail. In two bounds I was upon him.

With a despairing cry the man tried to twist himself from my grasp, and fought with the strength of a tiger to get away, and be would have, had Hanson not seized him from behind and held him in an iron grip.

"What is the matter, man?" I asked, when he had quieted.

"O God! didn't you see it, didn't you see it?" he cried.

"No, see what?"

"I don't know what it was. Something horrible, that made me want to jump overboard to forget it! Looked like a lot of drowned people, all fish-eaten and bloated, beckoning me from the water. God, how it frightened me." His voice fell almost to a whisper, and he shuddered and cast an apprehensive glance over his shoulder at the remembrance.

We took him below, where I poured him out a glass of spirits to steady his nerves, and where the bright cabin light seemed to comfort him.

The remainder of the night passed peacefully and at six in the morning I turned in.

I was very tired after my all night vigil and soon dropped into a dreamless slumber, from which I did not awaken until three in the afternoon.

When I rolled over and looked at my watch I was surprised at the lateness of the hour and quickly dressed, wondering why I had not been called.

Everything seemed unusually quiet and a strange foreboding of evil stole over me as I mounted the companion-way stairs. This quickly turned into a sort of terror when I saw that no one was at the wheel and the deck was absolutely deserted.

I called loudly several times, but the creak of the boom against the mast and the shrill scream of a sea gull, wheeling in flight overhead, were the only answers I received.

I rushed to the forecastle scuttle and peered below. No one was there. I rummaged through every part of the vessel, but not a soul was aboard! What had become of my companions?

With a lonesome feeling I ran on deck, glad to escape the increasing gloom of the cabin.

For the first time I noticed that one of the boats was gone. I scanned the sea far and near with my glasses, but no boat met my gaze—the straight azure line of the horizon stood out boldly against the lighter blue of the sky, unbroken.

With a curse I turned my attention to the compass and saw that the schooner was miles off her course, and I had no idea how long she had been running thus.

There had been no entry in the log for the day, so I worked out my position and found that I was still one hundred and twenty-five miles from my destination, due to the fact that I had been running, evidently most of the day, at right angles to my original course.

Having set the bow once more in the right direction I went below again to light up and get something to eat, intending to spend the night at the wheel.

When I returned, however, the wind had dropped to almost nothing and at last ceased altogether.

I sat in the cock-pit for awhile, smoking, but at last went to my stateroom to read until the wind should freshen.

I read for several hours and had just laid my book down to look at the barometer when a peculiar sound on deck attracted my attention. I imagined that a man was walking up and down overhead. I listened intently. Yes, there it was again, nearer now and more distinct. I held my breath for a minute. The sound continued—tramp, tramp, up and down, up and down. The man, if man it was, evidently had water in his boots, for at every step I could hear the sough and ooze of water, and at every turn in his beat I heard it pattering on the deck.

In a frenzy of foolish fear and nervous apprehension, I rushed up to see what it was.

But all my fright was for nothing, for no one was there.

A smiling moon lit up a peaceful sea, the shadows rode slowly back and forth across the deck, and the boats swung noiselessly in their davits.

I surveyed the tranquil scene for several minutes and then, with a laugh at my own cowardice, went below to my book.

I had no sooner taken it up, though, than the noise which had previously startled me was resumed—Tramp, tramp, tramp. I started up and listened. The steps ceased for a minute, and I heard a deep groan, followed by a sigh as though from one in agony. Then the steps continued.

My heart was pounding wildly and the cold perspiration stood in heavy beads upon my forehead.

With a superhuman effort, I again went on deck. There was nothing there to cause alarm—everything was the same as before.

Waiting for a few minutes, I went back to my book.

As I neared my door the light in my room was suddenly extinguished and I was left in utter darkness except for the rays of the moon which filtered through the sky-light and port-holes and fell in odd-shaped patches on the wall.

At first a dread of the supernatural stole over me and I was for turning back, but upon reflection decided that a draught had blown my lamp out.

I lit it again and it burned as brightly as ever.

So nervous was I by this time that I locked and bolted my door.

I then attempted to finish the story I was reading, but my mind kept continually reverting to that terrible sound, and I was constantly on the alert for it to begin again.

Suddenly the ring knob of my door dropped with a sharp click, almost causing my heart to stop.

I looked at it intently for a second. Good God! it was turning! So was the bolt knob.

Petrified with fear and astonishment, I lay there for a moment, watching it as it slowly and deliberately turned. Then I sprang for the door. With all my strength, and I am no weakling, I strove to twist it back, I even bent the ring in my hand, but with irresistible force it began to open inward, very slowly. I flung my weight on it and braced myself against the bunk behind me, but to no avail. Slowly it forced me back, and at the same time the lamp was extinguished again.

With a hoarse sob of fear I loosened my grip on the door and let it swing unhampered, slowly inward, while I hurriedly struck a match to light the lamp again. The little point of flame flared up for a second, but immediately went out.

At the same time an icy hand seemed to touch me from behind, and I heard a low, deep moan issuing from the darkness.

In a frenzy of fear I endeavored to run from the gruesome cabin out into the starry night. But some unexplainable, undefinable thing held me at the door, and, strive as I would, I could not pass. I groped back to the bunk.

My foot suddenly came in contact with something on the floor and I tripped and fell flat across it. It seemed to be a big bunch of seaweed and was all wet and slimy.

I hurriedly jumped to my feet, drew away from it, and lit another match. This time it burned long enough for me to see what I had fallen over.

It was seaweed, but was all tangled and gnarled around what appeared to be the fish-eaten and bloated corpse of a man. At the same time the gruesome thing reared itself into a standing position and moved toward me. The match went out, but by the light of the moon I beheld its terrible and fearsome features as it advanced, peering out of the tangle of yellow kelp at me with its empty sockets.

I shuddered with horror and drew my sheath knife, striking out wildly, but the awful apparition did not stop, though I struck home repeatedly.

My brain reeled, and I fell senseless to the cabin floor.

When I recovered consciousness the sun was streaming in upon me through the skylight.

How I welcomed its warm, generous, yellow light to drive away the awful darkness.

And how glad I was when I went on deck, after my cold breakfast of ham and bread, to hear the water gurgling alongside and find a gentle morning breeze wafting me steadily southward.

At three, that afternoon, I put in behind the breakwater at San Pedro and managed to let go an anchor and get down my headsails alone.

Keith, who had grown anxious about me and had been keeping watch from the veranda of the South Coast Yacht Club, on the bluff, was alongside in a launch almost as soon as the chain had rattled through the hawse pipe.

It certainly felt good to feel his strong hand-clasp and hear his friendly voice.

He told me that the men, terrified at the prospect of spending another night aboard, had overpowered the mate, put him into one of the boats, and slipped away, while I was asleep, and that they had been picked up by a lumber schooner and brought into San Pedro. And thus ended my most terrible experience.

We have since discovered that the mainmast of the *Morpheus* was one which had been in the Norwegian barque *Victory*, when she foundered off the Golden Gate in 1899, carrying all hands to the bottom. Perhaps this is an explanation.

Keith has had a new mast put in, anyway.

The Giant

Walter de la Mare

Peter lived with his aunt, and his sister Emma, in a small house near Romford. His aunt was a woman of very fair complexion, her heavy hair was golden-brown, her eyes blue; on work days she wore a broad print apron. His sister Emma helped her aunt in the housework as best she could, out of school-time. She would sometimes play at games with Peter, but she cared for few in which her doll could take no part. Still, Peter knew games which he might play by himself; and although sometimes he played with Emma and her doll, yet generally they played apart, she alone with her doll, and he with people of his own imagining.

The rose-papered room above the kitchen (being the largest room upstairs) was his aunt's bedroom. There Emma also slept, in a little bed near the window. For, although in the great double bed was room enough, (her aunt being but a middle-sized woman,) yet the other pillow was always smooth and undinted, and that half the bed always undisturbed. On May-day primroses were strewn there, and a sprig of mistletoe at Christmas.

On a bright morning in July (for notwithstanding the sun shone fierce in the sky, yet a random wind tempered his heat), Peter went out to sit under the shadow of the wall to read his book in the garden. But when he opened the door to go out, something seemed strange to him in the garden. Whether it was the garden itself that looked or sounded strange, or himself and his thoughts that were different from usual, he could not tell. He stood on the doorstep and looked out across the grass. He wrinkled up his eyes because of the fervid sunshine that glanced bright even upon the curved blades of grass. And, while he looked across towards the foot of the garden, almost without his knowing it his eyes began to travel up from the ground, up along the trees, till he was looking into the cloudless skies. He quickly averted his eyes, with water brimming over, it was so bright above. But yet, again, as he looked across, slowly his gaze wandered up from the ground into the dark blue. He fumbled the painted covers of his book and sat down on the doorstep. He could hear the neighbouring chickens clucking and scratching in the dust, and sometimes a voice in one of the gardens spoke out in the heat. But he could not read his book for glancing out of his eye along the garden. And suddenly, with a frown, he opened the door and ran back into the kitchen.

Emma was in the bedroom making the great bed. Peter climbed upstairs and began to talk to her, and while he talked drew gradually nearer and nearer to the window. And then he walked quickly away, and took hold of the brass knob of the bedpost.

"Why don't you look out of the window, Emmie?" said he.

"I'm a-making the bed, Peter, don't you see?" said Emma.

"You can see Mrs. Watts feeding the chickens," said Peter.

Emma drew aside the window-blind and looked out. Peter stood still, watching her intently.

"She's gone in now, and they are all pecking in the dust," said Emma.

"Can you see the black-and-white pussycat on our fence, Emmie?" said Peter in a soft voice.

Emma looked down towards the poplar-trees at the foot of the garden.

"No," she said; "and the sparrows are pecking up the crumbs I shook out of the tablecloth, so she can't be in our garden at all."

Emma turned away from the window, and set to dusting the looking-glass, unheeding her grave reflexion. Peter watched her in silence awhile.

"But, Emmie, didn't you see anything else at the bottom of the garden?" he said. But he said it in so small a voice that Emma, busy at her work, did not hear him.

In the evening of that day Peter and his aunt went out to water the mignonette and the sweet-williams, and the nasturtiums in the garden. There were slipper sweet peas there, also, and lad's love, and tall hollyhocks twice as high as himself, swaying, indeed, their topmost flower-cups above his aunt's brown head. And Peter carried down the pots of water to his aunt, and watered the garden, too, with his small rose-pot. Yet he could not forbear glancing anxiously and timidly towards the poplars, and following up with his eye the gigantic shape of his fancy that he found there.

"Aren't the trees sprouting up tall, auntie?" said he, standing close beside her.

"That they are, Peter," said his aunt. "Now some for the middle bed, my man, though I'm much afeard the rose-bush is done for with blight: time it blossomed long since."

"How high are the trees, auntie?" said Peter.

"Why, surely they're a good lump higher than the house; they do grow wonderful fast," said his aunt, stooping to pluck up a weed from the bed.

"How high is the house, auntie?" said Peter, bending down beside her.

"Bless me! I can't tell you that," said she, glancing up; "ask Mr. Ash there in his garden. Good-evening, Mr. Ash: here's my little boy asking me how high the house is,—they do ask questions, to be sure."

"Well," said Mr. Ash, narrowing his eye, over the fence, "I should think, ma'am, it were about thirty foot high; say thirty-five foot to the rim of the chimney-pot."

"Is that as high as the trees?" said Peter.

"Now, which trees might you be meaning, my friend?" said Mr. Ash.

"You mean those down by the fence yonder, don't you, Peter?" said his aunt. "Poplars, aren't they? That's what he means, Mr. Ash."

"Well," said Mr. Ash, pointing the stem of his pipe towards them, "if you ask me, they poplars must be a full forty foot high, and mighty well they've growed, too, seeing as how I saw 'em planted."

Peter watched Mr. Ash attentively, as he stood there looking over the fence towards the poplar-trees. But his aunt began to talk of other matters, so that Mr. Ash said no more on the subject. Yet he did not appear to have descried anything out of the common there.

Now the evening was darkening; already a lamp was shining at an upper window, and the crescent moon had become bright in the west. Peter stayed close beside his aunt; sometimes peeping from behind her skirts towards the trees, glancing from root to foliage, to crown, and thence into the shadowy skies, whence daylight was fast withdrawing. By-and-by his aunt began to feel the chill of the night air. She bade Mr. Ash good-night, and went into the house with Peter. Soon Peter heard Mr. Ash scraping his boots upon the stones. Presently after he also went in, and shut his door, leaving the gardens silent now.

At this time Peter was making a rabbit-hutch out of a sugar-box; but tonight he had no relish for the work, and sat down with a book, while Emma learned her spelling, repeating the words to herself.

"Auntie," said Peter, looking up when the clock had ceased striking, "if Satan was to come in our garden, would he be like a man, or is he little, like a hunchback?"

"Dearie me! what'll these stories put into his head next? Why, Peter, God would not let him come up into the world like that, not to hurt His dear children. But if they are bad, wicked children, and grown-up folk too for that matter, then God goes away angry, and the Spirit is grieved too. Why, my pretty, in pictures he has great dark wings, just as the angels' are beautiful and bright; but the good angels watch and guard little children and all good people."

"Then he's just as big as a man in the pictures, like Mr. Ash, not a—"

"Aunt Elizabeth has heaps of pictures of him in a book, auntie, with all the wicked angels crowding round," said Emma; "but he's much taller than Mr. Ash, like a giant, and they are all standing up in the sky, and—"

"Yes, Emmie, that's in the book. I daresay," said her aunt, frowning at Emma, and nodding her head. "But come and sit on auntie's lap, dearie; why, he looks quite scared, poor pigeon, with his stories. Auntie will tell you about little Snowwhite, shall she?—about little Snowwhite and the dwarfs?"

Peter said nothing, though his lip trembled; and albeit he asked no more questions, yet he did not attend to the story of Snowwhite.

At the beginning of the next day, Peter woke soon after the dawning, and getting out of bed peered through the glass of his window, down the garden. The flowers were not yet unfolded in the misty air. There was no movement nor sound anywhere. The trees leaned motionless in the early morning. But towering implacable against the rosy east stood that gigantic spectre of his imagination, secret and terrific there. And Peter with a sob ran back quickly to bed.

However, he mentioned nothing of his thoughts during the day, eating his breakfast, and going to school as usual. But when he reached school he had forgotten his lessons, and was kept in. Even there, alone in the vacant schoolroom, he could not learn his returned lessons, because of all his vivid fears passing to and fro in his mind. As the afternoon decreased, hour by hour, towards evening, he began to hate the memory of night and bedtime. He lingered on, seeking any excuse for light and company, until Emma spoke roughly to him. "Leave off worrying, Peter, do! How you do worry!"

At last, when even his aunt grew vexed at his disobedience, Peter begged her for a light to go to bed by. At first she refused, laughing at his timidity. But, in the end, with importunities he persuaded her; and she gave him a piece of candle in his room, to be burned in a little water, in order that when he was asleep, and the burning wick should fall low, then the water would rush in and extinguish it.

It was far in the night, just when the flame of the candle leapt out into darkness with a hiss, that Peter woke from a dream, and sat up trembling in his bed. He had dreamed of a street in the distance, whither a giant became a speck, and the eye was strained in vain. Even yet he saw its undimmed length retreating back unimaginably. And, as if impelled by an influence inscrutable, he got out silently and drew back the muslin window-blind. In the clear, dark air he saw the row of poplar trees; he saw that gigantic shade of fear abiding there, uplifted as with a threat, and the trembling stars of the heavens about him for a head-dress.

Peter cried out in terror of the sight, hiding his eyes in his hands. And while he stood sobbing bitterly, scarcely able to take breath, his ear caught a sound in the room like the wintry shaking of dry reeds at the brink of a pool. At this new sound he caught back his sobs; his scalp seemed to creep upon his head. He looked out between his fingers towards the bed; and he saw there an Angel standing, whose face was white and steadfast as silver, and whose eyes were pure as the white flame of the Holy Ones. His wings were to him as a covering of perfect brightness, his feet hovering in the silentness of the little room. Peter, his tears dried upon his face, could not bear to gaze long upon that steadfast figure angelical; yet it seemed as if he was now indeed come out of a dreadful vision into the pure and safe light of day; and when presently the visitant was vanished away, he went back into his still warm bed, his fear more than half abated, and fell asleep.

In the morning, when he looked out of the window, a gentle rustling rain was falling, clear in the reflected cloud-light of the sun. He could hear the waterdrops running together and dripping down from leaf to leaf. He heard the sparrows chirping upon the housetop, the remote crowing of a cock. And the poplar-trees were swaying their leafy tops in the cool air, as if they also had awakened refreshed from the evil perils of a dream.

The Gray Cat

A. C. Benson

The knight Sir James Leigh lived in a remote valley of the Welsh Hills. The manor house, of rough grey stone, with thick walls and mullioned windows, stood on a rising ground; at its foot ran a little river, through great boulders. There were woods all about; but above the woods, the bare green hills ran smoothly up, so high, that in the winter the sun only peeped above the ridge for an hour or two; beyond the house, the valley wound away into the heart of the hills, and at the end a black peak looked over. The place was very sparsely inhabited; within a close of ancient yew trees stood a little stone church, and a small parsonage smothered in ivy, where an old priest, a cousin of the knight, lived. There were but three farms in the valley, and a rough track led over the hills, little used, except by drovers. At the top of the pass stood a stone cross; and from this point you could see the dark scarred face of the peak to the left, streaked with snow, which did not melt until the summer was far advanced.

Sir James was a silent sad man, in ill health; he spoke little and bore his troubles bitterly; he was much impoverished, through his own early carelessness, and now so feeble in body that he had small hope of repairing the fortune he had lost. His wife was a wise and loving woman, who, though she found it hard to live happily in so lonely a place with a sickly husband, met her sorrows with a cheerful face, visited her poorer neighbours, and was like a ray of sunlight in the gloomy valley. They had one son, a boy Roderick, now about fifteen; he was a bright and eager child, who was happy enough, taking his life as he found it—and indeed he had known no other. He was taught a little by the priest; but he had no other schooling, for Sir James would spend no money except when he was obliged to do so. Roderick had no playmates, but he never found the time to be heavy; he was fond of long solitary rambles on the hills, being light of foot and strong.

One day he had gone out to fish in the stream, but it was bright and still, and he could catch nothing; so at last he laid his rod aside in a hollow place beneath the bank, and wandered without any certain aim along the stream. Higher and higher he went, till he found, looking about him, that he was as high as the pass; and then it came into his mind to track the stream to its source. The Manor was now out of sight, and there was nothing round him but the high green hills, with here and there a sheep feeding. Once a kite came out and circled slowly in the sun, pouncing like a plummet far down the glen; and still Roderick went onwards till he saw that he was at the top of the lower hills, and that the only thing higher than him was the peak itself. He saw now that the stream ran out of a still black pool some way in front of him, that lay under the very shadow of the dark precipice, and was fed by the snows that melted from the face. It was surrounded by rocks that lay piled in confusion. But the whole place wore an air that was more than desolate; the peak itself had a cruel look, and there was an intent silence, which was only broken, as he gazed, by the sound of rocks falling loudly from the face of the hill and thundering down. The sun warned him that he had gone far enough; and he determined to go homewards, half pleased at his discovery, and half relieved to quit so lonely and grim a spot.

That evening, when he sate with his father and mother at their simple meal, he began to say where he had been. His father heard him with little attention, but when Roderick described the dark pool and the sharp front of the peak he asked him abruptly how near he had gone to the pool. Roderick said that he had seen it from a distance, and then Sir James said somewhat sharply that he must not wander so far, and that he was not to go near that place again. Roderick was surprised at this, for his father as a rule interfered little with what he did; but he did not ask his father the reason, for there was something peevish, even harsh, in his tone. But afterwards, when he went out with his mother, leaving the knight to his own gloomy thoughts, as his will and custom was, his mother said with some urgency, "Roderick, promise me not to go to the pool again; it has an evil name, and is better left to itself." Roderick was eager to know the story of the place, but his mother would not tell him—only she would have him promise; so he promised, but complained that he would rather have had a reason given for his promise; but his mother, smiling and holding his hand, said that it should be enough for him to please her by doing her will. So Roderick gave his promise again, but was not satisfied.

The next day Roderick was walking in the valley and met one of the farmers, a young good-humoured man, who had always been friendly with the boy, and had often been to fish with him; Roderick walked beside him, and told him that he had followed the stream nearly to the pool, when the young farmer, with some seriousness, asked him how near he had been to the water. Roderick was surprised at the same question that his father had asked being asked again, and told him that he had but seen it from a hill-top near, adding, "But what is amiss with the place, for my father and mother have made me promise not to go there again?"

The young farmer said nothing for a moment, but seemed to reflect; then he said that there were stories about the place, stories that perhaps it was foolish to believe, but he went on to say that it was better to be on the safe side in all things, and that the place had an evil fame. Then Roderick with childish eagerness asked him what the stories were; and little by little the farmer told him. He said that something dwelt near or in the pool, it was not known what, that had an enmity to the life of man; that twice since he was a boy a strange thing had happened there; a young shepherd had come by his death at the pool, and was found lying in the water, strangely battered; that, he said, was long before Roderick was born; then he added, "You remember old Richard the shepherd?" "What!" said Roderick, "the old strange man that used to go about muttering to himself, that the boys threw stones at?" "Yes," said the farmer, "the very same. Well, he was not always so—I remember him a strong and cheerful man; but once when the sheep had got lost in the hills, he would go to the pool because he thought he heard them calling there, though we prayed him not to go. He came back, indeed, bringing no sheep, but an altered and broken man, as he was thenceforth and as you knew him; he had seen something by the pool, he could not say what, and had had a sore strife to get away." "But what sort of a thing is this?" said Roderick. "Is it a beast or a man, or what?"

"Neither," said the farmer very gravely. "You have heard them read in the church of the evil spirits who dwelt with men, and entered their bodies, and it was sore work even for the Lord Christ to cast them forth; I think it is one of these who has wondered thither; they say he goes not far from the pool, for he cannot abide the cross on the pass, and the church bell gives him pains." And then the farmer looked at Roderick and said, "You know that they ring the bell all night on the feast of All Souls?" "Yes," said Roderick, "I have heard it ring." "Well, on that night alone," said the farmer, "they say that spirits have power upon men, and come abroad to do them hurt; and so they ring the bell, which the spirits cannot listen to—but, young master, it is ill to talk of these things, and Christian men should not even think of them; but as I said, though Satan has but little power over the baptized soul, yet even so, says the priest, he can enter in, if the soul be willing to admit him,—and so I say, avoid the place! it may be that these are silly stories to affright folk, but it is ill to touch pitch; and no good can be got by going to the pool, and perhaps evil;—and now I think I have told you enough and more than enough." For Roderick was looking at him pale and with wide open eyes.

Is it strange that from that day the thing that Roderick most desired was to see the pool and what dwelt there? I think not; when hearts are young and before trouble has laid its heavy hand upon them, the hard and cruel things of life, wounds, blows, agonies, terrors, seen only in the mirrors of another spirit, are but as a curious and lively spectacle that feeds the mind with wonder. The stories to which Roderick had listened in church of men that were haunted by demons seemed to him but as dim and distant experiences on which he would fain look; and the fainter the thought of his promise grew, the stronger grew his desire to see for himself.

In the month of June, when the heart is light, and the smell of the woods is fresh and sharp, Roderick's father and mother were called to go on a journey, to see an ancient friend who was thought to be dying. The night before they set off Roderick had a strange dream; it seemed to him that he wandered over bare hillsides, and came at last to the pool; the peak rose sharp and clear, and the water was very black and still; while he gazed upon it, it seemed to be troubled; the water began to spin round and round, and bubbling waves rose and broke on the surface. Suddenly a hand emerged from the water, and then a head, bright and unwetted, as though the water had no power to touch it. Roderick saw that it was a man of youthful aspect and commanding mien; he waded out to the shore and stood for a moment looking round him; then he beckoned Roderick to approach, looking at him kindly, and spoke to him gently, saying that he had waited for him long. They walked together to the crag, and then, in some way that Roderick could not clearly see, the man opened a door into the mountain, and Roderick saw a glimmering passage within. The air came out laden with a rich and heavy fragrance, and there was a faint sound of distant music in the hill. The man turned and looked upon Roderick as though inviting him to enter; but Roderick shook his head and refused, saying that he was not ready; at which the man stepped inside with a smile, half of pity, and the door was shut.

Then Roderick woke with a start and wished that he had been bold enough to go within the door; the light came in serenely through the window, and he heard the faint piping of awakening birds in the dewy trees. He could not sleep, and presently dressed himself and went down. Soon the household was awake, for the knight was to start betimes; Roderick sate at the early meal with his father and mother. His father was cumbered with the thought of the troublesome journey, and asked many questions about the baggage; so Roderick said little, but felt his mother's eyes dwell on his face with love. Soon after they rode away; Roderick stood at the door to see them go, and there was so eager and bright a look in his face that his mother was somehow troubled, and almost called him to her to make him repeat his promise, but she feared that he would feel that she did not trust him, and therefore put the thought aside; and so they rode away, his mother waving her hand till they turned the corner by the wood and were out of sight.

Then Roderick began to consider how he would spend the day, with a half-formed design in his mind; when suddenly the temptation to visit the pool came upon him with a force that he had neither strength nor inclination to resist. So he took his rod, which might seem to be an excuse, and set off rapidly up the stream. He was surprised to find how swiftly the hills rose all about him, and how easily he went; very soon he came to the top; and there lay the pool in front of him, within the shadow of the peak, that rose behind it very clear and sharp. He hesitated no longer, but ran lightly down the slope, and next moment he was on the brink of the pool. It lay before him very bright and pure, like a jewel of sapphire, the water being of a deep azure blue; he went all round it. There was no sign of life in the water; at the end nearest the cliff he found a little cool runnel of water that bubbled into the pool from the cliffs. No grass grew round about it, and he could see the stones sloping down and becoming more beautiful the deeper they lay, from the pure tint of the water.

He looked all round him; the moorland quivered in the bright hot air, and he could see far away the hills lie like a map, with blue mountains on the horizon, and small green valleys where men dwelt. He sate down by the pool and he had a thought of bathing in the water; but his courage did not rise to this, because he felt still as though something sate in the depths that would not show itself, but might come forth and drag him down; so he sate at last by the pool, and presently he fell asleep.

When he woke he felt somewhat chilly; the shadow of the peak had come round, and fell on the water; the place was still as calm as ever, but looking upon the pool he had an obscure sense as though he were being watched by an unclosing eye; but he was thirsting with the heat; so he drew up, in his closed hands, some of the water, which was very cool and sweet; and his drowsiness came upon him, and again he slept.

When next he woke it was with a sense of delicious ease, and the thought that someone who loved him was near him stroking his hand. He looked up, and there close to his side sate very quietly what gave him a shock of surprise. It was a great gray cat, with soft abundant fur, which turned its yellow eyes upon him lazily, purred, and licked his hand; he caressed the cat, which arched its back and seemed pleased to be with him, and presently leapt upon his knee. The soft warmth of the fur against his hands, and the welcoming caresses of this fearless wild creature pleased him greatly; and he sate long in quiet thought, taking care not to disturb the cat, which, whenever he took his hand away, rubbed against him as though to show that it was pleased at his touch. But at last he thought that he must go homewards, for the day began to turn to the west. So he put the cat off his knee and began to walk to the top of the pass, as it was quicker to follow the road. For awhile the cat accompanied him, sometimes rubbing against his leg and sometimes walking in front, but looking round from time to time as though to consult his pleasure.

Roderick began to hope that it would accompany him home, but at a certain place the cat stopped, and would go no farther. Roderick lifted it up, but it leapt from him as if displeased, and at last he left it reluctantly. In a moment he came within sight of the cross in the hilltop, so that he saw the road was near. Often he looked round and saw the great cat regarding him as though it were sorry to be left; till at last he could see it no more.

He went home well pleased, his head full of happy thoughts; he had gone half expecting to see some dreadful thing, but had found instead a creature who seemed to love him.

The next day he went again; and this time he found the cat sitting by the pool; as soon as it saw him, it ran to him with a glad and yearning cry, as though it had feared he would not return; to-day it seemed brighter and larger to look upon; and he was pleased that when he returned by the stream it followed him much farther, leaping lightly from stone to stone; but at a certain place, where the valley began to turn eastward, just before the little church came in sight, it sate down as before and took its leave of him.

The third day he began to go up the valley again; but while he rested in a little wood that came down to the stream, to his surprise and delight the cat sprang out of a bush, and seemed more than ever glad of his presence. While he sate fondling it, he heard the sound of footsteps coming up the path; but the cat heard the sound too, and as he rose to see who was coming, the cat sprang lightly into a tree beside him and was hidden from his sight. It was the old priest on his way to an upland farm, who spoke fondly to Roderick, and asked him of his father and mother. Roderick told him that they were to return that night, and said that it was too bright to remain indoors and yet too bright to fish; the priest agreed and after a little more talk rose to go, and as his manner was, holding Roderick by the hand, he blessed him, saying that he was growing a tall boy. When he was gone,—and Roderick was ashamed to find how eager he was that the priest should go,—he called low to the cat to come back; but the cat came not, and though Roderick searched the tree into which it had sprung, he could find no sign of it, and supposed that it had crept into the wood.

That evening the travellers returned, the knight seeming cheerful, because the vexatious journey was over; but Roderick was half ashamed to think that his mind had been so full of his new plaything that he was hardly glad to see his parents return. Presently his mother said, "You look very bright and happy, dear child," and Roderick, knowing that he spoke falsely, said that he was glad to see them again; his mother smiled and asked what he had been doing, and he said that he had wandered on the hills, for it was too bright to fish; his mother looked at him for a moment, and he knew in his heart that she wondered if he had kept his promise; but he thought of his secret, and looked at her so straight and full that she asked him no further questions.

The next day he woke feeling sad, because he knew that there would be no chance to go to the pool. He went to and fro with his mother, for she had many little duties to attend to. At last she said, "What are you thinking of, Roderick? You seem to have little to say to me." She said it laughingly; and Roderick was ashamed, but said that he was only thinking; and so bestirred himself to talk. But late in the day he went a little alone through the wood, and reaching the end of it, looked up to the hill, kissing his hand towards the pool as a greeting to his friend; and as he turned, the cat came swiftly and lovingly out of the wood to him; and he caught it up in his arms and clasped it close, where it lay as if contented.

Then he thought that he would carry it to the house, and say nothing as to where he had found it; but hardly had he moved a step when the cat leapt from him and stood as though angry. And it came into Roderick's mind that the cat was his secret friend, and that their friendship must somehow be unknown; but he loved it even the better for that.

In the weeks that followed, the knight was ill and the lady much at home; from time to time Roderick saw the cat; he could never tell when it would visit him; it came and went unexpectedly, and always in some lonely and secret place. But gradually Roderick began to care for nothing else; his fishing and his riding were forgotten, and he began to plan how he might be alone, so that the cat would come to him. He began to lose his spirits and to be dull without it, and to hate the hours when he could not see it; and all the time it grew or seemed to grow stronger and sleeker; his mother soon began to notice that he was not well; he became thin and listless, but his eyes were large and bright; she asked him more than once if he were well, but he only laughed. Once indeed he had a fright; he had been asleep under a hawthorn in the glen on a hot July day; and waking saw the cat close to him, watching him intently with yellow eyes, as though it were about to spring upon him; but seeing him awake, it came wheedling and fondling him as often before; but he could not forget the look in its eyes, and felt grave and sad.

Then he began to be troubled with dreams; the man whom he had seen in his former dream rising from the pool was often with him—sometimes he led him to pleasant places; but one dream he had, that he was bathing in the pool, and caught his foot between the rocks and could not draw it out. Then he heard a rushing sound, and looking round saw that a great stream of water was plunging heavily into the pool, so that it rose every moment, and was soon up to his chin. Then he saw in his dream that the man sate on the edge of the pool and looked at him with a cold smile, but did not offer to help; till at last when the water touched his lips, the man rose and held up his hand; and the stream ceased to run, and presently his foot came out of the rock easily, and he swam ashore but saw no one.

Then it came to the autumn, and the days grew colder and shorter, and he could not be so much abroad; he felt, too, less and less disposed to stir out, and it now began to be on his mind that he had broken his promise to his mother; and for a week he saw nothing of the cat, though he longed to see it. But one night, as he went to bed, when he had put out his light, he saw that the moon was very bright; and he opened the window and looked out, and saw the gleaming stream and the grey valley; he was turning away, when he heard a light sound of the scratching of claws, and presently the cat sprang upon the window-sill and entered the room. It was now cold and he got into bed, and the cat sprang upon his pillow; and Roderick was so glad that the cat had returned that while he caressed it he talked to it in low tones. Suddenly came a step at the door, and a light beneath it, and his mother with a candle entered the room. She stood for a moment looking, and Roderick became aware that the cat was gone. Then his mother came near, thinking that he was asleep, and he sate up. She said to him, "Dear child, I heard you speaking, and wondered whether you were in a dream," and she looked at him with an anxious gaze. And he said, "Was I speaking, mother? I was asleep and must have spoken in a dream." Then she said, "Roderick, you are not old enough yet to sleep so uneasily—is all well, dear child?" And Roderick, hating to deceive his mother, said, "How should not all be well?" So she kissed him and went quietly away, but Roderick heard her sighing.

Then it came at last to All Souls' Day; and Roderick, going to his bed that night, had a strange dizziness and cried out, and found the room swim round him. Then he got up into his bed, for he thought that he must be ill, and soon fell asleep; and in his sleep he dreamed a dreadful dream. He thought that he lay on the hills beside the pool;

and yet he was out of the body, for he could see himself lying there. The pool was very dark, and a cold wind ruffled the waves. And again the water was troubled, and the man stepped out; but behind him came another man, like a hunchback, very swarthy of face, with long thin arms, that looked both strong and evil. Then it seemed as if the first man pointed to Roderick where he lay and said, "You can take him hence, for he is mine now, and I have need of him," adding, "Who could have thought it would be so easy?" and then he smiled very bitterly. And the hunchback went towards himself; and he tried to cry out in warning, and straining woke; and in the chilly dawn he saw the cat sit in his room, but very different from what it had been. It was gaunt and famished and the fur was all marred; its yellow eyes gleamed horribly, and Roderick saw that it hated him, he knew not why; and such fear came upon him that he screamed out, and as he screamed the cat rose as if furious, twitching its tail and opening its mouth; but he heard steps without, and screamed again, and his mother came in haste into the room, and the cat was gone in a moment, and Roderick held out his hands to his mother, and she soothed and quieted him, and presently with many sobs he told her all the story.

She did not reproach him, nor say a word of his disobedience, the fear was too urgent upon her; she tried to think for a little that it was the sight of some real creature lingering in a mind that was wrought upon by illness; but those were not the days when men preferred to call the strange afflictions of body and spirit, the sad scars that stain the fair works of God, by reasonable names. She did not doubt that by some dreadful hap her own child had somehow crept within the circle of darkness, and she only thought of how to help and rescue him; that he was sorry and that he did not wholly consent was her hope.

So she merely kissed and quieted him, and then she told him that she would return anon and he must rest quietly; but he would not let her leave him, so she stood in the door and called a servant softly. Sir James was long abed, for he had been in ill-health that day, and she gave word that someone must be found at once and go to call the priest, saying that Roderick was ill and she was uneasy. Then she came back to the bed, and holding Roderick's hand she said that he must try to sleep. Roderick said to her, "Mother, say that you forgive me." To which she only replied, "Dear child, do I not love you better than all the world? Do not think of me now, only ask help of God." So she sate with his hand in both of her own, and presently he fell asleep; but she saw that he was troubled in his dreams, for he groaned and cried out often; and now through the window she heard the soft tolling of the bell of the church, and she knew that a contest must be fought out that night over the child; but after a sore passage of misery, and a bitter questioning as to why one so young and innocent should thus be bound with evil bonds, she found strength to leave the matter in the Father's hands, and to pray with an eager hopefulness.

But the time passed heavily and still the priest did not arrive; and the ghostly terror was so sore on the child that she could bear it no longer and awakened him. And he told her in broken words of the terrible things that had oppressed him; sore fightings and struggles, and a voice in his ear that it was too late, and that he had yielded himself to the evil. And at last there came a quiet footfall on the stair, and the old priest himself entered the room, looking anxious, yet calm, and seeming to bring a holy peace with him.

Then she bade the priest sit down; and so the two sate by the bedside, with the solitary lamp burning in the chamber; and she would have had Roderick tell the tale, but he covered his face with his hands and could not. So she told the tale herself to the priest, saying, "Correct me, Roderick, if I am wrong"; and once or twice the boy corrected her, and added a few words to make the story plain, and then they sate awhile in silence, while the terrified looks of the mother and her son dwelt on the old priest's strongly lined face; yet they found comfort in the smile with which he met them.

At length he said, "Yes, dear lady and dear Roderick, the case is plain enough—the child has yielded himself to some evil power, but not too far, I think; and now must we meet the foe with all our might. I will abide here with the boy; and, dear lady, you were better in your own chamber, for we know not what will pass; if there were need I would call you." Then the lady said, "I will do as you direct me, Father, but I would fain stay." Then he said, "Nay, but there are things on which a Christian should not look, lest they should daunt his faith—so go, dear lady, and help us with your prayers." Then she said, "I will be below; and if you beat your foot thrice upon the floor, I will come. Roderick, I shall be close at hand; only be strong, and all shall be well." Then she went softly away.

Then the priest said to Roderick, "And now, dear son, confess your sin and let me shrive you." So Roderick made confession, and the priest blessed him: but while he blessed him there came the angry crying of a cat from somewhere in the room, so that Roderick shuddered in his bed. Then the priest drew from his robe a little holy book, and with a reverence laid it under Roderick's hand; and he himself took his book of prayers and said, "Sleep now, dear son, fear not." So Roderick closed his eyes, and being very weary slept. And the old priest in a low whisper said the blessed psalms. And it came near to midnight; and the place that the priest read was, *Thou shalt not be afraid for any terror by night, nor for the arrow that flieth by day; for the pestilence that walketh in darkness, nor for the sickness that destroyeth in the noonday;* and suddenly there ran as it were a shiver through his bones, and he knew that the time was come. He looked at Roderick, who slept wearily on his bed, and it seemed to him as though suddenly a small and shadowy thing, like a bird, leapt from the boy's mouth and on to the bed; it was like a wren, only white, with dusky spots upon it; and the priest held his breath; for now he knew that the soul was out of the body, and that unless it could return uninjured into the limbs of the child, nothing could avail the boy; and then he said quietly in his heart to God that if He so willed He should take the boy's life, if only his soul could be saved.

Then the priest was aware of a strange and horrible thing; there sprang softly on to the bed the form of the great gray cat, very lean and angry, which stood there, as though ready to spring upon the bird, which hopped hither and thither, as though careless of what might be. The priest cast a glance upon the boy, who lay rigid and pale, his eyes shut, and hardly seeming to breathe, as though dead and prepared for burial. Then the priest signed the cross and said "*In Nomine*"; and as the holy words fell on the air, the cat looked fiercely at the bird, but seemed to shrink into itself; and then it slipped away.

Then the priest's fear was that the bird might stray further outside of his care; and yet he dared not try and wake the boy, for he knew that this was death, if the soul was thrust apart from the body, and if he broke the unseen chain that bound them; so he waited and prayed. And the bird hopped upon the floor; and then presently the priest saw the cat draw near again, and in a stealthy way; and now the priest himself was feeling weary of the strain, for he seemed to be wrestling in spirit with something that was strong and strongly armed. But he signed the cross again and said faintly "*In Nomine*"; and the cat again withdrew.

Then a dreadful drowsiness fell upon the priest, and he thought that he must sleep. Something heavy, leaden-handed, and powerful seemed to be busy in his brain. Meanwhile the bird hopped upon the window-sill and stood as if preparing its wings for a flight. Then the priest beat with his foot upon the floor, for he could no longer battle. In a moment the lady glided in, and seemed as though scared to find the scene of so fierce an encounter so still and quiet. She would have spoken, but the priest signed her to be silent, and pointed to the boy and to the bird; and then she partly understood. So they stood in silence, but the priest's brain grew more numb; though he was aware of a creeping blackness that seemed to overshadow the bird, in the midst of which glared two bright eyes. So with a sudden effort he signed the cross, and said

"*In Nomine*" again; and at the same moment the lady held out her hand; and the priest sank down on the floor; but he saw the bird raise its wings for a flight, and just as the dark thing rose, and, as it were, struck openmouthed, the bird sailed softly through the air, alighted on the lady's hand, and then with a light flutter of wings on to the bed and to the boy's face, and was seen no more; at the same moment the bells stopped in the church and left a sweet silence. The black form shrank and slipped aside, and seemed to fall on the ground; and outside there was a shrill and bitter cry which echoed horribly on the air; and the boy opened his eyes, and smiled; and his mother fell on his neck and kissed him. Then the priest said, "Give God the glory!" and blessed them, and was gone so softly that they knew not when he went; for he had other work to do. Then mother and son had great joy together.

But the priest walked swiftly and sternly through the wood, and to the church; and he dipped a vessel in the stoup of holy water, turning his eyes aside, and wrapped it in a veil of linen. Then he took a lantern in his hand, and with a grave and fixed look on his face he walked sadly up the valley, putting one foot before another, like a man who forced himself to go unwilling. There were strange sounds on the hillside, the crying of sad birds, and the beating of wings, and sometimes a hollow groaning seemed to come down the stream. But the priest took no heed, but went on heavily till he reached the stone cross, where the wind whistled dry in the grass. Then he struck off across the moorland. Presently he came to a rise in the ground; and here, though it was dark, he seemed to see a blacker darkness in the air, where the peak lay.

But beneath the peak he saw a strange sight; for the pool shone with a faint white light, that showed the rocks about it. The priest never turned his head, but walked thither, with his head bent, repeating words to himself, but hardly knowing what he said.

Then he came to the brink; and there he saw a dreadful sight. In the water writhed large and luminous worms, that came sometimes up to the surface, as though to breathe, and sank again. The priest knew well enough that it was a device of Satan's to frighten him; so he delayed not; but setting the lantern down on the ground, he stood. In a moment the lantern was obscured as by the rush of batlike wings. But the priest took the veil off the vessel; and holding it up in the air, he let the water fall in the pool, saying softly, "Lord, let them be bound!"

But when the holy water touched the lake, there was a strange sight; for the bright worms quivered and fell to the depth of the pool; and a shiver passed over the surface, and the light went out like a flickering lamp. Then there came a foul yelling from the stones; and with a roar like thunder, rocks fell crashing from the face of the peak; and then all was still.

Then the priest sate down and covered his face with his hands, for he was sore spent; but he rose at length, and with grievous pain made his slow way down the valley, and reached the parsonage house at last.

Roderick lay long between life and death; and youth and a quiet mind prevailed.

Long years have passed since that day; all those that I have spoken of are dust. But in the window of the old church hangs a picture in glass which shows Christ standing, with one lying at his feet from whom he had cast out a devil; and on a scroll are the words, DE • ABYSSIS • TERRAE • ITERUM • REDUXISTI • ME, the which may be written in English, *Yea, and brought est me from the deep of the earth again.*

The Great Power

Henry Oyen

Of course, there is no reason why you should believe this story. Judging by all rational standards, the tale is quite impossible in this day and age. If the Society for the Discovery and Exploitation of Psychical Phenomena ever has it brought to its attention it may stop and ponder awhile. Otherwise, it is expected to meet with little credence.

You can hear the story told almost any sunny day, if you will linger in the little 'dobe squares or along the roads that are in the vicinage of Ildefonse, where the air is so dry and light that there is nothing to breathe for, and there is sun, and sun, and the only material things are the dark, clear-cut shadows on the light sand. Sometimes you will hear it in the sleepy, drone-toned patois of the peon; another time it will be in the matter-of-fact tone of the white citizen. But always, always, whether it be Gringo or Mexicano who opens his heart and tells you the story, it will be accompanied by such apology as opens this tale: "Of course you will scoff, señor, but it is all the truth."

San Miguel—a hundred dirty, red 'dobe houses, an old mission, and a great square—lies to the south and west of Ildefonse, on the very edge of the never-changing desert of yellow sands. At Ildefonse there are boards and sidewalks, and some of the houses have even floors in them; but at Miguel this is all left behind and there is only the atmosphere of the old 'dobes with the clay floors, the crumbling mission, and absolutely naught to suggest the year or the century.

Bradley, the northern doctor, came to Miguel because of many things, according to the people of the village. He was a bank robber, this blue-eyed man of the North; he had killed a man; he had weak lungs; he was there to write of the old mission; to let the modern world of the eastern and northern states know how near they were to the seventeenth century and the miracles of the church. So said the people, and Bradley laughed.

The reason for Bradley's presence in Miguel was quite inconsequential and trivial. Miguel was two hundred miles from the railroad. So Bradley came.

There was peace and rest, long sunny days and cool nights, during which there was nothing to do but sit in a long chair and soak in the joy of living, and this is what Bradley needed. But the fact which is of importance is that it was at Miguel that Bradley met Meta.

Bradley had dreamed of Meta for the better half of his life. He had dreamed of her while a boy at school; she had followed him through his medical studies, to Germany, where his education was completed, and all through the rest of his thirty-one years. He went to balls where the women were by all accorded the palm for beauty and found himself wondering why none of them were like Meta. He was entirely practical, was Bradley, but Meta was in his dreams for a good share of the time, else he would have been married long ago.

When she looked out of a wide-windowed 'dobe court and laughed, Bradley knew why he had come to Miguel.

There was no need for an introduction. He knew her at once; she knew him. It was as if they had walked together for much of their lives.

"Meta," said Bradley after her. Her voice was the voice of the Dream Meta.

"My heart's heart," said Meta, in the extravagant phrases of her people. And they laughed. Bradley was holding her hand. And Bradley knew then that for him there was no longer any trail that led back to the North. There was nothing any more, save the lazy sun, the clear-cut shadows, the drowse of the 'dobes,—and Meta.

This discovery in itself was nothing so remarkable, for many a man of the North has found in the eyes of the girls of Meta's people that for which he searched long and vainly among the maids of his own North. Many men have done so—and forgotten. Bradley was different. Bradley established himself permanently in Miguel. Bradley was a doctor, and there was scope for doctors in and around this part of the land.

Bradley practised little. Wherein was there sense of hurrying and worrying to build up a practice that would yield a professional reputation and eventually riches, when here, in a sun-washed land of bright colors, was ease and content with little price of purchase? Why work, when in the end there was nothing, after all, save Meta? It was delightfully simple. This feeling comes quickly to men in the sand land.

In the daytime Bradley was one of the few Americanos of the new quarter of the town as a matter of form. He dressed for dinner and kept his face clean and his clothes white. But when the shadows of the 'dobe houses grew long in the plaza and the cool hush of night called the people from within the doors, Meta and her lover sat on the roof bench of the 'dobe house and communed in the tongue which is peculiar neither to Saxon or Castilian. Sometimes Meta sang the love songs of her own tongue, and then the people on the roofs two houses away heard a strong, subdued voice go haltingly through the chorus. Sometimes Bradley sang, sometimes "Forever," and again "Vanity." But whoever it was that sang, the song had to do with the same theme; it was Them, only two of them, for whom the world was made—there were only two people in the universe worth a single moment's thought.

Then, one day, Bradley was called away to professional duty, and Meta was left alone to wait for the return of her lover. It was to Sangre De Cristo that Bradley went. Sangre De Cristo is on the other side of the untrailed desert from Miguel. The road around is five days long, and no man was there alive who could say he had journeyed through the sands since the wells were dried up.

There was a distemper of some kind at Sangre De Cristo. Was it possible that it was the Little Plague? Pray the good saint whose picture hung on the mission wall that it was not. But would the great doctor from the North come with his great wisdom and bag of medicines to look upon the faces of the sick at Sangre De Cristo and make them well? It was the old padre who sent the word. The professional instinct was developed strong in Bradley.

"I must go, dear heart," he said to Meta. "It will not lie long. If you need me, call for me, and I will hear; I know I will."

The conditions at Sangre De Cristo were much worse than the messenger had told. There was much fever there, the people were stark with fright, and the sanitation was awful. Bradley had enough of the northern energy left to do many things in a short time. He divided the people of the village into two classes—the sound and the unsound. He commissioned the venerable padre as chief nurse, and devoted himself to the simplified problem of preventing one class from falling ill, and keeping the other from dying with too great a frequency.

But the peons were slow to think and slower to act. They were safe now. Of course, the señor of The Medicines was here. They had no further concern in the matter, the señor be blessed a thousand times. So they resigned themselves, like children, to the care of Bradley. Bradley was almost alone, for the padre was old and feeble. It was a week before he had affaire adjusted so that he might sleep with an easy conscience. It was a week later before the people were whipped into such shape that it was worth the Doctor's while to take off his clothes when going to sleep. Then he retired to his bed in the old mission to gather up two weeks' lost sleep in one night.

Possibly there was something in the quiet blue night air of the old mission house, the air of rest and sleep in walls three hundred years old, that oppressed Bradley. Perhaps there was something in the wind that came over the yellow sands from Miguel.

Bradley found himself sitting upright in the middle of the night, uncertain whether he had slept or not. He was talking to himself and his first conscious words were: "That cursed messenger!"

The plague was at Miguel, and he was cursing the man who bore the message of the padre. The man must have been infected himself. The thing was all clear to Bradley. It had not come to him with a shock. He but awoke and knew that the fact was impressed upon his mind. He was perfectly wide-awake, sane, and in possession of his senses. He knew positively, the plague was at Miguel, and he arose and dressed hurriedly, for the message of the night was thumping in his head and Meta was among the stricken. It all came to him in the little 'dobe room as plainly as if it had been spoken, and he was not surprised in the least.

Bradley was a confirmed scoffer at matters spiritualistic. His professional education had made this certain. He was eminently practical, but there was no denying a thing such as this. The plague was at Miguel and Meta was stricken. It was as if some one had entered the room, spoken the news quietly, and departed, leaving naught behind him to show that he had been there but the memory of the words.

"But, señor, how do you know this?" gasped the padre. "There is no messenger, and we have no despatch wire strung thus far."

"Never mind, Father," said Bradley; "get me a horse and get it for me quick."

"But, señor, you cannot go so, alone, with only one horse. The way around the mountain is long and hard."

"Get me the horse; I'm in a hurry." The little padre bustled around patiently. He was not to be denied, this man in a hurry.

Bradley took a bottle of water, a piece of dried meat, his little bag, and mounted.

"Be good, Padre," he called out, sharply.

"Adios, my son, may the good saints ride with you," answered the old priest. But he called out in anguish when Bradley turned his horse's head out on the yellow sands straight toward Miguel.

The evening of the second day a man, gray and drawn, came staggering into the plaza of Miguel. The people clustered around, discussing with many motions and in excited tones the sickness which had stricken their people, just as Bradley knew they would be.

"Señor!" they called. The man looked up, and they saw it was the face of the northern doctor, with years of age suddenly added to it.

"Señor, señor, the blessed saints are truly good! The plague is here! We sent a messenger for you but yesterday—but you are here ere he could have reached you. What—"

Bradley had never stopped. He knew they were babbling at him and blessing him as their savior, but he kept on, straight to the sick bed in the house with the roof bench. *She* was there, and ill, just as he knew she would be. She looked up and smiled happily.

"I called for you, my heart," she said, weakly. "And I heard, I heard you," replied the practical-minded Bradley.

"But, señor, how did you come?" queried an old man. "Not surely by the road around the mountain, for that is a five-days' ride and she was stricken but yesterday—at sundown. And from the desert you—"

"From the desert I came," said Bradley.

"Not from Sangre De Cristo?"

"From Sangre De Cristo."

"But señor, it is a three-days' ride, and you must have water every twelve hours."

"I came in two days and part of one night," was Bradley's answer. "I watered—my horse and I—at Lagua de Cuato."

The villagers looked at each other and at Bradley, queerly.

"Señor," said one, softly, "there has been no water in Lagua de Cuato for four years."

"Señores," said Bradley, unhesitatingly, "I watered—I and my horse—there this morning."

But they went later and found the lake with its bottom powder dry, just as it had been for four years, with Bradley's horse dead in the gray dust—and it is that which makes the story so utterly impossible.

The Green Robe

R. H. Benson

The old priest was silent for a moment. The song of a great bee boomed up out of the distance and ceased as the white bell of a flower beside me drooped suddenly under his weight.

"I have not made myself clear," said the priest again. "Let me think a minute." And he leaned back.

We were sitting on a little red-tiled platform in his garden, in a sheltered angle of the wall. On one side of us rose the old irregular house, with its latticed windows, and its lichened roofs culminating in a bell-turret; on the other I looked across the pleasant garden where great scarlet poppies hung like motionless flames in the hot June sunshine, to the tall living wall of yew, beyond which rose the heavy green masses of an elm in which a pigeon lamented, and above all a tender blue sky. The priest was looking out steadily before him with great childlike eyes that shone strangely in his thin face under his white hair. He was dressed in an old cassock that showed worn and green in the high lights.

"No," he said presently, "it is not faith that I mean; it is only an intense form of the gift of spiritual perception that God has given me; which gift indeed is common to us all in our measure. It is the faculty by which we verify for ourselves what we have received on authority and hold by faith. Spiritual life consists partly in exercising this faculty. Well, then, this form of that faculty God has been pleased to bestow upon me, just as He has been pleased to bestow on you a keen power of seeing and enjoying beauty where others perhaps see none; this is called artistic perception. It is no sort of credit to you or to me, any more than is the color of our eyes, or a faculty for mathematics, or an athletic body.

"Now in my case, in which you are pleased to be interested, the perception occasionally is so keen that the spiritual world appears to me as visible as what we call the natural world. In such moments, although I generally know the difference between the spiritual and the natural, yet they appear to me simultaneously, as if on the same plane. It depends on my choice as to which of the two I see the more clearly.

"Let me explain a little. It is a question of focus. A few minutes ago you were staring at the sky, but you did not see the sky. Your own thought lay before you instead. Then I spoke to you, and you started a little and looked at me; and you saw me, and your thought vanished. Now can you understand me if I say that these sudden glimpses that God has granted me, were as though when you looked at the sky, you saw both the sky and your thought at once, on the same plane, as I have said? Or think of it in another way. You know the sheet of plate-glass that is across the upper part of the fireplace in my study. Well, it depends on the focus of your eyes, and your intention, whether you see the glass and the fire-plate behind, or the room reflected in the glass. Now can you imagine what it would be to see them all at once? It is like that." And he made an outward gesture with his hands.

"Well," I said, "I scarcely understand. But please tell me, if you will, your first vision of that kind."

"I believe," he began, "that when I was a child the first clear vision came to me, but I only suppose it from my mother's diary. I have not the diary with me now, but there is an entry in it describing how I said I had seen a face look out of a wall and had run indoors from the garden; half frightened, but not terrified. But I remember nothing of it myself, and my mother seems to have thought it must have been a waking dream; and if it were not for what has happened to me since perhaps I should have thought it a dream too. But now the other explanation seems to me more likely. But the first clear vision that I remember for myself was as follows:

"When I was about fourteen years old I came home at the end of one July for my summer holidays. The pony-cart was at the station to meet me when I arrived about four o'clock in the afternoon; but as there was a short cut through the woods, I put my luggage into the cart, and started to walk the mile and a half by myself. The field path presently plunged into a pine wood, and I came over the slippery needles under the high arches of the pines with that intense ecstatic happiness of home-coming that some natures know so well. I hope sometimes that the first steps on the other side of death may be like that. The air was full of mellow sounds that seemed to emphasise the deep stillness of the woods, and of mellow lights that stirred among the shadowed greenness. I know this now, though I did not know it then. Until that day although the beauty and the color and sound of the world certainly affected me, yet I was not conscious of them, any more than of the air I breathed, because I did not then know what they meant. Well, I went on in this glowing dimness, noticing only the trees that might be climbed, the squirrels and moths that might be caught, and the sticks that might be shaped into arrows or bows.

"I must tell you, too, something of my religion at that time. It was the religion of most well-taught boys. In the foreground, if I may put it so, was morality: I must not do certain things; I must do certain other things. In the middle distance was a perception of God. Let me say that I realised that I was present to Him, but not that He was present to me. Our Saviour dwelt in this middle distance, one whom I fancied ordinarily tender, sometimes stern. In the background there lay certain mysteries, sacramental and otherwise. These were chiefly the affairs of grown-up people. And infinitely far away, like clouds piled upon the horizon of a sea, was the invisible world of heaven whence God looked at me, golden gates and streets, now towering in their exclusiveness, now on Sunday evenings bright with a light of hope, now on wet mornings unutterably dreary. But all this was uninteresting to me. Here about me lay the tangible enjoyable world—this was reality: there in a misty picture lay religion, claiming, as I knew, my homage, but not my heart. Well; so I walked through these woods, a tiny human creature, yet greater, if I had only known it, than these giants of ruddy bodies and arms, and garlanded heads that stirred above me.

"My path presently came over a rise in the ground; and on my left lay a long glade, bordered by pines, fringed with bracken, but itself a folded carpet of smooth rabbit-cropped grass, with a quiet oblong pool in the centre, some fifty yards below me.

"Now I cannot tell you how the vision began; but I found myself, without experiencing any conscious shock, standing perfectly still, my lips dry, my eyes smarting with the intensity with which I had been staring down the glade, and one foot aching with the pressure with which I had rested upon it. It must have come upon me and enthralled me so swiftly that my brain had no time to reflect. It was no work, therefore, of the imagination, but a clear and sudden vision. This is what I remember to have seen.

"I stood on the border of a vast robe; its material was green. A great fold of it lay full in view, but I was conscious that it stretched for almost unlimited miles. This great green robe blazed with embroidery. There were straight lines of tawny work on either side which melted again into a darker green in high relief. Right in the centre lay a pale agate stitched delicately into the robe with fine dark stitches; overhead the blue lining of this silken robe arched out. I was conscious that this robe was vast beyond conception, and that I stood as it were in a fold of it, as it lay stretched out on some unseen floor. But, clearer than any other thought, stood out in my mind the certainty that this robe had not been flung down and left, but that it clothed a Person. And even as this thought showed itself a ripple ran along the high relief in dark green, as if the wearer of the robe had just stirred. And I felt on my face the breeze of His motion. And it was this I suppose that brought me to myself.

"And then I looked again, and all was as it had been the last time I had passed this way. There was the glade and the pool and the pines and the sky overhead, and the Presence was gone. I was a boy walking home from the station, with dear delights of the pony and the air-gun, and the wakings morning by morning in my own carpeted bedroom, before me.

"I tried, however, to see it again as I had seen it. No, it was not in the least like a robe; and above all where was the Person that wore it? There was no life about me, except my own, and the insect life that sang in the air. and the quiet meditative life of the growing things. But who was this Person I had suddenly perceived? And then it came upon me with a shock, and yet I was incredulous. It could not be the God of sermons and long prayers who demanded my presence Sunday by Sunday in His little church, that God Who watched me like a stern father. Why religion, I thought, told me that all was vanity and unreality, and that rabbits and pools and glades were nothing compared to Him who sits on the great white throne.

"I need not tell you that I never spoke of this at home. It seemed to me that I had stumbled upon a scene that was almost dreadful, that might be thought over in bed, or during an idle lonely morning in the garden, but must never be spoken of, and I can scarcely tell you when the time came that I understood that there was but one God after all."

The old man stopped talking. And I looked out again at the garden without answering him, and tried myself to see how the poppies were embroidered into a robe, and to hear how the chatter of the starlings was but the rustle of its movement, the clink of jewel against jewel, and the moan of the pigeon the creaking of the heavy silk, but I could not. The poppies flamed and the birds talked and sobbed, but that was all.

The Haunted Cap

George W. Kelley

Valor had earned for Colonel Pearson his rank in the Confederate service. His left cheek was marked by a star-like depression, where a bullet had entered at Chancellorsville, and his right was seamed by a long gash, left by a sabre at Aldie.

Four years after the war, one April evening, he was entertaining a guest at his residence on the left bank of the James, not many miles from Richmond. The chill air from the valley drove them from the verandah into the library, where the visitor eagerly listened to the Colonel's reminiscences of Stonewall Jackson.

"Speaking of Jackson," said the Colonel, "reminds me of this Union cap. It has a strange history." As he spoke he took from a shelf, where it rested among numerous other relics of the war, a dark-blue cap, with leather visor, such as was worn by privates in the Federal army. It was faded and stained, and the right half of the visor was broken and bent down. Through the middle of the band on the left side was a round hole, a trifle larger than a dime. There was no lining, but in the centre of the crown on the inside was a round, black wooden button.

"By hundreds of soldiers in Georgia and North Carolina," said the Colonel, "this is known as the 'Haunted Cap.' It was worn by a soldier in the 119th New York Volunteers, and was taken from his body at Chancellorsville by James Ashby of the 44th Georgia."

His guest having expressed a desire to hear the story, Colonel Pearson continued:

Ashby was among the first to enter the service of his State. He was not a planter nor the son of a planter—neither wealthy nor the heir to wealth. He had nothing to do with bringing about secession—perhaps opposed it—but the moment the war began he was in the ranks.

In many respects he was a rare type. In camp, on the march or under fire, he was equally happy and cheerful, and gave cheer to others. No mishap was a disaster, no wound serious. He never questioned nor complained.

In action there was not a more reliable man in the army. Always cool and steadfast, he would stand until ordered to retire, and he shot to hurt. He never fought behind cover if he could better see his mark in the open. When wounded, he disagreed with the surgeons as to the time he ought to stay under their care. At Malvern Hill a bullet cut a furrow across the crown of his head, yet he was in second Bull Run, and was there wounded in the arm. He was in line again at Sharpsburg—or Antietam, as your people call it—and later shared in our victory at Fredericksburg.

On May 2, '63, he was in the flanking columns of Jackson at Chancellorsville. You know about the battle—how Howard, with his right unprotected, was surprised, and most of the Eleventh Corps driven from their works and the field. Here and there a few men in the retreating line would make a stand for a moment and endeavor to rally. Ashby noticed a Federal soldier, as cool as he, taking slow aim, and realized that he was the intended victim of the Minié ball soon to fly. It came, piercing his hat. Now it was his turn, and the Federal soldier fell. As Ashby went by in the advance, he took this cap from the man he had shot. The bullet had entered the forehead, through the cap band. This clean hole has since been made by wearing away the broken edges of the rent. When killed, the soldier had his cap turned quarter way round, with the visor over the right ear, which accounts for the perforation being on the left side.

It was not uncommon for the soldiers on both sides to retain some trophy taken from the enemy, and so the cap which Ashby showed his comrades aroused no comment until one day he strolled down the company street, wearing it, and walking with a sort of mock military swagger.

That night he was the talk of the camp and was spoken of in a changed way. While some treated the performance lightly, saying that Ashby was joking, others could discern no element of fun. No one would say he was mentally affected, but if not what could be his purpose? For kind, brave, lovable Ashby to do such a thing seemed more than strange.

The next day, though Ashby did not wear the cap, he showed it to many, calling attention to the rent in the band, and relating how it was made. Indeed, he neglected no opportunity to do this, until men dreaded to meet him and give him occasion for exhibiting his trophy and telling its grim story.

Another night Ashby was the talk of the camp, and an element of dread entered into the discussion—fear for Ashby, or of something indefinable. If not out of his mind, something evil possessed him—an evil notion, if nothing worse. Darkness will give a direction to thoughts which in daylight would take some other course, and in the shades made by the camp fires some of the soldiers wandered mentally into strange realms. The opinion became general that the spirit of the dead Union soldier was plaguing Ashby. Others, more profound, reasoned that there had developed in the

Georgian the instinct which prompts the savage to take and keep the scalp of his victim as a token of his prowess.

Though no one had yet spoken to Ashby on the subject, he had overheard remarks which told him of the sensation he had made. The next day he again strolled through the camp wearing the cap. He had made the bullet-hole round, thus enlarging it, and turned the cap to the right so that the hole came in the centre of his forehead, and the white skin could be seen shining through.

Staring eyes and frowns met him at every turn. He stopped when he heard from one man, holding the attention of a knot of others, the remark:

"Ashby has gone too far with this foolishness. If he won't stop it, we'll take the cap away from him."

Ashby touched the arm of the speaker and said:

"Bill, you mustn't get mad and have a tantrum. I'm not harming any one."

"Yes, you are, Jim; that's jest what's the matter; you're harming yourself. The boys don't like what you're doing, and that feeling will grow till they don't like you."

"Now, boys, let's be reasonable," said Ashby. "Sit down, and we'll talk this over."

With a feeling of relief that the disagreeable matter seemed about to be settled, the dozen men sat down, and in a moment another dozen gathered, and, the news flying that Ashby was being called to account, others came, until half the regiment was assembled.

Ashby remained standing. When the eager crowd looked ready he raised his hand, but before he could utter a word Bill interrupted, saying:

"Now, Jim, I don't like to break in on you, but you must take that cap off while you talk. You know we don't want to see it anyway, and it's kind of crowdin' things to keep it on while you're talkin' about it. All we can see is that round white spot on your forehead. For God's sake, Jim, take it off."

"Take it off!" "Throw it away!" "Take it off!" came from all directions.

Ashby faced the throng with his old-time gay and happy look. And he was happy, for the time he had been waiting for had come. He listened with a smile to Bill's pleading, but when the demands for the removal of the cap were made in angry tones, he threw back his shoulders, and looked defiant. Then he bowed and smiled and dropped the cap at his feet.

"Now, Jim Ashby," said Bill, "I want to say one word more for the boys. We've never had any difference with you before—we couldn't. You're the only man in this regiment that every other man likes. But we can't bear this cap business. Some right ugly notion has got into your head, and no good can come of it. Surely no good is got foolin' with a dead man's things. I'm not afraid of much of anything, myself, but my flesh creeps every time I think of that cap. You shot the man that wore it in a fair fight—that's all right—but it can't be right to go paradin' around in the cap of a man you killed. It don't show respect for him. I wish you would let us have it, Jim, and we'll bury it with all the honors, and fire a salute. That's all I've got to say."

This speech was received with hearty applause, and then all turned to Ashby.

"Boys," said he, "Bill has said just what I thought he would, and I judge from your applause that you think as he does. Now, the trouble is, you're all superstitious. I'm not. You're afraid that after a man is dead he may come back to plague you. I've known you to charge up to a battery and face canister by the bucketful, and after dark have been afraid to go over that same ground, because there were dead men there. When those men were firing cannon at you by daylight, you didn't fear them or their guns, but after they were dead and the sun gone down, you shook all over.

"But I don't believe a man dies at all. He gets through here, and we call it death. I believe he's left these parts, but you have a fear that the soul still has a hold on folks on earth. That cap is nothing to me—only so much cloth with a hole through it. To you it's more. You seem to feel that the man who used to wear it owns it now. Now, boys, don't be childish. I won't wear the cap if it troubles anybody. I allow I only put it on today to stir you up, and get a chance to say what I have."

A dismal silence followed. Ashby looked over the crowd, and at the cap which he was turning in his hands. Then he held up the relic as if to throw it to his comrades for their disposal. Instead he placed it under his arm, saying, with a smile, "No more now, boys; we'll call this gathering adjourned," and walked away.

Excitement of a feverish sort spread through the camp, a few days later, when a story was started that Ashby was wearing the cap at times in his tent, and that some strange power possessed it. Four men said they had seen him put the cap on his head, visor to the front, and that in three minutes it had turned quarter way round, bringing the visor over the right ear and the bullet-hole in the middle of the forehead.

This story confirmed the fears of all who had wished Ashby to give up the grewsome relic, while those who, like himself, professed no belief in supernatural influences, declared of course that he was working a joke.

While the sincerity of the four men who had seen the cap turn on Jim's head was unquestioned, many made enquiries directly of him. To all he answered that the cap did revolve as stated, and furthermore, that it had done so a good many times. To doubters he expressed a willingness for investigation, and suggested that the next day, at noon, he would meet all who desired to be there in the company street, and would then put the cap on, and let others do so if they wished, and all could examine it.

Five hundred men were gathered when Ashby appeared next day. He wore his Confederate hat, but held so all could see it the now famous Haunted Cap. He mounted a box and looked slowly over his audience. Excepting a dozen or so in front, every man looked as if a death lottery were to be drawn, and he feared his name would be announced. No one moved, and all were silent, with fear and awe written on their faces. In contrast was Ashby's happy smile, and the dozen men at his feet were smiling also. To them this was an entertainment—a diversion from the monotony of life in camp—while to the others it seemed reckless toying with a dread mystery, a bold defiance of powers unknown.

Ashby raised the cap to the level of his shoulder, saying:

"Boys, you have all heard of the strange freaks of this Yankee cap. I want you to see for yourselves. When I put it on it turns around to just the place it was when the poor fellow who wore it got killed. Perhaps some of you would like to look it over." And he tossed it into the crowd.

A screeching shell would not have created so much commotion. No one took his eyes off the quick-sailing cap, and there was a stampede in the line of its flight. With all the dodging, the cap struck a man full in the breast. He leaped away with an oath, and all near drew aside, leaving the cap on the ground in the midst of a wide circle of frightened soldiers. Ashby laughed aloud.

One of the sceptics made his way through the crowd, picked up the cap and returned with it to the little group around the speaker. Each in turn and collectively, they examined it with much care and deliberation. In a half-disappointed way they offered it to those outside, who shook their heads, and it was then passed back to Ashby, who watched the proceedings with an air of indifference.

Ashby gave the cap a vigorous shake, and then slowly put it on his head, using both hands, holding the visor in his left, while he smoothed down his hair with the right, drawing the latter out as the cap settled down. The broken half of the visor hung down over his right eye, giving him an uncanny, one-eyed look.

"Now, watch!" he exclaimed, putting his hands behind him.

They did watch, and many of them wished for months after that they had not. No one could perceive any motion, either of Ashby or of the cap, but at the end of a minute it was clearly perceptible to all that the cap had moved toward the right at least an inch.

In less than another minute, Ashby's right eye coming into view and the bullet-hole beginning to transit the white skin of his forehead sent a chill through the blood of the watchers. Every man was breathless. Had a shriek or scream or any sudden utterance of alarm been made, or even a strong gust of wind swept by, they would have fallen in fright or rushed away in panic.

The cap still moved. No one saw the motion any more than one sitting across the room can see the steady move of the minute hand of a clock. Yet in three minutes the visor of the cap was over Ashby's right ear, and the bullet-hole in the centre of his forehead, and there it stopped.

Ashby removed the cap, saying: "Boys, shall we try it again?" The moving away of the spectators gave him a negative answer. Those veterans of many battles were afraid.

As he jumped to the ground, one of the men standing near asked to look at the cap again. Ashby at once handed it out, and the soldiers who had carefully examined it before scrutinized it critically. It was evident from their speech and manner that they did not detect any sign of human agency in the cap's movement.

When they banded it back Ashby remarked:

"The boys are worrying about something they can't account for. Why should a full-grown man be afraid of a thing because it's strange, or has some merely guessed-at connection with some other existence?"

"That's all right, Jim," said the sergeant of his company. "We men right here are no more afraid of that cap than you are. I'd be willing to wear it every day, and let it whirl, but the boys are different. They are afeard it'll bring you harm, and they can't spare you right now. So why not put the thing out of sight, and stop the worrying?"

"Oh, I'm not going to plague them any more," replied Ashby, putting the cap under his coat, "perhaps they'll never see this cap again."

Soon camp was broken, and Lee's army took up its march toward Pennsylvania, and the cap was only a memory among Ashby's comrades. Its story spread, however, and in distant camps the "Haunted Cap" afforded food for thought and tale. As the surface of a pond becomes smooth again where a stone has fallen, while around and beyond extend widening rings of disturbance, so the career of the cap seemed to end in the camp of its origin, while the legends connected with it grew and expanded in regions more remote. As told by the soldiers fifty miles away, the ghostly form of a Federal private was seen standing on the box with Ashby, while a spirit hand was plainly observed turning the cap on his head.

A little after noon on the first of July, part of Ewell's corps entered on the plain north of the village of Gettysburg, and was at once engaged with the Eleventh Corps of the Army of the Potomac. On the ridge to the right had been close, desperate fighting since early morn. There and on the plain the Union line now gave way, for it could not withstand the new enemy from the north, and, a little later, the approach of Gordon from the east. The Federal troops did not yield a step, however, without a struggle, and the combat was sharp and constant.

Ashby was in his place, and his cool, deliberate fire indicated that he was increasing the casualties of the enemy. Just as the entire Union line was forced back to the houses and streets of Gettysburg, he took from under his coat the "Haunted Cap" and put it on, the visor over his right ear and the bullet-hole in the middle of his forehead.

The men about him were aghast. It was no time or place for entreaty or objection, and without speech, they shrank away and left him fighting alone. But he did not appear to miss the strengthening touch of comrades; his rifle spoke as frequently as before, and he did not lag in the advance.

As the soldiers in blue surged through the village streets to reach the safety of the hills beyond, their retreat covered by a few regiments holding the outer buildings and checking our rapid advance, Ashby, still somewhat apart from his fellows, staggered a little, and then fell on his face. All the men near were at once about him. He was dead, shot in the forehead, and the bullet had gone through the hole in the cap-band.

He had made the supreme test and had failed. He had not conquered or dispelled the superstition of his comrades. Their fears had been realized. The evil they dreaded had befallen.

When Ashby was buried his fellow-soldiers nearly came to blows over his grave. No one wished the cap buried with him, but some wanted it buried by itself—and buried deep. Only one, a man who had not shared the prevailing fear at the exhibition in camp, wished to save it, and after much persuasion was allowed to take it, making solemn promise that no one should see it or be troubled with it in any way.

While on our retreat to the Potomac, I learned of an officer of Ashby's regiment of the "Haunted Cap." I sought out the soldier who had it, and became its possessor, together with its story, as you have heard it.

It was not till long afterward, when arranging this collection of relics, that I gave the matter another serious thought. Then one evening, sitting here in the firelight, I mentally reviewed the strange tale of the "Haunted Cap," watching it as it hung on that nail, almost expecting to see it turn as it had done on Ashby's head. That there *was* a mystery connected with it I felt sure, and I resolved to solve it if possible.

I accordingly wrote to friends and army associates in Georgia, letters of the same tenor, enquiring into the antecedents of Ashby, and to officers of the 119th New York, with a view of establishing, if possible, the identity of the private shot by Ashby at Chancellorsville, but making no allusion in either set to the cap legend.

In due time I received numerous letters from different parts of Georgia, where my enquiries had been transmitted, but only two or three were from persons who knew Ashby. All the others gave marvellous versions of the "Haunted Cap," but no two alike. One said:

"Jeems Ashby wore a cap like what we used on the guns, only larger, and one day it egsploded and bleu him into a milyon pieces." And another averred: "He stole a cap and it spun round on his head like a top till he got dizzy and died. That's the truth. There was sperits in it."

But one letter gave me all the facts I could ask for—the birthplace of Ashby, his parentage, where he attended school, his apprenticeship to a working jeweller in Atlanta, and that he was considered one of the most skilful in that line when he enlisted.

This information came the very day I made a discovery. I was examining the cap inch by inch, holding it by this wooden button on the inside, when the button seemed to part or move between my thumb and finger, but when I let go of it, it looked as solid as before. I could see no mark or break indicating a separation, and after running the point of my knife over every part, I was about to lay it aside, when it occurred to me to twist the top. I held it firmly by the bottom edge, and then twisted my thumb and finger over the top part, first to the left, as if to unscrew it, and then, as it did not yield, to the right. The top part came suddenly off, but, my finger slipping, flew back with a little snap. I did it again with more care—as I do now—and you see the button is in two pieces connected by a fine wire spring which, fully drawn, allows the top to be removed an inch. Furthermore, the spring is so adjusted that when the top closes against the bottom it turns to the left into a socket from which it cannot be removed except by a turn to the right. Observe, too, that one side of the top is thinner than the other and that the spring is fastened nearer that edge than the centre.

I spent the rest of the day experimenting. I made this band to pass over my head and fasten to this other around my neck. On the top of the band is a button which is gashed on the under side.

Putting the cap on with my left hand, with the right, while making the motion of smoothing down my hair, I disengage the spring button and insert the thin lower edge of its top into the gash of the button on the band. The slightest movement of eyebrows or scalp causes the spring to turn the cap until the visor is over my right ear, and the bullet hole in the centre of the forehead.

The Colonel placed the cap upon his head as he spoke, and went through the motions described, while his guest watched with interest the working of the ingenious contrivance.

"That seemed a long three minutes," he continued, as he finished the demonstration, "but it required hours of practice to get the results you have seen."

"It only remained for me to find out how Ashby had contrived to fasten the button to the top of his head. You will remember I told you that at Malvern Hill a bullet cut a furrow across his crown. I learned, after much inquiry, that the course of the bullet was marked by a slight ridge, with little bunches or hummocks. All was clear now. Ashby had so manipulated one of these bunches that he could insert the top of the button under it."

When the Colonel uttered the host word of this remarkable story, his Northern visitor grasped his hand, saying:

"Colonel Pearson, your common-sense and persistence solved this seeming mystery in the simplest manner. The cap remains just what Ashby said it was—so much cloth, with a hole through it."

"Yes, perhaps so," replied the Colonel, slowly, "perhaps so, but the fact remains that Ashby received his death through that bullet-hole. A mere coincidence, perhaps? Well—perhaps. I wish you would read this letter, though, and think about it. I did not receive it till I thought I had dispelled all the mystery."

The letter was from a private of the 119th New York, and was as follows:

Col. W. A. Pearson,

Dear Sir:—Your letter of enquiry has reached me, after traveling pretty nearly over all New York State. You know the soldiers are pretty well scattered now.

I can give particulars of only one comrade killed at Chancellorsville. His name was Gustav Kling, and he was next to me in the firing line, and next to him was Carl Wirth. When Jackson stampeded our right we tried to hold our line, but it was no use. Wirth and I had stopped firing and had begun to retire, when Gustav said, “There’s a good fighting rebel, and he’s a good shot. I’ve been watching him. But I’m a fair shot, too.” With that he took careful aim, and we watched, but the rebel he didn’t fall, but at once leveled his rifle and Gustav fell dead.

I can see now just how he looked. His cap was turned round one side. He had broken the visor, and it hung down over his eyes, so he pushed It round to the right.

After the battle I found his body and helped bury it. He was shot through the forehead.

Now I am going to tell you something that Carl Wirth and I have talked over a hundred times, or more, but have never mentioned to others:

When we were pushed back to the houses, at Gettysburg, the lines were pretty close together, and a little ahead of Dole’s brigade was a fine-looking Georgian, firing coolly, and evidently picking his men. I turned to Wirth, and said, “There’s the fellow who shot Gustav.” We both raised to fire, but before we could there was a report right between us, and the Georgian fell. And it was just like the report of the rifle Gustav carried when he was killed. It made a peculiar noise, different from ours, and we knew the sound well. It seemed to burn powder slower, and gave a sort of whistle or shriek, more like a rocket than the usual crack, and it was a most unearthly sound.

It was that familiar rifle shriek that sounded in our ears at Gettysburg when the man fell. Carl and I looked at each other. He was whiter than a sheet, and I felt I was the same.

We turned and ran. But then, I am not superstitious—and there were other reasons for running.

Colonel Pearson’s guest stopped reading at this point, and began to think, as requested by the Colonel. And he is still thinking.

How It Happened

Arthur Conan Doyle

She was a writing medium. This is what she wrote:—

I can remember some things upon that evening most distinctly, and others are like some vague, broken dreams. That is what makes it so difficult to tell a connected story. I have no idea now what it was that had taken me to London and brought me back so late. It just merges into all my other visits to London. But from the time that I got out at the little country station everything is extraordinarily clear. I can live it again—every instant of it.

I remember so well walking down the platform and looking at the illuminated clock at the end which told me that it was half-past eleven. I remember also my wondering whether I could get home before midnight. Then I remember the big motor, with its glaring headlights and glitter of polished brass, waiting for me outside. It was my new thirty-horse-power Robur, which had only been delivered that day. I remember also asking Perkins, my chauffeur, how she had gone, and his saying that he thought she was excellent.

"I'll try her myself," said I, and I climbed into the driver's seat.

"The gears are not the same," said he. "Perhaps, sir, I had better drive."

"No; I should like to try her," said I.

And so we started on the five-mile drive for home.

My old car had the gears as they used always to be in notches on a bar. In this car you passed the gear-lever through a gate to get on the higher ones. It was not difficult to master, and soon I thought that I understood it. It was foolish, no doubt, to begin to learn a new system in the dark, but one often does foolish things, and one has not always to pay the full price for them. I got along very well until I came to Claystall Hill. It is one of the worst hills in England, a mile and a half long and one in six in places, with three fairly sharp curves. My park gates stand at the very foot of it upon the main London road.

We were just over the brow of this hill, where the grade is steepest, when the trouble began. I had been on the top speed, and wanted to get her on the free; but she stuck between gears, and I had to get her back on the top again. By this time she was going at a great rate, so I clapped on both brakes, and one after the other they gave way. I didn't mind so much when I felt my footbrake snap, but when I put all my weight on my side-brake, and the lever clanged to its full limit without a catch, it brought a cold sweat out of me. By this time we were fairly tearing down the slope. The lights were brilliant, and I brought her round the first curve all right. Then we did the second one, though it was a close shave for the ditch. There was a mile of straight then with the third curve beneath it, and after that the gate of the park. If I could shoot into that harbour all would be well, for the slope up to the house would bring her to a stand.

Perkins behaved splendidly. I should like that to be known. He was perfectly cool and alert. I had thought at the very beginning of taking the bank, and he read my intention.

"I wouldn't do it, sir," said he. "At this pace, it must go over and we should have it on the top of us."

Of course he was right. He got to the electric switch and had it off, so we were in the free; but we were still running at a fearful pace. He laid his hands on the wheel.

"I'll keep her steady," said he, "if you care to jump and chance it. We can never get round that curve. Better jump, sir."

"No," said I; "I'll stick it out. You can jump if you like."

"I'll stick it with you, sir," said he.

If it had been the old car I should have jammed the gear-lever into the reverse, and seen what would happen. I expect she would have stripped her gears or smashed up somehow, but it would have been a chance. As it was, I was helpless. Perkins tried to climb across, but you couldn't do it going at that pace. The wheels were whirring like a high wind and the big body creaking and groaning with the strain. But the lights were brilliant, and one could steer to an inch. I remember thinking what an awful and yet majestic sight we should appear to any one who met us. It was a narrow road, and we were just a great, roaring, golden death to any one who came in our path.

We got round the corner with one wheel three feet high upon the bank. I thought we were surely over, but after staggering for a moment she righted and darted onwards. That was the third corner and the last one. There was only the park gate now. It was facing us, but, as luck would have it, not facing us directly. It was about twenty yards to the left up the main road into which we ran. Perhaps I could have done it, but I expect that the steering-gear had been jarred when we ran on the bank. The wheel did not turn easily. We shot out of the lane. I saw the open gate on the left. I whirled round my wheel with all the strength of my wrists. Perkins and I threw our bodies across, and then the next instant, going at fifty miles an hour, my right front wheel struck full on the right-hand pillar of my own gate. I heard the crash, I was conscious of flying through the air, and then—and then—!

When I became aware of my own existence once more I was among some brushwood in the shadow of the oaks upon the lodge side of the drive. A man was standing beside me. I imagined at first that it was Perkins, but when I looked again I saw that it was Stanley, a man whom I had known at college some years before, and for whom I had a really genuine affection. There was always something peculiarly sympathetic to me in Stanley's personality; and I was proud to think that I had some similar influence upon him. At the present moment I was surprised to see him, but I was like a man in a dream, giddy and shaken and quite prepared to take things as I found them without questioning them.

"What a smash!" I said. "Good Lord, what an awful smash!"

He nodded his head, and even in the gloom I could see that he was smiling the gentle, wistful smile which I connected with him.

I was quite unable to move. Indeed, I had not any desire to try to move. But my senses were exceedingly alert. I saw the wreck of the motor lit up by the moving lanterns. I saw the little group of people and heard the hushed voices. There were the lodge-keeper and his wife, and one or two more. They were taking no notice of me, but were very busy round the car. Then suddenly I heard a cry of pain.

"The weight is on him. Lift it easy," cried a voice.

"It's only my leg!" said another one, which I recognised as Perkins's. "Where's master?" he cried.

"Here I am," I answered, but they did not seem to hear me. They were all bending over something which lay in front of the car.

Stanley laid his hand upon my shoulder, and his touch was inexpressibly soothing. I felt light and happy, in spite of all.

"No pain, of course?" said he.

"None," said I.

"There never is," said he.

And then suddenly a wave of amazement passed over me. Stanley! Stanley! Why, Stanley had surely died of enteric at Bloemfontein in the Boer War!

"Stanley!" I cried, and the words seemed to choke my throat—"Stanley, you are dead."

He looked at me with the same old gentle, wistful smile.

"So are you," he answered.

In the Court of the Dragon

Robert W. Chambers

> Oh, thou who burn'st in heart for those who burn
> In Hell, whose fires thyself shall feed in turn;
> How long be crying—"Mercy on them, God!"
> Why, who art thou to teach and He to learn?

In the Church of St. Barnabé vespers were over; the clergy left the altar; the little choir-boys flocked across the chancel and settled in the stalls. A Suisse in rich uniform marched down the south aisle, sounding his staff at every fourth step on the stone pavement; behind him came that eloquent preacher and good man, Monseigneur C——.

My chair was near the chancel rail. I now turned toward the west end of the church. The other people between the altar and the pulpit turned too. There was a little scraping and rustling while the congregation seated itself again; the preacher mounted the pulpit stairs, and the organ voluntary ceased.

I had always found the organ-playing at St. Barnabé highly interesting. Learned and scientific it was, too much so for my small knowledge, but expressing a vivid if cold intelligence. Moreover, it possessed the French quality of taste: taste reigned supreme, self-controlled, dignified and reticent.

To-day, however, from the first chord I had felt a change for the worse, a sinister change. During vespers it had been chiefly the chancel organ which supported the beautiful choir, but now and again, quite wantonly as it seemed, from the west gallery where the great organ stands, a heavy hand had struck across the church at the serene peace of those clear voices. It was something more than harsh and dissonant, and it betrayed no lack of skill. As it recurred again and again, it set me thinking of what my architect's books say about the custom in early times to consecrate the choir as soon as it was built, and that the nave, being finished sometimes half a century later, often did not get any blessing at all: I wondered idly if that had been the case at St. Barnabé, and whether something not usually supposed to be at home in a Christian church might have entered undetected and taken possession of the west gallery. I had read of such things happening, too, but not in works on architecture.

Then I remembered that St. Barnabé was not much more than a hundred years old, and smiled at the incongruous association of mediaeval superstitions with that cheerful little piece of eighteenth-century rococo.

But now vespers were over, and there should have followed a few quiet chords, fit to accompany meditation, while we waited for the sermon. Instead of that, the discord at the lower end of the church broke out with the departure of the clergy, as if now nothing could control it.

I belong to those children of an older and simpler generation who do not love to seek for psychological subtleties in art; and I have ever refused to find in music anything more than melody and harmony, but I felt that in the labyrinth of sounds now issuing from that instrument there was something being hunted. Up and down the pedals chased him, while the manuals blared approval. Poor devil! whoever he was, there seemed small hope of escape!

My nervous annoyance changed to anger. Who was doing this? How dare he play like that in the midst of divine service? I glanced at the people near me: not one appeared to be in the least disturbed. The placid brows of the kneeling nuns, still turned towards the altar, lost none of their devout abstraction under the pale shadow of their white head-dress. The fashionable lady beside me was looking expectantly at Monseigneur C——. For all her face betrayed, the organ might have been singing an Ave Maria.

But now, at last, the preacher had made the sign of the cross, and commanded silence. I turned to him gladly. Thus far I had not found the rest I had counted on when I entered St. Barnabé that afternoon.

I was worn out by three nights of physical suffering and mental trouble: the last had been the worst, and it was an exhausted body, and a mind benumbed and yet acutely sensitive, which I had brought to my favourite church for healing. For I had been reading "The King in Yellow."

"The sun ariseth; they gather themselves together and lay them down in their dens." Monseigneur C—— delivered his text in a calm voice, glancing quietly over the congregation. My eyes turned, I knew not why, toward the lower end of the church. The organist was coming from behind his pipes, and passing along the gallery on his way out, I saw him disappear by a small door that leads to some stairs which descend directly to the street. He was a slender man, and his face was as white as his coat was black. "Good riddance!" I thought, "with your wicked music! I hope your assistant will play the closing voluntary."

With a feeling of relief, with a deep, calm feeling of relief, I turned back to the mild face in the pulpit and settled myself to listen. Here, at last, was the ease of mind I longed for.

"My children," said the preacher, "one truth the human soul finds hardest of all to learn; it has nothing to fear. It can never be made to see that nothing can really harm it."

"Curious doctrine!" I thought, "for a Catholic priest. Let us see how he will reconcile that with the Fathers."

"Nothing can really harm the soul," he went on, in, his coolest, clearest tones, "because—"

But I never heard the rest; my eye left his face, I knew not for what reason, and sought the lower end of the church. The same man was coming out from behind the organ, and was passing along the gallery *the same way*. But there had not been time for him to return, and if he had returned, I must have seen him. I felt a faint chill, and my heart sank; and yet, his going and coming were no affair of mine. I looked at him: I could not look away from his black figure and his white face. When he was exactly opposite to me, he turned and sent across the church straight into my eyes, a look of hate, intense and deadly: I have never seen any other like it; would to God I might never see it again! Then he disappeared by the same door through which I had watched him depart less than sixty seconds before.

I sat and tried to collect my thoughts. My first sensation was like that of a very young child badly hurt, when it catches its breath before crying out.

To suddenly find myself the object of such hatred was exquisitely painful: and this man was an utter stranger. Why should he hate me so? Me, whom he had never seen before? For the moment all other sensation was merged in this one pang: even fear was subordinate to grief, and for that moment I never doubted; but in the next I began to reason, and a sense of the incongruous came to my aid.

As I have said, St. Barnabé is a modern church. It is small and well lighted; one sees all over it almost at a glance. The organ gallery gets a strong white light from a row of long windows in the clere-story, which have not even colored glass.

The pulpit being in the middle of the church, it followed that, when I was turned toward it, whatever moved at the west end could not fail to attract my eye. When the organist passed it was no wonder that I saw him: I had simply miscalculated the interval between his first and his second passing. He had come in that last time by the other side-door. As for the look which had so upset me, there had been no such thing, and I was a nervous fool.

I looked about. This was a likely place to harbour supernatural horrors! That clear-cut, reasonable face of Monseigneur C——, his collected manner and easy, graceful gestures, were they not just a little discouraging to the notion of a gruesome mystery? I glanced above his head, and almost laughed. That flyaway lady supporting one corner of the pulpit canopy, which looked like a fringed damask table-cloth in a high wind, at the first attempt of a basilisk to pose up there in the organ loft, she would point her gold trumpet at him, and puff him out of existence! I laughed to myself over this conceit, which, at the time, I thought very amusing, and sat and chaffed myself and everything else, from the old harpy outside the railing, who had made me pay ten centimes for my chair, before she would let me in (she was more like a basilisk, I told myself, than was my organist with the anaemic complexion): from that grim old dame, to, yes, alas! Monseigneur C—— himself. For all devoutness had fled. I had never yet done such a thing in my life, but now I felt a desire to mock.

As for the sermon, I could not hear a word of it for the jingle in my ears of

> The skirts of St. Paul has reached.
> Having preached us those six Lent lectures,
> More unctuous than ever he preached:

keeping time to the most fantastic and irreverent thoughts.

It was no use to sit there any longer: I must get out of doors and shake myself free from this hateful mood. I knew the rudeness I was committing, but still I rose and left the church.

A spring sun was shining on the Rue St. Honoré, as I ran down the church steps. On one corner stood a barrow full of yellow jonquils, pale violets from the Riviera, dark Russian violets, and white Roman hyacinths in a golden cloud of mimosa. The street was full of Sunday pleasure-seekers. I swung my cane and laughed with the rest. Some one overtook and passed me. He never turned, but there was the same deadly malignity in his white profile that there had been in his eyes. I watched him as long as I could see him. His lithe back expressed the same menace; every step that carried him away from me seemed to bear him on some errand connected with my destruction.

I was creeping along, my feet almost refusing to move. There began to dawn in me a sense of responsibility for something long forgotten. It began to seem as if I deserved that which he threatened: it reached a long way back—a long, long way back. It had lain dormant all these years: it was there, though, and presently it would rise and confront me. But I would try to escape; and I stumbled as best I could into the rue de Rivoli, across the Place de la Concorde and on to the Quai. I looked with sick eyes upon the sun, shining through the white foam of the fountain, pouring over the backs of the dusky bronze river-gods, on the far-away Arc, a structure of amethyst mist, on the countless vistas of gray stems and bare branches faintly green. Then I saw him again coming down one of the chestnut alleys of the Cours la Reine.

I left the river side, plunged blindly across to the Champs Elysées and turned toward the Arc. The setting sun was sending its rays along the green sward of the Rond-point: in the full glow he sat on a bench, children and young mothers all about him. He was nothing but a Sunday lounger, like the others, like myself. I said the words almost aloud, and all the while I gazed on the malignant hatred of his face. But he was not looking at me. I crept past and dragged my leaden feet up the Avenue. I knew that every time I met him brought him nearer to the accomplishment of his purpose and my fate. And still I tried to save myself.

The last rays of sunset were pouring through the great Arc. I passed under it, and met him face to face. I had left him far down the Champs Elysées, and yet he came in with a stream of people who were returning from the Bois de Boulogne. He came so close that he brushed me. His slender frame felt like iron inside its loose black covering. He showed no signs of haste, nor of fatigue, nor of any human feeling. His whole being expressed one thing: the will, and the power to work me evil.

In anguish I watched him where he went down the broad crowded Avenue, that was all flashing with wheels and the trappings of horses and the helmets of the Garde Republicaine.

He was soon lost to sight; then I turned and fled. Into the Bois, and far out beyond it—I know not where I went, but after a long while as it seemed to me, night had fallen, and I found myself sitting at a table before a small café. I had wandered back into the Bois. It was hours now since I had seen him. Physical fatigue and mental suffering had left me no power to think or feel. I was tired, so tired! I longed to hide away in my own den. I resolved to go home. But that was a long way off.

I live in the Court of the Dragon, a narrow passage that leads from the rue de Rennes to the rue du Dragon.

It is an "Impasse"; traversable only for foot passengers. Over the entrance on the rue de Rennes is a balcony, supported by an iron dragon. Within the court tall old houses rise on either side, and close the ends that give on the two streets. Huge gates, swung back during the day into the walls of the deep archways, close this court, after midnight, and one must enter then by ringing at certain small doors on the side. The sunken pavement collects unsavory pools. Steep stairways pitch down to doors that open on the court. The ground floors are occupied by shops of second-hand dealers, and by iron workers. All day long the place rings with the clink of hammers and the clang of metal bars.

Unsavory as it is below, there is cheerfulness, and comfort, and hard, honest work above.

Five flights up are the ateliers of architects and painters, and the hiding-places of middle-aged students like myself who want to live alone. When I first came here to live I was young, and not alone.

I had to walk a while before any conveyance appeared, but at last, when I had almost reached the Arc de Triomphe again, an empty cab came along and I took it.

From the Arc to the rue de Rennes is a drive of more than half an hour, especially when one is conveyed by a tired cab horse that has been at the mercy of Sunday fête makers.

There had been time before I passed under the Dragon's wings to meet my enemy over and over again, but I never saw him once, and now refuge was close at hand.

Before the wide gateway a small mob of children were playing. Our concierge and his wife walked among them, with their black poodle, keeping order; some couples were waltzing on the side-walk. I returned their greetings and hurried in.

All the inhabitants of the court had trooped out into the street. The place was quite deserted, lighted by a few lanterns hung high up, in which the gas burned dimly.

My apartment was at the top of a house, halfway down the court, reached by a staircase that descended almost into the street, with only a bit of passage-way intervening, I set my foot on the threshold of the open door, the friendly old ruinous stairs rose before me, leading up to rest and shelter. Looking back over my right shoulder, I saw *him,* ten paces off. He must have entered the court with me.

He was coming straight on, neither slowly, nor swiftly, but straight on to me. And now he was looking at me. For the first time since our eyes encountered across the church they met now again, and I knew that the time had come.

Retreating backward, down the court, I faced him. I meant to escape by the entrance on the Rue du Dragon. His eyes told me that I never should escape.

It seemed ages while we were going, I retreating, he advancing, down the court in perfect silence; but at last I felt the shadow of the archway, and the next step brought me within it. I had meant to turn here and spring through into the street. But the shadow was not that of an archway; it was that of a vault. The great doors on the rue du Dragon were closed. I felt this by the blackness which surrounded me, and at the same instant I read it in his face. How his face gleamed in the darkness, drawing swiftly nearer! The deep vaults, the huge closed doors, their cold iron clamps were all on his side. The thing which he had threatened had arrived: it gathered and bore down on me from the fathomless shadows; the point from which it would strike was his infernal eyes. Hopeless, I set my back against the barred doors and defied him.

There was a scraping of chairs on the stone floor, and a rustling as the congregation rose. I could hear the Suisse's staff in the south aisle, preceding Monseigneur C—— to the sacristy.

The kneeling nuns, roused from their devout abstraction, made their reverence and went away. The fashionable lady, my neighbor, rose also, with graceful reserve. As she departed her glance just flitted over my face in disapproval.

Half dead, or so it seemed to me, yet intensely alive to every trifle, I sat among the leisurely moving crowd, then rose too and went toward the door.

I had slept through the sermon. Had I slept through the sermon? I looked up and saw him passing along the gallery to his place. Only his side I saw; the thin bent arm in its black covering looked like one of those devilish, nameless instruments which lie in the disused torture-chambers of mediaeval castles.

But I had escaped him, though his eyes had said I should not. *Had* I escaped him? That which gave him the power over me came back out of oblivion, where I had hoped to keep it. For I knew him now. Death and the awful abode of lost souls, whither my weakness long ago had sent him—they had changed him for every other eye, but not for mine. I had recognized him almost from the first; I had never doubted what he was come to do; and now I knew while my body sat safe in the cheerful little church, he had been hunting my soul in the Court of the Dragon.

I crept to the door; the organ broke out overhead with a blare. A dazzling light filled the church, blotting the altar from my eyes. The people faded away, the arches, the vaulted roof vanished. I raised my seared eyes to the fathomless glare, and I saw the black stars hanging in the heavens: and the wet winds from the lake of Hali chilled my face.

And now, far away, over leagues of tossing cloud-waves, I saw the moon dripping with spray; and beyond, the towers of Carcosa rose behind the moon.

Death and the awful abode of lost souls, whither my weakness long ago had sent him, had changed him for every other eye but mine. And now I heard *his voice*, rising, swelling, thundering through the flaring light, and as I fell, the radiance increasing, increasing, poured over me in waves of flame. Then I sank into the depths, and I heard the King in Yellow whispering to my soul: "It is a fearful thing to fall into the hands of the living God!"

The Invisible Eye

Erckmann-Chatrian

I

It was about this time, said Christian, poor as a church rat, I had taken shelter in the roof-loft of an old house in the rue des Minnesängers, at Nuremberg.

I had nestled myself in an angle of the roof. The slates served me for walls, and the roof-tree for a ceiling: I had to walk over my straw mattress to reach the window; but this window commanded a magnificent view, for it overlooked both city and country beyond. From it I watched cats gravely walking along the gutter, storks with beak-loads of frogs, carrying food to their devouring young ones; pigeons with their tails spread fan-like, whirling above the depths of the streets below.

In the evening, when the church-bells called the people to the *Angelus*, resting my elbows on the edge of the roof, I listened to their melancholy song, and watched the windows lit up one by one; the good townsmen, smoking their pipes on the pavement; the young girls, in short red petticoats, and with their pitchers under their arms, laughing and chatting about the fountain of Saint Sébalt. Insensibly all these objects faded from my view; the bats came abroad in the dim air, and I lay me down to sleep in the midst of the soft quietude.

The old second-hand dealer, Toubec, knew the road up to my little den as well as I knew it myself, and was not afraid of climbing the ladder. Every week his goat's head, surmounted by a rusty wig, pushed up the trap-door, his fingers clutched the edge of the floor, and in a noisy tone he cried:

"Well, well, Master Christian, have we anything new?"

To which I answered:

"Come in: why the deuce don't you come in? I'm just finishing a little landscape, and want to have your opinion of it."

Then his long thin spine lengthened itself out, until his head touched the roof; and the old fellow laughed silently.

I must do justice to Toubec: he never bargained with me. He bought all my pictures at 15 florins apiece, one with the other, and sold them again at 40. He was an honest Jew.

This kind of existence was beginning to please me, and I was every day finding in it some new charm, when the good city of Nuremberg was agitated by a strange and mysterious event.

Not far from my garret-window, a little to the left, rose the *auberge* of the *Bœuf-gras,* an old public-house much frequented by the country-people. Three or four waggons, loaded with sacks or casks, were always standing before its doors; for before going to market, the countrymen used to take their nip of wine there.

The gable of this *auberge* was conspicuous for the peculiarity of its form: it was very narrow, sharply pointed, and its edges were cut like the teeth of a saw; grotesque carvings ornamented the cornices and framework of its windows. But what was most remarkable was that the house which faced it reproduced exactly the same carvings and ornaments; every detail had been minutely copied, even to the support of the signboard, with its iron volutes and spirals.

It might have been said that those two ancient buildings reflected one another; only that, behind the *auberge,* grew a tall oak, the dark foliage of which served to bring into bold relief the forms of the roof, while the neighbouring house stood bare against the sky. For the rest, the *auberge* was as noisy and animated as the other house was silent. On the one side was to be seen, going in and coming out, an endless crowd of drinkers, singing, stumbling, cracking their whips; over the other, solitude reigned.

Once or twice a day, at most, the heavy door of the silent house opened to give egress to a little old woman, her back bent into a half-circle, her chin long and pointed, her dress clinging to her limbs, an enormous basket under her arm, and one hand tightly clutched upon her chest.

The physiognomy of this old woman had struck me more than once; her little green eyes, her skinny pinched-up nose, the large flower-pattern on her shawl, dating back a hundred years, at least, the smile that wrinkled her cheeks till they looked like two cockades, and the lace trimming of her bonnet hanging down upon her eyebrows,—all this appeared to me strange, interested me, and made me strongly desire to learn who this old woman was, and what she did in her great lonely house.

I had imagined her as passing there an existence of good works and pious meditation. But one day, when I had stopped in the street to look at her, she turned sharply round and darted at me a look, the horrible expression of which I know not how to describe, and made three or four hideous grimaces at me; then dropping again her doddering head, she drew her large shawl about her, the ends of which trained after her on the ground, and slowly entered her heavy door, behind which I saw her disappear.

"That's an old mad-woman," I said to myself; "a malicious cunning old mad-woman! I ought not to have allowed myself to be so interested in her. But I'll try and recall her abominable grimace—Toubec will give me 15 florins for it willingly."

This way of treating the matter was far from satisfying my mind, however. The old woman's horrible glance pursued me everywhere; and more than once, while scaling the perpendicular ladder of my lodging-hole, feeling my clothes caught in a nail, I trembled from head to foot, believing that the old woman had seized me by the tails of my coat for the purpose of pulling me down backwards.

Toubec, to whom I related the story, far from laughing at it, received it with a serious air.

"Master Christian," he said, "if the old woman means you harm, take care; her teeth are small, sharp-pointed, and wonderfully white, which is not natural at her age. She has the Evil Eye! Children run away at her approach, and the people of Nuremberg call her Flédermausse!"[1]

I admired, generally, the Jew's clear-sightedness, and what he had told me made me reflect a good deal; but at the end of a few weeks, having often met Flédermausse without harmful consequences, my fears died away and I thought no more of her.

Now, it happened one night, when I was lying sound asleep, I was awaked by a strange harmony. It was a kind of vibration, so soft, so melodious, that the murmur of a light breeze through foliage can convey but a feeble idea of its gentle nature. For a long time I listened to it, my eyes wide open, and holding my breath the better to hear it.

At length, looking towards the window, I saw two wings beating against the glass. I thought, at first, that it was a bat imprisoned in my chamber; but the moon was shining clearly, and the wings of a magnificent night-moth, transparent as lace, were designed upon its radiant disc. At times their vibrations were so rapid as to hide them from my view; then, for awhile they would lie in repose, extended on the glass pane, their delicate articulations made visible anew.

This vaporous apparition in the midst of the universal silence, opened my heart to the tenderest emotions; it seemed to me that a sylphid, pitying my solitude, had come to see me; and this idea brought the tears into my eyes.

"Have no fear, gentle captive,—have no fear!" I said to it; "your confidence shall not be betrayed. I will not retain you against your wishes; return to heaven—to liberty!"

1. Flitter-mouse, bat.

And I opened the window.

The night was calm. Thousands of stars glittered in space. For a moment I contemplated this sublime spectacle, and the words of prayer rose naturally to my lips. But judge of my amazement when, lowering my eyes, I saw a man hanging from the iron stanchion supporting the signboard of the *Bœuf-gras;* the hair in disorder, the arms stiff, the legs straightened to a point, and throwing their gigantic shadow the whole length of the street!

The immobility of this figure, in the moonlight, had something frightful in it. I felt my tongue grow icy cold, and my teeth chattered. I was about to utter a cry; but, by what mysterious attraction I know not, my eyes were drawn towards the opposite house, and there I dimly distinguished the old woman, in the midst of the heavy shadow, squatting at her window and contemplating the hanging body with diabolical satisfaction.

I became giddy with terror; my whole strength deserted me, and I fell down in a heap insensible.

I do not know how long I lay unconscious. On coming to myself I found that it was broad day. The mists of night, entering my garret, had dropped their fresh moisture on my hair. Mingled and confused noises rose from the street below. I looked out from my window.

The burgomaster and his secretary were standing at the door of the *Bœuf-gras;* they remained there a long time. People came and went, stopped to look, then passed on their way. Women of the neighbourhood, sweeping in front of their houses, looked from a distance towards the public-house and chatted with each other. At length a stretcher, on which lay a body covered with a woollen cloth, was brought out of the *auberge* and carried away by two men, who passed down the street, children, on their way to school, following them as they went.

Everybody else retired.

The window in front of the house remained open still; a fragment of rope dangled from the iron support of the signboard. I had not dreamed—I had really seen the night-moth on my window-pane—then the suspended body—then the old woman!

In the course of that day Toubec paid me his weekly visit.

"Anything to sell, Master Christian?" he cried, as his big nose became visible above the edge of the floor, which it seemed to shave.

I did not hear him. I was seated on my only chair, my hands upon my knees, my eyes fixed on vacancy before me. Toubec, surprised at my immobility, repeated in a louder tone, "Master Christian!—Master Christian!" then, stepping up to me, tapped me smartly on the shoulder.

"What's the matter?—what's the matter?" he asked.

"Ah! is that you, Toubec?"

"Well, it's pleasant for me to think so! Are you ill?"

"No,—I was thinking."

"What the deuce about?"

"The man who was hung—"

"Aha!" cried the old broker; "you saw the poor fellow, then? What a strange affair! The third in the same place!"

"The third?"

"Yes, the third. I ought to have told you about it before; but there's still time—for there's sure to be a fourth, following the example of the others, the first step only making the difficulty."

This said, Toubec seated himself on a box, struck a light with the flint and steel, lit his pipe and sent out a few puffs of tobacco-smoke with a thoughtful air.

"Good faith!" said he, "I'm not timid; but if anyone were to ask me to sleep in that room, I'd rather go and hang myself somewhere else! Nine or ten months back," he continued, "a wholesale furrier, from Tubingen, put up at the *Bœuf-gras*. He called for supper; ate well, drank well, and was shown up to bed in the room on the third floor they call the 'green chamber'; and the next day they found him hanging from the stanchion of the signboard.

"So much for number one, about which there was nothing to be said. A proper report of the affair was drawn up, and the body of the stranger was buried at the bottom of the garden. But about six weeks afterwards came a soldier from Neustadt; he had his discharge, and was congratulating himself on his return to his village. All the evening he did nothing but empty mugs of wine and talk of his cousin, who was waiting his return to marry him. At last they put him to bed in the green chamber, and, the same night, the watchman passing along the rue des Minnesängers noticed something hanging from the signboard-stanchion. He raised his lantern; it was the soldier, with his discharge-papers in a tin box hanging on his left thigh, and his hands planted smoothly on the outer seams of his trousers, as if he had been on parade!

"It was certainly an extraordinary affair! The burgomaster declared it was the work of the devil. The chamber was examined; they replastered its walls. A notice of the death was sent to Neustadt, in the margin of which the clerk wrote—'Died suddenly of apoplexy.'

"All Nuremberg was indignant against the landlord of the *Bœuf-gras,* and wished to compel him to take down the iron stanchion of his signboard, on the pretext that it put dangerous ideas in peoples' heads. But you may easily imagine that old Nikel Schmidt didn't listen with that ear.

" 'That stanchion was put there by my grandfather,' he said; 'the sign of the *Bœuf-gras* has hung on it, from father to son, for a hundred and fifty years; it does nobody any harm, not even the hay-carts that pass under it, because it's more than thirty feet high up; those who don't like it have only to look another way, and then they won't see it.'

"People's excitement gradually cooled down, and for several months nothing new happened. Unfortunately, a student of Heidelberg, on his way to the University, came to the *Bœuf-gras* and asked for a bed. He was the son of a pastor.

"Who could suppose that the son of a pastor would take into his head the idea of hanging himself to the stanchion of a public-house sign, because a furrier and a soldier had hung themselves there before him? It must be confessed, Master Christian, that the thing was not very probable—it would not have appeared more likely to you than it did tome. Well—"

"Enough! enough!" I cried; "it is a horrible affair. I feel sure there is some frightful mystery at the bottom of it. It is neither the stanchion nor the chamber—"

"You don't mean that you suspect the landlord?—as honest a man as there is in the world, and belonging to one of the oldest families in Nuremberg?"

"No, no! heaven keep me from forming unjust suspicions of any one; but there are abysses into the depths of which one dares not look."

"You are right," said Toubec, astonished at my excited manner; "and we had much better talk of something else. By-the-by, Master Christian, "what about our landscape, the view of the Sainte-Odille?"

The question brought me back to actualities. I showed the broker the picture I had just finished. The business was soon settled between us, and Toubec, thoroughly satisfied, went down the ladder, advising me to think no more of the student of Heidelberg.

I would very willingly have followed the old broker's advice, but when the devil mixes himself in our affairs he is not easily shaken off.

II

In the midst of solitude, all these events came back to my mind with frightful distinctness.

The old woman, I said to myself, is the cause of all this; she alone has planned these crimes, she alone has carried them into execution; but by what means? Has she had recourse to cunning only, or really to the intervention of the invisible powers?

I paced my garret, a voice within me crying, "It is not without purpose that Heaven has permitted you to see Flédermausse watching the agony of her victim; it was not without design that the poor young man's soul came to wake you in the form of a night-moth! No! all this has not been without purpose. Christian, Heaven imposes on you a terrible mission; if you fail to accomplish it, fear yourself that you may fall into the toils of the old woman! Perhaps in this moment she is laying her snares for you in the darkness!"

During several days these frightful images pursued me without cessation. I could not sleep; I found it impossible to work; the brush fell from my hand, and, shocking to confess, I detected myself at times complacently contemplating the dreadful stanchion. At last, one evening, unable any longer to bear this state of mind, I flew down the ladder four steps at a time, and went and hid myself beside Fledermausse's door, for the purpose of discovering her fatal secret.

From that time there was never a day that I was not on the watch, following the old woman like her shadow, never losing sight of her; but she was so cunning, she had so keen a scent, that without even taming her head she discovered that I was behind her, and knew that I was on her track. But nevertheless, she pretended not to see me—went to the market, to the butcher's, like a simple housewife; only she quickened her pace and muttered to herself as she went.

At the end of a month I saw that it would be impossible for me to achieve my purpose by these means, and this conviction filled me with an inexpressible sadness.

"What can I do?" I asked myself. "The old woman has discovered my intentions, and is thoroughly on her guard. I am helpless. The old wretch already thinks she sees me at the end of the cord!"

At length, from repeating to myself again and again the question, "What can I do?" a luminous idea presented itself to my mind.

My chamber overlooked the house of Flédermausse, but it had no dormer window on that side. I carefully raised one of the slates of my roof, and the delight I felt on discovering that by this means I could command a view of the entire antique building can hardly be imagined.

"At last I've got you!" I cried to myself; "you cannot escape me now! From here I shall see everything—the goings and comings, the habits of the weazel in her hole!

You will not suspect this invisible eye—this eye that will surprise the crime at the moment of its inception! Oh, Justice! it moves slowly, but it comes!"

Nothing more sinister than this den could be looked on—a large yard, paved with moss-grown flagstones; a well in one corner, the stagnant water of which was frightful to behold; a wooden staircase leading up to a railed gallery, from the balustrade of which hung the tick of an old mattress; to the left, on the first floor, a drain-stone indicated the kitchen; to the right, the upper windows of the house looked into the street. All was dark, decaying, and dank-looking.

The sun penetrated only for an hour or two during the day the depths of this dismal sty; then the shadows again spread over it—the light fell in lozenge shapes upon the crumbling walls, on the mouldy balcony, on the dull windows. Clouds of motes danced in the golden rays that not a motion of the air came to disturb.

Oh, the whole place was worthy of its mistress!

I had hardly made these reflections when the old woman entered the yard on her return from market. First, I heard her heavy door grate on its hinges, then Flédermausse, with her basket, appeared. She seemed fatigued—out of breath. The border of her bonnet hung down upon her nose as, clutching the wooden rail with one hand, she mounted the stairs.

The heat was suffocating. It was exactly one of those days when insects of every kind—the crickets, the spiders, and the mosquitoes—fill old buildings with their grating noises and subterranean borings.

Flédermausse crossed the gallery slowly, like a ferret that feels itself at home. For more than a quarter of an hour she remained in the kitchen, then came out and turned her mattress-tick, swept the stones a little, on which a few straws had been scattered; at last she raised her head, and with her green eyes carefully scrutinised every portion of the roof from which I was observing her.

By what strange intuition did she suspect anything? I know not; but I gently lowered the uplifted slate into its place, and gave over watching for the rest of that day.

The day following Flédermausse appeared to be reassured. A jagged ray of light fell into the gallery; passing this, she caught a fly, and delicately presented it to a spider established in an angle of the roof.

The spider was so large that, in spite of the distance, I saw it descend round by round of its ladder, then, gliding along one thread, like a drop of venom, seize its prey from the fingers of the dreadful old woman, and remount rapidly. Flédermausse watched it attentively; then her eyes half-closed, she sneezed, and cried to herself in a jocular tone:

"Bless you, beauty!—bless you!"

For six weeks I could discover nothing as to the power of Flédermausse: sometimes I saw her peeling potatoes, sometimes spreading her linen on the balustrade. Sometimes I saw her spin; but she never sang, as old women usually do, their quivering voices going so well with the humming of their spinning-wheel. Silence reigned about her. She had no cat—the favourite company of old maids; not a sparrow ever flew down into her yard; in passing over which the pigeons seemed to hurry their flight. It was as if everything was afraid of her look.

The spider alone took pleasure in her society.

I now look back with wonder at my patience during those long hours of observation; nothing escaped my attention, nothing was indifferent to me at the least sound I lifted my slate. Mine was a boundless curiosity stimulated by an indefinable fear.

Toubec complained.

"What the devil are you doing with your time, Master Christian?" he would say to me. "Formerly, you had something ready for me every week; now, hardly once in a month. Oh, you painters! people may well say, 'Idle as a painter!' As soon as they have a few kreutzer before them, they put their hands in their pockets and go to sleep!"

I myself was beginning to lose courage. With all my watching and spying, I had discovered nothing extraordinary. I was inclining to think that the old woman might not be so dangerous after all—that I had been wrong, perhaps, to suspect her. In short, I tried to find excuses for her. But one fine evening while, with my eye to the opening in the roof, I was giving myself up to these charitable reflections, the scene abruptly changed.

Flédermausse passed along her gallery with the swiftness of a flash of light. She was no longer herself: she was erect, her jaws knit, her look fixed, her neck extended; she moved with long strides, her grey hair streaming behind her.

"Oh, oh!" I said to myself, "something is going on—attention!"

But the shadows of night descended on the big house, the noises of the town died out, and all became silent. I was about to seek my bed when, happening to look out of my skylight, I saw a light in the window of the green chamber of the *Bœuf-gras*—a traveller was occupying that terrible room!

All my fears were instantly revived. The old woman's excitement explained itself—she scented another victim!

I could not sleep at all that night. The rustling of the straw of my mattress, the nibbling of a mouse under the floor, sent a chill through me. I rose and looked out of my window—I listened. The light I had seen was no longer visible in the green chamber.

During one of these moments of poignant anxiety—whether the result of illusion or of reality—I fancied I could discern the figure of the old witch, likewise watching and listening.

The night passed, the dawn showed grey against my window-panes, and, slowly increasing, the sounds and movements of the re-awakened town arose. Harassed with fatigue and emotion, I at last fell asleep; but my repose was of short duration, and by eight o'clock I was again at my post of observation.

It appeared that Flédermausse had passed a night no less stormy than mine had been; for, when she opened the door of the gallery I saw that a livid pallor was upon her cheeks and skinny neck. She had nothing on but her chemise and a flannel petticoat: a few locks of rusty grey hair fell upon her shoulders. She looked up musingly towards my garret; but she saw nothing—she was thinking of something else.

Suddenly she descended into the yard, leaving her shoes at the top of the stairs. Doubtless her object was to assure herself that the outer door was securely fastened. She then hurried up the stairs, taking three or four steps at a time. It was frightful to see! She rushed into one of the side rooms, and I heard the sound of a heavy box-lid fall. Then Flédermausse reappeared in the gallery, dragging with her a lay-figure the size of life—and this figure was dressed like the unfortunate student of Heidelberg!

With surprising dexterity the old woman suspended this hideous object to a beam of the over-hanging roof, then went down into the yard, to contemplate it from that point of view. A peal of grating laughter broke from her lips—she hurried up the stairs, and rushed down again, like a maniac; and every time she did this she burst into new fits of laughter.

A sound was heard by the outer door; the old woman sprang to the figure, snatched it from its fastening, and carried it into the house; then she reappeared and leant over the balcony, with outstretched neck, glittering eyes, and eagerly-listening ears. The sound passed away—the muscles of her face relaxed, she drew a long breath. The passing of a vehicle had alarmed the old witch.

She then, once more, went back into her chamber, and I heard the lid of the box close heavily.

This strange scene utterly confounded all my ideas. What could that lay-figure mean?

I became more watchful and attentive than ever. Flédermausse went out with her basket, and I watched her to the top of the street; she had resumed her air of tottering agedness, walking with short steps, and from time to time half-turning her head, so as to enable herself to look behind out of the corner of her eyes. For five long hours she remained abroad, while I went and came from my spying place incessantly, meditating all the while—the sun heating the slates above my head till my brain was almost scorched.

I saw at his window the traveller who occupied the green chamber at the *Bœuf-gras;* he was a peasant of Nassau, wearing a three-cornered hat, a scarlet waistcoat, and having a broad laughing countenance. He was tranquilly smoking his Ulm pipe, and unsuspecting anything. I felt impelled to call out to him, "My good fellow, be on your guard! Don't let yourself be fascinated by the old woman!—don't trust yourself!" But he could not have understood a word of what I had said to him, even if he had heard me.

About two o'clock Flédermausse came back. The sound of her door opening echoed to the end of the passage. Presently she appeared alone, quite alone, in the yard, and seated herself on the lowest step of the gallery-stairs. She placed her basket at her feet and drew from it, first several bunches of herbs, then some vegetables—then a three-cornered hat, a scarlet velvet waistcoat, a pair of plush breeches, and a pair of thick worsted stockings—the complete costume of a peasant of Nassau!

I reeled with giddiness—flames passed before my eyes.

I remembered those precipices that drew one towards them with irresistible power—wells that have had to be filled up because of persons throwing themselves into them—trees that have had to be cut down because of people hanging themselves upon them—the contagion of suicide and theft and murder, which at various times has taken possession of people's minds, by means well understood; that strange inducement, for example, which makes people yawn because they see others yawn—kill themselves because others kill themselves. My hair rose upon my head with horror!

But how could this Flédermausse—a creature so mean and wretched—have made discovery of so profound a law of nature? How had she found the means of turning it to the use of her sanguinary instincts? This I could neither understand nor imagine. Without more reflection, however, I resolved to turn the fatal law against her, and by its power to drag her into her own snare. So many innocent victims called for vengeance!

I began at once. I hurried to all the old clothes-dealers in Nuremberg; and by the evening I arrived at the *Bœuf-gras,* with an enormous parcel under my arm.

Nikel Schmidt had long known me. I had painted the portrait of his wife, a fat and comely dame.

"What!—Master Christian!" he cried, shaking me by the hand, "to what happy circumstance do I owe the pleasure of this visit?"

"My dear Mr. Schmidt, I feel a very strong desire to pass the night in that room of yours up yonder."

We were on the doorstep of the *auberge,* and I pointed up to the green chamber. The good fellow looked suspiciously at me.

"Oh! don't be afraid," I said, "I've no desire to hang myself."

"I'm glad of it! I'm glad of it! for, frankly, I should be sorry—an artist of your talent. When do you want the room, Master Christian?"

"To-night."

"That's impossible—it's occupied."

"The gentleman can have it at once, if he likes," said a voice behind us; "*I* shan't stay in it."

We turned in surprise. It was the peasant of Nassau; his large three-cornered hat pressed down upon the back of his neck, and his bundle at the end of his travelling-stick. He had learned the story of the three travellers who had hung themselves.

"Such chambers!" he cried, stammering with terror; "it's—it's murdering people to put them into such!—you—you deserve to be sent to the galleys!"

"Come, come, calm yourself," said the landlord; "you slept there comfortably enough last night."

"Thank heaven! I said my prayers before going to rest, or where should I be now?—where should I be now?"

And he hurried away, raising his hands to heaven.

"Well," said Master Schmidt, stupefied, "the chamber is empty, but don't go into it to do me an ill-turn."

"I should be doing myself a much worse one," I replied.

Giving my parcel to the servant-girl, I went and seated myself provisionally among the guests who were drinking and smoking.

For a long time I had not felt more calm, more happy to be in the world. After so many inquietudes, I was approaching my end—the horizon seemed to grow lighter. I know not by what formidable power I was being led on. I lit my pipe, and with my elbow on the table and a jug of wine before me, listened to the hunting-chorus from "Der Freischütz," played by a band of *Zigeuners* from Schwattz-Wald. The trumpet, the hunting-horn, the hautbois, turn by turn plunged me into vague reverie; and sometimes rousing myself to look at the old woman's house, I seriously asked myself whether all that had happened to me was more than a dream. But when the watchman came, to request us to vacate the room, graver thoughts took possession of my mind, and I followed, in meditative mood, the little servant-girl who preceded me with a candle in her hand.

III

We mounted the winding flight of stairs to the third story; arrived there, she placed the candle in my hand, and pointed to a door.

"That's it," she said, and hurried back down the stairs as fast as she could go.

I opened the door. The green chamber was like all other inn bedchambers; the ceiling was low, the bed was high. After casting a glance round the room, I stepped across to the window.

Nothing was yet noticeable in Flédermausse's house, with the exception of a light, which shone at the back of a deep obscure bedchamber,—a nightlight, doubtless.

"So much the better," I said to myself, as I reclosed the window curtains; "I shall have plenty of time."

I opened my parcel, and from its contents put on a woman's cap with a broad frilled border; then, with a piece of pointed charcoal, in front of the glass, I marked my forehead with a number of wrinkles. This took me a full hour to do; but after I had put on a gown and a large shawl, I was afraid of myself: Flédermausse herself was looking at me from the depths of the glass!

At that moment the watchman announced the hour of eleven. I rapidly dressed the lay-figure I had brought with me like the one prepared by the old witch. I then drew apart the window curtains.

Certainly, after all I had seen of the old woman—her infernal cunning, her prudence, and her address—nothing ought to have surprised even me; yet I was positively terrified.

The light, which I had observed at the back of her room, now cast its yellow rays on her lay-figure, dressed like the peasant of Nassau, which sat huddled up on the side of the bed, its head dropped upon its chest, the large three-cornered hat drawn down over its features, its arms pendent by its sides, and its whole attitude that of a person plunged in despair.

Managed with diabolical art, the shadow permitted only a general view of the figure, the red waistcoat and its six rounded buttons alone caught the light; but the silence of night, the complete immobility of the figure, and its air of terrible dejection, all served to impress the beholder with irresistible force; even I myself, though not in the least taken by surprise, felt chilled to the centre of my bones. How would it have been, then, with a poor countryman taken completely off his guard? He would have been utterly overthrown; he would have lost all control of will, and the spirit of imitation would have done the rest.

Scarcely had I drawn aside the curtains than I discovered Flédermausse on the watch behind her window-panes.

She could not see me. I opened the window softly, the window over the way softly opened too; then the lay-figure appeared to rise slowly and advance towards me; I did the same, and seizing my candle with one hand, with the other threw the casement wide open.

The old woman and I were face to face; for, overwhelmed with astonishment, she had let the lay-figure fall from her hands. Our two looks crossed with an equal terror.

She stretched forth a finger, I did the same; her lips moved, I moved mine; she heaved a deep sigh and leant upon her elbow, I rested in the same way.

How frightful the enacting of this scene was I cannot describe; it was made up of delirium, bewilderment, madness. It was a struggle between two wills, two intelligences, two souls, one of which sought to crush the other; and in this struggle I had the advantage. The dead struggled with me.

After having for some seconds imitated all the movements of Flédermausse, I drew a cord from the folds of my petticoat and tied it to the iron stanchion of the signboard.

The old woman watched me with open mouth. I passed the cord round my neck. Her tawny eyeballs glittered; her features became convulsed:

"No, no!" she cried, in a hissing tone; "No!"

I proceeded with the impassibility of a hangman.

The Flédermausse was seized with rage.

"You're mad! you're mad!" she cried, springing up and clutching wildly at the sill of the window; "You're mad!"

I gave her no time to continue. Suddenly blowing out my light, I stooped like a man preparing to make a vigorous spring, then seizing my lay-figure, slipped the cord about its neck and hurled it into the air.

A terrible shriek resounded through the street, and then all was silent again.

Perspiration bathed my forehead. I listened a long time. At the end of a quarter of an hour I heard far off—very far off—the cry of the watchman, announcing to the inhabitants of Nuremberg that midnight had struck.

"Justice is at last done," I murmured to myself; "the three victims are avenged. Heaven forgive me!"

This was five minutes after I had heard the last cry of the watchman, and when I had seen the old witch, drawn by the likeness of herself, a cord about her neck, hanging from the iron stanchion projecting from her house, I saw the thrill of death run through her limbs, and the moon, calm and silent, rose above the edge of the roof, and threw upon her dishevelled head its cold pale rays.

As I had seen the poor young student of Heidelberg, I now saw Flédermausse.

The next day all Nuremberg knew that "the Bat" had hung herself. It was the last event of the kind in the rue des Minnesängers.

The Island

Maurice Baring

"Perhaps we had better not land after all," said Lewis as he was stepping into the boat; "we can explore this island on our way home."

"We had much better land now," said Stewart; "we shall get to Teneriffe to-morrow in any case. Besides, an island that's not on the chart is too exciting a thing to wait for."

Lewis gave in to his younger companion, and the two ornithologists, who were on their way to the Canary Islands in search of eggs, were rowed to shore.

"They had better fetch us at sunset," said Lewis as they landed.

"Perhaps we shall stay the night," responded Stewart.

"I don't think so," said Lewis; but after a pause he told the sailors that if they should be more than half an hour late they were not to wait, but to come back in the morning at ten. Lewis and Stewart walked from the sandy bay up a steep basaltic cliff which sloped right down to the beach.

"The island is volcanic," said Stewart.

"All the islands about here are volcanic," said Lewis. "We shan't be able to climb much in this heat," he added.

"It will be all right when we get to the trees," said Stewart. Presently they reached the top of the cliff. The basaltic rock ceased and an open grassy incline was before them covered with myrtle and cactus bushes; and further off a thick wood, to the east of which rose a hill sparsely dotted with olive trees. They sat down on the grass, panting. The sun beat down on the dry rock; there was not a cloud in the sky nor a ripple on the emerald sea. In the air there was a strange aromatic scent; and the stillness was heavy.

"I don't think it can be inhabited," said Lewis.

"Perhaps it's merely a volcanic island cast up by a sea disturbance," suggested Stewart.

"Look at those trees," said Lewis, pointing to the wood in the distance.

"What about them?" asked Stewart.

"They are oak trees," said Lewis. "Do you know why I didn't want to land?" he asked abruptly. "I am not superstitious, you know, but as I got into the boat I distinctly heard a voice calling out: 'Don't land!'"

Stewart laughed. "I think it was a good thing to land," he said. "Let's go on now."

They walked towards the wood, and the nearer they got to it the more their surprise increased. It was a thick wood of large oak trees which must certainly have been a hundred years old. When they had got quite close to it they paused.

"Before we explore the wood," said Lewis, "let us climb the hill and see if we can get a general view of the island."

Stewart agreed, and they climbed the hill in silence. When they reached the top they found it was not the highest point of the island, but only one of several hills, so that they obtained only a limited view. The valleys seemed to be densely wooded, and the oak wood was larger than they had imagined. They laid down and rested and lit their pipes.

"No birds," remarked Lewis, gloomily.

"I haven't seen one—the island is extraordinarily still," said Stewart. The further they had penetrated inland the more oppressive and sultry the air had become; and the pungent aroma they had noticed directly was stronger. It was like that of mint, and yet it was not mint; and although sweet it was not agreeable. The heat seemed to weigh even on Stewart's buoyant spirits, for he sat smoking in silence, and no longer urged Lewis to continue their exploration.

"I think the island is inhabited," said Lewis, "and that the houses are on the other side. There are some sheep and some goats on that hill opposite. Do you see?"

"Yes," said Stewart, "I think they are mouflon, but I don't think the island is inhabited all the same." No sooner were the words out of his mouth than he started, and rising to his feet, cried: "Look there!" and he pointed to a thin wreath of smoke which was rising from the wood. Their languor seemed to leave them, and they ran down the hill and reached the wood once more. Just as they were about to enter it Lewis stooped and pointed to a small plant with white flowers and three oval-shaped leaves rising from the root.

"What's that?" he asked Stewart, who was the better botanist of the two. The flowers were quite white, and each had six pointed petals.

"It's a kind of garlic, I think," said Stewart. Lewis bent down over it. "It doesn't smell," he said. "It's not unlike moly (*Allium flavum*), only it's white instead of yellow, and the flowers are larger. I'm going to take it with me." He began scooping away the earth with a knife so as to take out the plant by the roots. After he had been working for some minutes he exclaimed: "This is the toughest plant I've ever seen; I can't get it out." He was at last successful, but as he pulled the root he gave a cry of surprise.

"There's no bulb," he said. "Look! only a black root."

Stewart examined the plant. "I can't make it out," he said.

Lewis wrapped the plant in his handkerchief and put it in his pocket. They entered the wood. The air was still more sultry here than outside, and the stillness even more oppressive. There were no birds and not a vestige of bird life.

"This exploration is evidently a waste of time as far as birds are concerned," remarked Lewis. At that moment there was a rustle in the undergrowth, and five pigs crossed their path and disappeared, grunting. Lewis started, and for some reason he could not account for, shuddered; he looked at Stewart, who appeared unconcerned.

"They are not wild," said Stewart. They walked on in silence. The place and its heavy atmosphere had again affected their spirits. When they spoke it was almost in a whisper. Lewis wished they had not landed, but he could give no reason to himself for his wish. After they had been walking for about twenty minutes they suddenly came on an open space and a low white house. They stopped and looked at each other.

"It's got no chimney!" cried Lewis, who was the first to speak. It was a one-storeyed building, with large windows (which had no glass in them) reaching to the ground, wider at the bottom than at the top. The house was overgrown with creepers; the roof was flat. They entered in silence by the large open doorway and found themselves in a low hall. There was no furniture and the floor was mossy.

"It's rather like an Egyptian tomb," said Stewart, and he shivered. The hall led into a further room, which was open in the centre to the sky, like the *impluvium* of a Roman house. It also contained a square basin of water, which was filled by water bubbling from a lion's mouth carved in stone. Beyond the *impluvium* there were two smaller rooms, in one of which there was a kind of raised stone platform. The house was completely deserted and empty. Lewis and Stewart said little; they examined the house in silent amazement.

"Look," said Lewis, pointing to one of the walls. Stewart examined the wall and noticed that there were traces on it of a faded painted decoration.

"It's like the wall paintings at Pompeii," he said.

"I think the house is modern," remarked Lewis. "It was probably built by some eccentric at the beginning of the nineteenth century, who did it up in Empire style."

"Do you know what time it is?" said Stewart, suddenly. "The sun has set and it's growing dark."

"We must go at once," said Lewis, "we'll come back here to-morrow." They walked on in silence. The wood was dim in the twilight, a fitful breeze made the trees rustle now and again, but the air was just as sultry as ever. The shapes of the trees seemed fantastic and almost threatening in the dimness, and the rustle of the leaves was like a human moan. Once or twice they seemed to hear the grunting of pigs in the undergrowth and to catch sight of bristly backs.

"We don't seem to be getting any nearer the end," said Stewart after a time. "I think we've taken the wrong path." They stopped. "I remember that tree," said Stewart, pointing to a twisted oak; "we must go straight on from there to the left." They walked on and in ten minutes' time found themselves once more at the back of the house. It was now quite dark.

"We shall never find the way now," said Lewis. "We had better sleep in the house." They walked through the house into one of the furthest rooms and settled themselves on the mossy platform. The night was warm and starry, the house deathly still except for the splashing of the water in the basin.

"We shan't get any food," Lewis said.

"I'm not hungry," said Stewart, and Lewis knew that he could not have eaten anything to save his life. He felt utterly exhausted and yet not at all sleepy. Stewart, on the other hand, was overcome with drowsiness. He lay down on the mossy platform and fell asleep almost instantly. Lewis lit a pipe; the vague forebodings he had felt in the morning had returned to him, only increased tenfold. He felt an unaccountable physical discomfort, an inexplicable sensation of uneasiness. Then he realised what it was. He felt there was someone in the house besides themselves, someone or something that was always behind him, moving when he moved, and watching him. He walked into the *impluvium*, but heard nothing and saw nothing. There were none of the thousand little sounds, such as the barking of a dog, or the hoot of a night-bird, which generally complete the silence of a summer night. Everything was uncannily still. He returned to the room. He would have given anything to be back on the yacht, for besides the physical sensation of discomfort and of the something watching him he also felt the unmistakable feeling of impending danger that had been with him nearly all day.

He lay down and at last fell into a doze. As he dozed he heard a subdued noise, a kind of buzzing, such as is made by a spinning wheel or a shuttle on a loom, and more strongly than ever he felt that he was being watched. Then all at once his body seemed to grow stiff with fright. He saw someone enter the room from the *impluvium*. It was a dim, veiled figure, the figure of a woman. He could not distinguish her features, but he had the impression that she was strangely beautiful; she was bearing a cup in her hands, and she walked towards Stewart and bent over him, offering him the cup.

Something in Lewis prompted him to cry out with all his might: "Don't drink! Don't drink!" He heard the words echoing in the air, just as he had heard the voice in the boat; he felt that it was imperative to call out, and yet he could not: he was paralysed; the words would not come. He formed them with his lips, but no sound came. He tried with all his might to rise and scream, and he could not move. Then a sudden cold faintness came upon him, and he remembered no more till he woke and found the sun shining brightly. Stewart was lying with eyes closed, moaning loudly in his sleep.

Lewis tried to wake him. He opened his eyes and stared with a fixed, meaningless stare. Lewis tried to lift him from the platform, and then a horrible thing happened. Stewart struggled violently and made a snarling noise, which froze the blood in Lewis's veins. He ran out of the house with cold beads of sweat on his forehead. He ran through the wood to the shore, and there he found the boat. He rowed back to the yacht and fetched some quinine. Then, together with the skipper, the steward, and some other sailors, he returned to the ominous house. They found it empty. There was no trace of Stewart. They shouted in the wood till they were hoarse, but no answer broke the heavy stillness.

Then sending for the rest of the crew, Lewis organised a regular search over the whole island. This lasted till sunset, and they returned in the evening without having found any trace of Stewart or of any other human being. In the night a high wind rose, which soon became a gale; they were obliged to weigh anchor so as not to be dashed against the island, and for twenty-four hours they underwent a terrific tossing. Then the storm subsided as quickly as it had come.

They made for the island once more and reached the spot where they had anchored three days before. There was no trace of the island. It had completely disappeared.

When they reached Teneriffe the next day they found that everybody was talking of the great tidal wave which had caused such great damage and destruction in the islands.

The Island

Alice Brown

John Haddon went down with one of the first passenger ships "*spurlos versenkt*" and, after varying tragedy and bewilderment, survived, and I was told by an intimate friend of us both the extraordinary impression the catastrophe and the rescue had stamped upon his memory. I never for a moment believed we were to accept the tale as anything but the sad overflow of disaster left in a mind submerged and then bared by the receding tide. I was convinced, and this without surprise, that Haddon had suffered shock and never recovered from it, that he would be moved by unhealthy or at least disturbing recollections to the end of his mortal time. And then I met him face to face, when we were both going over, the next year, on business connected with the Allies, and he came straight to me and made himself known. I'd heard he was on board, and had expected to see a man not quite rectilinear in his relation to other normal things, twisted by the fire and ice of what he had been through. But there walked up to me on deck a fine, keen, bronzed athlete with far-seeing blue eyes and an extraordinarily sweet smile on resolute lips.

"I'm Haddon," said he. "I know who you are. Wentworth has talked about you."

So at once we were cronies, beginning a good number of steps further on from our common acquaintance with Wentworth, and being warmly ready to continue. We ate and lounged together and had long subdued talks when we ran through the dangerous dark, a black speck on a blacker waste. We didn't mention shipwreck or the perils of the sea. Although he was such a daylight sort of person, with nothing even of the haze of fancy about him, I understood that was the thing which should be tabu. But one night when we were talking the dark away, he brought a thrill into my breath by himself grazing what I thought that danger line and in as commonplace a manner as if he had been describing a stroll on Broadway.

"You know," he said, "I went down in the *Artemisia*." (That name will serve.)

"Yes," I said, gulping, "Wentworth told me."

"He didn't need to," said Haddon, with a little laugh. "Of course we were all pretty well known, by name, at least. We were very much in the public eye—necessarily. You can't find yourself the victim of a hellish tragedy and not continue to be a marked man throughout your natural life. Did Wentworth tell you what really happened to me?"

"He told me you were one of the last picked up," I said. I was in a fever of wanting to say the right thing, knowing what even a word might recall to him. "He said it wasn't apparent exactly how you were saved, how you'd kept afloat so long, or what the live-preserver was—"

"He knew perfectly well what it was," said Haddon, in a brusque but indulgent kindliness. "So do you, only you can't account for it and so you don't want to mention it and go wrong. Don't mince matters. You needn't. I don't."

"Well," said I desperately, "he said the life-belt hadn't belonged to the *Artemisia* at all, but that old tramp, the *Elsinore*, that was lost a dozen years ago."

"Precisely," said Haddon. "That was what happened, and it's never been explained and never will be, except by me, and if you don't believe what I say you'll be no better for my opening up to you. Did Wentworth tell you I took that trip on the *Artemisia* just because Amy Lake was going over and I was in love with her and couldn't let her go alone?"

"No," said I, a little shocked that Wentworth's reticence on so fine an issue could be suspected for a moment. "He didn't mention her."

"No, of course not," said Haddon. "I knew it, really. But that was the fact. Did you know Amy Lake?"

I had seen her once and never forgotten her, a tall sweet creature in light grays, a winter outfit that made her look appropriately like some fleet, fine animal, through an invulnerable yet sensitive strength adapted to rigors and winter snows. She had come into a vociferous tea-room for a minute, and drunk her sip or two with a healthy relish and gone away again, leaving a blankness over all our talk and a duller atmosphere.

"I was in love with her, of course," said Haddon quietly.

The tone was an implication that he didn't really need to say it to a person of ordinary penetration. I took it acquiescently. I thought so, too. She was one of the women who, without challenging the senses, leave such an impression of beauty and harmony that all men not of the roughest type can at least see why some men should adore them.

"I hoped," he said, "I should have opportunities on the voyage such as I'd never had, get nearer her, you know, understand her a little and let her see I was trying to. We'd always been separated by a lot of things before, other people, relatives, the general gregariousness of what they call society, and after the war began, the whole terrible business. That, of course, did bring us together in essentials. We were both getting ready to go over to England and being hindered in ways you can guess. But somehow we didn't talk much about ourselves; the desperate big thing overpowered us and prevented it. But on that voyage we began to take each other for granted. We recognized—I did, as a matter of course, and I very soon guessed she did—we recognized we'd got more to say to each other than all the other passengers—and the world, for that matter—had to say to either of us. We saw at last our interests—our spiritual interests, you must let me say—were identical. I like to tell you this because I want you to see how the things that happened afterward, after the sinking, were founded on what came legitimately all along. I should be ashamed to keep it to myself as something sacred when it might start out a writing person like you into charting certain facts that ought to be common possessions if we're ever going to believe in the sanity and security of the universe again. We'd talked, that last night, about the Island you see from Innishmore. You know about it."

"I hadn't thought of it for years," I said, "until Wentworth reminded me, and then I knew I'd heard a particularly sweet ballad singer sing about it, and I remembered a line or two."

"Yes," said Haddon. "Amy remembered more than that. She'd copied the whole ballad, and sang it to me in a purling little whisper. Of course, when I came to life again after the *Artemisia* devilment, I looked up every word there is about the Island. There isn't much. You're most likely to see it from Innishmore, but not only from there but when you're at sea off the Irish coast. One of you writing persons says it's seen only in certain lights or moods of the mind." Now Haddon's voice took on the measured carefulness of one quoting from another who perhaps wrote in a style foreign to his own homespun speech. "It is an island that is sometimes actually seen. But mostly it isn't there. And when it is there it is almost always when the traveler is setting out for far shores and his heart is full of longing to return. Some might think it the embodiment of his longings. Some might call it a mirage of hope. It is believed also that not only is the island visible in beatific or passionately sorrowful states of mind, but that it actually does exist in the Atlantic, though again it is withdrawn. Whether it is a sort of amaranthine flower of the past no one knows, or whether the mind, projecting into the future, creates a jewel of its own in a waste of sea. You can imagine," Haddon concluded, dropping his tone of heedful recollection, "how an emigrant, starting out from the old country in the days of the longer voyage, saw it in the sunset light, all golden turrets and shimmering mists."

"They called it, didn't they," I asked, "the paradise of the pagan Irish?"

"It is the paradise of more than the pagan and more than the Irish," said he. "It's a stepping stone, a refuge—well!"

That last word held an infinity of meanings. It seemed to draw pitying attention to the guidebook childishness which accounts for things and stops contented and his own happier estate now that he knew.

"The next day," he said, "that noon, that luncheon—but I won't talk about that."

"No," I put in hastily. I wanted to spare him the rehearsal of the tragedy. I had an unreasoned feeling he'd go all to pieces if he tried to travel that watery road again and tell what the sea had done to him.

"But after luncheon," he went on, "I couldn't find her, and for some reason I didn't understand then I was desperately anxious to. You see the time began to look so short, and however closely I might be able to tie up our destinies and plans over there, it wouldn't be the same as that shipboard solitude. Besides, I felt as if we should be caught up and whirled round in such a sea of bigger things that my own paltry desires would have to wait indefinitely, as if there'd be no question but I should want them to wait. Everything would be war. Well, I went on deck and I saw her there before me not ten paces away, and she turned to me smiling, and—it came. I've never had any heart to talk about the sensations of the minute because, for me, they all involved her. The whole thing was connected with her, as if a colossal power had risen up, hostile to her, and had accepted that tremendous destruction as a condition of its being able to destroy her with it. I felt as if I were leaping, the whole of me, to get to her before we were separated forever, and yet maybe I didn't move before I was crushed and suffocated and snuffed out. That part of it is where my brain fails me. I didn't know, I don't know now, where my consciousness stopped, whether I did struggle and it went on faintly and faded out at last, or whether I was hit. When I came to myself I simply was alive, delightfully alive, and in another place. It was an Island, for there was the sea. It had the verdure of the British Isles, but its atmosphere was unlike anything I'd seen. And there was Amy close in front of me, and we laughed, we were so glad, and she said to me:

"'The Island!'

"'Do you think so?' I asked, for it looked more beautiful than the song, and was really so impalpable in spite of its reality that I couldn't fit it into any previous conception.

"'But look,' she said, 'all that golden mist. And the towers. They're not real towers. They're sunlight, don't you think?'

"'Oh, yes, they're real enough,' I said. 'Don't you see how they come out of the rock itself?'

"'That's not rock,' said she. 'It's as misty as the towers.'

"'Well, it's solid, too,' I said, and then I realized we were talking absurdly. We were simply trying to fit old expressions to new uses, and the real fact was also that our eyes were giving us more data than our minds could use."

"How did she look?" I asked. "Amy?"

I had to call her that. The strange thing that had happened to her seemed to remove her absolutely from ordinary customs of speech.

"Why," he said, "that's the queer part of it. She was herself, and yet different. I was amazed at her. I puzzled over her. She was beautiful, you understand, more beautiful than ever. That was it. I at once got the idea I'd never seen the real Amy, and this was she. Maybe I was different, too, for she said to me suddenly—and laughed—'How nice you look!' But I don't know."

"I mean," I ventured, though it seemed a childish thing to insist on, "what did she wear? The same things she had on when you saw her on the deck?"

"That's it," said he. "That's the big puzzle. Wentworth asked me that, and though I've almost hammered my head to think, I couldn't tell him. Whatever it was, it was beautiful. And familiar. Beyond that I don't know. And I don't know about the other people either."

"Oh, there were other people?" I asked.

"Scores of 'em, and all busy, and for a while all hurrying and talking. It was evidently a time of unusual excitement. For there were ships coming in—sail boats, beauties—and people landing from them. And everybody was met and evidently made to feel it was tremendously nice they'd come, and there was a good deal of laughing and relief. That's it. There was relief in the air, as if there'd been a cloudburst and now the sun was out and people were saying to one another, 'It didn't do any damage, after all.'"

"And did you really think you were on the fabulous Island?" I asked.

I wanted to pin him down to as literal fact as he could manage.

He laughed.

"Not for an instant," he answered, "then. Amy'd said so, you remember, and I partially agreed, but it was only because we were so light-hearted we said the first things that came into our heads. Really, I was perfectly sure we were on the coast of Ireland. I assumed that, without a doubt. And when things had quieted down a little and our passengers were dispersing, going off by ones and twos with the Island people, I went up to the Tall Man—"

"Who was he?" I interrupted.

"I don't know. I never even heard his name."

"You don't assume," I hesitated, "it was—" and this was the only way I could end—"some one supernatural?"

"Bless you, no," said he. "I call him the Tall Man simply because he was tall and I don't know his name. And he was most certainly some one in authority. I went up to him and said, 'Can we hire any sort of conveyance to take us to Queenstown or somewhere else where we can get passage for England?'

"And he looked at me, a long look, and smiled. And then I knew. But I didn't dare look at Amy. I thought it might frighten her, you see. But I might have known. She'd guessed it from the first. She took my hand, and we stood there like two children, not in any way distressed, but coming out of a wood-path to an open door, a little curious and pretty excited.

"'Don't you see, John?' said Amy. 'Don't you know?'

"And then I said it. My voice sounded strange to me.

"'Am I—dead?'

"For the minute I forgot her. I rather think the soul has to face that one thing alone, and now it was my turn to face it.

"'Yes,' said Amy. It was the most commonplace 'yes' you ever heard. She might have been encouraging a child, after he'd come out of some bad business like an anaesthetic. 'Now let's get to work. Isn't there something,' she said to the Tall Man, 'we can do?'

"He was immensely pleased with her. She seemed to have been clever in accepting it and adapting herself, as you might say.

"'Yes,' he said, 'there are lots of things you can do.'—And I've got to break off right here and say I don't know whether those were his actual words. But it was the sense of them. And then he looked doubtful and queer. 'The fact is,' he said, 'I'm not sure, you know, whether you're both going to stay.'

"'Oh, you mean,' said Amy—and when it comes to her I could swear to every word—'you're not sure whether we're both dead.' It seems astonishing to me, the way she used that word we hate so, lightly, you know, as if it meant something rather warm and pleasant. And then she snatched at my hand and held it tight. 'We've got to be,' she said. 'If one of us is, the other's got to be, too.'

"'I know,' he said. He seemed to understand perfectly. 'And it may be so. But I have a kind of a doubt—' and then he seemed to recall himself and remember he mustn't say more than he actually knew. 'Anyway,' he went on, 'it doesn't matter, and for the present, at least, you're on the Island. And you've come at a time of a good deal of anxiety for us—'

"'How can you have anxieties,' said Amy, 'if you're all dead?'

"He smiled at her.

"'Aren't you anxious?' he asked.

"And that reminded her.

vOf course,' she said. 'Why, I hadn't thought. I'd forgotten them—father and mother. But they'll be hearing—oh, think how it'll come to them. In an instant, maybe a cable message, maybe a line in a newspaper. Oh, how horrible of me to be happy for a minute!'

"'That's it,' he said. 'You've got to be anxious so long as you love anything on the earth—that is, while the earth's in the state it is now. And we're anxious about England.'

"'Then you're English,' I asked, 'all of you.'

"'No, no,' he said. 'But we used to belong to her, you see, we were a part of her. I mean, the actual Island. And those old birth bonds hold. Why, look at me. I'—he smiled at Amy—as if he must indulge her—'I died, we'll say—and I don't mind the word—a long, long time ago, and yet I never've been willing to leave here.'

"'Could you leave?' Amy asked him quickly. I think she saw herself hurrying back to America for a minute—invisible herself, maybe—a minute of comfort for her father and mother. 'Is it permitted?'

"'Oh, yes,' he said, 'anything's permitted. The things that wouldn't be permitted you simply don't want to do. But there's no particular pleasure in elbowing about among the others—the ones that are, so to speak, alive. (I'm using all your terms. It's simpler.) Besides, you realize that when you're dead (your term again, you see!) your place is among the dead. And people keep coming to us—just as you've come—and there are the drowned ships. We have as much fun getting them into dry dock and setting them afloat again as we have in receiving the drowned sailors.'

"'Were those the ships?' Amy put in quickly, and he nodded at her.

"'Yes,' he said, 'those were the good drowned boats that didn't want to go down and are mighty glad to get up again and feel the hand of man on them, man that made them. You don't suppose a boat can't love its creator do you? the one that shaped and guided her?'

"'But,' said Amy, 'if all those lost ships were on the ocean, we couldn't have helped seeing them and running into them. Or,' said she—and I can tell you she wrinkled her eyebrows at him. You know that way she had—'aren't they real ships, or only the souls of ships? Just as I suppose we're souls now and our bodies are off there in the sea?'

"She could meet it all, without a quiver. I couldn't. I didn't want to think of my body's being out there, fathoms down. But the Tall Man was smiling at her with that look he had for her and not once for me. No wonder!

"'You're going too fast now,' he said. 'I can't help you. I mustn't. You'll know it all in time.'

"Then he turned suddenly to a green walk that led up to one of the misty temples. I call 'em temples. What do I know? I don't know what they were used for ordinarily, nor how they were built, nor whether, if you struck 'em, they would hurt your hand. I only know they were outlines, a sort of enchanting outline that made you contented and pleased when you looked at it. And a lot of people were going toward it—not our *Artemisia* crowd, but the others, those that had met us and been kind.

"'I told you we are anxious,' said the Tall Man. 'That's a sign of it. It means we've got to talk things over.'

"He was moving away, as he spoke. I saw he was suddenly in a hurry—anxious, like the rest.

"'Oh,' said Amy, 'mayn't we come?'

"He stopped and looked at us, kindly, but a little doubtfully.

"'Why, yes,' he said then. 'I think so. Nobody ever does come—so soon. But you're different. At least, one of you is.'

"And then I began to understand it was he meant when he said maybe we couldn't both stay there, and I held to Amy's hand and made up my mind I'd never let it go. And she held mine just as tight. She'd had the same thought, you see, and she was determined, too. But she was tremendously interested—curious, in a darling kind of way—about the Island and it made her audacious, even.

"'Then we'll come,' she said to him. 'Let us go along behind you, and of course if the others don't like our being there they'll say so.'

"He smiled in that indulgent way he had, and I gathered from it he knew if he vouched for us it would be enough and that he was somebody very important in relation to the others, and he walked away and we followed.

"Well, we went along, and when we got inside what I call the temple—and after we were once there the walls didn't look like walls any more—it was just a large place,—when we were among the others we lost him and then saw him later, up on a kind of dais where they went to speak. At least it must have been a place higher than the rest of the temple—there I go, you see, calling it a temple!—or else the ones that spoke looked taller than the rest."

"Were they sitting?" I asked him, "the audience, I mean?"

"I'm not sure," he said. His voice sounded troubled. I could believe he was finding it more and more disturbing, as time went on, to realize how inexorably his memory of the event was losing its clear edges, growing less distinct. "I seem to remember them standing. I can't repeat the words of their discussion, but I do remember the sense of it. That will never leave me. They were in a state of anxiety, as he had said, and trying to see whether something couldn't be done. They were all perfectly agreed; that wasn't the ground of discussion. They were pulling together absolutely, and the point they were after was whether they couldn't make themselves known, as an island, you see, a possession, to England. They were doing all they could to help, receiving the dead and that kind of thing, and God knows what else. They may have been fighting the submarines, for all I know, with their invisible fleet. But they wanted England to know they were there, safeguarding when they could and comforting all the time. And then it came over me with a great rush that England not only had her daughter colonies, fighting for her, the cubs as brave as the lion, but she had her invisible colonies, too. They were round her like a guard of not mere human steel, but heavenly fire. Amy saw it, and we looked at each other and felt we'd begun to understand the universe a little bit, not the surface of things we'd been stumbling over up to now.

"But I had a thought I didn't like. Logic, reason, you know what a nasty way they have of putting a heavy hand on the curb of your high horse.

"'But,' I said, 'if England's got invisible cohorts fighting for her, Germany must have the same kind. And they'd be pretty formidable, those old scalawags, Barbarossa and his horsemen and the whole gang.'

"'I don't think so,' said Amy. 'When we die, we see things differently. They must have got something out of being dead, just as we have, and they've been dead centuries and we only—is it weeks or minutes? I don't believe Kultur looks very attractive, even to a German, if he's got out of his skin and begun to look with the eyes of his spirit. No, they wouldn't help Germany. They'd see she mustn't win. They'd know it would only be prolonging her childish bluff and brutishness. What they'd want most would be to have her humbled so she'd see she'd got to crawl up out of her slime. But

England—well, you know what you said on shipboard. That no matter what England had done in the past, to other nations and her own poor, it happens now she's right.'

"And as I looked at Amy and saw how alive she was, how eager, how understanding, how perfectly able to weave her past into the strange present and make them equally alive, my fear came over me that she was to stay here and, unless I was somehow let to hocus fate, I was to go. I hadn't dropped her hand and now I clutched it tighter and drew her away.

" 'Come,' I said, 'we must find some place of our own.'

"She was still thinking about the heavenly cohorts fighting for their earthly mothers, and though she didn't resist me she evidently went on in that same groove.

" 'Just think,' she said as we went out together, 'what it must be for the dead Germans, not bound, as we are, to a just and wonderful cause. They've got to know they can't help. It wouldn't be permitted. They can only pray and suffer shame.'

"I didn't answer. I saw before us a long alley, made by slender trees that seemed to throw a green light across the path, one to another, in an enchanting kind of way. The trees themselves were opaque gems and the light through them was pulsating and clear. I wish I could describe it to you. But I can't. You'll see those things sometime. (So shall I—again. And mighty soon, too. I'm as sure of that as I am we're sitting here tonight. That's why I take it as I do—not having her, you know.) I hurried Amy along the path so fast we seemed to skim the ground without touching it. Don't you know that dream we have of floating? You just give a little push with a tiptoe, and you're above the ground, willing yourself to go. And while we hurried, not breathlessly, but with a pleasurable sensation as if nothing nicer could happen to us than wafting along a green path, I had the queerest sensation that the path was ours, that nobody'd used it or even seen it before. And we came out on an open space with trees round it—not slender, like the path trees but big, round, populous, with spaces in them and coverts for a million birds. A green city, that's what each tree was, all full of plots and courts and alleys under dancing leaves."

"Were there birds?" I asked. Every time he stopped for a minute I felt as if he might actually break the thread and leave me lost on my bewildered way.

Again he was perplexed and troubled.

"About the birds," he said. "I've thought of that. And I can't be sure. I tell myself it couldn't have been so happy if there hadn't been birds. A tree like a green city and no birds to live in it—that's desolation. I think I heard them. Actually I do think so. Only they weren't songs I can remember. Except one. I've thought it might have been the skylark, not just an English lark, you know, but Shelley's." He laughed a little here, as if he could allow himself an occasional tender romancing over the inexhaustible riches of the place.

"And I did hear the sea, softly lapping on the shore. Well, I made Amy sit down with me and I held her hands, thinking all the time how tight I must cling to them to keep something—destiny or what we call life—from dragging me away from her. And then I told her about my fear. She was to stay, I told her, and I was to go. She looked at me seriously and I was plunged deeper and deeper in my misery to find she knew at once it was to be. But whereas I was distracted she was grave and—different. Calm, perhaps—that was it—as if she saw the end of things I was only guessing out from the beginning. But I had my plan.

"'Now,' I said to her, 'we're here alone. We've escaped from them all, and they're too busy to think of us. And this is our place. We must build us a house and live here—stay absolutely by ourselves, so nobody'll be reminded of us.'

"'It won't do any good,' said she, very grave, but not unhappy as I was. And then she laughed a little as if she liked me tremendously and wanted me to have my way, even for a minute or two, to soften things for me afterward and she said, 'Still, it won't do any harm.'

"Then all the strength I'd got came up in me—I don't know whether it was will or muscle—and I made up my mind I'd show the Powers I was as strong as They were, and I said:

"'Very well then, we'll build our house.'

"I got up and so did she, and we went to work. And to this day I don't know whether we talked about the house and what sort it should be, or how we found material, or whether we actually worked. I seem to remember tools of some sort and going round whistling and Amy's singing and her reminding me of old jokes and our agreeing we'd been so silly 'way back before we came here not to have been married the first day we met.

"'For we knew then,' said Amy. 'Not that it makes any difference now.'

"And suddenly the house was built and we stood looking at it. And it wasn't walled with mist like the Islanders' temple, but it was a good deal like some of the old houses we'd seen and talked about on shipboard. It was palpable to the eye and the touch—oh, you never'll understand me here; I can't express myself—and yet it was different. We loved it. When I looked at it I forgot my fear and Amy seemed to put aside her sad certainties. And I got daring and wished for the moon, and the moon came. Do you know, I never've looked it up to see if there was a moon at that particular time because I'd rather think it was our moon, the moon of our thoughts. And we stood at a window, looking at it—I must tell you about that window, though, before I forget. I'd wanted a 'magic casement,' like Keats's

opening on the foam
Of perilous seas, in faery lands forlorn."

And, if you'll believe me, I got it. Don't ask me what it looked like. I simply got it, that's all. And we knew it was that window and no other. And it was while we stood there looking at our world that she said to me:

"'You like to stay in the house, don't you? You'd rather do it than explore the Island.'

"I felt sulky, just because of my fear.

"'Yes,' I said. 'It's our house. We'd better stay in it—while we can.'

"The last words I hadn't meant to say. I didn't like to remind her of my fear.

"'Yes,' she said, 'you stay in the house because you think they won't find us when they want us. But they will.'

"Then she called me a name I won't tell you. But sometime I shall hear it.

"I didn't see why, if the Island itself wasn't visible to passing ships, our house should necessarily be visible to the Islanders themselves. There were queer rules here, I told her. We didn't know just what would obtain. But all the time I knew there was nothing in it and so did she. She began to talk, quietly.

"'You've heard the sounds, haven't you, even when we're in our house?'

"'I've heard the sea,' I told her.

"I'd made up my mind that was all I'd own to.

"'You've heard more,' said she. I could see she was terribly sorry for me now, not so much for herself because she'd begun to learn the end of things, and besides she saw some kinds of grief are of no use. 'We both have. We've heard their music—and their bugles—sometimes I think when we heard the bugles we ought to have gone. I suppose that was when more ships came in and brought more—dead.'

"I believe then I began to cry. Anyway I had a feeling of breaking up and going all to pieces, and as we do sometimes in nightmare I began to say the same thing over and over. 'For God's sake!' that was what I kept saying, and though I never could finish I knew she understood perfectly well what I was trying to pray. Not to leave me, that was what I was praying to her, whatever they said or did to her, not to leave me. And her face began to grow fainter and fainter, though she bent over me—I felt I was on my knees crying to her—she bent over me to give me the sight of it to the last. And it's my one best thing in life now to remember her hands held mine tighter and tighter and wouldn't let them go. And then there was a great clanging in my ears—I thought it was the Islanders summoning me to tell me I'd got to part from her, and I began to have a queer pain and misery. And I woke up. And there were two men I'd never seen, and I knew instantly the worst had happened. I'd been rescued and Amy was dead."

"About the life-preserver?" said I, because I knew we could never come back to this again and that was the most mysterious thing of all to me. "I couldn't understand—"

He got up and shook himself a little, as if he cast off the dust of old perplexities.

"You never will," he said. "You'll have to do as I do: believe it and accept it and be satisfied not to understand. The amount of the matter was that when I got on my feet I hunted out the boat that picked me up. I had a feeling that among so many incredible things they might have found Amy, too, and seen her dear body later than I did. But they hadn't. Only, just as I was going over the side, the captain followed me, and he said:

"'That was a queer thing about your life-belt. It was off the old *Elsinore*. How'd you come by it?'

"'Why,' I said, 'I didn't come by it. There wasn't any time for life-belts.'

"'But you had it on,' said he, '*Elsinore*, marked plain. I commanded that ship once myself.'

"'Then where is it?' said I.

"'I've got it down here below,' he said, and he went off to fetch it. But he came back in ten minutes or so, and he was more puzzled than I was. I'd seen the Island fleet, you remember. 'It can't be found,' said he, 'high nor low. But we shall come on it. I'll send it to you.'

"But he never did. I knew he wouldn't. He's written me once or twice about it. I believe it scares him, rather."

"But it doesn't scare you," I ventured.

"I should say not," he said. He laughed a little. "Some things I know. Nothing scares me now."

Jerry Bundler

W. W. Jacobs

It wanted a few nights to Christmas, a festival for which the small market town of Torchester was making extensive preparations. The narrow streets which had been thronged with people were now almost deserted; the cheap-jack from London, with the remnant of breath left him after his evening's exertions, was making feeble attempts to blow out his naphtha lamp, and the last shops open were rapidly closing for the night.

In the comfortable coffee-room of the old Boar's Head, half a dozen guests, principally commercial travellers, sat talking by the light of the fire. The talk had drifted from trade to politics, from politics to religion, and so by easy stages to the supernatural. Three ghost stories, never known to fail before, had fallen flat; there was too much noise outside, too much light within. The fourth story was told by an old hand with more success; the streets were quiet, and he had turned the gas out. In the flickering light of the fire, as it shone on the glasses and danced with shadows on the walls, the story proved so enthralling that George, the waiter, whose presence had been forgotten, created a very disagreeable sensation by suddenly starting up from a dark corner and gliding silently from the room. "That's what I call a good story," said one of the men, sipping his hot whisky. "Of course it's an old idea that spirits like to get into the company of human beings. A man told me once that he travelled down the Great Western with a ghost and hadn't the slightest suspicion of it until the inspector came for tickets. My friend said the way that ghost tried to keep up appearances by feeling for it in all its pockets and looking on the floor was quite touching. Ultimately it gave it up and with a faint groan vanished through the ventilator."

"That'll do, Hirst," said another man.

"It's not a subject for jesting," said a little old gentleman who had been an attentive listener. "I've never seen an apparition myself, but I know people who have, and I consider that they form a very interesting link between us and the afterlife. There's a ghost story connected with this house, you know."

"Never heard of it," said another speaker, "and I've been here some years now."

"It dates back a long time now," said the old gentleman. "You've heard about Jerry Bundler, George?"

"Well, I've just 'eard odds and ends, sir," said the old waiter, "but I never put much count to 'em. There was one chap 'ere what said 'e saw it, and the gov'ner sacked 'im prompt."

"My father was a native of this town," said the old gentleman, "and knew the story well. He was a truthful man and a steady churchgoer, but I've heard him declare that once in his life he saw the appearance of Jerry Bundler in this house."

"And who was this Bundler?" inquired a voice.

"A London thief, pickpocket, highwayman—anything he could turn his dishonest hand to," replied the old gentleman; "and he was run to earth in this house one Christmas week some eighty years ago. He took his last supper in this very room, and after he had gone up to bed a couple of Bow Street runners, who had followed him from London but lost the scent a bit, went upstairs with the landlord and tried the door. It was stout oak, and fast, so one went into the yard, and by means of a short ladder got onto the window-sill, while the other stayed outside the door. Those below in the yard saw the man crouching on the sill, and then there was a sudden smash of glass, and with a cry he fell in a heap on the stones at their feet. Then in the moonlight they saw the white face of the pickpocket peeping over the sill, and while some stayed in the yard, others ran into the house and helped the other man to break the door in. It was difficult to obtain an entrance even then, for it was barred with heavy furniture, but they got in at last, and the first thing that met their eyes was the body of Jerry dangling from the top of the bed by his own handkerchief."

"Which bedroom was it?" asked two or three voices together.

The narrator shook his head. "That I can't tell you; but the story goes that Jerry still haunts this house, and my father used to declare positively that the last time he slept here the ghost of Jerry Bundler lowered itself from the top of his bed and tried to strangle him."

"That'll do," said an uneasy voice. "I wish you'd thought to ask your father which bedroom it was."

"What for?" inquired the old gentleman.

"Well, I should take care not to sleep in it, that's all," said the voice, shortly.

"There's nothing to fear," said the other. "I don't believe for a moment that ghosts could really hurt one. In fact my father used to confess that it was only the unpleasantness of the thing that upset him, and that for all practical purposes Jerry's fingers might have been made of cotton wool for all the harm they could do."

"That's all very fine," said the last speaker again; "a ghost story is a ghost story, sir; but when a gentleman tells a tale of a ghost in the house in which one is going to sleep, I call it most ungentlemanly!"

"Pooh! nonsense!" said the old gentleman, rising; "ghosts can't hurt you. For my own part, I should rather like to see one. Good night, gentlemen."

"Good night," said the others. "And I only hope Jerry'll pay you a visit," added the nervous man as the door closed.

"Bring some more whisky, George," said a stout commercial; "I want keeping up when the talk turns this way."

"Shall I light the gas, Mr. Malcolm?" said George.

"No; the fire's very comfortable," said the traveller. "Now, gentlemen, any of you know any more?"

"I think we've had enough," said another man; "we shall be thinking we see spirits next, and we're not all like the old gentleman who's just gone."

"Old humbug!" said Hirst. "I should like to put him to the test. Suppose I dress up as Jerry Bundler and go and give him a chance of displaying his courage?"

"Bravo!" said Malcolm, huskily, drowning one or two faint "Noes." "Just for the joke, gentlemen."

"No, no! Drop it, Hirst," said another man.

"Only for the joke," said Hirst, somewhat eagerly. "I've got some things upstairs in which I am going to play in the *Rivals*—knee-breeches, buckles, and all that sort of thing. It's a rare chance. If you'll wait a bit I'll give you a full-dress rehearsal, entitled, 'Jerry Bundler; or, The Nocturnal Strangler.'"

"You won't frighten us," said the commercial, with a husky laugh.

"I don't know that," said Hirst, sharply; "it's a question of acting, that's all. I'm pretty good, ain't I, Somers?"

"Oh, you're all right—for an amateur," said his friend, with a laugh.

"I'll bet you a level sov. you don't frighten me," said the stout traveller.

"Done!" said Hirst. "I'll take the bet to frighten you first and the old gentleman afterwards. These gentlemen shall be the judges."

"You won't frighten us, sir," said another man, "because we're prepared for you; but you'd better leave the old man alone. It's dangerous play."

"Well, I'll try you first," said Hirst, springing up. "No gas, mind."

He ran lightly upstairs to his room, leaving the others, most of whom had been drinking somewhat freely, to wrangle about his proceedings. It ended in two of them going to bed.

"He's crazy on acting," said Somers, lighting his pipe. "Thinks he's the equal of anybody almost. It doesn't matter with us, but I won't let him go to the old man. And he won't mind so long as he gets an opportunity of acting to us."

"Well, I hope he'll hurry up," said Malcolm, yawning; "it's after twelve now."

Nearly half an hour passed. Malcolm drew his watch from his pocket and was busy winding it, when George, the waiter, who had been sent on an errand to the bar, burst suddenly into the room and rushed towards them.

"'E's comin', gentlemen," he said breathlessly.

"Why, you're frightened, George," said the stout commercial, with a chuckle.

"It was the suddenness of it," said George, sheepishly; "and besides, I didn't look for seein' 'im in the bar. There's only a glimmer of light there, and 'e was sitting on the floor behind the bar. I nearly trod on 'im."

"Oh, you'll never make a man, George," said Malcolm.

"Well, it took me unawares," said the waiter. "Not that I'd have gone to the bar by myself if I'd known 'e was there, and I don't believe you would either, sir."

"Nonsense!" said Malcolm. "I'll go and fetch him in."

"You don't know what it's like, sir," said George, catching him by the sleeve. "It ain't fit to look at by yourself, it ain't, indeed. It's got the—*What's that?*"

They all started at the sound of a smothered cry from the staircase and the sound of somebody running hurriedly along the passage. Before anybody could speak, the door flew open and a figure bursting into the room flung itself gasping and shivering upon them.

"What is it? What's the matter?" demanded Malcolm. "Why, it's Mr. Hirst." He shook him roughly and then held some spirit to his lips. Hirst drank it greedily and with a sharp intake of his breath gripped him by the arm.

"Light the gas, George," said Malcolm.

The waiter obeyed hastily. Hirst, a ludicrous but pitiable figure in knee-breeches and coat, a large wig all awry and his face a mess of grease paint, clung to him, trembling.

"Now, what's the matter?" asked Malcolm.

"I've seen it," said Hirst, with a hysterical sob. "O Lord, I'll never play the fool again, never!"

"Seen what?" said the others.

"Him—it—the ghost—anything!" said Hirst, wildly.

"Rot!" said Malcolm, uneasily.

"I was coming down the stairs," said Hirst. "Just capering down—as I thought—it ought to do. I felt a tap—"

He broke off suddenly and peered nervously through the open door into the passage.

"I thought I saw it again," he whispered. "Look—at the foot of the stairs. Can you see anything?"

"No, there's nothing there," said Malcolm, whose own voice shook a little. "Go on. You felt a tap on your shoulder—"

"I turned round and saw it—a little wicked head and a white dead face. Pah!"

"That's what I saw in the bar," said George. "'Orrid it was—devilish!"

Hirst shuddered, and, still retaining his nervous grip of Malcolm's sleeve, dropped into a chair.

"Well, it's a most unaccountable thing," said the dumbfounded Malcolm, turning round to the others. "It's the last time I come to this house."

"I leave to-morrow," said George. "I wouldn't go down to that bar again by myself, no, not for fifty pounds!"

"It's talking about the thing that's caused it, I expect," said one of the men; "we've all been talking about this and having it in our minds. Practically we've been forming a spiritualistic circle without knowing it."

"Hang the old gentleman!" said Malcolm, heartily. "Upon my soul, I'm half afraid to go to bed. It's odd they should both think they saw something."

"I saw it as plain as I see you, sir," said George, solemnly. "P'raps if you keep your eyes turned up the passage you'll see it for yourself."

They followed the direction of his finger, but saw nothing, although one of them fancied that a head peeped round the corner of the wall.

"Who'll come down to the bar?" said Malcolm, looking round.

"You can go, if you like," said one of the others, with a faint laugh; "we'll wait here for you."

The stout traveller walked towards the door and took a few steps up the passage. Then he stopped. All was quite silent, and he walked slowly to the end and looked down fearfully towards the glass partition which shut off the bar. Three times he made as though to go to it; then he turned back, and, glancing over his shoulder, came hurriedly back to the room.

"Did you see it, sir?" whispered George.

"Don't know," said Malcolm, shortly. "I fancied I saw something, but it might have been fancy. I'm in the mood to see anything just now. How are you feeling now, sir?"

"Oh, I feel a bit better now," said Hirst, somewhat brusquely, as all eyes were turned upon him. "I dare say you think I'm easily scared, but you didn't see it."

"Not at all," said Malcolm, smiling faintly despite himself.

"I'm going to bed," said Hirst, noticing the smile and resenting it. "Will you share my room with me, Somers?"

"I will with pleasure," said his friend, "provided you don't mind sleeping with the gas on full all night."

He rose from his seat, and bidding the company a friendly good-night, left the room with his crestfallen friend. The others saw them to the foot of the stairs, and having heard their door close, returned to the coffee-room.

"Well, I suppose the bet's off?" said the stout commercial, poking the fire and then standing with his legs apart on the hearthrug; "though, as far as I can see, I won it. I never saw a man so scared in all my life. Sort of poetic justice about it, isn't there?"

"Never mind about poetry or justice," said one of his listeners; "who's going to sleep with me?"

"I will," said Malcolm, affably.

"And I suppose we share a room together, Mr. Leek?" said the third man, turning to the fourth.

"No, thank you," said the other, briskly; "I don't believe in ghosts. If anything comes into my room I shall shoot it."

"That won't hurt a spirit, Leek," said Malcolm, decisively.

"Well the noise'll be like company to me," said Leek, "and it'll wake the house too. But if you're nervous, sir," he added, with a grin, to the man who had suggested sharing his room, "George'll be only too pleased to sleep on the door-mat inside your room, I know."

"That I will, sir," said George, fervently; "and if you gentlemen would only come down with me to the bar to put the gas out, I could never be sufficiently grateful."

They went out in a body, with the exception of Leek, peering carefully before them as they went. George turned the light out in the bar and they returned unmolested to the coffee-room, and, avoiding the sardonic smile of Leek, prepared to separate for the night.

"Give me the candle while you put the gas out, George," said the traveller.

The waiter handed it to him and extinguished the gas, and at the same moment all distinctly heard a step in the passage outside. It stopped at the door, and as they watched with bated breath, the door creaked and slowly opened. Malcolm fell back open-mouthed, as a white, leering face, with sunken eyeballs and close-cropped bullet head, appeared at the opening.

For a few seconds the creature stood regarding them, blinking in a strange fashion at the candle. Then, with a sidling movement, it came a little way into the room and stood there as if bewildered.

Not a man spoke or moved, but all watched with a horrible fascination as the creature removed its dirty neckcloth and its head rolled on its shoulder. For a minute it paused, and then, holding the rag before it, moved towards Malcolm.

The candle went out suddenly with a flash and a bang. There was a smell of powder, and something writhing in the darkness on the floor. A faint, choking cough, and then silence. Malcolm was the first to speak. "Matches," he said, in a strange voice. George struck one. Then he leapt at the gas and a burner flamed from the match. Malcolm touched the thing on the floor with his foot and found it soft. He looked at his companions. They mouthed inquiries at him, but he shook his head. He lit the candle, and, kneeling down, examined the silent thing on the floor. Then he rose swiftly, and dipping his handkerchief in the water-jug, bent down again and grimly wiped the white face. Then he sprang back with a cry of incredulous horror, pointing at it. Leek's pistol fell to the floor and he shut out the sight with his hands, but the others, crowding forward, gazed spell-bound at the dead face of Hirst.

Before a word was spoken the door opened and Somers hastily entered the room. His eyes fell on the floor. "Good God!" he cried. "You didn't—"

Nobody spoke.

"I told him not to," he said, in a suffocating voice. "I told him not to. I told him—"

He leaned against the wall, deathly sick, put his arms out feebly, and fell fainting into the traveller's arms.

Jikininki

Lafcadio Hearn

Once, when Musō Kokushi, a priest of the Zen sect, was journeying alone through the province of Mino, he lost his way in a mountain-district where there was nobody to direct him. For a long time he wandered about helplessly; and he was beginning to despair of finding shelter for the night, when he perceived, on the top of a hill lighted by the last rays of the sun, one of those little hermitages, called *anjitsu*, which are built for solitary priests. It seemed to be in ruinous condition; but he hastened to it eagerly, and found that it was inhabited by an aged priest, from whom he begged the favor of a night's lodging. This the old man harshly refused; but he directed Musōto a certain hamlet, in the valley adjoining where lodging and food could be obtained.

Musō found his way to the hamlet, which consisted of less than a dozen farm-cottages; and he was kindly received at the dwelling of the headman. Forty or fifty persons were assembled in the principal apartment, at the moment of Musō's arrival; but he was shown into a small separate room, where he was promptly supplied with food and bedding. Being very tired, he lay down to rest at an early hour; but a little before midnight he was roused from sleep by a sound of loud weeping in the next apartment. Presently the sliding-screens were gently pushed apart; and a young man, carrying a lighted lantern, entered the room, respectfully saluted him, and said:—

"Reverend Sir, it is my painful duty to tell you that I am now the responsible head of this house. Yesterday I was only the eldest son. But when you came here, tired as you were, we did not wish that you should feel embarrassed in any way: therefore we did not tell you that father had died only a few hours before. The people whom you saw in the next room are the inhabitants of this village: they all assembled here to pay their last respects to the dead; and now they are going to another village, about three miles off,—for by our custom, no one of us may remain in this village during the night after a death has taken place. We make the proper offerings and prayers;—then we go away, leaving the corpse alone. Strange things always happen in the house where a corpse has thus been left: so we think that it will be better for you to come away with us. We can find you good lodging in the other village. But perhaps, as you are a priest, you have no fear of demons or evil spirits; and, if you are not afraid of being left alone with the body, you will be very welcome to the use of this poor house. However, I must tell you that nobody, except a priest, would dare to remain here tonight."

Musō made answer:—

"For your kind intention and your generous hospitality, I and am deeply grateful. But I am sorry that you did not tell me of your father's death when I came;—for, though I was a little tired, I certainly was not so tired that I should have found difficulty in doing my duty as a priest. Had you told me, I could have performed the service before your departure. As it is, I shall perform the service after you have gone away; and I shall stay by the body until morning. I do not know what you mean by your words about the danger of staying here alone; but I am not afraid of ghosts or demons: therefore please to feel no anxiety on my account."

The young man appeared to be rejoiced by these assurances, and expressed his gratitude in fitting words. Then the other members of the family, and the folk assembled in the adjoining room, having been told of the priest's kind promises, came to thank him,—after which the master of the house said:—

"Now, reverend Sir, much as we regret to leave you alone, we must bid you farewell. By the rule of our village, none of us can stay here after midnight. We beg, kind Sir, that you will take every care of your honorable body, while we are unable to attend upon you. And if you happen to hear or see anything strange during our absence, please tell us of the matter when we return in the morning."

All then left the house, except the priest, who went to the room where the dead body was lying. The usual offerings had been set before the corpse; and a small Buddhist lamp—*tōmyō*—was burning. The priest recited the service, and performed the funeral ceremonies,—after which he entered into meditation. So meditating he remained through several silent hours; and there was no sound in the deserted village. But, when the hush of the night was at its deepest, there noiselessly entered a Shape, vague and vast; and in the same moment Musō found himself without power to move or speak. He saw that Shape lift the corpse, as with hands, devour it, more quickly than a cat devours a rat,—beginning at the head, and eating everything: the hair and the bones and even the shroud. And the monstrous Thing, having thus consumed the body, turned to the offerings, and ate them also. Then it went away, as mysteriously as it had come.

When the villagers returned next morning, they found the priest awaiting them at the door of the headman's dwelling. All in turn saluted him; and when they had entered, and looked about the room, no one expressed any surprise at the disappearance of the dead body and the offerings. But the master of the house said to Musō:—

"Reverent Sir, you have probably seen unpleasant things during the night: all of us were anxious about you. But now we are very happy to find you alive and unharmed. Gladly we would have stayed with you, if it had been possible. But the law of our village, as I told you last evening, obliges us to quit our houses after a death has taken place, and to leave the corpse alone. Whenever this law has been broken, heretofore, some great misfortune has followed. Whenever it is obeyed, we find that the corpse and the offerings disappear during our absence. Perhaps you have seen the cause."

Then Musō told of the dim and awful Shape that had entered the death-chamber to devour the body and the offerings. No person seemed to be surprised by his narration; and the master of the house observed:—

"What you have told us, reverend Sir, agrees with what has been said about this matter from ancient time."

Musō then inquired:—

"Does not the priest on the hill sometimes perform the funeral-service for your dead?"

"What priest?" the young man asked.

"The priest who yesterday evening directed me to this village," answered Musō. "I called at his *anjitsu* on the hill yonder. He refused me lodging, but told me the way here."

The listeners looked at each other, as in astonishment; and, after a moment of silence, the master of the house said:—

"Reverend Sir, there is no priest and there is no *anjitsu* on the hill. For the time of many generations there has not been any resident-priest in this neighbourhood."

Musō said nothing more on the subject; for it was evident that his kind hosts supposed him to have been deluded by some goblin. But after having bidden them farewell, and obtained all necessary information as to his road, he determined to look again for the hermitage on the hill, and so to ascertain whether he had really been deceived. He found the *anjitsu* without any difficulty; and, this time, its aged occupant invited him to enter. When he had done so, the hermit humbly bowed down before him, exclaiming:—"Ah! I am ashamed!—I am very much ashamed!—I am exceedingly ashamed!"

"You need not be ashamed for having refused me shelter," said Musō. "You directed me to the village yonder, where I was very kindly treated; and I thank you for that favour."

"I can give no man shelter," the recluse made answer;—and it is not for the refusal that I am ashamed. I am ashamed only that you should have seen me in my real shape,—for it was I who devoured the corpse and the offerings last night before your eyes . . . Know, reverend Sir, that I am a *jikininki*,[1]—an eater of human flesh. Have pity upon me, and suffer me to confess the secret fault by which I became reduced to this condition.

"A long, long time ago, I was a priest in this desolate region. There was no other priest for many leagues around. So, in that time, the bodies of the mountain-folk who died used to be brought here,—sometimes from great distances,—in order that I might repeat over them the holy service. But I repeated the service and performed the rites only as a matter of business;—I thought only of the food and the clothes that my sacred profession enabled me to gain. And because of this selfish impiety I was reborn, immediately after my death, into the state of a *jikininki*.[2] Since then I have been obliged to feed upon the corpses of the people who die in this district: every one of them I must devour in the way that you saw last night... Now, reverend Sir, let me beseech you to perform a Ségaki-service[2] for me: help me by your prayers, I entreat you, so that I may be soon able to escape from this horrible state of existence". . .

No sooner had the hermit uttered this petition than he disappeared; and the hermitage also disappeared at the same instant. And Musō Kokushi found himself kneeling alone in the high grass, beside an ancient and moss-grown tomb of the form called *go-rin-ishi*,[3] which seemed to be the tomb of a priest.

4

1. Literally, a man-eating goblin. The Japanese narrator gives also the Sanskrit term, "Râkshasa"; but this word is quite as vague as *jikininki*, since there are many kinds of Râkshasas. Apparently the word *jikininki* signifies here one of the *Baroman-Rasetsu-Gaki*,—forming the twenty-sixth class of pretas enumerated in the old Buddhist books.

2. A *Ségaki*-service is a special Buddhist service performed on behalf of beings supposed to have entered in the condition of gaki (pretas), or hungry spirits.

3. Literally, "five-circle [or 'five-zone'] stone." A funeral monument consisting of five parts superimposed,—each of a different form,—symbolising the five mystic elements: Ether, Air, Fire, Water, Earth.

Jubal, the Ringer

Fitz-James O'Brien

I

High in the brown belfry of the old Church of Saint Fantasmos sat Jubal the Ringer, looking over the huge town that lay spread below. A great black net-work of streets stretched far away on every side—the sombre web of intertwisted human passions and interests, in which, year after year, many thousand souls had been captured and destroyed.

Sleeping hills with clear-cut edges rose all about the dark town, which seemed to be lying at the bottom of a vast purple goblet, whose rim, touched with the whiteness of approaching day, looked as if they were brimming with the foam of some celestial wine. Deep in the distance rolled a long river, musical through the night, and shaking back the moon-beams from its bosom as if in play.

It was an old belfry, the belfry of Saint Fantasmos. It sprang from a vaulted arch with four groinings, which hung directly over the altar, so that one above in the bell-room could see, through the cracks in the stone ceiling, the silver lamps that lit the shrine, the altar-railings, the priest, the penitents below. Old flat mosses clung to the weather-beaten sides of the belfry, and the winds went in and out through it wheresoever they willed. From the very summit, which was pointed, there arose a tall iron rod, on which stood a golden cock, with head erect to catch the morning breeze, with feathers spread to bask in the morning sun. A golden cock, I said: alas! golden no longer. Wind and weather had used him badly, and he had moulted all his splendor. Battered, and gray, and rusty, with draggled tail and broken beak, he was no more the brave cock that he had been of yore. He had a malevolent and diabolical aspect. He looked as if he had made a compact with the demons of the night.

How blame him, if he had ceased to be an amiable cock? For years he had done his duty bravely to the town in all weathers, telling the points of the wind with unerring sagacity. The winds furious at having their secrets betrayed, would often steal softly down upon him in the disguise of a delicate breeze, and then burst upon him with the roar of a lion, in the hope of tumbling him from his sentinel's post. But they never caught him, for he was then young and agile, and he glided round at the slightest breath, so that the winds never could succeed in coming upon his broadside, but went off howling with anger to sea, where they wrecked ships, and buried them under the waves.

But the town neglected the poor cock, and he was never regilded or repaired, so that in time his pivots grew rusty, and he could no longer move with his former agility. Then the storms persecuted him, and the Equinox came down on him savagely twice a year, and buffeted him so that he thought his last hour was come; and those who passed by Saint Fantasmos on those ternpestuous nights heard him shrieking with rage, through the wild aerial combats, till thinking it the voice of a demon high up in the clouds, they crossed themselves, and hurried home to bed.

So the cock, and the belfry, and Jubal the Ringer grew old together; but Jubal was the oldest of all, for the human heart ages more quickly than stone or copper, and the storms that assail it are fiercer and sharper than the winds or the rains.

II

Jubal sat in the window of the belfry, looking over the black town, and moaning to himself. The day had not yet risen, but was near at hand.

"This morn," he said, shaking his long hair, which was already sprinkled with gray, "this morn she will be wed. This morn she will stand in front of the altar below, the light from the silver lamps shining on her white forehead, that I love better than the moon; and her lover will put the gold ring upon her finger, and the priest will bless her with lifted hands, while I, through the cracks in the vaulted ceiling, will behold all this: I, who adore her: I who have loved her for years, and followed her with my eyes as she wandered through the fields in May, toying with the hawthorn hedges, herself more fragrant, whiter, purer than the blossoms which she gathered. I, who used to spend the early dawn traversing the woods, gathering the red wild strawberries while the silver dews still lay upon them, in order that I might place them secretly at her door! Ah! she never knew how in the cold winter nights I sat in the fork of the apple-tree outside her chamber-window, watching her light, and gazing on her shadow as it fell upon the blind. Sometimes the shadow would seem to lengthen, and come across the walk and climb the tree, and, I would strive to fold it in my arms, as if it was my beloved in person; but it would suddenly recoil and elude me, and I could do nothing but kiss the branches where it had fallen, with my cold lips.

"One day, she went to gather white and yellow water-lilies, that swam on the surface of a pond. She held a long crook in her hand, with which she reached out and endeavored to bring them to shore. But they were cunning and slippery, and did not wish to be captured, by even so fair a maid as she; so when her crook touched them, they ducked their pearly and golden crests under the waters and escaped, coming up again all dripping and shining, and seemed to laugh at the eager girl. Being vexed at this, she stretched out her crook still farther, when the treacherous bank gave way, and my Agatha went down into the deep pond. I was near—I was always near her, though she knew it not—and I plunged in, and sought her amid the loathsome weeds. I brought her to shore, and chafed her fair forehead, and revived her. Then when she had recovered, I said to her: 'I am Jubal, the Ringer: I love you Agatha: will you make my lonely life happy forever?' With a look of wild horror she broke from me, and fled to her home.

"And I am despised, and she weds another. While the blessings are being given, and the church is white with orange-wreaths, and the poor wait in the porch for the nuptial bounty, I, who adore her, must sit aloft in this old belfry, and ring out jubilant chimes for the wedded pair.

"Aha! they know not Jubal, the Ringer. I can work the spells my mother worked, and I know the formulas that compel spirits. Agatha, thou false one, and thou, smooth-cheeked lover, who dreamst perhaps of her now, and thou, sacred priest, who givest away to another that which belongs to me, beware, for ye shall perish!"

Then Jubal laughed horribly, and spread his arms out as if he would embrace the night, and muttered certain strange sentences that were terrible to hear.

As he muttered, there came from the west a huge cloud of bats, that fastened themselves against the sides of the old belfry, and there was one for every stone, they were so numerous. And presently a ceaseless clicking resounded through the turret, as if myriads of tiny laborers were plying their pick-axes; a hail of falling fragments of mortar tinkled continually on the tin roofing of the Church of St. Fantasmos; and the bats seemed to eat into the crevices of the old belfry, as if they were about to sleep forever in its walls.

Presently the day rose. The sun-beams poured over the edges of the hills as the molten gold pours from the caldron of a worker in metals. The streets began to pulse with the first throbs of life, and Jubal, the Ringer, laughed aloud, for not a single bat was visible. The entire multitude had buried themselves in the walls of the belfry.

III

The street leading to the Church of St. Fantasmos was by nine o'clock as gay as the enamelled pages of a pope's missal. The road was strewn with flowers, and the people crushed the tender lily of the valley and the blue campanula and the spiced carnation under their feet. In and out between the throng of loiterers ran persons bearing boughs of the yellow laburnum in full blossom, until the way seemed arabesqued with gold. The windows on either side were filled with smiling faces, that pressed against the panes, like flowers pressing toward the light against conservatory casements. The linen of the maidens' caps was white as snow, and their cheeks were rose-red; and each jostled the other so as better to see the wedding procession of the fair Agatha and her gallant lover on its way to the altar of St. Fantasmos.

Presently the marriage cavalcade came by. It was like a page from a painted book. Agatha was so fair and modest; the bridegroom was so manly; the parents were so venerable with their white locks, and their faces lit with the beautiful sun-set of departing life.

As the procession passed beneath the windows, bunches of ribbons and flowers and bits of gay-colored paper, on which amorous devices were written, were flung to the bride and bridegroom by the bystanders; and a long murmur swelled along the street, of "God protect them, for they are beautiful and good!" And this lasted until they entered the gates of the church, where it was taken up by the poor people of the town who awaited them there. So, with benedictions falling upon them thick as the falling leaves of autumn, they passed into the Church of St. Fantasmos; but as they gained the threshold the bride looked up to the belfry, and there she fancied she beheld a man's head glaring at her with two fiery eyes, so that she shuddered and looked away. The next instant she looked up again, but the head was gone.

The people who were not invited to the ceremony loitered in the yard without, intending to accompany the bride home when the sacred rite was concluded, and cheer her by the way with songs composed in her honor. While they waited, the chimes in the belfry began to peal.

"How now!" cried one. "It is too soon for the chimes to peal. The couple are not yet married."

"What can Jubal be dreaming of?" said a second.

"Listen," cried a third; "did you ever hear such discords. Those are not wedding chimes. It is the music of devils."

A terrible fear suddenly fell over the multitude as they listened. Louder and louder swelled the colossal discords of the bells. The clouds were torn with these awful dissonances; the skies were curdled with the groans, the shrieks, the unnatural thunders that issued from the belfry.

The people below crossed themselves, and muttered to one another that there was a devil in the turret.

There was a devil in the turret, for Jubal was no longer man. With his eyes fixed on the crack in the vaulted ceiling, through which he saw the marriage ceremony proceeding, and his sinewy arms working with superhuman strength the machinery that moved the bells, he seemed the incarnation of a malevolent fiend. His hair stood erect; his eyes burned like fire-balls; and a white foam rose continually to his lips, and breaking into flakes, floated to the ground.

Still the terrible peals went on. The tortured bells swung now this way, now that, yelled forth a frightful diapason of sound that shook the very earth. Faster and faster Jubal tolled their iron tongues. Louder and louder grew the brazen clamor. The huge beams that supported the chimes cracked and groaned. The air, beaten with these violent sounds, swelled into waves that became billows, that in turn became mountains, and surged with irresistible force against the walls of the turret. The cock on the summit shivered and shrieked, as if the equinoxes of ten thousand years had been let loose on him at the same moment. The stones in the walls trembled, and from between their crevices vomited forth dust and mortar. The whole turret shook from base to apex.

Suddenly the people below beheld a vast cloud of bats issue from between the stones of the belfry and fly toward the west.

Then it appeared as if the bells spent their last strength in one vast accumulated brazen howl, that seemed to split the skies. The turret rocked twice, then toppled. Down through the vaulted arch, crushing it in as if it had been glass; down through the incensed air that filled the aisle, on priest and bride and bridegroom and parents and friends, came a white blinding mass of stone and mortar, and the next instant there was nothing but a cloud of dust slowly rising, a splash of blood here and there, that the dry stones soaked in, and one battered human head with long hair, half-visible through the mass of ruin. It was Jubal dead, but also Jubal avenged.

When on the ensuing October the wild equinoxes came like a horde of Cossacks over the hills, to make their last assault upon the golden cock, they found neither bird nor belfry, and the mischief they did that night at sea, out of mere spite, was, the legend says, incredible.

Jumbee

Henry S. Whitehead

Mr. Granville Lee, a Virginian of Virginians, coming out of the World War with a lung wasted and scorched by mustard gas, was recommended by his physician to spend a winter in the spice-and-balm climate of the Lesser Antilles—the lower islands of the West Indian archipelago. He chose one of the American islands, St. Croix, the old Santa Cruz—Island of the Holy Cross—named by Columbus himself on his second voyage; once famous for its rum.

It was to Jaffray Da Silva that Mr. Lee at last turned for definite information about the local magic; information which, after a two months' residence, accompanied with marked improvement in his general health, he had come to regard as imperative, from the whetting glimpses he had received of its persistence on the island.

Contact with local customs, too, had sufficiently blunted his inherited sensibilities, to make him almost comfortable, as he sat with Mr. Da Silva on the cool gallery of that gentleman's beautiful house, in the shade of forty years' growth of bougainvillea, on a certain afternoon. It was the restful gossipy period between five o'clock and dinnertime. A glass jug of foaming rum-swizzel stood on the table between them.

"But tell me, Mr. Da Silva," he urged, as he absorbed his second glass of the cooling, mild drink, "have you ever, actually, been confronted with a 'Jumbee'?—ever really seen one? You say, quite frankly, that you believe in them!"

This was not the first question about Jumbees that Mr. Lee had asked. He had consulted planters; he had spoken of the matter of Jumbees with courteous, intelligent, colored storekeepers about the town, and even in Christiansted, St. Croix's other and larger town on the north side of the island. He had even mentioned the matter to one or two coal-black sugar-field laborers; for he had been on the island just long enough to begin to understand—a little—the weird jargon of speech which Lafcadio Hearn, when he visited St. Croix many years before, had not recognised as "English"!

There had been marked differences in what he had been told. The planters and storekeepers had smiled, though with varying degrees of intensity, and had replied that the Danes had invented Jumbees, to keep their estate-laborers indoors after nightfall, thus ensuring a proper night's sleep for them, and minimising the depredations upon growing crops. The laborers whom he had asked had rolled their eyes somewhat, but, it being broad daylight at the time of the enquiries, they had broken their impassive gravity with smiles, and sought to impress Mr. Lee with their lofty contempt for the beliefs of their fellow blacks, and with queerly phrased assurances that Jumbee is a figment of the imagination.

Nevertheless, Mr. Lee was not satisfied. There was something here that he seemed to be missing—something extremely interesting, too, it appeared to him; something very different from "Bre'r Rabbit" and similar tales of his own remembered childhood in Virginia.

Once, too, he had been reading a book about Martinique and Guadeloupe, those ancient jewels of France's crown, and he had not read far before he met the word "Zombi." After that, he knew, at least, that the Danes had not "invented" the Jumbee. He heard, though vaguely, of the laborer's belief that Sven Garik, who had long ago gone back to his home in Sweden, and Garrity, one of the smaller planters now on the island, were "wolves"! Lycanthropy, animal-metamorphosis, it appeared, fanned part of this strange texture of local belief.

Mr. Jaffray Da Silva was one-eighth African. He was, therefore, by island usage, "colored," which is as different from being "black" in the West Indies as anything that can be imagined. Mr. Da Silva had been educated in the continental European manner. In his every word and action, he reflected the faultless courtesy of his European forbears. By every right and custom of West Indian society, Mr. Da Silva was a colored gentleman, whose social status was as clear-cut and definite as a cameo.

These islands are largely populated by persons like Mr. Da Silva. Despite the difference in their status from what it would be in North America, in the islands it has its advantages—among them that of logic. To the West Indian mind, a man whose heredity is seven-eighths derived from gentry, as like as not with authentic coats-of-arms, is entitled to be treated accordingly. That is why Mr. Da Silva's many clerks, and everybody else who knew him, treated him with deference, addressed him as "sir," and doffed their hats in continental fashion when meeting; salutes which, of course, Mr. Da Silva invariably returned, even to the humblest, which is one of the marks of a gentleman anywhere.

Jaffray Da Silva shifted one thin leg, draped in spotless white drill, over the other and lighted a fresh cigarette.

"Even my friends smile at me, Mr. Lee," he replied, with a tolerant smile, which lightened for an instant his melancholy, ivory-white countenance. "They laugh at me more or less because I admit I believe in Jumbees. It is possible that everybody with even a small amount of African blood possesses that streak of belief in magic and the like. I seem, though, to have a peculiar aptitude for it! It is a matter of experience with me, sir, and my friends are free to smile at me if they wish. Most of them—well, they do not admit their beliefs as freely as I, perhaps!"

Mr. Lee took another sip of the cold swizzel. He had heard how difficult it was to get Jaffray Da Silva to speak of his "experiences," and he suspected that under his host's even courtesy lay that austere pride which resents anything like ridicule, despite that tolerant smile.

"Please proceed, sir," urged Mr. Lee, and was quite unconscious that he had just used a word which, in his native South, is reserved for gentlemen of pure Caucasian blood.

"When I was a young man," began Mr. Da Silva, "about 1894; there was a friend of mine named Hilmar Iversen, a Dane, who lived here in the town, up near the Moravian Church on what the people call 'Foun'-Out Hill.' Iversen had a position under the government, a clerk's job, and his office was in the Port. On his way home he used to stop here almost every afternoon for a swizzel and a chat. We were great friends, close friends. He was then a man a little past fifty, a butter-tub of a fellow, very stout, and, like many of that build he suffered from heart attacks.

"One night a boy came here for me. It was eleven o'clock, and I was just hanging the mosquito-net on my bed, ready to turn in. The servants had all gone home, so went to the door myself, in shirt and trousers, and carrying a lamp; to see what was wanted—or, rather, I knew perfectly well what it was—a messenger to tell me Iversen was dead!"

Mr. Lee suddenly sat bolt-upright.

"How could you know that?" he enquired, his eyes wide. Mr. Da Silva threw away the remains of his cigarette.

"I sometimes know things like that," he answered, slowly. "In this case Iversen and I had been close friends for years. He and I had talked about magic and that sort of thing a great deal, occult powers, manifestations—that sort of thing. It is a very general topic here, as you may have seen. You would hear more of it if you continued to live here and settled into the ways of the island. In fact, Mr. Lee, Iversen and I had made a compact together. The one of us who 'went out' first, was to try to warn the other of it. You see, Mr. Lee, I had received Iversen's warning less than an hour before.

"I had been sitting out here on the gallery until ten o'clock or so. I was in that very chair you are occupying. Iversen had been having a heart arrack. I had been to see him that afternoon. He looked just as he always did when he was recovering from an attack. In fact he intended to return to his office the following morning. Neither of us, I am sure, had given a thought to the possibility of a sudden sinking spell. We had not even referred to our agreement.

"Well, it was about ten, as I've said, when all of a sudden I heard Iversen coming along through the yard below there, towards the house along that gravel path. He had, apparently, come through the gate from the Kongensgade—the King Street as they call it nowadays—and I could hear his heavy step on the gravel very plainly. He had a slight limp. 'Heavy crunch—light crunch; plod-plod—plod-plod'; old Iversen to the life; there was no mistaking his step. There was no moon that night. The half of a waning moon was due to show itself an hour and a half later, but just then it was virtually pitch-black down there in the garden.

"I got up out of my chair and walked over to the top of the steps. To tell you the truth, Mr. Lee, I rather suspected—have an aptitude for that sort of thing—that it was not Iversen himself; how shall I express it? I had the idea from somewhere inside me, that it was Iversen trying to keep our agreement. My instinct assured me that he had just died. I can not tell you how I knew it, but such was the case, Mr. Lee.

"So I waited, over there just behind you, at the top of the steps. The footfalls came along steadily. At the foot of the steps, out of the shadow of the hibiscus bushes, it was a trifle less black than farther down the path. There was a faint illumination, too, from a lamp inside the house. I knew that if it were Iversen, himself, I should be able to see him when the footsteps passed out of the deep shadow of the bushes. I did not speak.

"The footfalls came along towards that point, and passed it. I strained my eyes through the gloom, and I could see nothing. Then I knew, Mr. Lee, that Iversen had died, and that he was keeping his agreement.

"I came back here and sat down in my chair, and waited. The footfalls began to come up the steps. They came along the floor of the gallery, straight towards me. They stopped here, Mr. Lee, just beside me. I could *feel* Iversen standing here, Mr. Lee." Mr. Da Silva pointed to the floor with his slim, rather elegant hand.

"Suddenly, in the dead quiet, I could feel my hair stand up all over my scalp, straight and stiff. The chills started to run down my back, and up again, Mr. Lee. I shook like a man with the ague, sitting here in my chair.

"I said: 'Iversen, I understand! Iversen, I'm afraid!' My teeth were chattering like castanets, Mr. Lee. I said: 'Iversen, please go! You have kept the agreement. I am sorry I am afraid, Iversen. The flesh is weak. I am not afraid of you, Iversen, old friend. But you will understand, man! It's not ordinary fear. My intellect is all right, Iversen, but I'm badly panic-stricken, so please go, my friend.'

"There had been silence, Mr. Lee, as I said, before I began to speak to Iversen, for the footsteps had stopped here beside me. But when I said that, and asked my friend to go, I could feel that he went at once, and I knew that he had understood how I meant it! I was, suddenly, It was suddenly, Mr. Lee, as though there had never been any footsteps, if you see what I mean. It is hard to put into words. I daresay, if it had been one of the laborers, I should have been halfway to Christiansted through the estate, Mr. Lee, but I was not so frightened that I could not stand my ground.

"After I had recovered myself a little, and my scalp had ceased its pricking, and the chills were no longer running up and down my spine, I rose, and I felt extremely weary, Mr. Lee. It had been exhausting. I came into the house and drank a large tot of French brandy, and then I felt better, more like myself. I took my hurricane-lantern and lighted it and stepped down the path towards the gate leading to the Kongensgade. There was one thing I wished to see down there at the end of the garden. I wanted to see if the gate was fastened, Mr. Lee. It was that huge iron staple that you noticed, was in place. It has been used to fasten that old gate since some time in the eighteenth century, I imagine. I had not supposed anyone had opened the gate, Mr. Lee, but now I knew. There were no footprints in the gravel, Mr. Lee. I looked, carefully. The marks of the bush-broom where the house-boy had swept the path on his way back from closing the gate were undisturbed, Mr. Lee.

"I was satisfied, and no longer, even a little frightened. I came back here and sat down, and thought about my long friendship with old Iversen. I felt very sad to know that I should not see him again alive. He would never stop here again afternoon for a swizzel and a chat. About 11 o'clock I went inside the house and was preparing for bed when the rapping came at the front door. You see, Mr. Lee, I knew at once what it would mean.

"I went to the door, in shirt and trousers and stocking feet, carrying a lamp. We did not have electric light in those days. At the door stood Iversen's house-boy, a young fellow about eighteen. He was half-asleep, and very much upset. He 'cut his eyes' at me, and said nothing.

"'What is it, mon?' asked the boy.

" 'Mistress Iversen send ax yo' sir, please come to de house. Mr. Iversen die, sir.'

" 'What time Mr. Iversen die, mon—you hear?'

" 'I ain' able to say what o'clock, sir. Mistress Iversen come wake me where I sleep in a room in the yard, sir, an' sen' me please cahl you—I t'ink he die aboht an hour ago, sir.'

"I put on my shoes again, and the rest of my clothes, and picked up a St. Kitts supplejack—I'll get you one; it's one of those limber, grapevine walling sticks, a handy thing on a dark night—and started with the boy for Iversen's house.

"When we had arrived almost at the Moravian Church, I saw something ahead, near the roadside. It was then about eleven-fifteen, and the streets were deserted. What I saw made me curious to test something. I paused, and told the boy to run on ahead and tell Mrs. Iversen I would be there shortly. The boy started to trot ahead. He was pure black, Mr. Lee, but he went past what I saw without noticing it. He swerved a little away from it, and I think, perhaps, he slightly quickened his pace just at that point, but that was all."

"What did you see?" asked Mr. Lee, interrupting. He spoke a trifle breathlessly. His left lung was, as yet, far from being healed.

"The 'Hanging Jumbee,' " replied Mr. Da Silva, in his usual tones.

"Yes! There at the side of the road were three Jumbees. There's a reference to that in *The History of Stewart McCann*. Perhaps you've run across that, eh?"

Mr. Lee nodded, and Mr. Da Silva quoted:

"There they hung, though no ladder's rung
Supported their dangling feet.

"And there's another line in *The History*," he continued, smiling, "which describes a typical group of Hanging Jumbee:

"Maiden, man-child, and shrew.

"Well, there were the usual three Jumbees, apparently hanging in the air. It wasn't very light, but I could make out a boy of about twelve, a young girl, and a shriveled old woman—what the author of *The History of Stewart McCann* meant by the word 'shrew.' He told me himself, by the way, Mr. Lee, that he had put feet on his Jumbees mostly for the sake of a convenient rhyme—poetic licence! The Hanging Jumbee have no feet. It is one of their peculiarities. Their legs stop at the ankles. They have abnormally long, thin legs—African legs. They are always black, you know. Their feet—if they have them—are always hidden in a kind of mist that lies along the ground wherever one sees them. They shift and 'weave,' as a full-blooded African does—standing on one foot and resting the other—you've noticed that, of course—or scratching the supporting ankle with the toes of the other foot. They do not swing in the sense that they seem to be swung on a rope—that is not what it means; they do not twirl about. But they do—always—face the oncomer.

"I walked on, slowly, and passed them; and they kept their faces to me as they always do. I'm used to that. . . .

"I went up the steps of the house to the front gallery, and found Mrs. Iversen waiting for me. Her sister was with her, too. I remained sitting with them for the best part of an hour. Then two old black women who had been sent for, into the country, arrived. These were two old women who were accustomed to prepare the dead for burial. Then I persuaded the ladies to retire, and started to come home myself.

"It was a little past midnight, perhaps twelve-fifteen. I picked out my own hat from two or three of poor old Iversen's that were hanging on the rack, took my supplejack, and stepped out of the door onto the little stone gallery at the head of the steps.

"There are about twelve or thirteen steps from the gallery down to the street. As I started down them I noticed a third old black woman sitting, all huddled together, on the bottom step, with her back to me. I thought at once that this must be some old crone who lived with the other two—the preparers of the dead. I imagined that she had been afraid to remain alone in their cabin, and so had accompanied them into the town—they are like children, you know, in some ways—and that, feeling too humble to come into the house, she had sat down to wait on the step and had fallen asleep. You've heard their proverbs, have you not? There's one that exactly fits this situation that I had imagined: 'Cockroach no wear crockin' boot when he creep in fowl-house!' It means: 'Be very reserved when in the presence of your betters!' Quaint, rather! The poor souls!

"I started to walk down the steps towards the old woman. That scant half-moon had come up into the sky while I had been sitting with the ladies, and by its light everything was fairly sharply defined. I could see that old woman as plainly as I can see you now, Mr. Lee. In fact, I was looking directly at the poor creature as I came down the steps, and fumbling in my pocket for a few coppers for her—for tobacco and sugar, as they say! I was wondering, indeed, why she was not by this time on her feet and making one of their queer little bobbling bows—'cockroach bow to fowl,' as they might say! It seemed this old woman must have fallen into a very deep sleep, for she had not moved at all, although ordinarily she would have heard me, for the night was deathly still, and their hearing is extraordinarily acute, like a cat's, or a dog's. I remember that the fragrance from Mrs. Iversen's tuberoses, in pots on the gallery railing, was pouring out in a stream that night, 'making a greeting for the moon!' It was almost overpowering.

"Just as I was putting my foot on the fifth step, there came a tiny little puff of fresh breeze from somewhere in the hills behind Iversen's house. It rustled the dry fronds of a palm-tree that was growing beside the steps. I turned my head in that direction for an instant.

"Mr. Lee, when I looked back, down the steps, after what must have been a fifth of a second's inattention, that little old black woman who had been huddled up there on the lowest step, apparently sound asleep, was gone. She had vanished utterly—and, Mr. Lee, a little white dog, about the size of a French poodle, was bounding up the steps towards me. With every bound, a step at a leap, the dog increased in size. It seemed to swell out there before my very eyes.

"Then I was, really, frightened—thoroughly, utterly frightened. I knew if that 'animal' so much as touched me, it meant death, Mr. Lee—absolute, certain death. The little old woman was a 'sheen'—chien–of course. You know of lycanthropy—wolf change—of course. Well, this was one of our varieties of it. I do not know what it would be called, I'm sure. 'Canicanthropy,' perhaps. I don't know, but something—something first-cousin-once-removed from lycanthropy, and on the downward scale, Mr. Lee. The old woman was a were-dog!

"Of course, I had no time to think, only to use my instinct. I swung my supple-jack with all my might and brought it down squarely on that beast's head. It was only a step below me, then, and I could see the faint moonlight sparkle on the slaver about its mouth. It was then, it seemed to me, about the size of a medium-sized dog—nearly wolf size, Mr. Lee, and a kind of deathly white. I was desperate, and the force with which I struck caused me to lose my balance. I did not fall, but it required a moment or two for me to regain my equilibrium. When I felt my feet firm under me again, I looked about, frantically, on all sides, for the 'dog.' But it, too, Mr. Lee, like the old woman, had quite disappeared. I looked all about, you may well imagine, after that experience, in the clear, thin moonlight. For yards about the foot of the steps, there was no place—not even a small nook—where either the 'dog' or the old woman could have been concealed. Neither was on the gallery, which was only a few feet square, a mere landing.

"But there came to my ears, sharpened by that night's experiences, from far out among the plantations at the rear of Iversen's house, the pad-pad of naked feet. Someone—something—was running, desperately, off in the direction of the centre of the island, back into the hills, into the deep 'bush.'

"Then, behind me, out of the house onto the gallery rushed the two old women who had been preparing Iversen's body for its burial. They were enormously excited, and they shouted at me unintelligibly. I will have to render their words for you.

"'O, de Good Gahd protec' you, Marster Jaffray, sir—de Joombie, de Joombie! De "Sheen," Marster Jaffray! He go, sir?'

"I reassured the poor old souls, and went back home."

Mr. Da Silva fell abruptly silent. He did not move. Mr. Da Silva resumed, deliberately, after obtaining a light.

"You see, Mr. Lee, the West Indies are different from any other place in the world, I verily believe, sir. I've said so, anyhow, many a time, although I have never been out of the islands except when I was a young man, to Copenhagen. I've told you, exactly, what happened that particular night."

Mr. Lee heaved a sigh.

"Thank you, Mr. Da Silva, very much indeed, sir," said he, thoughtfully, and made as though to rise. His service wrist-watch indicated 6 o'clock.

"Let us have a fresh swizzel, at least, before you go," suggested Mr. Da Silva.

"We have a saying here in the island, that 'a man can't travel on one leg'! Perhaps you've heard it already."

"I have," said Mr. Lee.

"Knud, Knud! You hear, mon? Knud—tell Charlotte to mash up another bal' of ice—you hear? Quickly now," commanded Mr. Da Silva.

Lady Farquhar's Old Lady

A True Ghost Story

Mrs. Molesworth

"One that was a woman, sir; but, rest her soul, she's dead."

I myself have never seen a ghost (I am by no means sure that I wish ever to do so), but I have a friend whose experience in this respect has been less limited than mine. Till lately, however, I had never heard the details of Lady Farquhar's adventure, though the fact of there being a ghost story which she could, if she chose, relate with the authority of an eyewitness, had been more than once alluded to before me. Living at extreme ends of the country, it is but seldom my friend and I are able to meet; but a few months ago I had the good fortune to spend some days in her house, and one evening our conversation happening to fall on the subject of the possibility of so-called "supernatural" visitations or communications, suddenly what I had heard returned to my memory.

"By the bye," I exclaimed, "we need not go far for an authority on the question. You have seen a ghost yourself, Margaret. I remember once hearing it alluded to before you, and you did not contradict it. I have so often meant to ask you for the whole story. Do tell it to us now."

Lady Farquhar hesitated for a moment, and her usually bright expression grew somewhat graver. When she spoke, it seemed to be with a slight effort.

"You mean what they all call the story of 'my old lady,' I suppose," she said at last. "Oh yes, if you care to hear it, I will tell it you. But there is not much to tell, remember."

"There seldom is in *true* stories of the kind," I replied. "Genuine ghost stories are generally abrupt and inconsequent in the extreme, but on this very account all the more impressive. Don't you think so?"

"I don't know that I am a fair judge," she answered. "Indeed," she went on rather gravely, "my own opinion is that what you call *true* ghost stories are very seldom told at all."

"How do you mean? I don't quite understand you," I said, a little perplexed by her words and tone.

"I mean," she replied, "that people who really believe they have come in contact with—with anything of that kind, seldom care to speak about it."

"Do you really think so? do you mean that you feel so yourself?" I exclaimed with considerable surprise. "I had no idea you did, or I would not have mentioned the subject. Of course you know I would not ask you to tell it if it is the least painful or disagreeable to you to talk about it."

"But it isn't. Oh no, it is not nearly so bad as that," she replied, with a smile. "I cannot really say that it is either painful or disagreeable to me to recall it, for I cannot exactly apply either of those words to the thing itself. All that I feel is a sort of shrinking from the subject, strong enough to prevent my ever alluding to it lightly or carelessly. Of all things, I should dislike to have a joke made of it. But with you I have no fear of that. And you trust me, don't you? I don't mean as to truthfulness only; but you don't think me deficient in common sense and self-control—not morbid, or very apt to be run away with by my imagination?"

"Not the sort of person one would pick out as likely to see ghosts?" I replied. "Certainly not. You are far too sensible and healthy and vigorous. I can't, very readily, fancy you the victim of delusion of any kind. But as to ghosts—are they or are they not delusions? There lies the question! Tell us your experience of them, any way."

So she told the story I had asked for—told it in the simplest language, and with no exaggeration of tone or manner, as we sat there in her pretty drawing-room, our chairs drawn close to the fire, for it was Christmas time, and the weather was "seasonable." Two or three of Margaret's children were in the room, though not within hearing of us; all looked bright and cheerful, nothing mysterious. Yet notwithstanding the total deficiency of ghostly accessories, the story impressed me vividly.

"It was early in the spring of '55 that it happened," began Lady Farquhar; "I never forget the year, for a reason I will tell you afterwards. It is fully fifteen years ago now—a long time—but I am still quite able to recall the *feeling* this strange adventure of mine left on me, though a few details and particulars have grown confused and misty. I think it often happens so when one tries, as it were *too* hard, to be accurate and unexaggerated in telling over anything. One's very honesty is against one. I have not told it over many times, but each time it seems more difficult to tell it quite exactly; the impression left at the time was so powerful that I have always dreaded incorrectness or exaggeration creeping in. It reminds me, too, of the curious way in which a familiar word or name grows distorted, and then cloudy and strange, if one looks at it too long or thinks about it too much. But I must get on with my story. Well, to begin again. In the winter of '54-'55 we were living—my mother, my sisters, and I, that is, and from time to time my brother—in, or rather near, a quiet little village on the south coast of Ireland. We had gone there, before the worst of the winter began at home, for the sake of my health. I had not been as well as usual for some time (this was greatly owing, I believe, to my having lately endured unusual anxiety of mind), and my dear mother dreaded the cold weather for me, and determined to avoid it. I say that I had had unusual anxiety to bear, still it was not of a kind to render me morbid or fanciful. And what is even more to the point, my mind was perfectly free from prepossession or association in connection with the place we were living in, or the people who had lived there before us. I simply knew nothing whatever of these people, and I had no sort of fancy about the house—that it *was* haunted, or anything of that kind; and indeed I never heard that it was thought to be haunted. It did not look like it; it was just a moderate-sized, somewhat old-fashioned country, or rather sea-side, house, furnished, with the exception of one room, in an ordinary enough modern style. The exception was a small room on the bedroom floor, which, though not locked off (that is to say, the key was left in the lock outside), was not given up for our use, as it was crowded with musty old furniture, packed closely together, and all of a fashion many, many years older than that of the contents of the rest of the house. I remember some of the pieces of furniture still, though I think I was only once or twice in the room all the time we were there. There were two or three old-fashioned cabinets or bureaux; there was a regular four-post bedstead, with the gloomy curtains still hanging round it; and ever so many spider-legged chairs and rickety tables; and I rather think in one corner there was a spinet. But there was nothing particularly curious or attractive, and we never thought of meddling with the things or 'poking about,' as girls sometimes do; for we always thought it was by mistake that this room had not been locked off altogether, so that no one should meddle with anything in it.

"We had rented the house for six months from a Captain Marchmont, a half-pay officer, naval or military, I don't know which, for we never saw him, and all the negotiations were managed by an agent. Captain Marchmont and his family, as a rule, lived at Ballyreina all the year round—they found it cheap and healthy, I suppose—but this year they had preferred to pass the winter in some livelier neighbourhood, and they were very glad to let the house. It never occurred to us to doubt our landlord's being the owner of it: it was not till some time after we left that we learned that he himself was only a tenant, though a tenant of long standing. There were no people about to make friends with, or to hear local gossip from. There were no gentry within visiting distance, and if there had been, we should hardly have cared to make friends for so short a time as we were to be there. The people of the village were mostly fishermen and their families; there were so many of them, we never got to know any specially. The doctor and the priest and the Protestant clergyman were all newcomers, and all three very uninteresting. The clergyman used to dine with us sometimes, as my brother had had some sort of introduction to him when we came to Ballyreina; but we never heard anything about the place from him. He was a great talker, too; I am sure he would have told us anything he knew. In short, there was nothing romantic or suggestive either about our house or the village. But we didn't care. You see we had gone there simply for rest and quiet and pure air, and we got what we wanted.

"Well, one evening about the middle of March I was up in my room dressing for dinner, and just as I had about finished dressing, my sister Helen came in. I remember her saying as she came in, 'Aren't you ready yet, Maggie? Are you making yourself extra smart for Mr. Conroy?' Mr. Conroy was the clergyman; he was dining with us that night. And then Helen looked at me and found fault with me, half in fun of course, for not having put on a prettier dress. I remember I said it was good enough for Mr. Conroy, who was no favourite of mine; but Helen wasn't satisfied till I agreed to wear a bright scarlet neck-ribbon of hers, and she ran off to her room to fetch it. I followed her almost immediately. Her room and mine, I must, by the bye, explain, were at extreme ends of a passage several yards in length. There was a wall on one side of this passage, and a balustrade overlooking the staircase on the other. My room was at the end nearest the top of the staircase. There were no doors along the passage leading to Helen's room, but just beside her door, at the end, was that of the unused room I told you of, filled with the old furniture. The passage was lighted from above by a skylight—I mean, it was by no means dark or shadowy—and on the evening I am speaking of, it was still clear daylight. We dined early at Ballyreina; I don't think it could have been more than a quarter to five when Helen came into my room. Well, as I was saying, I followed her almost immediately, so quickly that as I came out of my room I was in time to catch sight of her as she ran along the passage, and to see her go into her own room. Just as I lost sight of her—I was coming along more deliberately, you understand—suddenly, how or when exactly I cannot tell, I perceived *another* figure walking along the passage in front of me. It was a woman, a little thin woman, but though she had her back to me, something in her gait told me she was not young. She seemed a little bent, and walked feebly. I can remember her dress even now with the most perfect distinctness. She had a gown of gray clinging stuff, rather scanty in the skirt, and one of those funny little old-fashioned black shawls with a sewed-on border, that you seldom see nowadays. Do you know the kind I mean? It was a narrow, shawl-pattern border, and there was a short tufty black fringe below the border. And she had a gray poke bonnet, a bonnet made of silk 'gathered' on to a large stiff frame; 'drawn' bonnets they used to be called. I took in all these details of her dress in a moment, and even in that moment I noticed too that the materials of her clothes looked *good*, though so plain and old-fashioned. But somehow my first impulse when I saw her was to call out, 'Fraser, is that you?' Fraser was my mother's maid: she was a young woman, and not the least like the person in front of me, but I think a vague idea rushed across my mind that it might be Fraser dressed up to trick the other servants. But the figure took no notice of my exclamation; it, or she, walked on quietly, not even turning her head round in the least; she walked slowly down the passage, seemingly quite unconscious of my presence, and, to my extreme amazement, disappeared into the unused room. The key, as I think I told you, was always turned in the lock—that is to say, the door was locked, but the key was left in it; but the old woman did not seem to me to unlock the door, or even to turn the handle. There seemed no obstacle in her way: she just quietly, as it were, walked *through* the door. Even by this time I hardly think I felt *frightened*. What I had seen had passed too quickly for me as yet to realise its strangeness. Still I felt perplexed and vaguely uneasy, and I hurried on to my sister's room. She was standing by the toilet-table, searching for the ribbon. I think I must have looked startled, for before I could speak she called out, 'Maggie, whatever is the matter with you? You look as if you were going to faint.' I asked her if she had heard anything, though it was an inconsistent question, for to *my* ears there had been no sound at all. Helen answered, 'Yes:' a moment before I came into the room she had heard the lock of the lumber-room (so we called it) door click, and had wondered what I could be going in there for. Then I told her what I had seen. She looked a little startled, but declared it must have been one of the servants.

"'If it is a trick of the servants,' I answered, 'it should be exposed'; and when Helen offered to search through the lumberroom with me at once, I was very ready to agree to it. I was so satisfied of the reality of what I had seen, that I declared to Helen that the old woman, whoever she was, must be in the room; it stood to reason that, having gone in, she *must* still be there, as she could not possibly have come out again without our knowledge.

"So, plucking up our courage, we went to the lumber-room door. I felt so certain that but a moment before, some one had opened it, that I took hold of the knob quite confidently and turned it, just as one always does to open a door. The handle turned, but the door did not yield. I stooped down to see why; the reason was plain enough: the door was still locked, locked as usual, and the key in the lock! Then Helen and I stared at each other: *her* mind was evidently recurring to the sound she had heard; what *I* began to think I can hardly put in words.

"But when we got over this new start a little, we set to work to search the room as we had intended. And we searched it thoroughly, I assure you. We dragged the old tables and chairs out of their corners, and peeped behind the cabinets and chests of drawers where no one *could* have been hidden. Then we climbed upon the old bedstead, and shook the curtains till we were covered with dust; and then we crawled under the valances, and came out looking like sweeps; but there was nothing to be found. There was certainly *no one* in the room, and by all appearances no one could have been there for weeks. We had hardly time to make ourselves fit to be seen when the dinner-bell rang, and we had to hurry downstairs. As we ran down we agreed to say nothing of what had happened before the servants, but after dinner in the drawing-room we told our story. My mother and brother listened to it attentively, said it was very strange, and owned themselves as puzzled as we. Mr. Conroy of course laughed uproariously, and made us dislike him more than ever. After he had gone we talked it over again among ourselves, and my mother, who hated mysteries, did her utmost to explain what I had seen in a matter-of-fact, natural way. Was I sure it was not only Helen herself I had seen, after fancying she had reached her own room? Was I quite certain it was not Fraser after all, carrying a shawl perhaps, which made her look different? Might it not have been this, that, or the other? It was no use. Nothing could convince me that I had *not* seen what I had seen; and though, to satisfy my mother, we cross-questioned Fraser, it was with no result in the way of explanation. Fraser evidently knew nothing that could throw light on it, and she was quite certain that at the time I had seen the figure, both the other servants were downstairs in the kitchen. Fraser was perfectly trustworthy; we warned her not to frighten the others by speaking about the affair at all, but we could not leave off speaking about it among ourselves. We spoke about it so much for the next few days, that at last my mother lost patience, and forbade us to mention it again. At least she *pretended* to lose patience; in reality I believe she put a stop to the discussion because she thought it might have a bad effect on our nerves, on mine especially; for I found out afterwards that in her anxiety she even went the length of writing about it to our old doctor at home, and that it was by his advice she acted in forbidding us to talk about it any more. Poor dear mother!

I don't know that it was very sound advice. One's mind often runs all the more on things one is forbidden to mention. It certainly was so with me, for I thought over my strange adventure almost incessantly for some days after we left off talking about it."

Here Margaret paused.

"And is that all?" I asked, feeling a little disappointed, I think, at the unsatisfactory ending to the "true ghost story."

"All!" repeated Lady Farquhar, rousing herself as if from a reverie, "all! oh, dear no. I have sometimes wished it had been, for I don't think what I have told you would have left any long-lasting impression on me. All! oh, dear no. I am only at the beginning of my story."

So we resettled ourselves again to listen, and Lady Farquhar continued:—

"For some days, as I said, I could not help thinking a good deal of the mysterious old woman I had seen. Still, I assure you, I was not exactly frightened. I was more puzzled—puzzled and annoyed at not being able in any way to explain the mystery. But by ten days or so from the time of my first adventure the impression was beginning to fade. Indeed, the day before the evening I am now going to tell you of, I don't think my old lady had been in my head at all. It was filled with other things. So, don't you see, the explaining away what I saw as entirely a delusion, a fancy of my own brain, has a weak point here; for *had* it been all my fancy, it would surely have happened *sooner*—at the time my mind really was full of the subject. Though even if it had been so, it would not have explained the curious coincidence of my 'fancy' with facts, actual facts of which at the time I was in complete ignorance. It must have been just about ten days after my first adventure that I happened one evening, between eight and nine o'clock, to be alone upstairs in my own room. We had dined at half-past five as usual, and had been sitting together in the drawing-room since dinner, but I had made some little excuse for coming upstairs; the truth being that I wanted to be alone to read over a letter which the evening post (there actually was an evening post at Ballyreina) had brought me, and which I had only had time to glance at. It was a very welcome and dearly-prized letter, and the reading of it made me very happy. I don't think I had felt so happy all the months we had been in Ireland as I was feeling that evening. Do you remember my saying I never forget the year all this happened? It was the year '55 and the month of March, the spring following that first dreadful 'Crimean winter,' and news had just come to England of the Czar's death, and every one was wondering and hoping and fearing what would be the results of it. I had no very near friends in the Crimea, but of course, like every one else, I was intensely interested in all that was going on, and in this letter of mine there was told the news of the Czar's death, and there was a good deal of comment upon it. I had read my letter—more than once, I daresay—and was beginning to think I must go down to the others in the drawing-room. But the fire in my bedroom was very tempting; it was burning so brightly, that though I had got up from my chair by the fireside to leave the room, and had blown out the candle I had read my letter by, I yielded to the inclination to sit down again for a minute or two to dream pleasant dreams and think pleasant thoughts. At last I rose and turned towards the door—it was standing wide open, by the bye. But I had hardly made a step from the fireplace when I was stopped short by what I saw. Again the same strange indefinable feeling of not knowing how or when it had come there, again the same painful sensation of perplexity (not yet amounting to fear) as to whom or what it was I saw before me. The room, you must understand, was perfectly flooded with the firelight; except in the corners, perhaps, every object was as distinct as possible. And the object I was staring at was not in a corner, but standing there right before me—between me and the open door, alas!—in the middle of the room. It was the old woman again, but this time with her face towards me, with a look upon it, it seemed to me, as if she were conscious of my presence. It is very difficult to tell over thoughts and feelings that can hardly have taken any time to pass, or that passed almost simultaneously. My *very* first impulse this time was, as it had been the first time I saw her, to explain in some natural way the presence before me. I think this says something for my common sense, does it not? My mind did not readily desert matters of fact, you see. I did not think of Fraser this time, but the thought went through my mind, 'She must be some friend of the servants who comes in to see them of an evening. Perhaps they have sent her up to look at my fire.' So at first I looked up at her with simple inquiry. But as I looked my feelings changed. I realised that this was the same being who had appeared so mysteriously once before; I recognised every detail of her dress; I even noticed it more acutely than the first time—for instance, I recollect observing that here and there the short tufty fringe of her shawl was stuck together, instead of hanging smoothly and evenly all round. I looked up at her face. I cannot now describe the features beyond saying that the whole face was refined and pleasing, and that in the expression there was certainly nothing to alarm or repel. It was rather wistful and beseeching, the look in the eyes anxious, the lips slightly parted, as if she were on the point of speaking. I have since thought that if *I* had spoken, if I *could* have spoken—for I did make one effort to do so, but no audible words would come at my bidding—the spell that bound the poor soul, this mysterious wanderer from some shadowy borderland between life and death, might have been broken, and the message that I now believe burdened her delivered. Sometimes I wish I could have done it; but then, again—oh no! a *voice* from those unreal lips would have been too awful—flesh and blood could not have stood it. For another instant I kept my eyes fixed upon her without moving; then there came over me at last with an awful thrill, a sort of suffocating gasp of horror, the consciousness, the actual realisation of the fact that this before me, this *presence*, was no living human being, no dweller in our familiar world, not a woman, but a ghost! Oh, it was an awful moment! I pray that I may never again endure another like it. There is something so indescribably frightful in the feeling that we are on the verge of being tried *beyond* what we can bear, that ordinary conditions are slipping away from under us, that in another moment reason or life itself must snap with the strain; and all these feelings I then underwent. At last I moved, moved backwards from the figure. I dared not attempt to *pass* her. Yet I could not at first turn away from her. I stepped backwards, facing her still as I did so, till I was close to the fireplace. Then I turned sharply from her, sat down again on the low chair still standing by the hearth, resolutely forcing myself to gaze into the fire, which was blazing cheerfully, though conscious all the time of a terrible fascination urging me to look round again to the middle of the room. Gradually, however, now that I no longer *saw* her, I began a little to recover myself. I tried to bring my sense and reason to bear on the matter. 'This being,' I said to myself, 'whoever and whatever she is, *cannot harm* me. I am under God's protection as much at this moment as at any moment of my life. All creatures, even disembodied spirits, if there be such, and this among them, if it be one, are under His control. *Why* should I be afraid? I am being tried; my courage and trust are being tried to the utmost: let me prove them, let me keep my own self-respect, by mastering this cowardly, unreasonable terror.' And after a time I began to feel stronger and surer of myself. Then I rose from my seat and turned towards the door again; and oh, the relief of seeing that the way was clear; my terrible visitor had disappeared! I hastened across the room, I passed the few steps of passage that lay between my door and the staircase, and hurried down the first flight in a sort of suppressed agony of eagerness to find myself again safe in the living human companionship of my mother and sisters in the cheerful drawing-room below. But my trial was not yet over, indeed it seemed to me afterwards that it had only now reached its height; perhaps he strain on my nervous system was now beginning to tell, and my powers of endurance were all but exhausted. I cannot say if it was so or not. I can only say that my agony of terror, of horror, of absolute *fear*, was far past describing in words, when, just as I reached the little landing at the foot of the first short staircase, and was on the point of running down the longer flight still before me, I saw *again*, coming slowly up the steps, as if to meet me, the ghostly figure of the old woman. It was too much. I was reckless by this time; I could not stop. I rushed down the staircase, brushing past the figure as I went: I use the word intentionally—I did *brush* past her, I *felt* her. This part of my experience was, I believe, quite at variance with the sensations of orthodox ghost-seers; but I am really telling you all I was conscious of.

"Then I hardly remember anything more; my agony broke out at last in a loud shrill cry, and I suppose I fainted. I only know that when I recovered my senses I was in the drawing-room, on the sofa, surrounded by my terrified mother and sisters. But it was not for some time that I could find voice or courage to tell them what had happened to me; for several days I was on the brink of a serious illness, and for long afterwards I could not endure to be left alone, even in the broadest daylight."

Lady Farquhar stopped. I fancied, however, from her manner that there was more to tell, so I said nothing; and in a minute or two she went on speaking.

"We did not stay long at Ballyreina after this. I was not sorry to leave it; but still, before the time came for us to do so, I had begun to recover from the most painful part of the impression left upon me by my strange adventure. And when I was at home again, far from the place where it had happened, I gradually lost the feeling of horror altogether, and remembered it only as a very curious and inexplicable experience. Now and then even, I did not shrink from talking about it, generally, I think, with a vague hope that somehow, some time or other, light might be thrown upon it. Not that I ever expected, or could have believed it possible, that the supernatural character of the adventure could be explained away; but I always had a misty fancy that sooner or later I should find out *something* about my old lady, as we came to call her; who she had been and what her history was."

"And did you?" I asked eagerly.

"Yes, I did," Margaret answered. "To some extent, at least, I learnt the explanation of what I had seen. This was how it was: nearly a year after we had left Ireland I was staying with one of my aunts, and one evening some young people who were also visiting her began to talk about ghosts, and my aunt, who had heard something of the story from my mother, begged me to tell it. I did so, just as I have now told it to you. When I had finished, an elderly lady who was present, and who had listened very attentively, surprised me a little by asking the name of the house where it happened. 'Was it Ballyreina?' she said. I answered 'Yes,' wondering how she knew it, for I had not mentioned it.

" 'Then I can tell you whom you saw,' she exclaimed; 'it must have been one of the old Miss Fitzgeralds—the eldest one. The description suits her exactly.'

"I was quite puzzled. We had never heard of any Fitzgeralds at Ballyreina. I said so to the lady, and asked her to explain what she meant. She told me all she knew. It appeared there had been a family of that name for many generations at Ballyreina. Once upon a time—a long-ago once upon a time—the Fitzgeralds had been great and rich; but gradually one misfortune after another had brought them down in the world, and at the time my informant heard about them the only representatives of the old family were three maiden ladies already elderly. Mrs. Gordon, the lady who told me all this, had met them once, and had been much impressed by what she heard of them. They had got poorer and poorer, till at last they had to give up the struggle, and sell, or let on a long lease, their dear old home, Ballyreina. They were too proud to remain in their own country after this, and spent the rest of their lives on the Continent, wandering about from place to place. The most curious part of it was that nearly all their wandering was actually *on foot*. They were too poor to afford to travel much in the usual way, and yet, once torn from their old associations, the travelling mania seized them; they seemed absolutely unable to rest. So on foot, and speaking not a word of any language but their own, these three desolate sisters journeyed over a great part of the Continent. They visited most of the principal towns, and were well known in several. I daresay they are still remembered at some of the places they used to stay at, though never for more than a short time together. Mrs. Gordon had met them somewhere, I forget where, but it was many years ago. Since then she had never heard of them; she did not know if they were alive or dead; she was only certain that the description of my old lady was exactly like that of the eldest of the sisters, and that the name of their old home was Ballyreina. And I remember her saying, 'If ever a heart was buried in a house, it was that of poor old Miss Fitzgerald.'

"That was all Mrs. Gordon could tell me," continued Lady Farquhar; "but it led to my learning a little more. I told my brother what I had heard. He used often at that time to be in Ireland on business; and to satisfy me, the next time he went he visited the village of Ballyreina again, and in one way and another he found out a few particulars. The house, you remember, had been let to us by a Captain Marchmont. He, my brother discovered, was not the owner of the place, as we had naturally imagined, but only rented it on a very long lease from some ladies of the name of Fitzgerald. It had been in Captain Marchmont's possession for a great many years at the time he let it to us, and the Fitzgeralds, never returning there even to visit it, had come to be almost forgotten. The room with the old-fashioned furniture had been reserved by the owners of the place to leave some of their poor old treasures in—relics too cumbersome to be carried about with them in their strange wanderings, but too precious, evidently, to be parted with. We, of course, never could know what may not have been hidden away in some of the queer old bureaux I told you of. Family papers of importance, perhaps; possibly some ancient love-letters, forgotten in the confusion of their leave-taking; a lock of hair, or a withered flower, perhaps, that she, my poor old lady, would fain have clasped in her hand when dying, or have had buried with her. Ah, yes; there must be many a pitiful old story that is never told."

Lady Farquhar stopped and gazed dreamily and half sadly into the fire.

"Then Miss Fitzgerald *was* dead when you were at Ballyreina?" I asked.

Margaret looked up with some surprise.

"Did I not say so?" she exclaimed. "That was the point of most interest in what my brother discovered. He could not hear the exact date of her death, but he learnt with certainty that she was dead—had died, at Geneva I think, some time in the month of March in the previous year; *the same month, March '55, in which I had twice seen the apparition at Ballyreina*."

This was my friend's ghost story.

The Lady Tantivy

Rosa Mulholland

Had I been napping? My head had fallen back, and my cap was awry. I had been in the garden all the afternoon gathering roses for *pot-pourri*, hoping that the absent might one day return to enjoy it, and thankful for occupation, as the summer days were long and lonesome in this remote spot, this great unpeopled house. When one is tired one easily falls asleep. But, then, how could I have been awakened by the horn of a coach?

Yet there it came again. Even in these days of extraordinary enterprise, who would run a coach through our out-of-the-world bit of country—a solitude leading, as one might say, from nowhere to nowhere else?

I put my cap straight and stood at the window, while again, louder and clearer, sounded the unusual music on the summer evening air. I left my sitting-room and stood at the open door of the great hall and looked out. Between mountainous walls of dark trees poured an avenue of sunshine across that bend in the hills where the sun was setting. Not from that side was the sound coming; but there again—tantivy—tantivy—tantivy! from the winding road that skirts the long miles of downs lying between as and shire. My ears strained to catch the cheerful echo, and I wished I were a passenger by that coach out into the lively world. But another blast of the bugle and the roll of quick coming wheels, startlingly near, assured me that the coach in question had turned in at our gates, and was posting towards me.

I stepped forward and strained my neck to see the first appearance of the vehicle as it rounded the corner of the broad drive; and here it came, speeding towards the house, as fine a specimen of a four-in-hand as ever was turned out in style by a coaching club. It was covered with passengers on the outside, and faces were looking laughingly out of the windows. They had all the air of gay ladies and gentlemen out for amusement. As they drove up with a long flourishing blast of the horn, I was struck by the eccentricity of the dress of this coaching company: the men in peculiarly shaped hats, high-collared coats and tight waists, the ladies with immense bonnets and scanty skirts. The horses were foaming, and I thought of the stables without grooms, nobody about but an old gardener and myself, and one woman-servant. I advanced a step, but nobody seemed looking at me, or even to perceive me. When the coach stopped a gentleman descended from the box-seat, opened the door of the coach, and handed out a lady, closed the door again, conducted her to the hall-door steps, left her there, and immediately remounted to his own seat. The driver gathered up the reins, the horn was blown, and the horses started. In a few moments the coach was out of sight, the sound of the retreating bugle grew fainter and fainter, and the lady remained standing on the doorsteps, alone and with her back to me.

When the horn was no longer audible she turned round, and came tripping up the steps, a charming young figure, her white muslin gown crisp and fresh with little frills and furbelows such as I had seen in pictures of my grandmother's days. Her blue sash and the little silk bag of the color of forget-me-nots that hung from her waist had a coquettish grace, matching the curve of her long slender neck, round which golden ringlets clung, and the arch smile on her rose-mouth and in the eyes that were looking up at me. Her head-dress, a peculiar basket-like object, hung from her arm, as did a long, slim, white scarf of some silken fabric.

"I am coming to spend a night with you," she said, so sweetly that I was captivated at once. "I have travelled from what would seem to you a distance—"

"Pray come in, though I cannot promise you much in the way of entertainment," I said. "I am only caretaker in the home of my relative, who is abroad—unfortunately." My sigh, and the word "unfortunately" would, I hoped, remind her of the misfortunes of our house, of which she had probably heard.

"I know all about it," she answered. "I am a member of the family. As I said, I have come a long way, according to your ideas, to spend a night with you. Will you take me all over the old house, and talk to me about the family? I am more interested than I can tell you in the fortunes of my kindred."

"But, my dear child," I said, "where have you come from, if I may ask, and—pardon me—but how am I to know?"

"That I am not a robber? Sit up, and watch all night—you and your servant and the old gardener. I am only one girl against the three of you. But, cousin, give me better treatment than this. You need have no doubt of me."

I felt ashamed of what she had seen in my eyes, and, wondering still at her reticence, I ran over in my mind an outline of the various far-out branches of the family tree, trying to guess which of them had dropped me this blossom. I could not recall that any of my distant cousins owned a daughter of her age.

"No," she said, seeming, as before, to answer my thought, "you cannot place me among our relatives, and I do not intend to enlighten you to-night. To-morrow you shall know more about me. In the meantime, take me round the old garden before the daylight goes, and tell me everything you can about the present-day family."

I thought "present-day" a curious term to use, but noticing that she replied to my questions without informing me as to the point, I put on my cloak and gathered up my skirts, and led the way through the dewy alleys of green to the great old garden, which had of late become almost a wilderness. As we went she put her arm through mine, and with a curious thrill I noticed that I did not feel her do so, but only saw the action.

"You know, I dare say, that the present owner of this house is in trouble and in exile?" I explained.

"About a will," she remarked.

"An ancient will and title-deed. The documents were lost a hundred years ago."

"A hundred and nine years to the day," she replied, smiling at me.

"You are singularly accurate," I said; "but the chief thing that matters is the loss."

"How have they got on without it for a hundred years?"

"There was no one to dispute their right; but within the last few years a distant relative has sprung up and laid claim to what he declares was the inheritance of his grandfather. He pretends that the lost will was made in favour of this ancestor. He has succeeded in so far that he has got the estate into Chancery, and my cousin, having first been impoverished by years of law expenditure, has had to quit his old home with his wife and children, and is living almost in poverty in an obscure part of France."

I spoke with tears, and the bright eyes of my companion flashed sunshine into my face.

"You are tenderly attached to your cousin?"

"You may say so. My own story is an unhappy one, and when I became a widow I should have been homeless had not Geoffry Wetherwilder taken me in. I have lived in the family for years, and even now, when they have had to give up everything, he has contrived to secure me a shelter as caretaker of the Hall."

"Worthy Wetherwilders, both of you," said the girl, who also claimed to be a Wetherwilder, and she stooped to gather a splendid rose of the old, almost obsolete oriflamme, which was just in flower all over the Maiden's Bower, close to the French rosary. "How well I remember this rose!" and she kissed it.

"You have been here before!" I exclaimed in astonishment.

"Have I not! The happiest hours of my short life were spent in this garden."

"Really!"

"'Twas this rose that Geoffry Wetherwilder gave me, the evening—just such a June evening as this—when he told me he loved me; just a hundred and eight years ago."

I stared at her, and laughed. "What are you saying?" I asked impatiently.

"Perhaps I am talking poetry," she said; "may not one do so in such a spot, on such an evening, and after?"

Her eyes roved over the garden, taking in all its beauties, and with a look behind their youthful brightness, of age and memory, which amazed and perplexed me.

"Talk as you please," I said, but I began to feel her uncanny.

"I have only a short time to be with you," she said quickly. "Let us enjoy it. I have been very happy in this place, though not so happy as we are now—I and my beloved. But love never forgets, and the things and places associated with it are eternally sweet. I shall take him these roses, and even in the place where we are now—"

I was trying to believe that here, in the days before I came to Wetherwilder Hall, this creature's romance had been enacted, though her apparent youth made folly of the idea. But I was growing quite bewildered by her looks and words, and was glad when she consented to leave the fading glories and the fragrance of the garden and to return with me indoors.

My handmaiden had provided a hasty supper—one or two light dishes, a sweetmeat, and grapes, coffee and shortbread. A great silver candelabra, with wax candles alight, stood in the middle of the round table in my sitting-room, which overlooked the garden, beyond which the great mounds of the trees were black against a golden stretch of sky. The flames of the candles hung like flowers in the air, for the gold sky-gleam was still at least equal with them in power of light within the room, and both together filled the place with a kind of mystic glamour.

We sat down to table, but I was too much excited to eat, and my guest, though plates were placed before her, seemed to behave as if they contained nothing but air. However, I had become afraid of observing her too closely, so quickly did she apprehend my thought, and I allowed myself to drift with her humour.

After supper she protested that she must see the old house, and so we proceeded upstairs just as the newly burnished moon-silver began to struggle in the sky with the sun-gold which was rusting away into darkness down west among wildernesses of grotesque-seeming ink-black oak woods. The white glory poured down the wide way of the great staircase as we went up; corridors, passages, and unused chambers lay beyond and above. I felt that I would rather have remained downstairs, but my companion hurried on, looking round here, and peeping in there, as if truly revisiting places that were dear and familiar to her.

She lingered only about a minute in each spot until we came to a small music-room, all brown with polished wood, without curtains or carpet, and hung round with musical instruments, some of them very old, an accumulation of years. Violin, guitar, mandolina, tambourine, cymbals, all were there, and an old-fashioned spinnet and a harp held place of honour in the middle of the floor.

With an air of rapture she stepped a-tiptoe across the floor, stretched her long delicate arm to take down the guitar from its hanging place, and slipping a faded blue ribbon that dangled from it over her head, she perched herself on a carved wooden stool, and sung with the most exquisite grace a soft, cooing love-song, the like of which for sweetness I had never listened to. When the piercing melody ceased she looked up at me, and never shall I forget the beauty of her as she did so, with the moonlight that struck through the narrow window just touching her face and shoulder. Her song sung, she replaced the guitar on the wall, and turning to me with a little laugh signed to me that she desired to quit the chamber.

Proceeding with our visitation we made little pause till we reached another small room, one which had been for generations a kind of schoolroom or study for the young people of the family. It was lined with books, and a table with drawers stood in the middle of the floor. Here had many a lesson been learned, and many a lecture listened to. Again, as in the music-room, the stranger's look of recognition became rapturous, as she walked round the rows of books with her eyes close to them, though I could scarcely imagine that the twilight from the window enabled her to read the titles of them.

Suddenly she drew forth from a corner, where it had evidently lain hid behind others, a small vellum-covered volume, and with a laugh of delight turned its pages over with a rapid hand, then placed it in mine with an eager movement, saying:

"Take it, cousin, and to-morrow look into it. It will explain away your perplexity."

I was growing weary of following her, of my ignorance of who she was and why she was here; and my wits were oppressed by the consciousness of something about her which I found quite unintelligible. I longed to be alone, that away from the fascination of her presence I might think the matter over, and arrive at some conclusion regarding her. I was, therefore, much relieved when she suddenly announced that she would retire for the night.

"Give me the yellow chamber," she said with her charming imperiousness.

I knew that my maiden had prepared for her a smaller room and nearer to my own, and remarked that she might perhaps feel lonesome in the greater apartment, which was situated at the other end of the house. But she reiterated her request, which was rather, indeed, a demand. In a short time the statelier chamber was made ready for her, and I accompanied her there. The yellow hangings on the bed and windows were let down and shaken out, but she would not allow the blinds to be drawn or the windows closed.

It is a splendid old room, the walls completely panelled in oak, the darkness of which is relieved by the gold-color of the furniture. She bade me good-night, bending to kiss me, but I did not feel her lips, and experienced again that uncanny thrill at finding my sense of touch unaffected by her nearness. I last saw her standing therewith her graceful arms extended dismissing me. Two candles were burning in the tall silver candlesticks on the dressing-table; the moon, full-orbed and glorious, shone out of the lovely green-grayness of the sky of a midsummer midnight, filling the framework of one window, while the other window showed the startling black fretwork formed by the huge boughs of a hundred-year-old chestnut tree against the silvery cloud-light. Between these and the flames of the candles the young slight figure stood, aerial in its lightness and grace, the face radiant with intelligence, the eyes of a brightness which seemed strange by such light as there was, the moon's soft ray making a luminous ring round her hair. She kissed her hand to me with a smile that is still in my heart; and then I closed the door and retreated to my own quarters, glad to escape, and feeling indescribably limp and overdone.

I did not find my brain cleared by solitude as immediately and effectively as I had hoped, and felt unable to do anything but huddle myself up in bed with a sense of the most utter prostration. After half an hour's rest I sat up and lit my candle, polished my spectacles, and opened the vellum-covered book which the stranger had handed to me. But whether from fatigue or for some other reason, I could not read a word of the contents, and soon consigned myself once more to repose and darkness.

Sleep took me by surprise, and I knew no more till I wakened with a thin clear sound in my ears, curiously familiar as the repetition of something I had been aware of very lately. It was the lively sound of a coach-horn blown from a distance. Again it came lightly, and again and again more faintly on the air,—tantivy, tantivy, tantivy! The great cedar outside flung its boughs about in the breeze, and their rustling drowned the retreating music. I sat up, and saw that the light of a midsummer dawn was gilding the edges of the window-blinds.

I dressed hurriedly, and feeling a strange reluctance to visiting the yellow chamber, I wakened my maid-servant and directed her to make me a strong cup of tea, which I swallowed nervously. The maid was a sturdy country wench, devoid of imagination, and she smiled at my discomfiture.

"It's my belief you won't find her, ma'am," she said. "They gay friends of hers called for her and took her off, early. I heard the coachin'-horn an hour ago, comin' an' comin', and goin' an' goin'. I put my head out of the winda, and I saw the coach, and the waft of her white gownd gettin' into it; and the whole caravan went clatterin' down the drive and out of sight among the trees just as the sun was risin. And I wouldn't be frettin' for her, if I was you, ma'am, for she's a queer kind of a visitor, takin' people short and givin' them trouble, and then goin' off without as much as saying good morning to them!"

"Come up stairs with me, Jenny, that I may assure myself she is gone," I said.

We entered the room. The windows still stood wide open, but their dark woodwork framed the brilliant sunshine and blue sky of a June morning. Rooks were cawing in the huge chestnut, which threw half the room into transparent shadow. The room was empty of its occupant of the night before. The bed had not been lain in, and everything stood undisturbed, as I had left it with her in it. And yet there was a change, for one of the panels in the wooded wall stood open as a door, showing a deep recess like a cupboard, about five feet above the level of the floor.

Thrilling with expectation of I knew not what, I looked into the open recess, and putting in my hand drew forth an Indian box containing some old yellow papers, the miniature of a girl, which was a faithful portrait of my late guest, and a few jewels in old-fashioned settings. Having read the papers, I telegraphed at once to Geoffry Wetherwilder, and to his solicitor, and both arrived as quickly as steam could carry them. The papers found proved to be the long-lost will, so urgently needed for the welfare of our family.

It was long before I ventured to relate to my cousin, or to his man of business, the story of the finding of the document as I have set it down here. When I did so each received my communication characteristically. The solicitor laughed and tapped his forehead with an amused glance at me. "Don't tell that monstrous tale again, my dear lady," he said, "for I can't undertake to defend you from the consequences."

He accepted as quite natural the finding of the papers behind a sliding panel, but the rest he put down to a dream.

Geoffry, on the contrary, heard my story with the most serious attention, and received it as truth in all its details. He had the Celtic strain in him which readily responds to a message from the unknown. The spiritual side of his nature was deeply stirred, and having been made suddenly very happy just when his fortunes looked darkest, the heart in him turned gratefully, like my own, to the lovely visitant from another state of being, who had taken thought of him and his, and restored them to their own.

"Don't say a word of it to Vanda, however," he said, speaking of his wife, who was already on her joyful way home, with her little children. "The thought of such an occurrence in the house would be an everlasting terror to her." And the mistress of Wetherwilder remains in ignorance of the story to this day.

The vellum-covered book proved to be a diary kept in disjointed, schoolgirl fashion. Inside the cover was written, "Elsinore Wetherwilder, aged seventeen to-day. Called by some impertinent cousins 'the Lady Tantivy,' because she loves riding to hunt, and in a four-in-hand coach." And after this was added in a masculine youthful hand: "and sometimes even insists upon blowing the horn!"

The first entry was of an earlier date than the inscription on the cover:

"This week I have arrived at Wetherwilder Hall. It is a change indeed for an orphan girl leaving her convent school with no family or relatives to receive her. What should I have done, where should I have gone, had not the dear old squire arrived at Avignon, and put me in his portmanteau and carried me home? Really, and really home. And such a home!

"I am wild with delight. I have a ready-made mother, and the big-boy cousins are brothers to me. And the best of it is they are all as happy as I am, for the Wetherwilders had no daughter until I came."

Various girlish and pretty writings followed, filling up a year. In the first winter, this:

"The snow is deep, yet the ball came off. The squire gave me a wonder of a white satin dress. My head is turned with flatteries. The duke proposed to me, but I should have refused him had he been king of the world, and that though he is a very goodly gentleman. It is Geoffry that I love, and never another man than Geoffry. If Geoffry does not love me, then will I back to my convent at Avignon and cover up this golden hair with a nun's veil—"

The next summer:

"This evening Geoffry told me that he loved me. It was in the garden among the oriflamme roses. I knew it before, but it was sweet to hear it—"

In the following autumn:

"I have been trying to plague Geoffry. He is so sweet-tempered one can hardly do it. I have hidden the will and documents he was showing me yesterday. I have put them behind the sliding panel in the yellow chamber, where I am now installed. As all his inheritance depends on them, he will be rather in a fright. I will tease him for a while, and then make amends by being ever so kind to him."

No more. Each time I close the little book, which I always keep by me with the miniature, I think I hear the faint horn blowing that announced the coming and going of my Lady Tantivy. She will never come again. When we meet, it must be that I shall go to her. Time and place are delusions. I am very old now, and as I gaze over the trees into the great space out of which she came in her ever-young delightfulness, my heart grows young and is glad.

The Last Ascent

E. R. Punshon

The extraordinary rapidity with which a successful airman may achieve fame was well shown in the case of my friend, Radcliffe Thorpe. One week known merely to a few friends as a clever young engineer, the next his name was on the lips of the civilised world. His first success was followed by a series of remarkable feats, of which his flight above the Atlantic, his race with the torpedo-boat-destroyers across the North Sea, and his sensational display during the military manœuvres on Salisbury Plain, impressed his name and personality firmly upon the fickle mind of the public, and explains the tremendous excitement caused by his in explicable disappearance during the great aviation meeting at Attercliffe, near London, towards the end of the summer.

Few people, I suppose, have forgotten the facts. For some time previously he had been devoting himself more especially to ascending to as great a height as possible. He held all the records for height, and it was known that at Attercliffe he meant to endeavour to eclipse his own achievements.

It was a lovely day, not a breath of wind stirring, not a cloud in the sky. We saw him start. We saw him fly up and up in great sweeping spirals. We saw him climb higher and ever higher into the azure space. We watched him, those of us whose eyes could bear the strain, as he dwindled to a dot and a speck, till at last he passed beyond sight.

It was a stirring thing to see a man thus storm, as it were, the walls of Heaven and probe the very mysteries of space. I remember I felt quite annoyed with someone who was taking a cinematograph record. It seemed such a sordid, business-like thing to be doing at such a moment.

Presently the aeroplane came into sight again and was greeted with a sudden roar of cheering.

"He is doing a glide down," someone cried excitedly, and though someone else declared that a glide from such a height was unthinkable and impossible, yet it was soon plain that the first speaker was right.

Down through unimaginable thousands of feet, straight and swift swept the machine, making such a sweep as the eagle in its pride would never have dared. People held their breath to watch, expecting every moment some catastrophe. But the machine kept on an even keel, and in a few moments I joined with the others in a wild rush to the field at a little distance where the machine, like a mighty bird, had alighted easily and safely.

But when we reached it we doubted our own eyes, our own sanity. There was no sign anywhere of Radcliffe Thorpe!

No one knew what to say; we looked blankly at our neighbours, and one man got down on his hands and knees and peered under the body of the machine as if he suspected Radcliffe of hiding there. Then the chairman of the meeting, Lord Fallowfield, made a curious discovery.

"Look," he said in a high, shaken voice, "the steering wheel is jammed!"

It was true. The steering wheel had been carefully fastened in one position, and the lever controlling the planes had also been fixed so as to hold them at the right angle for a downward glide. That was strange enough, but in face of the mystery of Radcliffe's disappearance little attention was paid it.

Where, then, was its pilot? That was the question that was filling everybody's mind. He had vanished as utterly as vanishes the mist one sees rising in the sunshine.

It was supposed he must have fallen from his seat, but as to how that had happened, how it was that no fragment of his body or his clothing was ever found, above all, how it was that his aeroplane had returned, the engine cut off, the planes secured in correct position, no even moderately plausible explanation was ever put forward.

The loss to aeronautics was felt to be severe. From childhood Radcliffe had shown that, in addition to this, he had a marked aptitude for drawing, usually held at the service of his profession, but now and again exercised in producing sketches of his friends.

Among those who knew him privately he was fairly popular, though not, perhaps, so much so as he deserved; certainly he had a way of talking "shop" which was a trifle tiring to those who did not figure the world as one vast engineering problem, while with women he was apt to be brusque and short-mannered.

My surprise, then, can be imagined when, calling one afternoon on him and having to wait a little, I had noticed lying on his desk a crayon sketch of a woman's face. It was a very lovely face, the features almost perfect, and yet there was about it something unearthly and spectral that was curiously disturbing.

"Smitten at last?" I asked jestingly, and yet aware of a certain odd discomfort.

When, he saw what I was looking at he went very pale.

"Who is it?" I asked.

"Oh, just—someone!" he answered.

He took the sketch from me, looked at it, frowned and locked it away. As he seemed unwilling to pursue the subject, I went on to talk of the business I had come about, and I congratulated him on his flight of the day before in which he had broken the record for height. As I was going he said:

"By the way, that sketch—what did you think of it?"

"Why, that you had better be careful," I answered, laughing; "or you'll be falling from your high estate of bachelordom."

He gave so violent a start, his face expressed so much of apprehension and dismay, that I stared at him blankly. Recovering himself with an effort, he stammered out:

"It's not—I mean—it's an imaginary portrait."

"Then," I said, amazed in my turn, "you've a jolly sight more imagination than anyone ever credited you with."

The incident remained in my mind. As a matter of fact, practical Radcliffe Thorpe, absorbed in questions of strain and ease, his head full of cylinders and wheels and ratchets and the Lord knows what else, would have seemed to me the last man on earth to create that haunting, strange, unearthly face, human in form, but not in expression.

It was about this time that Radcliffe began to give so much attention to the making of very high flights. His favourite time was in the early morning, as soon as it was light. Then in the chill dawn he would rise and soar and wing his flight high and ever higher, up and up, till the eye could no longer follow his ascent.

I remember he made one of these strange, solitary flights when I was spending the weekend with him at his cottage near the Attercliffe Aviation Grounds.

I had come down from town somewhat late the night before, and I remember that just before we went to bed we went out for a few minutes to enjoy the beauty of a perfect night. The moon was shining in a clear sky, not a sound or a breath disturbed the sublime quietude; in the south one wondrous star gleamed low on the horizon. Neither of us spoke; it was enough to drink in the beauty of such rare perfection, and I noticed how Radcliffe kept his eyes fixed upwards on the dark blue vault of space.

"Are you longing to be up there?" I asked him jestingly.

He started and flushed, and he then went very pale, and to my surprise I saw that he was shivering.

"You are getting cold," I said. "We had better go in."

He nodded without answering, and, as we turned to go in, I heard quite plainly and distinctly a low, strange laugh, a laugh full of a honeyed sweetness that yet thrilled me with great fear.

"What's that?" I said, stopping short.

"What?" Radcliffe asked.

"Someone laughed," I said, and I stared all round and then upwards. "I thought it came from up there," I said in a bewildered way, pointing upwards.

He gave me an odd look and, without answering, went into the cottage. He had said nothing of having planned any flight for the next morning; but in the early morning, the chill and grey dawn, I was roused by the drumming of his engine. At once I jumped up out of bed and ran to the window.

The machine was raising itself lightly and easily from the ground. I watched him wing his god-like way up through the still, soft air till he was lost to view. Then, after a time, I saw him emerge again from those immensities of space. He came down in one long majestic sweep, and alighted in a field a little way away from the house, leaving the aeroplane for his mechanics to fetch up presently.

"Hullo!" I greeted him. "Why didn't you tell me you were going up?"

As I spoke I heard plainly and distinctly, as plainly as ever I heard anything in my life, that low, strange laugh, that I had heard before, so silvery sweet and yet somehow so horrible.

"What's that?" I said, stopping short and staring blankly upwards, for, absurd though it seems, that weird sound seemed to come floating down from an infinite height above us.

"Not high enough," he muttered like a man in an ecstacy. "Not high enough yet."

He walked away from me then without another word. When I entered the cottage he was seated at the table sketching a woman's face the same face I had seen in that other sketch of his, spectral, unreal, and lovely.

"What on earth—?" I began.

"Nothing on earth," he answered in a strange voice. Then he laughed and jumped up, and tore his sketch across.

He seemed quite his old self again, chatty and pleasant, and with his old passion for talking "shop." He launched into a long explanation of some scheme he had in mind for securing automatic balancing.

I never told anyone about that strange, mocking laugh, in fact, I had almost forgotten the incident altogether when something brought every detail back to my memory. I had a letter from a person who signed himself "George Barnes."

Barnes, it seemed, was the operator who had taken the pictures of that last ascent, and as he understood I had been Mr. Thorpe's greatest friend, he wanted to see me. Certain expressions in the letter aroused my curiosity. I replied. He asked for an appointment at a time that was not very convenient, and finally I arranged to call at his house one evening.

It was one of those smart little six-room villas of which so many have been put up in the London suburbs of late. Barnes was buying it on the instalment system, and I quite won his heart by complimenting him on it. But for that, I doubt if anything would have come of my visit, for he was plainly nervous and ill at ease and very repentant of ever having said anything. But after my compliment to the house we got on better.

"It's on my mind," he said; "I shan't be easy till someone else knows."

We were in the front room where a good fire was burning—in my honour, I guessed, for the apartment had not the air of being much used. On the table were some photographs. Barnes showed them me. They were enlargements from those he had taken of poor Radcliffe's last ascent.

"They've been shown all over the world," he said. "Millions of people have seen them."

"Well?" I said.

"But there's one no one has seen no one except me."

He produced another print and gave it to me. I glanced at it. It seemed much like the others, having been apparently one of the last of the series, taken when the aeroplane was at a great height. The only thing in which it differed from the others was that it seemed a trifle blurred.

"A poor one," I said; "it's misty."

"Look at the mist," he said.

I did so. Slowly, very slowly, I began to see that that misty appearance had a shape, a form. Even as I looked I saw the features of a human countenance and yet not human either, so spectral was it, so unreal and strange. I felt the blood run cold in my veins and the hair bristle on the scalp of my head, for I recognised beyond all doubt that this face on the photograph was the same as that Radcliffe had sketched. The resemblance was absolute, no one who had seen the one could mistake the other.

"You see it?" Barnes muttered, and his face was almost as pale as mine.

"There's a woman," I stammered, "a woman floating in the air by his side. Her arms are held out to him."

"Yes," Barnes said. "Who was she?"

The print slipped from my hands and fluttered to the ground. Barnes picked it up and put it in the fire. Was it fancy or, as it flared up, and burnt and was consumed, did I really hear a faint laugh floating downwards from the upper air?

"I destroyed the negative," Barnes said, "and I told my boss something had gone wrong with it. No one has seen that photograph but you and me, and now no one ever will."

The Last Man's Club

Robert M. Clutch

"The Property of the Last Man."

Emotion choked the voice of the old man as he slowly spelled the words from the age-worn label which still clung raggedly to a bottle covered with the dust of many years. A mist came before his eyes as he held the old wine up to the light and a sigh escaped his lips as he placed it back on the table.

And this was the end! A long table, with thirty-eight plates, from which no one would eat; thirty-eight chairs, upon which no one would sit; a lonely old man seated at the head of a lonely board, drinking to the memory of his friends, all of whom he had survived.

How sad and how different from the joyous occasion which marked their organization this night sixty-four years before! He could see it just as it happened—thirty-nine young men, in the first flush of their manhood, clinking their glasses around a festive board, wild songs, gay pranks, and all joking about the poor old Last Man to be. It was youth joking about Time; hot blood and inexperience ridiculing halting footsteps and wisdom.

He recalled how they had gathered around at the midnight hour, raised their glasses high in the air and had drunk to him. And now he was to drink to them—drink of the old wine, which they had sealed with solemn rites—to take from the glass a delicious quaff and a sad memory, as he toasted their names one by one.

He recalled them all, the whole thirty-eight, beginning with active young manhood and ending with decrepit old age, as one by one in the different periods of their lives they had passed away. For five years, he remembered, they had remained intact. Then the first man died. There was a vacant chair at their next anniversary dinner, and a name was toasted in silence.

Another lapse of time, then a second went, then a third. One had mysteriously disappeared, one had been murdered, two were drowned, three killed on the railroad, and one had cheated the aims of the club by taking his own life. And then came the War of the Rebellion. They were twenty-seven when the great struggle began, but four years later, when it was ended, only nineteen men answered to their names at the following anniversary dinner and the memory of the others was toasted in silence.

The roll of the living grew smaller and that of the dead larger as year after year the survivors met. From young men they had slipped into middle life and from middle life they had become old. And now he was the Last Man. The honor was—

He stopped. The clock had begun to strike twelve. The hour for dissolving the Last Man's Club had arrived.

He listened reverently until the last lingering echo died out. Then he broke the seal of the bottle. With trembling hand he raised the glass to the tapering neck and inclined the bottle so that the crimson liquid bubbled out. He set the bottle on the bible, held the glass up to the light and looked at it. Then he glanced down the length of the table until his eyes rested on a vacant chair. For a few seconds he remained silent. A flush mantled his wrinkled cheeks. A light kindled his eyes. His bent form straightened up. He brought the glass down to the level of his lips, raised it again and inclined it toward the chair upon which his eyes were fastened.

Then, in a voice trembling with emotion, he called aloud the first man's name. It was the voice of friendship ringing out across nearly three generations of time—the voice of the Last Man toasting the first.

The second man's name was called out in. the same quavering voice, the glass inclined toward another vacant chair, then the third and fourth. Then two little spots glowed out on the old man's cheeks as he drank. His eyes snapped and sparkled under his bushy white brows. He became joyous, careless. He cackled and chuckled in mirth as he called his old comrades by name. More than once he made reference to some joke that had been buried and forgotten in the dim past.

The glass was emptied and filled again and again. The names were called out, incidents were delved into from the forgotten past as the old man conversed with the imaginary pictures of the men whose memory he was keeping alive.

He stopped and strained his eyes. "Why—why, there's Joe. Poor old Joe. See, Joe, I'm toastin' your mem'ry. Your mem'ry, Joe. I'm the—

"And there's Dick! Dick who was killed at Gettysburg. Killed with his hands on the colors. But I'd know you anywheres. Know you even if you didn't have your uniform on. Here's to you, Dick; here's to—"

He stopped and began to sing a song in a low, cracked voice. It was a strange old song, one musty with the flavor of olden days, with queer rhymings and funny sayings. The old man's voice rose higher, his eyes sparkled brighter, his cheeks grew more flushed. Suddenly his voice became husky, rose to a screech, broke to a whisper, and stopped.

The bottle was more than half emptied now, but still the old man kept at his solemn task. Now they were all toasted. Thirty-eight times had he raised the glass in the air, thirty-eight times had he sipped of the old wine to their memory, thirty-eight times had he called their names one by one. Thirty-eight gleams of joy, thirty-eight pangs of sorrow and it was all over. The Last Man's Club was no more.

A sense of sadness crept over him. He sat down in his chair wearily, and uttered a long-drawn sigh as his head dropped slowly on his bosom. Then the room grew dim and he closed his eyes.

A wild chorus, a confusion of familiar sounds, and a few bars of an old song awakened him. He jumped up, blinked in the light, and looked around him. The song fell upon his ears like the melody of an old poem. It awakened a whole flood of emotion in the old man's soul that held him spell-bound. He listened again. The sound came swelling from all sides, flooding his mind with reminiscences which almost made him weep. It was their drinking song, sung with a full chorus before Death had begun to step in nearly sixty years ago.

He looked down the table and gave a sudden start. He looked again. Was he dreaming? He rubbed his eyes to make sure.

Before him, seated around the board, were the thirty-eight men whose memory he had just toasted.

They were all singing—singing the same old song in the way he could never forget. It was like the voice of Yesterday reaching forth into the Present. He cleared his throat, took a long breath, and joined wildly in with the chorus. He sang the song through and stopped exhausted. He fought for his breath, gulped down a draught of wine, and rested. Then he glanced down the line of men seated around the board, looked at his own place, and stared. It was vacant! His chair was empty. It was the only unoccupied one around the board. He could not understand. He looked again. They were toasting him—The Last Man.

Weakly, he staggered over to the table. With palsied hand, he filled his glass as they did theirs, held it high in the air, and drank. The sides of the room slowly heaved before his eyes; the table became an indistinct streak of white; the thirty-eight guests blurred into two gray lines; then everything turned black. His glass fell from his hand and crashed against the chair. He reeled and swayed for a moment, extended both hands pleadingly towards the table, smiled, then fell heavily to the floor.

They found him there the next morning. The roll of the Last Man's Club was complete. He had gone to join them.

The Man from Honolulu

Lawrence William Pedrose

Cap Cavanaugh gravely wagged a forefinger.

"I have," he stated, "aboard my yacht in the harbor, a man who can swim Elliot Bay."

He spoke quietly, but had a bombshell been exploded amidst the group on the Arctic Club veranda, it would not have caused a greater sensation. From every side came gasps of incredulity, and a dozen chairs loudly scraped the floor, as their owners turned to stare at the speaker.

It was the evening following Turns Cavil's unsuccessful attempt to swim Seattle's harbor, in which effort that world-famous athlete had lost his life. Cap. Cavanaugh had returned but that morning from a cruise of the Friendly Islands, and as he always brought back from such trips a fund of rare good stories, the boys at the club were wont to single him out and start him yarning. The talk had finally gotten round to the tragedy of the day before, and when it is remembered that many athletes had attempted the four-mile swim from Seattle to the downtown wharves, without one having accomplished the feat, it will be understood why everyone hung breathlessly on the words of a well-known man like Cap. Cavanaugh.

"Yes," he reiterated in the same even voice, "I have a man who can swim the harbor—in fact, he can cross it and return without pausing to rest. If that five-hundred dollar purse which was put up for Turns Cavil, the professional, still stands—and the man of whom I speak is only an amateur—I think I can persuade him to take the risk.

"He is a Hawaiian, and claims to be of royal blood. His name is Kahmee—something; but we call him 'the Duke,' for short. I picked him up in Honolulu. He is well educated and very intelligent; but you know how it is with those brown men—nobody in the islands will give them employment entailing responsibility when whites can be had. I saw him do a few stunts in the surf and offered him a job as A. B., so he could get to the States. He jumped at the chance.

"Every evening, during the run up, he entertained us with stories. There was one in particular that I remember well, and, for a barefaced lie, it outdoes anything I ever before heard. The Duke, though, sticks to it and swears it is true, and he tells it with such evident sincerity that he almost convinces one.

"One night, a Cockney sailor told a tale of pelagic sealing with a Russian ship among the Aleutians, and when he had finished, the Duke began to question him about the seals.

"It is an established fact, you know, that the fur seal, or otariidae, as it is known scientifically, because it has ears and belongs to the otter family, spends a greater part of the year in the warm waters near the Equator and makes the long migration into the Arctic for the breeding season.

"When the Duke mentioned this, the Cockney got sarcastic and wanted to know what a nigger knew about it; whereupon the Duke quietly replied that he knew seals better than any other living man, because he had been with them on one of their annual migrations into the north and lived with them for several months. At this the Cockney flared up and called the Duke 'a blyme liar,' so I sent him below to cool off. It was then the Duke told his weird story.

"He said that when he was a kid of four, he was lost overboard one night from one of those Hawaiian native boats during a gale off the islands. He outlived the storm (you know how those little brown kids can swim; it seems as though they are born for the water), and when morning came, found himself out of sight of land and in the midst of a herd of seals, one of which took a fancy to him and adopted him.

"The seals were on their way to the Arctic, but so gradual was the change in temperature of the water as they slowly forged north, that the kid never noticed it. He had had on no clothing to begin with, and Nature soon padded him out with blubber like the seals till he was as roly-poly as any of them. Also, he grew a coat of silky fur, which extended from his neck to the tips of his toes.

"He says the first real discomfort he experienced was when the herd reached the ice-floes. It was a long time before he could accustom himself to sitting on the ice—"

At this point, an explosion of laughter greeted the narrator. He waited till it had subsided, then went on:

"The first month after the herd reached its breeding grounds, the bleak shores of the Aleutians, was a happy one for the kid. He had an abundance of food and all the baby seals for playmates. For hours at a stretch, he says, he used to take them in his arms and slide down the ice-hummocks, or disport with them in the water, playing games the like of which human beings never dreamed.

"Then came the fur hunters, sailing ships filled with big, black-bearded men, who drove the seals inland when they caught them sleeping on the shore or ice-fields and ruthlessly slaughtered them.

"The kid quickly learned to fear the hunters, and, because of his keener senses, became lookout for the herd, perching himself for hours at a time upon some ice-ridge and keeping watch out over the fog banks for the spars of the ships.

"He says he has a hazy recollection of a dark, gloomy day, when he was standing guard as usual, and the hunters slipped up on them in skin canoes under cover of the fog. Caught unawares, the herd bolted inland, the hunters pursuing with club and spear, and soon the ice for acres around was dyed red with the slaughter.

"Only a few of the seals escaped, and the kid managed to get away with these; but they would have nothing more to do with him, no doubt blaming him for the slaughter of their companions, so he left them and struck off by himself. Alone, he wandered from island to island, meeting with many adventures and many times narrowly escaping the hunters, till he at last came upon another herd that would take him in.

"A few weeks later, when the seals returned to the waters of his home, the kid followed, there to be picked up by a tribe of his own people and adopted by the chief.

"As he grew up, his remarkable ability to handle himself in the water, even in that land of wonderful swimmers, won him fame; but when he reached manhood, he waned, as an attraction and had to hunt for work. By being taken up by a college-bred Englishman—one of those wastrel remittancemen, you understand—he got an education, till today he is as choice in his use of English as a professor.

"He is only twenty-three now, and as fine a specimen of manhood as I have ever seen. He's quite fair skinned, too, and would pass for a Frenchman or Spaniard any time. I'll bring him up tomorrow night and introduce him. He is every inch a gentleman, and I am sure you will like him."

Cap. Cavanaugh concealed a yawn, glanced at his watch, rose, and with a "good-night, all," sauntered into the club house.

For a long while, the group on the veranda stared at one another in awed silence, then:

"It's impossible!" exploded Patterson, the sporting-news editor of a morning newspaper, and everyone looked queerly at him. "A human being couldn't have had those adventures!"

"I don't know about that," put in Snelling, a friend of Cap. Cavanaugh's and a man whose word carried considerable weight around the club. "I know Cap. quite well, and I am sure that the tales he tells are pretty near true."

Most were inclined to view the story as a yarn of the baldest Munchausen type, but when the crowd broke up, half an hour later, all had resolved to be on hand the following evening and meet the Duke.

The Arctic Club has a very liberal-minded membership, made up, for the larger part, of business men about town, and it opened wide its arms to Cap. Cavanaugh's prodigy, Duke Kahmee.

The Duke proved to be a rather likable young fellow, well dressed, well mannered and not at all forward. Most of the Hawaiians I had ever seen were short, stocky-built fellows who closely resembled the negro type; but the Duke was more like a white man. He was tall—over six feet—slender, and had a pantherlike gracefulness of carriage that suggested great strength. He had thick black hair and clean-cut features, while his firm, yet sensually-thick lips, when parted, revealed two even rows of snow-white teeth.

I could find but one fault with him—that was a vanity of dress that he affected. So extremely high was the white collar he wore that it concealed his whole neck, reaching to a point just below his ears; but so naturally did he wear it, that, under the spell of his personality, one was willing to forgive him it. I liked him from the start, and inside of an hour we had become friends.

I persuaded him to tell the story of his adventures among the seals, and he gave it almost word for word as had Cap. Cavanaugh. I must admit he was convincing. Even Patterson, who bore the nickname of "Old Unbelief," accepted it with the comment: "Highly improbable, but possible—yes, sir, possible."

Later we took the Duke down to the club natatorium and let him inspect the tank with a view to giving us an exhibition of his skill in the near future, little thinking that we would that very night see it demonstrated.

T. Henry Treat, a personal friend of Cap. Cavanaugh's, was standing on the slippery tiling at the deep-water end of the tank, explaining its construction to the Duke, who stood on the other side, when, turning to a swimming device which was swung to the rafters, his foot slipped, precipitating him into the water.

As the pool at that hour was closed to bathers, no attendants were on hand, and Treat, being unable to swim, sank. I cast round for a swimming belt, intending to jump in and help him, but suddenly the Duke shot past me, cleaved the air, and struck the water at the spot where Treat had last appeared.

Almost before the rest of us comprehended his move, he rose again, several yards out, supporting the form of the now unconscious clubman.

It was an hour before Treat was able to walk without assistance. He departed for the Laurels, his palatial home out on the Sound, insisting upon the Duke's going along as his guest for a few days.

The Duke had changed into dry clothes which had been furnished by the club members, but—and it caused me to wonder at the time—he stubbornly refused to exchange his bedraggled collar for one of mine. I did not insist, knowing that he could have his own soon sent up from the yacht.

Before he left, though, he promised he would swim the harbor the following Sunday, rain or shine, and we all voted him a good sport.

As Sunday was but two days away, preparations for the exhibition were immediately begun. Patterson saw to it that the newspapers made much of the Duke, so when Sunday dawned, excitement throughout the city was rife.

Large crowds thronged the two sides of the harbor when the hour announced for the swim arrived. Cap. Cavanaugh's yacht, with the Duke aboard, steamed to the West Side, where Turns Cavil had made his fatal start; and along with a few of the boys from the club, I was fortunate enough to be aboard. Also, to add interest to the gathering, Treat had brought along his family, which included Ruth, his daughter, a girl of twenty, with whom I was on close terms.

With many pangs of jealousy—for I, too, was an ardent admirer of Ruth and had reasons to believe that my suit was favored—I noticed an intimacy that had sprung up between her and the Duke during their short two days' acquaintance. I could not believe that she would ever marry a brown man, but he was a fine fellow, and I was conscious of a vague uneasiness. I think I began harboring a feeling of antagonism toward him from that moment.

When he came on deck, the Duke presented a striking picture. Unlike other swimmers, he wore a black garment that reached from the tips of his toes to the top of his head, leaving only his face and hands uncovered. The upper part of the garment was a hood which he had drawn low over his forehead, and he appeared more like a character one would expect to see on the stage or at a fancy-dress ball than at a swimming exhibition. Truly he resembled a very imp of shadow as he stood poised on the bow of the yacht, slender, his body as symmetrically formed as a girl's.

He made but one stipulation: that no boats follow him. As the sky was fast becoming overcast with dark dark clouds, Cap. Cavanaugh and the press boats acquiesced with considerable reluctance. Then, with a wave of his hand and a nodding smile, the Duke took a header into the bay, cutting the water without a splash, and a moment later his black head appeared many rods out. Nor did he head out the Sound, as other swimmers had done, to make allowance for the incoming tide, but darted in a straight line for the crowded wharves across the harbor.

To add to his difficulty, when he was a few hundred yards out, the squall that had been threatening, struck, and soon white-capped waves were sweeping the bay. Immediately the yacht put out to escort him, but he raised an arm and vigorously shook his head; and an instant later, even the spyglasses that had been trained on him constantly from the start, lost him among the waves.

Fifteen, thirty, forty-five minutes, an hour dragged slowly by, and the suspense was becoming unbearable, when suddenly a great screeching of whistles came from the tugs and other boats across the harbor.

The Duke had reached his goal!

Everyone aboard the yacht glanced at his watch, and a murmur of astonishment went up.

The Duke had done the four miles in the almost unbelievable time of seventy minutes!

Several men hastened ashore to telephone for verification, and they came back with the startling intelligence that the Duke already was far out on the return trip, having reported at the goal and left immediately after.

Ruth was the first to make him out as he approached. As he drew near, a rousing cheer went up. He was swimming strongly, and acknowledged the ovation with a playful dive, a wave of his hand and a broad grin.

To everyone's surprise, he refused assistance on reaching the yacht, springing lightly aboard, apparently not the least wearied. He hastened below to change into his clothes, and the yacht steamed back to her anchorage.

When the Duke appeared again on deck, Ruth took possession of him. She was radiant and-showed such a marked personal interest in him that, to conceal my disgust, I took myself off to another part of the boat.

Of course the Duke was lionized for the rest of that week, and I was certain I detected a strut in his walk, which he did not have when he first came. Also, he assumed an attitude of confidant proprietorship toward Ruth, and I avoided them as much as possible, to hide my growing antipathy for him.

At the end of the second week, there became rampant at the club, a rumor that Ruth and he were engaged and that the date for the wedding was to be set in the near future. Then, to cap the climax, as it were, the Treats invited me down for a few days, and the invitation was couched in such terms that I could not refuse.

When I reached the Laurels, I saw that the gossips had not erred; Ruth and the Duke were as devoted as a pair of doves. He trailed her round so closely that he gave me not one moment alone with her.

Several affairs, a dance, a picnic and a clam-bake, had been arranged, and I joined in the fun with a will, if without heart, and believed I concealed my feelings quite well. I was hurt deeply, but I said nothing of it.

The afternoon of my arrival, the Duke gave a private exhibition of his swimming and his performance was truly wonderful. As before, he wore the black suit with the hood, and when asked why, replied that he had found black to be the color best adapted to swimming, and that the hood held in place his hair, which was long and heavy and would otherwise annoy him.

He went through a maze of intricate movements, performing with ease every feat I had ever heard of being done by swimmers before. With watch in hand, I timed one of his underwater swims, and I gasped with astonishment when he stayed under a full four minutes. It was marvelous, staggering to the imagination.

Out on the lawn that evening, he entertained us with stories. He was a born narrator, and when he talked, everyone within sound of his smooth, silky voice, felt the power of his personality and hung on his words in thrilled silence.

There was one tale he told that deeply impressed us all. It was about a superstitious belief current among the Islands that when a child is born on the water it oftimes takes on the ways of a fish, sometimes even to the extreme of being deformed with webbed fingers and toes and like peculiarities. So strong is the native's faith in this tradition, the Duke declared, that, to appease the wrath of the God of Storms, they often return to the waves, a child born on them. He said he was positive he was born at sea, as he was so much at home in the water, and in conclusion laughingly raised his hands to show that he was "not webbed."

I could not stay near and see Ruth throw herself at this brown man, charming though I had to admit he was, so I strode down on to the beach to be alone with my thoughts, resolved to return to the city on the twelve o'clock boat that very night.

It was eleven o'clock when I returned to the house. Everyone seemed to have retired, so I slipped round to the rear.

Owing to its having been built on the edge of a bluff overlooking the Sound, in the rear, the second story of the house was the ground floor, the veranda, which the library and several bedrooms faced, extending across the back.

I stepped into the library to get my bag and there found Treat waiting up for me. Without explaining why, I said I was going and he gripped my shoulder in such a fatherly manner that I gulped. I realized then that he understood how things were with me, and though he said nothing, I knew that he favored me rather than the Duke for a son-in-law. His hands were tied, however, for Ruth was a girl of strong will and used to having her own way.

He paused in the library door and followed me with gloomy eyes as, too overcome with my emotions to speak, I turned down the moonlit porch. I know I walked like a man in a trance, for I was stunned; all the joy seemed to have been blotted out of my life.

I had gotten half way to the steps, when a reflection of the moon in a window as I passed, suddenly broke in upon my reflections and made me pause. The curtain had fallen away from the window, and as I peered into the room, I recognized it as the bathroom of the Duke's suite.

Feeling guiltily like a peeping Tom, I was about to pass on, when my eye fell on the bathtub, which was close to the window.

I started violently.

The tub was plainly revealed, and I noticed that it was full of water. Peering closer, I saw myriad bubbles rising at one end, and, as one fascinated, I watched them.

Slowly, the outlines of a form in the water below revealed themselves. I caught my breath, and, for a moment, my heart stopped beating, while my hair rose on end. I shuddered.

In the tub, with all but his feet submerged, lay the Duke, and the toes that stuck up were covered with short, silky gray fur and joined to one another by a film-like skin similar to the webs of a duck's foot.

Drawn as by a magnet, my eyes followed the obscure lines of the body till they came to his neck. Then, suddenly, my knees went weak and, with eyes sticking out and jaw sagging, I leaned against the window and stared.

Both sides of the Duke's neck, from his collarbones to a point an inch below his ears, were opening and closing with the regularity of his breathing; and each time the muscles expanded, a thick, dark-red fringe appeared in each of the openings, while a large bubble and many smaller ones streamed from his lips and rose to the surface.

I understood then why the Duke was "so much at home in the water"—*he had gills like a fish!*

My bag fell from my nerveless fingers, and with a hand pressed to my throat in an endeavor to hold back the screech of laughter that struggled for expression, I turned, wide-eyed with terror, and staggered back to where Treat still leaned against the library door.

The Man Who Did Things Twice

Don Mark Lemon

Of commanding figure and soldierly bearing, with deep-set gray eyes, hollow, cadaverous cheeks, and moustache and hair an intense blue black, his singular personality alone had anywhere and at all times attracted special attention to the man; but coupled with this distinguished personality, and singling him out as remarkable in the highest degree, was the fact that he lived in duplicate.

Thus—if on Monday he arose early, breakfasted on coffee, toast, and eggs, afterwards retired to his rooms to occupy himself until noon at his desk; then, after partaking of lunch, quit his rooms to ramble about the city, giving alms to the old blind organwoman, going up and down particular streets and through particular quarto's, thence back to his hotel, to his dinner, to his desk after dinner, and finally to bed—on Tuesday he would go through precisely the same régime; arising early, breakfasting on coffee, toast, and eggs; afterwards retiring to his desk, thence to lunch, to his rambles up and down those particular streets and through those particular quarters that he had visited on Monday, giving alms to the old blind organwoman; thence back to his hotel, to dinner, to his desk and papers; finally to bed.

On Wednesday he perhaps would spend the day quite differently, arising late, going out on horseback for the entire day, attending the theatre at night, and to bed at midnight or later; but howsoever he spent Wednesday, Thursday—or the day following—was sure to be a repetition down to the smallest detail.

Friday would see commenced a new series of action for Saturday to duplicate.

He was the echo—as it were—of himself, and a consummate echo at that, for time and time again he had been watched to see whether he would not make some mistake or fail in his series of duplication, but whenever it was possible for an act to be duplicated he never had been known to fail in its duplication; and, indeed, he had grown so shrewd in the matter that he never did on one day what could not reasonably be duplicated upon the next—if that succeeding day was to be a duplication of the preceding one, and not the beginning of a new series of action.

That this man should deliberately go about living as if his soul were a stereoscope, and life, to be appreciated, must be like the stereoscopic picture, double, was generally considered an astonishing thing; and, besides, it seemed such a reprehensible waste of energy, time, and money.

To fall from his horse upon a Wednesday at a particular crossing, bruising his body and spraining his wrist, was bad enough; but to repeat the accident at that particular crossing upon the following day was a pure waste of energy. To lose a half-hour on Friday by coming down to the depot too early was perhaps an error of calculation; but to repeat the action on the following Saturday was a waste of time. To visit his tailor on Monday and order a new suit of clothing was nothing reprehensible; but to drop in on the following day at precisely the same minute and order a similar suit of clothing could be nothing less than a waste of money.

It was this trait of duplicating all his expenditures that had first attracted attention to the man's singular character. And, indeed, one who coolly and voluntarily paid all his bills twice over was certain, sooner or later, to have minute notice taken of himself and his comings and goings.

Not only was Henry Hobart's character remarkable, but it had an element of danger as well. Any enemy could have committed a series of duplicate crimes or misdemeanors about the city of Weston and The Man Who Did Things Twice would have come under instant suspicion as the guilty party. But evidently Henry Hobart was without enemies; one might add, without friends. His was the best known face, but lie the least known man, in the cultured little city of Weston. Not that his character was such as to repel the advance of friendship, but simply that he drew around perhaps a gentle and kindly nature, an almost impenetrable cloak of reserve.

It may have been that the man's mind was divided, one half acting normally and consistently, whilst the other half drove him each alternate day to imitate his conduct of the preceding day, as a little impish boy imitates the actions of one going before him in the street. Or perhaps he was merely eccentric. But there seemed something more than eccentricity in his conduct when, upon a certain Saturday, he deliberately returned and allowed a vicious dog to bite him in the manner that it had bit him some twenty-four hours before. Such conduct could arise from nothing less than methodical madness.

Living his own life in his own reserved way, cultured and studious, troubling no one, offending none; doubly liberal in his expenditures and never pressed for means, steadfast in his chosen eccentricity—if such it were—and in his face and manner no questioning doubt of himself, perhaps in time Henry Hobart had been accepted like any other man, the curious had ceased to be curious, and his mysterious character, without any further or deeper scrutiny, had become one of the mysteries of human life, had not the man been suddenly struck down as by an invisible hand and the appalling mystery of his death heightened tenfold the mystery of his life.

On a Tuesday morning, at fifteen minutes of ten o'clock, an attendant was summoned by the call-bell to room Sixty-Three of the Sumner House, and upon obeying the call found Henry Hobart struggling in the throes of a strange and unnatural death.

The Man Who Did Things Twice, half-dressed, standing in the centre of his outer room, was battling with the invisible air about him for breath, or, as the attendant put it later, "Like he was fightin' with something that weren't there."

The hotel was aroused, Doctor Thiel was hastily summoned from his office on the next floor, and everything was done that science could suggest or despair persuade, yet in less than ten minutes Henry Hobart lay dead on the floor, within his stilled brain hidden the profound mystery of his life, and still echoing in the death room his one strangled cry ere death sealed his blue lips—*To-morrow!*

It was a strange case, a questionable case, a frightful case, but beyond all it proved a baffling case, for the police came, removed the body to the morgue, intimating death by poison or other foul play, and examined the rooms and overhauled the possessions of the dead man, but who the deceased was, who his kindred or what his former residence, or the cause of his death, they could not discover. The scholarly tomes that filled his shelves bore no signatures or bookmarks, and private papers of any kind there were none. The autopsy made the same day—afternoon—upon the body of the deceased failed to discover any poison, and Doctor Thiel's belief that the man had been strangled seemed without support, as no foreign substance or growth of any kind was found in the windpipe or air passages.

Nevertheless, Doctor Thiel was firm and blunt: "The man was strangled," he maintained. "Make the best of that, gentlemen, and then go to your dinners."

One thing only seemed certain, one tiling only was undisputed,—The Man Who Did Things Twice, with severed windpipe and autopsy-marred body, would not duplicate his own death upon the morrow. He had come to his death on a Tuesday, a Tuesday with which—had he lived—he would have begun a new course of action to be duplicated on Wednesday. But he had died, and now for once The Man Who Did Things Twice would fail in his eccentricity. Perhaps for that his spirit would be troubled.

Next morning, while the attendant who had been first on the death scene of the previous day was holding forth at length on the tragedy with certain servant-cronies, the call-bell suddenly rang and the hand of the call dial spun around and pointed to number Sixty-Three.

The man hastened to obey the summons, not noticing that the hands of the hall clock pointed to fifteen minutes of ten, nor delaying to recollect what guest occupied room Sixty-Three. The tragedy of the preceding day had been the event of his life, and he had not as yet descended to the trifles of his daily routine.

As he tapped briskly at the door of room Sixty-Three and put his hand upon the knob to enter, it suddenly came over him that he had done precisely such a thing before. That at about that time of some other morning he had been summoned by the call-bell to room Sixty-Three—had knocked, turned the knob, entered—and a loud cry, a shout thick with horror, broke from the man's lips, and he reeled back into the hallway.

There before him, in the centre of the fateful room, half-dressed, battling with the invisible air, with blue lips and protruding eyes, stood The Man Who Did Things Twice.

The ominous, ghostly hush that followed the frightened attendant's cry was quickly broken by the hurry of many feet, and soon again the hotel was aroused and again Doctor Thiel bent over the prostrate and dying Henry Hobart.

Outside and distantly could be heard the clang of the fire-bells, but in the room of death all was sudden silence, all were hushed by the frightful, ghostly thought that the scene before them had been enacted before—the dying man with his discolored face and struggling hands, the physician bending over him, the alarmed, pitying faces of the gathered guests, and the frightened servants huddled in the background. *And the man must die—die as he had died!*

They looked on, and waited. Then the end came, and Doctor Thiel, arising, said, "He is dead!" He had uttered those words once before and under like conditions. And the guests and the servants spoke together in horrified whispers, as they had done before; then the assembly broke up and the hallway was cleared, as before!

There was something immeasurably painful about it all, to live a thing over in that frightful way, to be, as it were, mere puppets at a show, and one day to be to another day as a reflection in a mirror.

For a time those who had witnessed both tragedies seemed to live in a kind of trance, and moved about and whispered together like beings in a dream; but finally the natural reasserted itself, and then curiosity seized them.

What was the meaning of it? Henry Hobart had died and his body had been mutilated by the surgeon's knife. How, then, had he died a second time and his body shown no marks of the knife? Had they been deceived by a ghost? No: there in room Sixty-Three lay the dead man—flesh and blood—and seven blocks away, resting on a marble slab, with the water dripping continually on it, lay the other body of Henry Hobart—The Man Who Did Things Twice.

A sudden doubt came into the mind of Doctor Thiel, a misgiving that frightened him. Was that other body—that autopsy-marred body—still resting quietly on its slab at the morgue? Or—

Hastily quitting the hotel, he hurried towards the morgue, and suddenly came up against an insurmountable blank wall of mystery. The morgue was a heap of charred ruin and smoldering, steaming ashes, and *if* the autopsy-marred body of Henry Hobart had been lying on its slab during the period of the fire, then it had been totally consumed, and that other body up at the hotel was that of a second Henry Hobart; but, if the autopsy-marred body of Henry Hobart had *not* been lying quietly on its slab during the raging of the fire, then, in God's name, who and what was he who had died up at the Sumner House that morning?

The Man with the Nose

Rhoda Broughton

[The details of this little story are of course imaginary, but the main incidents are, to the best of my belief, facts. They happened twenty, or more than twenty years ago.]

I

"Let us get a map and see what places look pleasantest?" says she.

"As for that," reply I, "on a map most places look equally pleasant."

"Never mind; get one!"

I obey.

"Do you like the seaside?" asks Elizabeth, lifting her little brown head and her small happy white face from the English sea-coast, along which her forefinger is slowly travelling.

"Since you ask me, distinctly *no*," reply I, for once venturing to have a decided opinion of my own, which during the last few weeks of imbecility I can be hardly said to have had. "I broke my last wooden spade five and twenty years ago. I have but a poor opinion of cockles—sandy red-nosed things, are not they? and the air always makes me bilious."

"Then we certainly will not go there," says Elizabeth, laughing. "A bilious bridegroom! alliterative but horrible! None of our friends show the least eagerness to lend us their country house."

"Oh that God would put it into the hearts of men to take their wives straight home, as their fathers did," say I, with a cross groan.

"It is evident, therefore, that we must go somewhere," returns she, not heeding the aspiration contained in my last speech, making her forefinger resume its employment, and reaching Torquay.

"I suppose so," say I, with a sort of sigh; "for once in our lives we must resign ourselves to having the finger of derision pointed at us by waiters and landlords."

"You shall leave your new portmanteau at home, and I will leave all my best clothes, and nobody will guess that we are bride and bridegroom; they will think that we have been married—oh, ever since the world began" (opening her eyes very wide).

I shake my head. "With an old portmanteau and in rags we shall still have the mark of the beast upon us."

"Do you mind much? do you hate being ridiculous?" asks Elizabeth, meekly, rather depressed by my view of the case; "because if so, let us go somewhere out of the way, where there will be very few people to laugh at us."

"On the contrary," return I, stoutly, "we will betake ourselves to some spot where such as we do chiefly congregate—where we shall be swallowed up and lost in the multitude of our fellow-sinners." A pause devoted to reflection. "What do you say to Killarney?" say I, cheerfully.

"There are a great many fleas there, I believe," replies Elizabeth, slowly; "flea-bites make large lumps on me; you would not like me if I were covered with large lumps."

At the hideous ideal picture thus presented to me by my little beloved I relapse into inarticulate idiocy; emerging from which by-and-by, I suggest "The Lakes?" My arm is round her, and I feel her supple body shiver though it is mid July, and the bees are booming about in the still and sleepy noon garden outside.

"Oh—no—no—not *there*!"

"Why such emphasis?" I ask gaily; "more fleas? At this rate, and with this *sine qua non*, our choice will grow limited."

"Something dreadful happened to me there," she says, with another shudder. "But indeed I did not think there was any harm in it—I never thought anything would come of it."

"What the devil was it?" cry I, in a jealous heat and hurry; "what the mischief *did* you do, and why have not you told me about it before?"

"I did not do much," she answers meekly, seeking for my hand, and when found kissing it in timid deprecation of my wrath; "but I was ill—very ill—there; I had a nervous fever. I was in a bed hung with a chintz with a red and green fern-leaf pattern on it. I have always hated red and green fern-leaf chintzes ever since."

"It would be possible to avoid the obnoxious bed, would not it?" say I, laughing a little. "Where does it lie? Windermere? Ulleswater? Wastwater? Where?"

"We were at Ulleswater," she says, speaking rapidly, while a hot color grows on her small white cheeks—"Papa, mamma, and I; and there came a mesmeriser to Penrith, and we went to see him—everybody did—and he asked leave to mesmerise me—he said I should be such a good medium—and—and—I did not know what it was like. I thought it would be quite good fun—and—and—I let him."

She is trembling exceedingly; even the loving pressure of my arms cannot abate her shivering.

"Well?"

"And after that I do not remember anything—I believe I did all sorts of extraordinary things that he told me—sang and danced, and made a fool of myself—but when I came home I was very ill, very—I lay in bed for five whole weeks, and—and was off my head, and said odd and wicked things that you would not have expected me to say—that dreadful bed! shall I ever forget it?"

"We will not go to the Lakes," I say, decisively, "and we will not talk any more about mesmerism."

"That is right," she says, with a sigh of relief, "I try to think about it as little as possible; but sometimes, in the dead black of the night, when God seems a long way off, and the devil near, it comes back to me so strongly—I feel, do not you know, as if he were *there*—somewhere in the room, and I *must* get up and follow him."

"Why should not we go abroad?" suggest I, abruptly turning the conversation.

"Why, indeed?" cries Elizabeth, recovering her gaiety, while her pretty blue eyes begin to dance. "How stupid of us not to have thought of it before; only *abroad* is a big word. *What* abroad?"

"We must be content with something short of Central Africa," I say, gravely, "as I think our £150 would hardly take us that far."

"Wherever we go, we must buy a dialogue book," suggests my little bride elect, "and I will learn some phrases before we start."

"As for that, the Anglo-Saxon tongue takes one pretty well round the world," reply I, with a feeling of complacent British swagger, putting my hands in my breeches pockets.

"Do you fancy the Rhine?" says Elizabeth, with a rather timid suggestion; "I know it is the fashion to run it down nowadays, and call it a cocktail river; but—but—after all it cannot be so very contemptible, or Byron could not have said such noble things about it."

"The castled crag of Drachenfels
Frowns o'er the wide and winding Rhine,
Whose breast of waters broadly swells
Between the banks which bear the vine,"

say I, spouting. "After all, that proves nothing, for Byron could have made a silk purse out of a sow's ear."

"The Rhine will not do then?" says she, resignedly, suppressing a sigh.

"On the contrary, it will do admirably: it is a cocktail river, and I do not care who says it is not," reply I, with illiberal positiveness; " but everybody should be able to say so from their own experience, and not from hearsay: the Rhine let it be, by all means."

So the Rhine it is.

II

I have got over it; we have both got over it tolerably, creditably; but, after all, it is a much severer ordeal for a man than a woman, who, with a bouquet to occupy her hands, and a veil to gently shroud her features, need merely be prettily passive. I am alluding, I need hardly say, to the religious ceremony of marriage, which I flatter myself I have gone through with a stiff sheepishness not unworthy of my country. It is a three-days-old event now, and we are getting used to belonging to one another, though Elizabeth still takes off her ring twenty times a day to admire its bright thickness; still laughs when she hears herself called "Madame." Three days ago, we kissed all our friends, and left them to make themselves ill on our cake, and criticise our bridal behaviour, and now we are at Brussels, she and I, feeling oddly, joyfully free from any chaperone. We have been mildly sight-seeing—very mildly, most people would say, but we have resolved not to take our pleasure with the railway speed of Americans, or the hasty sadness of our fellow Britons. Slowly and gaily we have been taking ours. To-day we have been to visit Wiertz's pictures. Have you ever seen them, oh reader? They are known to comparatively few people, but if you have a taste for the unearthly terrible—if you wish to sup full of horrors, hasten thither. We have been peering through the appointed peep-hole at the horrible cholera picture—the man buried alive by mistake, pushing up the lid of his coffin, and stretching a ghastly face and livid hands out of his winding—sheet towards you, while awful grey-blue coffins are piled around, and noisome toads and giant spiders crawl damply about. On first seeing it, I have reproached myself for bringing one of so nervous a temperament as Elizabeth to see so haunting and hideous a spectacle; but she is less impressed than I expected—less impressed than I myself am.

"He is very lucky to be able to get his lid up," she says, with a half-laugh; "we should find it hard work to burst our brass nails, should not we? When you bury me, dear, fasten me down very slightly, in case there may be some mistake."

And now all the long and quiet July evening we have been prowling together about the streets. Brussels is the town of towns for *flâner*-ing—have been flattening our noses against the shop windows, and making each other imaginary presents. Elizabeth has not confined herself to imagination however; she has made me buy her a little bonnet with feathers—"in order to look married," as she says, and the result is such a delicious picture of a child playing at being grown up, having practised a theft on its mother's wardrobe, that for the last two hours I have been in a foolish ecstacy of love and laughter over her and it. We are at the "Bellevue," and have a fine suite of rooms, *au premier*, evidently specially devoted to the English, to the gratification of whose well-known loyalty the Prince and Princess of Wales are simpering from the walls. Is there any one in the three kingdoms who knows his own face as well as he knows the faces of Albert Victor and Alexandra? The long evening has at last sudden into night—night far advanced—night melting into earliest day. All Brussels is asleep. One moment ago I also was asleep, soundly as any log. What is it that has made me take this sudden headlong plunge out of sleep into wakefulness? Who is it that is clutching at and calling upon me? What is it that is making me struggle mistily up into a sitting posture, and try to revive my sleep-numbed senses? A summer night is never wholly dark; by the half light that steals through the closed *persiennes* and open windows I see my wife standing beside my bed; the extremity of terror on her face, and her fingers digging themselves with painful tenacity into my arm.

"Tighter, tighter!" she is crying, wildly. "What are you thinking of? You are letting me go!"

"Good heavens!" say I, rubbing my eyes, while my muddy brain grows a trifle clearer. "What is it? What has happened? Have you had a nightmare?"

"You saw him," she says, with a sort of sobbing breathlessness; "you know you did! You saw him as well as I."

"I!" cry I, incredulously—"not I. Till this second I have been fast asleep. *I* saw nothing."

"You did!" she cries, passionately. "You know you did. Why do you deny it? You were as frightened as I?"

"As I live," I answer, solemnly, "I know no more than the dead what you are talking about; till you woke me by calling me and catching hold of me, I was as sound asleep as the seven sleepers."

"Is it possible that it can have been a dream?" she says, with a long sigh, for a moment loosing my arm, and covering her face with her hands. "But no—in a dream I should have been somewhere else, but I was *here*—here—on that bed, and he stood *there* (pointing with her forefinger)—just there, between the foot of it and the window!"

She stops, panting.

"It is all that brute Wiertz," say I, in a fury. "I wish I had been buried alive myself, before I had been fool enough to take you to see his beastly daubs."

"Light a candle," she says, in the same breathless way, her teeth chattering with fright. "Let us make sure that he is not hidden somewhere in the room?"

"How could he be?" say I, striking a match; "the door is locked."

"He might have got in by the balcony," she answers, still trembling violently.

"He would have had to have cut a very large hole in the *persiennes*," say I, half-mockingly. "See, they are intact and well fastened on the inside."

She sinks into an arm-chair, and pushes her loose soft hair from her white face.

"It *was* a dream then, I suppose?"

She is silent for a moment or two, while I bring her a glass of water, and throw a dressing-gown round her cold and shrinking form.

"Now tell me, my little one," I say, coaxingly, sitting down-at her feet, "what it was—what you thought you saw?"

"*Thought* I saw!" echoes she, with indignant emphasis, sitting upright, while her eyes sparkle feverishly. "I am as certain that I saw him standing there as I am that I see that candle burning—that I see this chair—that I see you."

"*Him*! but who is *him*?"

She falls forward on my neck, and buries her face in my shoulder.

"That—dreadful—man!" she says, while her whole body is one tremor.

"*What* dreadful man?" cry I, impatiently.

She is silent.

"Who was he?"

"I do not know."

"Did you ever see him before?"

"Oh, no—no, never! I hope to God I may never see him again!"

"What was he like?"

"Come closer to me," she says, laying hold of my hand with her small and chilly fingers; "stay *quite* near me, and I will tell you" (after a pause)—"he had a *nose*!"

"My dear soul," cry I, bursting out with a loud laugh in the silence of the night, "do not most people have noses? Would not he have been much more dreadful if he had had *none*?"

"But it was such a nose!" she says, with perfect trembling gravity.

"A bottle nose?" suggest I, still cackling.

"For heaven's sake, don't laugh!" she says, nervously; "if you had seen his face, you would have been as little disposed to laugh as I."

"But his nose?" return I, suppressing my merriment; "what kind of nose was it? See, I am as grave as a judge."

"It was very prominent," she answers, in a sort of awe-struck half-whisper, "and very sharply chiselled; the nostrils very much cut out." A little pause. "His eyebrows were one straight black line across his face, and under them his eyes burnt like dull coals of fire, that shone and yet did not shine; they looked like dead eyes, sunken, half extinguished, and yet sinister."

"And what did he do?" ask I, impressed, despite myself, by her passionate earnestness; "when did you first see him?"

"I was asleep," she said—"at least I thought so—and suddenly I opened my eyes, and he was *there—there*"—pointing again with trembling finger—"between the window and the bed."

"What was he doing? Was he walking about?"

"He was standing as still as stone—I never saw any live thing so still—*looking* at me; he never called or beckoned, or moved a finger, but his eyes *commanded* me to come to him, as the eyes of the mesmeriser at Penrith did." She stops, breathing heavily. I can hear her heart's loud and rapid beats.

"And you?" I say, pressing her more closely to my side, and smoothing her troubled hair.

"I *hated* it," she cries excitedly; "I loathed it—abhorred it. I was ice-cold with fear and horror, but—I felt myself going to him."

"Yes?"

"And then I shrieked out to you, and you came running, and caught fast hold of me, and held me tight at first—quite tight—but presently I felt your hold slacken—slacken—and though I *longed* to stay with you, though I was *mad* with fright, yet I felt myself pulling strongly away from you—going to him; and he—he stood there always looking—looking—and then I gave one last loud shriek, and I suppose I awoke—and it was a dream!"

"I never heard of a clearer case of nightmare," say I stoutly; "that vile Wiertz! I should like to see his whole *Musée* burnt by the hands of the hangman to-morrow."

She shakes her head. "It had nothing to say to Wiertz; what it meant I do not know, but—"

"It meant nothing," I answer, reassuringly, "except that for the future we will go and see none but good and pleasant sights, and steer clear of charnel-house fancies."

III

Elizabeth is now in a position to decide whether the Rhine is a cocktail river or no, for she is on it, and so am I. We are sitting, with an awning over our heads, and little wooden stools under our feet. Elizabeth has a small sailor's hat and blue ribbon on her head. The river breeze has blown it rather awry; has tangled her plenteous hair; has made a faint pink stain on her pale cheeks. It is some fete day, and the boat is crowded. Tables, countless camp-stools, volumes of black smoke pouring from the funnel, as we steam along. "Nothing to the Caledonian Canal!" cries a burly Scotchman in leggings, speaking with loud authority, and surveying with an air of contempt the eternal vine-clad slopes, that sound so well, and look so *sticky* in reality. "Cannot hold a candle to it!" A rival bride and bridegroom opposite, sitting together like love-birds under an umbrella, looking into each other's eyes instead of at the Rhine scenery.

"They might as well have staid at home, might not they?" says my wife, with a little air of superiority. "Come, we are not so bad as that, are we?"

A storm comes on: hailstones beat slantwise and reach us—stone and sting us right under our awning. Everybody rushes down below, and takes the opportunity to feed ravenously. There are few actions more disgusting than eating *can* be made. A handsome girl close to us—her immaturity evidenced by the two long tails of black hair down her back—is thrusting her knife half way down her throat.

"Come on deck again," says Elizabeth, disgusted and frightened at this last sight. "The hail was much better than this!"

So we return to our camp-stools, and sit alone under one mackintosh in the lashing storm, with happy hearts and empty stomachs.

"Is not this better than any luncheon?" asks Elizabeth, triumphantly, while the rain drops hang on her long and curled lashes.

"Infinitely better," reply I, madly struggling with the umbrella to prevent its being blown inside out, and gallantly ignoring a species of gnawing sensation at my entrails.

The squall clears off by and by, and we go steaming, steaming on past the unnumbered little villages by the water's edge with church spires and pointed roof, past the countless rocks with their little pert castles perched on the top of them, past the tall, stiff poplar rows. The church bells are ringing gaily as we go by. A nightingale is singing from a wood. The black eagle of Prussia droops on the stream behind us, swish-swish through the dull green water. A fat woman who is interested in it leans over the back of the boat, and by some happy effect of crinoline displays to her fellow-passengers two yards of thick white cotton legs. She is, fortunately for herself, unconscious of her generosity.

The day steals on; at every stopping place more people come on. There is hardly elbow room; and, what is worse, almost everybody is drunk. Rocks, castles, villages, poplars, slide by, while the paddles churn always the water, and the evening draws greyly on. At Bingen a party of big blue Prussian soldiers, very drunk, "glorious" as Tam o' Shanter, come and establish themselves close to us. They call for Lager Beer; talk at the tip-top of their strong voices; two of them begin to spar; all seem inclined to sing. Elizabeth is frightened. We are two hours late in arriving at Biebrich. It is half an hour more before we can get ourselves and our luggage into a carriage and set off along the winding road to Wiesbaden. "The night is chilly, but not dark." There is only a little shabby bit of a moon, but it shines as hard as it can. Elizabeth is quite worn out, her tired head droops in uneasy sleep on my shoulder. Once she wakes up with a start.

"Are you sure that it meant nothing?" she asks, looking me eagerly in my face; "do people often have such dreams?"

"Often, often," I answer, reassuringly.

"I am always afraid of falling asleep now," she says, trying to sit upright and keep her heavy eyes open, "for fear of seeing him standing there again. Tell me, do you think I shall? Is there any chance, any probability of it?"

"None, none!"

We reach Wiesbaden at last, and drive up to the Hotel des Quatre Saisons. By this time it is full midnight. Two or three men are standing about the door. Morris, the maid, has got out—so have I, and I am holding out my hand to Elizabeth, when I hear her give one piercing scream, and see her with ash-white face and starting eyes point with her forefinger—

"There he is!——there!—there!"

I look in the direction indicated, and just catch a glimpse of a tall figure, standing half in the shadow of the night, half in the gaslight from the hotel. I have not time for more than one cursory glance, as I am interrupted by a cry from the bystanders, and turning quickly round, am just in time to catch my wife, who falls in utter insensibility into my arms. We carry her into a room on the ground floor; it is small, noisy, and hot, but it is the nearest at hand. In about an hour she reopens her eyes. A strong shudder makes her quiver from head to foot.

"Where is he?" she says, in a terrified whisper, as her senses come slowly back. "He is somewhere about—somewhere near. I feel that he is!"

"My dearest child, there is no one here but Morris and me," I answer, soothingly. "Look for yourself. See."

I take one of the candles and light up each corner of the room in succession.

"You saw him!" she says, in trembling hurry, sitting up and clenching her hands together. "I know you did—I pointed him out to you—you *cannot* say that it was a dream *this* time."

"I saw two or three ordinary looking men as we drove up," I answer, in a commonplace, matter-of-fact tone. "I did not notice anything remarkable about any of them; you know the fact is, darling, that you have had nothing to eat all day, nothing but a biscuit, and you are over-wrought, and fancy things."

"Fancy!" echoes she, with strong irritation. "How you talk! Was I ever one to fancy things? I tell you that as sure as I sit here—as sure as you stand there—I saw him—*him*—the man I saw in my dream, if it was a dream. There was not a hair's breadth of difference between them—and he was looking at me—looking—"

She breaks off into hysterical sobbing.

"My dear child!" say I, thoroughly alarmed, and yet half angry, "for God's sake do not work yourself up into a fever: wait till to-morrow, and we will find out who he is, and all about him; you yourself will laugh when we discover that he is some harmless bagman."

"Why not *now*?" she says, nervously; "why cannot you find out *now—this minute*?"

"Impossible! Everybody is in bed! Wait till to-morrow, and all will be cleared up."

The morrow comes, and I go about the hotel, inquiring. The house is so full, and the data I have to go upon are so small, that for some time I have great difficulty in making it understood to whom I am alluding. At length one waiter seems to comprehend.

"A tall and dark gentleman, with a pronounced and very peculiar nose? Yes; there has been such a one, certainly, in the hotel, but he left at 'grand matin' this morning; he remained only one night."

"And his name?"

The garçon shakes his head. "That is unknown, monsieur; he did not inscribe it in the visitor's book."

"What countryman was he?"

Another shake of the head. "He spoke German, but it was with a foreign accent."

"Whither did he go?"

That also is unknown. Nor can I arrive at any more facts about him.

IV

A fortnight has passed; we have been hither and thither; now we are at Lucerne. Peopled with better inhabitants, Lucerne might well do for Heaven. It is drawing towards eventide, and Elizabeth and I are sitting, hand in hand, on a quiet bench, under the shady linden trees, on a high hill up above the lake. There is nobody to see us, so we sit peaceably hand in hand. Up by the still and solemn monastery we came, with its small and narrow windows, calculated to hinder the holy fathers from promenading curious eyes on the world, the flesh, and the devil, tripping past them in blue gauze veils: below us grass and green trees, houses with high-pitched roofs, little dormer-windows, and shutters yet greener than the grass; below us the lake in its rippleless peace, calm, quiet, motionless as Bethesda's pool before the coming of the troubling angel.

"I said it was too good to last," say I, doggedly, "did not I, only yesterday? Perfect peace, perfect sympathy, perfect freedom from nagging worries—when did such a state of things last more than two days?"

Elizabeth's eyes are idly fixed on a little steamer, with a stripe of red along its side and a tiny puff of smoke from its funnel, gliding along and cutting a narrow white track on Lucerne's sleepy surface.

"This is the fifth false alarm of the gout having gone to his stomach within the last two years," continue I, resentfully. "I declare to Heaven, that if it has not really gone there this time, I'll cut the whole concern."

Let no one cast up their eyes in horror, imagining that it is my father to whom I am thus alluding; it is only a great uncle by marriage, in consideration of whose wealth and vague promises I have dawdled professionless through twenty-eight years of my life.

"You *must* not go," says Elizabeth, giving my hand an imploring squeeze. "The man in the Bible said, 'I have married a wife, and therefore I cannot come'; why should it be a less valid excuse nowadays?"

"If I recollect rightly, it was considered rather a poor one even then," reply I, dryly.

Elizabeth is unable to contradict this, she therefore only lifts two pouted lips (Monsieur Taine objects to the redness of English women's mouths, but I do not) to he kissed, and says, "Stay." I am good enough to comply with her unspoken request, though I remain firm with regard to her spoken one.

"My dearest child," I say, with an air of worldly experience and superior wisdom, "kisses are very good things—in fact there are few better—but one cannot live upon them."

"Let us try," she says, coaxingly.

"I wonder which would get tired first?" I say, laughing. But she only goes on pleading, "Stay, stay."

"How *can* I stay?" I cry impatiently; "you talk as if I *wanted* to go! Do you think it is any pleasanter to me to leave you than to you to be left? But you know his disposition, his rancorous resentment of fancied neglects. For the sake of two days' indulgence, must I throw away what will keep us in ease and plenty to the end of our days?"

"I do not care for plenty," she says, with a little petulant gesture. "I do not see that rich people are any happier than poor ones. Look at the St. Clairs; they have £40,000 a year, and she is a miserable woman, perfectly miserable, because her face gets red after dinner."

"There will be no fear of our faces getting red after dinner," say I, grimly, "for we shall have no dinner for them to get red after."

A pause. My eyes stray away to the mountains. Pilatus on the right, with his jagged peak and slender snow-chains about his harsh neck; hill after hill rising silent, eternal, like guardian spirits standing hand in hand around their child, the lake. As I look, suddenly they have all flushed, as at some noblest thought, and over all their sullen faces streams an ineffable rosy joy—a solemn and wonderful effulgence, such as Israel saw reflected from the features of the Eternal in their prophet's transfigured eyes. The unutterable peace and stainless beauty of earth and sky seem to lie softly on my soul. "Would God I could stay! Would God all life could be like this!" I say devoutly, and the aspiration has the reverent earnestness of a prayer.

"Why do you say, '*Would God?*' " she cries, passionately, "when it lies with yourself. Oh my dear love" (gently sliding her hand through my arm, and lifting wetly-beseeching eyes to my face), "I do not know why I insist upon it so much—I cannot tell you myself—I dare say I seem selfish and unreasonable—but I feel as if your going now would be the end of all things—as if—" She breaks off suddenly.

"My child," say I, thoroughly distressed, but still determined to have my own way, "you talk as if I were going for ever and a day; in a week, at the outside, I shall be back, and then you will thank me for the very thing for which you now think me so hard and disobliging."

"Shall I?" she answers, mournfully. "Well, I hope so."

"You will not be alone, either; you will have Morris."

"Yes."

"And every day you will write me a long letter, telling me every single thing that you do, say, and think?"

"Yes."

She answers me gently and obediently; but I can see that she is still utterly unreconciled to the idea of my absence.

"What is it that you are afraid of?" I ask, becoming rather irritated. "What do you suppose will happen to you?"

She does not answer; only a large tear falls on my hand, which she hastily wipes away with her pocket handkerchief, as if afraid of exciting my wrath.

"Can you give me any good reason why I *should* stay?" I ask, dictatorially.

"None—none—only—stay—stay!"

But I am resolved *not* to stay. Early the next morning I set off.

V

The time it is not a false alarm; this time it really has gone to his stomach, and, declining to be dislodged thence, kills him. My return is therefore retarded until after the funeral and the reading of the will. The latter is so satisfactory, and my time is so fully occupied with a multiplicity of attendant business, that I have no leisure to regret the delay. I write to Elizabeth, but receive no letters from her. This surprises and makes me rather angry, but does not alarm me. "If she had been ill, if anything had happened, Morris would have written. She never was great at writing, poor little soul. What dear little babyish notes she used to send me during our engagement; perhaps she wishes to punish me for my disobedience to her wishes. Well, now she will see who was right." I am drawing near her now; I am walking up from the railway station at Lucerne. I am very joyful as I march along under an umbrella, in the grand broad shining of the summer afternoon. I think with pensive passion of the last glimpse I had of my beloved—her small and wistful face looking out from among the thick fair fleece of her long hair—winking away her tears and blowing kisses to me. It is a new sensation to me to have any one looking tearfully wistful over my departure. I draw near the great glaring Schweizerhof, with its colonnaded, tourist-crowded porch; here are all the pomegranates as I left them, in their green tubs, with their scarlet blossoms, and the dusty oleanders in a row. I look up at our windows; nobody is looking out from them; they are open, and the curtains are alternately swelled out and drawn in by the softly-playful wind. I run quickly upstairs and burst noisily into the sitting-room. Empty, perfectly empty! I open the adjoining door into the bedroom, crying, "Elizabeth! Elizabeth!" but I receive no answer. Empty too. A feeling of indignation creeps over me as I think, "Knowing the time of my return, she might have managed to be indoors." I have returned to the silent sitting-room, where the only noise is the wind still playing hide-and-seek with the curtains. As I look vacantly round my eye catches sight of a letter lying on the table. I pick it up mechanically and look at the address. Good heavens! what can this mean? It is my own, that I sent her two days ago, unopened, with the seal unbroken. Does she carry her resentment so far as not even to open my letters? I spring at the bell and violently ring it. It is answered by the waiter who has always specially attended us.

"Is madame gone out?"

The man opens his mouth and stares at me.

"Madame! Is monsieur then not aware that madame is no longer at the hotel?"

"*What*?"

"On the same day as monsieur, madame departed."

"*Departed*!" Good God! what are you talking about?"

"A few hours after monsieur's departure—I will not be positive as to the exact time, but it must have been between one and two o'clock as the midday *table d'hôte* was in progress—a gentleman came and asked for madame—"

"Yes—be quick."

"I demanded whether I should take up his card, but he said 'No,' that was unnecessary, as he was perfectly well known to madame; and, in fact, a short time afterwards, without saying anything to anyone, she departed with him."

"And did not return in the evening?"

"No, monsieur; madame has not returned since that day."

I clench my hands in an agony of rage and grief. "So this is it! With that pure child-face, with that divine ignorance—only three weeks married—this is the trick she has played me!" I am recalled to myself by a compassionate suggestion from the garçon.

"Perhaps it was the brother of Madame."

Elizabeth has no brother, but the remark brings back to me the necessity of self-command. "Very probably," I answer, speaking with infinite difficulty. "What sort of looking gentleman was he?"

"He was a very tall and dark gentleman with a most peculiar nose—not quite like any nose that I ever saw before—and most singular eyes. Never have I seen a gentleman who at all resembled him."

I sink into a chair, while a cold shudder creeps over me as I think of my poor child's dream—of her fainting fit at Wiesbaden—of her unconquerable dread of and aversion from my departure. And this happened twelve days ago! I catch up my hat, and prepare to rush like a madman in pursuit.

"How did they go?" I ask incoherently; "by train?—driving?—walking?"

"They went in a carriage."

"What direction did they take? Whither did they go?"

He shakes his head. "It is not known."

"It *must* be known," I cry, driven to frenzy by every second's delay. "Of course the driver could tell; where is he?—where can I find him?"

"He did not belong to Lucerne, neither did the carriage; the gentleman brought them with him."

"But madame's maid," say I, a gleam of hope flashing across my mind; "did she go with her?"

"No, monsieur, she is still here; she was as much surprised as monsieur at madame's departure."

"Send her at once," I cry eagerly; but when she comes I find that she can throw no light on the matter. She weeps noisily and says many irrelevant things, but I can obtain no information from her beyond the fact that she was unaware of her mistress's departure until long after it had taken place, when, surprised at not being rung for at the usual time, she had gone to her room and found it empty, and on inquiring in the hotel, had heard of' her sudden departure; that, expecting her to return at night, she had sat up waiting for her till two o'clock in the morning, but that, as I knew, she had not returned, neither had anything since been heard of her.

Not all my inquiries, not all my cross-questionings of the whole staff of the hotel, of the visitors, of the railway officials, of nearly all the inhabitants of Lucerne and its environs, procure me a jot more knowledge. On the next few weeks I look back as on a hellish and insane dream. I can neither eat nor sleep; I am unable to remain one moment quiet; my whole existence, my nights and my days, are spent in seeking, seeking. Everything that human despair and frenzied love can do is done by me. I advertise, I communicate with the police, I employ detectives; but that fatal twelve days' start forever baffles me. Only on one occasion do I obtain one tittle of information. In a village a few miles from Lucerne the peasants, on the day in question, saw a carriage driving rapidly through their little street. It was closed, but through the windows they could see the occupants—a dark gentleman, with the peculiar physiognomy which has been so often described, and on the opposite seat a lady lying apparently in a state of utter insensibility. But even this leads to nothing.

Oh, reader, these things happened twenty years ago; since then I have searched sea and land, but never have I seen my little Elizabeth again.

The Marble Hands

Bernard Capes

We left our bicycles by the little lych-gate and entered the old churchyard. Heriot had told me frankly that he did not want to come; but at the last moment, sentiment or curiosity prevailing with him, he had changed his mind. I knew indefinitely that there was something disagreeable to him in the place's associations, though he had always referred with affection to the relative with whom he had stayed here as a boy. Perhaps she lay under one of these greening stones.

We walked round the church, with its squat, shingled spire. It was utterly peaceful, here on the brow of the little town where the flowering fields began. The bones of the hill were the bones of the dead, and its flesh was grass. Suddenly Heriot stopped me. We were standing then to the north-west of the chancel, and a gloom of motionless trees over-shadowed us.

"I wish you'd just look in there a moment," he said, "and come back and tell me what you see."

He was pointing towards a little bay made by the low boundary wall, the green floor of which was hidden from our view by the thick branches and a couple of interposing tombs, huge, coffer-shaped, and shut within rails. His voice sounded odd; there was a "plunging" look in his eyes, to use a gambler's phrase. I stared at him a moment, followed the direction of his hand; then, without a word, stooped under the heavy, brushing boughs, passed round the great tombs, and came upon a solitary grave.

It lay there quite alone in the hidden bay—a strange thing, fantastic and gruesome. There was no headstone, but a bevelled marble curb, without name or epitaph, enclosed a gravelled space from which projected two hands. They were of white marble, very faintly touched with green, and conveyed in that still, lonely spot a most curious sense of reality, as if actually thrust up, deathly and alluring, from the grave beneath. The impression grew upon me as I looked, until I could have thought they moved stealthily, consciously, turning in the soil as if to greet me. It was absurd, but—I turned and went rather hastily back to Heriot.

"All right. I see they are there still," he said; and that was all. Without another word we left the place and, remounting, continued our way.

Miles from the spot, lying on a sunny downside, with the sheep about us in hundreds cropping the hot grass, he told me the story:

"She and her husband were living in the town at the time of my first visit there, when I was a child of seven. They were known to Aunt Caddie, who disliked the woman. I did not dislike her at all, because, when we met, she made a favourite of me. She was a little pretty thing, frivolous and shallow; but truly, I know now, with an abominable side to her. She was inordinately vain of her hands; and indeed they were the loveliest things, softer and shapelier than a child's. She used to have them photographed, in fifty different positions; and once they were exquisitely done in marble by a sculptor, a friend of hers. Yes, those were the ones you saw. But they were cruel little hands, for all their beauty. There was something wicked and unclean about the way in which she regarded them.

"She died while I was there, and she was commemorated by her own explicit desire after the fashion you saw. The marble hands were to be her sole epitaph, more eloquent than letters. They should preserve her name and the tradition of her most exquisite feature to remoter ages than any crumbling inscription could reach. And so it was done.

"That fancy was not popular with the parishioners, but it gave me no childish qualms. The hands were really beautifully modelled on the originals, and the originals had often caressed me. I was never afraid to go and look at them, sprouting like white celery from the ground.

"I left, and two years later was visiting Aunt Caddie a second time. In the course of conversation I learned that the husband of the woman had married again—a lady belonging to the place—and that the hands, only quite recently, had been removed. The new wife had objected to them—for some reason perhaps not difficult to understand—and they had been uprooted by the husband's order.

"I think I was a little sorry—the hands had always seemed somehow personal to me—and, on the first occasion that offered, I slipped away by myself to see how the grave looked without them. It was a close, lowering day, I remember, and the churchyard was very still. Directly, stooping under the branches, I saw the spot, I understood that Aunt Caddie had spoken prematurely. The hands had not been removed so far, but were extended in their old place and attitude, looking as if held out to welcome me. I was glad; and I ran and knelt, and put my own hands down to touch them. They were soft and cold like dead meat, and they closed caressingly about mine, as if inviting me to pull—to pull.

"I don't know what happened afterwards. Perhaps I had been sickening all the time for the fever which overtook me. There was a period of horror, and blankness—of crawling, worm-threaded immurements and heaving bones—and then at last the blessed daylight."

Heriot stopped, and sat plucking at the crisp pasture.

"I never learned," he said suddenly, "what other experiences synchronised with mine. But the place somehow got an uncanny reputation, and the marble hands were put back. Imagination, to be sure, can play strange tricks with one."

THE MASQUE OF THE RED DEATH

EDGAR ALLAN POE

THE "RED DEATH" HAD LONG DEVASTATED THE COUNTRY. NO PESTILENCE HAD EVER been so fatal, or so hideous. Blood was its Avatar and its seal—the redness and the horror of blood. There were sharp pains, and sudden dizziness, and then profuse bleeding at the pores, with dissolution. The scarlet stains upon the body and especially upon the face of the victim, were the pest ban which shut him out from the aid and from the sympathy of his fellow-men. And the whole seizure, progress and termination of the disease, were the incidents of half an hour.

But the Prince Prospero was happy and dauntless and sagacious. When his dominions were half depopulated, he summoned to his presence a thousand hale and light-hearted friends from among the knights and dames of his court, and with these retired to the deep seclusion of one of his castellated abbeys. This was an extensive and magnificent structure, the creation of the prince's own eccentric yet august taste. A strong and lofty wall girdled it in. This wall had gates of iron. The courtiers, having entered, brought furnaces and massy hammers and welded the bolts. They resolved to leave means neither of ingress or egress to the sudden impulses of despair or of frenzy from within. The abbey was amply provisioned. With such precautions the courtiers might bid defiance to contagion. The external world could take care of itself. In the meantime it was folly to grieve, or to think. The prince had provided all the appliances of pleasure. There were buffoons, there were improvisatori, there were ballet-dancers, there were musicians, there was Beauty, there was wine. All these and security were within. Without was the "Red Death."

It was toward the close of the fifth or sixth month of his seclusion, and while the pestilence raged most furiously abroad, that the Prince Prospero entertained his thousand friends at a masked ball of the most unusual magnificence.

It was a voluptuous scene, that masquerade. But first let me tell of the rooms in which it was held. There were seven—an imperial suite. In many palaces, however, such suites form a long and straight vista, while the folding doors slide back nearly to the walls on either hand, so that the view of the whole extent is scarcely impeded. Here the case was very different; as might have been expected from the duke's love of the *bizarre*. The apartments were so irregularly disposed that the vision embraced but little more than one at a time. There was a sharp turn at every twenty or thirty yards, and at each turn a novel effect. To the right and left, in the middle of each wall, a tall and narrow Gothic window looked out upon a closed corridor which pursued the windings of the suite. These windows were of stained glass whose color varied in accordance with the prevailing hue of the decorations of the chamber into which it opened. That at the eastern extremity was hung, for example, in blue—and vividly blue were its windows. The second chamber was purple in its ornaments and tapestries, and here the panes were purple. The third was green throughout, and so were the casements. The fourth was furnished and lighted with orange—the fifth with white—the sixth with violet. The seventh apartment was closely shrouded in black velvet tapestries that hung all over the ceiling and down the walls, falling in heavy folds upon a carpet of the same material and hue. But in this chamber only, the color of the windows failed to correspond with the decorations. The panes here were scarlet—a deep blood color. Now in no one of the seven apartments was there any lamp or candelabrum, amid the profusion of golden ornaments that lay scattered to and fro or depended from the roof. There was no light of any kind emanating from lamp or candle within the suite of chambers. But in the corridors that followed the suite, there stood, opposite to each window, a heavy tripod, bearing a brazier of fire, that projected its rays through the tinted glass and so glaringly illumined the room. And thus were produced a multitude of gaudy and fantastic appearances. But in the western or black chamber the effect of the fire-light that streamed upon the dark hangings through the blood-tinted panes, was ghastly in the extreme, and produced so wild a look upon the countenances of those who entered, that there were few of the company bold enough to set foot within its precincts at all.

It was in this apartment, also, that there stood against the western wall, a gigantic clock of ebony. Its pendulum swung to and fro with a dull, heavy, monotonous clang; and when the minute-hand made the circuit of the face, and the hour was to be stricken, there came from the brazen lungs of the clock a sound which was clear and loud and deep and exceedingly musical, but of so peculiar a note and emphasis that, at each lapse of an hour, the musicians of the orchestra were constrained to pause, momentarily, in their performance, to harken to the sound; and thus the waltzers perforce ceased their evolutions; and there was a brief disconcert of the whole gay company; and, while the chimes of the clock yet rang, it was observed that the giddiest grew pale, and the more aged and sedate passed their hands over their brows as if in confused revery or meditation. But when the echoes had fully ceased, a light laughter at once pervaded the assembly; the musicians looked at each other and smiled as if at their own nervousness and folly, and made whispering vows, each to the other, that the next chiming of the clock should produce in them no similar emotion; and then, after the lapse of sixty minutes (which embrace three thousand and six hundred seconds of the Time that flies), there came yet another chiming of the clock, and then were the same disconcert and tremulousness and meditation as before.

But, in spite of these things, it was a gay and magnificent revel. The tastes of the duke were peculiar. He had a fine eye for colors and effects. He disregarded the *decora* of mere fashion. His plans were bold and fiery, and his conceptions glowed with barbaric lustre. There are some who would have thought him mad. His followers felt that he was not. It was necessary to hear and see and touch him to be *sure* that he was not.

He had directed, in great part, the moveable embellishments of the seven chambers, upon occasion of this great *fete*; and it was his own guiding taste which had given character to the masqueraders. Be sure they were grotesque. There were much glare and glitter and piquancy and phantasm—much of what has been since seen in "Hernani." There were arabesque figures with unsuited limbs and appointments. There were delirious fancies such as the madman fashions. There were much of the beautiful, much of the wanton, much of the *bizarre*, something of the terrible, and not a little of that which might have excited disgust. To and fro in the seven chambers there stalked, in fact, a multitude of dreams. And these—the dreams—writhed in and about, taking hue from the rooms, and causing the wild music of the orchestra to seem as the echo of their steps. And, anon, there strikes the ebony clock which stands in the hall of the velvet. And then, for a moment, all is still, and all is silent save the voice of the clock. The dreams are stiff-frozen as they stand. But the echoes of the chime die away—they have endured but an instant—and a light, half-subdued laughter floats after them as they depart. And now again the music swells, and the dreams live, and writhe to and fro more merrily than ever, taking hue from the many tinted windows through which stream the rays from the tripods. But to the chamber which lies most westwardly of the seven, there are now none of the maskers who venture; for the night is waning away; and there flows a ruddier light through the blood-colored panes; and the blackness of the sable drapery appals; and to him whose foot falls upon the sable carpet, there comes from the near clock of ebony a muffled peal more solemnly emphatic than any which reaches *their* ears who indulge in the more remote gaieties of the other apartments.

But these other apartments were densely crowded, and in them beat feverishly the heart of life. And the revel went whirlingly on, until at length there commenced the sounding of midnight upon the clock. And then the music ceased, as I have told; and the evolutions of the waltzers were quieted; and there was an uneasy cessation of all things as before. But now there were twelve strokes to be sounded by the bell of the clock; and thus it happened, perhaps that more of thought crept, with more of time, into the meditations of the thoughtful among those who revelled. And thus too, it happened, perhaps, that before the last echoes of the last chime had utterly sunk into silence, there were many individuals in the crowd who had found leisure to become aware of the presence of a masked figure which had arrested the attention of no single individual before. And the rumor of this new presence having spread itself whisperingly around, there arose at length from the whole company a buzz, or murmur, expressive of disapprobation and surprise—then, finally, of terror, of horror, and of disgust.

In an assembly of phantasms such as I have painted, it may well be supposed that no ordinary appearance could have excited such sensation. In truth the masquerade license of the night was nearly unlimited; but the figure in question had out-Heroded Herod, and gone beyond the bounds of even the prince's indefinite decorum. There are chords in the hearts of the most reckless which cannot be touched without emotion. Even with the utterly lost, to whom life and death are equally jests, there are matters of which no jest can be made. The whole company, indeed, seemed now deeply to feel that in the costume and bearing of the stranger neither wit nor propriety existed. The figure was tall and gaunt, and shrouded from head to foot in the habiliments of the grave. The mask which concealed the visage was made so nearly to resemble the countenance of a stiffened corpse that the closest scrutiny must have had difficulty in detecting the cheat. And yet all this might have been endured, if not approved, by the mad revellers around. But the mummer had gone so far as to assume the type of the Red Death. His vesture was dabbled in *blood*—and his broad brow, with all the features of the face, was besprinkled with the scarlet horror.

When the eyes of Prince Prospero fell upon this spectral image (which with a slow and solemn movement, as if more fully to sustain its *role*, stalked to and fro among the waltzers) he was seen to be convulsed, in the first moment with a strong shudder either of terror or distaste; but, in the next, his brow reddened with rage.

"Who dares?" he demanded hoarsely of the courtiers who stood near him—"who dares insult us with this blasphemous mockery? Seize him and unmask him—that we may know whom we have to hang at sunrise, from the battlements!"

It was in the eastern or blue chamber in which stood the Prince Prospero as he uttered these words. They rang throughout the seven rooms loudly and clearly—for the prince was a bold and robust man, and the music had become hushed at the waving of his hand.

It was in the blue room where stood the prince, with a group of pale courtiers by his side. At first, as he spoke, there was a slight rushing movement of this group in the direction of the intruder, who, at the moment was also near at hand, and now, with deliberate and stately step, made closer approach to the speaker. But from a certain nameless awe with which the mad assumptions of the mummer had inspired the whole party, there were found none who put forth hand to seize him; so that, unimpeded, he passed within a yard of the prince's person; and, while the vast assembly, as if with one impulse, shrank from the centres of the rooms to the walls, he made his way uninterruptedly, but with the same solemn and measured step which had distinguished him from the first, through the blue chamber to the purple—through the purple to the green—through the green to the orange—through this again to the white—and even thence to the violet, ere a decided movement had been made to arrest him. It was then, however, that the Prince Prospero, maddening with rage and the shame of his own momentary cowardice, rushed hurriedly through the six chambers, while none followed him on account of a deadly terror that had seized upon all. He bore aloft a drawn dagger, and had approached, in rapid impetuosity, to within three or four feet of the retreating figure, when the latter, having attained the extremity of the velvet apartment, turned suddenly and confronted his pursuer. There was a sharp cry—and the dagger dropped gleaming upon the sable carpet, upon which, instantly afterwards, fell prostrate in death the Prince Prospero. Then, summoning the wild courage of despair, a throng of the revellers at once threw themselves into the black apartment, and, seizing the mummer, whose tall figure stood erect and motionless within the shadow of the ebony clock, gasped in unutterable horror at finding the grave cerements and corpse-like mask which they handled with so violent a rudeness, untenanted by any tangible form.

And now was acknowledged the presence of the Red Death. He had come like a thief in the night. And one by one dropped the revellers in the blood-bedewed halls of their revel, and died each in the despairing posture of his fall. And the life of the ebony clock went out with that of the last of the gay. And the flames of the tripods expired. And Darkness and Decay and the Red Death held illimitable dominion over all.

The Mezzotint

M. R. James

Some time ago I believe I had the pleasure of telling you the story of an adventure which happened to a friend of mine by the name of Dennistoun, during his pursuit of objects of art for the museum at Cambridge.

He did not publish his experiences very widely upon his return to England; but they could not fail to become known to a good many of his friends, and among others to the gentleman who at that time presided over an art museum at another University. It was to be expected that the story should make a considerable impression on the mind of a man whose vocation lay in lines similar to Dennistoun's, and that he should be eager to catch at any explanation of the matter which tended to make it seem improbable that he should ever be called upon to deal with so agitating an emergency. It was, indeed, somewhat consoling to him to reflect that he was not expected to acquire ancient MSS. for his institution; that was the business of the Shelburnian Library. The authorities of that institution might, if they pleased, ransack obscure corners of the Continent for such matters. He was glad to be obliged at the moment to confine his attention to enlarging the already unsurpassed collection of English topographical drawings and engravings possessed by his museum. Yet, as it turned out, even a department so homely and familiar as this may have its dark corners, and to one of these Mr. Williams was unexpectedly introduced.

Those who have taken even the most limited interest in the acquisition of topographical pictures are aware that there is one London dealer whose aid is indispensable to their researches. Mr. J. W. Britnell publishes at short intervals very admirable catalogues of a large and constantly changing stock of engravings, plans, and old sketches of mansions, churches, and towns in England and Wales. These catalogues were, of course, the ABC of his subject to Mr. Williams: but as his museum already contained an enormous accumulation of topographical pictures, he was a regular, rather than a copious, buyer; and he rather looked to Mr. Britnell to fill up gaps in the rank and file of his collection than to supply him with rarities.

Now, in February of last year there appeared upon Mr. Williams' desk at the museum a catalogue from Mr. Britnell's emporium, and accompanying it was a typewritten communication from the dealer himself. This latter ran as follows:

DEAR SIR,

We beg to call your attention to No. 978 in our accompanying catalogue, which we shall be glad to send on approval.

Yours faithfully,
J. W. BRITNELL

To turn to No. 978 in the accompanying catalogue was with Mr. Williams (as he observed to himself) the work of a moment, and in the place indicated he found the following entry:

978.—Unknown. Interesting mezzotint: View of a manor-house, early part of the century. 15 by 10 inches; black frame. £2 2s.

It was not specially exciting, and the price seemed high. However, as Mr. Britnell, who knew his business and his customer, seemed to set store by it, Mr. Williams wrote a postcard asking for the article to be sent on approval, along with some other engravings and sketches which appeared in the same catalogue. And so he passed without much excitement of anticipation to the ordinary labors of the day.

A parcel of any kind always arrives a day later than you expect it, and that of Mr. Britnell proved, as I believe the right phrase goes, no exception to the rule. It was delivered at the museum by the afternoon post of Saturday, after Mr. Williams had left his work, and it was accordingly brought round to his rooms in college by the attendant, in order that he might not have to wait over Sunday before looking through it and returning such of the contents as he did not propose to keep. And here he found it when he came in to tea, with a friend.

The only item with which I am concerned was the rather large, black-framed mezzotint of which I have already quoted the short description given in Mr. Britnell's catalogue. Some more details of it will have to be given, though I cannot hope to put before you the look of the picture as clearly as it is present to my own eye. Very nearly the exact duplicate of it may be seen in a good many old inn parlours, or in the passages of undisturbed country mansions at the present moment. It was a rather indifferent mezzotint, and an indifferent mezzotint is, perhaps, the worst form of engraving known. It presented a full-face view of a not very large manor-house of the last century, with three rows of plain sashed windows with rusticated masonry about them, a parapet with balls or vases at the angles, and a small portico in the centre. On either side were trees, and in front a considerable expanse of lawn. The legend "A. W. F. sculpsit" was engraved on the narrow margin; and there was no further inscription. The whole thing gave the impression that it was the work of an amateur. What in the world Mr. Britnell could mean by affixing the price of £2 2s. to such an object was more than Mr. Williams could imagine. He turned it over with a good deal of contempt; upon the back was a paper label, the left-hand half of which had been torn off. All that remained were the ends of two lines of writing; the first had the letters *—ngley Hall*; the second, *—ssex*.

It would, perhaps, be just worth while to identify the place represented, which he could easily do with the help of a gazetteer, and then he would send it back to Mr. Britnell, with some remarks reflecting upon the judgement of that gentleman.

He lighted the candles, for it was now dark, made the tea, and supplied the friend with whom he had been playing golf (for I believe the authorities of the University I write of indulge in that pursuit by way of relaxation); and tea was taken to the accompaniment of a discussion which golfing persons can imagine for themselves, but which the conscientious writer has no right to inflict upon any non-golfing persons.

The conclusion arrived at was that certain strokes might have been better, and that in certain emergencies neither player had experienced that amount of luck which a human being has a right to expect. It was now that the friend—let us call him Professor Binks—took up the framed engraving and said:

"What's this place, Williams?"

"Just what I am going to try to find out," said Williams, going to the shelf for a gazetteer. "Look at the back. Somethingley Hall, either in Sussex or Essex. Half the name's gone, you see. You don't happen to know it, I suppose?"

"It's from that man Britnell, I suppose, isn't it?" said Binks. "Is it for the museum?"

"Well, I think I should buy it if the price was five shillings," said Williams, "but for some unearthly reason he wants two guineas for it. I can't conceive why. It's a wretched engraving, and there aren't even any figures to give it life."

"It's not worth two guineas, I should think," said Binks, "but I don't think it's so badly done. The moonlight seems rather good to me; and I should have thought there *were* figures, or at least a figure, just on the edge in front."

"Let's look," said Williams. "Well, it's true the light is rather cleverly given. Where's your figure? Oh, yes! Just the head, in the very front of the picture."

And indeed there was—hardly more than a black blot on the extreme edge of the engraving—the head of a man or woman, a good deal muffled up, the back turned to the spectator, and looking towards the house.

Williams had not noticed it before.

"Still," he said, "though it's a cleverer thing than I thought, I can't spend two guineas of museum money on a picture of a place I don't know."

Professor Binks had his work to do, and soon went; and very nearly up to Hall time Williams was engaged in a vain attempt to identify the subject of his picture. "If the vowel before the *ng* had only been left, it would have been easy enough," he thought, "but as it is, the name may be anything from Guestingley to Langley, and there are many more names ending like this than I thought; and this rotten book has no index of terminations."

Hall in Mr. Williams's college was at seven. It need not be dwelt upon; the less so as he met there colleagues who had been playing golf during the afternoon, and words with which we have no concern were freely bandied across the table—merely golfing words, I would hasten to explain.

I suppose an hour or more to have been spent in what is called common-room after dinner. Later in the evening some few retired to Williams's rooms, and I have little doubt that whist was played and tobacco smoked. During a lull in these operations Williams picked up the mezzotint from the table without looking at it, and handed it to a person mildly interested in art, telling him where it had come from, and the other particulars which we already know.

The gentleman took it carelessly, looked at it, then said, in a tone of some interest:

"It's really a very good piece of work, Williams; it has quite a feeling of the romantic period. The light is admirably managed, it seems to me, and the figure, though it's rather too grotesque, is somehow very impressive."

"Yes, isn't it?" said Williams, who was just then busy giving whisky and soda to others of the company, and was unable to come across the room to look at the view again.

It was by this time rather late in the evening, and the visitors were on the move. After they went Williams was obliged to write a letter or two and clear up some odd bits of work. At last, some time past midnight, he was disposed to turn in, and he put out his lamp after lighting his bedroom candle. The picture lay face upwards on the table where the last man who looked at it had put it, and it caught his eye as he turned the lamp down. What he saw made him very nearly drop the candle on the floor, and he declares now if he had been left in the dark at that moment he would have had a fit. But, as that did not happen, he was able to put down the light on the table and take a good look at the picture. It was indubitable—rankly impossible, no doubt, but absolutely certain. In the middle of the lawn in front of the unknown house there was a figure where no figure had been at five o'clock that afternoon. It was crawling on all fours towards the house, and it was muffled in a strange black garment with a white cross on the back.

I do not know what is the ideal course to pursue in a situation of this kind, I can only tell you what Mr. Williams did. He took the picture by one corner and carried it across the passage to a second set of rooms which he possessed. There he locked it up in a drawer, sported the doors of both sets of rooms, and retired to bed; but first he wrote out and signed an account of the extraordinary change which the picture had undergone since it had come into his possession.

Sleep visited him rather late; but it was consoling to reflect that the behaviour of the picture did not depend upon his own unsupported testimony. Evidently the man who had looked at it the night before had seen something of the same kind as he had, otherwise he might have been tempted to think that something gravely wrong was happening either to his eyes or his mind. This possibility being fortunately precluded, two matters awaited him on the morrow. He must take stock of the picture very carefully, and call in a witness for the purpose, and he must make a determined effort to ascertain what house it was that was represented. He would therefore ask his neighbour Nisbet to breakfast with him, and he would subsequently spend a morning over the gazetteer.

Nisbet was disengaged, and arrived about 9:30. His host was not quite dressed, I am sorry to say, even at this late hour. During breakfast nothing was said about the mezzotint by Williams, save that he had a picture on which he wished for Nisbet's opinion. But those who are familiar with University life can picture for themselves the wide and delightful range of subjects over which the conversation of two Fellows of Canterbury College is likely to extend during a Sunday morning breakfast. Hardly a topic was left unchallenged, from golf to lawn-tennis. Yet I am bound to say that Williams was rather distraught; for his interest naturally centred in that very strange picture which was now reposing, face downwards, in the drawer in the room opposite.

The morning pipe was at last lighted, and the moment had arrived for which he looked. With very considerable—almost tremulous—excitement he ran across, unlocked the drawer, and, extracting the picture—still face downwards—ran back, and put it into Nisbet's hands.

"Now," he said, "Nisbet, I want you to tell me exactly what you see in that picture. Describe it, if you don't mind, rather minutely. I'll tell you why afterwards."

"Well," said Nisbet, "I have here a view of a country-house—English, I presume—by moonlight."

"Moonlight? You're sure of that?"

"Certainly. The moon appears to be on the wane, if you wish for details, and there are clouds in the sky."

"All right. Go on. I'll swear," added Williams in an aside, "there was no moon when I saw it first."

"Well, there's not much more to be said," Nisbet continued. "The house has one—two—three rows of windows, five in each row, except at the bottom, where there's a porch instead of the middle one, and—"

"But what about figures?" said Williams, with marked interest.

"There aren't any," said Nisbet, "but—"

"What! No figure on the grass in front?"

"Not a thing."

"You'll swear to that?"

"Certainly I will. But there's just one other thing."

"What?"

"Why, one of the windows on the ground-floor—left of the door—is open."

"Is it really so? My goodness! he must have got in," said Williams, with great excitement; and he hurried to the back of the sofa on which Nisbet was sitting, and, catching the picture from him, verified the matter for himself.

It was quite true. There was no figure, and there was the open window. Williams, after a moment of speechless surprise, went to the writing-table and scribbled for a short time. Then he brought two papers to Nisbet, and asked him first to sign one—it was his own description of the picture, which you have just heard—and then to read the other which was Williams's statement written the night before.

"What can it all mean?" said Nisbet.

"Exactly," said Williams. "Well, one thing I must do—or three things, now I think of it. I must find out from Garwood"—this was his last night's visitor—"what he saw, and then I must get the thing photographed before it goes further, and then I must find out what the place is."

"I can do the photographing myself," said Nisbet, "and I will. But, you know, it looks very much as if we were assisting at the working out of a tragedy somewhere. The question is, has it happened already, or is it going to come off? You must find out what the place is. Yes," he said, looking at the picture again, "I expect you're right: he has got in. And if I don't mistake, there'll be the devil to pay in one of the rooms upstairs."

"I'll tell you what," said Williams: "I'll take the picture across to old Green" (this was the senior Fellow of the College, who had been Bursar for many years). "It's quite likely he'll know it. We have property in Essex and Sussex, and he must have been over the two counties a lot in his time."

"Quite likely he will," said Nisbet, "but just let me take my photograph first. But look here, I rather think Green isn't up today. He wasn't in Hall last night, and I think I heard him say he was going down for the Sunday."

"That's true, too," said Williams, "I know he's gone to Brighton. Well, if you'll photograph it now, I'll go across to Garwood and get his statement, and you keep an eye on it while I'm gone. I'm beginning to think two guineas is not a very exorbitant price for it now."

In a short time he had returned, and brought Mr. Garwood with him. Garwood's statement was to the effect that the figure, when he had seen it, was clear of the edge of the picture, but had not got far across the lawn. He remembered a white mark on the back of its drapery, but could not have been sure it was a cross. A document to this effect was then drawn up and signed, and Nisbet proceeded to photograph the picture.

"Now what do you mean to do?" he said. "Are you going to sit and watch it all day?"

"Well, no, I think not," said Williams. "I rather imagine we're meant to see the whole thing. You see, between the time I saw it last night and this morning there was time for lots of things to happen, but the creature only got into the house. It could easily have got through its business in the time and gone to its own place again; but the fact of the window being open, I think, must mean that it's in there now. So I feel quite easy about leaving it. And besides, I have a kind of idea that it wouldn't change much, if at all, in the daytime. We might go out for a walk this afternoon, and come in to tea, or whenever it gets dark. I shall leave it out on the table here, and sport the door. My skip can get in, but no one else."

The three agreed that this would be a good plan; and, further, that if they spent the afternoon together they would be less likely to talk about the business to other people; for any rumour of such a transaction as was going on would bring the whole of the Phasmatological Society about their ears.

We may give them a respite until five o'clock.

At or near that hour the three were entering Williams's staircase. They were at first slightly annoyed to see that the door of his rooms was unsported; but in a moment it was remembered that on Sunday the skips came for orders an hour or so earlier than on weekdays. However, a surprise was awaiting them. The first thing they saw was the picture leaning up against a pile of books on the table, as it had been left, and the next thing was Williams's skip, seated on a chair opposite, gazing at it with undisguised horror. How was this? Mr. Filcher (the name is not my own invention) was a servant of considerable standing, and set the standard of etiquette to all his own college and to several neighbouring ones, and nothing could be more alien to his practice than to be found sitting on his master's chair, or appearing to take any particular notice of his master's furniture or pictures. Indeed, he seemed to feel this himself. He started violently when the three men were in the room, and got up with a marked effort. Then he said:

"I ask your pardon, sir, for taking such a freedom as to set down."

"Not at all, Robert," interposed Mr. Williams. "I was meaning to ask you some time what you thought of that picture."

"Well, sir, of course I don't set up my opinion against yours, but it ain't the pictur I should 'ang where my little girl could see it, sir."

"Wouldn't you, Robert? Why not?"

"No, sir. Why, the pore child, I recollect once she see a Door Bible, with pictures not 'alf what that is, and we 'ad to set up with her three or four nights afterwards, if you'll believe me; and if she was to ketch a sight of this skelinton here, or whatever it is, carrying off the pore baby, she would be in a taking. You know 'ow it is with children, 'ow nervish they git with a little thing and all. But what I should say, it don't seem a right pictur to be laying about, sir, not where anyone that's liable to be startled could come on it. Should you be wanting anything this evening, sir? Thank you, sir."

With these words the excellent man went to continue the round of his masters, and you may be sure the gentlemen whom he left lost no time in gathering round the engraving. There was the house, as before under the waning moon and the drifting clouds. The window that had been open was shut, and the figure was once more on the lawn: but not this time crawling cautiously on hands and knees. Now it was erect and stepping swiftly, with long strides, towards the front of the picture. The moon was behind it, and the black drapery hung down over its face so that only hints of that could be seen, and what was visible made the spectators profoundly thankful that they could see no more than a white dome-like forehead and a few straggling hairs. The head was bent down, and the arms were tightly clasped over an object which could be dimly seen and identified as a child, whether dead or living it was not possible to say. The legs of the appearance alone could be plainly discerned, and they were horribly thin.

From five to seven the three companions sat and watched the picture by turns. But it never changed. They agreed at last that it would be safe to leave it, and that they would return after Hall and await further developments.

When they assembled again, at the earliest possible moment, the engraving was there, but the figure was gone, and the house was quiet under the moonbeams. There was nothing for it but to spend the evening over gazetteers and guide-books. Williams was the lucky one at last, and perhaps he deserved it. At 11:30 p.m. he read from Murray's *Guide to Essex* the following lines:

> 16-1/2 miles, *Anningley*. The church has been an interesting building of Norman date, but was extensively classicized in the last century. It contains the tomb of the family of Francis, whose mansion, Anningley Hall, a solid Queen Anne house, stands immediately beyond the churchyard in a park of about 80 acres. The family is now extinct, the last heir having disappeared mysteriously in infancy in the year 1802. The father, Mr. Arthur Francis, was locally known as a talented amateur engraver in mezzotint. After his son's disappearance he lived in complete retirement at the Hall, and was found dead in his studio on the third anniversary of the disaster, having just completed an engraving of the house, impressions of which are of considerable rarity.

This looked like business, and, indeed, Mr. Green on his return at once identified the house as Anningley Hall.

"Is there any kind of explanation of the figure, Green?" was the question which Williams naturally asked.

"I don't know, I'm sure, Williams. What used to be said in the place when I first knew it, which was before I came up here, was just this: old Francis was always very much down on these poaching fellows, and whenever he got a chance he used to get a man whom he suspected of it turned off the estate, and by degrees he got rid of them all but one. Squires could do a lot of things then that they daren't think of now. Well, this man that was left was what you find pretty often in that country—the last remains of a very old family. I believe they were Lords of the Manor at one time. I recollect just the same thing in my own parish."

"What, like the man in *Tess o' the Durbervilles*?" Williams put in.

"Yes, I dare say; it's not a book I could ever read myself. But this fellow could show a row of tombs in the church there that belonged to his ancestors, and all that went to sour him a bit; but Francis, they said, could never get at him—he always kept just on the right side of the law—until one night the keepers found him at it in a wood right at the end of the estate. I could show you the place now; it marches with some land that used to belong to an uncle of mine. And you can imagine there was a row; and this man Gawdy (that was the name, to be sure—Gawdy; I thought I should get it—Gawdy), he was unlucky enough, poor chap! to shoot a keeper. Well, that was what Francis wanted, and grand juries—you know what they would have been then—and poor Gawdy was strung up in double-quick time; and I've been shown the place he was buried in, on the north side of the church—you know the way in that part of the world: anyone that's been hanged or made away with themselves, they bury them that side. And the idea was that some friend of Gawdy's—not a relation, because he had none, poor devil! he was the last of his line: kind of *spes ultima gentis*—must have planned to get hold of Francis's boy and put an end to *his* line, too. I don't know—it's rather an out-of-the-way thing for an Essex poacher to think of—but, you know, I should say now it looks more as if old Gawdy had managed the job himself. Booh! I hate to think of it! have some whisky, Williams!"

The facts were communicated by Williams to Dennistoun, and by him to a mixed company, of which I was one, and the Sadducean Professor of Ophiology another. I am sorry to say that the latter when asked what he thought of it, only remarked: "Oh, those Bridgeford people will say anything"—a sentiment which met with the reception it deserved.

I have only to add that the picture is now in the Ashleian Museum; that it has been treated with a view to discovering whether sympathetic ink has been used in it, but without effect; that Mr. Britnell knew nothing of it save that he was sure it was uncommon; and that, though carefully watched, it has never been known to change again.

Midnight House

William Fryer Harvey

I had often seen the name on the ordnance map, and had as often wondered what sort of a house it was.

If I had had the placing, it should have been among pine woods in some deep, waterless valley, or else in the Fens by a sluggish tidal river, with aspens whispering in a garden half choked by poisonous evergreens.

I might have placed it in a cathedral city, in a sunless alley overlooking the narrow strip of graveyard of a church no longer used; a house so surrounded by steeple and belfry that every sleeper in it would wake at midnight, aroused by the clamorous insistence of the chimes.

But the Midnight House of cold reality, that I had found by chance on the map when planning a walking tour that never came into being, was none of these. I saw no more than an inn on an old coaching road that crossed the moors as straight as an arrow, keeping to the hill-tops, so that I guessed it to be Roman.

Men have a certain way of living in accordance with their name that one often looks for in vain with places. The Pogsons will never produce a poet, whatever may be the fame they may achieve as lawyers, journalists, or sanitary engineers; but Monckton-in-the-Forest, through which I passed last week, is a railway junction and nothing more, in the middle of a bare plain; not a stone remains of the once famous priory that gave to the place its name.

I expected then to be disappointed, but for some reason or other I made a resolve, if ever chance should leave me within twenty miles of the inn, to spend a night in Midnight House.

I could not have chosen a better day. It was late in November and warm—too warm I had found for the last five-mile tramp across the heather. I had seen no one since noon, when a keeper on the distant skyline had tried in vain to make me understand that I was trespassing; and now at dusk I stood again on the high road with Midnight House below me in the hollow.

It would be hard to picture a more desolate scene—bare hills rising on every side to the dull, lead sky above; at one's feet heather, burnt black after last spring's firing, broken in places by patches of vivid emerald that marked the bogs.

The building of stone, roofed with heavy, lichen-covered flags, formed three sides of a square, the centre of which was evidently used as a farm-yard.

Nowhere was there sign of life; half the windows were shuttered, and, though the dim light of afternoon was fast waning, I saw no lamp in the tap-room, by the door which overlooked the road.

I knocked, but no one answered; and, growing impatient at the delay, walked round to the back of the house, only to be greeted by the savage barking of a collie, that tugged frantically at the chain which fastened it to the empty barrel that served it as kennel. The noise was at any rate sufficient to bring out the woman of the house, who listened stolidly to my request for a night's lodging, and then to my surprise refused me.

They were busy, she said, and had no time to look after visitors. I was not prepared for this. I knew that there were beds at the inn; it was used at least once a year by the men who rented the shooting, and I had not the slightest inclination for another ten-mile tramp along roads I did not know. A drop of rain on my cheek clenched the matter; grudgingly the woman saw reason in my arguments and finally consented to take me in. She showed me into the dining-room, lit the fire, and left me with the welcome news that the ham and eggs would be ready in half an hour's time.

The room in which I found myself was of some size, panelled half-way up to the ceiling, though the natural beauty of the wood had been recently spoiled by a coat of drab-colored paint.

The windows were, as usual, firmly shut; and from the musty smell I gathered that it was little used. Half a dozen sporting prints hung on the walls; over the mantelpiece was a cheap German engraving representing the death of Isaac; on the sideboard were two glass cases, containing a heron and two pied blackbirds, both atrociously stuffed; while above that piece of hideous Victorian furniture, two highly colored portraits of the Duke and Duchess of York gazed smilingly upon the patriarch.

Altogether the room was not a cheerful one, and I was relieved to find a copy of *East Lynne* lying on the horsehair sofa. Most inns contain the book; the fourteen chapters which I have read represent as many evenings spent alone in wayside hostelries.

Just before six the woman came in to lay the table. From my chair, in the shadow by the fireside I watched her unobserved. She moved slowly; the simplest action was performed with a strange deliberation, as if her mind, half bent upon something else, found novelty in what before was commonplace. The expression of her face gave no clue to her thoughts. I saw only that her features were strong and hard.

As soon as the meal was upon the table she left the room, without having exchanged a word; and feeling unusually lonely, I sat down to make the best of the ham and eggs and the fifteenth chapter of *East Lynne*.

The food was good enough, better than I had expected; but for some reason or other my spirits were no lighter when, the table having been cleared, I drew up my chair to the fire and filled my pipe.

"If this house is not already haunted," I said to myself, "it is certainly time it were so," and I began to pass in review a whole procession of ghosts without finding one that seemed really suited to the place.

At half-past nine, and the hour was none too soon, the woman reappeared with a candle, and intimated gruffly that she would show me my room. She stopped opposite a door at the end of a corridor to the left of the stair head. "You had better wedge the windows, if you want to sleep with them open; people complain a deal about their rattling." I thanked her and bade her good night.

I was spared at least the horror of a four-poster, though the crimson-canopied erection, which occupied at least a quarter of the room, seemed at first sight to be little better. There was no wardrobe, but in its place a door, papered over with the same material as the walls and, at first sight, indistinguishable from them, opened into a closet, empty save for a row of hooks and lighted by a single window.

I noticed that neither of the doors had keys, and that a red velvet bell-pull by the bed was no longer fastened to its wire, but hung useless from a nail driven into one of the beams of the ceiling.

I am in the habit of securely bolting my door whenever I spend a night away from home, a piece of common prudence which nothing less than an awful fright from a sleep-walker taught me twenty years ago.

To do so was on this occasion impossible, but I dragged a heavy chest across the door which led into the passage, placing the water-jug against the inner one, in case the wind should blow it open in the night: then, after wedging the window with my pocket-knife, I got into bed, but not to sleep. Twice I heard the clock outside strike the hour, twice the half-hour, vet, late as it was, the house seemed still awake. Distant footsteps echoed down the stone passages; once I caught the crash of broken crockery—never the sound of a voice. At length I fell asleep, with the same feeling of unaccountable depression that had dogged me since sundown still upon me.

I had in truth walked far too far that day to receive the inestimable boon of the weary, a dim consciousness of annihilation. Instead I tramped again over dream moors with a Baedeker in my hand, trying in vain to find the valley of the shadow.

I came at last to a mountain tarn, filled with brown peat water; on the marge a huge ferry-boat was drawn up, on which crowds of men, women, and children were embarking. The boat at last was full and we were putting off, the heavy sails filling before a wind which never ruffled the surface of the water, when someone cried that there was still another to come, pointing as he spoke to an old man who stood on the shore madly gesticulating. An argument followed, some in the boat saying that it was too late to put back, others that the man would perish with cold if we left him there on the shelterless moor. But we were too eager to see the valley of the shadow, and the steersman held on his course. As we left him, a sudden change came across the old man's features; the mask of benevolence vanished; we saw only a face of such utter malignancy that the children in fright ran whimpering to their mothers.

In the boat they whispered his name, how he was a man for ever seeking to gain entrance to the ferry, that he might accomplish some awful purpose, and in joy at our escape a strange song was raised, which rose and fell like the music of a running stream.

I was awakened by the sound of rain upon the window; the water in the brook outside had already risen and was making itself heard, but with a sound so soothingly monotonous that I was soon asleep again.

Again I dreamed. This time I was a citizen of a great leaguered city. The once fertile plain that stretched from the walls to the dim horizon lay ravaged by the armies that had swept over it. The sun was sinking as a crowd of half-starved wretches came to the western gate, clamouring to come in. They were the peasants, caught between the besieging hosts and the frowning barriers of the city that had no food for mouths other than its own. As I stood at the postern to the right of main gate with a little knot of companions, a man approached who at once attracted our attention. He was a huge fellow, in the prime of life, straight as a tree, and strong enough to carry an ox. He came up to our leader and asked to be let in. "I have travelled day and night for twelve months," he said, "that I might fight by your side." The last sally had cost us dear and we were short of men such as he. "Come in and welcome," said the captain of the guard at last. He had already taken a key from his breast and was unlocking the postern, when I cried out. Something in the man's face I had recognized; it was that of the old man who had tried to get into the ferry. "He's a spy!" I shouted. "Lock the gates, for God's sake! Shut the window, or he'll climb in!"

I jumped out of bed with my own words ringing in my ears. Some window at any rate required shutting; it was the one in the cupboard opening out of my room. Wind had come with the rain and the sash had been loosened. The air was no longer close and the clouds were lifting, scudding over the moon. I craned out my neck, drinking in the cool night air. As I did so, I noticed an oblong patch of light on the roadway; it came from an upper window at the opposite end of the building; now and then the patch was crossed by a shadow. The people of the inn kept strangely late hours.

I did not at once go back to bed, but, stiff and sore, drew up a chair to the window with pillows and a couple of blankets, and there I sat for fully half an hour, listening to the howling of the dog, a wail of utter weariness far too dismal for the moon alone to have awakened. Then it suddenly turned into an angry growl, and I caught the sound of distant hoofs upon the road. At the same time the shadow reappeared upon the blind, the window was pulled up, and the hard, sour face of my landlady peered out into the darkness.

Evidently she was expecting someone. A minute later a horse, that had been hard ridden, drew up steaming before the door; its rider dismounted.

"Leave the beast to me," said the woman from the window, in a voice hardly raised above a whisper. "I'll see that it's made all right in the stable. Come straight upstairs; it's the third room on the right."

The man took up what seemed to be a heavy bag and, leaving his horse, passed on up the stair. I heard him stumble at the step on the landing and swear beneath his breath. Just then the clock struck three. I began to wonder if any mischief were brewing in Midnight House.

I have only the vaguest recollection of what happened between then and dawn. My attempts to obtain sleep were not as great as the struggles I made to free myself from the awful nightmares that took possession of me as soon as I began to lose consciousness. All I knew was that there was a spirit of evil abroad, an ugly, horrible spirit, that was trying to enter the house; and that every one seemed to be blind to its true nature, seemed to be helping it to gain its end. That was the lurid background of my dreams. One thing alone I remember clearly, a long-drawn-out cry, real and no wild fantasy, that came out of the night to die away into nothingness.

When I got up in the morning soon after nine, I had a splitting headache that made me resolve to be less ready in future to sample strange beds and stranger inns.

I entered the dining-room to find myself no longer alone. A tall, middle-aged man, with a look about him as if he had passed anything but a restful night, was seated at the table. He had just finished breakfast, and rose to go as I took my place. He wished me a curt good morning and left the room. I hurried over my meal, paid my bill to the same impassive-faced woman, the only occupant of the house I had seen, and shouldering my rucksack, set out along the road. I walked on for two miles, until I had nearly reached the summit of a steep incline, and was hesitating over which of three roads to take, when, turning round, I saw the stranger approaching.

As soon as his horse had overtaken me I asked him the way.

"By the by," I said, "can you tell me anything about that inn? It's the gloomiest house I ever slept in. Is it haunted?"

"Not that I know of. How can a house be haunted when there are no such things as ghosts?"

Something in the ill-concealed superiority of the tone in which he replied made me look at him more closely. He seemed to read my thoughts. "Yes, I'm the doctor," he said, "and precious little I get out of the business, I can tell you. You are not looking out for a quiet country practice yourself, I suppose? I don't think a night's work like this last's would tempt you."

"I don't know what it was," I said, "but, if I was to hazard a guess, I should say some singularly wicked man must have died in the inn last night."

He laughed out loud. "You're rather wide of the mark, for the fact is I have been helping to usher into the world another pretty innocent. As things turned out, the child did not live above half an hour, not altogether to the mother's sorrow, I should judge. People talk pretty freely in the country. There's nothing else to do; and we all know each others' affairs. It might have come into the world in better circumstances, certainly; but after all is said and done, we shan't have much to complain of if we can keep the birth-rate from falling any lower. What was it last year? Some appallingly low figure, but I can't remember the actual one. Yes, I've always been interested in statistics. They can explain nearly everything."

I was not quite so sure.

THE MONSTRANCE

ARTHUR MACHEN

Then it fell out in the sacring of the Mass that right as the priest heaved up the Host there came a beam redder than any rose and smote upon it, and then it was changed bodily into the shape and fashion of a Child having his arms stretched forth, as he had been nailed upon the Tree.—*Old Romance*

SO FAR THINGS WERE GOING VERY WELL INDEED. THE NIGHT WAS THICK AND BLACK AND cloudy, and the German force had come three-quarters of their way or more without an alarm. There was no challenge from the English lines; and indeed the English were being kept busy by a high shell-fire on their front. This had been the German plan; and it was coming off admirably. Nobody thought that there was any danger on the left; and so the Prussians, writhing on their stomachs over the ploughed field, were drawing nearer and nearer to the wood. Once there they could establish themselves comfortably and securely during what remained of the night; and at dawn the English left would be hopelessly enfiladed—and there would be another of those movements which people who really understand military matters call "readjustments of our line."

The noise made by the men creeping and crawling over the fields was drowned by the cannonade, from the English side as well as the German. On the English centre and right things were indeed very brisk; the big guns were thundering and shrieking and roaring, the machine guns were keeping up the very devil's racket; the flares and illuminating shells were as good as the Crystal Palace in the old days, as the soldiers said to one another. All this had been thought of and thought out on the other side. The German force was beautifully organized. The men who crept nearer and nearer to the wood carried quite a number of machine guns in bits on their backs; others of them had small bags full of sand; yet others big bags that were empty. When the wood was reached the sand from the small bags was to be emptied into the big bags; the machine-gun parts were to be put together, the guns mounted behind the sandbag redoubt, and then, as Major Von und Zu pleasantly observed, "the English pigs shall to gehenna-fire quickly come."

The major was so well pleased with the way things had gone that he permitted himself a very low and guttural chuckle; in another ten minutes success would be assured. He half turned his head round to whisper a caution about some detail of the sandbag business to the big sergeant-major, Karl Heinz, who was crawling just behind him. At that instant Karl Heinz leapt into the air with a scream that rent through the night and through all the roaring of the artillery. He cried in a terrible voice, "The Glory of the Lord!" and plunged and pitched forward, stone dead. They said that his face as he stood up there and cried aloud was as if it had been seen through a sheet of flame.

"They" were one or two out of the few who got back to the German lines. Most of the Prussians stayed in the ploughed field. Karl Heinz's scream had frozen the blood of the English soldiers, but it had shot to pieces; hardly a score of them returned. The rest of the force were attended to by an English burying party. According to custom the dead men were searched before they were buried, and some singular relics of the campaign were found upon them, but nothing so singular as Karl Heinz's diary.

He had been keeping it for some time. It began with entries about bread and sausage and the ordinary incidents of the trenches; here and there Karl wrote about an old grandfather, and a big china pipe, and pine woods and roast goose. Then the diarist seemed to get fidgety about his health. Thus:

> *April 17.*—Annoyed for some days by murmuring sounds in my head. I trust I shall not become deaf, like my departed uncle Christopher.
> *April 20.*—The noise in my head grows worse; it is a humming sound. It distracts me; twice I have failed to hear the captain and have been reprimanded.
> *April 22.*—So bad is my head that I go to see the doctor. He speaks of tinnitus, and gives me an inhaling apparatus that shall reach, he says, the middle ear.
> *April 25.*—The apparatus is of no use. The sound is now become like the booming of a great church bell. It reminds me of the bell at St. Lambart on that terrible day of last August.
> *April 26.*—I could swear that it is the bell of St. Lambart that I hear all the time. They rang it as the procession came out of the church.

The man's writing, at first firm enough, begins to straggle unevenly over the page at this point. The entries show that he became convinced that he heard the bell of St. Lambart's Church ringing, though (as he knew better than most men) there had been no bell and no church at St. Lambart's since the summer of 1914. There was no village either—the whole place was a rubbish-heap.

Then the unfortunate Karl Heinz was beset with other troubles.

May 2.—I fear I am becoming ill. To-day Joseph Kleist, who is next to me in the trench, asked me why I jerked my head to the right so constantly. I told him to hold his tongue; but this shows that I am noticed. I keep fancying that there is something white just beyond the range of my sight on the right hand.

May 3.—This whiteness is now quite clear, and in front of me. All this day it has slowly passed before me. I asked Joseph Kleist if he saw a piece of newspaper just beyond the trench. He stared at me solemnly—he is a stupid fool—and said, "There is no paper."

May 4.—It looks like a white robe. There was a strong smell of incense today in the trench. No one seemed to notice it. There is decidedly a white robe, and I think I can see feet, passing very slowly before me at this moment while I write.

There is no space here for continuous extracts from Karl Heinz's diary. But to condense with severity, it would seem that he slowly gathered about himself a complete set of sensory hallucinations. First the auditory hallucination of the sound of a bell, which the doctor called *tinnitus*. Then a patch of white growing into a white robe, then the smell of incense. At last he lived in two worlds. He saw his trench, and the level before it, and the English lines; he talked with his comrades and obeyed orders, though with a certain difficulty; but he also heard the deep boom of St. Lambart's bell, and saw continually advancing towards him a white procession of little children, led by a boy who was swinging a censer. There is one extraordinary entry: "But in August those children carried no lilies; now they have lilies in their hands. Why should they have lilies?"

It is interesting to note the transition over the border line. After May 2 there is no reference in the diary to bodily illness, with two notable exceptions. Up to and including that date the sergeant knows that he is suffering from illusions; after that he accepts his hallucinations as actualities. The man who cannot see what he sees and hear what he hears is a fool. So he writes: "I ask who is singing 'Ave Maria Stella.' That blockhead Friedrich Schumacher raises his crest and answers insolently that no one sings, since singing is strictly forbidden for the present."

A few days before the disastrous night expedition the last figure in the procession appeared to those sick eyes.

The old priest now comes in his golden robe, the two boys holding each side of it. He is looking just as he did when he died, save that when he

> walked in St. Lambart there was no shining round his head. But this is illusion and contrary to reason, since no one has a shining about his head. I must take some medicine.

Note here that Karl Heinz absolutely accepts the appearance of the martyred priest of St. Lambart as actual, while he thinks that the halo must be an illusion; and so he reverts again to his physical condition.

The priest held up both his hands, the diary states, "as if there were something between them. But there is a sort of cloud or dimness over this object, whatever it may be. My poor Aunt Kathie suffered much from her eyes in her old age."

One can guess what the priest of St. Lambart carried in his hands when he and the little children went out into the hot sunlight to implore mercy, while the great resounding bell of St. Lambart boomed over the plain. Karl Heinz knew what happened then; they said that it was he who killed the old priest and helped to crucify the little child against the church door. The baby was only three years old. He died calling piteously for "mummy" and "daddy."

And those who will may guess what Karl Heinz saw when the mist cleared from before the monstrance in the priest's hands. Then he shrieked and died.

Mrs. Ponsonby's Dream

B. M. Croker

I would not spend another such a night
Though 'twere to bring a world of happy days.

Richard III

One winter's day sixty years ago, when the climate of Ireland, in spite of what aged people declare to the contrary, was quite as moist as it is now, a tall, erect, dark woman stood watching the rain stream down the windows of a front drawing-room in Mountjoy Square. She wore her hair in bands, and was dressed in a puce tabinet gown, with a low neck, and very tight long sleeves-in fact, the fashion of both coiffure and sleeves would be deemed *á la mode* at present—and her expression of sullen discontent with the weather is, in these latitudes, never out of date.

As she yawned and drummed upon the panes with a much beringed hand, the door opened, and another lady, older and plainer than herself, wearing a massive beaver bonnet, a damp pelisse, and carrying a heavy morocco box, hurried into the room.

"It's turned out shockingly wet," she exclaimed, "so I took a hackney coach from the Bank. I fetched your diamonds, you see, and I've ordered the brown posters for the Britzka tomorrow."

"And I was hoping that you could not get them," said her sister peevishly, turning round as she spoke.

"La, Sally, what freak have you got now?"—setting down the jewel-case, and staring with eyes of dismay.

"It's no freak, my good Nancy, but a dream—a warning, and I never felt so ill-disposed to spend a week at Williamsfort since I was born."

"Gracious patience, Sal! but Richard will be sorely put out if you fail him."

"I suppose he will," glancing at an open letter in her hand, which was a great cumbersome affair, the size of a pocket-handkerchief, bearing a red seal and a nobleman's frank. It was not from her lover, but from her only brother—a wealthy bachelor—and said:

DEAR SAL,

The Emersons, Hamiltons, and Moores, and six men are coming on Tuesday for the Assizes and ball. I should expect you, as usual, to play hostess. Order post-horses in time, and I'll send a pair to meet you at the thirteenth milestone. Don't be later than three o'clock—we dine at four.

Your affectionate brother,

R. Connor

P.S.—Pray bring the oysters from Jury's and oblige.

"Nancy," said her sister, suddenly sitting down, "tell me honestly, do you believe in dreams?"

"In dreams—no—but I must confess that I think there is something in cup-tossing."

"Pooh—that is rare folly! Pray, did you never have a dream that haunted you, and terrified you, and made you ill at ease?"

"Nay, I'm a sound sleeper, and the worst thing I ever dreamt was, that I was married," and she wheezed and giggled ridiculously.

"And that means a death," remarked Mrs. Ponsonby. "Well, I had an awful experience last night, and you know how poorly I was today, and thought not to rise. I believe I have received a warning not to go to Williamsfort," solemnly nodding her head.

"La, my dear sister Sally, what talk is this for a sensible creature like yourself! I do protest you are joking."

"At least, you shall listen and judge, my good Nancy. I dreamt that I drove up to the house a little late. The door was opened by a strange young man, with a dark sinister face. I immediately asked for old John, and he replied that he was dead—had died very suddenly—whereupon I felt mightily shocked and upset. But I noticed that all the time this wretch was speaking to me, and assisting me to alight, his eyes were resolutely fastened on the jewelled clasps of my furred travelling pelisse. At last Richard appeared in a vast flurry, and confirmed the ill news of poor John's death—assured me that the company were all assembled, and hurried me off to dress. I wore my crimson velvet, all my diamonds, and even my stomacher, to do dear Dick honour, and went downstairs, still sorely discomposed, though I had frequent recourse to my smelling-salts. At dinner—which was, as usual, well cooked and served—I was always catching the new butler's gaze whenever I looked up; his attention appeared to be riveted on me and my jewels. After the gentlemen had joined us, which was not until late, we played cards, and I lost nigh twenty-three guineas at Faro to my Lady Susan. It's my belief she cheats—see how real was my dream."

Miss Nancy nodded her head, but made no remark.

"We retired late. I lay in the lattice chamber, which, you know, has a separate passage, and a dressing-room opening into both room and passage. Well, I locked one door, but not the one communicating with the dressing-closet—and presently went to bed. I was just dozing off, when I heard soft, stealthy steps in the passage. The handle turned, but the door was fast. In a few seconds the dressing-room was entered very cautiously, and then the door into my room. Through my eyelashes I watched the new butler creep in, and by the firelight I saw him approach the bed on tip-toe, a long knife in his hand; and then, thank Heaven, I awoke! My heart was beating so terribly fast that I never closed an eye the whole night, and more than once I felt about to swoon."

"It certainly sounds as real as a true tale," said her sister slowly. "But it was only the potted boar's head you had for supper!" she added soothingly.

"It was a solemn warning, I'll swear; and I'm in more than half a mind to send an excuse to Dick, and say I have a bad attack of the vapours."

"Do not, sister Sally; if you disoblige Richard for a mere dream, he will be mortally incensed. He likes to see you at the head of the table; your celebrated jewels make a rare show; and you are still a very personable and agreeable woman. I tell you that if old John has gone, we would have had tidings of his death. Of course, there is no new butler; and really, sister, you amaze me—you are generally so brave! That time the mail-coach upset in the snowdrift, you never minded one bit, whilst I was screaming like a Gib cat."

Mrs. Ponsonby had not another word to say; she was sensible of derision in her sister's looks; Nancy's sound commonsense carried the day, and so restored her confidence and dispelled her presentiments, that the next afternoon saw the widow depart in her own carriage, along with her best gowns, her diamonds, and her maid.

It was nearly four o'clock when a pair of smoking horses trotted up the long winding avenue to Williamsfort. Mrs. Ponsonby, having constantly consulted her watch, was in a fever of nervousness, for her brother was punctuality itself, and would be seriously put out by her tardy arrival. The door was opened; she gave a little stifled cry—for the dark man of her dream stood on the threshold! She felt inclined to shriek, but after a pause faintly inquired for "old John—where is he?"

"He is dead, your ladyship; he was taken suddenly five days ago," was the glib reply, "and buried on Monday—"

Mr. Connor now appeared, and formerly conducted his sister into the house; but she felt so weak that she could scarcely crawl into a sitting-room, and when she had found a seat, burst into tears, and piteously demanded another pair of horses, and permission to return to town within half an hour.

Her brother instantly administered his panacea for all ills, from nerves to toothache—a glass of old port; and as the lady recovered her voice and her composure, listened to her story in crimson amazement.

"'Tis true that old John died very suddenly—of gout to the stomach; but this new fellow has excellent testimonials. However, lock all your doors tonight, Sal, and when you hear a sound ring your bell—we will keep guard—and you will be as safe as if you were in a church. Now burry and dress, my good Sally; the company are waiting, and the Judge, know, is hungry, and so am!"

Everything fell out precisely as in Mrs. Ponsonby's dream. She occupied the isolated lattice chamber. She noticed the butler's persistent contemplation of her diamonds. She lost heavily at Faro—and Lady Susan won. Pale enough after her journey and money losses, the hostess at last retired, and having dismissed her maid—who complained of the megrims, and flatly declined to sleep in the dressing-room—locked an doors, and went to bed.

About one o'clock, as she lay wide awake, her expectant ear caught stealthy footsteps, then a handle turned. She sprang out on the floor, tore at her bell, and then fainted. Meanwhile, Mr. Connor and his friends rushed headlong towards her room, and discovered, half concealed in a dark corner in the passage, the new butler, in his stockinged feet, carrying a basket of wood.

"What"—string of fashionable oaths—"are you doing up here?" demanded his master, taking him roughly by the collar.

"The servant-maids were tired, and asked me to carry up firing to the rooms," was the ready reply.

"Firing! at one in the morning?" giving the basket an angry kick.

Out fell the wood, and out fell a long glittering knife—which spoke for itself.

The younger men now hurried the culprit downstairs, and locked him securely in his own apartment, intending to deliver him over the next morning into the arms of the law.

But when they went to open the door and hand the new butler (and old burglar) to the police, it was discovered that the bird had flown! A sheet fluttering from the window was all that remained of the realisation of Mrs. Ponsonby's Dream.

The Music on the Hill

Saki

Sylvia Seltoun ate her breakfast in the morning-room at Yessney with a pleasant sense of ultimate victory, such as a fervent Ironside might have permitted himself on the morrow of Worcester fight. She was scarcely pugnacious by temperament, but belonged to that more successful class of fighters who are pugnacious by circumstance. Fate had willed that her life should be occupied with a series of small struggles, usually with the odds slightly against her, and usually she had just managed to come through winning. And now she felt that she had brought her hardest and certainly her most important struggle to a successful issue. To have married Mortimer Seltoun, "Dead Mortimer" as his more intimate enemies called him, in the teeth of the cold hostility of his family, and in spite of his unaffected indifference to women, was indeed an achievement that had needed some determination and adroitness to carry through; yesterday she had brought her victory to its concluding stage by wrenching her husband away from Town and its group of satellite watering-places and "settling him down," in the vocabulary of her kind, in this remote wood-girt manor farm which was his country house.

"You will never get Mortimer to go," his mother had said carpingly, "but if he once goes he'll stay; Yessney throws almost as much a spell over him as Town does. One can understand what holds him to Town, but Yessney—" and the dowager had shrugged her shoulders.

There was a sombre almost savage wildness about Yessney that was certainly not likely to appeal to town-bred tastes, and Sylvia, notwithstanding her name, was accustomed to nothing much more sylvan than "leafy Kensington." She looked on the country as something excellent and wholesome in its way, which was apt to become troublesome if you encouraged it overmuch. Distrust of town-life had been a new thing with her, born of her marriage with Mortimer, and she had watched with satisfaction the gradual fading of what she called "the Jermyn-Street-look" in his eyes as the woods and heather of Yessney had closed in on them yesternight. Her will-power and strategy had prevailed; Mortimer would stay.

Outside the morning-room windows was a triangular slope of turf, which the indulgent might call a lawn, and beyond its low hedge of neglected fuchsia bushes a steeper slope of heather and bracken dropped down into cavernous combes overgrown with oak and yew. In its wild open savagery there seemed a stealthy linking of the joy of life with the terror of unseen things. Sylvia smiled complacently as she gazed with a School-of-Art appreciation at the landscape, and then of a sudden she almost shuddered.

"It is very wild," she said to Mortimer, who had joined her; "one could almost think that in such a place the worship of Pan had never quite died out."

"The worship of Pan never has died out," said Mortimer. "Other newer gods have drawn aside his votaries from time to time, but he is the Nature-God to whom all must come back at last. He has been called the Father of all the Gods, but most of his children have been stillborn."

Sylvia was religious in an honest, vaguely devotional kind of way, and did not like to hear her beliefs spoken of as mere aftergrowths, but it was at least something new and hopeful to hear Dead Mortimer speak with such energy and conviction on any subject.

"You don't really believe in Pan?" she asked incredulously.

"I've been a fool in most things," said Mortimer quietly, "but I'm not such a fool as not to believe in Pan when I'm down here. And if you're wise you won't disbelieve in him too boastfully while you're in his country."

It was not till a week later, when Sylvia had exhausted the attractions of the woodland walks round Yessney, that she ventured on a tour of inspection of the farm buildings. A farmyard suggested in her mind a scene of cheerful bustle, with churns and flails and smiling dairymaids, and teams of horses drinking knee-deep in duck-crowded ponds. As she wandered among the gaunt grey buildings of Yessney manor farm her first impression was one of crushing stillness and desolation, as though she had happened on some lone deserted homestead long given over to owls and cobwebs; then came a sense of furtive watchful hostility, the same shadow of unseen things that seemed to lurk in the wooded combes and coppices. From behind heavy doors and shuttered windows came the restless stamp of hoof or rasp of chain halter, and at times a muffled bellow from some stalled beast. From a distant comer a shaggy dog watched her with intent unfriendly eyes; as she drew near it slipped quietly into its kennel, and slipped out again as noiselessly when she had passed by. A few hens, questing for food under a rick, stole away under a gate at her approach. Sylvia felt that if she had come across any human beings in this wilderness of barn and byre they would have fled wraith-like from her gaze. At last, turning a corner quickly, she came upon a living thing that did not fly from her. A stretch in a pool of mud was an enormous sow, gigantic beyond the town-woman's wildest computation of swine-flesh, and speedily alert to resent and if necessary repel the unwonted intrusion. It was Sylvia's turn to make an unobtrusive retreat. As she threaded her way past rickyards and cowsheds and long blank walls, she started suddenly at a strange sound—the echo of a boy's laughter, golden and equivocal. Jan, the only boy employed on the farm, a tow-headed, wizen-faced yokel, was visibly at work on a potato clearing half-way up the nearest hill-side, and Mortimer, when questioned, knew of no other probable or possible begetter of the hidden mockery that had ambushed Sylvia's retreat. The memory of that untraceable echo was added to her other impressions of a furtive sinister "something" that hung around Yessney.

Of Mortimer she saw very little; farm and woods and trout-streams seemed to swallow him up from dawn till dusk. Once, following the direction she had seen him take in the morning, she came to an open space in a nut copse, further shut in by huge yew trees, in the centre of which stood a stone pedestal surmounted by a small bronze figure of a youthful Pan. It was a beautiful piece of workmanship, but her attention was chiefly held by the fact that a newly cut bunch of grapes had been placed as an offering at its feet. Grapes were none too plentiful at the manor house, and Sylvia snatched the bunch angrily from the pedestal. Contemptuous annoyance dominated her thoughts as she strolled slowly homeward, and then gave way to a sharp feeling of something that was very near fright; across a thick tangle of undergrowth a boy's face was scowling at her, brown and beautiful, with unutterably evil eyes. It was a lonely pathway, all pathways round Yessney were lonely for the matter of that, and she sped forward without waiting to give a closer scrutiny to this sudden apparition. It was not till she had reached the house that she discovered that she had dropped the bunch of grapes in her flight.

"I saw a youth in the wood today," she told Mortimer that evening, "brown-faced and rather handsome, but a scoundrel to look at. A gipsy lad, I suppose."

"A reasonable theory," said Mortimer, "only there aren't any gipsies in these parts at present."

"Then who was he?" asked Sylvia, and as Mortimer appeared to have no theory of his own she passed on to recount her finding of the votive offering.

"I suppose it was your doing," she observed; "it's a harmless piece of lunacy, but people would think you dreadfully silly if they knew of it."

"Did you meddle with it in any way?" asked Mortimer.

"I—I threw the grapes away. It seemed so silly," said Sylvia, watching Mortimer's impassive face for a sign of annoyance.

"I don't think you were wise to do that," he said reflectively. "I've heard it said that the Wood Gods are rather horrible to those who molest them."

"Horrible perhaps to those that believe in them, but you see I don't," retorted Sylvia.

"All the same," said Mortimer in his even, dispassionate tone, "I should avoid the woods and orchards if I were you, and give a wide berth to the horned beasts on the farm."

It was all nonsense, of course, but in that lonely wood-girt spot nonsense seemed able to rear a bastard brood of uneasiness.

"Mortimer," said Sylvia suddenly, "I think we will go back to Town some time soon."

Her victory had not been so complete as she had supposed; it had carried her on to ground that she was already anxious to quit.

"I don't think you will ever go back to Town," said Mortimer. He seemed to be paraphrasing his mother's prediction as to himself.

Sylvia noted with dissatisfaction and some self-contempt that the course of her next afternoon's ramble took her instinctively clear of the network of woods. As to the horned cattle, Mortimer's warning was scarcely needed, for she had always regarded them as of doubtful neutrality at the best: her imagination unsexed the most matronly dairy cows and turned them into bulls liable to "see red" at any moment. The ram who fed in the narrow paddock below the orchards she had adjudged, after ample and cautious probation, to be of docile temper; today, however, she decided to leave his docility untested, for the usually tranquil beast was roaming with every sign of restlessness from corner to corner of his meadow. A low, fitful piping, as of some reedy flute, was coming from the depth of a neighbouring copse, and there seemed to be some subtle connection between the animal's restless pacing and the wild music from the wood. Sylvia turned her steps in an upward direction and climbed the heather-clad slopes that stretched in rolling shoulders high above Yessney. She had left the piping notes behind her, but across the wooded combes at her feet the wind brought her another kind of music, the straining bay of hounds in full chase. Yessney was just on the outskirts of the Devon-and-Somerset country, and the hunted deer sometimes came that way. Sylvia could presently see a dark body, breasting hill after hill, and sinking again and again out of sight as he crossed the combes, while behind him steadily swelled that relentless chorus, and she grew tense with the excited sympathy that one feels for any hunted thing in whose capture one is not directly interested. And at last he broke through the outermost line of oak scrub and fern and stood panting in the open, a fat September stag carrying a well-furnished head. His obvious course was to drop down to the brown pools of Undercombe, and thence make his way towards the red deer's favoured sanctuary, the sea. To Sylvia's surprise, however, he turned his head to the upland slope and came lumbering resolutely onward over the heather. "It will be dreadful," she thought, "the hounds will pull him down under my very eyes." But the music of the pack seemed to have died away for a moment, and in its place she heard again that wild piping, which rose now on this side, now on that, as though urging the failing stag to a final effort. Sylvia stood well aside from his path, half hidden in a thick growth of whortle bushes, and watched him swing stiffly upward, his flanks dark with sweat, the coarse hair on his neck showing light by contrast. The pipe music shrilled suddenly around her, seeming to come from the bushes at her very feet, and at the same moment the great beast slewed round and bore directly down upon her. In an instant her pity for the hunted animal was changed to wild terror at her own danger; the thick heather roots mocked her scrambling efforts at flight, and she looked frantically downward for a glimpse of oncoming hounds. The huge antler spikes were within a few yards of her, and in a flash of numbing fear she remembered Mortimer's warning, to beware of horned beasts on the farm. And then with a quick throb of joy she saw that she was not alone; a human figure stood a few paces aside, knee-deep in the whortle bushes.

"Drive it off!" she shrieked. But the figure made no answering movement.

The antlers drove straight at her breast, the acrid smell of the hunted animal was in her nostrils, but her eyes were filled with the horror of something she saw other than her oncoming death. And in her ears rang the echo of a boy's laughter, golden and equivocal.

My Enemy and Myself

Vincent O'Sullivan

In the garden, when I was a child, I used to stare for hours at the white roses. In these there was for me a certain strangeness, which was yet quite human; for I know that I was full of sorrow if I found the petals strewn over the hushed grass. I had a terror of great waters, wild and lonely; I saw an austere dignity in the moon shining on a flat sea; things, cordage and broken spars, cast ashore by the ocean, told me wonderful, sad tales. And because my head was thick with thoughts, I had little speech; and for this I was laughed at and called stupid: "He was always a dull child, murmured my mother, bending over me, when I, in the crisis of a fever, was on the point of embarking for a vague land. As I grew older, I still dwelt within my soul, a satisfied prisoner: the complaint of huge trees in a storm; the lash and surge of breakers on an iron coast; the sound of certain words; the sight of dim colors which blend sometimes in gray sunsets; the heavy scent of some exquisite poisonous flower; a contemplation of youthful forms engaged in an unruly game;—ah! in these things also I found perfect sensation and ecstacy. Still, my tongue held to its old stubbornness: I was ever delayed by a habit of commonplace speech, a shame at exposing my thoughts. In time I won a cloud of easy acquaintance; but my awkwardness in conversation, my tendency to be maladroit,—call it what you like! always stepped between when I was about to make a friend. Then, at last, came Jacquette.

I remember that she was playing a composition by Chopin, a curious black-colored thing, when I first came into her company; and now, even as I write, when our love is over, I hear that sombre music again. But the important matter is, that here was the person I had been seeking so long; here was the mind to meet with my mind; with her I could, at length, get out of myself (as we now say); become free. All the dear thoughts which had for years dwelt with me in close privateness, I gave to her; all my desires, all my mean hopes. Ah! the merry airs we had then: her bright laughter which, as wind, drove glumness, as foam, before it! I think I tired her of my enthusiasms and decisions; but it was so sweet to have some one to listen and understand, and she never would admit that she was tired. Nay! one morning in the apple-orchard, when the wind was turning her hair to the sunshine, she kissed me very prettily on the mouth.

After that, I forget how long it was till I came in one night and found my enemy sitting with her at the fireside. He was not my enemy then, mind you: indeed, I thought him a nice, pleasant creature, with a mighty handsome face. We became familiar: he seemed to like me, and I was sure I had gained another friend. The months glided by, and we three came to sitting together late of nights: he and Jacquette, the wise people, silent, gazing at each other; I, the fool, in the middle, talking in a youthful, impassioned way. Once I paused suddenly, and looked up, and caught a somewhat contemptuous smile peeping from the corners of Jacquette's mouth and dancing in her eyes; while he, for an answer, fell a-laughing into her face. Of course, I must have wearied them both, *bored them* (as we say) to desperation; but I was a very young man, with all the warmth and admiration of the young; and in the time of youth, a woman is always older than a man. Besides, I loved her so much, and I had such strange pleasure in loving her, that I think it was rather cruel of her to laugh.

"Why did you laugh at me?" I asked, when I was twisting a garland of wild roses for her hair.

"Oh, I didn't laugh!" she exclaimed. "Or if I did," she added, looking down with a tooth on her lip, "it must have been because I was so pleased to hear you saying beautiful words to us—poor ignorant things!"

The next day I had an affair of great importance in the town where I lived, so I told Jacquette that on account of this affair I could not go down, as my custom was, to her cottage by the sea, that night. But as the day waned, and the night closed in, I became the thrall of a longing to hear her singing voice, to play fantastic music with her delightfully. Thus it came about that it was nearly eleven o'clock when I reached the shore, and hearkened to the calling sea. There was a note of melancholy, almost a sob, in the noise of it to-night: and that, taken with a monstrous depression, filled me strangely with a desire to die—to give up life at this point! I saw a light in Jacquette's bedroom, but the rest of the little house was dark; and I was turning away, when my hand chanced to strike the door-handle, which I pushed, and found the door not locked. Let me go in! (thinks I): I shall sit awhile and dream of Jacquette, and a few chords touched softly on the piano will tell my love I am dreaming of her. Here (perhaps you will say!) I was wrong: but I was ready to welcome a servant's company, or, in spite of his growing offensiveness, my enemy's, should I find him there, rather than be alone with my saddening thoughts. The room I chose to sit in, because there was a dying fire in it, was just under Jacquette's bedroom; and ere I had sat a minute, I became conscious of voices in the room above. As soon as I made out the man's voice, a thousand serpents seemed literally to eat their way into my brain, turning my vision red; and I lay for an hour, may-be, on the carpet, fainting, and stricken, and dazed. Now, at last, after an hour I was myself, or rather more than myself, with every nerve tight as a fiddle-string, still seeing red, as I unclasped the long jack-knife, which the Greek sailor had given me, and laid it in the hollow of my hand.

I knew that it would dawn by three o'clock, so I stood quite still, only moving my tongue over my dry lips, and shaking my head to keep a sweat from running into my eyes. A cat cried in the road, and the breakers thundered against the rocks.

A little before dawn, while it was yet dark, I heard a murmur of low voices—her voice and my enemy's; and then the man came down the stairs.

"Good night, my sweet love!" said Jacquette.

"O my darling, good night!" came from my enemy, and so he banged the door behind him.

One moment I paused to peer through the window, and make sure of my man. Then I fetched a run, and was on him like a panther, holding him close, with his hot breath scorching my face. Coming on him from behind, as I did, the middle finger of my left hand struck his eye, and now, as I pressed, the eye bulged out.

"My friend," he groaned, "for Christ's sake, have pity!"

"To hell with your friendship!" I said. "Much pity you had for my honour!" says I, and with that I let him have the knife in his throat, and the blood spurted over my hands hot and sticky. As soon as I could get free of his clutch, I looked up at Jacquette's bedroom window, and there she was, sure enough! in her nightdress, with the blind in her hand, gazing out. Straight up to her room I went, and flung open the door. She turned to me gray and whingeing.

"My little love—," she began.

I put my hands on my hips and spat hard into her face. Then I tramped down stairs and out of the lonely cottage.

I had not the least fear of detection: the servants slept in an out-house, and the place was too desolate for any chance passenger. I stood triumphing by the corpse of my enemy; but even as I looked the moon shewed from a rift of cloud, lighting the blood, and the hue left by violent death in the features, and I ran for my life from that hideous one-eyed thing.

I came to the town, and to a house where I lay constantly, about four o'clock, in a curious trembling fit. I bathed my head and hands, however, in a heavy perfume, and then became strangely calm, and fell to thinking of the rightness of the deed. Just there was the consoling thought: certainly I had done a murder, but in doing it I had delivered punishment to a traitress and her paramour. Now that the thing was over, it was clearly my duty to forget all about it as soon as possible; and this I set myself to do, aided by a cigarette and a novel of the ingenious Miss Jane Austen. I had succeeded in my aim, I was clear-minded and very serene, when of a sudden something heavy fell against the door of my room.

"At this hour?" I murmured in surprise, and went to the door.

A body that nearly knocked me down, the dead body of a man, fell into the room, and lay, face downward, on the carpet. Then I did the one act I shall never cease to regret: From a movement of kindness, pity, curiosity, what you will! I bent down and turned over the corpse. Slowly the thing got to its feet; and my enemy, with a dry gaping wound in his throat, and his eye hanging from its socket by a bit of skin, stood before me, face to face.

"O God, have mercy!" I screamed, and beat on the wall with my hands; and again and again:—"God have mercy!"

"You do well to ask God for mercy," says my enemy; "for you will not get much from men." He stood by the fire-place.

"I beg of you," I said, in a low, passionate voice, "I beg of you, by all you find dear, for the sake of our old friendship, to leave this place, to let me go free."

He shook his head. "For Jacquette's sake?" He laughed harshly.

"My friend," I said to my enemy, "for Christ's sake, have pity!"

"Pity you?" says he in a jeer. "You!"

As I looked at him, I was stung into strong fury. My eyes clung to the wound in his throat, and my fingers ached to close in it—to misuse it, to maul it.

But as I sprang at him, he gave a shriek that woke the town; a shriek of fear too, let me think it at this last, like to that of a lost soul when the gates of hell have closed behind for ever: and when the people of the house rushed in, they found me kneeling by his dead body, with my knife in my enemy's throat, and his new blood, bright and wet, on my hands.

They will hang me because I loved Jacquette.

The 9:30 Up-Train

Sabine Baring-Gould

In a well-authenticated ghost story, names and dates should be distinctly specified. In the following story I am unfortunately able to give only the year and the month, for I have forgotten the date of the day, and I do not keep a diary. With regard to names, my own figures as a guarantee as that of the principal personage to whom the following extraordinary circumstances occurred, but the minor actors are provided with fictitious names, for I am not warranted to make their real ones public. I may add that the believer in ghosts may make use of the facts which I relate to establish his theories, if he finds that they will be of service to him—when he has read through and weighed well the startling account which I am about to give from my own experiences.

On a fine evening in June, 1860, I paid a visit to Mrs. Lyons, on my way to the Hassocks Gate Station, on the London and Brighton line. This station is the first out of Brighton.

As I rose to leave, I mentioned to the lady whom I was visiting that I expected a parcel of books from town, and that I was going to the station to inquire whether it had arrived.

"Oh!" said she, readily, "I expect Dr. Lyons out from Brighton by the 9:30 train; if you like to drive the pony chaise down and meet him, you are welcome, and you can bring your parcel back with you in it."

I gladly accepted her offer, and in a few minutes I was seated in a little low basket-carriage, drawn by a pretty iron-grey Welsh pony.

The station road commands the line of the South Downs from Chantonbury Ring, with its cap of dark firs, to Mount Harry, the scene of the memorable battle of Lewes. Woolsonbury stands out like a headland above the dark Danny woods, over which the rooks were wheeling and cawing previous to settling themselves in for the night. Ditchling beacon—its steep sides gashed with chalk-pits—was faintly flushed with light. The Clayton windmills, with their sails motionless, stood out darkly against the green evening sky. Close beneath opens the tunnel in which, not so long before, had happened one of the most fearful railway accidents on record.

The evening was exquisite. The sky was kindled with light, though the sun was set. A few gilded bars of cloud lay in the west. Two or three stars looked forth—one I noticed twinkling green, crimson, and gold, like a gem. From a field of young wheat hard by I heard the harsh, grating note of the corncrake. Mist was lying on the low meadows like a mantle of snow, pure, smooth, and white; the cattle stood in it to their knees. The effect was so singular that I drew up to look at it attentively. At the same moment I heard the scream of an engine, and on looking towards the downs I noticed the up-train shooting out of the tunnel, its red signal lamps flashing brightly out of the purple gloom which bathed the roots of the hills.

Seeing that I was late, I whipped the Welsh pony on, and proceeded at a fast trot.

At about a quarter mile from the station there is a turnpike—an odd-looking building, tenanted then by a strange old man, usually dressed in a white smock, over which his long white beard flowed to his breast. This toll-collector—he is dead now—had amused himself in bygone days by carving life-size heads out of wood, and these were stuck along the eaves. One is the face of a drunkard, round and blotched, leering out of misty eyes at the passers-by; the next has the crumpled features of a miser, worn out with toil and moil; a third has the wild scowl of a maniac; and a fourth the stare of an idiot.

I drove past, flinging the toll to the door, and shouting to the old man to pick it up, for I was in a vast hurry to reach the station before Dr. Lyons left it. I whipped the little pony on, and he began to trot down a cutting in the greensand, through which leads the station road.

Suddenly, Taffy stood still, planted his feet resolutely on the ground, threw up his head, snorted, and refused to move a peg. I "gee-uped," and "tshed," all to no purpose; not a step would the little fellow advance. I saw that he was thoroughly alarmed; his flanks were quivering, and his ears were thrown back. I was on the point of leaving the chaise, when the pony made a bound on one side and ran the carriage up into the hedge, thereby upsetting me on the road. I picked myself up, and took the beast's head. I could not conceive what had frightened him; there was positively nothing to be seen, except a puff of dust running up the road, such as might be blown along by a passing current of air. There was nothing to be heard, except the rattle of a gig or tax-cart with one wheel loose: probably a vehicle of this kind was being driven down the London road, which branches off at the turnpike at right angles. The sound became fainter, and at last died away in the distance.

The pony now no longer refused to advance. It trembled violently, and was covered with sweat.

"Well, upon my word, you have been driving hard!" exclaimed Dr. Lyons, when I met him at the station.

"I have not, indeed," was my reply; "but something has frightened Taffy, but what that something was, is more than I can tell."

"Oh, ah!" said the doctor, looking round with a certain degree of interest in his face; "so you met it, did you?"

"Met what?"

"Oh, nothing;—only I have heard of horses being frightened along this road after the arrival of the 9:30 up-train. Flys never leave the moment that the train comes in, or the horses become restive—a wonderful thing for a fly-horse to become restive, isn't it?"

"But what causes this alarm? I saw nothing!"

"You ask me more than I can answer. I am as ignorant of the cause as yourself. I take things as they stand, and make no inquiries. When the flyman tells me that he can't start for a minute or two after the train has arrived, or urges on his horses to reach the station before the arrival of this train, giving as his reason that his brutes become wild if he does not do so, then I merely say, 'Do as you think best, cabby,' and bother my head no more about the matter."

"I shall search this matter out," said I resolutely. "What has taken place so strangely corroborates the superstition, that I shall not leave it uninvestigated."

"Take my advice and banish it from your thoughts. When you have come to the end, you will be sadly disappointed, and will find that all the mystery evaporates, and leaves a dull, commonplace residuum. It is best that the few mysteries which remain to us unexplained should still remain mysteries, or we shall disbelieve in supernatural agencies altogether. We have searched out the arcana of nature, and exposed all her secrets to the garish eye of day, and we find, in despair, that the poetry and romance of life are gone. Are we the happier for knowing that there are no ghosts, no fairies, no witches, no mermaids, no wood spirits? Were not our forefathers happier in thinking every lake to be the abode of a fairy, every forest to be a bower of yellow-haired sylphs, every moorland sweep to be tripped over by elf and pixie? I found my little boy one day lying on his face in a fairy-ring, crying: 'You dear, dear little fairies, I *will* believe in you, though papa says you are all nonsense.' I used, in my childish days, to think, when a silence fell upon a company, that an angel was passing through the room. Alas! I now know that it results only from the subject of weather having been talked to death, and no new subject having been started. Believe me, science has done good to mankind, but it has done mischief too. If we wish to be poetical or romantic, we must shut our eyes to facts. The head and the heart wage mutual war now. A lover preserves a lock of his mistress's hair as a holy relic, yet he must know perfectly well that for all practical purposes a bit of rhinoceros hide would do as well—the chemical constituents are identical. If I adore a fair lady, and feel a thrill through all my veins when I touch her hand, a moment's consideration tells me that phosphate of lime No. 1 is touching phosphate of lime No. 2—nothing more. If for a moment I forget myself so far as to wave my cap and cheer for king, or queen, or prince, I laugh at my folly next moment for having paid reverence to one digesting machine above another."

I cut the doctor short as he was lapsing into his favourite subject of discussion, and asked him whether he would lend me the pony-chaise on the following evening, that I might drive to the station again and try to unravel the mystery.

"I will lend you the pony," said he, "but not the chaise, as I am afraid of its being injured should Taffy take fright and run up into the hedge again. I have got a saddle."

Next evening I was on my way to the station considerably before the time at which the train was due.

I stopped at the turnpike and chatted with the old man who kept it. I asked him whether he could throw any light on the matter which I was investigating. He shrugged his shoulders, saying that he "knowed nothink about it."

"What! Nothing at all?"

"I don't trouble my head with matters of this sort," was the reply. "People *do* say that something out of the common sort passes along the road and turns down the other road leading to Clayton and Brighton; but I pays no attention to what them people says."

"Do you ever hear anything?"

"After the arrival of the 9:30 train I does at times hear the rattle as of a mail-cart and the trot of a horse along the road; and the sound is as though one of the wheels was loose. I've a been out many a time to take the toll; but, Lor' bless 'ee! them sperits—if sperits them be—don't go for to pay toll."

"Have you never inquired into the matter?"

"Why should I? Anythink as don't go for to pay toll don't concern me. Do ye think as I knows 'ow many people and dogs goes through this heer geatt in a day? Not I—them don't pay toll, so them's no odds to me."

"Look here, my man!" said I. "Do you object to my putting the bar across the road, immediately on the arrival of the train?"

"Not a bit! Please yersel'; but you han't got much time to lose, for theer comes thickey train out of Clayton tunnel."

I shut the gate, mounted Taffy, and drew up across the road a little way below the turnpike. I heard the train arrive—I saw it puff off. At the same moment I distinctly heard a trap coming up the road, one of the wheels rattling as though it were loose. I repeat deliberately that I *heard* it—I cannot account for it—but, though I heard it, yet I saw nothing whatever.

At the same time the pony became restless, it tossed its head, pricked up its ears, it started, pranced, and then made a bound to one side, entirely regardless of whip and rein. It tried to scramble up the sand-bank in its alarm, and I had to throw myself off and catch its head. I then cast a glance behind me at the turnpike. I saw the bar bent, as though someone were pressing against it; then, with a click, it flew open, and was dashed violently back against the white post to which it was usually hasped in the day-time. There it remained, quivering from the shock.

Immediately I heard the rattle—rattle—rattle—of the tax-cart. I confess that my first impulse was to laugh, the idea of a ghostly tax-cart was so essentially ludicrous; but the *reality* of the whole scene soon brought me to a graver mood, and, remounting Taffy, I rode down to the station.

The officials were taking their ease, as another train was not due for some while; so I stepped up to the stationmaster and entered into conversation with him. After a few desultory remarks, I mentioned the circumstances which had occurred to me on the road, and my inability to account for them.

"So that's what you're after!" said the master somewhat bluntly. "Well, I can tell you nothing about it; sperits don't come in my way, saving and excepting those which can be taken inwardly; and mighty comfortable warming things they be when so taken. If you ask me about other sorts of sperits, I tell you flat I don't believe in 'em, though I don't mind drinking the health of them what does."

"Perhaps you may have the chance, if you are a little more communicative," said I.

"Well, I'll tell you all I know, and that is precious little," answered the worthy man. "I know one thing for certain—that one compartment of a second-class carriage is always left vacant between Brighton and Hassocks Gate, by the 9:30 up-train."

"For what purpose?"

"Ah! that's more than I can fully explain. Before the orders came to this effect, people went into fits and that like, in one of the carriages."

"Any particular carriage?"

"The first compartment of the second-class carriage nearest to the engine. It is locked at Brighton, and I unlock it at this station."

"What do you mean by saying that people had fits?"

"I mean that I used to find men and women a-screeching and a-hollering like mad to be let out; they'd seen some'ut as had frightened them as they was passing through the Clayton tunnel. That was before they made the arrangement I told y' of."

"Very strange!" said I meditatively.

"Wery much so, but true for all that. I don't believe in nothing but sperits of a warming and cheering nature, and them sort ain't to be found in Clayton tunn'l to my thinking."

There was evidently nothing more to be got out of my friend. I hope that he drank my health that night; if he omitted to do so, it was his fault, not mine.

As I rode home revolving in my mind all that I had heard and seen, I became more and more settled in my determination to thoroughly investigate the matter. The best means that I could adopt for so doing would be to come out from Brighton by the 9:30 train in the very compartment of the second-class carriage from which the public were considerately excluded.

Somehow I felt no shrinking from the attempt; my curiosity was so intense that it overcame all apprehension as to the consequences.

My next free day was Thursday, and I hoped then to execute my plan. In this, however, I was disappointed, as I found that a battalion drill was fixed for that very evening, and I was desirous of attending it, being somewhat behindhand in the regulation number of drills. I was consequently obliged to postpone my Brighton trip.

On the Thursday evening about five o'clock I started in regimentals with my rifle over my shoulder, for the drilling ground—a piece of furzy common near the railway station.

I was speedily overtaken by Mr. Ball, a corporal in the rifle corps, a capital shot and most efficient in his drill. Mr. Ball was driving his gig. He stopped on seeing me and offered me a seat beside him. I gladly accepted, as the distance to the station is a mile and three-quarters by the road, and two miles by what is commonly supposed to be the short cut across the fields.

After some conversation on volunteering matters, about which Corporal Ball was an enthusiast, we turned out of the lanes into the station road, and I took the opportunity of adverting to the subject which was uppermost in my mind.

"Ah! I have heard a good deal about that," said the corporal. "My workmen have often told me some cock-and-bull stories of that kind, but I can't say has 'ow I believed them. What you tell me is, 'owever, very remarkable. I never 'ad it on such good authority afore. Still, I can't believe that there's hanything supernatural about it."

"I do not yet know what to believe," I replied, "for the whole matter is to me perfectly inexplicable."

"You know, of course, the story which gave rise to the superstition?"

"Not I. Pray tell it me."

"Just about seven years agone—why, you must remember the circumstances as well as I do—there was a man druv over from I can't say where, for that was never exact-ly hascertained,—but from the Henfield direction, in a light cart. He went to the Station Inn, and throwing the reins to John Thomas, the ostler, bade him take the trap and bring it round to meet the 9:30 train, by which he calculated to return from Brighton. John Thomas said as 'ow the stranger was quite unbeknown to him, and that he looked as though he 'ad some matter on his mind when he went to the train; he was a queer sort of a man, with thick grey hair and beard, and delicate white 'ands, jist like a lady's. The trap was round to the station door as hordered by the arrival of the 9:30 train. The ostler observed then that the man was ashen pale, and that his 'ands trembled as he took the reins, that the stranger stared at him in a wild habstracted way, and that he would have driven off without tendering payment had he not been respectfully reminded that the 'orse had been given a feed of hoats. John Thomas made a hobservation to the gent relative to the wheel which was loose, but that hobservation met with no corresponding hanswer. The driver whipped his 'orse and went off. He passed the turnpike, and was seen to take the Brighton road hinstead of that by which he had come. A workman hobserved the trap next on the downs above Clayton chalk-pits. He didn't pay much attention to it, but he saw that the driver was on his legs at the 'ead of the 'orse. Next morning, when the quarrymen went to the pit, they found a shattered taxcart at the bottom, and the 'orse and driver dead, the latter with his neck broken. What was curious, too, was that an 'andkerchief was bound round the brute's heyes, so that he must have been driven over the edge blindfold. Hodd, wasn't it? Well, folks say that the gent and his tax-cart pass along the road every hevening after the arrival of the 9:30 train; but I don't believe it; I ain't a bit superstitious—not I!"

Next week I was again disappointed in my expectation of being able to put my scheme in execution; but on the third Saturday after my conversation with Corporal Ball, I walked into Brighton in the afternoon, the distance being about nine miles. I spent an hour on the shore watching the boats, and then I sauntered round the Pavilion, ardently longing that fire might break forth and consume that architectural monstrosity. I believe that I afterwards had a cup of coffee at the refreshment-rooms of the station, and capital refreshment-rooms they are, or were—very moderate and very good. I think that I partook of a bun, but if put on my oath I could not swear to the fact; a floating reminiscence of bun lingers in the chambers of memory, but I cannot be positive, and I wish in this paper to advance nothing but reliable facts. I squandered precious time in reading the advertisements of baby-jumpers—which no mother should be without—which are indispensable in the nursery and the greatest acquisition in the parlour, the greatest discovery of modern times, etc., etc. I perused a notice of the advantage of metallic brushes, and admired the young lady with her hair white on one side and black on the other; I studied the Chinese letter commendatory of Horniman's tea and the inferior English translation, and counted up the number of agents in Great Britain and Ireland. At length the ticket-office opened, and I booked for Hassocks Gate, second class, fare one shilling.

I ran along the platform till I came to the compartment of the second-class carriage which I wanted. The door was locked, so I shouted for a guard.

"Put me in here, please."

"Can't there, s'r; next, please, nearly empty, one woman and baby."

"I particularly wish to enter *this* carriage," said I.

"Can't be, lock'd, orders, comp'ny," replied the guard, turning on his heel.

"What reason is there for the public's being excluded, may I ask?"

"Dn'ow, 'spress ord'rs—c'n't let you in; next caridge, pl'se; now then, quick, pl'se."

I knew the guard and he knew me—by sight, for I often travelled to and fro on the line, so I thought it best to be candid with him. I briefly told him my reason for making the request, and begged him to assist me in executing my plan. He then consented, though with reluctance.

"'Ave y'r own way," said he; "only if an'thing 'appens, don't blame me!"

"Never fear," laughed I, jumping into the carriage.

The guard left the carriage unlocked, and in two minutes we were off.

I did not feel in the slightest degree nervous. There was no light in the carriage, but that did not matter, as there was twilight. I sat facing the engine on the left side, and every now and then I looked out at the downs with a soft haze of light still hanging over them. We swept into a cutting, and I watched the lines of flint in the chalk, and longed to be geologising among them with my hammer, picking out "shepherds' crowns" and sharks' teeth, the delicate rhynconella and the quaint ventriculite. I remembered a not very distant occasion on which I had actually ventured there, and been chased off by the guard, after having brought down an avalanche of chalk debris in a manner dangerous to traffic whilst endeavouring to extricate a magnificent ammonite which I found, and—alas! left—protruding from the side of the cutting. I wondered whether that ammonite was still there; I looked about to identify the exact spot as we whizzed along; and at that moment we shot into the tunnel.

There are two tunnels, with a bit of chalk cutting between them. We passed through the first, which is short, and in another moment plunged into the second.

I cannot explain how it was that *now*, all of a sudden, a feeling of terror came over me; it seemed to drop over me like a wet sheet and wrap me round and round.

I felt that *someone* was seated opposite me—someone in the darkness with his eyes fixed on me.

Many persons possessed of keen nervous sensibility are well aware when they are in the presence of another, even though they can see no one, and I believe that I possess this power strongly. If I were blindfolded, I think that I should know when anyone was looking fixedly at me, and I am certain that I should instinctively know that I was not alone if I entered a dark room in which another person was seated, even though he made no noise. I remember a college friend of mine, who dabbled in anatomy, telling me that a little Italian violinist once called on him to give a lesson on his instrument. The foreigner—a singularly nervous individual—moved restlessly from the place where he had been standing, casting many a furtive glance over his shoulder at a press which was behind him. At last the little fellow tossed aside his violin, saying—

"I can note give de lesson if someone weel look at me from behind! Dare is somebodee in de cupboard, I know!"

"You are right, there is!" laughed my anatomical friend, flinging open the door of the press and discovering a skeleton.

The horror which oppressed me was numbing. For a few moments I could neither lift my hands nor stir a finger. I was tongue-tied. I seemed paralysed in every member. I fancied that I *felt* eyes staring at me through the gloom. A cold breath seemed to play over my face. I believed that fingers touched my chest and plucked at my coat. I drew back against the partition; my heart stood still, my flesh became stiff, my muscles rigid.

I do not know whether I breathed—a blue mist swam before my eyes, and my head span.

The rattle and roar of the train dashing through the tunnel drowned every other sound.

Suddenly we rushed past a light fixed against the wall in the side, and it sent a flash, instantaneous as that of lightning, through the carriage. In that moment I saw what I shall never, never forget. I saw a face opposite me, livid as that of a corpse, hideous with passion like that of a gorilla.

I cannot describe it accurately, for I saw it but for a second; yet there rises before me now, as I write, the low broad brow seamed with wrinkles, the shaggy, overhanging grey eyebrows; the wild ashen eyes, which glared as those of a demoniac; the coarse mouth, with its fleshy lips compressed till they were white; the profusion of wolf-grey hair about the cheeks and chin; the thin, bloodless hands, raised and half-open, extended towards me as though they would clutch and tear me.

In the madness of terror, I flung myself along the seat to the further window.

Then I felt that *it* was moving slowly down, and was opposite me again. I lifted my hand to let down the window, and I touched something: I thought it was a hand—yes, yes! it *was* a hand, for it folded over mine and began to contract on it. I felt each finger separately; they were cold, dully cold. I wrenched my hand away. I slipped back to my former place in the carriage by the open window, and in frantic horror I opened the door, clinging to it with both my hands round the window-jamb, swung myself out with my feet on the floor and my head turned from the carriage. If the cold fingers had but touched my woven hands, mine would have given way; had I but turned my head and seen that hellish countenance peering out at me, I must have lost my hold.

Ah! I saw the light from the tunnel mouth; it smote on my face. The engine rushed out with a piercing whistle. The roaring echoes of the tunnel died away. The cool fresh breeze blew over my face and tossed my hair; the speed of the train was relaxed; the lights of the station became brighter. I heard the bell ringing loudly; I saw people waiting for the train; I felt the vibration as the brake was put on. We stopped; and then my fingers gave way. I dropped as a sack on the platform, and then, then—not till then—I awoke. There now! from beginning to end the whole had been a frightful dream caused by my having too many blankets over my bed. If I must append a moral—Don't sleep too hot.

No. 17

E. Nesbit

I YAWNED. I COULD NOT HELP IT. BUT THE FLAT, INEXORABLE VOICE WENT ON.

"Speaking from the journalistic point of view—I may tell you, gentlemen, that I once occupied the position of advertisement editor to the *Bradford Woollen Goods Journal*—and speaking from that point of view, I hold the opinion that all the best ghost stories have been written over and over again; and if I were to leave the road and return to a literary career I should never be led away by ghosts. Realism's what's wanted nowadays, if you want to be up-to-date."

The large commercial paused for breath.

"You never can tell with the public," said the lean, elderly traveller; "it's like in the fancy business. You never know how it's going to be. Whether it's a clockwork ostrich or Sometite silk or a particular shape of shaded glass novelty or a tobacco-box got up to look like a raw chop, you never know your luck."

"That depends on who you are," said the dapper man in the comer by the fire. "If you've got the right push about you, you can make a thing go, whether it's a clockwork kitten or imitation meat, and with stories, I take it, it's just the same-realism or ghost stories. But the best ghost story would be the realest one, I think."

The large commercial had got his breath.

"I don't believe in ghost stories, myself," he was saying with earnest dullness; "but there was rather a queer thing happened to a second cousin of an aunt of mine by marriage—a very sensible woman with no nonsense about her. And the soul of truth and honour. I shouldn't have believed it if she had been one of your flighty, fanciful sort."

"Don't tell us the story," said the melancholy man who travelled in hardware; "you'll make us afraid to go to bed."

The well-meant effort failed. The large commercial went on, as I had known he would; his words overflowed his mouth, as his person overflowed his chair. I turned my mind to my own affairs, coming back to the commercial room in time to hear the summing up.

"The doors were all locked, and she was quite certain she saw a tall, white figure glide past her and vanish. I wouldn't have believed it if—" And so on *da capo*, from "if she hadn't been the second cousin" to the "soul of truth and honour."

I yawned again.

"Very good story," said the smart little man by the fire. He was a traveller, as the rest of us were; his presence in the room told us that much. He had been rather silent during dinner, and afterwards, while the red curtains were being drawn and the red and black cloth laid between the glasses and the decanters and the mahogany, he had quietly taken the best chair in the warmest comer. We had got our letters written and the large traveller had been boring for some time before I even noticed that there was a best chair and that this silent, bright-eyed, dapper, fair man had secured it.

"Very good story," he said; "but it's not what I call realism. You don't tell us half enough, sir. You don't say when it happened or where, or the time of year, or what color your aunt's second cousin's hair was. Nor yet you don't tell us what it was she saw, nor what the room was like where she saw it, nor why she saw it, nor what happened afterwards. And I shouldn't like to breathe a word against anybody's aunt by marriage's cousin, first or second, but I must say I like a story about what a man's seen *himself*."

"So do I," the large commercial snorted, "when I hear it."

He blew his nose like a trumpet of defiance.

"But," said the rabbit-faced man, "we know nowadays, what with the advance of science and all that sort of thing, we know there aren't any such things as ghosts. They're hallucinations; that's what they are—hallucinations."

"Don't seem to matter what you call them," the dapper one urged. "If you see a thing that looks as real as you do yourself, a thing that makes your blood run cold and turns you sick and silly with fear—well, call it ghost, or call it hallucination, or call it Tommy Dodd; it isn't the *name* that matters."

The elderly commercial coughed and said, "You might call it another name. You might call it—"

"No, you mightn't," said the little man, briskly; "not when the man it happened to had been a teetotal Bond of Joy for five years and is to this day."

"Why don't you tell us the story?" I asked.

"I might be willing," he said, "if the rest of the company were agreeable. Only I warn you it's not that sort-of-a-kind-of-a-somebody fancied-they-saw-a-sort-of-a-kind-of-a-something-sort of a story. No, sir. Everything I'm going to tell you is plain and straightforward and as clear as a time-table-clearer than some. But I don't much like telling it, especially to people who don't believe in ghosts."

Several of us said we did believe in ghosts. The heavy man snorted and looked at his watch. And the man in the best chair began.

"Tum the gas down a bit, will you? Thanks. Did any of you know Herbert Hatteras? He was on this road a good many years. No? Well, never mind. He was a good chap, I believe, with good teeth and a black whisker. But I didn't know him myself. He was before my time. Well, this that I'm going to tell you about happened at a certain commercial hotel. I'm not going to give it a name, because that sort of thing gets about, and in every other respect it's a good house and reasonable, and we all have our living to get. It was just a good ordinary, old-fashioned commercial hotel, as it might be this. And I've often used it since, though they've never put me in that room again. Perhaps they shut it up after what happened.

"Well, the beginning of it was, I came across an old school-fellow; in Boulter's Lock one Sunday it was, I remember. Jones was his name, Ted Jones. We both had canoes. We had tea at Marlow, and we got talking about this and that and old times and old mates; and do you remember Jim, and what's become of Tom, and so on. Oh, you know. And I happened to ask after his brother, Fred by name. And Ted turned pale and almost dropped his cup, and he said, 'You don't mean to say you haven't heard?' 'No,' says I, mopping up the tea he'd slopped over with my handkerchief. 'No; what?' I said.

" 'It was horrible,' he said. 'They wired for me, and I saw him afterwards. Whether he'd done it himself or not, nobody knows; but they'd found him lying on the floor with his throat cut.' No cause could be assigned for the rash act, Ted told me. I asked him where it had happened, and he told me the name of this hotel—I'm not going to name it. And when I'd sympathised with him and drawn him out about old times and poor old Fred being such a good old sort and all that, I asked him what the room was like. I always like to know what the places look like where things happen.

"No, there wasn't anything specially rum about the room, only that it had a French bed with red curtains in a sort of alcove; and a large mahogany wardrobe as big as a hearse, with a glass door; and, instead of a swing-glass, a carved, black-framed glass screwed up against the wall between the windows, and a picture of 'Belshazzar's Feast' over the mantelpiece. I beg your pardon?" He stopped, for the heavy commercial had opened his mouth and shut it again.

"I thought you were going to say something," the dapper man went on. "Well, we talked about other things and parted, and I thought no more about it till business brought me to—but I'd better not name the town either—and I found my firm had marked this very hotel—where poor Fred had met his death, you know—for me to put up at. And I had to put up there too, because of their addressing everything to me there. And, anyhow, I expect I should have gone there out of curiosity.

"No. I didn't believe in ghosts in those days. I was like you, sir," he nodded amiably to the large commercial.

"The house was very full and we were quite a large party in the room—very pleasant company, as it might be tonight; and we got talking of ghosts—just as it might be us. And there was a chap in glasses, sitting just over there, I remember—an old hand on the road he was; and he said, just as it might be any of you, 'I don't believe in ghosts, but I wouldn't care to sleep in Number Seventeen, for all that'; and, of course, we asked him why. 'Because,' said he, very short, 'that's why.'

"But when we'd persuaded him a bit, he told us.

"'Because that's the room where chaps cut their throats,' he said.

"'There was a chap called Bert Hatteras began it. They found him weltering in his gore. And since that every man that's slept there's been found with his throat cut.'

"I asked him how many had slept there. 'Well, only two beside the first,' he said; 'they shut it up then.' 'Oh, did they?' said I. 'Well, they've opened it again. Number Seventeen's my room!'

"I tell you those chaps looked at me.

"'But you aren't going to sleep in it?' one of them said. And explained that I didn't pay half a dollar for a bedroom to keep awake in.

"'I suppose it's press of business has made them open it up again,' the chap in spectacles said. 'It's a very mysterious affair. There's some secret horror about that room that we don't understand,' he said, 'and I'll tell you another queer thing. Every one of those poor chaps was a commercial gentleman. That's what I don't like about it. There was Bert Hatteras—he was the first, and a chap called Jones-Frederick Jones, and then Donald Overshaw—a Scotchman he was and travelled in child's underclothing.'

"Well, we sat there and talked a bit, and if I hadn't been a Bond of Joy, I don't know that I mightn't have exceeded, gentlemen—yes, positively exceeded for the more I thought about it the less I liked the thought of Number Seventeen. I hadn't noticed the room particularly, except to see that the furniture had been changed since poor Fred's time. So I just slipped out, by-and-by and I went out to the little glass case under the arch where the booking-clerk sits—just like here, that hotel was—and I said, 'Look here, miss; haven't you another room empty except seventeen?'

"'No,' she said; 'I don't think so.'

"'Then what's that?' I said, and pointed to a key hanging on the board, the only one left.

"'Oh,' she said, 'that's sixteen.'

" 'Anyone in sixteen?' I said. 'Is it a comfortable room?'

" 'No,' said she. 'Yes; quite comfortable. It's next door to yours—much the same class of room.'

" 'Then I'll have sixteen, if you've no objection,' I said, and went back to the others, feeling very clever.

"When I went up to bed I locked my door, and, though I didn't believe in ghosts, I wished seventeen wasn't next door to me, and I wished there wasn't a door between the two rooms, though the door was locked right enough and the key in my side. I'd only got the one candle besides the two on the dressing-table, which I hadn't lighted; and I got my collar and tie off before I noticed that the furniture in my new room was the furniture out of Number Seventeen; French bed with red curtains, mahogany wardrobe as big as a hearse, and the carved mirror over the dressing-table between the two windows, and 'Belshazzar's Feast' over the mantelpiece. So that, though I'd not got the room where the commercial gentlemen had cut their throats, I'd got the *furniture* out of it. And for a moment I thought that was worse than the other. When I thought of what the furniture could tell, if it could speak—

"It was a silly thing to do—but we're all friends here and I don't mind owning up—I looked under the bed and I looked inside the hearse-wardrobe and I looked in a sort of narrow cupboard there was, where a body could have stood upright—"

"A body?" I repeated.

"A man, I mean. You see, it seemed to me that either these poor chaps had been murdered by someone who hid himself in Number Seventeen to do it, or else there was something there that frightened them into cutting their throats; and upon my soul, I can't tell you which idea I liked least!"

He paused, and filled his pipe very deliberately. "Go on," someone said. And he went on.

"Now, you'll observe," he said, "that all I've told you up to the time of my going to bed that night's just hearsay. So I don't ask you to believe it—though the three coroners' inquests would be enough to stagger most chaps, I should say. Still, what I'm going to tell you now's my part of the story—what happened to me myself in that room." He paused again, holding the pipe in his hand, unlighted.

There was a silence, which I broke.

"Well, what *did* happen?" I asked.

"I had a bit of a struggle with myself," he said. "I reminded myself it was not that room, but the next one that it had happened in. I smoked a pipe or two and read the morning paper, advertisements and all. And at last I went to bed. I left the candle burning, though, I own that."

"Did you sleep?" I asked.

"Yes. I slept. Sound as a top. I was awakened by a soft tapping on my door. I sat up. I don't think I've ever been so frightened in my life. But I made myself say, 'Who's there?' in a whisper. Heaven knows I never expected anyone to answer. The candle had gone out and it was pitch-dark. There was a quiet murmur and a shuffling outside. And no one answered. I tell you I hadn't expected anyone to. But I cleared my throat and cried out, 'Who's there?' in a real out-loud voice. And 'Me, sir,' said a voice. 'Shaving-water, sir; six o'clock, sir.'

"It was the chambermaid."

A movement of relief ran round our circle.

"I don't think much of your story," said the large commercial.

"You haven't heard it yet," said the story-teller, dryly. "It was six o'clock on a winter's morning, and pitch-dark. My train went at seven. I got up and began to dress. My one candle wasn't much use. I lighted the two on the dressing-table to see to shave by. There wasn't any shaving-water outside my door, after all. And the passage was as black as a coal-bole. So I started to shave with cold water; one has to sometimes, you know. I'd gone over my face and I was just going lightly round under my chin when I saw something move in the looking-glass. I mean something that moved was reflected in the looking-glass. The big door of the wardrobe had swung open and by a sort of double reflection I could see the French bed with the red curtains. On the edge of it sat a man in his shirt and trousers—a man with black hair and whiskers, with the most awful look of despair and fear on his face that I've ever seen or dreamt of. I stood paralysed, watching him in the mirror. I could not have turned round to save my life. Suddenly he laughed. It was a horrid, silent laugh, and showed all his teeth. They were very white and even. And the next moment he had cut his throat from ear to ear, there before my eyes. Did you ever see a man cut his throat? The bed was all white before."

The story-teller had laid down his pipe, and he passed his hand over his face before he went on.

"When I could look round I did. There was no one in the room. The bed was as white as ever. Well, that's all," he said, abruptly, "except that now, of course, I understood how these poor chaps had come by their deaths. They'd all seen this horror—the ghost of the first poor chap, I suppose—Bert Hatteras, you know; and with the shock their hands must have slipped and their throats got cut before they could stop themselves.

Oh! by the way, when I looked at my watch it was two o'clock; there hadn't been any chambermaid at all. I must have dreamed that. But I didn't dream the other. Oh! and one thing more. It was the same room. They hadn't changed the room, they'd only changed the number. *It was the same room*!"

"Look here," said the heavy man; "the room you've been talking about. My room's sixteen. And it's got that same furniture in it as what you describe, and the same picture and all."

"Oh, has it?" said the story-teller, a little uncomfortable, it seemed. "I'm sorry. But the cat's out of the bag now, and it can't be helped. Yes, it was this house I was speaking of. I suppose they've opened the room again. But you don't believe in ghosts; you'll be all right."

"Yes," said the heavy man, and presently got up and left the room.

"He's gone to see if he can get his room changed, you see if he hasn't," said the rabbit-faced man; "and I don't wonder."

The heavy man came back and settled into his chair.

"I could do with a drink," he said, reaching to the bell.

"I'll stand some punch, gentlemen, if you'll allow me," said our dapper story-teller. "I rather pride myself on my punch. I'll step out to the bar and get what I need for it."

"I thought he said he was a teetotaller," said the heavy traveller when he had gone. And then our voices buzzed like a hive of bees. When our story-teller came in again we turned on him-half-a-dozen of us at once—and spoke.

"One at a time," he said gently. "I didn't quite catch what you said."

"We want to know," I said, "how it was—if seeing that ghost made all those chaps cut their throats by startling them when they were shaving—how was it *you* didn't cut *your* throat when you saw it?"

"I should have," he answered, gravely, "without the slightest doubt—I should have cut my throat, only," he glanced at our heavy friend, "I always shave with a safety razor. I travel in them," he added, slowly, and bisected a lemon.

"But—but," said the large man, when he could speak through our uproar, "I've gone and given up my room."

"Yes," said the dapper man, squeezing the lemon; "I've just had my things moved into it, it's the best room in the house. I always think it worth while to take a little pains to secure it."

On the Turn of a Coin

Cleveland Moffett

Down the corridor, walking carefully, came four hospital attendants, holding the stretcher resting on two large wheels, rolling noiselessly. The operation was over. On the stretcher lay a young woman, unconscious. Her face was beautiful, but white as the covering sheets, and her head was wound with bandages. She breathed faintly through parted lips.

Out of the operating-room came the surgeon who had finished his work, and with him his assistants, young men in blouses and black caps, most of them wearing pointed beards. An odor of carbolic acid followed them.

"Poor girl," said one, as he watched the stretcher turn into one of the wards. "I wonder if she'll speak before she dies."

"It will be better for her assassin if she doesn't," said another.

Then they went off to various duties. Last of all came Auguste Caseau, hurrying and behindhand, as usual. He had risen late, had reached the hospital late, and had had no breakfast. Of all the medical students at the Lariboisière Hospital there was none more popular than Caseau, but the pleasures of Paris at night often made him neglect his duties of the day. In the present instance he did not know who the young woman was whom he had just seen under the knife, nor had he any idea how her skull had been crushed with such frightful wounds. All he knew was that she had remarkable beauty and was doomed to die.

He was hurrying off to a neighboring café when a stranger waiting at the door touched his arm. The man's eyes were eager, he spoke with ill-concealed excitement and seemed like one who had gone many hours without sleep.

"Tell me," he said, "did she speak?"

Caseau shook his head, looking at the man suspiciously.

"Can she live?"

"God knows, the doctor took sixteen pieces of bone out of her head."

"Holy Mother, sixteen pieces of bone!"

Caseau was walking meantime toward the café, and the man followed him. His eagerness for information betrayed an interest in the case that argued some special knowledge, and Caseau was curious. "Will you drink?" he said, when they had taken seats at a table.

The stranger called for absinthe and drained his glass quickly. "I must ask one more question, my friend," he said. "Tell me where were the wounds on this girl's head—were they on the back?"

"They were," assented Caseau, who had ordered his breakfast.

"Were there none in front, none on the forehead nor on the face?"

Caseau shook his head. "There were none."

"How strange," muttered the man. "She was facing him when . . ."

"Facing whom?" asked Caseau sharply, and the question seemed to bring the man to his senses.

"Pardon me; I forgot that you do not know. I have been through so much for the last twelve hours that I am dazed. Do you believe in occult things, hallucinations and so on?"

Caseau was only in his second year, and the lectures on hallucinations did not begin until the third, so he answered guardedly.

"That depends," he said, with an air of holding knowledge in reserve. He questioned with his eyes, and for the first time appeared sympathetic. The man ordered another absinthe.

"I will tell you about it," he said. "I shall go mad unless I tell some one. In the first place, let me assure you that usually I am the most matter-of-fact man in Paris; I never get angry, I never get excited, but last night—" He paused and a little shiver ran over him.

"But last night," repeated Caseau encouragingly.

"It was about nine o'clock, and I was walking up the Rue Fontaine with my hat off because the night was hot, and whistling because business had been good. You see I am a grocer down on the Street of the Four Winds. When I reached the corner of the Rue Breda, where I live, I stopped in a little cake-shop to buy some sweets for my wife. Then I hurried upstairs, two at a time, for I was eager to see her. Our apartment is on the fifth floor, looking out on the Rue Fontaine, and a balcony runs along the windows where my wife keeps flowers growing. It is a nice place to sit summer evenings, and I expected to find her there.

"Imagine my surprise, then, on opening the door, to find the apartment quite dark, except for the glow of the little night-lamp from the bedroom at the end of the corridor. And instead of seeing my wife come running to meet me, all smiles, I found absolute stillness in the place, stillness and darkness. In that moment, as I stood with the door ajar, and my hand on the knob, there came over me a creeping sense of fear, something I had never known before. It seemed to me that some great danger was lurking in the air, that some evil presence was near me. So strong was this feeling that, acting on the first impulse, I stepped back on to the landing outside and closed the door behind me.

"In an instant, however, my reason reasserted itself, and ashamed of my weakness I opened the door again, closed it sharply behind me, and double-locked it. Then hanging my hat on a hook at one side I started down the corridor. There was a distance of twenty feet that I had to traverse before reaching the bedroom, and I assure you that I never in my life endured such torture as I felt in taking those few steps. At first it was a fear for myself that held me back, but presently this was superseded by a horrible sickening fear for my wife. I saw it was she whose life was threatened, or had been threatened, for the conviction grew upon me that I had come too late. When I was half-way down the corridor, I clutched the wall with one hand and pressed the other to my brow, which was throbbing with frightful fancies. They say that drowning men see strange things as death comes on, but no drowning man, I am sure, ever saw a vision more distinct than came to me there of my poor wife."

By this time Caseau was listening intently.

"She is a beautiful woman, I beg you to believe, and I saw her as plainly as I see you now, stretched on the bed, her face as lovely as ever in its setting of dark hair, only very pale. But there were wounds, dreadful wounds, on the back of the head, from which the pillow was stained crimson."

"But this was only the vision?" put in Caseau.

"Yes, a vision. God grant you may never have one. I was unable to move, afraid to speak. I seemed rooted to the floor.

"Finally my will conquered, and I staggered into the bedroom. With an awful fascination my eyes sought the bed, around which were drawn the red curtains. On the side toward me, on a little table, burned the night lamp. Everything in the room seemed as usual—there was no sign that ill had come—yet I cannot tell you with what feelings I stepped forward and drew apart the curtains. My wife lay there apparently sleeping, her lovely face turned toward me, and the pillow beneath her head as white as her hand that pressed it. With a sigh of relief I sank into a chair. At that moment I was startled to hear, behind the curtains, a gasping sob, and then a burst of hysterical weeping. Hurrying to the bedside I besought my wife to be calm, assuring her that I was there to protect her.

"At last my wife recovered sufficiently to explain her fright as well as she was able to do so. She had dined alone about six o'clock and about seven had given Amandine, our servant, permission to go out for the evening. Then she had spent a little time tidying up the apartment, and about half-past seven had settled down to read in the room where we have our library. This room faces on the Rue Breda. In front of this room there is a short stretch of balcony, which ends in an iron partition that separates it from the balcony of the house adjoining, which is No. 4. It would be possible for a man to climb over this partition and step from one balcony to the other.

"As my wife read she must have dozed, for presently, although her back was turned to the window, she seemed to see a man of large stature standing on the balcony outside and peering into the room. This man had bushy red hair and eyes of the palest blue—eyes that frightened her. Presently he withdrew stealthily, climbed over the partition, and peered into a window of No. 4. Once again he drew back, seemed to hesitate, smiled with a grim humor and noiselessly drawing a coin from his pocket spun it in the air and caught it deftly in his open palm. Then moving closer to the window for better light he nodded, put the coin back in his pocket and forthwith entered the room where my wife sat, passing easily through the long, door-like halves of the window, that were swung wide open.

"Spellbound, my wife watched the man, who paid no heed to her, but made his way at once to the bedroom, she following in mortal terror. Approaching the bed he noticed that its curtains were drawn and paused a moment, casting his eyes about him as if in search for something. Near the fireplace lay a heavy brass poker which he picked up, returning with it to the bedside. Breathless my wife watched as he put aside the curtains. A woman lay there sleeping, with her face turned away, but my wife thought it was herself. She saw the man lift the poker as if to strike, at which the woman lying in the bed started and looked toward him. At this my wife's terror burst the bonds in her throat and she cried aloud.

"Of course it was only fancy, a dream, if you like, something that was not real, for the next instant she was alone in the room. But the effect was most distressing. Do what she would she could not drive from her mind the face of that tawny-haired assassin, with his pale blue eyes. It seemed to her that he was still near her with murderous purpose. In vain, lamp in hand, she searched the apartment, and tried to convince herself that nothing was there; in vain she closed and bolted the windows opening on the balcony. That sense of nameless fear pursued her still; and whichever way she turned it seemed to her that an enemy was crouching behind her, waiting his chance to spring or strike.

"Finally she went to bed, hoping that sleep would give her some relief; but she could not sleep, she could not get her thoughts out of the morbid channel in which they were running. So, anxious, restless, sick at heart, she had waited for me to come, and my coming, alas, brought her only added terrors, for my strange delay at the door, my opening it twice and closing it, then my long pause and silence in the corridor, instead of the cheery greeting I was wont to give her, made her sure that it was not I at all, but some intruder come to do her harm, some prowling assailant of the night, perhaps the very man whose eyes and fiery hair had frightened her so in the vision.

"Then, realizing that it was her husband who was there, the man who loved her, and that there was no danger at all, she burst into the fit of hysterical sobbing from which I had such difficulty in calming her."

"You are preventing me from eating my breakfast, sir, with your queer story," said Caseau. "And besides, I can't see what it has to do with the young woman who has just been operated on."

"Let me finish," said the man, "let me finish. We hardly slept all night, for our fears persisted in spite of the knowledge that no harm had befallen. I made matters worse by foolishly telling my wife of the fright I had experienced on entering the apartment, and my vision of the murdered woman. You will remember particularly that the wounds were on the back of the head, and you tell me that is where they really were."

"That is where they were on the woman in the hospital, but she is not your wife?"

"No, thank heaven, but you know who she is?"

"Not I," said Caseau. "I got in too late to learn any details."

"She is Marie Gagnol, who occupied the apartment adjoining ours in No. 4, Rue Breda."

"My God!" exclaimed Caseau.

Just then one of the other students came in from the hospital. "She's dead," he said. "She never spoke. But they are going to try an important experiment on her. Dr. Rosseau thinks she closed her eyes with fright at the very moment when she saw the murderer, and never opened them since. He's going to test his new apparatus for getting the last image recorded on the retina. If he succeeds it will be a new triumph for the hospital and for science."

"Gentlemen," said the stranger impressively, "if the doctor's experiment succeeds I believe on my soul that it will also be a triumph for justice."

That afternoon Dr. Rosseau made the experiment, with brilliant success; it was one of the first demonstrations of the possibilities of colored photography. Registered in the sensitive film of the dead woman's eyes, was found the distinct image of a man of unusual size, who clutched in his hands an uplifted poker. The man's hair was red, his eyes a pale blue.

Two months later such a man died under the knife on the Place de la Roquette. He had been arrested, convicted and condemned on the sole evidence of a pair of lifeless eye-balls, supported by the testimony of a woman who had never seen him except in a vision. On the eve of his execution he made a full confession. He stated that the murder was a chance crime, prompted only by greed. He had reached the balcony running in front of Nos. 2 and 4 Rue Breda by using a rope hung from the roof. He declared that for about five minutes while he was standing outside he had hesitated whether to enter the apartment of No. 2 or No. 4. He had rested the decision on the turn of a coin.

Only a Dream

H. Rider Haggard

Footprints—footprints—the footprints of one dead. How ghastly they look as they fall before me! Up and down the long hall they go, and I follow them. *Pit, pat* they fall, those unearthly steps, and beneath them starts up that awful impress. I can see it grow upon the marble, a damp and dreadful thing.

Tread them down; tread them out; follow after them with muddy shoes, and cover them up. In vain. See how they rise through the mire! Who can tread out the footprints of the dead?

And so on, up and down the dim vista of the past, following the sound of the dead feet that wander so restlessly, stamping upon the impress that will not be stamped out. Rave on, wild wind, eternal voice of human misery; fall, dead footsteps, eternal echo of human memory; stamp, miry feet; stamp into forgetfulness that which will not be forgotten.

And so on, on to the end.

Pretty ideas these for a man about to be married, especially when they float into his brain at night like ominous clouds into a summer sky, and he is going to be married to-morrow. There is no mistake about it—the wedding, I mean. To be plain and matter-of-fact, why there stand the presents, or some of them, and very handsome presents they are, ranged in solemn rows upon the long table. It is a remarkable thing to observe when one is about to make a really satisfactory marriage how scores of unsuspected or forgotten friends crop up and send little tokens of their esteem. It was very different when I married my first wife, I remember, but then that marriage was not satisfactory—just a love-match, no more.

There they stand in solemn rows, as I have said, and inspire me with beautiful thoughts about the innate kindness of human nature, especially the human nature of our distant cousins. It is possible to grow almost poetical over a silver teapot when one is going to be married to-morrow. On how many future mornings shall I be confronted with that teapot? Probably for all my life; and on the other side of the teapot will be the cream jug, and the electroplated urn will hiss away behind them both. Also the chased sugar basin will be in front, full of sugar, and behind everything will be my second wife.

"My dear," she will say, "will you have another cup of tea?" and probably I shall have another cup.

Well, it is very curious to notice what ideas will come into a man's head sometimes. Sometimes something waves a magic wand over his being, and from the recesses of his soul dim things arise and walk. At unexpected moments they come, and he grows aware of the issues of his mysterious life, and his heart shakes and shivers like a lightning-shattered tree. In that drear light all earthly things seem far, and all unseen things draw near and take shape and awe him, and he knows not what is true and what is false, neither can he trace the edge that marks off the Spirit from the Life. Then it is that the footsteps echo, and the ghostly footprints will not be stamped out.

Pretty thoughts again! and how persistently they come! It is one o'clock and I will go to bed. The rain is falling in sheets outside. I can hear it lashing against the window panes, and the wind wails through the tall wet elms at the end of the garden. I could tell the voice of those elms anywhere; I know it as well as the voice of a friend. What a night it is; we sometimes get them in this part of England in October. It was just such a night when my first wife died, and that is three years ago. I remember how she sat up in her bed.

"Ah! those horrible elms," she said; "I wish you would have them cut down, Frank; they cry like a woman," and I said I would, and just after that she died, poor dear. And so the old elms stand, and I like their music. It is a strange thing; I was half broken-hearted, for I loved her dearly, and she loved me with all her life and strength, and now—I am going to be married again.

"Frank, Frank, don't forget me!" Those were my wife's last words; and, indeed, though I am going to be married again to-morrow, I have not forgotten her. Nor shall I forget how Annie Guthrie (whom I am going to marry now) came to see her the day before she died. I know that Annie always liked me more or less, and I think that my dear wife guessed it. After she had kissed Annie and bid her a last good-bye, and the door had closed, she spoke quite suddenly: "There goes your future wife, Frank," she said; "you should have married her at first instead of me; she is very handsome and very good, and she has two thousand a year; *she* would never have died of a nervous illness." And she laughed a little, and then added:

"Oh, Frank dear, I wonder if you will think of me before you marry Annie Guthrie. Wherever I am I shall be thinking of you."

And now that time which she foresaw has come, and Heaven knows that I have thought of her, poor dear. Ah! those footsteps of one dead that will echo through our lives, those woman's footprints on the marble flooring which will not be stamped out. Most of us have heard and seen them at some time or other, and I hear and see them very plainly to-night. Poor dead wife, I wonder if there are any doors in the land where you have gone through which you can creep out to look at me to-night? I hope that there are none. Death must indeed be a hell if the dead can see and feel and take measure of the forgetful faithlessness of their beloved. Well, I will go to bed and try to get a little rest. I am not so young or so strong as I was, and this wedding wears me out. I wish that the whole thing were done or had never been begun.

What was that? It was not the wind, for it never makes that sound here, and it was not the rain, since the rain has ceased its surging for a moment; nor was it the howling of a dog, for I keep none. It was more like the crying of a woman's voice; but what woman can be abroad on such a night or at such an hour—half-past one in the morning?

There it is again—a dreadful sound; it makes the blood turn chill, and yet has something familiar about it. It is a woman's voice calling round the house. There, she is at the window now, and rattling it, and, great heavens! she is calling me.

"Frank! Frank! Frank!" she calls.

I strive to stir and unshutter that window, but before I can get there she is knocking and calling at another.

Gone again, with her dreadful wail of "Frank! Frank!" Now I hear her at the front door, and, half mad with a horrible fear, I run down the long, dark hall and unbar it. There is nothing there—nothing but the wild rush of the wind and the drip of the rain from the portico. But I can hear the wailing voice going round the house, past the patch of shrubbery. I close the door and listen. There, she has got through the little yard, and is at the back door now. Whoever it is, she must know the way about the house. Along the hall I go again, through a swing door, through the servants' hall, stumbling down some steps into the kitchen, where the embers of the fire are still alive in the grate, diffusing a little warmth and light into the dense gloom.

Whoever it is at the door is knocking now with her clenched fist against the hard wood, and it is wonderful, though she knocks so low, how the sound echoes through the empty kitchens.

There I stood and hesitated, trembling in every limb; I dared not open the door. No words of mine can convey the sense of utter desolation that overpowered me. I felt as though I were the only living man in the whole world.

"*Frank*! *Frank*!" cries the voice with the dreadful familiar ring in it. "Open the door; I am so cold. I have so little time."

My heart stood still, and yet my hands were constrained to obey. Slowly, slowly I lifted the latch and unbarred the door, and, as I did so, a great rush of air snatched it from my hands and swept it wide. The black clouds had broken a little overhead, and there was a patch of blue, rain-washed sky with just a star or two glimmering in it fitfully. For a moment I could only see this bit of sky, and by degrees I made out the accustomed outline of the great trees swinging furiously against it, and the rigid line of the coping of the garden wall beneath them. Then a whirling leaf hit me smartly on the face, and instinctively I dropped my eyes on to something that as yet I could not distinguish—something small and black and wet.

"What are you?" I gasped. Somehow I seemed to feel that it was not a person—I could not say, "*Who* are you?"

"Don't you know me?" wailed the voice, with the far-off familiar ring about it. "And I mayn't come in and show myself. I haven't the time. You were so long opening the door, Frank, and I am so cold—oh, so bitterly cold! Look there, the moon is coming out, and you will be able to see me. I suppose that you long to see me, as I have longed to see you."

As the figure spoke, or rather wailed, a moonbeam struggled through the watery air and fell on it. It was short and shrunken, the figure of a tiny woman. Also it was dressed in black and wore a black covering over the whole head, shrouding it, after the fashion of a bridal veil. From every part of this veil and dress the water fell in heavy drops.

The figure bore a small basket on her left arm, and her hand—such a poor thin little hand—gleamed white in the moonlight. I noticed that on the third finger was a red line, showing that a wedding-ring had once been there. The other hand was stretched towards me as though in entreaty.

All this I saw in an instant, as it were, and as I saw it, horror seemed to grip me by the throat as though it were a living thing, for as the voice had been familiar, so was the form familiar, though the churchyard had received it long years ago. I could not speak—I could not even move.

"Oh, don't you know me yet?" wailed the voice; "and I have come from so far to see you, and I cannot stop. Look, look," and she began to pluck feverishly with her poor thin hand at the black veil that enshrouded her. At last it came off, and, as in a dream, I saw what in a dim frozen way I had expected to see—the white face and pale yellow hair of my dead wife. Unable to speak or stir. I gazed and gazed. There was no mistake about it, it was she, ay, even as I had last seen her, white with the whiteness of death, with purple circles round her eyes and the grave-cloth yet beneath her chin. Only her eyes were wide open and fixed upon my face; and a lock of the soft yellow hair had broken loose, and the wind tossed it.

"You know me now, Frank—don't you, Frank? It has been so hard to come and see you, and so cold! But you are going to be married to-morrow, Frank; and I promised—oh, a long time ago—to think of you when you were going to be married wherever I was, and I have kept my promise, and I have come from where I am and brought a present with me. It was bitter to die so young! I was so young to die and leave you, but I had to go. Take it—take it; be quick, I cannot stay any longer. *I could not give you my life, Frank, so I have brought you my death—take it*!"

The figure thrust the basket into my hand, and as it did so the rain came up again, and began to obscure the moonlight.

"I must go, I must go," went on the dreadful, familiar voice, in a cry of despair. "Oh, why were you so long opening the door? I waited to talk to you before you married Annie; and now I shall never see you again—never! never! never! I have lost you for ever! ever! ever!"

As the last wailing notes dies away the wind came down with a rush and a whirl and the sweep as of a thousand wings, and threw me back into the house, bringing the door to with a crash after me.

I staggered into the kitchen, the basket in my hand, and set it on the table. Just then some embers of the fire fell in, and a faint little flame rose and glimmered on the bright dishes on the dresser, even revealing a tin candlestick, with a box of matches by it. I was well-nigh mad with the darkness and fear, and, seizing the matches, I struck one, and held it to the candle. Presently it caught, and I glanced round the room. It was just as usual, just as the servants had left it, and above the mantelpiece the eight-day clock ticked away solemnly. While I looked at it it struck two, and in a dim fashion I was thankful for its friendly sound.

Then I looked at the basket. It was of very fine white plaited work with black bands running up it, and a chequered black-and-white handle. I knew it well. I have never seen another like it. I bought it years ago at Medeira, and gave it to my poor wife.

Ultimately it was washed overboard in a gale in the Irish Channel. I remember that it was full of newspapers and library books, and I had to pay for them. Many and many is the time that I have seen that identical basket standing there on that very kitchen table, for my dear wife always used it to put flowers in, and the shortest cut from that part of the garden where her roses grew was through the kitchen. She used to gather the flowers, and then come in and place her basket on the table, just where it stood now, and order the dinner.

All this passed through my mind in a few seconds as I stood there with the candle in my hand, feeling indeed half dead, and yet with my mind painfully alive. I began to wonder if I had gone asleep, and was the victim of a nightmare. No such thing. I wish it had only been a nightmare. A mouse ran out along the dresser and jumped on to the floor, making quite a crash in the silence.

What was in the basket? I feared to look, and yet some power within me forced me to it. I drew near to the table and stood for a moment listening to the sound of my own heart. Then I stretched out my hand and slowly raised the lid of the basket.

"I could not give you my life, so I have brought you my death!" Those were her words. What could she mean—what could it all mean? I must know or I should go mad. There it lay, whatever it was, wrapped up in linen.

Ah, heaven help me! It was a small bleached human skull!

A dream! After all, only a dream by the fire, but what a dream. And I am to be married to-morrow.

Can I be married to-morrow?

The Other Sense

J. S. Fletcher

Oct. 21st.—They have told me to-day, with obvious reluctance, and in the kindest fashion, that I am to go to-morrow to the house of a Dr. Schreiber, in whose care I am to remain until I am restored to health. Restored to health!—my God! I am as healthy a lad of nineteen (I believe) as any one would wish to meet; certainly I have no recollection of any illness beyond a dose of measles when I was seven, and a very slight touch of scarlet fever a few years ago. Restored to health!—no, that is merely their kind way of putting it. What they really mean is: I am to go and live with this Dr. Schreiber, whoever he may be, until he, and they, and the doctors whom they have brought to see so often lately, think I am—*sane*.

That, of course, is the real truth. I have often wondered as I have grown up out of my lonely childhood towards manhood, how strange it is that what seems so easy to the child about truth-telling seems so difficult to the man—I am beginning to understand. All the same, it would have been much more to my taste if my guardian and his wife had said to me, "Angus, we're very, very sorry, but the doctors and we don't think everything is as it should be with your intellect, and Dr. Schreiber is a famous mental specialist, and—" so on.

But then—equally, of course—they couldn't have said that to me if they really believe that I *am* mad. And they do. *I* know—I have seen them not once, but a thousand times since I came here to London from Alt-na-Shiel two years ago (when shall I see it again, and the mists on the mountains!), watching me as country folk watch the freaks at a fair. There is a puzzled look which comes into their faces; their brows knit, and their lips are slowly compressed, or pursed up, and—if they think I do not see them—*they look at each other and shake their heads and sigh.*

I cannot think of more than three things which should make them believe me mad. One is that I am very fond of solitude, liking to be left to myself as much as I can. Another is that I think a great deal—just as I read a great deal—and that I sometimes frown at my thoughts, sometimes smile at them, sometimes laugh, long and loud, at them. Perhaps, when Major Kennedy and Mrs. Kennedy and I are alone after dinner, he reading *The Times* and she busied with her knitting, behaviour of this sort on my part may seem strange—it is only now occurring to me that it may. Certainly I have seen the Major drop his newspaper and jump—literally *jump*—in his arm-chair when, thinking of something that amused me, I have indulged in a sudden peal of laughter—yet why should one not laugh whenever one sees or thinks of something to laugh at? But I have found that a great many of the people whom I have met in London only laugh when a sort of signal is given.

Those are two reasons. The only other reason I can think of is that I have told them once or twice—just as I told the doctors whom they have at times brought to see me—that I can *see* things which, I find out, most other people do not or cannot see. The first time I told them, for instance, of the spirit which I have seen a score or so of times at Alt-na-Shiel, they stared at me as if I were telling them lies, and they both looked curiously uncomfortable. Now, my old nurse, Margaret Lang, never looked uncomfortable when I told her of these things, neither did Dugald Graeme, my father's old body-servant. They seemed to realize and to understand my meaning.

I have been thinking to-day (since I heard what my guardian and his wife had to tell me—he, poor man, in his stiff military-modelled sentences, and she more by tears than by words) about my life as a child and afterwards as a boy. Alt-na-Shiel is in one of the loneliest glens of the Strathern Mountains—a very great way indeed from the railways. There my father—Angus MacIntyre, like myself—went to live just after he was married to my mother, and there my mother died just after I was born. My father was a man of books, and after my mother's death he thought of nothing but books. Margaret Lang—helped by Dugald Graeme—brought me up, but after I was able to walk, my real nurse and mother was the open air. I used to sit out—anywhere—all day long, content to see the sky, and hear the countryside sounds, and smell the heather and the gorse and the bracken. And I cannot remember, looking back, when it was that I did not see things that other people did not see. I was never afraid of anything that I ever saw.

I have gone on *seeing* ever since—now, usually, at long intervals. When I was seventeen my father died, and it was found that Major Kennedy, a distant connection, was to be my guardian, and that I was to live with him until my twenty-first year. That is why I am now writing this in my journal in my own room in Major Kennedy's house in Bayswater—and why I am to-morrow to take up my residence with Dr. Schreiber at Wimbledon Common. Possibly I am writing it because, for anything I know, this may be my last day of complete liberty. I do not know what the rules are in these private mad-houses—if this to which I am going is such a place.

If I may speak frankly to myself in these pages, I must say that I cannot see why I should be considered at all mentally afflicted. I am, as things go, fairly well educated;

fond as I am of solitude, I am fond of games, especially of football, golf, and tennis; I am certainly very strong in body, and of rude health. And as for my appetite . . .

However, they say I suffer from occasional delusions. We shall see.

II

Oct. 23rd.—I came here—to Dr. Schreiber's house—yesterday afternoon, accompanied by Dr. Wilkinson, one of the two doctors who have been to see me so often lately. The parting between the Kennedys and myself made me think of the conventional descriptions of boys going to school. Major Kennedy shook hands with me at least six times, and Mrs. Kennedy cried. Dr. Wilkinson and I talked football all the way from Bayswater to Wimbledon, and I found out that he got his Blue at Oxford—I forget in what year.

Just before we got to Wimbledon Common I thought I would have a little straightforward conversation with Dr. Wilkinson.

"Look here, sir," I said. "You, in common with Dr. Gordon and Major and Mrs. Kennedy, think I am a little mad?"

"I think that a few months' residence with Dr. Schreiber will turn you out as fit as a fiddle," he replied.

"Why do most people give an evasive answer when it would be much simpler to tell the truth in one word?" I asked him.

"Ah, why don't they?" he answered. "I've often wondered that myself."

"Or, again," said I, "how is it that people who happen through no fault of their own to possess a certain faculty, or certain faculties, which other people—most people—do not possess, are invariably considered to be—queer?"

He shook his head, and I relapsed into such a profound and cogitative silence that at last he asked me what I was thinking about.

"I was thinking, sir," I replied, "how admirably you would have filled the *rôle* of those physicians of the Middle Ages who, whenever powerful monarchs or statesmen wanted to get rid of any person inimical to them, were ever ready to testify to their madness and to enclose them within a dungeon or an oubliette, or—"

"Well, you'll not find Dr. Schreiber's place much of a dungeon, my boy!" he said, laughing. "Here we are, so you can see for yourself."

I got out of the brougham and looked about me. This house is an old-fashioned structure of red brick, covered over with climbing plants, and it stands in the midst of a bright green lawn, the flower-beds and borderings of which are just now cheerful with a profusion of autumn blooms. There is not a suspicion of anything prison-like about it—on the contrary, its appearance suggests freedom and liberty. My first glance at it forced me to set up a comparison between it and Bayswater.

Dr. Schreiber came out to meet us. He is a youngish man—perhaps thirty-five, perhaps forty—tall, muscular, broad-shouldered, bronzed, cheery. I should have taken him for one of the sweller sort of professional cricketers rather than for what I was led to believe him—a private mad-house keeper. He welcomed me in a very friendly way, and after Dr. Wilkinson had gone volunteered to show me round the house and grounds. I was somewhat astonished to find no one about, except servants in the house and a gardener sweeping up fallen leaves on the lawn.

"Where, sir," I asked, "are the rest of us?"

"The rest of whom?" he inquired, looking surprised.

"The rest of your other mad folk," I answered. "I am sent here because they think me mad."

He laughed—burst, rather, into laughter—and slapped my shoulders.

"Oh, hang all that, old chap!" he said. "There's no one here but you, myself, my assistant, Pollard, who's a real good sort, and the servants. You're as free as air here, and if I don't give you a first-class time it won't be my fault."

Later we fell to talking about golf. To-day, after he had been to visit his patients—he seems to have a pretty extensive practice—we managed to get a full round in before dusk came on. He beat me by two up and one to play.

III

Oct. 27th.—I have been very happy here so far—much happier, I believe—nay, am sure, than I have ever been since I left Alt-na-Shiel. Life is very pleasant in this house, and with Dr. Schreiber. He is very different, I think, to all other men I have ever met. I have beer with him frequently to visit some of his poorer patients—it seemed to me that he laughs them out of their complaints. I do not mean that he laughs at them, but that his cheeriness is infectious, and lifts them out of themselves. He is certainly a great man—a big *human.*

Last night, after dinner, he and I were playing billiards, and somehow—I do not know how—we reached the question of what those other people call my delusion. We sat down—this was the first time I had ever spoken of it to him—and I told him of some things which I had seen—especially of the ghost (if it is a ghost) of the parish clerk of Ardnashonach. Instead of looking as if he could scarcely believe his ears (as

Major Kennedy looks), or shaking his head (as Dr. Wilkinson did), he listened most intently, and asked me a lot of questions. Not questions about myself, which is what I detest, but sensible questions.

"And they aren't delusions, you know," I said at the end. "I *have* seen these things—*seen* them! You believe me?"

"Yes," he said, "I do. Look here—if you ever *see* anything while you're here, just come that minute and tell me. Now, then, we've time for another hundred before bed."

IV

Nov. 4th.—I have been examining this old house inside and out with some interest since Dr. Schreiber told me, a day or two ago, that it was once (a century or more ago) the residence of a famous statesman. It is, I think, Early Georgian, and has the most delightful rooms, many of which are panelled in oak to a considerable height. There is one, now used as a dining-room, but formerly the library, which attracts me more than all the rest. It has four high narrow windows overlooking the garden, and with its quaint old oak furniture (which Dr. Schreiber took over from his predecessor in the practice, a man named Turrell, who was, he says, one of the cleverest men of his day) it makes a picture of color and distinction. There is an old oak long settle near the deep fireplace in which I shall love to sit when the winter really settles in—if it ever does in this soft-aired, sunny south, so different to the far-away north.

V

Nov. 17th.—Something has happened.

That seems a trite enough thing to write down, but the three words, after all, mean much, followed by an explanation. The truth is, my curious sense (extra sense, I suppose), has manifested itself again. I believe the last time was five years ago, when I saw the fairies near the church of Dalnarossie.

Yesterday afternoon, about five o'clock, Dr. Schreiber having gone to London, and Mr. Pollard to visit a patient across the Common, I was alone in the dining-room, and sitting in the corner of the long settle. There was no light in the room except that of the fire, which had burnt itself down to that clear glow which fires get on sharp, frosty afternoons of late autumn. I had spent most of the time since lunch reading a curious old book which I had found in Dr. Schreiber's study the day before, and was leaning back against the cushions of the long settle with my eyes closed—thinking of what I had read, and enjoying the quiet of the shadowy, scarcely-lighted room—when

I suddenly *felt* that I was not alone. The feeling was so strong, so acute, that for a full minute I remained quiescent. At last I opened my eyes, knowing without doubt that I was going to see something.

What I saw was this:

There stood upon the big, square hearthrug, within a few feet of me, a young man whom I judged to be of about my own age—perhaps a little older. He was tall, he stooped slightly, and he was spare of figure. His attire was modern—a black morning coat and vest and dark, striped trousers—and he stood with his hands in his pockets, after the fashion affected by Eton boys—somewhat slouchingly. His head was bent forward, and at first I could not see his face, but he presently turned a little, and the glow of the fire fell on it. I knew then that I was regarding a ghost.

The face confirmed me in my belief that this was—had been, I should say—a young man of say, nineteen years of age. It was a sad, uneasy face—a face whereon were many signs of anxiety, trouble, perplexity—and it was curiously old. It was not a strong face—the chin was small and delicate; the mouth amiable, but weak; the eyes, big and blue, were the eyes of a child—and there was a frightened expression in them.

I sat perfectly still, watching. The figure remained in an irresolute position—fidgeting on the hearthrug for a minute or so—then it walked slowly to the window, stood looking out into the garden awhile, then came back to the hearthrug, lingered there a minute more, and finally crossed the room and opened the door. I followed it through the doorway on the instant; the servants had already lighted the hall lamp, and the hall was clearly illuminated. And the hall was empty. There was no figure there.

I told Dr. Schreiber all this after we had finished our usual game of billiards last night. He listened with the gravest attention to everything I said, and when I had finished merely remarked:

"Angus, if you should ever see this apparition, or whatever it may be, again, do not be afraid to tell me at once."

VI

Nov. 22nd.—I have seen the ghost of the young man again.

This afternoon I went out to stroll about the neighbourhood, and in the course of my wanderings turned into Wimbledon churchyard. I was walking aimlessly about the paths, looking at the tombstones and wondering if they had any unusual names or quaint epitaphs upon them, when I suddenly saw the apparition again, standing at the side of a grave which lay at the chancel end of the church. It was attired exactly as before, and stood in a similar fashion, slightly slouching, with its hands in the pockets of its trousers. The face was just as sad and troubled as ever, and had the same air of perplexity. The big, blue, childish eyes turned from the grave to the headstone, and from the headstone to the grave, as if trying to read something on the one or to see something on the other. Then they stared all round the churchyard—wonderingly.

I drew nearer, and looked at the inscription on the tombstone by which the ghost stood—in fact, I approached to within a few feet of the ghost itself. It seemed to me that it saw me—but only looked at me in the casual, uninterested way in which strangers regard each other.

The inscription was short and simple:

Here lieth the body of Major-General Sir Arthur Debenham, K.C.B.; born January 15th, 1831; died October 4th, 1892. Also that of Florence Georgiana, his wife; born September 12th, 1834; died February 7th, 1893. Also in memory of their only child, Everard; born August 12th, 1874; died July 20th, 1893, at Hudiksvall, Sweden, where he is interred.

When I looked round again the apparition had disappeared.

I came straight back to Dr. Schreiber's house, and happened to catch him just coming in. After I had told him of this second appearance he remained silent for some time, and at last, without making any comment, asked me to go with him into the garden. He approached the gardener, an oldish man, who was at work there before Dr. Schreiber took over the practice.

"Gregson," he said, "you've lived a long time about here, haven't you?"

"Man and boy, five-and-fifty years, sir," replied Gregson.

"Did you ever know Major-General Sir Arthur Debenham?"

"Know the old General, sir? I should think I did!—why, he lived not half a mile from here. I knew 'em all. Why, the young gentleman, poor Mr. Everard, he lived here in this very house with your predecessor, Dr. Turrell, for some months after Lady Debenham died. Dr. Turrell and him was a-travelling on the Continent when Mr. Everard died, sir."

"What was the matter with him—with Mr. Everard?"

"Matter, sir? Why, what I calls a galloping consumption. He was a weak, white-faced lad always, and he got a deal worse after he came to live with the doctor. That was why they went to foreign parts—to see if it would do him any good."

"Why did he come to live with Dr. Turrell—had he no relations of his own that he could go to?"

"They did say, sir, that he'd neither kith nor kin. Dr. Turrell had been the old General's doctor, and Lady Debenham's too—he was about the only friend they had hereabouts, sir. They were a bit queer, the old gentleman and his wife—eccentric, as they term it."

"Was the General rich?"

Gregson scratched his head.

"Well, I should say he was a warm man, sir—always considered to be so, anyway. Kept his carriage, and so on," he answered.

After a few more questions we went away. But I have since been asking more questions of Gregson and of the house-keeper. Their description of Everard Debenham is that of the apparition of the young man whose ghost I have now seen on two occasions.

VII

Nov. 28th.—I think that even Major Kennedy will now believe that I possess some curious power of seeing the usually unseen.

Yesterday afternoon, at two o'clock, Dr. Schreiber, Mr. Pollard, and myself were lunching in the dining-room when I suddenly saw the ghost enter. It came in very quietly—in its usual half-slouching attitude, and immediately upon entering the room halted and stood looking about it in an irresolute manner. The expression of the face was, if anything, more anxious than ever, and the eyes were almost miserable in their perplexity.

My companions saw me lay down my knife and fork and look towards the door with a fixed expression.

"What is it, Angus?" inquired Dr. Schreiber.

"It is here again," I answered, knowing that Mr. Pollard was by this time acquainted with the matter.

"Where is it?"

"Standing between you and the door. It looks as if it did not know where to go, or what to do, or as if it were seeking somebody or something."

"Watch it closely, then, and tell us what happens."

Then I began to report the ghost's movements to them.

"It has walked over to the window and is standing there, looking out into the garden . . . now it has come to the hearthrug, and is staring into the fire . . . and now it is going out of the room again. . . ."

"Follow it," said Dr. Schreiber.

The three of us left the table and followed the ghost out of the room. This time it did not disappear—instead, it turned to the right along the hall and went into Dr. Schreiber's study.

"What is it doing?" asked the doctor, when we got within.

"It is standing in front of your desk, looking at your writing-chair. It seems more perplexed than ever: Now it has gone round to the hearth and is looking all along the mantelpiece as if it wanted to find something . . . now it is leaving the room."

"Follow it."

The ghost went out through the hall into the garden—we three close upon its heels. It stood on the step outside the door for a moment, looking very dejected; then moved slowly away across the garden and walked round the lawn in the centre once or twice. It now slouched more than ever, and its head hung forward as if it were in trouble or pain. Suddenly it turned away by a side path towards a part of the garden given up to trees and shrubs. I described its further movements to my companions.

"It is walking up that little path which leads to the summer-house . . . now it has entered the summer-house . . . it is standing there looking just as lost, perplexed, troubled as ever . . . now it . . . ah!"

"What do you see, Angus?" asked the doctor.

"It has gone—disappeared," I replied.

We turned back to the house.

"What do you think of that, Pollard?" said Dr. Schreiber.

"Queer!" replied Mr. Pollard.

Nobody said anything more just then, and very soon afterwards the two doctors went out together. An hour later they returned with a carpenter and his assistant and a couple of men who looked like navvies. Dr. Schreiber asked me to come with them, and then led the way to the summer-house. When we arrived there he addressed the carpenter.

"I want the floor of this place removed, and the soil beneath excavated until I tell the men to stop," he said. "Do it at once."

It did not take much time for the carpenter and his men to take up the floor, which was formed of squares of pine wood, easily detachable.

Then the men began to dig.

There is no necessity to write down the details of this gruesome search. We found the body of the young man whose ghost I had seen so many times. It was dressed just as the ghost was dressed. Gregson at once identified it as that of Everard Debenham.

Dr. Schreiber has communicated with the Home Office, the police, and the coroner.

VIII

Nov. 30th.—The coroner's inquest is just over. The expert from the Home Office, a famous doctor, says that Everard Debenham was poisoned, and the jury have returned a verdict of wilful murder against Dr. Turrell, to whom, it seems, all General Debenham 's estate was left in the event of Everard 's death if that took place previous to his marriage and the birth of children. We hear that Dr. Turrell has been arrested at Edinburgh, where he had gone to live after selling his practice to Dr. Schreiber.

IX

March 21st.—*Alassio, Italy.*—On arriving here this afternoon we found the English newspapers, and learnt from them that Dr. Turrell was hanged at Wandsworth Gaol last week, and that he left a full confession. There are also articles commenting upon the strange circumstances under which the crime was discovered.

But there was nothing strange about them to me.

Over the Wires

Mrs. H. D. Everett

Ernest Carrington, captain in the "Old Contemptibles," was in England on his first leave from the front. There he had a special errand, hoping to trace a family of the name of Regnier, which had been swept away in the exodus from Belgium, then of recent date. Two old people, brother and sister, harmless folk who had shown him the kindest hospitality before their home was wrecked and burned; and with them their niece Isabeau, who was his chosen love and his betrothed wife. He had endured agonies in these last weeks, receiving no news of them though he fully believed they had escaped to England: it was more than strange that Isabeau did not write, as she knew his address, though he was ignorant of hers.

A friend in London had made inquiry for him where the thronging refugees were registered and their needs dealt with, but nothing seemed to be known of the Regniers. Now he would be on the spot, and could himself besiege the authorities. Hay might have been lukewarm over the quest, but it seemed impossible that he, Carrington, could fail. His friend Hay, with whom he was to have stayed, had just been transferred from Middlesex to the coast defence of Scotland, but had placed at Carrington's disposal his small flat, and the old family servant who was caretaker.

The flat was a plain little place, but it seemed luxurious indeed to Carrington that first evening, in sharp contrast to his recent experiences roughing it in the campaign. His brain was still in a whirl after the hurried journey, and it was too late to embark upon his quest that night; but the next morning, the very next morning, he would begin the search for Isabeau.

Only one item in Hay's room demands description. There was a telephone installation in one corner; and twice while Carrington's dinner was being served, there came upon it a sharp summons, answered first by the servant, and; secondly by himself. Major Hay was wanted, and it had to be detailed how Major Hay had departed upon sudden orders for Scotland only that morning.

Now the meal was over and cleared away, and the outer door closed, shutting Carrington in for the night. Left alone, his thoughts returned to the channel in which they had flowed for many days and nights. Isabeau his Isabeau: did the living world still hold his lost treasure, and under what conditions and where? And—maddening reflection—what might she not have suffered of privation, outrage, while he was held apart by his soldier's duty, ignorant, impotent to succour! He could picture her as at their last meeting when they exchanged tokens, the light in her eyes, the sweetness of her lips: the image was perfect before him, down to every fold of her white dress, and every ripple of her hair. His own then, pledged to him, and now vanished into blank invisibility and silence. What could have happened: what dread calamity had torn her from him? Terrible as knowledge might be when gained, it was his earnest prayer that he might know.

A groan burst from his lips, and he cried out her name in a passion of appeal.

"Isabeau, where are you? Speak to me, dead or alive!"

Was it in answer that the telephone call began to ring?—not sharply and loudly, like those demands for Major Hay, but thin and faint like their echo. But without doubt it rang, and Carrington turned to the instrument and took down the receiver.

"Yes," he called back. "What is it?"

Great Heaven! it was Isabeau's voice that answered, a voice he could but just hear, as it seemed to be speaking from far away. "Ernest—Ernest," she cried, "have you forgotten me? I have forgotten many things since I was tortured, but not you—never you."

"I am here, my darling. I have come to England seeking you, with no other thought in mind. Tell me, for God's sake, where I can find you. Can I come to-night?"

There was a pause, and then the remote voice began again, now a little stronger and clearer.

"Ernest—is it really you! I can die happy, now you tell me that you love me still. That is all I wanted, just the assurance. All I may have in this world—now."

"Darling, of course I love you: you are all in all to me. Where are you speaking from? Tell me, and I will come?"

"No, no: it is all I wanted, what you have just said. It will be easy now to die. I could never have looked you in the face again—after—I am not fit. But soon I shall be washed clean. What does it say—washed? And they gave them white robes—!"

The voice failed, dying away, and when Carrington spoke there was no answer. He called to her by name, begging her to say if she was in London or where, but either the connection, had been cut off, or she did not hear. Then after an interval he rang up the exchange. Who was it who had just used the line? But the clerk was stupid or sleepy, thought there had been no call, but was only just on after the shift, and could not say.

It was extraordinary, that she could know where he was to be found that night, and call to him. And how was it that the voice had ceased without giving him a clue? But surely, surely, it would come again.

To seek his bed, tired as he was, seemed now to be impossible. He waited in the living-room, sometimes pacing up and down, sometimes sitting moodily, his head bent on his hands: could he rest or sleep when a further call might come, and, if unheard, a chance be lost. And a call did come a couple of hours later; the same thin reedy vibration of the wire. In a moment he was at the instrument, the receiver at his ear, and again it was Isabeau's voice that spoke.

"Ernest, can you hear me? Will you say it over again: say that you love me still, in spite of all?"

"Dearest, I love you with all my heart and soul. And I entreat you to tell me where you are, so that I can find you."

"You will be told—quite soon. They are so kind—the people here, but they want to know my name. I cannot tell them any more than Isabeau; I have forgotten what name came after. What was my name when you knew me?"

"My darling, you were Isabeau Regnier. And you were living at Martel, with your old uncle Antoine Regnier, and his sister, Mademoiselle Elise. Surely you remember?"

"Yes; yes. I remember now. I remember all. I was Isabeau Regnier then, and now I am lost—lost—lost! Poor old uncle Antoine! They set him up against the wall and shot him, because they said he resisted; and they dragged the Tante and me away. But the Tante could not go fast enough to please them. They stabbed her in the back with their bayonets, and left her bleeding and moaning, lying in the road to die. Oh, if only they had killed me too. Don't ask me—never ask me—what they did to me!"

"Do not think of it, Isabeau dearest. Think only that I have come to seek you, and that you are safe in England and will be my wife. But I must know where you are, and when I can come to see you."

"I will tell you some time, but not now. The nurse says I must not go on talking; that I am making myself more ill. She's wrong, for it cannot make me ill to speak to you; but I must do as I am bidden. Tell me that you love me; just once again. That you love what I was: you cannot love what I have become."

"Darling, I loved you then, I love you now, and shall love you always. But tell me—you must tell me where—"

She did not answer. This seemed to be the end, for, though he still watched and listened, the wire did not vibrate again that night, nor for many following hours.

He did not spend those hours in inaction. He was early at the London office, and then took the express to Folkestone, but at neither place was there knowledge of the name of Regnier. Nor had he better fortune at the other seaports, which he visited the day following. But where there had been such thronging numbers, despite the organisation vigilance, was it wonderful that a single name had dropped unnoted? And if what had been told him was correct, about the murder of her uncle and aunt, she must have reached England alone.

His next resort was to a private inquiry-office, and there an appointment was arranged for him at three o'clock on Friday afternoon.

He had arrived in London on the Monday, and it was on Monday evening and night that those communications from Isabeau came over the wire. Each of the following nights, Tuesday, Wednesday, and Thursday, he had spent in Hay's rooms, but from the installed telephone there was no sound or sign.

No sign came until mid-day on Friday, when he was just debating whether to go out to lunch, or have it brought to him from the service down below. The thin, echo-like call sounded again, and he was at once at the receiver.

"Isabeau! Is it you? Speak!"

"Yes, it is I." It was Isabeau's voice that answered, and yet her voice with a difference: it was firmer and clearer than on Monday night, although remote—so remote!

"Where are you? Tell me, that I may come to you. I am seeking you everywhere."

"I do not know where I am. It is all strange and new. But I rejoice in this: I have left behind what was soiled. I would tell you more, but something stops the words. I want you to do something for me: I have a fancy. You have done much, dear Ernest, but this is one thing more."

"What is it, dearest? You have only to ask."

"Go to the end of this street at two o'clock. That is in an hour from now; and wait there till I pass by. I shall not look as I used to do, but I will give you a flower—"

Here the voice failed; he could scarcely distinguish the last words. Strange, that one thing could be said and not another, never what he craved to know. But in an hour he would see her—speak to her, and their separation would be at an end. Not as she used to look! Did she mean changed by what she had suffered? But not so changed, surely, that he would not know, that she would need to identify herself by the gift of a flower. And was the change she spoke of, of the body or the mind? A chill doubt as to the latter, which had assailed him before, crept over him again. But even if it were so, there would be means of healing. She was ill now, shaken by what she had suffered: with love and care, and returning health, all would be well.

He was punctual at the place of appointment. A draughty corner this street-end; but what did he, campaign-hardened, care for chill winds, or for the flying gusts of rain? The passers-by were few for a London street; but each one was carefully scrutinized and each umbrella looked under—that is, if a woman carried it. There was not one, however, that remotely resembled Isabeau. Taxis went by, now and then horse-drawn vehicles; presently a funeral came up the crossing street. A glass hearse with a coffin in it, probably a woman's coffin by its size. A cross of violets lay upon it within, but a couple of white wreaths had been placed outside, next to the driver's seat. A hired brougham was the only following.

They had done better to put the wreaths under shelter, but perhaps no one was in charge who greatly cared. As the cortège came level with the corner, a sharper gust than before, tore a white spray from the exposed wreath, and whirled it over towards him; it struck him on the chest, and fell on the wet pavement at his feet. He stooped to pick it up: he loved flowers too well to see it trodden in the mud: and as he did so, a great fear for the first time pierced him through. What might it not signify, this funeral flower? But no, death was not possible: scarcely an hour ago he had heard her living voice.

He waited long at the rendezvous, the flower held in his hand, but no one resembling her came by. Then, chilled and dispirited, but still holding the flower, he turned back to his lodging. It was time and over for his appointment at the inquiry office, but the rain had soaked him through, and he must change to a dry coat.

The servant met him as he came in.

"A letter for you, sir. I am sorry for the delay. You should have had it before, but it must have been brushed off the table and not seen. I found it just now on the floor."

Could it be from Isabeau?—but no, the address was not in her writing. Carrington tore it open: it was from the Belgian central office, and bore date two days bade.

"We have at last received information respecting Mademoiselle Regnier. A young woman who appeared to have lost her memory, was charitably taken in by Mrs. Duckworth, in whose house she has remained through a recent serious illness, the hospitals being over full. She recovered memory last night, and now declares her name to be Isabeau Regnier, formerly of Martel. Mrs. Duckworth's address is 18, Silkmore Gardens, S. Kensington, and you will doubtless communicate with her."

Here at last was the information so long vainly sought, and it must have been from the Kensington house that Isabeau telephoned, though her voice sounded like a long-distance call. He would go thither at once; his application to the inquiry office was no longer needed: but still there was a chill at his heart as he looked at the white flower.

Was some deep-down consciousness aware, in spite of his surface ignorance; and had it begun to whisper of the greater barrier which lay between?

As he approached the house in Silkmore Gardens, he might have noticed that a servant was going from room to room, drawing up blinds that had been lowered. At the door he asked for Mrs. Duckworth.

"I am not sure if my mistress can see you, sir," was the maid's answer. "She has been very much upset."

"Will you take in my card, and say my business is urgent. I shall be grateful if she will spare me even five minutes. I am a friend of Mademoiselle Regnier's."

Carrington was shown into a sitting-room at the back of the house, with windows to the ground and a vision of greenery beyond. It was not long before Mrs. Duckworth came to him; she wore a black gown, and looked as if she had been weeping.

"You knew Isabeau Regnier," she began with a certain abruptness. "Are you the Ernest of whom she used to speak?"

"I am. She is my affianced wife, so you see I inquire for her by right. I have been searching for her in the utmost distress, and until now in vain. I have but just heard that you out of your charity took her in, also that she has been ill. May I see her now, to-day?"

The lady's eyes filled again with tears, and she shrank back.

"Ah, you do not know what has happened. O, how sad, how dreadful to have to tell you! Isabeau is dead."

"What, just now, within this hour? She was speaking to me on the telephone only at mid-day."

"No—there is some mistake. That is impossible. She died last Tuesday, and was buried this afternoon. Her coffin left the house at a quarter before two, and my husband went with it to the cemetery. I would have gone too, only that I have been ill."

At first he could only repeat her words: "Dead—Tuesday—Isabeau dead!" She was frightened by the look of his face—the look of a man who is in close touch with despair.

"Oh, I'm so sorry. Oh do sit down, Mr. Carrington. This has been too much for you."

He sank into a chair, and she went hurriedly out, and returned with a glass in her hand.

"Drink this: nay, you must. I am sorry; oh, I am sorry. I wish my husband were here; he would tell you all about it better than I. It has been a grief to us all, to every one in the house; we all grew fond of her. And we began quite to hope she would get well. When she came to us her memory was a blank, except for the wrong that had been done her. That seemed to have blotted out all that was behind, except her love for Ernest—you. But she said she could never look Ernest in the face again, and she wanted to be lost. She took an interest in things here after a while, and she was kind and helpful, like a daughter in the house—we have no children. And then her illness came on again; it was something the matter with the brain, caused by the shock she had sustained. She was very ill, but we could not get her into any hospital, all were too full. But she had every care with us, you may be sure of that, and I think she was happier to be here to the last. So it went on, up and down, sometimes a little better, sometimes worse. Last Monday evening delirium set in. She fancied Ernest was here—you—and she was talking to you all the time. It was as if she heard you answering."

"Have you a telephone installed? Could she get up and go to the telephone?"

"We have a telephone—yes, certainly. But she had not strength enough to leave her bed, and the installation is downstairs in the study."

"I declare to you on my most solemn word that she spoke to me over the telephone—twice on Monday night, and once to-day. It is beyond comprehension. Can you tell me what she said, speaking as she thought to Ernest?"

"She asked you to remind her of her forgotten name. We did not get Regnier till then, nor Martel where she lived; it was as if she heard the words spoken by you. I wrote at once to the organising people to say we had found out: I had no idea then that her death was so near. With the recollection of her name came back—horrors, and she was telling them to you. It seems she lived with an old uncle and aunt: would that be right for the girl you knew? They shot her uncle, the Germans did, when they burnt the house, and stabbed her poor old aunt and left her to die. I can show you a photograph of Isabeau, if that will help to identify. It is only an amateur snapshot, taken in our garden, at the time she was so much better, and, we hoped, recovering. It is very like her as she was then."

Mrs. Duckworth opened the drawer of a cabinet, and took out a small square photograph of a girl in a white dress sitting under a tree, and looking out of the picture with sad appealing eyes.

Carrington looked at it, and at first he could not speak. Presently he said, answering a question of Mrs. Duckworth's:

"Yes, there can be no doubt."

He had heard enough. Mrs. Duckworth would fain have asked further about the marvel of the voice, but he got up to take leave.

"I will come again if you will permit," he said. "Another day I shall be able to thank you better for all you did for her—for all your kindness. You will then tell me where she is laid, and let me take on myself—all expense. Now I must be alone."

There was ready sympathy in the little woman's face; tears were running down, though her words of response were few. Carrington still held the photograph.

"May I take this?" he said, and she gave an immediate assent. Then he pressed the hand she held out in farewell, and in another moment was gone.

The sequel to this episode is unknown. Carrington sat long that night with the picture before him, the pathetic little picture of his lost love; and cried aloud to her in his solitude: "Isabeau, speak to me, come to me. Death did not make it impossible before: why should it now? Do not think I would shrink from you or fear you. Nothing is in my heart but a great longing—a great love—a great pity. Speak again—speak!"

But no answer came. The telephone in the corner remained silent, and that curious far-off tremor of the wire sounded for him no more.

A Penny Walk

John Colquhoun

The uniformed bell-boy bowed me politely into the street. He had been very attentive in showing me over the apartment, and I thanked him as courteously as possible. I fear, however, that my manner was not entirely the suavest, for, to tell the truth, I was in a most disagreeable humor. This was the twelfth apartment I had inspected that morning, and each one had seemed, for our purposes at least, a little less desirable than its predecessor. I had assured my wife, before she left for a week's visit at her mother's home, that I would find precisely the furnished apartment we needed, before her return. I was now half-way through the fourth day's profitless search, and the job was getting on my nerves.

A neighboring church-spire clock confirmed my inward feeling that lunch-time was at hand, so I walked to the near-by avenue, with its roaring elevated and clattering surface cars, and was soon busied in temporarily forgetting my troubles over a substantial meal. The respite was not of long duration, for, with the black coffee and accompanying cigar, came meditation—and with meditation a renewal of my perplexity. I had completely exhausted the list for the day, carefully compiled from advertisements in the papers and inquiries at numerous real-estate agencies, and was really at a loss to know where to turn. Perhaps the next morning's papers would have additional advertisements. But I felt that I ought not to waste the afternoon; although my previous exertions might fairly entitle me to half a day's rest. However, I could not justify myself in entirely abandoning the task even for half a day; so I racked my brains for some scheme by means of which I might discover pastures new.

Curiously enough, as I sat there engaged in unproductive speculation, my mind jumped back to a boyish recollection, which had no apparent connection with my train of thought. I recalled a most singular old gentleman who had visited us many years ago, and who used to claim that he had derived much amusement and experienced many strange adventures from a habit which he had acquired or originated, of taking what he called "penny walks." His method in pursuing this peculiar pastime was as follows:

He would start from his house, go to the nearest street-comer, and toss up a cent. If it came down "heads," he turned to the right; if "tails," to the left. In either case, he walked one block and then continued his progress by repeating the process at that and each subsequent street-corner. I smiled as I remembered how he would reel off a string of adventures and scrapes into which he claimed to have been thus led by the Goddess of Chance (or the penny), that would discount Baron Munchausen's most famous exploits.

We had none of us much faith in his tales or his "penny-walk" plan, being essentially matter-of-fact and unimaginative people. Nor do I think any of us had ever tried the scheme ourselves, considering it to be a very undignified and childish manner of obtaining amusement, and preferring, when we took the air, a straight-away five-mile constitutional.

Of a sudden it occurred to me, however, that here was a most ingenious and labor-saving device for experimenting with fortune. And incidentally, I reflected, it might result, by some outlandish freak of chance, in my securing the much-desired apartment. At any rate it seemed better than doing nothing at all in the matter of my quest, during the balance of the day. So regarding it as quite a satisfactory compromise between duty and disinclination, I speedily resolved to put my old friend's curious custom to the test.

Summoning the waiter, I paid my check and started forth with enthusiasm. At the door of the restaurant I took a handful of coins from my pocket to select the necessary copper. There were no pennies among them. But reflecting that one coin was as good as another for the purpose, I chose instead an old French silver coin which I had carried as a pocket-piece for some years. It had a particular value in my eyes as a pocket-piece, because it bore the date 1813, and I carried it principally because some of my more superstitious friends had informed me that to carry a pocket-piece with a "13" in the date, was to ensure misfortune. Now, I despise all such superstitious notions, and I always do all I can to show my utter contempt for fears resultant from them. I invariably cross between the carriages of a funeral procession whenever I get a chance to do so. I am President of a "Thirteen Club." I always walk under all the ladders that come in my way, and I even persuaded my wife to marry me on Friday. So it was with considerable satisfaction that I selected this particular coin for the purpose of my experiment, with the determination to do all that I could to "hoodoo" Fate.

I glanced up and down the street for the nearest corner. As far as I could determine with the eye, I was precisely in the middle of the block. Consequently the plan must be put in operation at once. I tossed up the coin and it came down "heads" in my open palm. I turned quickly to the right and walked to the corner. Here the coin directed me to the left, and I departed from the noisy avenue of the elevated and surface cars and turned into a quiet residence street.

I strolled leisurely along, keeping watch for any promising apartment house, but there was none on the block. At the next corner the coin indicated a turn to the right and I passed down the avenue parallel to the one which I had started from. Then another turn to the right, through a parallel residence street, equally apartment-houseless, brought me back to the noisy avenue of the elevated road, a block below the point at which I had left it. "Left" said the coin, and I went down the busy thoroughfare; left again and I passed away into a third quiet residence street, also unproductive. Then down the parallel avenue; and again back by the next residence street to the elevated highway, and once more left, down that thoroughfare.

I paused at this point in disgust. It was decidedly annoying to be taken with such geometrical regularity through parallel and successive cross-streets and to be returned so unerringly at regular intervals to the very street of all streets which possessed no possibilities in the line of my search. And I stood uncertainly on the corner for a moment or two, half inclined to end the experiment at once. But it finally occurred to me that I might better keep it up a little longer; so I decided to continue the operation until the repetitions had reached the much dreaded number thirteen, and if at that time nothing had developed, to abandon the scheme altogether.

I calculated that I had already made nine tosses. Four more remained therefore. So up went the coin again; down it came "heads" and once more I turned to the left into the residence street; the eleventh toss took me, as usual, down the parallel avenue, and the twelfth returned me with unfailing accuracy to the avenue of the elevated road. This was simply maddening, and I was becoming thoroughly exasperated. However, in accordance with my resolution, I made the thirteenth toss and proceeded down the detested avenue once more, following the relentless route forced upon me with such extraordinary persistence.

Now, if I were at all superstitious, I suppose I might have discovered in this somewhat remarkable repetition of chance an indication that I ought to continue the experiment indefinitely with a probability of eventual success. But I am not in the least afflicted with that weakness; consequently, all this simply impressed me as a series of very dreary coincidences, and I determined to put an end to them at once. So I replaced the coin in my pocket and glanced up at the street sign on the lamp-post to ascertain my whereabouts. The sign read, "18th St." Here was another tiresome coincidence. For the date on the coin was 1813 and the thirteenth toss had brought me to the corner of Eighteenth Street. It was becoming a sort of nuisance and I decided I would permit myself no further dalliance with such trivialities. Therefore, to show my contempt for my previous weakness, and to prove there was nothing at all singular in these happenings, I crossed under the elevated tracks and walked rapidly away down the street, in exactly the opposite direction from that which the coin had hitherto pointed out.

The first block contained nothing but disreputable tenements, stables and small shops. The second took on a better appearance, with respectable three-story brick dwellings. But in the third block I paused in surprise a few doors from the corner, before a decidedly good-looking, though somewhat old-fashioned apartment house. Instinctively I glanced at the house number on the glass transom over the door. It was 318. "How absurd!" I thought. "Everything runs to thirteens and eighteens." At this moment a smiling negro attendant, who had been seated just inside the door, observed me standing there and gazing up at the house. He ran quickly down the steps.

"May-be you was a-lookin' for a furnished apartment, sir," he said. "I got something I'd like to show you if you was."

There could be no possible reason for not looking at it, I reflected, despite this numerical foolishness of coincidence. For I recalled that this would be the thirteenth apartment I had seen that day. So I followed him up the steps at once, and much to my delight was soon engaged in inspecting just the sort of an apartment I had been hunting for. The rooms were large and airy, and the parlor and dining-room gave out upon some pretty back yards of private houses in the rear. And I was particularly pleased with the parlor furniture. It was all so delightfully old-fashioned and commodious. Indeed, the chairs and two spindle-legged sofas looked as if they might have been fifty years old, though all were in perfect repair. There was, too, an air of extreme neatness about the whole place, while the few ornaments and little pieces of bric-a-brac displayed unmistakable evidences of good taste.

A short interview with the superintendent resulted in business arrangements satisfactory to both sides, and I paid a month's rental and departed for the nearest telegraph office to wire the good news to my wife.

On her return to the city, she was as much pleased with the place as I had been, and we were soon snugly ensconced in our new quarters and enjoying its comforts. I believe my wife forgot to ask me how I found the place, and I concluded it was hardly necessary to tell her of the silly little coincidences. Besides, really, I reflected, it was not until I desisted from the tossing-up process that I had made any progress whatever.

My wife took especial delight in the quaint old parlor furniture and was never tired of admiring it and talking about it, and wishing that, when we were able to afford a home in the country, we might have similar furniture for our parlor there. One chair in particular caught her fancy. It was a large, high-backed rocker, with a broad seat and wide, cushioned arms. And it had curious bronze knobs at the ends of the arms and on the tops of the posts, which extended high up above the back. She often told me that she rarely sat anywhere else save in that chair during my absence at the office in the daytime, and I know that in the evenings it appeared to have an almost unaccountable fascination for her.

We made many conjectures as to where the furniture had come from, and who had formerly owned it. But ten years of city residence had proved the wisdom of never attempting to secure information from the employees of an apartment house unless you are prepared to gossip about all your neighbors. So we were content to rejoice in our good fortunes and ask no questions.

The pleasure we derived from the comforts of our new home was, however, much marred after a short months residence therein by a change in my wife's health which occasioned me considerable apprehension. She appeared to be suffering from no perceptible malady, at least so far as I could detect, nor, indeed, did she complain of feeling at all ill except that she admitted a strange loss of appetite for which she could not herself account. And this was the more incomprehensible because it was accompanied by a sensation which she described as being more like hunger than anything else. She would often talk in the morning, for instance, of how much she would relish a certain dish, and give instructions that it should be prepared for dinner that night. And yet, when the dinner hour arrived, she would be seized with a sudden aversion to all food, and it was with the greatest difficulty that she could be induced to eat more than the meagerest portion of anything. I questioned the servants closely about her conduct in this respect during my absence, and found that she rarely could be prevailed upon to eat more than a morsel at any time. I suggested various tonics and she consented to take them willingly enough, but they produced little or no beneficial effect. So that she began perceptibly to fall away in weight and to exhibit signs of weakness and lassitude which were most distressing to me, as she had hitherto been a woman of vigorous health and perfectly normal appetite.

My fears as to her physical condition were considerably augmented, moreover, by a remarkable change in her disposition. She was by nature of a most vivacious and cheerful temperament, never depressed, and always merry and full of pleasant chat.

Whereas now she rather avoided than sought conversation, although she was not irritable or fretful in any way. But it was extremely hard to arouse her interest in any of the occupations or pursuits which formerly afforded her entertainment or pleasure. I could never induce her to go out to dinner or the theatre. She even entirely ceased church-going, though she had been all her life an earnest and devout believer, and a faithful and constant attendant upon divine services. She retained her extraordinary fondness for the big rocking-chair, however, and would sit there by the hour at the window, rocking slowly back and forth and humming a little French chansonnette over and over again. I had never heard her sing this French song before, and asked her where she learned it. She could only vaguely answer that she supposed she must have learned it in childhood, though she could not remember where.

In spite of all this change she was not unhappy, but was entirely content with her life and surroundings. But I began to realize that she was living in a mental world of her own, from which all—even I—were excluded. I tried not to show her how much pain this caused me, but it was inexpressibly bitter to be deprived of the loving companionship and sympathetic interchange of idea and impression which had bound our lives so closely together.

As the symptoms grew worse rather than better, I called in our family physician, who had known my wife for fifteen years. He could discover no organic disease, and, although he questioned her most closely, was unable to elicit any information to assist him in assigning a cause for the peculiar malady which had taken possession of her. At his suggestion I employed an eminent specialist; but his examination produced no further light on the subject. Both doctors prescribed change of scene, and after much persuasion, I induced her to go with me to Atlantic City. We remained there only three days; for she grew perceptibly worse instead of better, and begged me so earnestly to take her back to our own little quiet home that I could not resist her entreaties.

She was now becoming so weak that she could not walk about the apartment without assistance, and I was fairly beside myself with grief and anxiety, and nearly wild at my inability to procure some adequate remedy for her illness. She began, too, to he possessed of hallucinations, as her strength diminished; and of these the most curious was that she repeatedly expressed a longing to see France once more; to go home to France to die. It was as if she had been born there and was now overcome with homesickness for the land of her birth. And yet she had never been abroad, and knew nothing of France beyond the casual knowledge possessed by ordinarily well-educated persons.

By this time her extraordinary fondness for the old arm-chair had become a mania so strong that she would not stir out of it all day long. And, if we had permitted it, she would have slept in it at night. Indeed, she often begged us to allow her to do so, and seemed much aggrieved when we refused to grant this request.

We had just succeeded in getting her off to her room after considerable trouble on that account one night, and I had remained by her bedside until she fell asleep; then I returned to the parlor. I was too miserable to read, and sat there absorbed in my sorrow for a long time, glowering occasionally at the old rocking-chair. For I had begun to hate it as much as my wife seemed to love it. To me it took on all the semblance of a deadly enemy, because of its close association with her illness. Yet, tonight, I felt impelled, for some unaccountable reason, to sit in it myself; and finally, after some angry mental demur, I rose almost involuntarily and, crossing the room, drew it a little away from the window and seated myself. It was comfortable enough. There could be no doubt of that; and I leaned back and spread out my arms on the wide armrests, as was my wife's custom. I had been seated there but a few moments, pondering over her unfortunate condition, when I began to think of her strange hallucinations in regard to France. And somehow they seemed not so inexplicable to me now. I really began to feel quite an understanding of them, and wondered if, after all, it might not a pleasant thing to die in the sunny, southern portion of that beautiful country.

With a violent start I came to myself in anger. "Curse the chair!" I ejaculated. "I believe it is making us all crazy."

It required a determined effort of the will to arouse myself; but I was now thoroughly enraged, and rising quickly I seized the huge brass knob at the end of the right arm of the chair and with a violent pull started to move it back to its usual place.

The tug was so sharp and sudden that, to my surprise, instead of moving the chair I only succeeded in pulling off the brass knob in my hand. Gazing at it in amazement, I discovered that it was hollow, and that a cotton plug had been inserted in the end. This I easily removed with my pocket-knife and then inverted the cylinder over the library table. A small sealed and addressed package fell out, followed by an old French gold coin and a little roll of thin writing paper. Unrolling the latter I found written thereon in a fine feminine hand, as even and regular as copper-plate, the following:—

To whomsoever Le Bon Dieu in his mercy may entrust my message:
I, Antoinette Burdeleau du Chateau-Roehamboullle, formerly of the
province of Languedoc in the south of France, do earnestly beseech you

to perform this slight devoir, the last request of a dying woman. You will have found with this letter a little packet all addressed for the sending. This packet may not be despatched before I am gone. Alas, that I must confess my loneliness! I have no friend to whom I may entrust it. Fearing that after my death the service might not be performed by menial hands, I am compelled to commend it in this manner to the kind offices of an unknown stranger. Reimburse the necessary expense of the sending from the Louis d'Or. It is my last, and has been kept for this employment. Expect no reply, for none will come. But accept the small trust, and the blessing of the departed shall reach you from beyond the grave and bring peace and welfare to your house.

Adieu! Receive my grateful salutations.

B. DU C-R

Then followed in a wavering and hardly legible hand:

C'est fini. I shall go home tonight.

I picked up the golden coin from the table and, turning it over, glanced casually at the date upon the other side. It was 1813.

Again I felt the sense of annoyance at the numerical coincidence, recalling my own pocket-piece and the experiences of the day on which I had first seen our present home. I had tried continually to obliterate the silly episode from my mind, because of conviction that persons who knew me less well than I knew myself might have accused me of superstition, had they known of my ridiculous performances on that occasion, which were after all only in the nature of a jest. But the events of that day would persist in recurring to me despite my wish to forget them, and especially since my wife's illness had I been plagued by this undesired recollection. And now this gold coin, with the ridiculous date, brought every detail of the day's walk back to my memory with surprising distinctness.

This was very exasperating, and I found every attempt to compose my mind quite useless. So, as sleep was impossible, I concluded to take a long walk to restore my mind to a more equable condition. I first replaced the knob in the arm of the chair, and mechanically thrusting the articles which it had contained in my coat pocket, sallied out.

The fresh night air was grateful and I walked along feeling a sense of relief from the exercise. As I turned into the broad avenue of the elevated road, which was brightly lighted and more pleasant to walk upon at night for that reason, I passed an "all-night" drug-store. The curious message and the packet in my pocket were fresh in my mind, and turning quickly into the store I had the package properly weighed and stamped, and deposited it in the branch post-office on the opposite corner. The performance of this slight task in a measure relieved me and, after a long walk, I returned home to enjoy the most refreshing sleep I had experienced in months.

The next morning I arose late, and when I came into the dining-room found my wife propped up in a chair at the table.

I succeeded in concealing my great surprise and delight at seeing her so wonderfully changed. For though she was still very weak, her whole manner was radically different, and she talked and laughed, though rather feebly, with quite her old spirit. It was as if some strange burden had been lifted from her. I could hardly believe the evidence of my senses, the transition was so complete. She ate a hearty breakfast with evident enjoyment, and chattered away like a magpie, and she was greatly amused because I had forgotten to look at the morning paper with my coffee,—an invariable habit of mine.

Suddenly she asked me, with a change of manner, if I would object to listening to a very strange dream she had had the night before. As a rule, I never allow people to tell me their dreams, not even my wife. I regard dreams as entirely useless and silly; and I'm sure I have enough of my own to forget, without being bothered by those of other people. But of course this was an exceptional occasion, so I readily consented.

"I dreamed," she said, "that a little old lady, with the sweetest face in the world,—but oh! such a sad face,—a was standing at the foot of my bed. She was dressed in quaint old-fashioned clothing such as you see in pictures of the ladies of the French nobility of one hundred years ago. I seemed to know her and yet not to know, and I seemed to be wide awake. Yet, I was not surprised to see her, and not at all afraid. She looked down at me with the very pleasantest smile and I thought she said:

" 'Sleep sweetly, poor child; I will trouble you no longer, for it is now accomplished.'

"And then I seemed to fall asleep, in my dream, as she stood there smiling. But all at once I woke up in reality and I heard our little cathedral clock strike twelve. Wasn't that odd?"

I started involuntarily, though I laughed and made light of the vision. For in a flash, as I recalled finding the letter and the other two articles in the chair the night before, I remembered that, as I was mailing the little packet, I had heard the near-by church clock striking the hour of midnight.

My wife recovered so rapidly that at the end of two weeks I sent her away to the country to complete the cure. I was quite lonesome without her and, one evening shortly after her departure, invited the superintendent of the building, who was a pleasant young bachelor, to join me in a cigar and a glass of wine. The wine made him quite talkative, and as I had been pondering considerably, though much against my better judgment, over my recent experiences connected with the apartment, I decided to ask him something about the former tenant or tenants. At first he was disinclined to give me any information. But, finally, I said at a hazard: "Was there ever a French lady here?"

At this he yielded, stating that, as I evidently knew something, I might better be told the whole story. He hoped, however, that I should not repeat the story, even to my wife, as it was a tale which the proprietor wished to have forgotten, fearing it might injure his chances of renting the apartment.

There had been, he told me, a very old French lady who occupied the apartment before our tenancy, and who went by the name of Madame Bardeleau. She had lived entirely alone there for some years, and never made any friendships with any of the other tenants, though she was always extremely polite when spoken to in the corridors or in the elevator. But there was something so reserved and distant about her manner that no one ventured to intrude upon the privacy which she evidently preferred. She went out every day and returned with one or two little parcels which were supposed to contain her supply of food, which she prepared herself over a little gas-stove. Toward the last part of her occupancy of the premises, however, she became so feeble that she was unable to go out, and then the grocer and the butcher called for orders, which, when filled, were sent up to her on the dumb-waiter, and for which she always paid in cash. One week she gave no orders whatever, though both tradesmen called every day. No one knew that anything was the matter, as she could be seen sitting in her old rocking-chair at the window, rocking back and forth, nearly all day, singing to herself, as had been her habit for some time. One morning her curtains were not raised, and, when the trades-people came, they got no response from her at all. An inspector for the gas company called that morning, for the purpose of taking a reading of the meter, but was unable to gain an entrance to her apartment. This started an inquiry which resulted in fears that she might be ill. And finally, no response being given to repeated knocks, the door was burst in. She was found dead in her old chair by the window.

The coroner reported that she died of inanition, and a subsequent search of the premises and interrogation of the tradesmen revealed the fact that she had purchased no food for over a week. No money or jewelry was found; but there was a brief note to the landlord asking that she be given proper burial, and that her furniture be sold to pay the expenses. The landlord complied with her request as to the burial, but instead of selling the furniture, decided to keep it and rent the apartment furnished.

There had been many rumors as to her former life, and the proprietor of a little French restaurant where she had been known to dine occasionally several years before she died, and who claimed to know something about her, said that she had come from a very old and distinguished family of the French nobility, though he either could not or would not reveal the name. It was generally believed that she had exhausted all her resources, and being too proud to let her poverty be known, or to appeal for assistance, had chosen to die as she did, of starvation.

I had listened to this narration with an interest greater than that inspired by ordinary curiosity, as may be imagined. But I concluded it wiser to say nothing as to my discovery in the chair; especially as the landlord wished the whole affair forgotten. It is always well to be on good terms with one's landlord. But a strange impulse prompted one question.

"Was she a very old lady?" I asked.

"You can easily figure that out for yourself," responded the superintendent. "Her memorandum of the inscription she desired placed on her tombstone stated that she was born in 1813."

The outer bell rang and the superintendent, being summoned to some duties in his office, departed.

Once more that feeling of annoyance over these ridiculous and I apparently unescapable coincidences! And this time I was more angry than ever at this tiresome number which continually intruded itself upon an otherwise tranquil and peaceful mind. I seized my hat and started out for a breath of fresh air. The night was too warm for walking, so, taking the elevated road to the ferry, I was soon seated on the upper deck of a boat enjoying the cool breezes of the bay. We were passing Liberty Island when I drew from my wallet the letter and the gold coin I had found in the chair, and from my little change pocket my old silver pocket-piece. I wrapped the two coins in the letter, tied the little parcel up tightly with a bit of string I found in my pocket, and dropped them gently over the railing into the water.

I wish to repeat that I am not a superstitious man, and it seemed to me entirely unnecessary that I should continue to burden myself with the possibility of such silly coincidences.

Perdita

Hildegarde Hawthorne

I. Alfalfa Ranch

Alfalfa Ranch, low, wide, with spreading verandas all overgrown by roses and woodbine, and commanding on all sides a wide view of the rolling alfalfa-fields, was a most bewitching place for a young couple to spend the first few months of their married life. So Jack and I were naturally much delighted when Aunt Agnes asked us to consider it our own for as long as we chose. The ranch, in spite of its distance from the nearest town, surrounded as it was by the prairies, and without a neighbor within a three-mile radius, was yet luxuriously fitted with all the modern conveniences. Aunt Agnes was a rich young widow, and had built the place after her husband's death, intending to live there with her child, to whom she transferred all the wealth of devotion she had lavished on her husband. The child, however, had died when only three years old, and Aunt Agnes, as soon as she recovered sufficient strength, had left Alfalfa Ranch, intending never to visit the place again. All this had happened nearly ten years ago, and the widow, relinquishing all the advantages her youth and beauty, quite as much as her wealth, could give her, had devoted herself to work amid the poor of New York.

At my wedding, which she heartily approved, and where to a greater extent than ever before she cast off the almost morbid quietness which had grown habitual with her, she seemed particularly anxious that Jack and I should accept the loan of Alfalfa Ranch, apparently having an old idea that the power of our happiness would somehow lift the cloud of sorrow which, in her mind, brooded over the place. I had not been strong, and Jack was overjoyed at such an opportunity of taking me into the country. High as our expectations were, the beauty of the place far exceeded them all. What color! What glorious sunsets! And the long rides we took, seeming to be utterly tireless in that fresh sweet air!

One afternoon I sat on the veranda at the western wing of the house. The veranda here was broader than elsewhere, and it was reached only by a flight of steps leading up from the lawn on one side, and by a door opposite these steps that opened into Jack's study. The rest of this veranda was enclosed by a high railing, and by wire nettings so thickly overgrown with vines that the place was always very shady. I sat near the steps, where I could watch the sweep of the great shadows thrown by the clouds that were sailing before the west wind. Jack was inside, writing, and now and then he would say something to me through the open window. As I sat, lost in delight at the beauty of the view and the sweetness of the flower-scented air, I marvelled that Aunt Agnes could ever have left so charming a spot. "She must still love it," I thought, getting up to move my chair to where I might see still further over the prairies, "and some time she will come back—" At this moment I happened to glance to the further end of the veranda, and there I saw, to my amazement, a little child seated on the floor, playing with the shifting shadows of the tangled creepers. It was a little girl in a daintily embroidered white dress, with golden curls around her baby head. As I still gazed, she suddenly turned, with a roguish toss of the yellow hair, and fixed her serious blue eyes on me.

"Baby!" I cried. "Where did you come from? Where's your mamma, darling?" And I took a step towards her.

"What's that, Silvia?" called Jack from within. I turned my head and saw him sitting at his desk.

"Come quick, Jack; there's the loveliest baby—" I turned back to the child, looked, blinked, and at this moment Jack stepped out beside me.

"Baby?" he inquired. "What on earth are you talking about, Silvia dearest?"

"Why, but—" I exclaimed. "There *was* one! How did she get away? She was sitting right there when I called."

"A *baby*!" repeated my husband. "My dear, babies don't appear and disappear like East-Indian magicians. You have been napping, and are trying to conceal the shameful fact."

"Jack," I said, decisively, "don't you suppose I know a baby when I see one? She was sitting right there, playing with the shadows, and I—It's certainly very queer!"

Jack grinned. "Go and put on your habit," he replied; "the horses will be here in ten minutes. And remember that when you have accounted for her disappearance, her presence still remains to be explained. Or perhaps you think Wah Sing produced her from his sleeve?"

I laughed. Wah Sing was our Chinese cook, and more apt, I thought, to put something up his sleeve than to take anything out.

"I suppose I *was* dreaming," I said, "though I could almost as well believe I had only dreamed our marriage."

"Or rather," observed Jack, "that our marriage had only dreamed us."

II. Shadows

About a week later I received a letter from Aunt Agnes. Among other things, chiefly relating to New York's slums, she said:

"I am in need of rest, and if you and Jack could put up with me for a few days, I believe I should like to get back to the old place. As you know, I have always dreaded a return there, but lately I seem somehow to have lost that dread. I feel that the time has come for me to be there again, and I am sure you will not mind me."

Most assuredly we would not mind her. We sat in the moonlight that night on the veranda, Jack swinging my hammock slowly, and talked of Aunt Agnes. The moon silvered the waving alfalfa, and sifted through the twisted vines that fenced us in, throwing intricate and ever-changing patterns on the smooth flooring. There was a hum of insects in the air, and the soft wind ever and anon blew a fleecy cloud over the moon, dimming for a moment her serene splendor.

"Who knows?" said Jack, lighting another cigar. "This may be a turning-point in Aunt Agnes's life, and she may once more be something like the sunny, happy girl your mother describes. She is beautiful, and she is yet young. It may mean the beginning of a new life for her."

"Yes," I answered. "It isn't right that her life should always be shadowed by that early sorrow. She is so lovely, and could be so happy. Now that she has taken the first step, there is no reason why she shouldn't go on."

"We'll do what we can to help her," responded my husband. "Let me fix your cushions, darling; they have slipped." He rose to do so, and suddenly stood still, facing the further end of the veranda. His expression was so peculiar that I turned, following the direction of his eyes, even before his smothered exclamation of "Silvia, look there!" reached me.

Standing in the fluttering moonlight and shadows was the same little girl I had seen already. She still wore white, and her tangled curls floated shining around her head. She seemed to be smiling, and slightly shook her head at us.

"What does it mean, Jack?" I whispered, slipping out of the hammock.

"How did she get there? Come!" said he, and we walked hastily towards the little thing, who again shook her head. Just at this moment another cloud obscured the moon for a few seconds, and though in the uncertain twilight I fancied I still saw her, yet when the cloud passed she was not to be found.

III. Perdita

Aunt Agnes certainly did look as though she needed rest. She seemed very frail, and the color had entirely left her face. But her curling hair was as golden as ever, and her figure as girlish and graceful. She kissed me tenderly, and kept my hand in hers as she wandered over the house and took long looks across the prairie.

"Isn't it beautiful?" she asked, softly. "Just the place to be happy in! I've always had a strange fancy that I should be happy here again some day, and now I feel as though that day had almost come. You are happy, aren't you, dear?"

I looked at Jack, and felt the tears coming to my eyes. "Yes, I am happy. I did not know one could be so happy," I answered, after a moment.

Aunt Agnes smiled her sweet smile and kissed me again. "God bless you and your Jack! You almost make me feel young again."

"As though you could possibly feel anything else," I retorted, laughing. "You little humbug, to pretend you are old!" and slipping my arm round her waist, for we had always been dear friends, I walked off to chat with her in her room.

We took a ride that afternoon, for Aunt Agnes wanted another gallop over that glorious prairie. The exercise and the perfect afternoon brought back the color to her cheeks.

"I think I shall be much better to-morrow," she observed, as we trotted home. "What a country this is, and what horses!" slipping her hand down her mount's glossy neck. "I did right to come back here. I do not believe I will go away again." And she smiled on Jack and me, who laughed, and said she would find it a difficult thing to attempt.

We all three came out on the veranda to see the sunset. It was always a glorious sight, but this evening it was more than usually magnificent. Immense rays of pale blue and pink spread over the sky, and the clouds, which stretched in horizontal masses, glowed rose and golden. The whole sky was luminous and tender, and seemed to tremble with light.

We sat silent, looking at the sky and at the shadowy grass that seemed to meet it. Slowly the color deepened and faded.

"There can never be a lovelier evening," said Aunt Agnes, with a sigh.

"Don't say that," replied Jack. "It is only the beginning of even more perfect ones."

Aunt Agnes rose with a slight shiver, "It grows chilly when the sun goes," she murmured, and turned lingeringly to enter the house. Suddenly she gave a startled exclamation. Jack and I jumped up and looked at her. She stood with both hands pressed to her heart, looking—

"The child again," said Jack, in a low voice, laying his hand on my arm.

He was right. There in the gathering shadow stood the little girl in the white dress. Her hands were stretched towards us, and her lips parted in a smile. A belated gleam of sunlight seemed to linger in her hair.

"Perdita!" cried Aunt Agnes, in a voice that shook with a kind of terrible joy. Then, with a stifled sob, she ran forward and sank before the baby, throwing her arms about her. The little girl leaned back her golden head and looked at Aunt Agnes with her great, serious eyes. Then she flung both baby arms round her neck, and lifted her sweet mouth—

Jack and I turned away, looking at each other with tears in our eyes. A slight sound made us turn back. Aunt Agnes had fallen forward to the floor, and the child was nowhere to be seen.

We rushed up, and Jack raised my aunt in his arms and carried her into the house. But she was quite dead. The little child we never saw again.

The Presence by the Fire

H. G. Wells

It never occurred to Reid that his wife lay dying until the very last day of her illness. He was a man of singularly healthy disposition, averse on principle to painful thoughts, and I doubt if in the whole of his married life his mind had dwelt for five minutes together on the possibility of his losing her.

They were both young, and intimate companions—such companions as many desire to be, and few become. And perhaps it was her sense of the value of this rare companionship that made her, when first her health declined, run many an avoidable risk rather than leave him to go his way alone.

He was sorry that she was ill, sorry she should suffer, and he missed her, as she lay upstairs, in a thousand ways; but though the doctor was mindful to say all the "preparatory" phrases of his profession, and though her sister spoke, as she conceived, quite plainly, it was as hard for him to understand that this was more than a temporary interruption of their life, as it would have been to believe that the sun would not rise again after to-morrow morning.

The day before she died he was restless, and after wandering about the house and taking a short walk, he occupied himself in planting out her evening primroses—a thing she had made a point of doing now for ten springs in succession. The garden she had always tended, he said, should not seem neglected when she came down again. He had rather his own work got in arrears than that this should happen.

The first realisation, when the doctor, finding all conventional euphemisms useless, told him the fact at last in stark, plain words, stunned him. Even then it is doubtful if he believed. He said not a word in answer, but the color left his face, and the lines about his mouth hardened. And he walked softly and with white, expressionless features into her room.

He stood in the doorway and stared for a minute at her thin little features, with the eyes closed and two little lines between the brows; then went and knelt by the bed and looked closely into her face. She did not move until he touched her hair and very softly whispered her name.

Then her eyes opened for a moment, and he saw that she knew him. Her lips moved, and it seemed that she whispered one of those foolish, tender little names that happy married folk delight in inventing for one another, and then she gathered her strength as if with an effort to speak distinctly. He bent mechanically and heard the last syllables of *au revoir.*

For a moment he did not clearly understand what the words were. That was all she said, and as for him, he answered not a word. He put his hand in hers, and she pressed it faintly and then more faintly. He kissed her forehead with dry lips, and the little lines of pain there faded slowly into peace.

For an hour they let him kneel, until the end had come; and all that time he never stirred. Then they had to tap his shoulder to rouse him from his rigour. He got up slowly, bent over her for a moment, looking down into her tranquil face, and then allowed them to lead him away.

That was how Reid parted from his wife, and for days after he behaved as a man who had been suddenly deprived of all initiative. He did no work; he went nowhere outside the house; he ate, drank and slept mechanically; and he did not even seem to suffer actively. For the most part, he sat stupidly at his desk or wandered about the big garden, looking with dull eyes at the little green buds that were now swiftly opening all about him. Not a soul ventured to speak to him of his loss, albeit those who did not know him might have judged his mood one of absolute apathy.

But nearly a week after the funeral the floodgates of his sorrow were opened. Quite suddenly the thing came upon him. Her sister heard him walk into the study and throw himself into a chair. Everything was still for a space, and then he sprang up again and she heard him wailing, "Mary! Mary!" and then he ran, sobbing violently and stumbling, along the passage to his room. It was grotesquely like a little child that had suddenly been hurt.

He locked his door: and her sister, fearing what might happen, went along the passage. She thought of rapping at the door, but on second thoughts she refrained. After listening awhile she went away.

It was long after the first violence of his grief had passed that Reid first spoke of his feelings. He who had been a matter-of-fact materialist was converted, I found, to a belief in immortality by the pitiless logic of her uncompleted life. But I think it was an imperfect, a doubting, belief even at the best. And to strengthen it, perhaps, he began to show a growing interest in the inquiries of those who are sifting whatever evidence there may be of the return of those who are dead.

"For I want my wife now," said he. "I want her in this life. I want her about me—her comfort, her presence. What does it matter that I shall meet her again when I am changed, and she is changed? It was the dear trivialities, the little moments, the touch of her hand, the sound of her voice in the room with me, her distant singing in the garden, and her footfall on the stairs. If I could believe that," he said, "if I could believe—"

And in that spirit it was that he kept to the old home, and would scarcely bear that a thing within or without should be altered in any way. The white curtains that had been there the last autumn hung dirty in the windows, and the little desk that had been her own in the study stood there still, with the pen thrown down as he fancied she had left it.

"Here, if anywhere," he said, "she is at home. Here, if anywhere, her presence lives."

Her sister left him when a housekeeper was obtained, and he went on living there alone, working little and communicating for the most part with these dead memories. After a time he loved nothing so much as to talk of her, and I think in those days that I was of service to him. He would take me about the house, pointing to this trivial thing and that, and telling me some little act of hers that he linked therewith. And he always spoke of her as one who still lived.

"She does" so and so, he would say; "she likes" so and so. We would pace up and down the rich lawn of his house. "My wife is particularly fond of those big white lilies," he would say, "and this year they are finer than ever." So the summer passed and the autumn came.

And one day late in the evening he came to me, walking round the house and tapping at the French window of my study, and as he came in out of the night I noticed how deadly white and sunken his face was and how bright his eyes.

"I have seen her," he said to me, in a low, clear voice. "She has visited me. I knew she was watching me and near me. I have felt her presence for weeks and weeks. And now she has come."

He was intensely excited, and it was some time before I could get any clear story from him.

He had been sitting by the tire in his study, musing, no doubt going over for the hundredth time, day by day and almost hour by hour as he was wont to do, one of the summer holidays they had spent together. He was staring, he said, into the glowing coals, and almost imperceptibly it was that there grew upon him the persuasion that he was not alone. The thought took shape slowly in his mind, but with a strange quality of absolute conviction, that she was sitting in the armchair in front of him, as she had done so often in the old days, and watching him a-dreaming. For a moment he did not dare to look up, lest he should find this a mere delusion.

Then slowly he raised his eyes. He was dimly aware of footsteps advancing along the passage as he did so. A wave of bitter disappointment swept over him as he saw the chair was empty, and this incontinently gave place to a tumult of surprise and joyful emotion. For he saw her—saw her distinctly. She was standing behind the chair, leaning over the back of it, and smiling the tender smile he knew so well. So in her life she had stood many a time and listened to him, smiling gently. The firelight played upon her face.

"I saw her as plainly as I see you," he said. "I saw the smile in her eyes, and my heart leapt out to her."

For a moment he was motionless, entranced, and with an instantaneous appreciation of the transitoriness of this appearance. Then suddenly the door opened, the shadows in the room rushed headlong, and the housemaid came in with his lamp lit and without the shade—a dazzling glare of naked flame. The yellow light splashed over the room and brought out everything clear and vivid.

By mere reflex action he turned his head at the sound of the door-handle, and forthwith turned it back again. But the face he had longed for so patiently had vanished with the shadows before the light. Everything was abruptly plain and material. The girl replenished the fire, moved the armchair on one side, and took away the scuttle lining to refill it with coals. A curious bashfulness made Reid pretend to make notes at his table until these offices were accomplished. Then he looked across the fireplace again, and the room was empty. The sense of her presence, too, had gone. He called upon her name again and again, rubbed his eyes, and tried to force her return by concentrating his mind upon her. But nothing availed. He could see her no more.

He allowed me to cross-examine him in the most detailed way upon this story. His manner was so sane, so convincing, and his honesty so indisputable, that I went to bed that night with my beliefs and disbeliefs greatly shaken. Hitherto I had doubted every ghost story I had heard; but here at last was one of a different quality. Indeed, I went to bed that night an unwilling convert to the belief in the phantasms of those who are dead and all that that belief implies.

My faith in Reid was confirmed by the fact that from late August, when this happened, until December he did not see the apparition again. Had it been an hallucination begotten of his own intense brooding it must inevitably have recurred. But it was presently to be proved beyond all question that the thing he saw was an exterior presence. Night after night he sat in his study, longing for the repetition of that strange experience; and at last, after many nights, he saw her for the second time.

It was earlier in the evening, but with the shorter winter days the room was already dark. Once more he looked into his study fire, and once more that fire glowed redly. Then there came the same sense of her presence, the same hesitation before he raised his eyes. But this time he looked over the chair at once and saw her without any flash of disappointment.

At the instant he felt not the faintest suspicion that his senses deceived him. For a moment he was dumb. He was seized with an intense longing to touch her hand. Then came into his head some half-forgotten story that one must speak first to a spirit. He leant forward.

"Mary!" he said very softly. But she neither moved nor spoke. And then suddenly it seemed that she grew less distinct.

"Mary!" he whispered, with a sudden pang of doubt. Her features grew unfamiliar.

Then suddenly he rose to his feet, and as he did so the making of the illusion was demonstrated. The high light on a vase that had been her check moved to the right; the shadow that had been her arm moved to the left.

Few people realise how little we actually see of what is before our eyes: a patch of light, a patch of shadow, and all the rest our memory and our imagination supply. A chance grouping of dim forms in the dusky firelit study had furnished all the suggestion his longing senses had required. His eyes and his heart and the humour of chance had cheated him.

He stood there staring. For a moment the disintegration of the figure filled him with a sense of grotesque horror and dismay. For a moment it seemed beyond the sanity of things. Then, as he realised the deception his senses had contrived, he sat down again, put his elbows on the table and buried his face in his hands.

About ten he came and told me. He told me in a clear hard voice, without a touch of emotion, recording a remarkable fact. "As I told you the other thing, it is only right that I should tell you this," he said.

Then he sat silently for a space. "She will come no more," he said at last. "She will come no more."

And suddenly he rose, and without a greeting, passed out into the night.

The Rocker

Oliver Onions

I

There was little need for the swart gipsies to explain, as they stood knee-deep in the snow round the bailiff of the Abbey Farm, what it was that had sent them. The unbroken whiteness of the uplands told that, and, even as they spoke, there came up the hill the dark figures of the farm men with shovels, on their way to dig out the sheep. In the summer, the bailiff would have been the first to call the gipsies vagabonds and roost-robbers; now . . . they had women with them too.

"The hares and foxes were down four days ago, and the liquid-manure pumps like a snow man," the bailiff said. . . . "Yes, you can lie in the laithes and welcome—if you can find 'em. Maybe you'll help us find our sheep too—"

The gipsies had done so. Coming back again, they had had some ado to discover the spot where their three caravans made a hummock of white against a broken wall.

The women—they had four women with them—began that afternoon to weave the mats and baskets they hawked from door to door; and in the forenoon of the following day one of them, the black-haired, soft-voiced quean whom the bailiff had heard called Annabel, set her babe in the sling on her back, tucked a bundle of long cane-loops under her oxter, and trudged down between eight-foot walls of snow to the Abbey Farm. She stood in the latticed porch, dark and handsome against the whiteness, and then, advancing, put her head into the great hall-kitchen.

"Has the lady any chairs for the gipsy woman to mend?" she asked in a soft and insinuating voice. . . .

They brought her the old chairs; she seated herself on a box in the porch; and there she wove the strips of cane in and out, securing each one with a little wooden peg and a tap of her hammer. The child remained in the sling at her back, taking the breast from time to time over her shoulder; and the silver wedding ring could be seen as she whipped the cane, back and forth.

As she worked, she cast curious glances into the old hall-kitchen. The snow outside cast a pallid, upward light on the heavy ceiling-beams; this was reflected in the polished stone floor; and the children, who at first had shyly stopped their play, seeing the strange woman in the porch—the nearest thing they had seen to gipsies before had been the old itinerant glazier with his frame of glass on his back—resumed it, but still eyed her from time to time. In the ancient walnut chair by the hearth sat the old, old lady who had told them to bring the chairs. Her hair, almost as white as the snow itself, was piled up on her head *à la Marquise*; she was knitting; but now and then she allowed the needle in the little wooden sheath at her waist to lie idle, closed her eyes, and rocked softly in the old walnut chair.

"Ask the woman who is mending the chairs whether she is warm enough there," the old lady said to one of the children; and the child went to the porch with the message.

"Thank you, little missie—thank you, lady dear—Annabel is quite warm," said the soft voice; and the child returned to the play.

It was a childish game of funerals at which the children played. The hand of Death, hovering over the dolls, had singled out Flora, the articulations of whose sawdust body were seams and whose boots were painted on her calves of fibrous plaster. For the greater solemnity, the children had made themselves sweeping trains of the garments of their elders, and those with cropped curls had draped their heads with shawls, the fringes of which they had combed out with their fingers to simulate hair—long hair, such as Sabrina, the eldest, had hanging so low down her back that she could almost sit on it. A cylindrical-bodied horse, convertible (when his flat head came out of its socket) into a locomotive, headed the sad *cortège*; then came the defunct Flora; then came Jack, the raffish sailor doll, with other dolls; and the children followed with hushed whisperings.

The youngest of the children passed the high-backed walnut chair in which the old lady sat. She stopped.

"Aunt Rachel—" she whispered, slowly and gravely opening very wide and closing very tight her eyes.

"Yes, dear?"

"Flora's dead!"

The old lady, when she smiled, did so less with her lips than with her faded cheeks. So sweet was her face that you could not help wondering, when you looked on it, how many men had also looked upon it and loved it. Somehow, you never wondered how many of them had been loved in return.

"I'm so sorry, dear," Aunt Rachel, who in reality was a great-aunt, said. "What did she die of this time?"

"She died of . . . Brown Titus . . . 'n now she's going to be buried in a grave as little as her bed."

"In a what, dear?"

"As little . . . dread . . . as little as my bed . . . you say it, Sabrina."

"She means, Aunt Rachel,

"Teach me to live that I may dread

The Grave as little as my bed,"

Sabrina, the eldest, interpreted.

"Ah! . . . But won't you play at cheerful things, dears?"

"Yes, we will, presently, Aunt Rachel; gee up, horse! . . . Shall we go and ask the chair-woman if she's warm enough?"

"Do, dears."

Again the message was taken, and this time it seemed as if Annabel, the gipsy, was not warm enough, for she gathered up her loops of cane and brought the chair she was mending a little way into the hall-kitchen itself. She sat down on the square box they used to cover the sewing machine.

"Thank you, lady dear," she murmured, lifting her handsome almond eyes to Aunt Rachel. Aunt Rachel did not see the long, furtive, curious glance. Her own eyes were closed, as if she was tired; her cheeks were smiling; one of them had dropped a little to one shoulder, as it might have dropped had she held in her arms a babe; and she was rocking, softly, slowly, the rocker of the chair making a little regular noise on the polished floor.

The gipsy woman beckoned to one of the children.

"Tell the lady, when she wakes, that I will tack a strip of felt to the rocker, and then it will make no noise at all," said the low and wheedling voice; and the child retired again.

The interment of Flora proceeded. . . .

An hour later Flora had taken up the burden of Life again. It was as Angela, the youngest, was chastising her for some offence, that Sabrina, the eldest, looked with wondering eyes on the babe in the gipsy's sling. She approached on tiptoe.

"May I look at it, please?" she asked timidly.

The gipsy set one shoulder forward, and Sabrina put the shawl gently aside, peering at the dusky brown morsel within.

"Sometime, perhaps—if I'm very careful—" Sabrina ventured diffidently, "—if I'm *very* careful—may I hold it?"

Before replying, the gipsy once more turned her almond eyes towards Aunt Rachel's chair. Aunt Rachel had been awakened for the conclusion of Flora's funeral, but her eyes were closed again now, and once more her cheek was dropped in that tender suggestive little gesture, and she rocked. But you could see that she was not properly asleep. . . . . It was, somehow, less to Sabrina, still peering at the babe in the sling, than to Aunt Rachel, apparently asleep, that the gipsy seemed to reply.

"You'll know some day, little missis, that a wean knows its own pair of arms," her seductive voice came.

And Aunt Rachel heard. She opened her eyes with a start. The little regular noise of the rocker ceased. She turned her head quickly; tremulously she began to knit again; and, as her eyes rested on the sidelong eyes of the gipsy woman, there was an expression in them that almost resembled fright.

II

They began to deck the great hall-kitchen for Christmas, but the snow still lay thick over hill and valley, and the gipsies' caravans remained by the broken wall where the drifts had overtaken them. Though all the chairs were mended, Annabel still came daily to the farm, sat on the box they used to cover the sewing machine, and wove mats. As she wove them, Aunt Rachel knitted, and from time to time fragments of talk passed between the two women. It was always the white-haired lady who spoke first, and Annabel made all sorts of salutes and obeisances with her eyes before replying.

"I have not seen your husband," Aunt Rachel said to Annabel one day. (The children at the other end of the apartment had converted a chest into an altar, and were solemnising the nuptials of the resurrected Flora and Jack, the raffish sailor-doll.)

Annabel made roving play with her eyes. "He is up at the caravans, lady dear," she replied. "Is there anything Annabel can bid him do?"

"Nothing, thank you," said Aunt Rachel.

For a minute the gipsy watched Aunt Rachel, and then she got up from the sewing machine box and crossed the floor. She leaned so close towards her that she had to put up a hand to steady the babe at her back.

"Lady dear," she murmured with irresistible softness, "your husband died, didn't he?"

On Aunt Rachel's finger was a ring, but it was not a wedding ring. It was a hoop of pearls.

"I have never had a husband," she said.

The gipsy glanced at the ring. "Then that is—?"

"That is a betrothal ring," Aunt Rachel replied.

"Ah! . . ." said Annabel.

Then, after a minute, she drew still closer. Her eyes were fixed on Aunt Rachel's, and the insinuating voice was very low.

"Ah! . . . And did *it* die too, lady dear?"

Again came that quick, half-affrighted look into Aunt Rachel's face. Her eyes avoided those of the gipsy, sought them, and avoided them again.

"Did what die?" she asked slowly and guardedly. . . .

The child at the gipsy's back did not need suck; nevertheless, Annabel's fingers worked at her bosom, and she moved the sling. As the child settled, Annabel gave Aunt Rachel a long look.

"Why do you rock?" she asked slowly.

Aunt Rachel was trembling. She did not reply. In a voice soft as sliding water the gipsy continued:

"Lady dear, we are a strange folk to you, and even among us there are those who shuffle the pack of cards and read the palm when silver has been put upon it, knowing nothing . . . But some of us *see*—some of us *see*."

It was more than a minute before Aunt Rachel spoke.

"You are a woman, and you have your babe at your breast now. . . . Every woman sees the thing you speak of."

But the gipsy shook her head. "You speak of seeing with the heart. I speak of eyes—these eyes."

Again came a long pause. Aunt Rachel had given a little start, but had become quiet again. When at last she spoke it was in a voice scarcely audible.

"That cannot be. I know what you mean, but it cannot be. . . . He died on the eve of his wedding. For my bridal clothes they made me black garments instead. It is long ago, and now I wear neither black nor white, but—" her hands made a gesture. Aunt Rachel always dressed as if to suit a sorrow that Time had deprived of bitterness, in such a tender and fleecy grey as one sees in the mists that lie like lawn over hedgerow and copse early of a midsummer's morning. "Therefore," she resumed, "your heart may see, but your eyes cannot see that which never was."

But there came a sudden note of masterfulness into the gipsy's voice.

"With my eyes—*these* eyes," she repeated, pointing to them.

Aunt Rachel kept her own eyes obstinately on her knitting needles. "None except I have seen it. It is not to be seen," she said.

The gipsy sat suddenly erect.

"It is not so. Keep still in your chair," she ordered, "and I will tell you when—"

It was a curious thing that followed. As if all the will went out of her, Aunt Rachel sat very still; and presently her hands fluttered and dropped. The gipsy sat with her own hands folded over the mat on her knees. Several minutes passed; then, slowly, once more that sweetest of smiles stole over Aunt Rachel's cheeks. Once more her head dropped. Her hands moved. Noiselessly on the rockers that the gipsy had padded with felt the chair began to rock. Annabel lifted one hand.

"*Dovo se li,*" she said. "It is there."

Aunt Rachel did not appear to hear her. With that ineffable smile still on her face, she rocked. . . .

Then, after some minutes, there crossed her face such a look as visits the face of one who, waking from sleep, strains his faculties to recapture some blissful and vanishing vision. . . .

"*Jal*—it is gone," said the gipsy woman.

Aunt Rachel opened her eyes again. She repeated dully after Annabel:

"It is gone."

"Ghosts," the gipsy whispered presently, "are of the dead. Therefore it must have lived."

But again Aunt Rachel shook her head. "It never lived."

"You were young, and beautiful? . . . "

Still the shake of the head. "He died on the eve of his wedding. They took my white garments away and gave me black ones. How then could it have lived?"

"Without the kiss, no. . . . But sometimes a woman will lie through her life, and at the graveside still will lie. . . . Tell me the truth."

But they were the same words that Aunt Rachel repeated: "He died on the eve of his wedding; they took away my wedding garments. . . ." From her lips a lie could hardly issue. The gipsy's face became grave. . . .

She broke another long silence.

"I believe," she said at last. "It is a new kind—but no more wonderful than the other. The other I have seen, now I have seen this also. Tell me, does it come to any other chair?"

"It was his chair; he died in it," said Aunt Rachel.

"And you—shall you die in it?"

"As God wills."

"Has . . . *other life* . . . visited it long?"

"Many years; but it is always small; it never grows."

"To their mothers babes never grow. They remain ever babes. . . . None other has ever seen it?"

"Except yourself, none. I sit here; presently it creeps into my arms; it is small and warm; I rock, and then . . . it goes."

"Would it come to another chair?"

"I cannot tell. I think not. It was his chair."

Annabel mused. At the other end of the room Flora was now bestowed on Jack, the disreputable sailor. The gipsy's eyes rested on the bridal party. . . .

"Yet another might see it—"

"None has."

"No; but yet. . . . The door does not always shut behind us suddenly. Perhaps one who has toddled but a step or two over the threshold might, by looking back, catch a glimpse. . . . What is the name of the smallest one?"

"Angela."

"That means 'angel'. . . Look, the doll who died yesterday is now being married. . . . It may be that Life has not yet sealed the little one's eyes. Will you let Annabel ask her if she sees what it is you hold in your arms?"

Again the voice was soft and wheedling. . . .

"No, Annabel," said Aunt Rachel faintly.

"Will you rock again?"

Aunt Rachel made no reply.

"Rock . . ." urged the cajoling voice.

But Aunt Rachel only turned the betrothal ring on her finger. Over at the altar Jack was leering at his new-made bride, past decency; and little Angela held the wooden horse's head, which had parted from its body.

"Rock, and comfort yourself—" tempted the voice.

Then slowly Aunt Rachel rose from her chair.

"No, Annabel," she said gently. "You should not have spoken. When the snow melts you will go, and come no more; why then did you speak? It was mine. It was not meant to be seen by another. I no longer want it. Please go."

The swarthy woman turned her almond eyes on her once more.

"You cannot live without it," she said as she also rose. . . .

And as Jack and his bride left the church on the redheaded horse, Aunt Rachel walked with hanging head from the apartment.

III

Thenceforward, as day followed day, Aunt Rachel rocked no more; and with the packing and partial melting of the snow the gipsies up at the caravans judged it time to be off about their business. It was on the morning of Christmas Eve that they came down in a body to the Abbey Farm to express their thanks to those who had befriended them; but the bailiff was not there. He and the farm men had ceased work, and were down at the church, practising the carols. Only Aunt Rachel sat, still and knitting, in the black walnut chair; and the children played on the floor.

A night in the toy-box had apparently bred discontent between Jack and Flora—or perhaps they sought to keep their countenances before the world; at any rate, they sat on opposite sides of the room, Jack keeping boon company with the lead soldiers, his spouse reposing, her lead-balanced eyes closed, in the broken clockwork motor-car. With the air of performing some vaguely momentous ritual, the children were kissing one another beneath the bunch of mistletoe that hung from the centre beam. In the intervals of kissing they told one another in whispers that Aunt Rachel was not very well, and Angela woke Flora to tell her that Aunt Rachel had Brown Titus also.

"Stay you here; I will give the lady dear our thanks," said Annabel to the group of gipsies gathered about the porch; and she entered the great hall-kitchen. She approached the chair in which Aunt Rachel sat.

There was obeisance in the bend of her body, but command in her long almond eyes, as she spoke.

"Lady dear, you must rock or you cannot live."

Aunt Rachel did not look up from her work.

"Rocking, I should not live long," she replied.

"We are leaving you."

"All leave me."

"Annabel fears she has taken away your comfort."

"Only for a little while. The door closes behind us, but it opens again."

"But for that little time, rock—"

Aunt Rachel shook her head.

"No. It is finished. Another has seen. . . . Say good-bye to your companions; they are very welcome to what they have had; and God speed you."

"They thank you, lady dear. . . . Will you not forget that Annabel saw, and rock?"

"No more."

Annabel stooped and kissed the hand that bore the betrothal hoop of pearls. The other hand Aunt Rachel placed for a moment upon the smoky head of the babe in the sling. It trembled as it rested there, but the tremor passed, and Annabel, turning once at the porch, gave her a last look. Then she departed with her companions.

That afternoon, Jack and Flora had shaken down to wedlock as married folk should, and sat together before the board spread with the dolls' tea-things. The pallid light in the great hall-kitchen faded; the candles were lighted; and then the children, first borrowing the stockings of their elders to hang at the bed's foot, were packed off early—for it was the custom to bring them down again at midnight for the carols. Aunt Rachel had their good-night kisses, not as she had them every night, but with the special ceremony of the mistletoe.

Other folk, grown folk, sat with Aunt Rachel that evening; but the old walnut chair did not move upon its rockers. There was merry talk, but Aunt Rachel took no part in it. The board was spread with ale and cheese and spiced loaf for the carol-singers; and the time drew near for their coming.

When at midnight, faintly on the air from the church below, there came the chiming of Christmas morning, all bestirred themselves.

"They'll be here in a few minutes," they said; "somebody go and bring the children down"; and within a very little while subdued noises were heard outside, and the lifting of the latch of the yard gate. The children were in their nightgowns, hardly fully awake; a low voice outside was heard giving orders; and then there arose on the night the carol.

"Hush!" they said to the wondering children; "listen! . . ."

It was the Cherry Tree Carol that rose outside, of how sweet Mary, the Queen of Galilee, besought Joseph to pluck the cherries for her Babe, and Joseph refused; and the voices of the singers, that had begun hesitatingly, grew strong and loud and free.

". . . and Joseph wouldn't pluck the cherries," somebody was whispering to the tiny Angela. . . .

"Mary said to Cherry Tree,
'Bow down to my knee,
That I may pluck cherries
For my Babe and me.' "

the carollers sang; and "Now listen, darling," the one who held Angela murmured. . . .

"The uppermost spray then
Bowed down to her knee;
'Thus you may see, Joseph,
These cherries are for me.'

"'O, eat your cherries, Mary,
Give them your Babe now;
O, eat your cherries, Mary,
That grew upon the bough.'"

The little Angela, within the arms that held her, murmured, "It's the gipsies, isn't it, mother?"

"No, darling. The gipsies have gone. It's the carol-singers, singing because Jesus was born."

"But, mother . . . it *is* the gipsies, isn't it? . . . 'Cos look . . ."

"Look where?"

"At Aunt Rachel, mother . . . The gipsy woman wouldn't go without her little baby, would she?"

"No, she wouldn't do that."

"Then has she *lent* it to Aunt Rachel, like I lend my new toys sometimes?"

The mother glanced across at Aunt Rachel, and then gathered the night-gowned figure more closely.

"The darling's only half awake," she murmured. . . . "Poor Aunt Rachel's sleepy too. . . ."

Aunt Rachel, her head dropped, her hands lightly folded as if about some shape that none saw but herself, her face again ineffable with that sweet and peaceful smile, was once more rocking softly in her chair.

The Rockery

E. G. Swain

The Vicar's garden at Stoneground has certainly been enclosed for more than seven centuries, and during the whole of that time its almost sacred privacy has been regarded as permanent and unchangeable. It has remained for the innovators of later and more audacious days to hint that it might be given into other hands, and still carry with it no curse that should make a new possessor hasten to undo his irreverence. Whether there can be warrant for such confidence, time will show. The experiences already related will show that the privacy of the garden has been counted upon both by good men and worse. And here is a story, in its way, more strange than any.

By way of beginning, it may be well to describe a part of the garden not hitherto brought into notice. That part lies on the western boundary, where the garden slopes down to a sluggish stream, hardly a stream at all, locally known as the Lode. The Lode bounds the garden on the west along its whole length, and there the moor-hen builds her nest, and the kingfisher is sometimes, but in these days too rarely, seen. But the centre of vision, as it were, of this western edge lies in a cluster of tall elms. Towards these all the garden paths converge, and about their base is raised a bank of earth, upon which is heaped a rockery of large stones lately overgrown with ferns.

Mr. Batchel's somewhat prim taste in gardening had long resented this disorderly bank. In more than one place in his garden had wild confusion given place to a park-like trimness, and there were not a few who would say that the change was not for the better. Mr. Batchel, however, went his own way, and in due time determined to remove the rockery. He was puzzled by its presence; he could see no reason why a bank should have been raised about the feet of the elms, and surmounted with stones; not a ray of sunshine ever found its way there, and none but coarse and uninteresting plants had established themselves. Whoever had raised the bank had done it ignorantly, or with some purpose not easy for Mr. Batchel to conjecture.

Upon a certain day, therefore, in the early part of December, when the garden had been made comfortable for its winter rest, he began, with the assistance of his gardener, to remove the stones into another place.

We do but speak according to custom in this matter, and there are few readers who will not suspect the truth, which is that the gardener began to remove the stones, whilst Mr. Batchel stood by and delivered criticisms of very slight value. Such strength, in fact, as Mr. Batchel possessed had concentrated itself upon the mind, and somewhat neglected his body, and what he called help, during his presence in the garden, was called by another name when the gardener and his boy were left to themselves, with full freedom of speech.

There were few of the stones rolled down by the gardener that Mr. Batchel could even have moved, but his astonishment at their size soon gave place to excitement at their appearance. His antiquarian tastes were strong, and were soon busily engaged. For, as the stones rolled down, his eyes were feasted, in a rapid succession, by capitals of columns, fragments of moulded arches and mullions, and other relics of ecclesiastical building.

Repeatedly did he call the gardener down from his work to put these fragments together, and before long there were several complete lengths of arcading laid upon the path. Stones which, perhaps, had been separated for centuries, once more came together, and Mr. Batchel, rubbing his hands in excited satisfaction, declared that he might recover the best parts of a Church by the time the rockery had been demolished.

The interest of the gardener in such matters was of a milder kind. "We must go careful," he merely observed, "when we come to the organ." They went on removing more and more stones, until at length the whole bank was laid bare, and Mr. Batchel's chief purpose achieved. How the stones were carefully arranged, and set up in other parts of the garden, is well known, and need not concern us now.

One detail, however, must not be omitted. A large and stout stake of yew, evidently of considerable age, but nevertheless quite sound, stood exposed after the clearing of the bank. There was no obvious reason for its presence, but it had been well driven in, so well that the strength of the gardener, or, if it made any difference, of the gardener and Mr. Batchel together, failed even to shake it. It was not unsightly, and might have remained where it was, had not the gardener exclaimed, "This is the very thing we want for the pump." It was so obviously "the very thing" that its removal was then and there decided upon.

The pump referred to was a small iron pump used to draw water from the lode. It had been affixed to many posts in turn, and defied them all to hold it. Not that the pump was at fault. It was a trifling affair enough. But the pumpers were usually garden-boys, whose impatient energy had never failed, before many days, to wriggle the pump away from its supports. When the gardener had, upon one occasion, spent half a day in attaching it firmly to a post, they had at once shaken out the post itself. Since, therefore, the matter was causing daily inconvenience, and the gardener becoming daily more concerned for his reputation as a rough carpenter, it was natural for him to exclaim, "This is the very thing." It was a better stake than he had ever used, and as had just been made evident, a stake that the ground would hold.

"Yes!" said Mr. Batchel, "it is the very thing; but can we get it up?" The gardener always accepted this kind of query as a challenge, and replied only by taking up a pick and setting to work, Mr. Batchel, as usual, looking on, and making, every now and then, a fruitless suggestion. After a few minutes, however, he made somewhat more than a suggestion. He darted forward and laid his hand upon the pick. "Don't you see some copper?" he asked quickly.

Every man who digs knows what a hiding place there is in the earth. The monotony of spade work is always relieved by a hope of turning up something unexpected. Treasure lies dimly behind all these hopes, so that the gardener, having seen Mr. Batchel excited over so much that was precious from his own point of view, was quite ready to look for something of value to an ordinary reasonable man. Copper might lead to silver, and that, in turn, to gold. At Mr. Batchel's eager question, therefore, he peered into the hole he had made, and examined everything there that might suggest the rounded form of a coin.

He soon saw what had arrested Mr. Batchel. There was a lustrous scratch on the side of the stake, evidently made by the pick, and though the metal was copper, plainly enough, the gardener felt that he had been deceived, and would have gone on with his work. Copper of that sort gave him no sort of excitement, and only a feeble interest.

Mr. Batchel, however, was on his hands and knees. There was a small irregular plate of copper nailed to the stake; without any difficulty he tore it away from the nails, and soon scraped it clean with a shaving of wood; then, rising to his feet, he examined his find.

There was an inscription upon it, so legible as to need no deciphering. It had been roughly and effectually made with a hammer and nail, the letters being formed by series of holes punched deeply into the metal, and what he read was:—

MOVE NOT THIS STAKE
NOV. 1, 1702

But to move the stake was what Mr. Batchel had determined upon, and the metal plate he held in his hand interested him chiefly as showing how long the post had been there. He had happened, as he supposed, upon an ancient landmark. The discovery, recorded elsewhere, of a well, near to the edge of his present lawn, had shown him that his premises had once been differently arranged. One of the minor antiquarian tasks he had set himself was to discover and record the old arrangement, and he felt that the position of this stake would help him. He felt no doubt of its being a point upon the western limit of the garden; not improbably marked in this way to show where the garden began, and where ended the ancient hauling-way, which had been secured to the public for purposes of navigation.

The gardener, meanwhile, was proceeding with his work. With no small difficulty he removed the rubble and clay which accounted for the firmness of the stake. It grew dark as the work went on, and a distant clock struck five before it was completed. Five was the hour at which the gardener usually went home; his day began early. He was not, however, a man to leave a small job unfinished, and he went on loosening the earth with his pick, and trying the effect, at intervals, upon the firmness of the stake. It naturally began to give, and could be moved from side to side through a space of some few inches. He lifted out the loosened stones, and loosened more. His pick struck iron, which, after loosening, proved to be links of a rusted chain. "They've buried a lot of rubbish in this hole," he remarked, as he went on loosening the chain, which, in the growing darkness, could hardly be seen. Mr. Batchel, meanwhile, occupied himself in a simpler task of working the stake to and fro, by way of loosening its hold. Ultimately it began to move with greater freedom. The gardener laid down his tool and grasped the stake, which his master was still holding; their combined efforts succeeded at once; the stake was lifted out.

It turned out to be furnished with an unusually long and sharp point, which explained the firmness of its hold upon the ground. The gardener carried it to the neighbourhood of the pump, in readiness for its next purpose, and made ready to go home. He would drive the stake to-morrow, he said, in the new place, and make the pump so secure that not even the boys could shake it. He also spoke of some designs he had upon the chain, should it prove to be of any considerable length. He was an ingenious man, and his skill in converting discarded articles to new uses was embarrassing to his master. Mr. Batchel, as has been said, was a prim gardener, and he had no liking for makeshift devices. He had that day seen his runner beans trained upon a length of old gas-piping, and had no intention of leaving the gardener in possession of such a treasure as a rusty chain. What he said, however, and said with truth, was that he wanted the chain for himself. He had no practical use for it, and hardly expected it to yield him any interest. But a chain buried in 1702 must be examined—nothing ancient comes amiss to a man of antiquarian tastes.

Mr. Batchel had noticed, whilst the gardener had been carrying away the stake, that the chain lay very loosely in the earth. The pick had worked well round it. He said, therefore, that the chain must be lifted out and brought to him upon the morrow, bade his gardener good night, and went in to his fireside.

This will appear to the reader to be a record of the merest trifles, but all readers will accept the reminder that there is no such thing as a trifle, and that what appears to be trivial has that appearance only so long as it stands alone. Regarded in the light of their consequences, those matters which have seemed to be least in importance, turn out, often enough, to be the greatest. And these trifling occupations, as we may call them for the last time, of Mr. Batchel and the gardener, had consequences which shall now be set down as Mr. Batchel himself narrated them. But we must take events in their order. At present Mr. Batchel is at his fireside, and his gardener at home with his family. The stake is removed, and the hole, in which lies some sort of an iron chain, is exposed.

Upon this particular evening Mr. Batchel was dining out. He was a good natured man, with certain mild powers of entertainment, and his presence as an occasional guest was not unacceptable at some of the more considerable houses of the neighbourhood. And let us hasten to observe that he was not a guest who made any great impression upon the larders or the cellars of his hosts. He liked port, but he liked it only of good quality, and in small quantity. When he returned from a dinner party, therefore, he was never either in a surfeited condition of body, or in any confusion of mind. Not uncommonly after his return upon such occasions did he perform accurate work. Unfinished contributions to sundry local journals were seldom absent from his desk. They were his means of recreation. There they awaited convenient intervals of leisure, and Mr. Batchel was accustomed to say that of these intervals he found none so productive as a late hour, or hour and a half, after a dinner party.

Upon the evening in question he returned, about an hour before midnight, from dining at the house of a retired officer residing in the neighbourhood, and the evening had been somewhat less enjoyable than usual. He had taken in to dinner a young lady who had too persistently assailed him with antiquarian questions. Now Mr. Batchel did not like talking what he regarded as "shop," and was not much at home with young ladies, to whom he knew that, in the nature of things, he could be but imperfectly acceptable. With infinite good will towards them, and a genuine liking for their presence, he felt that he had but little to offer them in exchange. There was so little in common between his life and theirs. He felt distinctly at his worst when he found himself treated as a mere scrap-book of information. It made him seem, as he would express it, de-humanised.

Upon this particular evening the young lady allotted to him, perhaps at her own request, had made a scrap-book of him, and he had returned home somewhat discontented, if also somewhat amused. His discontent arose from having been deprived of the general conversation he so greatly, but so rarely, enjoyed. His amusement was caused by the incongruity between a very light-hearted young lady and the subject upon which she had made him talk, for she had talked of nothing else but modes of burial.

He began to recall the conversation as he lit his pipe and dropped into his armchair. She had either been reflecting deeply upon the matter, or, as seemed to Mr. Batchel, more probable, had read something and half forgotten it. He recalled her questions, and the answers by which he had vainly tried to lead her to a more attractive topic. For example:

She: Will you tell me why people were buried at cross roads?

He: Well, consecrated ground was so, jealously guarded that a criminal would be held to have forfeited the right to be buried amongst Christian folk. His friends would therefore choose cross roads where there was set a wayside cross, and make his grave at the foot of it. In some of my journeys in Scotland I have seen crosses.

But the young lady had refused to be led into Scotland. She had stuck to her subject.

She: Why have coffins come back into use? There is nothing in our Burial Service about a coffin.

He: True, and the use of the coffin is due, in part, to an ignorant notion of confining the corpse, lest, like Hamlet's father, he should walk the earth. You will have noticed that the corpse is always carried out of the house feet foremost, to suggest a final exit, and that the grave is often covered with a heavy slab. Very curious epitaphs are to be found on these slabs.

But she was not to be drawn into the subject of epitaphs. She had made him tell of other devices for confining spirits to their prison, and securing the peace of the living, especially of those adopted in the case of violent and mischievous men. Altogether an unusual sort of young lady.

The conversation, however, had revived his memories of what was, after all, a matter of some interest, and he determined to look through his parish registers for records of exceptional burials. He was surprised at himself for never having done it. He dismissed the matter from his mind for the time being, and as it was a bright moonlight night he thought he would finish his pipe in the garden.

Therefore, although midnight was close at hand, he strolled complacently round his garden, enjoying the light of the moon no less than in the daytime he would have enjoyed the sun; and thus it was that he arrived at the scene of his labors upon the old rockery. There was more light than there had been at the end of the afternoon, and when he had walked up the bank, and stood over the hole we have already described, he could distinctly see the few exposed links of the iron chain. Should he remove it at once to a place of safety, out of the way of the gardener? It was about time for bed. The city clocks were then striking midnight. He would let the chain decide. If it came out easily he would remove it; otherwise, it should remain until morning.

The chain came out more than easily. It seemed to have a force within itself. He gave but a slight tug at the free end with a view of ascertaining what resistance he had to encounter, and immediately found himself lying upon his back with the chain in his hand. His back had fortunately turned towards an elm three feet away which broke his fall, but there had been violence enough to cause him no little surprise.

The effort he had made was so slight that he could not account for having lost his feet; and being a careful man, he was a little anxious about his evening coat, which he was still wearing. The chain, however, was in his hand, and he made haste to coil it into a portable shape, and to return to the house.

Some fifty yards from the spot was the northern boundary of the garden, a long wall with a narrow lane beyond. It was not unusual, even at this hour of the night, to hear footsteps there. The lane was used by railway men, who passed to and from their work at all hours, as also by some who returned late from entertainments in the neighbouring city.

But Mr. Batchel, as he turned back to the house, with his chain over one arm, heard more than footsteps. He heard for a few moments the unmistakable sound of a scuffle, and then a piercing cry, loud and sharp, and a noise of running. It was such a cry as could only have come from one in urgent need of help.

Mr. Batchel dropped his chain. The garden wall was some ten feet high and he had no means of scaling it. But he ran quickly into the house, passed out by the hall door into the street, and so towards the lane without a moment's loss of time.

Before he has gone many yards he sees a man running from the lane with his clothing in great disorder, and this man, at the sight of Mr. Batchel, darts across the road, runs along in the shadow of an opposite wall and attempts to escape.

The man is known well enough to Mr. Batchel. It is one Stephen Medd, a respectable and sensible man, by occupation a shunter, and Mr. Batchel at once calls out to ask what has happened. Stephen, however, makes no reply but continues to run along the shadow of the wall, whereupon Mr. Batchel crosses over and intercepts him, and again asks what is amiss. Stephen answers wildly and breathlessly, "I'm not going to stop here, let me go home."

As Mr. Batchel lays his hand upon the man's arm and draws him into the light of the moon, it is seen that his face is streaming with blood from a wound near the eye.

He is somewhat calmed by the familiar voice of Mr. Batchel, and is about to speak, when another scream is heard from the lane. The voice is that of a boy or woman, and no sooner does Stephen hear it than he frees himself violently from Mr. Batchel and makes away towards his home. With no less speed does Mr. Batchel make for the lane, and finds about half way down a boy lying on the ground wounded and terrified.

At first the boy clings to the ground, but he, too, is soon reassured by Mr. Batchel's voice, and allows himself to be lifted on to his feet. His wound is also in the face, and Mr. Batchel takes the boy into his house, bathes and plasters his wound, and soon restores him to something like calm. He is what is termed a call-boy, employed by the Railway Company to awaken drivers at all hours, and give them their instructions.

Mr. Batchel is naturally impatient for the moment he can question the boy about his assailant, who is presumably also the assailant of Stephen Medd. No one had been visible in the lane, though the moon shone upon it from end to end. At the first available moment, therefore, he asks the boy, "Who did this?"

The answer came, without any hesitation, "Nobody." "There was nobody there," he said, "and all of a sudden somebody hit me with an iron thing."

Then Mr. Batchel asked, "Did you see Stephen Medd?" He was becoming greatly puzzled.

The boy replied that he had seen Mr. Medd "a good bit in front," with nobody near him, and that all of a sudden someone knocked him down.

Further questioning seemed useless. Mr. Batchel saw the boy to his home, left him at the door, and returned to bed, but not to sleep. He could not cease from thinking, and he could think of nothing but assaults from invisible hands. Morning seemed long in coming, but came at last.

Mr. Batchel was up betimes and made a very poor breakfast. Dallying with the morning paper, rather than reading it, his eye was arrested by a headline about "Mysterious assaults in Elmham." He felt that he had mysteries of his own to occupy him and was in no mood to be interested in more assaults. But he had some knowledge of Elmham, a small town ten miles distant from Stoneground, and he read the brief paragraph, which contained no more than the substance of a telegram. It said, however, that three persons had been victims of unaccountable assaults. Two of them had escaped with slight injuries, but the third, a young woman, was dangerously wounded, though still alive and conscious. She declared that she was quite alone in her house and had been suddenly struck with great violence by what felt like a piece of iron, and that she must have bled to death but for a neighbour who heard her cries. The neighbour had at once looked out and seen nobody, but had bravely gone to her friend's assistance.

Mr. Batchel laid down his newspaper considerably impressed, as was natural, by the resemblance of these tragedies to what he had witnessed himself. He was in no condition, after his excitement and his sleepless night, to do his usual work. His mind reverted to the conversation at the dinner party and the trifle of antiquarian research it had suggested. Such occupation had often served him when he found himself suffering from a cold, or otherwise indisposed for more serious work. He would get the registers and collect what entries there might be of irregular burial. He found only one such entry, but that one was enough. There was a note dated All Hallows, 1702, to this effect:

> This day did a vagrant from Elmham beat cruelly to death two poor men who had refused him alms, and upon a hue and cry being raised, took his own life. He was buried in one Parson's Close with a stake through his body and his arms confined in chains, and stoutly covered in.

No further news came from Elmham. Either the effort had been exhausted, or its purpose achieved. But what could have led the young lady, a stranger to Mr. Batchel and to his garden, to hit upon so appropriate a topic? Mr. Batchel could not answer the question as he put it to himself again and again during the day. He only knew that she had given him a warning, by which, to his shame and regret, he had been too obtuse to profit.

The Room of Fear

Ella Scrysmour

Menzies Castle was a house of mourning! Sir John Baverie—delightful guest and most companionable of friends—was dead. Mollie, Lady Menzies, the youthful chatelaine of the historic house was red-eyed with weeping, as she flung herself into her husband's arms.

"Archie, I shall go mad if we stay here another day. It's too awful!"

Lord Menzies smoothed his wife's hair and fondled her tenderly. He was a gaunt man of forty-odd years, and his young wife was the apple of his eye.

"Little one, don't worry," he said quietly. "It's just a coincidence. You heard what the doctors said. Sir John died of heart failure and—"

"Yes," she broke in, "but so did Tom Estcourt. Tom—who was never ill in his life. And then Rosa Mullindon. No one could deny that Rosa was healthy enough—yet she died. And now dear old Sir John. I'm sure the Tower Room is haunted!"

"My dear Mollie, you really must not give way to such fancies. We live in the twentieth century, and rooms and places aren't haunted now. The Tower Room is perfectly safe, and it is only an extraordinary coincidence that on the three occasions it has been used as a bedchamber, its occupants have died of heart failure."

But little Mollie Menzies shook her head. She still believed in the uncanny.

"Look here," he said at last. "I'll sleep there myself, one day soon. You see, I shall be quite all right."

"No, no," cried his wife. "You mustn't—I'm so afraid, Archie, I—"

A bell clanged through the great hall. A second later the butler announced "Miss Shiela Crerar."

Lord Menzies smiled.

"All right, little girl. See your Psychic Detective. She has evidently agreed to take your case up for you."

Shiela came forward quickly.

"I was so sorry to hear of your trouble, Lady Menzies, and I do hope I shall be able to help you."

"You don't know how thankful I was to hear you were still staying with Lady Morven, Miss Crerar. She told me how wonderful you were over that peculiar affair at Duroch Lodge, and so I telephoned through on chance."

"And as it was only a matter of fifteen miles I motored here at once," finished Shiela with a smile.

"My husband, Miss Crerar. Now you must go, Archie, I can't possibly talk in front of you. You don't know how horribly material he is, Miss Crerar."

As soon as the two women were alone Lady Menzies began.

"There isn't a great deal to tell," she said thoughtfully. "I will show you over the Castle later on. The Tower Room is the oldest part of it, and dates from the tenth century. There were originally four stories to it, now nothing is left but the Tower Room itself, which is built on a higher level than the rest of the Castle. Underneath it are cellars, which were originally used as kitchens, I believe. The room was closed up in my husband's grandfather's time—it was supposed to be damp. About two years ago, the Earl had the door re-opened, and the room furnished as a studio for me. The light is excellent there for painting. That is my great hobby, you know."

"Well?" said Shiela interestedly.

"Well, there is no more to tell. I used the room constantly with no ill effect. A year ago this very month we had the entire west wing redecorated. There was a small house party here at the time, and I was rather pushed for room. I—I had the Tower Room fitted up as a bedroom for a distant cousin of mine." Her voice broke slightly. "I had known Tom Estcourt all my life. He was a sailor—a jolly, lighthearted fellow that nothing could upset. He slept in that room for three nights. He never complained about anything, on the fourth he was found dead in bed. It was 'just heart failure' the doctor said. A few weeks later Rosa Mullindon came to stay with me. She had been engaged to Tom, and expressed a desire to occupy the same room in which he died. We tried to dissuade her, but she urged us to give in to her wishes; she was broken-hearted over his death. I went in to her at eleven—she was quite happy, reading a book of his that had never been removed. Next morning she was dead. Everyone thought it was just a coincidence, and when the ceiling fell down in Sir John's bedroom, he it was who suggested sleeping in the Tower Room. He knew of the deaths of Tom and Rosa, and always laughed at me when I said that some uncanny influence must be at work. I told him there was plenty of room, and there was not the slightest necessity to use that horrible room, but he insisted. That was last night. He was as merry as could be, and made arrangements to be called earlier this morning, as he had arranged to play nine holes of golf with the minister before breakfast. When his man went in to call him, he was dead, had been dead for some hours. Dr Brown was sent for at once, and certified, as before, heart failure. He seemed dissatisfied with his own diagnosis, however, and phoned to Taynuilt for Dr Andrew, and to Oban for Professor Weymiss. They arrived an hour ago, and corroborated his verdict. Just heart failure, with no complications. But I am not satisfied, Miss Crerar."

"But it seems a very straightforward story," said Shiela. "So far it is strange that three deaths should have taken place there, but you say you used the room constantly as a studio with no ill effects?"

Lady Menzies held out her hands pathetically.

"That's the story," she said. "Sir John's relatives are very anxious that his body should be taken to England to his home there. It will leave by the night express tomorrow, so you can commence your investigations the day after. Meanwhile, the house is too sad to offer much entertainment. Sir John was very popular, you know."

"Please don't bother about me," said Shiela. "If you will let me go to my room I shall be quite happy with a book."

"Most of my guests left considerately this morning," went on Mollie, "and by lunch tomorrow the last one will have gone, so there will be a quiet house in which you can work. I'll take you to your room. We dine at seven."

When Shiela was alone she sat at her open window and drank in the balmy air. Her life was altered by the merest chance. So far she had been successful. Would she continue so?

On the following evening the minister held a brief service in the darkened death-chamber, and then the coffin was carried on stalwart shoulders to the ferry, where it was taken across the Loch to the nearest station—Taynuilt.

The castle was empty at last—Shiela its only guest. It was with mixed feelings she entered the Tower Room. In her heart she hoped that if some sinister influence was at work she would be able to discover it. But, on the whole, she felt rather sceptical, and thought Lady Menzies was distressing herself over nothing.

There was certainly nothing ghostly about the Tower Room. It was a long apartment, with a circular alcove at one end, lighted as well by large windows on either side. In the alcove was a glass door, which led down a short flight of steps to the garden and the cellars below. A huge stone hearth, with massive brass dogs, was built cornerwise across the room, which added considerably to its picturesque appearance.

There was neither cupboard nor recess, and nowhere where anyone could hide. Lady Menzies led the way down to the cellars. There was nothing even gloomy about these. They were lit by electricity, and the sandy floor was dry and clean. Both the Tower Room and the vaults seemed above reproach.

"I'll stay here all night," announced Shiela, when once they were in the Tower Room.

"No, no," gasped Lady Menzies. "I am sure it's not safe. I couldn't allow it—"

"Nonsense," smiled Shiela. "If I am to investigate, I must stay here. Now please don't worry. I promise you I shall be quite all right. Oh, there is a bell. Is it in working order?" and she pulled at an old-fashioned bell cord.

Immediately there clanged out a cracked and plaintive call, and a maid came scared into the room.

"It's all right, Sanders," said Lady Menzies. "Miss Crerar was trying the bell."

"Now," said Shiela, "if anything happens I'll peal the bell, and you can send someone in to me."

It was not without misgivings that Lady Menzies left her in the ill-fated room that night. But Shiela was very cheerful. The lights were full on and a fire burnt merrily, and as Lady Menzies shut the door after her, Shiela heard the muffled tones of the big grandfather clock outside strike eleven. She had really no preparations to make. She had no plan of campaign, for she didn't know what she was waiting for—what she expected even. However, she drew a chair close to the blazing fire and began to read.

The book was rather dull, and she dozed over it; the fire burned low, and suddenly she awoke with a start. The grandfather clock outside chimed the three-quarters. It must be a quarter to one! She had been asleep nearly an hour. She stretched her arms in delicious contentment, her mouth was wide open in a yawn, but even as the last silvery notes died away in the silence she became conscious of fear, fear of something intangible, and she realised she was shivering from head to foot. With an effort she relaxed her muscles, and her arms fell to her sides, but the effort left her weak and trembling. Her mouth was stiff with horror, and she closed it with a jerk.

She looked round the room—there was nothing to be seen—the lights shone steadily, and a faint glow came from the fast-dying embers. Suddenly her knees gave way under her, and she sank exhausted to the floor. The grandfather clock chimed again and in a mellow tone proclaimed the hour of one.

For fifteen minutes she had lain upon the floor in an uncontrollable fit of fear. She tried to reason with herself, but could scarcely command her thoughts. She was only conscious of one thing, one sensation—terror, a blind terror that was all the more hideous as its source was nameless.

There was no unreal quiet about the room—no ghostly calm. There was no strange light to be seen or unaccustomed cry to be heard. Everything was quite natural—there was absolutely nothing to account for her nervous state.

She managed to raise herself on one elbow, and was shocked to find the sweat pouring off her forehead, while her heart pumped painfully. She dragged herself to her chair and fell back exhausted into it. As the minutes passed so her terror increased until she felt suffocated. The grandfather clock chimed with monotonous regularity, and presently struck two. An hour and a quarter had passed! Shiela felt powerless to move—the minutes were the most awful in her life. The fire burnt lower still until the embers of wood became white and lifeless. Again and again the silvery chimes rent the air, but the girl was as if under a spell, and remained motionless, her eyes glazed with terror, her face white and drawn, and her limbs quaking.

Three o'clock—four! Already the grey dawn was creeping in through the curtained windows and the birds had commenced their morning song.

As the last stroke of four died away the nauseating pall that had hung over Shiela like an unwholesome garment lifted. She became aware of a sense of relief. Her limbs ceased trembling. She was weak, it was true, but she was clothed once more in her right mind. Tired and worn out with her vigil of terror, she flung herself on the bed and drew the eiderdown about her cold shoulders.

At eight tea was brought her by a frightened maid, who feared what she might find in that room of tragedy. But Shiela was sleeping peacefully, and there was no hint of mystery or horror.

She awoke lazily, and drank her tea greedily. She was tired and very thirsty. She looked round the room, and gradually the night's events unfolded themselves to her sleepy brain. She remembered the unholy terror she had suffered. From a quarter to one until four she had been within its awful grasp. She had suffered the tortures of the damned, yet there was nothing to account for it. She dressed slowly, and thought deeply. Yes, there must be something wrong with the room! She knew now that the doctor's verdict of heart failure was correct. The inmates had died of heart failure brought on by fear. But fear of what?

She tapped the walls; they were all solid stone, and gave out no hollow sound. She looked up the chimney; it was a very old-fashioned one, and she could see the glimmer of light beyond the gloom. It was a very puzzled Shiela that appeared at breakfast. Lady Menzies looked at her anxiously.

"How did you sleep?" she asked.

"When I got to bed—very well indeed. But I sat up rather late. I feel tired this morning."

"You saw nothing—heard nothing?"

"Nothing."

Her hostess seemed relieved, and spent the day with Shiela in the open air. They had a round of golf, and in the afternoon explored the glens and woods.

The second night she sat up as before. Again the room had no perceptible change, but as the last sound of the clock chiming the quarter to one broke the stillness, the same terror came over her. This time the fear was more intense. She experienced her old childish fears of the dark, but they were intensified a thousandfold. She was horribly frightened, she crouched down in a corner of the room as if waiting for some terrible doom. Her heart beat painfully—her throat was parched—her lips cracked. She tried to remonstrate with herself for her stupidity, but the ever present feeling of terror overwhelmed her. Her head was bent as if waiting for a blow—she anticipated the hideousness of pain.

Her wonderful will power was hardly strong enough to help her in her fears, and as she involuntarily gave way to them, her sufferings were more acute than before.

She made one more effort to reach the door, but her limbs refused to work, and she sank down, muttering incoherent gibberings. Time passed—she had lost the sense of where she was. Dimly she heard four silvery notes. Four o'clock! And as if by magic, the fear left her.

This time she felt weaker than on the previous night, and when the maid called her in the morning she was flushed and feverish, and said she would have her breakfast in bed.

Lady Menzies came in to see her, and realised at once that something had happened. Shiela, however, refused to tell her anything, and only announced that she intended going on with her investigations.

Three more nights passed, but the strain was growing too much for the girl. She grew to dread the days, because they would lead to the nights. She dreaded the nights, and longed for day to dawn. Every night, as regularly as clockwork, as soon as the clock chimed the quarter to one, the feeling of terror claimed her, and for hours she was in its cold embrace.

She was very reticent about her discovery, but Lady Menzies felt alarmed as she saw the roses fading from her cheeks, and the deep shadows under her eyes growing darker day by day.

The mystery remained unsolved. Try as she might, she could discover no reason for the paroxysms that oppressed her.

One day she asked Lord Menzies to send for Robert Moffat, a well-known chemical analyst of Glasgow. Carefully he examined the room, but could find not the slightest sign of poison or noxious gas concealed in the wallpapers or furniture. After a long examination he announced that there was absolutely nothing the matter with the room at all!

Then they brought an architect in to see if he could discover any secret chamber leading from the Tower Room, but his examinations only proved that the walls were quite solid.

A fortnight passed, and Shiela had become very nervy and restless. The nightly torment she went through was beginning to undermine her constitution. Each night left her weaker than the previous one; she began to suffer from palpitations of the heart, and experienced great pain when she breathed.

"I won't give in," she said to herself, between tightly clenched teeth. "I *will* master this stupid terror."

Although the fear was still intangible, it had become more real. She suffered actual physical pain at times. It varied in intensity, but, always sensitive to the slightest scratch, her sufferings at times were almost unbearable. Then came the night when her whole body felt as if it was on the rack. Her joints cracked—her muscles swelled, and when she woke in the morning, her arms were inflamed and sore.

She felt the time had come to speak of the terror she was going through. Lord Menzies looked grave.

"If there is anything supernatural at work, don't you think it would be wiser if I had the door blocked up again? The room needn't be used, and I think it would be wiser for you to give up this search."

"No," said Shiela, defiantly; "I am determined to get to the bottom of this mystery. I wonder if you would have the room entirely re-decorated?"

"Why, certainly, if you think it will make any difference."

"And the chimney swept?"

"Certainly."

The orders were given, and for a week Shiela slept in peace, and to some extent recovered her nerve.

When the room was finished, Shiela again insisted on sleeping there, but the horror was worse, if anything, than it was before. She felt the cold sweat running down her body; her hands were clammy and cold, and as the clock outside struck three, she realised she could no longer stand the strain. She dragged herself across the floor to the bell-pull—unconsciously her lips moved. "Stavordale! Stavordale! help me," she cried. A harsh bell clanged through the oaken corridors with startling suddenness. Lady Menzies stirred uneasily, and then woke to life.

"Archie—It's Miss Crerar; she's in danger," she cried. "Quickly—quickly."

But the servants were before her, and when she reached the Tower Room, Shiela was being carried out. She was quite stiff; her eyes were closed, and her breath came in short convulsive gasps. Tenderly she was placed on a settee, and brandy was forced between her tightly clenched teeth. She moaned slightly, and opened her eyes, and then fell into a rather restless sleep.

Lady Menzies watched by her side through the rest of the night, and in the morning, although she was much better, a doctor was sent for.

"Heart trouble," he said, quickly, when he first glanced at her, but after examination—"Very strange. She shows every sign of having a badly strained heart. Yet it is working quite normally now. I should say she has had some great shock. Plenty of rest and quiet, a light diet, and she will be quite all right in a couple of days."

About ten, Stavordale Hartland came over in a great state of excitement.

"Shiela—Miss Crerar?" he asked. "Is she ill?"

"Why, how did you know?" asked Lady Menzies in some surprise. "She is certainly not very well. She fainted last night, but there is not the slightest cause for alarm."

Stavordale's face whitened.

"It's damnable," he cried. "I beg your pardon, Lady Menzies, but it really is. It's perfectly mad of a child like Shiela to meddle with the unknown. When may I see her?" he asked eagerly.

"Tomorrow. She will be quite herself, I hope."

Next morning Stavordale arrived with an armful of flowers for Shiela. She smiled shyly as she took them.

"How did you know I was ill?" she asked.

"You told me yourself," he said, grimly.

"I did?" in some astonishment.

"Yes. I awoke and heard you calling me. 'Stavordale, Stavordale, help me,' you seemed to say. Oh, so distinctly that I thought for the moment you were still with us in the house. The horror in your voice nearly maddened me—I knew something was wrong. Little girl," he went on hoarsely, "if you called for me in distress, surely it proves you think of me sometimes? Won't you give all this up and be my wife?"

"Oh, I can't" she cried tremulously. "I—I can't. I have a mission to fulfil I can't explain. If you will only be patient—"

"Will you send for me if you ever want any help?" he pleaded. "I promise you I will be patient. I won't worry you any more—"

"If I ever need any help I will send for you," she said sweetly, and he had to be content with that.

"I am going to stay in the cellars under the Tower Room," announced Shiela a few days later. In vain they threatened—forbade—commanded.

"Won't you let someone watch with you?" pleaded Lady Menzies, but she refused all help.

At eleven she went down and turned the lights on full. It was rather chilly, and she buttoned up her coat and drew a rug round her shoulders. The hours passed slowly. One—two—three—four. At seven she went to her own room, and slept peacefully until late in the morning. The next night found her in the cellars again, but nothing disturbed her tranquillity. The cellars were obviously immune from the phenomena that haunted the upper chamber.

In desperation she fulfilled her promise to Stavordale and sent for him.

"I can't fathom this at all," she said. "I wonder if you and Lord Menzies would sit up with me tonight in the Tower Room? I want to see if the same fear will affect you both."

That night there were three watchers. It was very still, and there was a pleasant smell of cigar smoke in the room. They talked on all subjects but one—psychology was taboo. Lord Menzies was in the midst of a funny story when the clock chimed the quarter to one. He stopped in the middle of a word, his face whitened, and he stared at Shiela out of glassy eyes. Stavordale moved restlessly. Shiela had lost consciousness, fear the omnipotent held her within its thrall.

Lord Menzies staggered to his feet, and gasped in unnatural tones, "I'm stifling. Let's get out of this accursed place."

It took the united efforts of the three to force themselves out of the room. They staggered, supported each other, staggered again, and eventually reached the door.

The sweat was running down the two men's faces, and it was with a sigh of relief that they closed the door behind them. But as they reached the passage the terror left them.

"This is the end," said Lord Menzies dryly. "You don't sleep there again, young lady. Tomorrow I have the door bricked up. Why, it's worse than uncanny—it's unholy."

Next day Shiela went to the Tower Room. She was very disappointed. All the suffering she had gone through had been for nought. She had not discovered the sinister secret of the room. Already the furniture was gone, and the carpet had been taken away. The sunlight streamed in and its beams strayed into the passage beyond. Almost without thinking, she noticed the difference in the flooring. Out in the passage it was black and shining, slightly rough and uneven in places. In the Tower Room itself the floor was more even—newer, smoother.

"I wonder," she said to herself, and went in search of the earl.

"Before the door is bricked up," she said abruptly, "I wonder if you would try and prise up some of the flooring in the Tower Room?"

"Why?" he asked.

"I was looking at it just now, and the floor looks altogether newer than that outside. Surely if the Tower is the oldest part of the castle, and the original flooring is in the passage, the Tower Room ought to have still older boards?"

"Start at the door," she directed. "One of the boards looks quite loose there."

With great difficulty he succeeded in raising one of the narrow boards. Eagerly they peered underneath. A wooden step, black with age, worm-eaten, and uneven, met their astonished gaze. He prised open a second and a third board, and three more steps were laid bare before them.

"This room was on a lower level at one time," said Shiela in excitement. "Oh, have the floor all taken up, Lord Menzies."

With the help of some of the outdoor servants, the whole of the flooring was removed, and the original floor was open to view, some three and a half feet below; three stairs led down to it from the other portion of the house.

Shiela gazed at it uncomprehendingly. It was a very rough, uneven floor, great knots were in the wood, and in parts it was very frail. Here and there iron rings and rusty bolts were fixed to the ground. In one corner an iron slab was raised perhaps a foot from the ground. On the slab itself were fastened metal sockets in the shape of a boot. Shiela gazed at them curiously, and slipped her little feet into them.

"Whatever are they for?" she asked, and suddenly gave a cry of pain. "Oh, help me, Lord Menzies. I can't get out. Something is hurting me."

The earl bent over her. A rusty catch on one side still worked, and he opened the boot-shaped metal. Inside were sharp iron spikes that fell into position when the foot was slipped into the "boot"; but they were so cunningly fixed that they would not allow the feet to come out again, and the slightest movement gave the most excruciating pain.

Shiela was scared. "What is it?" she asked.

"Torture," he breathed.

He picked up an old and rusty pair of thumbscrews. "A torture chamber," he repeated, "and I should say one of the most horrible of its kind, yet I have never heard of it. Who used it—whether it was civil or religious—I don't know. It must have been complete in its terrors."

Blood stains on the floor had turned brown and rusty, but they were ominous reminders of the horrors of bygone days. In one corner lay a spiked iron club, rusted with blood. There was a rack fixed to the floor itself. Chains, clubs, iron masks with bloody spikes inside—the room was completely equipped for its dreadful purpose.

"It's horrible," said Shiela, shuddering. "I wonder I didn't think of the solution myself. This was a torture chamber, and probably always used at the dead of night."

"From about a quarter to one until four o'clock," put in Lord Menzies.

"Yes. It would be the most unlikely time for discovery. It was no doubt entirely secret. That is the reason you have no records of its existence. You see," she went on excitedly, "the hideous fear of the unhappy victims communicated itself to the very room. The walls, the wood, the bricks, were impregnated with wave upon wave of terror from the suffering ones. They retained it throughout the ages, and each night the terror that was once inflicted here, is let loose again at the hour it used to take place."

"But is such a thing possible?" asked the earl.

Shiela smiled. "It seems like it, doesn't it? What other explanation can you give? At any rate, may I suggest that you have the old floor taken away altogether?"

"Well?"

"Have the cavity between the old and new floors filled in, and destroy"—pointing with a shudder—"these."

"And you think that the room will be all right then?"

"I don't know. It seems possible."

"You will stay till it is all complete," urged Lady Menzies.

"With pleasure."

The work was set in motion at once, and in the course of excavations the workmen discovered a charred skeleton. The fingers were gone, and the way the bones were twisted proved only too plainly the pain that the unhappy creature must have suffered.

"May it rest in peace," said Lord Menzies, and he gave orders for its burial.

The hideous belts and torture instruments the earl caused to be thrown into the loch. He never found any records of the terrible place. He searched his own family histories, but never a sign or clue was given to point to its existence.

Shiela, Lord Menzies, and Stavordale Hartland stayed in the room the first night that the floor had been relaid. At a quarter to one they all became nervous, but the night passed with no ill effects. Clearly the Room of Fear no longer justified its name. The intangible horrors of the past had gone.

The sounds of agony, the horror and terror, the awe inspiring spectacles that had been absorbed into the very room itself, and that were nightly exuded from it, had gone never to return. The Torture Chamber was no more.

It was early September when Shiela once more boarded a train en route for Edinburgh.

Stavordale Hartland saw her off from Benderloch. She had stayed a couple of nights at Duroch Lodge after leaving Menzies Castle. As the guard waved his flag, Stavordale drew towards her, and instinctively their lips met. The whistle blew, and Shiela, blushing rosy red, slipped back into her corner seat, trembling with happiness.

Stavordale Hartland watched the train fade away in the distance. What mattered it that no smiling face leant out of the window and waved him a farewell? He pictured the rosy face in the corner, the tremulous lips, the downcast eyes. He was well content.

The Seaweed Room

Clarice Irene Clinghan

"This is the seaweed room," announced the housekeeper, putting a key into the lock; "it's been shut up for a long time, and will be a bit musty."

With this she threw open the stout oaken door, and we entered a square apartment, darkened by closed shutters, and heavy with a strong, pungent odor. As our guide raised a window and opened the blinds there was a rustling all about us as of the flight of pigeons. This was caused by the fluttering of quantities of dry seaweed which were festooned upon the walls, and over the doors and windows.

"That's nothing but common seaweed," said the good woman, noticing our interested glances. "It's used only as an ornament and to give character to the room. All the choice varieties are in these glass cases, and pressed in this pile of scrapbooks, with notes and explanations under 'em."

"Did Professor Linwood collect these specimens himself?" I asked.

"I suppose so. He used to go on long voyages to the tropics and come home laden with new varieties, and then he'd spend months classifying and arranging them. He was a diver in his younger days, and after that made contracts for lifting sunken vessels, or exploring old hulks that had money or merchandise on board. He'd put on his diving suit and go down with his men, I've heard tell, and many's the strange adventures he's had in ships at the bottom of the ocean—so he told me one day when he felt chatty. That's how he first took to collecting seaweeds; he ransacked the bottom of the sea to get specimens. But after his marriage he never seemed to care for it any more. But perhaps all this don't interest you—it's the seaweed you want. You can examine it as much as you like."

We did so and lingered long, held by the charm of this strange room, that was redolent with the mysteries of the great deep. We sat on a couch, talking in low tones and listening to the rustling seaweeds over our heads, our feet resting on some of the same material, which had been fashioned into a rude mat that covered the floor and also the divan on which we were seated.

The whole apartment was full of it in all forms and phases. A wreath of it surrounded the only portrait in the room—that of a young girl with frank pleasing eyes and a sweet mouth.

The housekeeper, who had excused herself for a few moments, now returned with tea and biscuits. As she poured the fragrant beverage into little fat cups we ventured to inquire who the original of the picture was.

"Mrs. Linwood, the professor's wife," replied the woman, giving a quick, apprehensive look at it over her shoulder.

"Then," replied my companion, "it's no wonder the professor took no more voyages after his marriage!"

"I said he collected no more seaweed, sir," responded the housekeeper. " He made one voyage directly after his marriage, and took his bride with him. The vessel was wrecked in a terrific storm and only a few of the passengers were saved. Mrs. Linwood was among the lost."

"That was an odd coincidence—that she should be lost and he be saved," I said, half questioningly.

"Well, sir, that leads up to the most peculiar story you ever heard. As long as the professor lived I never dared breathe it, but now he's gone I might relate a strange circumstance in connection with this room."

We encouraged her so much that the good woman began immediately.

"It was not until the professor was nearly sixty that he thought of taking a wife. Then he was very foolish, if I may be allowed to say it, for he fell in love with a little girl only eighteen, and he being rich, her parents favored the match, though she was much attached to a second cousin of hers, a young fellow in an importing house, poor, but with good prospects; and, as luck would have it, this cousin was on the same steamer that took the professor and his bride to China, he going there on business for his firm.

"It must have been hard for the two poor young things to be doomed to such a long voyage, under such circumstances, especially as the professor was of an intensely jealous disposition and forbade his wife to speak to her cousin.

"But, as I said, the vessel ran aground in a storm and sank almost immediately. Mrs. Linwood was drowned; and her husband came back a changed man, broken in mind and body. He had even lost his interest in his particular fad, and I have seen him shudder at the sight of a piece of seaweed. He locked up this room and I never saw him enter it again except on one notable occasion."

"What was that?" inquired my companion.

"Well, you see, not having his scientific studies to take up his mind, the poor man became very lonesome and morbid. He never wanted to be alone, and must needs have a houseful of company the whole time. This was easy, for he had a great many nephews and nieces, and they, with their friends, kept us in a state of commotion, especially during the holidays and in summer vacations.

"One Christmas eve, his favorite nephew, Jack Newton, came late in the evening, and to save my soul I didn't know where to put him to sleep. He was a merry, rollicking lad of seventeen, and he said he'd sleep in the attic—anywhere so that he got a chance at the dinner next day—always thinking of his stomach, like any healthy boy.

"The attic was out of the question. Suddenly a thought came to me, and I asked him if he'd mind sleeping in the seaweed room?

"'Just the thing—awfully jolly,' said the boy, giving me a squeeze that nearly broke my neck.

"'Then not a word to your uncle,' I said, as soon as I could speak.

"'Mum's the word,' said the boy with a wink.

"So I fixed him a bunk on this 'ere conch we're a-sitting on, and, as it was bitter cold, started a bit of fire in the grate. Then I locked him in and carried away the key, so if by some strange chance the professor should stray up there late in the evening he would find the key gone, and probably think it had been mislaid, for it usually hung on a nail beside the door.

"If I'd known the queer tricks of this room then as I do now, I'd never have locked the boy in.

"What happened during that night I get straight from Jack himself. It seems he went straight to sleep, and never woke till the faintest bit of daylight was stealing into his window. Then he was aroused, poor chap, by a low murmur of voices, and sitting up he saw on the hearth two figures talking together—one a girl with long black hair, and the other a young man who held her hands and was bending his face down to here. Both of 'em was dripping wet, and he could hear the trickle of the water as it fell on the big stone hearth they were standing on. Their faces were turned from him, but in the girl's hair was tangled a quantity of seaweed.

"Did I tell you Jack was a plucky little fellow? He was, to the backbone. He said to himself that what he saw was 'an optical delusion,' I believe he called it, that there was nobody but himself in the room—there couldn't be, because the door was locked. 'What do you want—who are you?' he cried, and with that jumped out of bed and came straight towards the two figures. As he advanced they retreated towards the window; and when he reached the window there wasn't anything there, though the window was shut except for a little space at the top.

"Well, Jack went back to bed and lay thinking it over for an hour, then fell asleep again. He was perfectly healthy, Jack was, and hadn't much idea of the supernatural.

"But now comes the strange part of it; for as he was dressing the next morning what did the boy find but a pool of salt water on the stone hearth, in that little hollow you can see from here that has been worn in it, and lying in it a bit of fresh seaweed, in which was tangled a long black hair! Then, as Jack told me, his own hair began to rise in good earnest, and he was scared.

"So that morning after breakfast he takes the bit of seaweed to his uncle and asks him if he'd ever seen any like it.

"The professor looked at the piece of wet weed, and his color went like the going out of a lighted taper. 'It's an uncommon variety,' he said, 'as it's never found except on the bodies of drowned people. Where did you get it, Jack!' And he looked at the boy wild-like, for I was a-watching of 'em from the passageway.

" 'I found it in my room,' blurted out the boy. 'There was a couple of people in there last night, uncle, dripping wet.'

" 'What do you mean?' gasped his uncle, looking at him strangely.

" 'Come and I'll show you,' he says, in spite of the fact that I was shaking my fist at him from the hallway. So together they went up to the seaweed room, I following to explain why I'd taken the liberty to lodge Jack there. But the professor never noticed me. He followed Jack into the room, white to the lips, and kneeling down examined the little pool of water on the hearth. 'It's sea water,' he whispered, after a moment. 'What did you see, boy? Tell me everything.'

" 'There's nothing much to tell, uncle,' went on Jack, in his straightforward way. 'The girl's hair was down her back all wet, and full of seaweed. And see! Here's a long black hair in the seaweed I found.'

"The professor looked, then gave a cry such as I hope never to hear again, and fell back on the floor unconscious. He came back to life, but never was well after it, and he died six weeks afterward. Before he went he became communicative, and the secret of his wife's death came out. He and his wife were in a small boat, the last to leave the sinking vessel, together with a few other passengers and one sailor. The professor, being a man of authority and a well-known seaman, was in charge of the boat. Just as they were pushing off they saw a figure clinging to the mast just above the water. It was Mrs. Linwood's cousin and former lover. At this she cried to her husband to put back to the ship and rescue him, and took on sent his danger that the demon of jealousy entered her husband's soul, and he swore it would be impossible to go back, and that to take another person into the boat would sink it. At that moment the mast disappeared, and as it did so the young man sprang into the sea, waving a farewell to his cousin. Then, with one look at the professor that he never forgot to his dying day, she, too, jumped overboard and probably sank immediately—at least, the body could not be recovered.

"Yes, it was a strange thing, those two coming back—if it was them—to this room; those who have book-learning can make it clear, perhaps, but I'm only an ignorant old woman and don't understand these deep things; I can only tell it to you just as it happened."

Self-Haunted

E. E. Kellett

I confess I did not like the look of that bed; though precisely *what* it was that I did not like was hard to tell. I looked at it in the candlelight again and again; and the oftener I looked at it the more ordinary it seemed—and the more dreadful.

"Come," I said to myself; "this is nonsense; we aren't in the Middle Ages. This isn't an Elizabethan four-poster; it's a nineteenth century iron Maple. A bicyclist, and object to a little roughing it! You've slept in many a worse affair before now."

But it was not *discomfort* that I feared.

Could it be that I was exhausted by my fifty miles of cycle-ride along the flat and easy Dutch roads? Were my nerves overstrung? If so, the cause and the effect were disproportionate; for I had done my two hundred miles in a day before now, and had felt no particular ill-effects. And to-night, till I entered this room, I had noticed nothing amiss in myself. Still, it must be so. My nerves must have been overwrought without my knowing it. A night's good sound sleep would restore them. But, a night in that bed—!

Let me not be so unjust to my Creator as to ascribe all that followed to accident. He who watches over the meanest of His creatures would never have permitted me to suffer such agonies but for some weakness, some collusion with evil, on my own part. I have seen since, though I did not see it at the time, that the events of that night were my own fault, and a punishment for my fault. During that afternoon, as I rested for an hour or so in the shade of a welcome tree, evil thoughts had come to me. *What* precisely they were I shall not tell, nor is it necessary to do so. Suffice it to say that I harboured them. At first appearing as it were from without, they were welcomed into my soul, and speedily became a fixed purpose. For the first time in my life I deliberately *resolved* upon a course of sin. I had opened the door to the powers of wickedness; and it is no wonder that they entered in. This story is a warning to those who are inclined to do the same.

The resolve was none the less fixed that, during the twenty mile ride I had made since, it had been completely forgotten. Action and open air had driven it from memory; yet it lay entrenched in the background of my mind, to emerge into fulfilment at the due time. And such an intention is itself a crime: whosoever hateth his brother is a murderer, whether the deed is actually performed or not.

But all this is the history of later reflection. I had no such thoughts when I entered my bedroom after a comfortable supper and a placid pipe, with just that pleasant amount of weariness in my body which promises a dreamless sleep. Never in my life had I felt less superstitious, less anxious as to my rest. Nevertheless, hardly had I entered the room when, at the sight of the bed of which I have spoken, a strange feeling of gloomy foreboding descended upon my soul like a pall.

A foolish impulse seized me to inspect the room. Foolish indeed, for one glance was enough to convince the most superstitious that there was nothing there. There was no tapestry, no dark corner, no dismal painting on the wall, no stain upon the floor. It was clean with all the cleanliness of Holland, and ordinary with all the tameness of modernity. A few prints of windmills and canals adorned or disfigured the walls. The romantic, the ghostly, could hardly seek a more unlikely abode than this most commonplace of chambers. As well look for a ghost in a jerry-built "model dwelling." I did not guess that I myself was the one supernatural element in the room: that such evil influences as were there I had myself brought I felt a strange sinking of the heart as I tried to reassure myself by gazing round those placid walls. I dragged a chest of drawers to the door, and turned the key doubly. The room must have been modern indeed to possess a door with a lock. As I turned the key, I heard someone laugh. My God, what a laugh! It combined all the tones of mockery with all the tones of exquisite anguish; as though it were the laugh of a demon in mortal torture enjoying the spectacle of another demon in even worse plight than himself. And I could have sworn it came from the bed!

For what seemed an age I stood paralysed with horror, while the cold sweat came out on my forehead. Thought, decision, were swallowed up in the one emotion of fear. But at last reason reasserted itself. I determined, though it cost me my life, to investigate that bed. Lighting a second candle, since the first was going low, I drew some consolation from the increased illumination in the room; and, approaching with a curious mixture of stealthiness and courage, I removed the counterpane from the bed, and turned down the blankets and sheets. There was nothing to be seen. Everything was precisely as it should be. The sheets were dry and clean—all, in fact, that the most timid of travellers could have desired; and yet—I turned away, half-despising myself for my fears; and, as I did so, I seemed to hear something—the crinkling sound as though someone were turning in the bed, and the half-sigh of semi-conscious exertion. I turned again; and unquestionably there was *somebody* there. An invisibility lay before me, a presence not to be seen but to be apprehended—perhaps to be felt; for the pillow bore an impress of a head, and the sheets were hollowed as if with the weight of a body. Horror-struck, incapable of thought or speech, I fell back into the corner of the room, gazing spell-bound at this horrible phenomenon, and listening with concentrated agony of premonition for the voice which should reveal its meaning. As I huddled into my corner, with my hands before me as if to ward off an invisible assailant, I observed again a motion in the bed. A something which I could not see appeared to rise into a sitting posture, to grasp at the sheets and blankets which I had removed, to bestow them around itself, and then with a sigh to fall into slumber once more. But not before it had reduced me, if possible, to still greater helplessness than ever; for, ere it finally appeared to lie down, a strange breathing sound emerged from a point above the pillow, and the candle, which I had left by the side of the bed, went out, and left me in darkness. The phantom had extinguished it; and I perceived clearly that here was a being that loved darkness rather than light, because its deeds were evil.

It has occurred to me since, as it has doubtless occurred to the reader, to wonder why I should have stayed in that room. Why did I not shriek for help? Why had I not, instead of barring the door, flung it wide open, to welcome the consolations of human company? It was certainly no dread of ridicule that restrained me, no consciousness that others, seeing nothing to terrify, would have judged me weak or lunatic. And yet it was a true instinct; for I see now that the coming contest was one that had to be fought by myself alone, either then or later. He who has paltered with the evil one must himself face him; *that* struggle, like the struggle of death, must be met in person, and none can give aid or consolation but the Divine Being Himself.

To describe my emotions as I sat huddled in my corner, apparently for hours, is neither an easy nor a profitable task. I prefer not to dwell upon that time of agony and fear, for even the memory of it is sufficient to bring the sweat to my brow and to stop the beating of my heart. How I lived through it I know not; and yet perhaps the chief horror of it all was the conviction that it would *not* kill me. Less dreadful would it have been had I but anticipated some manifestation the shock of which might be mortal; but I knew it was not to be

My mental changes were gradual, as were the changes of the *something* in the bed. Slowly—it may have been the process of hours—it seemed to me, as I gazed spell-bound and unwinking at the spot where horror lay, the invisible began to put on visibility. A gloomy twilight slowly diffused itself through the apartment, upon which my straining eyes seemed to make out a gradually condensing form, at first vaporous, shapeless, and hardly to be apprehended by the senses, but growing, with almost imperceptible degrees, into definiteness of outline. At length, as the unholy light in the room increased into intolerable and devilish brightness, I saw, as distinctly as ever I saw anything in my life, a face upon that pillow; and, oh, my God! if the invisible had been awful, the visible was more dreadful a thousand times. Every vile passion—lust, murder, revenge, cruelty, hate—was stamped upon that face in unmistakable characters, as though all the evil of which the human race is collectively capable had concentrated itself there. To my terror was added unutterable loathing; nor do I believe that the most criminal of men could have gazed upon that face without the intensest detestation; for he would verily have seen there the actual ugliness of sin itself, unveiled and unashamed.

The horrible eyes met mine; but I despair of conveying any idea of what I saw there. The ordinary man, who knows but ordinary vicious faces—who, for example, has seen the faces of a few typical murderers—has only the feeblest images on which to model his conceptions of utter unredeemed wickedness; and it was utter unredeemed wickedness that was before me. Yet even the most inconceivably villainous of faces has distinctive recognisable features; it retains the marks of heredity, it has its family likeness to the sweet face of a mother or the innocent face of a child. In the horrible visage before me, to my unutterable shame, I recognised *my own*. Those were my own eyes that glittered before me; it was my own mouth round whose corners writhed the horrible grin which terrified me; it was my own lips that seemed parted to utter some demoniac blasphemy. For a moment I gazed with an emotion almost more of astonishment than of fear: the certainty that this was myself, for a moment struggled with the surprise I felt at finding myself so horrible.

But in that face, beyond its identity, were two other noticeable things; two visions forcibly stamped themselves upon my brain, those of domination and of mockery. There was irresistible force, compelling obedience; and there was diabolic scorn. Both these convinced me that in that face there lived not only myself, but *something else*.

At length the irresistible force, the something else in that face which was not myself, began slowly to exert itself in influence upon me. I felt dragged towards the bed, and was as incapable of withstanding the impulse as the tides are incapable of withstanding the moon. Furious but helpless, I obeyed the force, and slowly, like a bird yielding to the fascination of the python, I drew near the bed. You who know what it is to be constrained to face a sight of horror—to watch the surgeon operate upon a well-loved child—to see in a once beautiful countenance the ravages of leprosy or lupus—may form some dim conception of the agonies of my involuntary advance; and at each step the horrible lips were distorted into a diabolic grin of malice. Yet my limbs obeyed the commanding impulse; and, after a journey of ages, I stood at the side of the bed. The awful face approached mine; the demonic arms outspread and clasped me; I was drawn, my body unresisting, but my soul straining helplessly backward, first upon the bed, and then into it. And then, with one more killing, freezing laugh, the phantom vanished; the unholy light extinguished itself; a sacred happy darkness supervened; and I was alone.

Alone! My God, the happiness, the bliss of loneliness! For perhaps a minute I enjoyed that bliss. My mind, exhausted with fearing, was incapable of dread, incapable of anything but rest. I thought of nothing, I saw nothing. Little did I know that my ghostly enemy, like the torturers of the Inquisition, was but sparing me that I might recover strength to endure worse torments. Perhaps it feared that unconsciousness would rob it of its prey, and left me, to return with seven demons worse than itself.

After a minute of heavenly lassitude, I was again recalled to the realities of things. As I lay on my right side, I felt, rather than heard, behind me the crinkling of the sheets, as though I were no longer alone in the bed. Slowly the something insinuated itself beside me; silently, impalpably, invisibly it drew itself into horrible proximity. I saw, I felt, I heard, nothing; but I *knew*. Behind me was a shapeless form, an invisible phantom, an imponderable incubus. Thus, while I panted and my heart beat like a hammer, we lay for what seemed hours. And then, out of the darkness, at my very ear, came the sound of breathing; and over my face wandered the foul touch of invisible hands. With mighty strainings I strove to move; the muscles in my arms cracked with my efforts to stir and at least face my foe; but in vain. I was tied as with the chains of catalepsy; motion was as impossible as to him who is being buried alive. One sound will save him; the soul almost bursts the body to utter it; but the sound is not uttered. My soul nearly left my body in its struggles to control it and compel it to motion; but no motion came.

I seemed not only to have all my senses in their fullest keenness; not only to hear, to feel, as I had never heard or felt before; but my mind seemed also to apprehend without the agency of sense. The barriers between the natural and the supernatural seemed to be removed; and I knew, not mediately but directly, that I was engaged in a mortal struggle with the evil one. Not merely did I feel the embrace of those arms, not merely did I hear the motion of the hands above me, but I had the direct consciousness of a spirit operating upon my soul, not through the ordinary channels, but as spirit wrestling with spirit. Prayer there was none, nor room for it. As the poet on the mountain-top does not need sound, and thought expires in emotion, so I, in this deadly soul-grapple, could find no place for imagination, for entreaty; the dread reality swallowed up all besides. Since then—but only after the lapse of years—I have been able to conceive, perhaps more intensely than the combatant himself, those fearful struggles of the old saints with the Tempter, which Bunyan has depicted for us in his story of Christian and Apollyon. Yet mine was no temptation; it was a desperate effort of some supernatural being to overcome me by the force of sheer terror, and to drag me, body and soul, with him into regions of torment, from which no escape should be possible; and, during the struggle, I felt, with no conceivable palliation, all the tortures of the damned, aggravated by all the horrors of anticipation.

Upon my soul lay a dead-weight of conscious weakness. I realised, every moment more intensely, the overmastering force of my assailant, and the certainty that whatever might be his aim he was likely to accomplish it. Slowly the contest became more and more frantic, and concentrated itself into actual vision. Phantoms danced before my eyes; demons grinned in my face; horrible laughter rang in my ears; the grip of the gruesome bat-like arms tightened round my throat; and every emotion of wonder, horror, and killing despair revelled confusedly in my mind. Conscious as I was that my only salvation depended upon my control of myself, I began to feel that the demonic foe was effecting a lodging within me, and was rapidly forming an alliance with the worse and weaker elements in my own soul. I was, and I knew it, about to be stormed and possessed by a demon; henceforward I was to be no longer a man but a demoniac; no longer to rule my actions in perfect sanity, but to wander to and fro among the tombs, dominated perhaps by a legion of devils. The horrible fear that such was to be my fate was a powerful aid to my ghastly visitant in bringing it about. Fearful was my struggle to retain the dominion over myself. "No," I seemed to hear myself saying, "while I live I will keep my most precious possession, the mastery over my own actions; I will never yield my will to its destroyer." Even as I spoke the struggle became fiercer; I seemed to feel myself interpenetrated with Satanic influences. As with a wave they threatened to overflow me; in a sort of swoon I reaped that my soul was passing beyond my control—nay, that it was passing away altogether, and that its place was being taken by a devilish power.

There are some who are pleased to laugh at the old stories of demoniacal possession; they speak of them as old wives' tales, as the legends of a decayed superstition. With such persons I do not argue; for I *know*. I can believe in the pangs suffered by the child when the demon, in obedience to a stronger, tore its way out of him; for I have felt the worse pangs of a demon striving to gain admission. I can well believe that even to-day men are possessed by devils—for, within a hair's breadth, I suffered that fate myself.

Do not tell me I am mad. I am as sane as any human being ever was; but the remembrance of my escape fills me with gratitude to God and with a consciousness how near, how very near, the legions of hell are to our hearts; eternally close by, to force an entrance, to contract alliances with our baser passions; to creep, or intrude, or climb into the fold.

For a long time I was sustained by that predominating instinct in man—the instinct to claim even his worst thoughts and actions as his own. I still retained a trembling grip upon free-will. I muttered to myself that I would still be a *person*; whether I sinned or did well the act should be mine, and not that of another. As I felt the accursed influence drawing nearer and nearer to the stronghold of my heart, I exclaimed inwardly that I would never yield it a willing obedience. But, slowly, it seemed to rise and sap the very fountains of the will. I felt my personality gliding out of my grasp. That dreadful doom was in truth to be mine—the doom of committing crimes for which men do not blame you, but of which they speak in tones of mingled horror and pity, and for which the punishment is not the hangman's rope but the strait waistcoat and the padded room. I was to be that lowest, that most unhappy of all God's creatures—the criminal not held responsible for his villanies, but spared, half in hatred, half in awe, as one with whom God alone is competent to deal.

Those stories, trust me, are true; the story of the Magdalen and of the Gadarene. But they are only half the truth. They tell us the blessed means by which the accursed lodger was driven out; they withhold from us in mercy that other narrative of the means by which he found an entrance; of the desperate strivings, the rackings, the loathing, the tears, the fatal surrender. Nor can I presume to rush in where the Evangelist feared to tread. Let me leave it, reader, to your imagination, to your pity; conscious that your imagination will be too weak to form an image of my sufferings, and your pity, though never so tender, too harsh, from happy ignorance, to sympathise. And God grant your ignorance may last!

The struggle was very long and weary—so long and weary that I fancy I shall carry its traces even beyond the grave. Nor do I claim any merit for the final victory; I am rather humbled by it, and willing to ascribe it to Him alone who is able to put down principalities and powers. When things were at their very worst—when the hot breath of my adversary wandered over my face like a destroying flame, and when I could hear his mocking laugh of expected triumph—then suddenly, whether by the direct unasked influence of the Almighty, or because in my last despair I found myself somehow enabled to pray—the battle swayed.

"Oh, God," I cried aloud, the spell of silence broken, "oh, God, suffer me at least to keep my own soul!"

As I spoke, the fiery hands were withdrawn; the lurid light vanished into welcome blackness; and then, as though my brain would endure no more, I ceased to know, and begin to fancy. The sheets hardened about me, as though changing into the oak-wood of a coffin; the bed seemed to whirl round and round; the dancing phantoms twisted and turned more rapidly before my eyes; the room swam about me; and I seemed to die. I was in my coffin below the earthy removed from human fellowship, horribly lonely. The smell of damp mould was in my nostrils, for I was dead, but conscious. And then exhausted nature could do no more; I sank into oblivion.

When I awoke, the sun was streaming through the windows, lighting up the commonplace room, with its pictures of Dutch landscapes and its dull and clean walls. There, against the door, stood the chest of drawers. Never was a room less ghostly. Without, the cheery voice of the landlord informed me that it was nine o'clock, and that my shaving-water had arrived. Yet, as wakefulness increased, my terrors grew. I summoned all my resolution, and with one spring left that bed of horrors. I scarcely stayed to pack my few belongings into my knapsack; hurriedly I cleared away the chest from the door and hastened downstairs. There must have been something in my appearance out of the ordinary, for the landlord stared at one aghast, and I heard him say to his wife, "Our lodger looks like one who has been in hell." I refused breakfast, flung a piece of gold upon the table, opened the door, by which my bicycle was standing, and, swiftly mounting, rode from that accursed house as though all the fiends of hell were at my heels.

SHARE AND SHARE ALIKE

ROBERT S. BARR

The quick must haste to vengeance taste,
For time is on his head;
But he can wait at the door of fate,
Though the stay be long and the hour be late
The dead.

MELVILLE HARDLOCK STOOD IN THE CENTER OF THE ROOM WITH HIS FEET WIDE APART and his hands in his trousers pockets, a characteristic attitude of his. He gave a quick glance at the door, and saw with relief that the key was in the lock, and that the bolt prevented anybody coming in unexpectedly. Then he gazed once more at the body of his friend, which lay in such a helpless-looking attitude upon the floor. He looked at the body with a feeling of mild curiosity, and wondered what there was about the lines of the figure on the floor that so certainly betokened death rather than sleep, even though the face was turned away from him. He thought, per haps, it might be the hand with its back to the floor and its palm toward the ceiling; there was a certain look of helplessness about that. He resolved to investigate the subject some time when he had leisure.

Then his thoughts turned toward the subject of murder. It was so easy to kill, he felt no pride in having been able to accomplish that much. But it was not everybody who could escape the consequences of his crime. It required an acute brain to plan after-events so that shrewd detectives would be baffled. There was a complacent conceit about Melville Hardlock, which was as much a part of him as his intense selfishness, and this conceit led him to believe that the future path he had outlined for himself would not be followed by justice.

With a sigh Melville suddenly seemed to realize that while there was no necessity for undue haste, yet it was not wise to be too leisurely in some things, so he took his hands from his pockets and drew to the middle of the floor a large Saratoga trunk. He threw the heavy lid open, and in doing so showed that the trunk was empty. Picking up the body of his friend, which he was surprised to note was so heavy and troublesome to handle, he with some difficulty doubled it up so that it slipped into the trunk. He piled on top of it some old coats, vests, newspapers, and other miscellaneous articles until the space above the body was filled. Then he pressed down the lid and locked it; fastening the catches at each end. Two stout straps were now placed around the trunk and firmly buckled after he had drawn them as tight as possible. Finally he damped the gum side of a paper label, and when he had pasted it on the end of the trunk, it showed the words in red letters, "S. S. Platonic, cabin, wanted." This done, Melville threw open the window to allow the fumes of chloroform to dissipate themselves in the outside air. He placed a closed, packed, and labeled port manteau beside the trunk, and a valise beside that again, which, with a couple of handbags, made up his luggage. Then he unlocked the door, threw back the bolt, and, having turned the key again from the outside, strode down the thickly-carpeted stairs of the hotel into the large pillared and marble-floored vestibule where the clerk's office was. Strolling up to the counter behind which stood the clerk of the hotel, he shoved his key across to that functionary, who placed it in the pigeon-hole marked by the number of his room.

"Did my friend leave for the West last night, do you know?"

"Yes," answered the clerk, "he paid his bill and left. Haven't you seen him since?"

"No," replied Hardlock.

"Well, he'll be disappointed about that, because he told me he expected to see you before he left, and would call up at your room later. I suppose he didn't have time. By the way, he said you were going back to England to-morrow. Is that so?"

"Yes, I sail on the Platonic. I suppose I can have my luggage sent to the steamer from here without further trouble?"

"Oh, certainly," answered the clerk; "how many pieces are there? It will be fifty cents each."

"Very well; just put that down in my bill with the rest of the expenses, and let me have it to night. I will settle when I come in. Five pieces of luggage altogether."

"Very good. You'll have breakfast to-morrow, I suppose?"

"Yes, the boat does not leave till nine o'clock."

"Very well; better call you about seven, Mr. Hardlock. Will you have a carriage?"

"No, I shall walk down to the boat. You will be sure, of course, to have my things there in time."

"Oh, no fear of that. They will be on the steamer by half-past eight."

"Thank you."

As Mr. Hardlock walked down to the boat next morning, he thought he had done rather a clever thing in sending his trunk in the ordinary way to the steamer. "Most people," he said to himself, "would have made the mistake of being too careful about it. It goes along in the ordinary course of business. If anything should go wrong it will seem incredible that a sane man would send such a pack age in an ordinary express wagon to be dumped about, as they do dump luggage about in New York."

He stood by the gangway on the steamer, watch ing the trunks, valises, and portmanteaus come on board.

"Stop!" he cried to the man, "that is not to go down in the hold; I want it. Don't you see it's marked 'wanted'?"

"It is very large, sir," said the man; "it will fill up a stateroom by itself."

"I have the captain's room," was the answer.

So the man flung the trunk down on the deck with a crash that made even the cool Mr. Hardlock shudder.

"Did you say you had the captain's room, sir?" asked the steward standing near.

"Yes."

"Then I am your bedroom steward," was the answer; "I will see that the trunk is put in all right."

The first day out was rainy but not rough; the second day was fair and the sea smooth. The second night Hardlock remained in the smoking room until the last man had left. Then, when the lights were extinguished, he went out on the upper deck, where his room was, and walked up and down smoking his cigar. There was another man also walking the deck, and the red glow of his cigar, dim and bright alternately, shone in the darkness like a glowworm.

Hardlock wished that he would turn in, whoever he was. Finally the man flung his cigar overboard and went down the stairway. Hardlock had now the dark deck to himself. He pushed open the door of his room and turned out the electric light. It was only a few steps from his door to the rail of the vessel high above the water. Dimly on the bridge he saw the shadowy figure of an officer walking back and forth. Hardlock looked over the side at the phosphorescent glitter of the water which made the black ocean seem blacker still. The sharp ring of the bell, betokening midnight, made Melville start as if a hand had touched him, and the quick beating of his heart took some moments to subside. "I've been smoking too much to-day," he said to himself. Then looking quickly up and down the deck, he walked on tiptoe to his room, took the trunk by its stout leather handle and pulled it over the ledge in the doorway. There were small wheels at the bottom of the trunk, but although they made the pulling of it easy, they seemed to creak with appalling loudness. He realized the fearful weight of the trunk as he lifted the end of it up on the rail. He balanced it there for a moment, and glanced sharply around him, but there was nothing to alarm him. In spite of his natural coolness, he felt a strange, haunting dread of some undefinable disaster, a dread which had been completely absent from him at the time he committed the murder. He shoved off the trunk before he had quite intended to do so, and the next instant he nearly bit through his tongue to suppress a groan of agony. There passed half a dozen moments of supreme pain and fear before he realized what had happened. His wrist had caught in the strap handle of the trunk, and his shoulder was dislocated. His right arm was stretched taut and helpless, like a rope holding up the frightful and ever-increasing weight that hung between him and the sea. His breast was pressed against the rail, and his left hand gripped the iron stanchion to keep himself from going over. He felt that his feet were slipping, and he set his teeth and gripped the iron with a grasp that was itself like iron. He hoped the trunk would slip from his useless wrist, but it rested against the side of the vessel, and the longer it hung the more it pressed the hard strap handle into his nerveless flesh. He had realized from the first that he dare not cry for help, and his breath came hard through his clenched teeth as the weight grew heavier and heavier. Then, with his eyes strained by the fearful pressure, and perhaps dazzled by the glittering phosphorescence running so swiftly by the side of the steamer far below, he seemed to see from out the trunk something in the form and semblance of his dead friend quivering like summer heat below him. Sometimes it was the shimmering phosphorescence, then again it was the wraith hovering over the trunk. Hardlock, in spite of his agony, wondered which it really was; but he wondered no longer when it spoke to him.

"Old friend," it said, "you remember our compact when we left England. It was to be 'share and share alike,' my boy 'share and share alike.' I have had my share. Come!"

Then on the still night air came the belated cry for help, but it was after the foot had slipped and the hand had been wrenched from the iron stanchion.

The Skeleton

Jerome K. Jerome

Jephson was always at his best when all other things were at their worst. It was not that he struggled in Mark Tapley fashion to appear most cheerful when most depressed; it was that petty misfortunes and mishaps genuinely amused and inspirited him. Most of us can recall our unpleasant experiences with amused affection; Jephson possessed the robuster philosophy that enabled him to enjoy his during their actual progress. He arrived drenched to the skin, chuckling hugely at the idea of having come down on a visit to a houseboat in such weather.

Under his warming influence, the hard lines on our faces thawed, and by supper time we were, as all Englishmen and women who wish to enjoy life should be, independent of the weather.

Later on, as if disheartened by our indifference, the rain ceased, and we took our chairs out on the deck, and sat watching the lightning, which still played incessantly. Then, not unnaturally, the talk drifted into a sombre channel, and we began recounting stories, dealing with the gloomy and mysterious side of life.

Some of these were worth remembering, and some were not. The one that left the strongest impression on my mind was a tale that Jephson told us.

I had just been relating a somewhat curious experience of my own. I met a man in the Strand one day that I knew very well, as I thought, though I had not seen him for years. We walked together to Charing Cross, and there we shook hands and parted. Next morning, I spoke of this meeting to a mutual friend, and then I learnt, for the first time, that the man had died six months before.

The natural inference was that I had mistaken one man for another, an error that, not having a good memory for faces, I frequently fall into. What was remarkable about the matter, however, was that throughout our walk I had conversed with the man under the impression that he was that other dead man, and, whether by coincidence or not, his replies had never once suggested to me my mistake.

As soon as I finished speaking, Jephson, who had been listening very thoughtfully, asked me if I believed in spiritualism "to its fullest extent."

"That is rather a large question," I answered. "What do you mean by 'spiritualism to its fullest extent'?"

"Well, do you believe that the spirits of the dead have not only the power of re-visiting this earth at their will, but that, when here, they have the power of action, or rather, of exciting to action. Let me put a definite case. A spiritualist friend of mine, a sensible and by no means imaginative man, once told me that a table, through the medium of which the spirit of a friend had been in the habit of communicating with him, came slowly across the room towards him, of its own accord, one night as he sat alone, and pinioned him against the wall. Now can any of you believe that, or can't you?"

"I could," Brown took it upon himself to reply; "but, before doing so, I should wish for an introduction to the friend who told you the story. Speaking generally," he continued, "it seems to me that the difference between what we call the natural and the supernatural is merely the difference between frequency and rarity of occurrence. Having regard to the phenomena we are compelled to admit, I think it illogical to disbelieve anything that we are not able to disprove."

"For my part," remarked MacShaugnassy, "I can believe in the ability of our spirit friends to give the quaint entertainments credited to them much easier than I can in their desire to do so."

"You mean," added Jephson, "that you cannot understand why a spirit, not compelled as we are by the exigencies of society, should care to spend its evenings carrying on a labored and childish conversation with a room full of abnormally uninteresting people."

"That is precisely what I cannot understand," MacShaugnassy agreed.

"Nor I, either," said Jephson. "But I was thinking of something very different altogether. Suppose a man died with the dearest wish of his heart unfulfilled, do you believe that his spirit might have power to return to earth and complete the interrupted work?"

"Well," answered MacShaugnassy, "if one admits the possibility of spirits retaining any interest in the affairs of this world at all, it is certainly more reasonable to imagine them engaged upon a task such as you suggest, than to believe that they occupy themselves with the performance of mere drawing-room tricks. But what are you leading up to?"

"Why to this," replied Jephson, seating himself straddle-legged across his chair, and leaning his arms upon the back. "I was told a story this morning at the hospital by an old French doctor. The actual facts are few and simple; all that is known can be read in the Paris police records of forty-two years ago.

"The most important part of the case, however, is the part that is not known, and that never will be known.

"The story begins with a great wrong done by one man unto another man. What the wrong was I do not know. I am inclined to think, however, it was connected with a woman. I think that because he who had been wronged hated him who had wronged with a hate such as does not often burn in a man's brain unless it be fanned by the memory of a woman's breath.

"Still that is only conjecture, and the point is immaterial. The man who had done the wrong fled, and the other man followed him. It became a point to point race, the first man having the advantage of a day's start. The course was the whole world, and the stakes were the first man's life.

"Travellers were few and far between in those days, and this made the trail easy to follow. The first man, never knowing how far or how near the other was behind him, and hoping now and again that he might have baffled him, would rest for a while. The second man, knowing always just how far the first one was before him, never paused, and thus each day the man who was spurred by Hate drew nearer to the man who was spurred by Fear.

At this town the answer to the never varied question would be:

"'At seven o'clock last evening, M'sieur.'

"'Seven—ah; eighteen hours. Give me something to eat, quick, while the horses are being put to.'

"At the next the calculation would be sixteen hours.

"Passing a lonely chalet, Monsieur puts his head out of the window:

"'How long since a carriage passed this way, with a tall, fair man inside?'

"'Such a one passed early this morning, M'sieur.'

"'Thanks, drive on, a hundred francs apiece if you are through the pass before daybreak.'

"'And what for dead horses, M'sieur?'

"'Twice their value when living.'

"One day the man who was ridden by Fear looked up, and saw before him the open door of a cathedral, and, passing in, knelt down and prayed. He prayed long and fervently, for men, when they are in sore straits, clutch eagerly at the straws of faith. He prayed that he might be forgiven his sin, and, more important still, that he might be pardoned the consequences of his sin, and be delivered from his adversary; and a few chairs from him, facing him, knelt his enemy, praying also.

"But the second man's prayer, being a thanksgiving merely, was short, so that when the first man raised his eyes, he saw the face of his enemy gazing at him across the chair tops, with a mocking smile upon it.

"He made no attempt to rise, but remained kneeling, fascinated by the look of joy that shone out of the other man's eyes. And the other man moved the high-backed chairs one by one, and came towards him softly.

"Then, just as the man who had been wronged stood beside the man who had wronged him, full of gladness that his opportunity had come, there burst from the cathedral tower a sudden clash of bells, and the man whose opportunity had come broke his heart and fell back dead, with that mocking smile of his still playing round his mouth.

"And so he lay there.

"Then the man who had done the wrong rose up and passed out, praising God.

"What became of the body of the other man is not known. It was the body of a stranger who had died suddenly in the cathedral. There was none to identify it, none to claim it.

"Years passed away, and the survivor in the tragedy became a worthy and useful citizen, and a noted man of science.

"In his laboratory were many objects necessary to him in his researches, and prominent among them, stood in a certain corner, a human skeleton. It was a very old and much-mended skeleton, and one day the long-expected end arrived, and it tumbled to pieces.

"Thus it became necessary to purchase another.

"The man of science visited a dealer he well knew; a little parchment-faced old man who kept a dingy shop, where nothing was ever sold, within the shadow of the towers of Notre Dame.

The little parchment-faced old man had just the very thing that Monsieur wanted—a singularly fine and well-proportioned "study." It should be sent round and set up in Monsieur's laboratory that very afternoon.

"The dealer was as good as his word. When Monsieur entered his laboratory that evening, the thing was in its place.

"Monsieur seated himself in his high-backed chair, and tried to collect his thoughts. But Monsieur's thoughts were unruly, and inclined to wander, and to wander always in one direction.

"Monsieur opened a large volume and commenced to read. He read of a man who had wronged another and fled from him, the other man following. Finding himself reading this, he closed the book angrily, and went and stood by the window and looked out. He saw before him the sun-pierced nave of a great cathedral, and on the stones lay a dead man with a mocking smile upon his face.

"Cursing himself for a fool, he turned away with a laugh. But his laugh was short-lived, for it seemed to him that something else in the room was laughing also. Struck suddenly still, with his feet glued to the ground, he stood listening for a while: then sought with starting eyes the corner from where the sound had seemed to come. But the white thing standing there was only grinning.

"Monsieur wiped the damp sweat from his head and hands, and stole out.

"For a couple of days he did not enter the room again. On the third, telling himself that his fears were those of a hysterical girl, he opened the door and went in. To shame himself, he took his lamp in his hand, and crossing over to the far corner where the skeleton stood, examined it. A set of bones bought for a hundred francs. Was he a child, to be scared by such a bogey!

"He held his lamp up in front of the thing's grinning head. The flame of the lamp flickered as though a faint breath had passed over it.

"The man explained this to himself by saying that the walls of the house were old and cracked, and that the wind might creep in anywhere. He repeated this explanation to himself as he recrossed the room, walking backwards, with his eyes fixed on the thing. When he reached his desk, he sat down and gripped the arms of his chair till his fingers turned white.

"He tried to work, but the empty sockets in that grinning head seemed to be drawing him towards them. He rose and battled with his inclination to fly screaming from the room. Glancing fearfully about him, his eye fell upon a high screen, standing before the door. He dragged it forward, and placed it between himself and the thing, so that he could not see it—nor it see him. Then he sat down again to his work. For awhile he forced himself to look at the book in front of him, but at last, unable to control himself any longer, he suffered his eyes to follow their own bent.

"It may have been an hallucination. He may have accidentally placed the screen so as to favour such an illusion. But what he saw was a bony hand coming round the corner of the screen, and, with a cry, he fell to the floor in a swoon.

"The people of the house came running in, and lifting him up, carried him out, and laid him upon his bed. As soon as he recovered, his first question was, where had they found the thing—where was it when they entered the room? and when they told him they had seen it standing where it always stood, and had gone down into the room to look again, because of his frenzied entreaties, and returned trying to hide their smiles, he listened to their talk about overwork, and the necessity for change and rest, and said they might do with him as they would.

"So for many months the laboratory door remained locked. Then there came a chill autumn evening when the man of science opened it again, and closed it behind him.

"He lighted his lamp, and gathered his instruments and books around him, and sat down before them in his high-backed chair. And the old terror returned to him.

"But this time he meant to conquer himself. His nerves were stronger now, and his brain clearer; he would fight his unreasoning fear. He crossed to the door and locked himself in, and flung the key to the other end of the room, where it fell among jars and bottles with an echoing clatter.

"Later on, his old housekeeper, going her final round, tapped at his door and wished him good night, as was her custom. She received no response, at first, and, growing nervous, tapped louder and called again; and at length an answering 'good night' came back to her.

"She thought little about it at the time, but afterwards she remembered that the voice that had replied to her had been strangely grating and mechanical. Trying to describe it, she likened it to such a voice as she would imagine coming from a statue.

"Next morning his door remained still locked. It was no unusual thing for him to work all night, and far into the next day, so no one thought to be surprised. When, however, evening came, and yet he did not appear, his servants gathered outside the room and whispered, remembering what had happened once before.

"They listened, but could hear no sound. They shook the door and called to him, then beat with their fists upon the wooden panels. But still no sound came from the room.

"Becoming alarmed, they decided to burst open the door, and, after many blows, it gave way and flew back, and they crowded in.

"He sat bolt upright in his high-backed chair. They thought at first he had died in his sleep. But when they drew nearer and the light fell upon him, they saw the livid marks of bony fingers round his throat; and in his eyes there was a terror such as is not often seen in human eyes."

The Spirit of the Dance

Julian Hawthorne

From the first I could not away with the sudden uprising and domination in me of a scene long past. It painted itself in deep and vivid colors. Set off against that loom and glow, the present seemed pallid and hardly real. For years I had not recalled it, but to-night, revived, no doubt, by my meeting with Traunce himself and attendant things, it came rolling in on me like the tides of a tropic sea, storming in my ears, flooding warm and keen through all my senses. Oh, that Eastern Star, and her wondrous dancing! And, throbbing through it, the delicious spell of the great Gothic master's music!

I think, though, that it was only when I crossed the threshold of the studio that I felt it in its fulness. The rest of the handsome and comfortable American home, with its handsome and comfortable American mistress, could have had small part in it. But at the studio she had abrogated her housewifely authority, and had left Traunce to handle it as he liked.

Probably he had not intended it, but there is a spiritual power in old associations and emotions; and then, here were the old furnishings and decorations—Oriental tiles and vases, weapons, tables, draperies. But, with these, there was something unseen which altered my pulse and breathing, and made the dead and gone visible.

Mrs. Traunce had taken an easy chair—the only American thing in the room—and had begun to sew. The baby, a little girl of three or four, with serious blue eyes and rose-leaf cheeks, sat at her feet, playing with a toy bear. The artist, hands in pockets, strolled about saying, in his leisurely, humorous, sad voice, things of no importance or sequence. I lounged against the teakwood cabinet, staring at the big bronze Buddha squatting yonder; he looked like old Keshub, thought I, and was sitting just where, six years ago, Keshub had sat, thumping his hand drum, in that other place. A pastil must have been burning somewhere, for I perceived the very scent of that former time. The lamp, hung from the ceiling over Mrs. Traunce's chair, imperfectly illuminated the rest of the large room. It seemed India once more—the ancient, hot, Eastern city, with its dusky thousands, its mysteries, sufferings, ignorance, wisdom, beauty, magic. We were in the heart of the native quarter, one story above the narrow street. Did not the Buddha blink and stir? Keshub, surely! Then where was the rana? O Eastern Star, are you with us still?

I cannot well distinguish, here, between the real and the imagined in what took place. We have all, perhaps, experienced such moods. Time and space are but representatives of spiritual states, and, before an intense access of memory or emotion, are dispelled, producing strange results.

We were examining an antique necklace which Traunce had brought from India. It lay sparkling snakelike on dark velvet in its shallow case.

"It may be a couple of thousand years old," he said.

"Baby have it for Fuz Wuz," said the little girl, stretching up her hand.

"No, darling; not nice for Baby," said Mrs. Traunce.

I glanced round over my shoulder, convinced that some one was bending over me; but there was, of course, nothing there.

"Beautiful workmanship," I remarked. "I suppose there are stories about it?"

"One of the legends is that it killed a Hindu princess," Traunce answered, smiling.

"Strangled her?"

"No, poison. The Borgias and their rings had predecessors. If you look close at this thing, you'll see minute needle-points in the links. They held the poison, or were smeared with it, something very subtle and strong. The least prick or abrasion was enough. I presume the way of it was, the rajah hung the necklace on the bosom of the doomed princess, and then folded her to his breast; and she died with his kiss on her lips."

"I cannot understand such people!" said Mrs. Traunce, with emphasis.

"You've never lived in India—thank goodness!" rejoined her husband. Meanwhile, in my ears there was a throbbing, reduplicating sound, very low and remote, but which made me, in spite of myself, turn my eyes aside to where the Buddha squatted in his corner. But Keshub was not tum-tumming on his hand drum; there was only a bronze Buddha.

"Of course," I said, for the sake of saying something, "the poison must have evaporated long since—ages since."

"I don't know. A month ago our Persian kitten, in my wife's lap, struck at it with her paw as we were examining it. She thought it a snake, maybe. It may have been coincidence, but she died that night, with symptoms of poisoning."

"Well, I detest India and everything in it," said good, sensible Mrs. Traunce, rising to put the necklace in its case, on the tabouret near by. "I wish you would throw the thing away."

The baby, sitting on the rug with her little bare legs outstretched, had put the bear between them, and was lecturing it. "If Fuz Wuz run away," quoth she, threatening with her small forefinger, "Baby smack it."

I felt uneasy. In spite of the warmth of the room, my hands were clammy and cold. I got up and moved hither and yon, to start my circulation.

"Have a cigarette," said Traunce; "here are some of the same kind that—"

He did not finish. As I inhaled the smoke, I fancied I knew why.

How, indeed, could a man who had loved, and had been loved by, that imperial creature, descend to his present condition? We three had often smoked those cigarettes together. Yet his eyes, meditatively following the sway and swing of the delicate clouds gathering in air from our lips, did not catch, as I did, a memory of the swinging, swaying movements of one who had danced before him as never woman had danced since the unnamed daughter of the Gileadite had come forth with timbrels from her father's house, to meet him returning victorious, to his despair. How could he who had known the embraces of that slender incarnation of fire and air take to his arms this commonplace, good-looking, domestic chattel? Yet he betrayed no traces of a consciousness of sacrilege or degradation. She was dead; but had she, too, forgotten? I exerted myself to gossip and laugh, but my uneasiness remained.

The smoke of the Oriental tobacco hung, a thin, blue cloud, in the half-gloom, and was slowly lifted into a vertical twist by the attraction of the pendent lamp. I had found a low divan in a corner, and, reclining there, was inadvertently following the movements of the baby, who had tied a string to the bear and was leading it on a journey to foreign countries. It struck me that the convoluted pillar of vapor had acquired clearer form and independent movement, and now, in the gliding motion of its approach to the baby, I recognized no other than Amra herself. The lamp, hanging between me and these two, though above them, produced the effect of a semitransparent veil, through which, obscurely, I observed them. The throbbing of Keshub's hand drum, on my right, which had intermitted, now became again faintly audible. Traunce and his wife, meanwhile, sitting together on the hither side of the light, were distinctly visible; yet my eyes passed over or through them as if they had been unsubstantial. They, obviously, were unconscious of what was taking place behind them. Traunce had taken his old violoncello from its box and was adjusting the bridge. The placid, regular in-and-out waving of Mrs. Traunce's hand in sewing, fell in with the rhythm of Keshub's drumming.

Amra crouched down before the child, who seemed to take her presence as a matter of course. Something, I could not see what, passed from the one to the other. Now, her slender brown hand holding the child's tiny white one, the two were advancing toward the tabouret on which lay exposed the antique necklace. The drumming became louder.

I understood the little girl's danger, but could not move or speak to prevent it. But the mother—apprised, it may be, by maternal instinct, which surpasses even clairvoyance in subtlety—turned in her seat at the last moment, and before the little fingers could close upon the glittering peril, had sprung to her baby and snatched her back. The tabouret was overturned, and the necklace fell to the floor with a crash. The mystic gates closed noiselessly; all was changed. I blundered forward like an awakened sleep-walker. Baby, whimpering a little, was being soothed on her mother's bosom. Traunce bent over the necklace on the rug.

"It's broken; the links have come apart," said he.

"I'm glad of it," exclaimed the mother resentfully. "Sweep the hateful thing up in the dust-pan, and throw it into the ash-barrel. My baby sha'n't be killed by your old Hindu rubbish! What if I hadn't turned round!"

Traunce made no rejoinder, and I was ashamed to look her in the face, lest she detect some vestige of my visions in my eyes. For that matter, however, Amra and Keshub now seemed more remote than Benares. The artist and I gingerly gathered up from the rug all we could find of the shattered serpent, and put the fragments in a place inaccessible to infancy, even when led by a spirit. Baby, restored to equanimity, was preparing to resume her place on the cushion at her mother's feet, when the latter, with an ejaculation of surprise, drew her back.

"What has the child got on her legs?" she exclaimed.

"Hello, that's odd!" muttered Traunce, lifting one of the soft little feet in his hand. "Silver anklets, such as the women wear in—H'm! And clasped on! How did she manage it? And where did she find them? I didn't know I had such things in the place—not small enough for her, at any rate. She didn't have 'em when we came in here. H'm!"

"Well, I'm going to take them off," said Mrs. Traunce. "Who knows—Ugh! It's uncanny."

But Baby objected so vehemently that their removal was postponed, and, as luck would have it, Traunce, in looking about the studio for some explanation of the presence of the anklets, happened upon an old Indian jar, in which was a handful of native ornaments of silver and copper. Baby must have found the anklets there and put them on. My secret was safe, and I felt relieved.

Mrs. Traunce resumed her sewing, and Traunce continued to tinker with his cello. I lighted another cigarette, and returned to the divan. I kept telling myself that perhaps, after all, I had simply fallen asleep. The Buddha was nothing but a bronze Buddha, and Amra had been dead and buried for six long years. I had fancied that I saw her—an apparition that resembled her—give Baby something, but I had not seen that it was the silver bangles. Why not be sensible, and let the painted jar account for them?

I wondered they did not send the child to bed; but she did not appear sleepy. She sat on her cushion, absorbed in the enterprise of fitting a silk jacket on her bear. She was charmingly pretty and lovable. Could anyone—could even the spirit of a dead woman who had been forgotten and supplanted—wish to injure her? But what other woman had there ever been to compare with Amra? And what death, in the midst of life and passion, so tragic as hers? Oh, that last night, how it remade itself before me! Her dying vows, murmured against his lips; his frantic grief, which had made me fear that he would follow her! And yet he, after scarce more than a year, returning to his country, could forget that poignant hour and its vows, and could love and marry yonder comely lump of clay! I regretted the accident which, acquainting me with his whereabouts, had led to my visiting him. There he sat, tinkering at his cello—the same cello, it must be, on which, that unforgettable night, he had played to Amra's dancing. What wonder if she stirred in her grave!

It was the notes of the cello that roused me from my abstraction. Traunce, having tuned it to his satisfaction, was drawing the bow across the strings.

"Shall I play something?" he asked. "What shall it be?"

"Play the first movement of the 'Moonlight Sonata.'" I spoke the words, yet I cannot affirm that the impulse to utter them came from my own will. For it was to the undulations of that marvelous music that Amra's curved feet had been moving when the serpent struck her, and her death-cry rang through the closing chords.

But Traunce's manner revealed no discomposure. "I'll try it; but I'm out of practice. How did it begin? Let me see!"

He had been a master of the art, and now, after a few uncertain sounds, the noble instrument began to sing with the harmonies of the most potent genius music has ever known.

He had not completed the opening bars before the illusion, or whatever it was, was surging over me once more in all its strength. Round me again had gathered the oppressive but fascinating dusk of Benares, with its odors and its murmurs, and its low-gabled, impending architecture. I had passed through the crevice-like street, winding snakewise amid the silent-stepping throng of figures naked, caftaned, or white-turbaned; now night-dark, now half lighted by oil-lamps glowing in the hollow of tiny booths filled with the yellow gleam of brass-work. I had reached the stuccoed building, crooked with age, on the corner, and felt my way up through the stifling obscurity to the door which, opening, revealed the wide, dim-lit room which Traunce called his studio. Dark, rich hues on all sides; the gleam of metals like bright thoughts in a gloomy mind; the bland sheen of ivory and jade; the faint scent of musk, as from the sweet body of the anointed Shulamite. On one side, old Keshub, impenetrable and impassive, his lean, brown limbs and dark face and beard hardly discernible below the globular whiteness of his turban; and on the other, Traunce, his cello between his knees. He drew a deep note from the strings, looked up, and nodded smilingly.

"Get a cigarette, old chap, and occupy your divan. You're just in time. Light of my soul, wilt thou dance?"

She uprose slowly from the cushions at his feet. Like the pillar of a fairy temple she stood, enwound in her glittering, translucent sari. The yellow gold of her earrings shone against the mellow dusk of her slender neck. Bracelets tinkled on her arms, and anklets at her naked feet. Her hair, evenly parted, curved past her cheeks, and was mounded midnight-black on the crown of her small head; beneath the level of her delicate, black brows opened long, imperial eyes, abysses of darkness and of light; and no carver of jewels ever wrought anything half so perfect as the fineness of her nostrils, the noble passion of her lips, the melting contour of her chin. Yet was her beauty of form and face less than the grace of her postures; and when she moved, music found a model which it might rival but not surpass.

She took her place on the Persian carpet, where the light from the pierced lantern softly touched her figure. It had the effect of the very moonlight which irradiates the first mood of Beethoven's sonata, twinkling along the ripples of his fairy sea. Like the waves of that sea, her bosom began to heave, and downward from her loins went sinuous changes of outline, while her arms rose, spread outward, and descended, smooth as the dip and soar of sea-gulls. As the inspiration of the music became stronger, the folds of the sari loosened, and were caught in the weaving of her hands, undulating in air around her like wreaths of mist. Keshub's low drumming, in its monotonous minor, throbbed in the ear like the beating of hearts oppressed with love. Love was the theme of all—love from the beginning to the end of things, beautiful and immortal, tender and insatiable. Its power stirred through Amra's polished limbs, beauty of the soul kindling beneath beauty of the flesh. It wrought in her like leaping flame, in vain suppressed. Like flame blown on by the wind, her body swayed and writhed on the stem of her supple waist, and the low clinking of silver at wrist and ankle lent a barbaric color to the silent speech of form. O Eastern Star, with the blood of princes in your veins, love was your life, your art, and your expression; and death, even then creeping toward the elastic treading of your fragrant feet, could but bring the utterance of love to its fulfilment! The voice of the cello rose in liquid yearnings. Facing the player, Amra lifted and flung open her arms, and the sari fell light as gossamer behind her on the floor. Love flowed from her face to his, from every matchless contour of her body; he laid aside the cello, dropped the bow, and rose. She stepped toward him.

Something had glided from the folds of Keshub's robe, and had slid in sluggish curves along the carpet. It was a small, brown thing, nearly invisible in the obscurity, which I, my senses overwrought by the spell of sound and motion, barely observed, and its deadly significance quite escaped me. It crept nearer, and lay coiled in the place where Amra's next step must fall. Keshub alone knew, and he sat watching, like an image of bronze. . . .

Years ago it had happened, where, on the banks of the Ganges, Benares stands dreaming of her mysterious past. To-night, in this land of new things, new dreams, new thought, the scene in every detail had been reproduced. The sight of my soul had been opened, and I looked into the regions of the soul. Strange! But less strange than that my mortal eyes continued to perform their office, so that I beheld simultaneously the actual contemporary scene, in the main wonderfully coinciding with the spiritual, but also, in certain incidents, diverging from it. Instead of confusing, this double consciousness seemed to clarify my perception and understanding.

Diverted from her play by her father's music, the little girl had dropped her bear and got to her feet. For her four years she was sturdy on her little legs; but her present manifestation was extraordinary. Her movements had a sort of infantile awkwardness and uncertainty, yet a sort of grace, too, given by nature and the childlike absence of self-consciousness. She was imitating, imperfectly, yet with marvelous spirit and feeling, the dance of Amra, as if a mirror had reflected the movements, while magically transforming the shape and stature. The baby face assumed a rapt and solemn expression, and at moments I scarce knew whether it were she or Amra that I beheld, so intimate was the transfusion of sentiment; but, again, she would become all baby-like when a failure to reproduce a gesture or a motion left her out of touch with her inspiration, causing her to frown and emit a little grunt of annoyance. But then, immediately, she would catch the clue once more, and her chubby arms would rise and fall, her body sway and turn, and her little feet, with the gleam and clink of their silver bangles, softly lift and replace themselves. From one point of view the performance was grotesque and laughable, but from another it was profoundly moving and impressive; I felt a meaning in it which I could but vaguely fathom, and a foreboding gradually grew in me of some sinister issue, I knew not what, which stirred the roots of my hair. This emotion was entirely distinct from that of the remembered tragedy which Amra herself was rehearsing.

Keshub, old Keshub, why do you drum so loudly, almost drowning the tones of the cello? Or is it the beating of my own heart in my ears? Beware the serpent—beware! Oh, Amra, Rana, Spirit of beauty and of retribution, of love and of jealousy, would you visit upon the innocent the wrongs of the dead past? It was long ago; will you not forgive and forbear, and be at peace? A little child, serious-eyed, and rose-leaf pure!

Dominated by the spell, I could lift neither hand nor foot, nor open my mouth in a cry of warning. But was it not incredible that Traunce and his wife remained totally unconscious of what impended? They saw nothing but the child, quaintly dancing to her father's music; heard nothing but the undulating strains of the sonata, weaving their magic over the fairyland of imagination. Of Amra, Keshub, the serpent—of the marvel and menace of the mystic life that is within life, of the fatal return of the circle upon itself—these two perceived and surmised nothing. Only the mother, pausing for a moment in her sewing to contemplate her baby's performance, murmured, half to herself: "She's an odd child; I hardly understand her myself sometimes! She never danced like that before; and who ever heard of anybody's dancing to the 'Moonlight Sonata'? It's like what one hears of those odalisk creatures in that horrible East of yours!" Then she took up her sewing again, and her capable, shapely hand resumed its out-and-back movement; and all the while that Wonder and Terror, overshadowing the child, controlling it, hovered portentous, a spiritual Vengeance! Sluggish and deadly, the serpent lay in the path.

But now Traunce, roused by his wife's words from his preoccupation, looked up; and as his eyes comprehended the movements of the child, I saw them dilate. He continued to play, but mechanically; the veil of memory was being withdrawn, though not the deeper veils. . . . Why did he not stop playing? Was he, too, spellbound, though ignorantly? Must murder be done upon the innocent, and none stir to prevent it? Look, man—the serpent! Another wave of that enchanted melody will bear the child upon its fangs!

No sound left my lips. But within my paralyzed body had begun a life-and-death struggle for freedom. Invisible to the outward eye, the desperate tension of it was instantly perceptible in the spiritual sphere. Suddenly it was as if I were in the mid-shriek of a storm, and assailed by a whirl of threatening shapes. The air darkened; but through broad rifts I caught glimpses of an appalling scenery far within the boundaries of the abysses of the soul. Subtle hands grasped fiercely at my heart, and clutched chokingly at the channels of my breath. Needles of fire flickered at my eyes, and the weight that bore down my limbs was as a mountain of iron. From a remote point in the horizon a dark cloud drove upon me, and assumed the form of Keshub; we grappled; he was corpse-cold, but of maniac strength; I called upon my soul, and felt him falter, and crumble in my hands like fetid clay. And there, before me, stood Amra, smiling inscrutably, with outstretched, inviting arms. "Yield, beloved, and take me to be thine forever."

Yes, I had loved her. In those days I would have given heaven for her embrace. And she had passed me by as one passes a dead tree in the pasture, with a heart fixed elsewhere. But, as she confronted me at this moment, her allurement seized upon me with a force compared with which all that had been before was like a fitful breeze. I believed that her promise would be kept—a soul for a soul. She took her place in the inmost of my heart. What concerned me the things of earth, since love could be immortal?

What is it that guides and saves a man in the supreme moments? Not his own will, but the presence in him of something sacred beyond his own reach, which blooms fragrant in the decay of his mortal strength, and breathes celestial messages.

So, in that moment, above the strength of my own will, as by the touch of an omnipotent hand, I was lifted up, and the chains fell from me. The vision of Amra shriveled and faded before me, and her dark retinue with her. I stepped quickly forward, and caught up the baby in my arms, just as she way about to set her naked foot on the poisonous thing that lay there. And there I stood, in the warm, familiar studio, holding her while substance and dream danced a reel in my brain. But the baby was sound asleep.

Mrs. Traunce dropped her sewing; Traunce stood up with a haggard look.

"What is it? What happened?" he faltered.

"The snake would have stung her," I said.

"The snake!" We all looked down at the carpet. There was no snake there; but in its place lay the jeweled head of the serpent necklace, with its poisoned needlepoints. We had overlooked it in gathering up the broken pieces of the ornament.

The mother took her baby from my arms. "Fancy her going to sleep right in the midst of dancing! Something must have hypnotised her—the sonata, maybe! I won't bring her here again; it's uncanny, I tell you."

"It's all right now; the curse is lifted." said I, with a slightly hysterical laugh.

"I'm going to put her in bed; good night," said she, at the door.

When we were alone, Traunce put a hand on my arm, and there was a perceptible tremor in it.

"Did you—have you anything to tell me?" he asked. "I fancied—"

I hesitated a moment. Then I shook my head and turned away.

"Ask the bronze Buddha," I said. "I know nothing."

Story of an Obstinate Corpse

Elia W. Peattie

Virgil Hoyt is a photographer's assistant up at St. Paul, and enjoys his work without being consumed by it. He has been in search of the picturesque all over the West and hundreds of miles to the north, in Canada, and can speak three or four Indian dialects and put a canoe through the rapids. That is to say, he is a man of adventure, and no dreamer. He can fight well and shoot better, and swim so as to put up a winning race with the Indian boys, and he can sit in the saddle all day and not worry about it to-morrow.

Wherever he goes, he carries a camera.

"The world," Hoyt is in the habit of saying to those who sit with him when he smokes his pipe, "was created in six days to be photographed. Man—and particularly woman—was made for the same purpose. Clouds are not made to give moisture nor trees to cast shade. They have been created in order to give the camera obscura something to do."

In short, Virgil Hoyt's view of the world is whimsical, and he likes to be bothered neither with the disagreeable nor the mysterious. That is the reason he loathes and detests going to a house of mourning to photograph a corpse. The bad taste of it offends him; but above all, he doesn't like the necessity of shouldering, even for a few moments, a part of the burden of sorrow which belongs to some one else. He dislikes sorrow, and would willingly canoe five hundred miles up the cold Canadian rivers to get rid of it. Nevertheless, as assistant photographer, it is often his duty to do this very kind of thing.

Not long ago he was sent for by a rich Jewish family to photograph the remains of the mother, who had just died. He was put out, but he was only an assistant, and he went. He was taken to the front parlor, where the dead woman lay in her coffin. It was evident to him that there was some excitement in the household, and that a discussion was going on. But Hoyt said to himself that it didn't concern him, and he therefore paid no attention to it.

The daughter wanted the coffin turned on end in order that the corpse might face the camera properly, but Hoyt said he could overcome the recumbent attitude and make it appear that the face was taken in the position it would naturally hold in life, and so they went out and left him alone with the dead.

The face of the deceased was a strong and positive one, such as may often be seen among Jewish matrons. Hoyt regarded it with some admiration, thinking to himself that she was a woman who had known what she wanted, and who, once having made up her mind, would prove immovable. Such a character appealed to Hoyt. He reflected that he might have married if only he could have found a woman with strength of character sufficient to disagree with him. There was a strand of hair out of place on the dead woman's brow, and he gently pushed it back. A bud lifted its head too high from among the roses on her breast and spoiled the contour of the chin, so he broke it off. He remembered these things later with keen distinctness, and that his hand touched her chill face two or three times in the making of his arrangements.

Then he took the impression, and left the house.

He was busy at the time with some railroad work, and several days passed before he found opportunity to develop the plates. He took them from the bath in which they had lain with a number of others, and went energetically to work upon them, whistling some very saucy songs he had learned of the guide in the Red River country, and trying to forget that the face which was presently to appear was that of a dead woman. He had used three plates as a precaution against accident, and they came up well. But as they developed, he became aware of the existence of something in the photograph which had not been apparent to his eye in the subject. He was irritated, and without attempting to face the mystery, he made a few prints and laid them aside, ardently hoping that by some chance they would never be called for.

However, as luck would have it,—and Hoyt's luck never had been good,—his employer asked one day what had become of those photographs. Hoyt tried to evade making an answer, but the effort was futile, and he had to get out the finished prints and exhibit them. The older man sat staring at them a long time.

"Hoyt," he said, "you're a young man, and very likely you have never seen anything like this before. But I have. Not exactly the same thing, perhaps, but similar phenomena have come my way a number of times since I went in the business, and I want to tell you there are things in heaven and earth not dreamt of—"

"Oh, I know all that tommy-rot," cried Hoyt, angrily; "but when anything happens I want to know the reason why and how it is done."

"All right," answered his employer, "then you might explain why and how the sun rises."

But he humored the young man sufficiently to examine with him the baths in which the plates were submerged, and the plates themselves. All was as it should be; but the mystery was there, and could not be done away with.

Hoyt hoped against hope that the friends of the dead woman would somehow forget about the photographs; but the idea was unreasonable, and one day, as a matter of course, the daughter appeared and asked to see the pictures of her mother.

"Well, to tell the truth," stammered Hoyt, "they didn't come out quite—quite as well as we could wish."

"But let me see them," persisted the lady. "I'd like to look at them anyhow."

"Well, now," said Hoyt, trying to be soothing, as he believed it was always best to be with women,—to tell the truth he was an ignoramus where women were concerned,—"I think it would be better if you didn't look at them. There are reasons why—" he ambled on like this, stupid man that he was, till the lady naturally insisted upon seeing the pictures without a moment's delay.

So poor Hoyt brought them out and placed them in her hand, and then ran for the water pitcher, and had to be at the bother of bathing her forehead to keep her from fainting.

For what the lady saw was this: Over face and flowers and the head of the coffin fell a thick veil, the edges of which touched the floor in some places. It covered the features so well that not a hint of them was visible. "There was nothing over mother's face!" cried the lady at length.

"Not a thing," acquiesced Hoyt. "I know, because I had occasion to touch her face just before I took the picture. I put some of her hair back from her brow."

"What does it mean, then?" asked the lady.

"You know better than I. There is no explanation in science. Perhaps there is some in—in psychology."

"Well," said the young woman, stammering a little and coloring, "mother was a good woman, but she always wanted her own way, and she always had it, too."

"Yes."

"And she never would have her picture taken. She didn't admire her own appearance. She said no one should ever see a picture of her."

"So?" said Hoyt, meditatively. "Well, she's kept her word, hasn't she?"

The two stood looking at the photographs for a time. Then Hoyt pointed to the open blaze in the grate.

"Throw them in," he commanded. "Don't let your father see them—don't keep them yourself. They wouldn't be agreeable things to keep."

"That's true enough," admitted the lady. And she threw them in the fire. Then Virgil Hoyt brought out the plates and broke them before her eyes.

And that was the end of it—except that Hoyt sometimes tells the story to those who sit beside him when his pipe is lighted.

A Sworn Statement

Being the Deposition of Mr. Audenried's Valet

Emma Dawson

This ae night, this ae night,
Every night and alle,
Fire and sleet and candle-light,
And Christ receive thy saule.
—Lykrwake Dirge

I first met Mr. Audenried through his advertising for a valet. I liked his appearance, and engaged with him at a lower salary than one of my experience and ability will usually work for. He was then living in a furnished house on Rincon Hill, whence he could see the bay. He sat for hours looking at it and writing verses. He had money, but was neither young nor strong, and seldom went out. He had been very handsome, was still fine-looking, with eyes that glowed with a lurid, internal fire.

There was one other person in the house, a quiet lady, yet one to be noticed and remembered. I pride myself on my discretion. It was nothing to me how many "Coralies" or "Camilles" existed. It was long before I alluded to her, though I met her in the upper hall, on the stairs, and sometimes found her in the room with my master and myself, or just outside the door, standing near, as if waiting for me to go. After a while, I got the notion that she did not like me, and it made it unpleasant. After long thinking it over, for I did not want to leave, I gave a month's notice.

"Why is this, Wilkins?" says Mr. Audenried. "If it is a question of wages, stay on. I like your quiet ways," says he. That is just what he says.

"To tell the truth, sir," I says, "it's not my pay—it's the lady, sir."

"What!" says he.

So then I told of her air of watchful dislike, and how I was not used to being spied upon, and that it was needless my recommendations could all show. He turned quite pale, so white that I thought Heaven forgive me if I 'd made trouble between them, for she looked sad enough anyway. He did not speak for a long while.

Then he muttered to himself: *"This* man, too!"

He made me tell him all over again. Then, after a pause, he says: "Find me another place, Wilkins, and help me move."

So I thought there was a quarrel. We did move from house to house, from street to street, from city to city, all through the State and to ethers near. Mr. Audenried never spoke of her, nor noticed her, but as soon as she came, as she always did come, he at once gave the order to start. He seemed to watch my face, and I fancied he knew in that way when she was about. I wondered what their story might be, and tried to make out from verses he wrote that time, but all I could get hold of were these:

PROPHETIC

Unto the garden's bloom close set
Of lily, larkspur, violet,
Sweet jasmine, rose, and mignonette
More beauty lending,
Fair Marguerite stands in the sun,
Plucks leaves from daisy, one by one,
While Faust, impatient, sees it done
And waits the ending.

See! on the garden-wall behind,
Their happy shadows plain defined,
Bent heads and eager hand, outlined
Like soft engraving;
And there athwart their fingers' pose
A shape whose presence neither knows.
Mephisto! 'T is his head that shows
A cock's plume waving!

Sometimes we rested a few days or weeks, sometimes went on, day after day, without stopping, but she was my master's shadow; she followed us everywhere. I used to try and puzzle out what their secret was. If it had been love, it must now be hate, I told myself, seeing how they often met and passed without a word. He did not appear to even see her.

We had come back to San Francisco, and it was nearing Christmas-time when I was first seized with my queer spells. We had taken another furnished house, far out and high upon Washington street. I thought we had got rid of the woman; but coming home late one afternoon I found her in the window, while my master had been looking over his writing-desk. Before him lay withered flowers, a ribbon, a lady's glove, and a photograph with some look of this persistent woman, but younger and handsomer.

I felt uneasy. Mr. Audenried sat with head on his hand, lost in thought. When I spoke he did not hear nor notice me until I put the medicine he had sent for into the hand in his lap. Then he did not know it at first, though in giving the parcel I touched his hand. Something about him I could not describe kept me an instant motionless in that position.

A stupor came over me. The carved ivory hourglass we had filled with Arizona sand from before the Casa Grande, our bright, thick Moqui blanket on the lounge, our foreign fur rugs, our Japanese fans, bronzes, and china—the whole room came and went as to one who is sleepy yet tries to keep awake. Again and again it vanished, reappearing enlarged to twice, three times, its size. Then it was lost in a mist, from which rose a different scene.

The chandelier had changed to long lines of lights, the pictures to great mirrors, and arches with banners and streamers. Devices in evergreen showed that it was Christmas Eve. I was aware of a rush and whirl of dancers, waltz-music, flowers, gay colors, and the scent of a sandal-wood fan; but I saw plainly only one woman, young, gay, lovely, but with a faint likeness to some one I had seen who was older and wretched. I rubbed my eyes, and when I opened them at the sound of my master's voice, it was the room I knew, with all its familiar objects, and he and I were there alone.

One day I met our quiet lady coming from Mr. Audenried's study, and found him there in a fainting-fit. As I was helping him across the hall to his bedroom I had the second of my odd attacks.

A dullness and vague fear troubled me. Our many-branched antlers, our lacquered-work and carved cabinets and great Chinese lantern, the stained-glass skylight, the big vase of pampas-grass, the open doors and windows, the sunny yard, with callas and geraniums in bloom, all wavered before me, went and came and vanished.

I saw a room with flowered chintz in curtains and furniture-covers, a glowing anthracite fire, and Christmas wreaths hanging in long windows looking on frost-bound garden and river. And the beautiful woman of the ball! Still young, but now unhappy, looking at me in despair. Both arms outstretched in an agony of entreaty, and tears rolling down her cheeks. Terribly distressed by her woe, I gave a cry of pity just as Mr. Audenried, gasping and falling on the bed, brought me back to him, to myself, and to his

Putting away his things for the night I found these verses in a woman's writing:

IN ABSENCE

In my black night no moonshine nor star-glimmer
On my long, weary path that leads Nowhere
I get no shimmer
Of that great glory our day knew.
I cannot think the world holds you;
It is not ours, this Land of Vague Despair—
I scarce can breathe its air.

I am as one whom some sweet tune, down dropping,
Has left half-stunned by silence like a blow;
Like one who, stopping
In drifting desert sands, looks back
Where sky slants down above his track,
To mark the tufted palm whose outlines show
An oasis below;

Like one whom winter wind and rain are blinding,
And storm-tossed billows bear from land away,
Who, no hope finding,
Should yield himself to bitter fate.
Can I do thisl Ah, God I too late—
Have I not felt thy dear, warm lips convey
Commands I must obey?

"Forget-me-not!" a kiss for every letter.
"Forget-me-not!" a kiss for every word.
It could not better
Have stamped Itself upon my soul
It passed beyond my own control.
All thought, all circumstance are by it stirred,
Invisible, unheard.

Though, like Francesca, ever falling, falling
Through dizzy space to endless depths afar,
Thy kiss recalling
Would charm me to forget my woe;
Of Heaven or Hell I should not know,
Nor as I passed see any blazing star,
Nor mark its rhythmic jar.

If such remembrance only—moon-reflection
On depths untried of my soul's unknown sea—
Mere recollection—
Could hold me spellbound by its sway,
What of your true kiss can I say?
Ah! that is wholly speechless ecstasy,—
No words for that could be!

I thought it might be I had myself grown nervous about the quiet lady, to have these crazy fits after seeing her, and I dreaded to have her come again. But it was not my place to urge Mr. Audenried to move, and he seemed tired of changing.

One evening he had a severe attack of palpitation of the heart, and called me in great haste. I had been wondering what had put him in such a flutter, when that lady opened the door and glanced round the room as if she had forgotten something, but did not come in. Mr. Audenried was so ill that he had to sit up in bed and have me hold him firmly, my hands pressing his breast and his back.

Again that strange dread and drowsiness fell on me like a cloud. My master's pearl combs, brushes, crystal jewel-box, with its glittering contents, and a bunch of violets in a wineglass on the bureau, his Japanese quilted silk dressing-gown thrown over a chair, embroidered slippers here, gay smoking-cap there, and a large lithograph of Modjeska, glimmered through a fog, came back, withdrew again.

The one high gas-burner became a full moon, the walls fell away; I stood out of doors in a summer night's dimness and stillness that make one feel lonely; grass, daisies, and buttercups underfoot, and overhead stars and endless space. The beautiful woman, worn and wild-looking, with flashing eyes, stood there in a threatening posture, calling down curses! I shrank in horror, though the vision lasted, as before, not more than a quarter of a second.

Mr. Audenried, wasted and wan, had grown so nervous that after this time he refused to be left alone, and above all, cautioned me to stay beside him on Christmas Eve.

"An unpleasant anniversary to me," he says.

The doctor advised him to change to a hotel, to have cheerful society. We moved to the Palace Hotel, and to divert his mind from its own horror Mr. Audenried gave a dinner-party in his rooms on Christmas Eve.

It was a wild night, just right for "Tam O'Shanter," which one of the gentlemen recited. The weather or my master's forced gayety made me gloomy. There was a raw Irish waiter to help, and once I went into the anteroom just in time to catch him about to season one of Mr. Audenried's private dishes from a bottle out of our Japanese cabinet. It was marked "Poison," but he could not read.

"What could possess you," I says, "to meddle with *that?*"

"Sure," he says, "the lady showed me which to take."

"The *lady!* What lady?" I says, trembling from head to foot.

"A dark lady," says he, "with a proud nose and mouth, and eyebrows in one long, heavy line."

I was horrified. I did not want to figure in a murder case. I liked Mr. Audenried too well to leave. I was too poor to lose a good place. I resolved to stay and protect him, but my heart beat faster. For my own safety I meant to say over the multiplication-table, and not get bewitched or entranced again. I told myself over and over, "She shall not outwit me."

The wind and rain beat against the windows, and I heard one of our guests singing "The Midnight Revellers":

"The first was shot by Carlist thieves
Three years ago in Spain;
The second was drowned in Alicante,
While I alone remain.
But friends I have, two glorious friends,
Two braver could not be;
And every night when midnight tolls
They meet to laugh with me!"

As I took in some wine, a gentleman was saying: "Too wild a story for such a commonplace background as San Francisco."

"One must be either commonplace or sated with horrors to say that," says Mr. Audenried. "What city has more or stranger disappearances and assassinations? There have been murders and suicides at all the hotels. Other cities surpass it in age, but none in crime and mystery."

It was a lively party. A love-song from one of the gentlemen turned the talk on love affairs, and I went in just as Mr. Audenried was saying: "Aaron Burr relied wholly on the fascination of his touch. I believe in the magnetism of touch; that it cannot only impart disease but sensations. Holding a sleeper's hand while I read, by no willpower of mine he dreamed of scenes I saw in my mind."

Trained servant as I am, I disgraced myself then. I dropped and broke some of our own bubble-like glasses I was carrying. I was so unnerved by this explanation of my queer turns. It flashed upon me how they had only come when I was touching him. I had heard a former master, a learned German, talk about his countryman Mesmer, and I understood that what had appeared to me in my spells was what Mr. Audenried was thinking of!

I could scarcely recover myself for the rest of the company's stay. I recollect no more about it, except that somebody played the flute till it seemed as if a twilight breeze sighed for being pent in our four walls and longed to join its ruder brother-winds outside; and that Mr. Audenried read these verses of his:

RONDEL

To-night, O friends! we meet "Kriss Kringle";
He comes, he comes when falls betwixt us
The chiming midnight-bells' soft klingle,
When, glad, we crowd round cheery ingle,
Or, lonely, grieve that joy has missed us;
Or, in cathedral gloom, pray Christus;
Or drain gay toasts where glasses jingle.
Though marshalled hosts of cares have tricked us,
In wine's Red Sea drown all and single—
"Christmas!"
Drown recollection that afflicts us—
Our bowls, like witches' caldrons, mingle
Too much of old Yule-tide that kissed us—
The bitter drink that Life has mixed us

Forget, and shout till rafters tingle—
"Christmas!"

The last guest had hardly gone when Mrs. Carnavon's card was brought up. This was an elderly lady we had met in our travels, who took an interest in Mr. Audenried's case, though a stranger. She came in, bright and chatty, and my master was so cheered up by it that he readily let me leave.

I did not want to go. I had not been drinking; I was well and in my right mind, but my whole skin seemed to draw up with a shiver and thrill as at some near terror. But he sent me to a druggist to have Mrs. Carnavon's vinaigrette refilled.

As I left the passage to our suite of rooms and turned into the long, lonesome hall, more dreary than ever in its vastness at this quiet, late hour, I saw a little way ahead our brunette stepping into the elevator. I fancied a mocking smile on her face as she looked back at me. I forgot the multiplication-table, whose fixed rules were to keep me in my senses. For the first time it struck me that she was the woman of my visions, grown older and sadder.

I hurried, but when I reached the door she had gone, and stout Mrs. Lisgar was coming up, like the change of figures in a pantomime. She was another mystery of mine; for her maid had told me Mrs. Lisgar and my master knew each other abroad, but were sworn foes now, neither of us knew why.

"I beg your pardon, Madam," I says; "did you see the lady who just went down? A handsome brunette, with eyebrows that join above a Roman nose, and a very short upper lip. Where did she go?"

Mrs. Lisgar swelled bigger and redder. "Has Mr. Audenried sent you to annoy me?" she says.

"Certainly not, Madam," says I. "But I saw her!—heavy, meeting eyebrows, scornful mouth, and—"

"Silence, sir!" she cried. "There was no one in the elevator. Don't you know you are speaking of my poor sister, dead for many years?"

In my confusion I gasped out at random: "Mrs. Carnavon is here. Do you know her?"

Mrs. Lisgar says: "She was my sister's most intimate friend. But you are either drunk or crazy. I was with her when she died in Arizona last week."

An awful suspicion seized me; a cold sweat broke out on my brow. I had not lost sight of Mr. Audenried's door. I bowed to Mrs. Lisgar and tried to hurry back, but a numbness in every limb weighed me down till I seemed to move as slowly as the bells that were striking twelve.

As I drew near, I heard angry voices inside, then a fearful groan, which seemed to die off in the distance. But I found every room in our suite vacant, except for my figure, which I caught glimpses of at every turn, staring out of the great mirrors, ghastly, haggard, with bloodshot eyes, and a strained look about the mouth, madly straying among the lights and flowers, tables with remnants of the feast, and the disordered chairs, which after such a revel have a queer air of life of their own.

A long window in the parlor stood wide open. Chilled with fright, with I don't know what vague thought, I ran and looked out. Six stories from the street, nothing to be seen outside but the night and storm, neither on the lighted pavement far below, nor among drifting clouds overhead! Nothing but impenetrable darkness then and afterward over Mr. Audenried's fate.

This is all I can tell of the well-known strange disappearance of my unhappy master. It is the truth, the whole truth and nothing but the truth.

The Terrible Old Man

H. P. Lovecraft

It was the design of Angelo Ricci and Joe Czanek and Manuel Silva to call on the Terrible Old Man. This old man dwells all alone in a very ancient house on Water Street near the sea, and is reputed to be both exceedingly rich and exceedingly feeble; which forms a situation very attractive to men of the profession of Messrs. Ricci, Czanek, and Silva, for that profession was nothing less dignified than robbery.

The inhabitants of Kingsport say and think many things about the Terrible Old Man which generally keep him safe from the attention of gentlemen like Mr. Ricci and his colleagues, despite the almost certain fact that he hides a fortune of indefinite magnitude somewhere about his musty and venerable abode. He is, in truth, a very strange person, believed to have been a captain of East India clipper ships in his day; so old that no one can remember when he was young, and so taciturn that few know his real name. Among the gnarled trees in the front yard of his aged and neglected place he maintains a strange collection of large stones, oddly grouped and painted so that they resemble the idols in some obscure Eastern temple. This collection frightens away most of the small boys who love to taunt the Terrible Old Man about his long white hair and beard, or to break the small-paned windows of his dwelling with wicked missiles; but there are other things which frighten the older and more curious folk who sometimes steal up to the house to peer in through the dusty panes. These folk say that on a table in a bare room on the ground floor are many peculiar bottles, in each a small piece of lead suspended pendulum-wise from a string. And they say that the Terrible Old Man talks to these bottles, addressing them by such names as Jack, Scar-Face, Long Tom, Spanish Joe, Peters, and Mate Ellis, and that whenever he speaks to a bottle the little lead pendulum within makes certain definite vibrations as if in answer. Those who have watched the tall, lean, Terrible Old Man in these peculiar conversations, do not watch him again. But Angelo Ricci and Joe Czanek and Manuel Silva were not of Kingsport blood; they were of that new and heterogeneous alien stock which lies outside the charmed circle of New England life and traditions, and they saw in the Terrible Old Man merely a tottering, almost helpless greybeard, who could not walk without the aid of his knotted cane, and whose thin, weak hands shook pitifully. They were really quite sorry in their way for the lonely, unpopular old fellow, whom everybody shunned, and at whom all the dogs barked singularly. But business is business, and to a robber whose soul is in his profession, there is a lure and a challenge about a very old and very feeble man who has no account at the bank, and who pays for his few necessities at the village store with Spanish gold and silver minted two centuries ago.

Messrs. Ricci, Czanek, and Silva selected the night of April 11th for their call. Mr. Ricci and Mr. Silva were to interview the poor old gentleman, whilst Mr. Czanek waited for them and their presumable metallic burden with a covered motor-car in Ship Street, by the gate in the tall rear wall of their host's grounds. Desire to avoid needless explanations in case of unexpected police intrusions prompted these plans for a quiet and unostentatious departure.

As prearranged, the three adventurers started out separately in order to prevent any evil-minded suspicions afterward. Messrs. Ricci and Silva met in Water Street by the old man's front gate, and although they did not like the way the moon shone down upon the painted stones through the budding branches of the gnarled trees, they had more important things to think about than mere idle superstition. They feared it might be unpleasant work making the Terrible Old Man loquacious concerning his hoarded gold and silver, for aged sea-captains are notably stubborn and perverse. Still, he was very old and very feeble, and there were two visitors. Messrs. Ricci and Silva were experienced in the art of making unwilling persons voluble, and the screams of a weak and exceptionally venerable man can be easily muffled. So they moved up to the one lighted window and heard the Terrible Old Man talking childishly to his bottles with pendulums. Then they donned masks and knocked politely at the weather-stained oaken door.

Waiting seemed very long to Mr. Czanek as he fidgeted restlessly in the covered motor-car by the Terrible Old Man's back gate in Ship Street. He was more than ordinarily tender-hearted, and he did not like the hideous screams he had heard in the ancient house just after the hour appointed for the deed. Had he not told his colleagues to be as gentle as possible with the pathetic old sea-captain? Very nervously he watched that narrow oaken gate in the high and ivy-clad stone wall. Frequently he consulted his watch, and wondered at the delay. Had the old man died before revealing where his treasure was hidden, and had a thorough search become necessary? Mr. Czanek did not like to wait so long in the dark in such a place. Then he sensed a soft tread or tapping on the walk inside the gate, heard a gentle fumbling at the rusty latch, and saw the narrow, heavy door swing inward. And in the pallid glow of the single dim street-lamp he strained his eyes to see what his colleagues had brought out of that sinister house which loomed so close behind. But when he looked, he did not see what he had expected; for his colleagues were not there at all, but only the Terrible Old Man leaning quietly on his knotted cane and smiling hideously. Mr. Czanek had never before noticed the color of that man's eyes; now he saw that they were yellow.

Little things make considerable excitement in little towns, which is the reason that Kingsport people talked all that spring and summer about the three unidentifiable bodies, horribly slashed as with many cutlasses, and horribly mangled as by the tread of many cruel boot-heels, which the tide washed in. And some people even spoke of things as trivial as the deserted motor-car found in Ship Street, or certain especially inhuman cries, probably of a stray animal or migratory bird, heard in the night by wakeful citizens. But in this idle village gossip the Terrible Old Man took no interest at all. He was by nature reserved, and when one is aged and feeble one's reserve is doubly strong. Besides, so ancient a sea-captain must have witnessed scores of things much more stirring in the far-off days of his unremembered youth.

The Terror by Night

Lewis Lister

Maynard disincumbered himself from his fishing-creel, stabbed the butt of his rod into the turf, and settled down in the heather to fill a pipe. All round him stretched the undulating moor, purple in the late summer sunlight. To the southward, low down, a faint haze told where the sea lay. The stream at his feet sang its queer, crooning moor-song as it rambled onward, chuckling to meet a bed of pebbles somewhere out of sight, whispering mysteriously to the rushes that fringed its banks of peat, deepening to a sudden contralto as it poured over granite boulders into a scum-flecked pool below.

For a long time the man sat smoking. Occasionally he turned his head to watch with keen eyes the fretful movements of a fly hovering above the water. Then a sudden dimple in the smooth surface of the stream arrested his attention. A few concentric ripples widened, travelled towards him, and were absorbed in the current. His lips curved into a little smile and he reached for his rod. In the clear water he could see the origin of the ripples; a small trout, unconscious of his presence, was waiting in its hover for the next tit-bit to float down stream. Presently it rose again.

"The odds are ten to one in your favour," said the man. "Let's see!"

He dropped on one knee and the cast leapt out in feathery coils. Once, twice it swished; the third time it alighted like thistledown on the surface. There was a tiny splash, a laugh, and the little greenheart rod flicked a trout high over his head. It was the merest baby—half-an-ounce, perhaps—and it fell from the hook into the herbage some yards from the stream.

"Little ass!" said Maynard. "That was meant for your big brother."

He recovered his cast and began to look for his victim. Without avail he searched the heather, and as the fateful seconds sped, at last laid down his rod and dropped on hands and knees to probe among the grass-stems.

For a while he hunted in vain, then the sunlight showed a golden sheen among some stones. Maynard gave a grunt of relief, but as his hand closed round it a tiny flutter passed through the fingerling; it gave a final gasp and was still. Knitting his brows in almost comical vexation, he hastened to restore it to the stream, holding it by the tail and striving to impart a life-like wriggle to its limpness.

"Buck up, old thing!" he murmured encouragingly. "Oh, buck up! You're all right, really you are!"

But the "old thing" was all wrong. In fact, it was dead.

Standing in the wet shingle, Maynard regarded the speckled atom as it lay in the palm of his hand.

"A matter of seconds, my son. One instant in all eternity would have made just the difference between life and death to you. And the high gods denied it you!"

On the opposite side of the stream, set back about thirty paces from the brink, stood a granite boulder. It was as high as a man's chest, roughly cubical in shape; but the weather and clinging moss had rounded its edges, and in places segments had crumbled away, giving foothold to clumps of fern and starry moor-flowers. On three sides the surrounding ground rose steeply, forming an irregular horseshoe mound that opened to the west. Perhaps it was the queer amphitheatrical effect of this setting that connected up some whimsical train of thought in Maynard's brain.

"It would seem as if the gods had claimed you," he mused, still holding the corpse. "You shall be a sacrifice—a burnt sacrifice to the God of Waste Places."

He laughed at the conceit, half-ashamed of his own childishness, and crossing the stream by some boulders, he brushed away the earth and weed from the top of the great stone. Then he retraced his steps and gathered a handful of bleached twigs that the winter floods had left stranded along the margin of the stream. These he arranged methodically on the cleared space; on the top of the tiny pyre he placed the troutlet.

"There!" he said, and smiling gravely struck a match. A faint column of smoke curled up into the still air, and as he spoke the lower rim of the setting sun met the edge of the moor. The evening seemed suddenly to become incredibly still, even the voice of the stream ceasing to be a sound distinct. A wagtail bobbing in the shallows fled into the waste. Overhead the smoke trembled upwards, a faint stain against a cloudless sky. The stillness seemed almost acute. It was as if the moor were waiting, and holding its breath while it waited. Then the twigs upon his altar crackled, and the pale flames blazed up. The man stepped back with artistic appreciation of the effect.

"To be really impressive, there ought to be more smoke," he continued.

Round the case of the stone were clumps of small flowers. They were crimson in color and had thick, fleshy leaves. Hastily, he snatched a handful and piled it on the fire. The smoke darkened and rose in a thick column; there was a curious pungency in the air.

Far off the church-bell in some unseen hamlet struck the hour. The distant sound, coming from the world of men and everyday affairs, seemed to break the spell. An ousel fluttered across the stream and dabbled in a puddle among some stones. Rabbits began to show themselves and frisk with lengthened shadows in the clear spaces. Maynard looked at his watch, half-mindful of a train to be caught somewhere miles away, and then, held by the peace of running water, stretched himself against the sloping ground.

The glowing world seemed peopled by tiny folk, living out their timid, inscrutable lives around him. A water-rat, passing bright-eyed upon his lawful occasion, paused on the border of the stream to consider the stranger, and was lost to view. A stagnant pool among some reeds caught the reflection of the sunset and changed on the instant into raw gold.

Maynard plucked a grass stem and chewed it reflectively, staring out across the purple moor and lazily watching the western sky turn from glory to glory. Over his head the smoke of the sacrifice still curled and eddied upwards. Then a sudden sound sent him on to one elbow—the thud of an approaching horse's hoofs.

"Moor ponies!" he muttered, and, rising, stood expectant beside his smoking altar.

Then he heard the sudden jingle of a bit, and presently a horse and rider climbed into view against the pure sky. A young girl, breeched, booted and spurred like a boy, drew rein, and sat looking down into the hollow.

For a moment neither spoke; then Maynard acknowledged her presence by raising his tweed hat. She gave a little nod.

"I thought it was somebody swaling—burning the heather." She considered the embers on the stone, and then her grey eyes travelled back to the spare, tweed-clad figure beside it.

He smiled in his slow way—a rather attractive smile.

"No. I've just concluded some pagan rites in connection with a small trout!" He nodded gravely at the stone. "That was a burnt sacrifice." With whimsical seriousness he told her of the trout's demise and high destiny.

For a moment she looked doubtful; but the inflection of breeding in his voice, the wholesome, lean face and humorous eyes, reassured her. A smile hovered about the corners of her mouth.

"Oh, is that it? I wondered . . ."

She gathered the reins and turned her horse's head.

"Forgive me if I dragged you out of your way," said Maynard, never swift to conventionality, but touched by the tired shadows in her eyes. The faint droop of her mouth, too, betrayed intense fatigue. "You look fagged. I don't want to be a nuisance or bore you, but I wish you'd let me offer you a sandwich. I've some milk here, too."

The girl looked round the ragged moor, brooding in the twilight, and half hesitated. Then she forced a wan little smile.

"I am tired, and hungry, too. Have you enough for us both?"

"Lots!" said Maynard. To himself he added: "And what's more, my child, you'll have a little fainting affair in a few minutes, if you don't have a feed."

"Come and rest for a minute," he continued aloud.

He spoke with pleasant, impersonal kindliness, and as he turned to his satchel she slipped out of the saddle and came towards him, leading her horse.

"Drink that," he said, holding out the cup of his flask. She drank with a wry little face, and coughed. "I put a little whisky in it," he explained. "You needed it."

She thanked him and sat down with the bridle linked over her arm. The color crept back into her cheeks. Maynard produced a packet of sandwiches and a pasty.

"I've been mooning about the moor all the afternoon and lost myself twice," she explained between frank mouthfuls. "I'm hopelessly late for dinner, and I've still got miles to go."

"Do you know the way now?" he asked

"Oh, yes! It won't take me long. My family are sensible, too, and don't fuss." She looked at him, her long-lashed eyes a little serious. "But you—how are you going to get home? It's getting late to be out on the moor afoot."

Maynard laughed.

"Oh, I'm all right, thanks!" He sniffed the warm September night. "I think I shall sleep here, as a matter of fact. I'm a gipsy by instinct—

"Give to me the life I love,
Let the lave go by me,
Give the jolly Heaven above—"

He broke off, arrested by her unsmiling eyes. She was silent a moment.

"People don't as a rule sleep out about here." The words came jerkily, as if she were forcing a natural tone into her voice.

"No?" He was accustomed to being questioned on his unconventional mode of life, and was prepared for the usual expostulations. She looked abruptly towards him.

"Are you superstitious?"

He laughed and shook his head.

"I don't think so. But what has that got to do with it?"

She hesitated, flushing a little.

"There is a legend—people about here say that the moor here is haunted. There is a Thing that hunts people to death!"

He laughed outright, wondering how old she was. Seventeen or eighteen, perhaps. She had said her people "didn't fuss." That meant she was left to herself to pick up all these old wives' tales.

"Really! Has anyone been caught?"

She nodded, unsmiling.

"Yes; old George Toms. He was one of Dad's tenants, a big purple-faced man, who drank a lot and never took much exercise. They found him in a ditch with his clothes all torn and covered with mud. He had been run to death; there was no wound on his body, but his heart was broken." Her thoughts recurred to the stone against which they leant, and his quaint conceit. "You were rather rash to go offering burnt sacrifices about here, don't you think? Dad says that stone is the remains of an old Phoenician altar, too."

She was smiling now, but the seriousness lingered in her eyes.

"And I have probably invoked some terrible heathen deity—Ashtoreth, or Pugm, or Baal! How awful!" he added, with mock gravity.

The girl rose to her feet.

"You are laughing at me. The people about here are superstitious, and I am a Celt, too. I belong here."

He jumped up with a quick protest.

"No, I'm not laughing at you. Please don't think that! But it's a little hard to believe in active evil when all around is so beautiful." He helped her to mount and walked to the top of the mound at her stirrup. "Tell me, is there any charm or incantation, in case—?" His eyes were twinkling, but she shook her fair head soberly.

"They say iron—cold iron—is the only thing it cannot cross. But I must go!" She held out her hand with half-shy friendliness. "Thank you for your niceness to me." Her eyes grew suddenly wistful. "Really, though, I don't think I should stay there if I were you. Please!"

He only laughed, however, and she moved off, shaking her impatient horse into a canter. Maynard stood looking after her till she was swallowed by the dusk and surrounding moor. Then, thoughtfully, he retraced his steps to the hollow.

A cloud lay across the face of the moon when Fear awoke Maynard. He rolled on to one elbow and stared round the hollow, filled with inexplicable dread. He was ordinarily a courageous man, and had no nerves to speak of; yet, as his eyes followed the line of the ridge against the sky, he experienced terror, the elementary, nauseating terror of childhood, when the skin tingles, and the heart beats at a suffocating gallop. It was very dark, but momentarily his eyes grew accustomed to it. He was conscious of a queer, pungent smell, horribly animal and corrupt.

Suddenly the utter silence broke. He heard a rattle of stones, the splash of water about him, realised that it was the brook beneath his feet, and that he, Maynard, was running for his life.

Neither then nor later did Reason assert herself. He ran without question or amazement. His brain—the part where human reasoning holds normal sway—was dominated by the purely primitive instinct of flight. And in that sudden rout of courage and self-respect one conscious thought alone remained. What ever it was that was even then at his heels, he must not see it. At all costs it must be behind him, and, resisting the sudden terrified impulse to look over his shoulder, he unbuttoned his tweed jacket and disengaged himself from it as he ran. The faint haze that had gathered round the full moon dispersed, and he saw the moor stretching before him, grey and still, glistening with dew.

He was of frugal and temperate habits, a wiry man at the height of his physical powers, with lean flanks and a deep chest.

At Oxford they had said he was built to run for his life. He was running for it now, and he knew it.

The ground sloped upwards after awhile, and he tore up the incline, breathing deep and hard; down into a shallow valley, leaping gorse bushes, crashing through whortle and meadow sweet, stumbling over peat-cuttings and the workings of forgotten tin-mines. An idiotic popular tune raced through his brain. He found himself trying to frame the words, but they broke into incoherent prayers, still to the same grotesque tune.

Then, as he breasted the flank of a boulder-strewn tor, he seemed to hear snuffling breathing behind him, and, redoubling his efforts, stepped into a rabbit hole. He was up and running again in the twinkling of an eye, limping from a twisted ankle as he ran.

He sprinted over the crest of the hill and thought he heard the sound almost abreast of him, away to the right. In the dry bed of a watercourse some stones were dislodged and fell with a rattle in the stillness of the night; he bore away to the left. A moment later there was Something nearly at his left elbow, and he smelt again the nameless, foetid reek. He doubled, and the ghastly truth flashed upon him. The Thing was playing with him! He was being hunted for sport— the sport of a horror unthinkable. The sweat ran down into his eyes.

He lost all count of time; his wrist watch was smashed on his wrist. He ran through a reeling eternity, sobbing for breath, stumbling, tripping, fighting a leaden weariness; and ever the same unreasoning terror urged him on. The moon and ragged skyline swam about him; the blood drummed deafeningly in his ears, and his eyeballs felt as if they would burst from their sockets. He had nearly bitten his swollen tongue in two falling over an unseen peat-cutting, and blood-flecked foam gathered on his lips.

God, how he ran! But he was no longer among bog and heather. He was running—shambling now—along a road. The loping pursuit of that nameless, shapeless Something sounded like an echo in his head.

He was nearing a village, but saw nothing save a red mist that swam before him like a fog. The road underfoot seemed to rise and fall in wavelike undulations. Still he ran, with sobbing gasps and limbs that swerved under his weight; at his elbow hung death unnamable, and the fear of it urged him on while every instinct of his exhausted body called out to him to fling up his hands and end it.

Out of the mist ahead rose the rough outline of a building by the roadside; it was the village smithy, half workshop, half dwelling. The road here skirted a patch of grass, and the moonlight, glistening on the dew, showed the dark circular scars of the turf where, for a generation, the smith's peat fires had heated the great iron hoops that tyred the wheels of the wains. One of these was even then lying on the ground with the turves placed in readiness for firing in the morning, and in the throbbing darkness of Maynard's consciousness a voice seemed to speak faintly the voice of a girl:

"There's a Thing that hunts people to death. But iron—cold iron—it cannot cross."

The sweat of death was already on his brow as he reeled sideways, plunging blindly across the uneven tufts of grass. His feet caught in some obstruction and he pitched forward into the sanctuary of the huge iron tyre—a spasm of cramp twisting his limbs up under him.

As he fell a great blackness rose around him, and with it the bewildered clamour of awakened dogs.

Dr. Stanmore came down the flagged path from the smith's cottage, pulling on his gloves. A big car was passing slowly up the village street, and as it came abreast the smithy the doctor raised his hat.

The car stopped, and the driver, a fair-haired girl, leant sideways from her seat.

"Good-morning, Dr. Stanmore! What's the matter here? Nothing wrong with any of Matthew's children, is there?"

The Doctor shook his head gravely.

"No, Lady Dorothy; they're all at school. This is no one belonging to the family—a stranger who was taken mysteriously ill last night just outside the forge, and they brought him in. It's a most queer case, and very difficult to diagnose—that is to say, to give a diagnosis in keeping with one's professional—er—conscience."

The girl switched off the engine, and took her hand from the brake-lever. Something in the doctor's manner arrested her interest.

"What is the matter with him?" she queried. "What diagnosis have you made, professional or otherwise?"

"Shock, Lady Dorothy; severe exhaustion and shock, heart strained, superficial lesions, bruises, scratches, and so forth. Mentally he is in a great state of excitement and terror, lapsing into delirium at times—that is really the most serious feature. In fact, unless I can calm him I am afraid we may have some brain trouble on top of the other thing. It's most mysterious!"

The girl nodded gravely, holding her underlip between her white teeth.

"What does he look like—in appearance, I mean? Is he young?"

The shadow of a smile crossed the doctor's

"Yes, Lady Dorothy—quite young, and very good-looking. He is a man of remarkable athletic build. He is calmer now, and I have left Matthew's wife with him while I slip out to see a couple of other patients."

Lady Dorothy rose from her seat and stepped down out of the car.

"I think I know your patient," she said. "In fact, I had taken the car to look for him, to ask him to lunch with us. Do you think I might see him for a minute? If it is the person I think it is I may be able to help you diagnose his illness."

Together they walked up the path and entered the cottage. The doctor led the way upstairs and opened a door. A woman sitting by the bed rose and dropped a curtsey.

Lady Dorothy smiled a greeting to her and crossed over to the bed. There, his face grey and drawn with exhaustion, with shadows round his closed eyes, lay Maynard; one hand lying on the counterpane opened and closed convulsively, his lips moved. The physician eyed the girl interrogatively.

"Do you know him?" he asked.

She nodded, and put her firm, cool hand over the twitching fingers.

"Yes," she said. "And I warned him. Tell me, is he very ill?"

"He requires rest, careful nursing, absolute quiet—"

"All that he can have at the Manor," said the girl softly. She met the doctor's eyes and looked away, a faint color tingeing her cheeks. "Will you go and telephone to father? I will take him back in the car now if he is well enough to be moved."

"Yes, he is well enough to be moved," said the doctor. "It is very kind of you. Lady Dorothy, and I will go and telephone at once. Will you stay with him for a little while?"

He left the room, and they heard his feet go down the narrow stairs. The cottage door opened and closed.

The two women, the old and the young, peasant and peer's daughter, looked at each other, and there was in their glance that complete under standing which can only exist between women.

"Do 'ee mind old Jarge Toms, my lady?"

Lady Dorothy nodded.

"I know, I know! And I warned him! They won't believe, these men! They think because they are so big and strong that there is nothing that can hurt them."

"'Twas the iron that saved un, my lady. 'Twas inside one of John's new tyres as was lyin' on the ground that us found un. Dogs barkin' wakened us up. But it'd ha' had un, else—" A sound downstairs sent her flying to the door. "'Tis the kettle, my lady. John's dinner spilin', an' I forgettin'."

She hurried out of the room and closed the door.

The sound of their voices seemed to have roused the occupant of the bed. His eyelids fluttered and opened; his eyes rested full on the girl's face. For a moment there was no consciousness in their gaze; then a whimsical ghost of a smile crept about his mouth.

"Go on," he said in a weak voice, "Say it!"

"Say what?" asked Lady Dorothy. She was suddenly aware that her hand was still on his, but the twitching fingers had closed about hers in a calm, firm grasp.

"Say 'I told you so'!"

She shook her head with a little smile.

"I told you that cold iron—"

"Cold iron saved me." He told her of the iron hoop on the ground outside the forge. "You saved me last night."

She disengaged her hand gently.

"I saved you last night since you say so. But in future—"

Someone was coming up the stairs. Maynard met her eyes with a long look.

"I have no fear," he said. "I have found something better than cold iron."

The door opened and the doctor came in. He glanced at Maynard's face and touched his pulse.

"The case is yours, Lady Dorothy!" he said with a little bow.

That Haunting Thing

Achmed Abdullah

Diana Manning was the very last woman to whom such a thing should have happened. For there was nothing about her in the least psychic or spiritual.

She was matter with a capital *M*, and sex with a capital *S*; $, rather, since hers was sex without the excuse of passion—sex dealing entirely and shamelessly with bank accounts, high power racing cars, diamonds, and vintage champagnes.

She was lovely, and she drove the hearts and the purses of men as a breath drives a thin sheet of flame.

Only her finger nails gave the mark of the east side tenement (she was a *née* Maggie Smith) where she had been born and bred; for they were too well kept, too highly polished, too perfectly manicured.

But men did not notice. They seldom looked farther than her hair which was like a sculptured reddish-bronze helmet, her low, smooth, ivory forehead, her short, delicately curved nose, her lips which were crimson like a fresh sword wound, her eyes which spoke of wondrous promises—and lied damnably.

Her life had been melodramatic—from the man's angle, be it understood, and not from her own since, sublimely evil, she was beyond the moralizing sense of bad and, of course, good.

There had been death in the trail of her shimmering gowns, suicide, ruin, the slime of the divorce courts, disgrace to more than one.

But she had never cared a whit.

She was always petting her own hard thoughts, puncturing the lives of strangers—who never remained strangers for long—with the dagger point of her personality, her greed, her evil; and men kept on fluttering around the red, burning candle which was her life, like silly willow flies.

Then more deaths, Requiems bought and paid for, and all that sort of thing.

Quite melodramatic. Incredibly, garishly so.

But—what will you?

It isn t always the woman who pays, stage and pulpit to the contrary. And if she *does* pay it's usually the man who endorses the note.

When she reached her home on the upper west side that Saturday night, she felt the *Thing* the moment she stepped across the threshold. She felt it shrouded, ambiguous, vague. But it was there. Very small at first. Hidden somewhere in the huge, square entrance hall and peeping in upon her mind.

She wondered what it was, and what it might be doing there.

So she called to her maid:

"Annette! Annette!"

She did not call to reassure herself. For the woman was not afraid. That was it exactly; she was not afraid from first to last. If she had been, she would have switched on the light.

But she did not. She left the flat in darkness. Deliberately.

And that, again, was strange since hitherto she had always hated darkness and half-light and seeping, graying shadow; had always wanted and gloried in full, orange bursts of color big, clustering, massive, cruel lights. She had just that sort of complexion pallid, you know, smooth, with her color rising evenly, dawn-hued and tender, and never in patches and blurry streaks.

"Annette! Annette!" she called again, a mere matter of habit; for she relied on her respectable, middle-aged Burgundian maid for anything and everything that troubled her, from wrestling with a cynical, inquisitive reporter to putting the correct quantity of ammonia in her bromo seltzers.

"Yes, *madame*," came the maid's sleepy voice.

"Has anybody called?"

"No, *madame*."

"But—"

She looked into the corner of the entrance hall. The *Thing* seemed to be crouching amongst the peacock-green cushions of the ottoman there.

"But, Annette—" she commenced again.

She did not complete the sentence. Somehow, it did not make any difference. The *Thing* was there.

And what did it matter how it had got in?

"I am coming, *madame*," said the maid.

"Never mind. Go to sleep. I'll undress myself. Good night, Annette!"

"Good night, *madame*!"

Diana Manning shrugged her shoulders, walked across the entrance hall, and put her hand on the door-knob of her boudoir. She said to herself that she would open the door quickly, slide in, and close it as quickly.

For she sensed, rather, she knew, that the *Thing* intended to follow her. It radiated energy and vigor and determination. A certain kindly determination that, just for a fleeting moment, touched in her the sense of awe.

But the moment she opened the door, the moment her lithe body slid from the darkness of the entrance hall into the creamy, silky, perfumed darkness of her boudoir, she knew that the *Thing* flitted in by her side. She felt it blow over her neck, her face, her breast, like a gust of wind.

It even touched her. It touched her *non*-physically. That is the only way to put it.

Nor was she afraid then. On the contrary, she felt rather sorry for the *Thing*. And that touched in her once more the sense of awe—naturally, since to feel sorry was to her a new sensation, since never before in all her life had she felt sorry for anything or anybody.

The result was that she began to hate the *Thing*—with cold, calculating hatred, hatred without fear.

She locked the windows and doors. Quite instinctively her hand brushed the tiny nacre button which controlled the Venetian chandelier. But she did not press it. She left the boudoir in darkness.

For she was familiar with every stick of furniture about the place. She knew the exact location of the great, carved, crimson-and-gold Spanish renaissance day bed between the window and the fireplace, the big buhl table in the center of the room, the smaller one, covered with a mass of bric-à-brac, between the two windows, the low divan running along the south wall and overlapping toward the fireplace, the three chairs at odd angles, the four little tabourets, and, in the northeast corner, the Chinese screen, inlaid with ivory and lac and jade, behind which she kept a small liquor chest. She knew the room, every inch of it, and could move about it, in spite of the darkness, like a cat.

The *Thing*, on the other hand, whatever it was, would find many pitfalls in the cluttered-up boudoir if it tried to get rambunctious.

These latter were the exact words with which Diana Manning expressed the thought to herself; in this very moment of awe and hatred. Remember—she was born and bred on the east side. Of course, since those days of sooty, sticky, grimy tenement chrysalis, she had learned to broaden her *a*'s and slur her *r*'s and to change the slang of the gutters for that of the race tracks.

But, somehow, she knew that the *Thing* would be more familiar with her earlier diction.

She lay down on the couch, staring into the darkness.

She had decided to watch carefully, to pounce upon the *Thing* suddenly and to throttle it.

For, somehow, the *Thing* had taken on the suggestion of deliberate, personal intention of an aggressive hostility—something which felt and hated, even suffered, yet which had no bodily reality.

The realization of it froze Diana into rigidity—not the rigidity of fear, but something far worse than fear, partaking of Fate—of she didn't know what.

She only knew that she must watch—then pounce and kill.

"I must have matters out with it," she thought. "One of us two is master in this room; it or I. And I can't afford to wait all night. At half past eleven young 'Bunny' Whipple is calling for me—"

Again, at the thought of Bunny Whipple, she felt that strange, hateful new sensation of awe blended with pity. The *Thing* was responsible for it the *Thing*!

How she hated it! She clenched her fists until the knuckles stretched white. What had the *Thing* to do with Bunny Whipple and—yes—with Bunny Whipple's little blue-eyed, golden-haired wife—the bride who—

Diana cut off the thought in mid-air and tossed it aside as if it were a soiled glove.

She watched more carefully than ever, her breath coming in short staccato bursts, her body tense and strained, her mind rigid. She tried to close her mind; she did not want the *Thing* to peep in upon it.

For right then she knew—she did not feel nor guess—she knew that the *Thing* had the trick of expanding and decreasing at will.

It made her angry. She did not consider it fair.

For it gave to the *Thing* the advantage of suddenly shrinking to the size of a pin point and hiding in a knot of the Tabriz rug which covered the floor and, immediately afterwards, of bloating into monstrous size, like a balloon, and floating toward the stuccoed ceiling like an immense soap bubble—hanging there looking down with that strange, hateful, rather kindly determination.

"Bunny Whipple's wife—" she thought again. "I saw her yesterday—and the silly little fool recognized me. She would have spoken to me had I given her the chance. Spoken to me as she wrote me—asking me to give her back her husband's love—*love*—"

Her mind formed the word, caressed it as if it were something futile and soft and naïve and laughable, like a ball of cotton or a tiny kitten—

The next moment, she whipped it aside with all her hard will. She sat up straight.

For, at the forming of the word, the *Thing* which a second earlier had been a pin-point sitting on the gilded edge of a Sèvres vase, bloated and stretched gigantically, leaped up, appeared to float, leaped again toward the ceiling as if trying to jerk it away from the cross beams.

Then, just as suddenly, it dropped on the floor. It lay there, roaring with laughter.

Diana did not hear the laughter. She felt it. She knew it.

Too, she knew exactly where it was; between the large buhl table and the divan. She'd get it and choke it while it lay there helpless with merriment.

She jumped from her couch, her fingers spread like a cat's claws.

"I'll get you you—you—*Thing*!" she said the words out loud. "I'll get you! I'll get you!"

Her voice rose in a shrill, tearing shriek—step by step, she approached the divan.

"I'll get you—get you—get you—"

"Madame! Madame! Did you call me?"

It was the maid s voice coming from the hall.

"No—no! Go to bed, Annette! Go to bed—do you hear me?" as the maid rattled the door-knob. "I don't want to be disturbed—"

"I beg your pardon, *madame*." Annette coughed discreetly. "I didn't know that anybody—thought you had come home alone—I—"

"Go to bed! At once!" Diana shrieked; then, the maid s footsteps pattering away, she fell on the couch, panting.

She was in a towering rage. She felt sure that if it had not been for the maid she could have pounced upon the *Thing* while it lay there on the floor, roaring with laughter.

Now the laughter had died out and the *Thing* had got away. It had shrunk into a tiny butterfly—that's how Diana felt it—which was beating its wings against the brass rod of the portières. But it was fluttering rather helplessly, blindly, as if it had lost some of its energy and vigor; and again Diana felt sorry and correspondingly her hatred grew. And her determination.

"I'll get you—you—"

She waited until her breath came more evenly, rose, walked noiselessly to the portières and rustled them.

The *Thing* was startled. Diana could feel the tiny wings flutter and beat. She could hear its terrible, straining effort to bloat into a huge soap-bubble and, not succeeding, to shrink into a pinpoint.

But something was making it impossible, and Diana knew what it was.

It was the fact that, in one of the hidden back cells of her brain, the thought of Bunny Whipple s silly little fool of a golden-haired wife had taken firm root, refused to budge.

So Diana kept the thought. She nursed it. It seemed like a bait, and she thrust it forward.

She spoke out loud, her face raised up to the portières:

"Silly little fool of a golden-haired bride!" and she added, out of subconscious volition: "Silly Bunny!"

She had spoken the last words caressingly, as a naughty boy speaks to a cat before he catches her and tweaks her tail, and the *Thing* was about to fall into the trap. For a second it hovered on the brass rod, seemed to wait, expectant, undecided.

Then it came down a few inches. It fluttered within reach of Diana's outstretched hand.

But when she closed her hand suddenly, viciously, it winged away again, breathless, frightened, but unharmed. It flew into the center of the room. It made a renewed terrible effort to bloat into a balloon.

And this time it succeeded—partly.

She did not feel exactly what shape it had assumed, but it was something amorphous, flabby, covered all over with soft bumps which were very beastly.

She followed, more determined than ever, and the *Thing* tried to leap into the air.

It had nearly succeeded when Diana, with quick presence of mind, thought again of Bunny Whipple and Bunny Whipple 's silly, golden-haired wife.

"She asks me to give her back Bunny's love—his love! God! Does the silly little fool think that Bunny loves me? Does she call that—love?"

This time it was Diana who burst into a roar of laughter, and the *Thing* stood still and listened, its head cocked on one side, stupid, ridiculous, foolish; and when Diana neared it, when it tried to fly, to hover, to swing in mid air, all it succeeded in doing was to move swiftly about the room, just an inch or two away from the woman s groping fingers.

Diana laughed again, for she knew that the *Thing* had lost its faculty of flying, that it would not be able to escape her for long with the chances all in her favor.

For the boudoir was cluttered with furniture, and she knew the location of every piece, while the *Thing* would lose itself, stumble, fall, and then—

"Wait! You just wait!" she whispered; and the *Thing* backing away from the center of the room toward the carved Chinese screen, she followed step by step, her fingers groping, clawing, the lust of the hunter in her eyes, in her heart.

"I'll throttle you—"

Then she reconsidered. To throttle so as to kill, she would have to measure her own strength exactly against the *Thing's* strength of resistance. And that would be hard.

For the *Thing* was non-physical. It had no body.

But it was sure to have a heart. She would stab that heart.

So she picked from the buhl table the jeweled Circassian dagger which she had admired the day before in a little shop on Lexington Avenue and which Bunny had given to her—with some very foolish remark, quite typical of him—she remembered. "I wish to God you'd kill yourself with it! Get out of my life—leave me in peace—me and Lottie—"

Lottie was the silly, golden-haired wife.

But when, dagger in hand, Diana took up the chase again, she was disappointed. For the *Thing* seemed as familiar with the room as she herself. It avoided sliding rugs, sharp-cornered buhl tables, tabourets and chairs placed at odd angles. It never as much as grazed a single one of the many brittle bits of bric-à-brac.

Once it chuckled as if faintly amused at some thing.

But Diana did not give up heart. She had made up her mind, and she was a hard woman—her soul a blending of diamond and fire-kissed steel.

"I'll get you!" and she thought of a new, better way. She would corner the *Thing*.

Again she advanced, slowly, cautiously, step by step, driving the *Thing* before her across the width of the room, always keeping uppermost in her mind the thought of Bunny Whipple and his silly fool of a golden-haired wife—the thought which was paralyzing the *Thing's* faculty of bloating and shrinking and flying.

The end came very suddenly.

Watching her chance, she had the *Thing* cornered, straight up against the inlaid Chinese screen.

It tried to shrink—to bloat—to fly—to get away.

But Diana had timed her action to the click of a second. She brought the dagger down—with all her strength—and the *Thing* crumpled, it gave, it was not.

There was just a sharp pain, a crimson smear, and a very soft voice from a far, starry, velvety distance.

"You have killed me, Diana!"

"Killed—whom? Who are you?"

"The evil in your soul, Diana! The evil—" then something which had been congealed seemed to turn fluid and alive and golden; something rose into a state that was too calm to be ecstasy.

The next morning, Bunny Whipple's silly, blue-eyed, golden-haired wife was sitting across from her husband at breakfast.

He was white and haggard and shaky. She looked at him, pity in her eyes.

"Have you seen the morning paper, Bunny?" she asked.

"No! Don't want to. More scandal about me, I guess—" he bit the words off savagely.

"Only—that—that woman—" she faltered.

"Diana Manning! All right! What about her?"

"She was found dead last night by her maid. She had stabbed herself through the heart with a Circassian dagger. The—the papers say that a smile was on her face—a happy, sweet smile as if—"

She picked up the *Star* and read the reporter's lyric outburst out loud:

"As if death had brought her happiness and salvation and a deep, calm, glorious fulfillment."

Bunny Whipple did not reply. He stared into his coffee cup.

Very suddenly he looked up. His wife had risen and walked around the table toward him.

She put her slim, white hands on his shoulders.

There were tears in her eyes—tears and a trembling question.

He drew her to him, and kissed her.

The Third Doctor

Claude N. Settles

The little cyclone heater in Doctor Stilman's office was roaring loudly. Outside, the blinding snow swirled and eddied in a driving wind, and entered even the smallest of crevices to lie in little drifts as if in defiant mockery to the efforts of the industrious stove. At the window stood the doctor looking out at the drifts as they piled higher and higher in the little narrow street. All day long it had been thus—and all the day before. The snow had come until everything was covered, yet the driving wind continued to bring it. The doctor was getting worried. There had been no calls for two days now,—something very unusual. The compulsory inertia was decidedly irksome. Here was his year drawing to a close,—the first year of his practice, which, as he had always been told, was the hardest. Truly, if there were to be any harder, he did not wish to experience them.

His reverie was suddenly disturbed, as he saw coming down the street, the stooped and bent figure of Squire Fenks, slowly and patiently plodding through the drifts. As was his custom, the old man was coming on his weekly trip for a chat with the doctor. He was the doctor's main stay. Long ago the young man would have "pulled stakes" and shaken Heesville dust from his feet but for the older man's advice and companionship. And now the young doctor's entire nature changed as he saw the old man coming to him through such weather as this. It was a foolish sacrifice, yet he appreciated it.

"Hello, Squire!" he called, "how d' you like this for winter weather?"

The old man only smiled and shook his head. He stamped his feet wearily on the pine block which was used for a doorstep and entered.

The doctor saw in an instant that the old man had not come to cheer him up. He was there merely from a sense of duty. The old man was not feeling well. Silently he drew forward the only armchair in the room and sank into it with something like a sigh.

"What's the trouble, Squire?" asked the doctor jokingly. "Did you have sauerkraut for dinner?"

The squire only smiled sheepishly.

"Sonny, you've got me so you can read me like a book, ain't ye?" Then the troubled look came once more into his face and he lapsed into silence. The doctor tried again to get him to talk, but it was of no avail. Monosyllables were his only answers, and even these were given with no intelligence. At last the doctor gave up and a long silence followed, until he grew restless once more. He went over to the old man and sat down beside him.

"Squire," he said kindly, "there's something seriously wrong. You're acting like some fourteen-year-old girl in love. I never did know you to moon around as you're doing tonight. Tell me what the trouble is."

He received no response. Reaching out, he laid his hand firmly on the old man's shoulder.

"Listen here," he exclaimed. "I've been here nearly a year, now, Squire—such a year as I never want to pass through again. I would never have gotten through if it hadn't been for you. I've always told you my troubles and you have always helped me to get around 'em. Every week you've come around here just to listen to my tale of woe and to cheer me up. Now it's my turn. 'Fess up. Here's where I pay back some honest debts."

The old man shuddered slightly, and raising his eyes, glanced quickly around the room. Not satisfied with that, he arose, and walking to the window, looked up and down the fast darkening street. With one more searching glance around the room, he sat down, industriously mopping his forehead with his red bandana. He reached out his hand and in an agitated manner grasped the doctor's knee.

"Doc," he cried eagerly, "are you superstitious?"

"Oh, it's along that line, is it? Seen a ghost, have you?" The doctor tried to laugh the old man out of his mood, but he was not in the mood himself. Moreover, the old man was keyed up to the point where he was determined that he would talk.

"I know you'll make fun of me, Doc, but I can't help it. Four years ago I would have laughed, too, but it's not funny now. No, it's not funny! Not now!" And he dropped his head forward in his hands and continued talking as if in a dream. "You laugh and say you're not superstitious. Everybody does. Everybody says that things just happened that way. That's the way they say things out loud, but way down deep inside, everybody knows that he's got some superstition; that there's some system or something that runs things. Doc," the old man roused up with a start, "did you know that people think this office is haunted?"

The doctor saw the old man's serious manner and refrained from smiling. "No, I don't think I ever heard of it. Why?"

"Well, we all thought we would never let you know, but I've changed my mind. I'm going to tell you all about it so you can look out—and get out if you want to.

"You see, the whole thing started when this shack was built. That's been four years ago. Old Doc Skibs was our doctor then and he wasn't much of a doctor. Folks always said it was his wife that did the curin' 'cause she was a witch. O' course I didn't believe nothin' in that—not then, though she did gather up an awful lot o' herbs. But anyway, old Doc Skibs, he was gettin' old and folks got so they didn't trust him much, and he was feeble and couldn't make the calls, and there was a sentiment come in that we ought to get a new doctor. But we couldn't get one. There was no place for one to come to. So they decided to build this shack; and they did. They started in just working now and then, and the old doctor's wife like to had a fit, she was that jealous. She couldn't see that the doctor was gettin' old. She thought it was spite work. Two times the shack caught fire, but we managed to save it both times. Then I guess the old lady Skibs kind of changed her tactics, 'cause pretty soon she got so she'd come by every day and she'd laugh and joke the boys 'bout the old shack and she'd say they couldn't get a man to stay in it more'n a year fer anything. When we'd ask her why, she'd just tell us to wait—we'd see, we'd see; and then she'd cackle kind o' crazy like and wouldn't say nothin' more. 'Not more'n a year,' she'd say, 'not more'n a year!'

"Well, we finished up the shack and 'tweren't long till we got a young doc, just out o' college, and say, he was a good one. He come here and everybody liked him. He was a friend to everyone, especially to the kids. And he done a lot of things for this town. Made 'em drain off that old frog pond that used to be down back of the depot, and he made old Hank Reynolds clean up his baker shop, and made Jim Rickey fix his dairy, and I don't know what he didn't do, 'sides doctorin' the people. He was here *just* a year." Here the old Squire paused, got up, and walked the length of the room. "And that damned old woman just grinned and nodded her head and kept sayin,' 'I told you so. I told you. *Just* a year. I told you.' That's all she'd say." The old man paced the room until he became quiet once more. Then he continued:

"It was Jim Rickey done it, over that dairy business. He shot Doc in the back one night when he was going over to see Kate Bundy's little baby. They caught Jim three days later and hung him up without ever thinkin' of a trial, but that didn't bring the doctor back. We'd ought to a-hung that damned—"

Here the old man choked and was silent. His companion waited expectantly. The sarcastic smile had faded from *his* face before the squire was half through. Now he was eager that the story go on.

"Doctor Signey came next, didn't he?" he prompted.

"Yes," the old man went on, "it was three or four months before we got anyone, but finally we did. He came from the same college as t'other one, and was just as good—only people didn't like him as well. He wasn't just as popular 'cause he wasn't just what he ought to be in some ways, and never went to church. But here's the big thing about it: *he was here just one year to the day.* It was the eighteenth of June, a year after he came here, that they found him, one morning, in a hotel room over to Seeville, layin' in the middle of the floor with a woman—both of them dead. There was a gun a-layin' between 'em and ye couldn't tell which one of 'em had done the shootin'. Both had been shot in the head at close range. Powder stains showed it. Nobody ever did find out who the woman was, nor how she got to town, no more'n if she'd dropped from the sky. Nobody ever seen her before at all. But that doesn't matter. What matters is that it was *just a year* both times, and both times old lady Skibs went around to everybody, grinning and sayin', 'I told ye so. None of 'em stays more'n a year.'

"Of course, everybody thought she had something to do with it both times, but we didn't know sure, and we couldn't prove nothin'. Then, too, we wanted to keep the thing hushed so's we could get another doctor. That's why we never told you the whole story. I'm tellin' you now, though, 'case it can't do no harm and it may do you some help. You can do just as you please, but I'd advise you to move and get away from here."

"Oh, pshaw, Squire, you're all worked up like the rest of the people, over nothing. Why, there's nothing behind all this. You admit, yourself, that the old woman had no direct connection with it, which only goes to show that the whole thing was a mere coincidence. Just because the other two doctors met a tragic death, doesn't mean that I must kick the bucket the same way. Yet—it does seem—rather strange—" he said slowly, trailing off into a deep study.

For a long time neither spoke. The doctor was more worried than he liked to admit. The squire broke the silence. "Don't you think you had better get out, Doc?"

He said it low, and with so much force that it sounded like a warning command. The doctor's worried look showed that he was thinking hard. He knew more than the squire thought he did.

"It all looks so crazy to me, Squire, yet—it might—be—"

"That's the trouble, Doc. As I said, there's nobody likes to believe in superstition. But take this into consideration: there's a chance that there might be somethin' to it. So don't you think you'd better come over to my house for tonight and tomorrow?"

"No," answered the doctor as he rose from the chair. "The whole thing seems like a blamed lot of foolishness when I look at it with common sense. Why, what would the fellows back home think if they heard I had run away from an office because I thought it was haunted?"

"Well, I hate to leave you, boy. I hope you have it right, but I'm very much afraid for you. I'm so much afraid that I'm going to say good-bye instead of good-night. Good-bye, Doc, I hope you're safe this time tomorrow." And the old man passed sorrowfully out into the storm, where the roaring wind fairly staggered him as he moved along in the deep drifts.

When he had gone, the doctor slowly proceeded to prepare his evening meal. The preparation was mere pastime. It was done from force of habit. When he sat down to eat he found he wanted nothing. The sight of everything disgusted him, and naturally, he felt disgusted with himself. Why should he let a little story like this bother him? There was nothing to it. But then, the squire had not told him all. He had made some things plain, which the doctor had never understood, though. The doctor remembered now. It was all as plain as day. A week or so after he had come to town he had been called out to see this old woman, this same old Mrs. Skibs. He never forgot how she cursed him and the way she screamed: "You'll see! You'll see! Just one year!" She died that night, and the neighbors, who had called him against the old lady's wishes, would tell him nothing. Now he had an explanation.

That death-bed scene kept running again and again through his mind. He paced the room, thinking. The more he thought, the more worried and depressed he became. The air seemed close and stifling. He must get out and away from there. The room itself and everything in it became a terror from which he must flee. He seized his hat and coat and started for the door. As he reached it, he hesitated. For the first time, he noticed the wind. He heard it raging in a perfect blizzard outside. Absentmindedly, he laid his hand upon the latch. In an instant it was wrenched from his grasp as if by some unseen force. It swung, as with a vengeance, and struck him full in the face, knocking him sprawling. In a second of time he was on his feet, terror fairly shaking his frame.

There are times when even the bravest of men lose their nerve. When brought to battle with the supernatural they become as children in the dark. This was the doctor's condition. He stood panic-stricken, waiting for the next blow, but none came. Nothing was there except the rushing icy wind and the blinding snow. Trembling, he cautiously closed the door and lighted the extinguished light. As he poked the fire to warm up the now chilled room he began to see his own foolishness. He laughed to himself, "I must have the jim-jams." He merely muttered, but the sound of his own voice made him shudder.

For a long time, he paced the floor, and finally, as a last resort, decided to go to bed. He undressed in the now cold room and shivering almost in a nervous fit, climbed in. There he lay in wide-eyed terror, his ears strained to every little sound. The creaking of a shutter; the sudden twang of a bedspring; everything set him to trembling anew. At last he could stand it no longer. He got up, dressed again, and once more walked the floor in agitation. He attempted to reason the whole thing out sensibly. Surely it was all absurd, this thing of *"just a year."* It was absolutely ridiculous. Even if there had been anything to it, there was no danger now. The old woman was dead and could have no more influence. Gradually, as the room became warmer, he became calmer, and at last he dozed.

When he awoke it was dark and he was utterly bewildered. The fire had gone out and the room was as still as death. Even the familiar ticking of his watch was not to be heard. He had forgotten to wind it. The silent darkness grew thicker around him and pressed in upon him like a weight. His breath began to come in short gasps as he felt some terrible something behind the blackness, which was slowly creeping upon him. He covered his head to stifle a scream. Oh, why had he not gone with the squire? Why not go yet? He uncovered his head and listened—listened for that invisible something which he knew not. He *must* get out and get away before he went mad. With a jerk, he flung back the covers and sprang out. He hastily lighted the light and started the fire, and gained some courage.

"No, I'm *not* going," he stamped his foot in self censure. "I'm a fool. I've got to stick now. Must be four o'clock. Two hours till daylight—God! wish I knew sure—damned old woman—I can see her yet, the night she died. She just kept screaming it 'I told ye, I told ye, *just a year.*' God! what if she gets me? What if she does?" he almost screamed.

Here he seemed to bring himself up with a jerk.

"I'm a damned fool. Never was superstitious before—very. She said *'just* a year.' Damn. I must have a sedative. I'll go crazy! I can see her yet. Old hag! Sedative—hydrocyanic acid—dilute—strongest known. Ugh! she was ugly! And my year's up at six o'clock!"

As he talked, he staggered to the shelves and took down a bottle and poured a glass full. In an abstracted manner he placed the bottle on the shelf and turned to the stove, muttering, "and she said *just* a year and mine's up at six o'clock—two hours."

Suddenly he sprang back in terror. "Lord God! look at the ants!"

Around the stove circled a dozen or more large black ants that had been thawed from the half rotten chunk of wood in the corner.

"Oh, I see," he exclaimed, as he saw where they came from. "What d'ye know about that? Ha!" He tipped the glass slowly, talking to himself the while. "Old rip! got two before me—thinks she'll get me. Folks think it, too. Think I'll be the third!"

A bit of the liquid ran from the tipped glass and fell upon an ant as it crawled stupidly along the half warm floor. The liquid had hardly touched it before the insect was dead.

"Huh! Dead! And I started to drink it! Concentrated!" The glass dropped from his nervous fingers and fell with a crash. In his sudden fright, his nerves broke down completely. He fairly screamed. "Damned old hag! She's after me! Concentrated hydrocyanic acid! Deadly poison! God! She almost made me drink it! She's after me! I must get out!"

Seizing his hat and coat, he rushed headlong from the shack, leaving the door wide open.

The next morning, the worried squire returned. He found the disordered room, the broken glass, the nice white drift of snow piled from the door to the now cold stove, and his heart sank. He knew the worst had come.

He went in to the telephone and called the neighbors and they all went in search. They found him in the stable behind his horse, lying as if asleep. A hoofprint on his big chest told the whole story, while lines of anguish, written over all his face, showed what a night he had spent. It was the face of an older man by ten years.

For some moments they looked on in silence, with bared heads. Then a husky, hollow sounding whisper came from one of the group:

"Boys, it's just a year—*just one year*—and he's the third," and he expressed the thoughts of the whole group when he added slowly, "I wonder if—it's—her!"

But no one answered.

Thirteen at Table

Lord Dunsany

In front of a spacious fireplace of the old kind, when the logs were well alight, and men with pipes and glasses were gathered before it in great easeful chairs, and the wild weather outside and the comfort that was within, and the season of the year—for it was Christmas—and the hour of the night, all called for the weird or uncanny, then out spoke the ex-master of foxhounds and told this tale.

I once had an odd experience too. It was when I had the Bromley and Sydenham, the year I gave them up—as a matter of fact it was the last day of the season. It was no use going on because there were no foxes left in the county, and London was sweeping down on us. You could see it from the kennels all along the skyline like a terrible army in grey, and masses of villas every year came skirmishing down our valleys. Our coverts were mostly on the hills, and as the town came down upon the valleys the foxes used to leave them and go right away out of the county and they never returned. I think they went by night and moved great distances. Well, it was early April and we had drawn blank all day, and at the last draw of all, the very last of the season, we found a fox. He left the covert with his back to London and its railways and villas and wire and slipped away towards the chalk country and open Kent. I felt as I once felt as a child on one summer's day when I found a door in a garden where I played left luckily ajar, and I pushed it open and the wide lands were before me and waving fields of corn.

We settled down into a steady gallop and the fields began to drift by under us, and a great wind arose full of fresh breath. We left the clay lands where the bracken grows and came to a valley at the edge of the chalk. As we went down into it we saw the fox go up the other side like a shadow that crosses the evening, and glide into a wood that stood on the top. We saw a flash of primroses in the wood and we were out the other side, hounds hunting perfectly and the fox still going absolutely straight. It began to dawn on me then that we were in for a great hunt; I took a deep breath when I thought of it; the taste of the air of that perfect spring afternoon as it came to one galloping, and the thought of a great run, were together like some old rare wine. Our faces now were to another valley, large fields led down to it, with easy hedges, at the bottom of it a bright blue stream went singing and a rambling village smoked, the sunlight on the opposite slopes danced like a fairy; and all along the top old woods were frowning, but they dreamed of spring. The field had fallen of and were far behind and my only human companion was James, my old first whip, who had a hound's instinct, and a personal animosity against a fox that even embittered his speech.

Across the valley the fox went as straight as a railway line, and again we went without a check straight through the woods at the top. I remember hearing men sing or shout as they walked home from work, and sometimes children whistled; the sounds came up from the village to the woods at the top of the valley. After that we saw no more villages, but valley after valley arose and fell before us as though we were voyaging some strange and stormy sea; and all the way before us the fox went dead up-wind like the fabulous Flying Dutchman. There was no one in sight now but my first whip and me; we had both of us got on to our second horses as we drew the last covert. Two or three times we checked in those great lonely valleys beyond the village, but I began to have inspirations; I felt a strange certainty within me that this fox was going on straight up-wind till he died or until night came and we could hunt no longer, so I reversed ordinary methods and only cast straight ahead, and always we picked up the scent again at once. I believe that this fox was the last one left in the villa-haunted lands and that he was prepared to leave them for remote uplands far from men, that if we had come the following day he would not have been there, and that we just happened to hit off his journey.

Evening began to descend upon the valleys, still the hounds drifted on, like the lazy but unresting shadows of clouds upon a summer's day; we heard a shepherd calling to his dog, we saw two maidens move towards a hidden farm, one of them singing softly; no other sounds, but ours, disturbed the leisure and the loneliness of haunts that seemed not yet to have known the inventions of steam and gun-powder.

And now the day and our horses were wearing out, but that resolute fox held on. I began to work out the run and to wonder where we were. The last landmark I had ever seen before must have been over five miles back, and from there to the start was at least ten miles more. If only we could kill! Then the sun set. I wondered what chance we had of killing our fox. I looked at James' face as he rode beside me. He did not seem to have lost any confidence, yet his horse was as tired as mine. It was a good clear twilight and the scent was as strong as ever, and the fences were easy enough, but those valleys were terribly trying, and they still rolled on and on. It looked as if the light would outlast all possible endurance both of the fox and the horses, if the scent held good and he did not go to ground, otherwise night would end it. For long we had seen no houses and no roads, only chalk slopes with the twilight on them, and here and there some sheep, and scattered copses darkening in the evening. At some moment I seemed to realise all at once that the light was spent and that darkness was hovering. I looked at James, he was solemnly shaking his head. Suddenly in a little wooded valley we saw climb over the oaks the red-brown gables of a queer old house; at that instant I saw the fox scarcely heading by fifty yards. We blundered through a wood into full sight of the house, but no avenue led up to it or even a path nor were there any signs of wheelmarks anywhere. Already lights shone here and there in windows. We were in a park, and a fine park, but unkempt beyond credibility; brambles grew everywhere. It was too dark to see the fox any more but we knew he was dead beat, the hounds were just before us—and a four-foot railing of oak. I shouldn't have tried it on a fresh horse the beginning of a run, and here was a horse near his last gasp. But what a run! an event standing out in a life-time, and the hounds close up on their fox, slipping into the darkness as I hesitated. I decided to try it. My horse rose about eight inches and took it fair with his breast, and the oak log flew into handfuls of wet decay,—it rotten with years. And then we were on a lawn, and at the far end of it the hounds were tumbling over their fox. Fox, hounds and light were all done together at the end of a twenty-mile point. We made some noise then, but nobody came out of the queer old house.

I felt pretty stiff as I walked round to the hall door with the mask and the brush, while James went with the hounds and the two horses to look for the stables. I rang a bell marvellously encrusted with rust, and after a long while the door opened a little way, revealing a hall with much old armour in it and the shabbiest butler that I have ever known.

I asked him who lived there. Sir Richard Arlen. I explained that my horse could go no further that night and that I wished to ask Sir Richard Arlen for a bed.

"O, no one ever comes here, sir," said the butler.

I pointed out that I had come.

"I don't think it would be possible, sir," he said.

This annoyed me, and I asked to see Sir Richard, and insisted until he came. Then I apologised and explained the situation. He looked only fifty, but a 'Varsity oar on the wall with the date of the early seventies made him older than that; his face had something of the shy look of the hermit; he regretted that he had not room to put me up. I was sure that this was untrue, also I had to be put up there, there was nowhere else within miles, so I almost insisted. Then to my astonishment he turned to the butler and they talked it over in an undertone. At last they seemed to think that they could manage it, though clearly with reluctance. It was by now seven o'clock and Sir Richard told me he dined at half past seven. There was no question of clothes for me other than those I stood in, as my host was shorter and broader. He showed me presently to the drawing-room and there he reappeared before half-past seven in evening dress and a white waistcoat. The drawing-room was large and contained old furniture, but it was rather worn than venerable; an aubusson carpet flapped about the floor, the wind seemed momently to enter the room, and old draughts haunted corners; stealthy feet of rats that were never at rest indicated the extent of the ruin that time had wrought in the wainscot; somewhere far off a shutter flapped to and fro, the guttering candles were insufficient to light so large a room. The gloom that these things suggested was quite in keeping with Sir Richard's first remark to me after he entered the room.

"I must tell you, sir, that I have led a wicked life. O, a very wicked life."

Such confidences from a man much older than oneself after one has known him for half an hour are so rare that any possible answer merely does not suggest itself. I said rather slowly, "O, really," and chiefly to forestall another such remark I said, "What a charming house you have."

"Yes," he said, "I have not left it for nearly forty years. Since I left the 'Varsity. One is young there, you know, and one has opportunities; but I make no excuses, no excuses." And the door slipping its rusty latch, came drifting on the draught into the room, and the long carpet flapped and the hangings upon the walls, then the draught fell rustling away and the door slammed to again.

"Ah, Marianne," he said, "we have a guest to-night. Mr. Linton. This is Marianne Gib." And everything became clear to me. "Mad," I said to myself, for no one had entered the room.

The rats ran up the length of the room behind the wainscot ceaselessly, and the wind unlatched the door again and the folds of the carpet fluttered up to our feet and stopped there, for our weight held it down.

"Let me introduce Mr. Linton," said my host. "Lady Mary Errinjer."

The door slammed back again. I bowed politely. Even had I been invited I should have humoured him, but it was the very least that an uninvited guest could do.

This kind of thing happened eleven times: the rustling, and the fluttering of the carpet and the footsteps of the rats, and the restless door, and then the sad voice of my host introducing me to phantoms. Then for some while we waited while I struggled with the situation; conversation flowed slowly. And again the draught came trailing up the room, while the flaring candles filled it with hurrying shadows. "Ah, late again, Cicely," said my host in his soft, mournful way. "Always late, Cicely." Then I went down to dinner with that man and his mind and the twelve phantoms that haunted it. I found a long table with fine old silver on it and places laid for fourteen. The butler was now in evening dress, there were fewer draughts in the dining-room, the scene was less gloomy there. "Will you sit next to Rosalind at the other end?" Richard said to me. "She always takes the head of the table. I wronged her most of all."

I said, "I shall be delighted."

I looked at the butler closely; but never did I see by any expression of his face, or by anything that he did, any suggestion that he waited upon less than fourteen people in the complete possession of all their faculties. Perhaps a dish appeared to be refused more often than taken, but every glass was equally filled with champagne. At first I found little to say, but when Sir Richard speaking from the far end of the table said, "You are tired, Mr. Linton?" I was reminded that I owed something to a host upon whom I had forced myself. It was excellent champagne, and with the help of a second glass I made the effort to begin a conversation with a Miss Helen Errold, for whom the place upon one side of me was laid. It came more easy to me very soon; I frequently paused in my monologue, like Mark Anthony, for a reply, and sometimes I turned and spoke to Miss Rosalind Smith. Sir Richard at the other end talked sorrowfully on; he spoke as a condemned man might speak to his judge, and yet somewhat as a judge might speak to one that he once condemned wrongly. My own mind began to turn to mournful things. I drank another glass of champagne, but I was still thirsty. I felt as if all the moisture in my body had been blown away over the downs of Kent by the wind up which we had galloped. Still I was not talking enough: my host was looking at me. I made another effort; after all I had something to talk about: a twenty-mile point is not often seen in a lifetime, especially south of the Thames. I began to describe the run to Rosalind Smith. I could see then that my host was pleased, the sad look in his face gave a kind of a flicker, like mist upon the mountains on a miserable day when a faint puff comes from the sea and the mist would lift if it could. And the butler refilled my glass very attentively. I asked her first if she hunted, and paused and began my story. I told her where we had found the fox and how fast and straight he had gone, and how I had got through the village by keeping to the road, while the little gardens and wire, and then the river, had stopped the rest of the field. I told her the kind of country that we crossed and how splendid it looked in the spring, and how mysterious the valleys were as soon as the twilight came, and what a glorious horse I had and how wonderfully he went.

I was so fearfully thirsty after the great hunt that I had to stop for a moment now and then, but I went on with my description of that famous run, for I had warmed to the subject, and after all there was nobody to tell of it but me except my old whipper-in, and "the old fellow's probably drunk by now," I thought. I described to her minutely the exact spot in the run at which it had come to me clearly that this was going to be the greatest hunt in the whole history of Kent. Sometimes I forgot incidents that had happened, as one well may in a run of twenty miles, and then I had to fill in the gaps by inventing. I was pleased to be able to make the party go off well by means of my conversation, and besides that the lady to whom I was speaking was extremely pretty: I do not mean in a flesh-and-blood kind of way, but there were little shadowy lines about the chair beside me that hinted at an unusually graceful figure when Miss Rosalind Smith was alive; and I began to perceive that what I first mistook for the smoke of guttering candles and a table-cloth waving in the draught was in reality an extremely animated company who listened, and not without interest, to my story of by far the greatest hunt that the world had ever known: indeed, I told them that I would confidently go further and predict that never in the history of the world would there be such a run again. Only my throat was terribly dry.

And then, as it seemed, they wanted to hear more about my horse. I had forgotten that I had come there on a horse, but when they reminded me it all came back; they looked so charming leaning over the table intent upon what I said, that I told them everything they wanted to know. Everything was going so pleasantly if only Sir Richard would cheer up. I heard his mournful voice every now and then—these were very pleasant people if only he would take them the right way. I could understand that he regretted his past, but the early seventies seemed centuries away and I felt sure that he misunderstood these ladies, they were not revengeful as he seemed to suppose. I wanted to show him how cheerful they really were, and so I made a joke and they all laughed at it, and then I chaffed them a bit, especially Rosalind, and nobody resented it in the very least. And still Sir Richard sat there with that unhappy look, like one that has ended weeping because it is vain and has not the consolation even of tears.

We had been a long time there and many of the candles had burned out, but there was light enough. I was glad to have an audience for my exploit, and being happy myself I was determined Sir Richard should be. I made more jokes and they still laughed good-naturedly; some of the jokes were a little broad perhaps but no harm was meant. And then,—I do not wish to excuse myself, but I had had a harder day than I ever had had before and without knowing it I must have been completely exhausted; in this state the champagne had found me, and what would have been harmless at any other time must somehow have got the better of me when quite tired out. Anyhow, I went too far, I made some joke,—I cannot in the least remember what,—that suddenly seemed to offend them. I felt all at once a commotion in the air; I looked up and saw that they had all arisen from the table and were sweeping towards the door. I had not time to open it, but it blew open on a wind; I could scarcely see what Sir Richard was doing because only two candles were left, I think the rest blew out when the ladies suddenly rose. I sprang up to apologise, to assure them—and then fatigue overcame me as it had overcome my horse at the last fence, I clutched at the table, but the cloth came away, and then I fell. The fall, and the darkness on the floor, and the pent-up fatigue of the day overcame me all three together.

The sun shone over glittering fields and in at a bedroom window, and thousands of birds were chanting to the spring, and there I was in an old four-poster bed in a quaint old panelled bedroom, fully dressed, and wearing long muddy boots; someone had taken my spurs and that was all. For a moment I failed to realise and then it all came back, my enormity and the pressing need of an abject apology to Sir Richard. I pulled an embroidered bell rope until the butler came; he came in perfectly cheerful and indescribably shabby. I asked him if Sir Richard was up, and he said he had just gone down, and told me to my amazement that it was twelve o'clock. I asked to be shown in to Sir Richard at once.

He was in his smoking-room. "Good morning," he said cheerfully the moment I went in. I went directly to the matter in hand. "I fear that I insulted some ladies in your house—" I began.

"You did indeed," he said, "You did indeed." And then he burst into tears and took me by the hand. "How can I ever thank you?" he said to me then. "We have been thirteen at table for thirty years and I never dared to insult them because I had wronged them all, and now you have done it and I know they will never dine here again." And for a long time he still held my hand, and then he gave it a grip and a kind of a shake which I took to mean "good-bye," and I drew my hand away then and left the house. And I found James in the stables with the hounds and asked him how he had fared, and James, who is a man of very few words, said he could not rightly remember, and I got my spurs from the butler and climbed on to my horse; and slowly we rode away from that queer old house, and slowly we wended home, for the hounds were footsore but happy and the horses were tired still. And when we recalled that the hunting season was ended we turned our faces to spring and thought of the new things that try to replace the old. And that very year I heard, and have often heard since, of dances and happier dinners at Sir Richard Arlen's house.

Thrawn Janet

Robert Louis Stevenson

The Reverend Murdoch Soulis was long minister of the moorland parish of Balweary, in the vale of Dule. A severe, bleak-faced old man, dreadful to his hearers, he dwelt in the last years of his life, without relative or servant or any human company, in the small and lonely manse under the Hanging Shaw. In spite of the iron composure of his features, his eye was wild, scared, and uncertain; and when he dwelt, in private admonitions, on the future of the impenitent, it seemed as if his eye pierced through the storms of time to the terrors of eternity. Many young persons, coming to prepare themselves against the season of the Holy Communion, were dreadfully affected by his talk. He had a sermon on 1st Peter, v. and 8th, "The devil as a roaring lion," on the Sunday after every seventeenth of August, and he was accustomed to surpass himself upon that text both by the appalling nature of the matter and the terror of his bearing in the pulpit. The children were frightened into fits, and the old looked more than usually oracular, and were, all that day, full of those hints that Hamlet deprecated. The manse itself, where it stood by the water of Dule among some thick trees, with the Shaw overhanging it on the one side, and on the other many cold, moorish hill-tops rising towards the sky, had begun, at a very early period of Mr. Soulis's ministry, to be avoided in the dusk hours by all who valued themselves upon their prudence; and guidmen sitting at the clachan alehouse shook their heads together at the thought of passing late by that uncanny neighbourhood. There was one spot, to be more particular, which was regarded with especial awe. The manse stood between the high-road and the water of Dule, with a gable to each; its back was towards the kirktown of Balweary, nearly half a mile away; in front of it, a bare garden, hedged with thorn, occupied the land between the river and the road. The house was two stories high, with two large rooms on each. It opened not directly on the garden, but on a causewayed path, or passage, giving on the road on the one hand, and closed on the other by the tall willows and elders that bordered on the stream. And it was this strip of causeway that enjoyed among the young parishioners of Balweary so infamous a reputation. The minister walked there often after dark, sometimes groaning aloud in the instancy of his unspoken prayers; and when he was from home, and the manse door was locked, the more daring schoolboys ventured, with beating hearts, to "follow my leader" across that legendary spot.

This atmosphere of terror, surrounding, as it did, a man of God of spotless character and orthodoxy, was a common cause of wonder and subject of inquiry among the few strangers who were led by chance or business into that unknown, outlying country. But many even of the people of the parish were ignorant of the strange events which had marked the first year of Mr. Soulis's ministrations; and among those who were better informed, some were naturally reticent, and others shy of that particular topic. Now and again, only, one of the older folk would warm into courage over his third tumbler, and recount the cause of the minister's strange looks and solitary life.

Fifty years syne, when Mr. Soulis cam' first into Ba'weary, he was still a young man—a callant, the folk said—fu' o' book-learnin' an' grand at the exposition, but, as was natural in sae young a man, wi' nae leevin' experience in religion. The younger sort were greatly taken wi' his gifts an' his gab; but auld, concerned, serious men and women were moved even to prayer for the young man, whom they took to be a self-deceiver, an' the parish that was like to be sae ill-supplied. It was before the days o' the Moderates—weary fa' them; but ill things are like guid—they baith come bit by bit, a pickle at a time; an' there were folk even then that said the Lord had left the college professors to their ain devices, an' the lads that went to study wi' them wad hae done mair an' better sittin' in a peat-bog, like their forbears o' the persecution, wi' a Bible under their oxter an' a speerit o' prayer in their heart. There was nae doubt, onyway, but that Mr. Soulis had been ower lang at the college. He was careful an' troubled for mony things besides the ae thing needful. He had a feck o' books wi' him—mair than had ever been seen before in a' that presbytery; and a sair wark the carrier had wi' them, for they were a' like to have smoored in the De'il's Hag between this an' Kilmackerlie. They were books o' divinity, to be sure, or so they ca'd them; but the serious were of opinion there was little service for sae mony, when the hale o' God's Word would gang in the neuk o' a plaid. Then he wad sit half the day, an' half the nicht forbye, which was scant decent—writin', nae less; an' first, they were feared he wad read his sermons; an' syne it proved he was writin' a book himsel', which was surely no' flttin' for ane o' his years an' sma' experience.

Onyway it behoved him to get an auld, decent wife to keep the manse for him an' see to his bit denners; an' he was recommended to an auld limmer—Janet M'Clour, they ca'd her—an' sae far left to himsel' as to be ower persuaded. There was mony advised him to the contrar, for Janet was mair than suspeckit by the best folk in Ba'weary. Lang or that, she had had a wean to a dragoon; she hadnae come forrit[1] for maybe thretty year; an' bairns had seen her mumblin' to hersel' up on Key's Loan in the gloamin', whilk was an unco time an' place for a God-fearin' woman. Howsoever, it was the laird himsel' that had first tauld the minister o' Janet; an' in thae days he wad hae gane a far gate to pleesure the laird. When folk tauld him that Janet was sib to the de'il, it was a' superstition by his way o' it; an' when they cast up the Bible to him an' the witch o' Endor, he wad threep it doun their thrapples that thir days were a' gane by, an' the de'il was mercifully restrained.

Weel, when it got about the clachan that Janet M'Clour was to be servant at the manse, the folk were fair mad wi' her an' him thegether; an' some o' the guid wives had nae better to dae than get round her door-cheeks and chairge her wi' a' that was ken't again' her, frae the sodger's bairn to John Tamson's twa kye. She was nae great speaker; folk usually let her gang her ain gate, an' she let them gang theirs, wi' neither Fair-guid-een nor Fair-guid-day: but when she buckled to, she had a tongue to deave the miller. Up she got, an' there wasna an auld story in Ba'weary but she gart somebody lowp for it that day; they couldnae say ae thing but she could say twa to it; till, at the hinder end, the guidwives up and claught hand o' her, an' clawed the coats aff her back, an' pu'd her doun the clachan to the water o' Dule, to see if she were a witch or no, soum or droun. The carline skirled till ye could hear her at the Hangin' Shaw, an' she focht like ten; there was mony a guidwife bure the mark o' her neist day an' mony a lang day after; an' just in the hottest o' the collieshangie, wha suld come up (for his sins) but the new minister.

"Women," said he (and he had a grand voice), "I charge you in the Lord's name to let her go."

Janet ran to him—she was fair wud wi' terror—an' clang to him, an' prayed him, for Christ's sake, save her frae the cummers; an' they, for their pairt, tauld him a' that was ken't, an' maybe mair.

"Woman," says he to Janet, "is this true?"

"As the Lord sees me," says she, "as the Lord made me, no a word o't. Forbye the bairn," says she, "I've been a decent woman a' my days."

"Will you," says Mr. Soulis, "in the name of God, and before me, His unworthy minister, renounce the devil and his works?"

1 "To come forrit"—to offer oneself as a communicant.

Weel, it wad appear that when he askit that, she gave a girn that fairly frichtit them that saw her, an' they could hear her teeth play dirl thegither in her chafts; but there was naething for't but the ae way or the ither; an' Janet lifted up her hand an' renounced the de'il before them a'.

"And now," says Mr. Soulis to the guidwives, "home with ye, one and all, and pray to God for His forgiveness."

An' he gied Janet his arm, though she had little on her but a sark, an' took her up the clachan to her ain door like a leddy o' the land; an' her screighin' and laughin' as was a scandal to be heard.

There were mony grave folk lang ower their prayers that nicht; but when the morn cam' there was sic a fear fell upon a' Ba'weary that the bairns hid theirsels, an' even the men-folk stood an' keekit frae their doors. For there was Janet comin' doun the clachan—her or her likeness, nane could tell—wi' her neck thrawn, an' her heid on ae side, like a body that has been hangit, an' a girn on her face like an unstreakit corp. By an' by they got used wi' it, an' even speered at her to ken what was wrang; but frae that day forth she couldnae speak like a Christian woman, but slavered an' played click wi' her teeth like a pair o' shears; an' frae that day forth the name o' God cam' never on her lips. Whiles she wad try to say it, but it michtna be. Them that kenned best said least; but they never gied that Thing the name o' Janet M'Clour; for the auld Janet, by their way o't, was in muckle hell that day. But the minister was neither to haud nor to bind; he preached about naething but the folk's cruelty that had gi'en her a stroke of the palsy; he skelpt the bairns that meddled her; an' he had her up to the manse that same nicht, an' dwalled there a' his lane wi' her under the Hangin' Shaw.

Weel, time gaed by: an' the idler sort commenced to think mair lichtly o' that black business. The minister was weel thocht o'; he was aye late at the writing, folk wad see his can'le doon by the Dule water after twal' at e'en; an' he seemed pleased wi' himsel' an' upsitten as at first, though a' body could see that he was dwining. As for Janet she cam' an' she gaed; if she didnae speak muckle afore, it was reason she should speak less then; she meddled naebody; but she was an eldritch thing to see, an' nane wad hae mistrysted wi' her for Ba'weary glebe.

About the end o' July there cam' a spell o' weather, the like o't never was in that countryside; it was lown an' het an' heartless; the herds couldnae win up the Black Hill, the bairns were ower weariet to play; an' yet it was gousty too, wi' claps o' het wund that rumm'led in the glens, and bits o' shouers that slockened naething. We aye thocht it but to thun'er on the morn; but the morn cam', an' the morn's morning, an' it was aye the same uncanny weather, sair on folks and bestial. O' a' that were the waur, nane suffered like Mr. Soulis; he could neither sleep nor eat, he tauld his elders; an' when he wasna writin' at his weary book, he wad be stravaguin' ower a' the country-side like a man possessed, when a' body else was blithe to keep caller ben the house.

Abune Hangin' Shaw, in the bield o' the Black Hill, there's a bit enclosed grund wi' an iron yett; an' it seems, in the auld days, that was the kirkyaird o' Ba'weary, and consecrated by the Papists before the blessed licht shone upon the kingdom. It was a great howff o' Mr. Soulis's, onyway; there he wad sit an' consider his sermons; an' indeed it's a bieldy bit. Weel, as he cam' ower the wast end o' the Black Hill ae day, he saw first twa, an' syne fower, an' syne seeven corbie craws fleein' round an' round abune the auld kirkyaird. They flew laigh an' heavy, an' squawked to ither as they gaed; an' it was clear to Mr. Soulis that something had put them frae their ordinar'. He wasna easy fleyed, an' gaed straucht up to the wa's; an' what suld he find there but a man, or the appearance o' a man, sittin' in the inside upon a grave. He was of a great stature, an' black as hell, an' his e'en were singular to see.[2] Mr. Soulis had heard tell o' black men, mony's the time; but there was something unco about this black man that daunted him. Het as he was, he took a kind o' cauld grue in the marrow o' his banes; but up he spak for a' that; an' says he: "My friend, are you a stranger in this place?" The black man answered never a word; he got upon his feet, an' begoud to hirsle to the wa' on the far side; but he aye lookit at the minister; an' the minister stood an' lookit back; till a' in a meenit the black man was ower the wa' an' rinnin' for the bield o' the trees. Mr. Soulis, he hardly kenned why, ran after him; but he was fair forjeskit wi' his walk an' the het, unhalesome weather; an' rin as he likit, he got nae mair than a glisk o' the black man amang the birks, till he won doun to the foot o' the hillside, an' there he saw him ance mair, gaun hap-step-an'-lowp ower Dule water to the manse.

Mr. Soulis wasnae weel pleased that this fearsome gangrel suld mak' sae free wi' Ba'weary manse; an' he ran the harder, an', wet shoon, ower the burn, an' up the walk; but the deil a black man was there to see. He stepped out upon the road, but there was naebody there; he gaed a' ower the gairden, but na, nae black man. At the hinder end, an' a bit feared, as was but natural, he lifted the hasp an' into the manse; an' there was Janet M'Clour before his een, wi' her thrawn craig, an' nane sae pleased to see him. An' he aye minded sinsyne, when first he set his een upon her, he had the same cauld and deidly grue.

---

2 It was a common belief in Scotland that the devil appeared as a black man. This appears in several witch trials, and I think in Law's "Memorials," that delightful storehouse of the quaint and grisly.

"Janet," says he, "have you seen a black man?"

"A black man?" quo' she. "Save us a'! Ye're no wise, minister. There's nae black man in a' Ba'weary."

But she didnae speak plain, ye maun understand; but yam-yammered, like a powney wi' the bit in its moo.

"Weel," says he, "Janet, if there was nae black man, I have spoken with the Accuser of the Brethren."

An' he sat down like ane wi' a fever, an' his teeth chittered in his heid.

"Hoots," says she, "think shame to yoursel', minister"; an' gied him a drap brandy that she keept aye by her.

Syne Mr. Soulis gaed into his study amang a' his books. It's a lang, laigh, mirk chalmer, perishin' cauld in winter, an' no' very dry even in the tap o' the simmer, for the manse stands near the burn. Sae doun he sat, an' thocht o' a' that had come an' gane since he was in Ba'weary, an' his hame, an' the days when he was a bairn an' ran daffin' on the braes; an' that black man aye ran in his heid like the owercome o' a sang. Aye the mair he thocht, the mair he thocht o' the black man. He tried the prayer, an' the words wadnae come to him; an' he tried, they say, to write at his book, but he could nae mak' nae mair o' that. There was whiles he thocht the black man was at his oxter, an' the swat stood upon him cauld as well-water; an' there was ither whiles when he cam' to himsel' like a christened bairn an' minded naething.

The upshot was that he gaed to the window an' stood glowrin' at Dule water. The trees are unco thick, an' the water lies deep an' black under the manse; an' there was Janet washin' the cla'es wi' her coats kilted. She had her back to the minister, an' he, for his pairt, hardly kenned what he was lookin' at. Syne she turned round, an' shawed her face; Mr. Soulis had the same cauld grue as twice that day afore, an' it was borne in upon him what folk said, that Janet was deid lang syne, an' this was a bogle in her clay-cauld flesh. He drew back a pickle and he scanned her narrowly. She was tramp-trampin' in the cla'es, croonin' to hersel'; and eh! Gude guide us, but it was a fearsome face. Whiles she sang louder, but there was nae man born o' woman that could tell the words o' her sang; an' whiles she lookit side-lang doun, but there was naething there for her to look at. There gaed a scunner through the flesh upon his banes; an' that was Heeven's advertisement. But Mr. Soulis just blamed himsel', he said, to think sae ill o' a puir, auld afflicted wife that hadnae a freend forbye himsel'; an' he put up a bit prayer for him an' her, an' drank a little caller water—for his heart rose again' the meat—an' gaed up to his naked bed in the gloamin'.

That was a nicht that has never been forgotten in Ba'weary, the nicht o' the seeventeenth o' August, seeventeen hun'er' an' twal'. It had been het afore, as I hae said, but that nicht it was better than ever. The sun gaed doun amang unco-lookin' clouds; it fell as mirk as the pit; no' a star, no' a breath o' wund; ye couldnae see your han' afore your face, an' even the auld folk cuist the covers frae their beds an' lay pechin' for their breath. Wi' a' that he had upon his mind, it was geyan unlikely Mr. Soulis wad get muckle sleep. He lay an' he tummled; the gude, caller bed that he got into brunt his very banes; whiles he slept, an' whiles he waukened; whiles he heard the time o' nicht, an' whiles a tyke yowlin' up the muir, as if somebody was deid; whiles he thocht he heard bogles claverin' in his lug, an' whiles he saw spunkies in the room. He behoved, he judged, to be sick; an' sick he was—little he jaloosed the sickness.

At the hinder end he got a clearness in his mind, sat up in his sark on the bedside, an' fell thinkin' ance mair o' the black man an' Janet. He couldnae weel tell how—maybe it was the cauld to his feet—but it cam' in upon him wi' a spate that there was some connection between thir twa, an' that either or baith o' them were bogles. An' just at that moment, in Janet's room, which was neist to his, there cam' a stramp o' feet as if men were wars'lin', an' then a loud bang; an' then a wund gaed reishling round the fower quarters o' the house; an' then a' was aince mair as seelent as the grave.

Mr. Soulis was feared for neither man nor deevil. He got his tinder-box, an' lit a can'le, an' made three steps o't ower to Janet's door. It was on the hasp, an' he pushed it open, an' keekit bauldly in. It was a big room, as big as the minister's ain, an' plenished wi' grand, auld, solid gear, for he had naething else. There was a fower-posted bed wi' auld tapestry; an' a braw cabinet o' aik, that was fu' o' the minister's divinity books, an' put there to be out o' the gate; an' a wheen duds o' Janet's lying here an' there about the floor. But nae Janet could Mr. Soulis see; nor ony sign o' a contention. In he gaed (an' there's few that wad hae followed him) an' lookit a' round, an' listened. But there was naething to be heard, neither inside the manse nor in a' Ba'weary parish, an' naething to be seen but the muckle shadows turnin' round the can'le. An' then a' at aince, the minister's heart played dunt an' stood stock-still; an' a cauld wund blew amang the hairs o' his heid. Whaten a weary sicht was that for the puir man's een! For there was Janet hangin' frae a nail beside the auld aik cabinet: her heid aye lay on her shouther, her een were steekit, the tongue projected frae her mouth, an' her heels were twa feet clear abune the floor.

"God forgive us all!" thocht Mr. Soulis; "poor Janet's dead."

He cam' a step nearer to the corp; an' then his heart fair whammled in his inside. For, by what cantrip it wad ill beseem a man to judge, she was hingin' frae a single nail an' by a single wursted thread for darnin' hose.

It's an awfu' thing to be your lane at nicht wi' siccan prodigies o' darkness; but Mr. Soulis was strong in the Lord. He turned an' gaed his ways oot o' that room, an' lockit the door ahint him; an' step by step, doon the stairs, as heavy as leed; an' set doon the can'le on the table at the stairfoot. He couldnae pray, he couldnae think, he was dreepin' wi' caul' swat, an' naething could he hear but the dunt-dunt-duntin' o' his ain heart. He micht maybe hae stood there an hour, or maybe twa, he minded sae little; when a' o' a sudden, he heard a laigh, uncanny steer upstairs; a foot gaed to an' fro in the chalmer whaur the corp was hingin'; syne the door was opened, though he minded weel that he had lockit it; an' syne there was a step upon the landin', an' it seemed to him as if the corp was lookin' ower the rail an' doun upon him whaur he stood.

He took up the can'le again (for he couldnae want the licht), an' as saftly as ever he could, gaed straucht out o' the manse an' to the far end o' the causeway. It was aye pit-mirk; the flame o' the can'le, when he set it on the grund, brunt steedy and clear as in a room; naething moved, but the Dule water seepin' an' sabbin' doun the glen, an' yon unhaly footstep that cam' ploddin' doun the stairs inside the manse. He kenned the foot ower weel, for it was Janet's; an' at ilka step that cam' a wee thing nearer, the cauld got deeper in his vitals. He commended his soul to Him that made an' keepit him; "and, O Lord," said he, "give me strength this night to war against the powers of evil."

By this time the foot was comin' through the passage for the door; he could hear a hand skirt alang the wa', as if the fearsome thing was feelin' for its way. The saughs tossed an' maned thegither, a lang sigh cam' ower the hills, the flame o' the can'le was blawn aboot; an' there stood the corp o' Thrawn Janet, wi' her grogram goun an' her black mutch, wi' the heid aye upon the shouther, an' the girn still upon the face o't—leevin', ye wad hae said—deid, as Mr. Soulis weel kenned—upon the threshold o' the manse.

It's a strange thing that the saul o' man should be that thirled into his perishable body; but the minister saw that, an' his heart didnae break.

She didnae stand there lang; she began to move again an' cam' slowly towards Mr. Soulis whaur he stood under the saughs. A' the life o' his body, a' the strength o' his speerit, were glowerin' frae his een. It seemed she was gaun to speak, but wanted words, an' made a sign wi' the left hand. There cam' a clap o' wund, like a cat's fuff;

oot gaed the can'le, the saughs skreighed like folk; and Mr. Soulis kenned that, live or die, this was the end o't.

"Witch, beldame, devil!" he cried, "I charge you, by the power of God, begone—if you be dead, to the grave—if you be damned, to hell."

An' at that moment the Lord's ain hand out o' the Heevens struck the Horror whaur it stood; the auld, deid, desecrated corp o' the witch-wife, sae lang keepit frae the grave an' hirsled round by de'ils, lowed up like a brunstane spunk an' fell in ashes to the grund; the thunder followed, peal on dirlin' peal, the rairin' rain upon the back o' that; an' Mr. Soulis lowped through the garden hedge, an' ran, wi' skelloch upon skelloch, for the clachan.

That same mornin', John Christie saw the Black Man pass the Muckle Cairn as it was chappin' six; before eicht, he gaed by the change-house at Knockdow; an' no' lang after, Sandy M'Lellan saw him gaun linkin' doun the braes frae Kilmackerlie. There's little doubt but it was him that dwalled sae lang in Janet's body; but he was awa' at last; an' sinsyne the de'il has never fashed us in Ba'weary.

But it was a sair dispensation for the minister; lang, lang he lay ravin' in his bed; an' frae that hour to this he was the man ye ken the day.

"To Let"

Alice Turner Curtis

On one of the streets leading from the park in the center of a town near Boston is a very attractive modern house with a history. It was built for the occupancy of a Mr. and Mrs. Leslie, whose mysterious deaths mark the beginning of this story.

The facts here recorded are just as I heard them. Indeed I was a resident of the town during the period in which these strange occurrences took place, and had a personal acquaintance with the people mentioned.

The Leslies had been married a year, were apparently happy, and were well and favorably known in the town. One morning a neighbor noticed that lights were burning in the Leslie house. He ran up the steps and rang the bell. There was no response, and after a few hours the neighbors decided that something was wrong inside, and that an entrance must be made at once. The front door was accordingly forced open, and as the men went in they could see into the room beyond the hall, the sitting-room. Mr. Leslie was sitting with a paper across his knees, apparently asleep, and on a couch near by lay his wife.

It took but a few moments to ascertain that both had been dead for some hours. Their faces were peaceful and composed; there were no signs of disturbance in the house.

Every possible inquiry was made. No trace of poison or of foul play could be found. Numberless theories were advanced, and the wonder and excitement over the tragic death of the young couple grew daily.

After some months their relatives removed the furnishings, and "To Let" appeared in the cottage windows. The house was immediately taken by a man from Boston, whose family consisted, beside himself, of his wife and two little girls. None of this family had heard the story of the Leslies, nor did they hear it until they had been in the cottage for some weeks.

One night, after they had occupied the dwelling for over a week, the man of the family was awakened by a sudden scream. His wife awoke at the same moment, and exclaimed: "One of the children must have the nightmare," but just then the two little girls rushed into the room, exclaiming, "What's the matter, mother? What are you screaming about?" Almost before they had finished speaking two more screams in quick succession rang through the house. The place was carefully searched, but no cause for the disturbance could be found.

The next night at about the same hour like sounds were heard. After that Mr. Weston made inquiries of the neighbors. None of them had been disturbed. One suggested that possibly a cat was shut up somewhere in the house and had made the noises heard, but a careful search of the entire premises failed to discover any such commonplace solution of the mysterious sounds.

A week passed without any recurrence of the midnight sounds, when one night Mrs. Weston awoke from a most terrible dream. She dreamed that she was lying upon the couch in the sitting-room. In front of her stood a young man who held a pillow in his hands. "I shall stifle you," he said clearly; "it's no use to struggle." Mrs. Weston dreamed that she tried to scream; that once, twice, three times she endeavored to rise from the couch to push away the pillow, but could not.

From this dream she awoke suddenly, and, as she lay endeavoring to overcome its impression, a gasping shriek, quickly followed by two more, awakened her husband, and again sent the little girls flying in terror to their mother's room.

This time Mrs. Weston held herself responsible for the terrible screams. "I've had a dreadful dream, and I suppose I screamed without knowing it," she said. She had hardly finished this explanation when again came the screams, the last dying away in a stifled moan.

The family was by this time thoroughly terrified. They had heard the story of the Leslies, and without waiting for further experiences in the house they moved at once.

Their story got about the town, with the result that the house was vacant for a year. Then a family, consisting of an elderly couple, Mr. and Mrs. Walters, and their son, a young man about twenty-five, moved in. The remainder of the story was told me by this son, and I will give it in his own words as nearly as possible:

"I wasn't afraid of any haunted house. My father was deaf, so it would take a reasonably loud scream to wake him, and my mother was a sensible woman. The house just suited us. We got nicely settled in a few weeks, and my elder brother and his wife came out from Boston to make us a visit. The first night they were there I stayed in town for the theater. The train I came out in left a few minutes after eleven, and I reached the house at about a quarter before twelve. I was nearly ready for bed when a shriek like that of a person struggling for his life sounded through the house. I hurried into the hall, and as I did so my brother opened his door. Before either of us could speak a second and a third scream followed. By this time even father's deaf ears had been penetrated, and we all sat up talking the matter over far into the night before we felt like sleep.

"In the end we decided not to mention the occurrence. We thought of several possible explanations of the noise. The next morning we made a careful examination of the house and surroundings. We made inquiries as to late trains, thinking we might have mistaken the shriek of an engine for a human voice; but all our conjectures led to nothing. We could find no satisfactory reason for the disturbance.

"I made inquiries about the Leslies, and found that many people believed that Leslie had stifled his wife, and then taken some subtle poison which left no trace; but there was no evidence to support this theory; no sign of poison had been found, no cause could be given for such an act, and nothing could explain the midnight screams. A week passed quietly, when one night my brother awakened our mother, telling her that his wife was ill. She had awakened from a bad dream almost suffocated, and my mother worked over her for some time before she was restored. She refused to tell her dream, but we were well assured that it was a repetition of Mrs. Weston's. The next morning my brother and his wife went to their home.

"I had one more experience in that house which I shall never forget. My father was to be out one night until midnight at the meeting of a society of which he was a member, and my mother and I decided to wait up for him.

"About eleven o'clock mother lay down on the couch and went to sleep. The room was brightly lighted, and I sat near the couch reading.

"Just as I heard my father come in I was startled by a sudden moan from my mother. I turned quickly toward the couch, and as I did so I saw plainly that the sofa pillow lay upon her face. I snatched it away, and awakened her with some little difficulty.

"Meantime my father had come into the room, and as he entered a scream, terrible in its nearness and intensity, rang out, thrilling us all with a sickening shock. We left the next day."

This finished his story. No explanation of these happenings has ever been given. The Leslies' death remains a mystery, and to explain the Presence that occupied this cottage after their death would be to account for a side of life which we barely touch and cannot comprehend.

The house is still to let.

Tom Toothacre's Ghost Story

Harriet Beecher Stowe

"What is it about that old house in Sherbourne?" said Aunt Nabby to Sam Lawson, as he sat drooping over the coals of a great fire one October evening.

Aunt Lois was gone to Boston on a visit; and, the smart spice of her scepticism being absent, we felt the more freedom to start our story-teller on one of his legends.

Aunt Nabby sat trotting her knitting-needles on a blue-mixed yarn stocking. Grandmamma was knitting in unison at the other side of the fire. Grandfather sat studying the *Boston Courier*. The wind outside was sighing in fitful wails, creaking the pantry-doors, occasionally puffing in a vicious gust down the broad throat of the chimney. It was a drizzly, sleety evening; and the wet lilac-bushes now and then rattled and splashed against the window as the wind moaned and whispered through them.

We boys had made preparation for a comfortable evening. We had enticed Sam to the chimney corner, and drawn him a mug of cider. We had set down a row of apples to roast on the hearth, which even now were giving faint sighs and sputters as their plump sides burst in the genial heat. The big oak back-log simmered and bubbled, and distilled large drops down amid the ashes; and the great hickory forestick had just burned out into solid bright coals, faintly skimmed over with white ashes. The whole area of the big chimney was full of a sleepy warmth and brightness just calculated to call forth fancies and visions. It only wanted somebody now to set Sam off; and Aunt Nabby broached the ever-interesting subject of haunted houses.

"Wal, now, Miss Badger," said Sam, "I ben over there, and walked round that 'are house consid'able; and I talked with Granny Hokum and Aunt Polly, and they've putty much come to the conclusion that they'll hev to move out on't. Ye see, these 'ere noises, they keep 'em awake nights; and Aunt Polly, she gets 'stericky; and Hannah Jane, she says, ef they stay in the house, *she* can't live with 'em no longer. And what can them lone women do without Hannah Jane? Why, Hannah Jane, she says these two months past she's seen a woman, regular, walking up and down the front hall between twelve and one o'clock at night; and it's jist the image and body of old Ma'am Tillotson, Parson Hokum's mother, that everybody know'd was a thunderin' kind o' woman, that kep' everything in a muss while she was alive. What the old critter's up to now there ain't no knowin'. Some folks seems to think it's a sign Granny Hokum's time's comin'. But Lordy massy! says she to me, says she, 'Why, Sam, I don't know nothin' what I've done, that Ma'am Tillotson should be set loose on me.' Anyway they've all got so narvy, that Jed Hokum has ben up from Needham, and is goin' to cart 'em all over to live with him. Jed, he's for hushin' on't up, 'cause he says it brings a bad name on the property.

"Wal, I talked with Jed about it; and says I to Jed, says I, 'Now, ef you'll take my advice, jist you give that 'are old house a regular overhaulin', and paint it over with tew coats o' paint, and that are'll clear 'em out, if anything will. Ghosts is like bed-bugs,—they can't stan' fresh paint,' says I. 'They allers clear out. I've seen it tried on a ship that got haunted.' "

"Why, Sam, do ships get haunted?"

"To be sure they do!—haunted the wust kind. Why, I could tell ye a story'd make your har rise on eend, only I'm 'fraid of frightening boys when they're jist going to bed."

"Oh! you can't frighten Horace," said my grandmother. "He will go and sit out there in the graveyard till nine o'clock nights, spite of all I tell him."

"Do tell, Sam!" we urged. "What was it about the ship?"

Sam lifted his mug of cider, deliberately turned it round and round in his hands, eyed it affectionately, took a long drink, and set it down in front of him on the hearth, and began:—

"Ye 'member I telled you how I went to sea down East, when I was a boy, 'long with Tom Toothacre. Wal, Tom, he reeled off a yarn one night that was 'bout the toughest I ever hed the pullin' on. And it come all straight, too, from Tom. 'Twa'n't none o' yer hearsay: 'twas what he seen with his own eyes. Now, there wa'n't no nonsense 'bout Tom, not a bit on't; and he wa'n't afeared o' the divil himse'f; and he ginally saw through things about as straight as things could be seen through. This 'ere happened when Tom was mate o' The Albatross, and they was a-runnin' up to the banks for a fare o' fish. The Albatross was as handsome a craft as ever ye see; and Cap'n Sim Witherspoon, he was skipper—a rail nice likely man he was. I heard Tom tell this 'ere one night to the boys on The Brilliant, when they was all a-settin' round the stove in the cabin one foggy night that we was to anchor in Frenchman's Bay, and all kind o' layin' off loose.

"Tom, he said they was having a famous run up to the Banks. There was a spankin' southerly, that blew 'em along like all natur'; and they was hevin' the best kind of a time, when this 'ere southerly brought a pesky fog down on 'em, and it grew thicker than hasty-puddin'. Ye see, that 'are's the pester o' these 'ere southerlies: they's the biggest fog-breeders there is goin'. And so, putty soon, you couldn't see half ship's length afore you.

"Wal, they all was down to supper, except Dan Sawyer at the wheel, when there come sich a crash as if heaven and earth was a-splittin', and then a scrapin' and thump bumpin' under the ship, and gin 'em sich a h'ist that the pot o' beans went rollin', and brought up jam ag'in the bulkhead; and the fellers was keeled over,—men and pork and beans kinder permiscus.

" 'The divil!' says Tom Toothacre, 'we've run down somebody. Look out, up there!'

"Dan, he shoved the helm hard down, and put her up to the wind, and sung out, 'Lordy massy! we've struck her right amidships!'

" 'Struck what?' they all yelled, and tumbled up on deck.

" 'Why, a little schooner,' says Dan. 'Didn't see her till we was right on her. She's gone down tack and sheet. Look! there's part o' the wreck a-floating off: don't ye see?'

"Wal, they didn't see, 'cause it was so thick you couldn't hardly see your hand afore your face. But they put about, and sent out a boat, and kind o' sarched round; but, Lordy massy! ye might as well looked for a drop of water in the Atlantic Ocean. Whoever they was, it was all done gone and over with 'em for this life, poor critters!

"Tom says they felt confoundedly about it; but what could they do? Lordy massy! what can any on us do? There's places where folks jest lets go 'cause they hes to. Things ain't as they want 'em, and they can't alter 'em. Sailors ain't so rough as they look: they's feelin' critters, come to put things right to 'em. And there wasn't one on 'em who wouldn't 'a' worked all night for a chance o' saving some' o' them poor fellows. But there't was, and 'twa'n't no use trying.

"Wal, so they sailed on: and by'm by the wind kind o' chopped round no'theast, and then come round east, and sot in for one of them regular east blows and drizzles that takes the starch out o' fellers more 'n a regular storm. So they concluded they might as well put into a little bay there, and come to anchor.

"So they sot an anchor-watch, and all turned in.

"Wal, now comes the particular curus part o' Tom's story; and it was more curus 'cause Tom was one that wouldn't 'a' believed no other man that had told it. Tom was one o' your sort of philosophers. He was fer lookin' into things, and wa'n't in no hurry 'bout believin'; so that this 'un was more 'markable on account of its bein' Tom that seen it than ef it had ben others.

"Tom says that night he hed a pesky toothache that sort o' kep' grumblin' and jumpin' so he couldn't go to sleep; and he lay in his bunk, a-turnin' this way and that, till long past twelve o'clock.

"Tom had a 'thwart-ship bunk where he could see into every bunk on board, except Bob Coffin's, and Bob was on the anchor-watch. Wal, he lay there, tryin' to go to sleep, hearin' the men snorin' like bullfrogs in a swamp, and watchin' the lantern a-swingin' back and forward; and the sou'westers and pea-jackets were kinder throwin' their long shadders up and down as the vessel sort o' rolled and pitched,—for there was a heavy swell on,—and then he'd hear Bob Coffin tramp, tramp, trampin' overhead,—for Bob had a pretty heavy foot of his own,—and all sort o' mixed up together with Tom's toothache, so he couldn't get to sleep. Finally, Tom, he bit off a great chaw o' 'baccy, and got it well sot in his cheek, and kind o' turned over to lie on't, and ease the pain. Wal, he says he laid a spell, and dropped off in a sort o' doze, when he woke in sich a chill his teeth chattered, and the pain came on like a knife, and he bounced over, thinking the fire had gone out in the stove.

"Wal, sure enough, he see a man a-crouching over the stove, with his back to him, a-stretchin' out his hands to warm 'em. He had on a sou'wester and a pea-jacket with a red tippet round his neck; and his clothes was drippin' as if he'd just come in from a rain.

"'What the divil!' says Tom. And he riz right up, and rubbed his eyes. 'Bill Bridges,' says he, 'what shine be you up to now?' For Bill was a master oneasy critter, and allers a-gettin' up and walkin' nights; and Tom, he thought it was Bill. But in a minute he looked over, and there, sure enough, was Bill, fast asleep in his bunk, mouth wide open, snoring like a Jericho ram's-horn. Tom looked round, and counted every man in his bunk, and then says he, 'Who the divil is this? for there's Bob Coffin on deck, and the rest is all here.'

"Wal, Tom wa'n't a man to be put under too easy. He hed his thoughts about him allers; and the fust he thought in every pinch was what to do. So he sot considerin' a minute, sort o' winkin' his eyes to be sure he saw straight, when, sure enough, there come another man backin' down the companion-way.

"'Wal, there's Bob Coffin, anyhow,' says Tom to himself. But no, the other man he turned: Tom see his face; and, sure as you live, it was the face of a dead corpse. Its eyes was sot, and it jest came as still across the cabin, and sot down by the stove and kind o' shivered, and put out its hands as if it was gettin' warm.

"Tom said that there was a cold air round in the cabin, as if an iceberg was comin' near, and he felt cold chills running down his back; but he jumped out of his bunk, and took a step forward. 'Speak!' says he. 'Who be you? and what do you want?'

"They never spoke, nor looked up, but kept kind o' shivering and crouching over the stove.

"'Wal,' says Tom, 'I'll see who you be, anyhow.' And he walked right up to the last man that come in, and reached out to catch hold of his coat-collar; but his hand jest went through him like moonshine, and in a minute he all faded away; and when he turned round the other one was gone too. Tom stood there, looking this way and that; but there warn't nothing but the old stove, and the lantern swingin', and the men all snorin' round in their bunks. Tom, he sung out to Bob Coffin. 'Hullo, up there!' says he. But Bob never answered, and Tom, he went up, and found Bob down on his knees, his teeth a-chatterin' like a bag o' nails, trying to say his prayers; and all he could think of was, 'Now I lay me,' and he kep' going that over and over. Ye see, boys, Bob was a drefful wicked, swearin' critter, and hadn't said no prayers since he was tew years old, and it didn't come natural to him. Tom give a grip on his collar, and shook him. 'Hold yer yawp,' said he. 'What you howlin' about? What's up?'

"'Oh, Lordy massy!' says Bob, 'we're sent for,—all on us,—there's been two on 'em: both on 'em went right by me!'

"Wal, Tom, he hed his own thoughts; but he was bound to get to the bottom of things, anyway. Ef 't was the devil, well and good—he wanted to know it. Tom jest wanted to hev the matter settled one way or t'other: so he got Bob sort o' stroked down, and made him tell what he saw.

"Bob, he stood to it that he was a-standin' right for'ard, a-leanin' on the windlass, and kind o' hummin' a tune, when he looked down, and see a sort o' queer light in the fog; and he went and took a look over the bows, when up came a man's head in a sort of sou'wester, and then a pair of hands, and catched at the bob-stay; and then the hull figger of a man riz right out o' the water, and clim up on the martingale till he could reach the jib-stay with his hands, and then he swung himself right up on to the bowsprit, and stepped aboard, and went past Bob, right aft, and down into the cabin. And he hadn't more 'n got down, afore he turned round, and there was another comin' in over the bowsprit, and he went by him, and down below: so there was two on 'em, jest as Tom had seen in the cabin.

"Tom he studied on it a spell, and finally says he, 'Bob, let you and me keep this 'ere to ourselves, and see ef it'll come again. Ef it don't, well and good: ef it does—why, we'll see about it.'

"But Tom he told Cap'n Witherspoon, and the Cap'n he agreed to keep an eye out the next night. But there warn't nothing said to the rest o' the men.

"Wal, the next night they put Bill Bridges on the watch. The fog had lifted, and they had a fair wind, and was going on steady. The men all turned in, and went fast asleep, except Cap'n Witherspoon, Tom, and Bob Coffin. Wal, sure enough, 'twixt twelve and one o'clock, the same thing came over, only there war four men 'stead o' two. They come in jes' so over the bowsprit, and they looked neither to right nor left, but clim down stairs, and sot down, and crouched and shivered over the stove jist like the others. Wal, Bill Bridges, he came tearin' down like a wild-cat, frightened half out o' his wits, screechin' 'Lord, have mercy! we're all goin' to the devil!' And then they all vanished.

"'Now, Cap'n, what's to be done?' says Tom. 'Ef these 'ere fellows is to take passage, we can't do nothin' with the boys: that's clear.'

"Wal, so it turned out; for, come next night, there was six on 'em come in, and the story got round, and the boys was all on eend. There wa'n't no doin' nothin' with 'em. Ye see, it's allers jest so. Not but what dead folks is jest as 'spectable as they was afore they's dead. These might 'a' been as good fellers as any aboard; but it's human natur'. The minute a feller's dead, why, you sort o' don't know 'bout him; and it's kind o' skeery hevin' on him round; and so't wa'n't no wonder the boys didn't feel as if they could go on with the vy'ge, ef these 'ere fellers was all to take passage. Come to look, too, there war consid'able of a leak stove in the vessel; and the boys, they all stood to it, ef they went farther, that they'd all go to the bottom. For, ye see, once the story got a-goin', every one on 'em saw a new thing every night. One on 'em saw the bait-mill a-grindin', without no hands to grind it; and another saw fellers up aloft, workin' in the sails. Wal, the fact war, they jest had to put about,—run back to Castine.

"Wal, the owners, they hushed up things the best they could; and they put the vessel on the stocks, and worked her over, and put a new coat o' paint on her, and called her "The Betsey Ann"; and she went a good vy'ge to the Banks, and brought home the biggest fare o' fish that had been for a long time; and she's made good vy'ges ever since; and that jest proves what I've been a-saying,—that there's nothin' to drive out ghosts like fresh paint."

The Tower

Barry Pain

In the billiard room of the Cabinet Club, shortly after midnight, two men had just finished a game. A third had been watching it from the lounge at the end of the room. The winner put up his cue, slipped on his coat, and with a brief "Good-night" passed out of the room. He was tall, dark, clean-shaven and foreign in appearance. It would not have been easy to guess his nationality, but he did not look English.

The loser, a fair-haired boy of twenty-five, came over to the lounge and dropped down by the side of the elderly man who had been watching the billiards.

"Silly game, ain't it, doctor?" he said cheerfully. The doctor smiled.

"Yes," he said, "Vyse is a bit too hot for you, Bill."

"A bit too hot for anything," said the boy. "He never takes any trouble; he never hesitates; he never thinks; he never takes an easy shot when there's a brilliant one to be pulled off. It's almost uncanny."

"Ah," said the doctor, reflectively, "it's a queer thing. You're the third man whom I heard say that about Vyse within the last week."

"I believe he's quite alright—good sort of chap, you know. He's frightfully clever too—speaks a lot of beastly difficult Oriental languages—does well at any game he takes up."

"Yes," said the doctor, "he is clever; and he is also a fool."

"What do you mean? He's eccentric, of course. Fancy his buying that rotten tower—a sweet place to spend Christmas in all alone, I don't think."

"Why does he say he's going there?"

"Says he hates the conventional Christmas, and wants to be out of it; says also that he wants to shoot duck."

"That won't do," said the doctor. "He may hate the conventional Christmas. He may, and probably will, shoot duck. But that's not his reason for going there."

"Then what is it?" asked the boy.

"Nothing that would interest you much, Bill. Vyse is one of the chaps that want to know too much. He's playing about in a way that every medical man knows to be a rotten, dangerous way. Mind, he may get at something; if the stories are true he has already got at a good deal. I believe it is possible for a man to develop in himself certain powers at a certain price."

"What's the price?"

"Insanity, often as not. Here, let's talk about something pleasanter. Where are you yourself going this Christmas, by the way?"

"My sister has taken compassion upon this lone bachelor. And you?"

"I shall be out of England," said the doctor. "Cairo, probably."

The two men passed out into the hall of the club.

"Has Mr. Vyse gone yet?" the boy asked the porter.

"Not yet, Sir William. Mr. Vyse is changing in one of the dressing rooms. His car is outside."

The two men passed the car in the street, and noticed the luggage in the tonneau. The driver, in his long leather coat, stood motionless beside it, waiting for his master. The powerful headlight raked the dusk of the street; you could see the paint on a tired woman's cheek as she passed through it on her way home at last.

"See his game?" said Bill.

"Of course," said the doctor. "He's off to the marshes and that blessed tower of his tonight."

"Well, I don't envy him—holy sort of amusement it must be driving all that way on a cold night like this. I wonder if the beggar ever goes to sleep at all?"

They had reached Bill's chambers in Jermyn Street.

"You must come in and have a drink," said Bill.

"Don't think so, thanks," said the doctor; "it's late, you know."

"You'd better," said Bill, and the doctor followed him in.

A letter and a telegram were lying on the table in the diminutive hall. The letter had been sent by messenger, and was addressed to Sir William Orsley, Bart., in a remarkably small handwriting. Bill picked it up, and thrust it into his pocket at once, unopened. He took the telegram with him into the room where the drinks had been put out, and opened it as he sipped his whisky-and-soda.

"Great Scot!" he exclaimed.

"Nothing serious, I hope," said the doctor.

"I hope not. I suppose all the children have got to have the measles some time or another; but it's just a bit unlucky that my sister's three should all go down with it just now. That does for her house-party at Christmas, of course."

A few minutes later, when the doctor had gone, Bill took the letter from his pocket and tore it open. A cheque fell from the envelope and fluttered to the ground. The letter ran as follows:

> DEAR BILL,—I could not talk to you tonight, as the doctor, who happens to disapprove of me, was in the billiard-room. Of course, I can let you have the hundred you want, and enclose it herewith with the utmost pleasure. The time you mention for repayment would suit me all right, and so would any other time. Suit your own convenience entirely.
>
> I have a favour to ask of you. I know you are intending to go down to the Leylands' for Christmas. I think you will be prevented from doing so. If that is the case, and you have no better engagement, would you hold yourself at my disposal for a week? It is just possible that I may want a man like you pretty badly. There ought to be plenty of duck this weather, but I don't know that I can offer any other attraction—Very sincerely yours,
>
> EDWARD VYSE.

Bill picked up the cheque and thrust it into the drawer with a feeling of relief. It was a queer invitation, he thought—funnily worded, with the usual intimations of time and place missing. He switched off the electric lights and went into his bedroom. As he was undressing a thought struck him suddenly.

"How the deuce," he said aloud, "did he know that I should be prevented from going to Polly's place?" Then he looked round quickly. He thought that he had heard a faint laugh just behind him. No one was there, and Bill's nerves were good enough. In twenty minutes he was fast asleep.

The cottage, built of grey stone, stood some thirty yards back from the road, from which it was screened by a shrubbery. It was an ordinary eight-roomed cottage, and it did well enough for Vyse and his servants and one guest—if Vyse happened to want a guest. There was a pleasant little walled garden of a couple of acres behind the cottage. Through a doorway in the further wall one passed into a stunted and dismal plantation, and in the middle of this rose the tower, far higher than any of the trees that surrounded it.

Sir William Orsley had arrived just in time to change before dinner. Talk at dinner had been of indifferent subjects—the queer characters of the village, and the chances of sport on the morrow. Bill had mentioned the tower, and his host had hastened to talk of other things. But now that dinner was over, and the man who had waited on them had left the room, Vyse of his own accord returned to the subject.

"Danvers is a superstitious ass," he observed, "and he's in quite enough of a funk about that tower as it is; that's why I wouldn't give you the whole story while he was in the room. According to the village tradition, a witch was burned on the site where the tower now stands, and she declared that where she burned the devil should have his house. The lord of the manor at that time, hearing what the old lady had said, and wishing to discourage house-building on that particular site, had it covered with a plantation, and made it a condition of his will that this plantation should be kept up."

Bill lit a cigar. "Looks like checkmate," he said. "However, seeing that the tower is actually there—"

"Quite so. This man's son came no end of a cropper, and the property changed hands several times. It was divided and sub-divided. I, for instance, only own about twenty acres of it. Presently there came along a scientific old gentleman and bought the piece that I now have. Whether he knew of the story, or whether he didn't, I cannot say, but he set to work to build the tower that is now standing in the middle of the plantation. He may have intended it as an observatory. He got the stone for it on the spot from his own quarry, but he had to import his labor, as the people in these parts didn't think the work healthy. Then one fine morning before the tower was finished they found the old gentleman at the bottom of his quarry with his neck broken."

"So," said Bill, "they say of course that the tower is haunted. What is it that they think they see?"

"Nothing. You can't see it. But there are people who think they have touched it and have heard it."

"Rot, ain't it?"

"I don't know exactly. You see, I happen to be one of those people."

"Then, if you think so, there's something in it. This is interesting. I say, can't we go across there now?"

"Certainly, if you like. Sure you won't have any more wine? Come along, then."

The two men slipped on their coats and caps. Vyse carried a lighted stable-lantern. It was a frosty moonlit night, and the path was crisp and hard beneath their feet. As Vyse slid back the bolts of the gate in the garden wall, Bill said suddenly, "By the way, Vyse, how did you know that I shouldn't be at the Leylands' this Christmas? I told you I was going there."

"I don't know. I had a feeling that you were going to be with me. It might have been wrong. Anyhow, I'm glad you're here. You are just exactly the man I want. We've only a few steps to go now. The path is ours. That cart-track leads away to the quarry where the scientific gentleman took the short cut to further knowledge. And here is the door of the tower."

They walked round the tower before entering. The night was so still that, unconsciously, they spoke in lowered voices and trod as softly as possible. The lock of the heavy door groaned and screeched as the key turned. The light of the lantern fell now on the white sand of the floor and on a broken spiral staircase on the further side. Far up above one saw a tangle of beams and the stars beyond them. Bill heard Vyse saying that it was left like that after the death in the quarry.

"It's a good solid bit of masonry," said Bill, "but it ain't a cheerful spot exactly. And, by jove! It smells like a menagerie."

"It does," said Vyse, who was examining the sand on the floor.

Bill also looked down at the prints in the sand. "Some dog's been in here."

"No," said Vyse, thoughtfully. "Dogs won't come in here, and you can't make them. Also, there were no marks on the sand when I left the place and locked the door this afternoon. Queer, isn't it?"

"But the thing's a blank impossibility. Unless, of course, we are to suppose that—"

He did not finish his sentence, and, if he had finished it, it would not have been audible. A chorus of grunting, growling and squealing broke out almost from under his feet, and he sprang backwards. It lasted for a few seconds, and then died slowly away.

"Did you hear that?" Vyse asked quietly.

"I should rather think so."

"Good; then it was not subjective. What was it?"

"Only one kind of beast makes that row. Pigs, of course—a whole drove of them. It sounded like they were in here, close to us. But as they obviously are not, they must be outside."

"But they are not outside," said Vyse. "Come and see."

They hunted the plantation through and through with no result, and then locked the tower door and went back to the cottage. Bill said very little. He was not capable of much self-analysis, but he was conscious of a sudden dislike of Vyse. He was angry that he had ever put himself under an obligation to this man. He had wanted the money for a gambling debt, and he had already repaid it. Now he saw Vyse in the light of a man from whom one should accept a kindness. The strange experience that he had just been through filled him with a loathing far more than with fear or wonder. There was something unclean and diabolical about the whole thing that made a decent man reluctant to question or investigate. The filthy smell of the brutes seemed still to linger in his nostrils. He was determined that on no account would he enter the tower again, and that as soon as he could find a decent excuse he would leave the place altogether.

A little later, as he sat before the log fire and filled his pipe, he turned to his host with a sudden question: "I say, Vyse, why did you want me to come down here? What's the meaning of it all?"

"My dear fellow," said Vyse, "I wanted you for the pleasure of your society. Now, don't get impatient. I also wanted you because you are the most normal man I know. Your confirmation of my experiences in the tower is most valuable to me. Also, you have good nerves, and, if you will forgive me for saying so, no imagination. I may want help that only a man with good nerves would be able to give."

"Why don't you leave that thing alone? It's too beastly."

Vyse laughed. "I'm afraid my hobby bores you. We won't talk about it. After all, there's no reason why you should help me?"

"Tell me just what it is you wanted."

"I wanted you if you heard this whistle"—he took an ordinary police whistle down from the mantelpiece—"any time tonight or tomorrow night, to come over to the tower at once and bring a revolver with you. The whistle would be a sign that I was in a tight place—that my life, in fact, was in danger. You see, we are dealing here with something preternatural, but it is also something material; in addition to other risks, one risks ordinary physical destruction. However, I could see that you were repelled by the sight and sound of those beasts, whatever they may be; and I can tell you from my own experience that the touch of them is even worse. There is no reason why you should bother yourself any further about the thing."

"You can take the whistle with you," said Bill. "If I hear it I will come."

"Thanks," said Vyse, and immediately changed the subject. He did not say why he was spending the night in the tower, or what it was he proposed to do there.

It was three in the morning when Bill was suddenly startled out of his sleep. He heard the whistle being blown repeatedly. He hurried on some clothes and dashed down into the hall, where his lantern lay all ready for him. He ran along the garden path and through the door in the wall until he got to the tower. The sound of the whistle had ceased now, and everything was horribly still. The door of the tower stood wide open, and without hesitation Bill entered, holding his lantern high.

The tower was absolutely empty. Not a sound was to be heard. Bill called Vyse by name twice loudly, and then again the awful silence spread over the place.

Then, as if guided by some unseen hand, he took the track that led to the quarry, well knowing what he would find at the bottom of it.

The jury assigned the death of Vyse as an accident, and said that the quarry should be fenced in. They had no explanation to offer of the mutilation of the face, as if by the teeth of some savage beast.

The Tragedy at the "Loup Noir"

Gladys Stern

The boy at the corner of the table flicked the ash of his cigar into the fire.

"Spiritualism is all rot!" he declared.

"I don't know," the host reflected thoughtfully. "One hears queer stories sometimes."

"Which reminds me—" started the Bore.

But before he could proceed any further the little French Judge ruthlessly cut him short.

"Bah!" Contempt and geniality were mingled in his tone. "Who are we, poor ignorant worms, that we should dare to say 'is' or 'is not'? Your Shakespeare, he was right! 'There are more things in heaven and earth, Horatio, than are dreamt of in your philosophy!' "

The faces of the four Englishmen instantly assumed that peculiarly stolid expression always called forth by the mention of Shakespeare.

"But Spiritualism—" started the host.

Again the little French Judge broke in:

"I who you speak, I myself know of an experience, of the most remarkable, to this day unexplained save by Spiritualism, Occultism, what you will! You shall hear! The case is one I conducted professionally some two years ago, though, of course, the events which I now tell in their proper sequence, came out only in the trial. I string them together for you, yes?"

The Bore, who fiercely resented any stories except his own, gave vent to a discontented grunt; the other three prepared to listen carefully. From the drawing-room, whither the ladies had retired after dinner, sounded the faraway strains of a piano. The little French Judge held out his glass for a crème de menthe; his eyes were sparkling with suppressed excitement; he gazed deep into the shining green liquid as if seeing therein a moving panorama of pictures, then he began:

On a dusky autumn evening, a young man, tall, olive-skinned, tramps along the road leading from Paris to Longchamps. He is walking with a quick, even swing. Now and again a hidden anxiety darkens his face.

Suddenly he branches off to the left; the path here is steep and muddy. He stops in front of a blurred circle of yellow light; by this can one faintly perceive the outlines of a building. Above the narrow doorway hangs a creaking sign which announces to all it may concern that this is the "Loup Noir," much sought after for its nearness to the racecourse and for its excellent *ménage*.

"*Voilà*!" mutters our friend.

On entering, he is met by the burly innkeeper, a shrewd enough fellow, who has seen something of life before settling down in Longchamps. The young man glances past him as if seeking some other face, then recollecting himself demands shelter for the night.

"I greatly fear—" began the innkeeper, then pauses, struck by an idea. "Holà, Gaston! Have monsieur and madame from number fourteen yet departed?"

"Yes, monsieur; already early this morning; you were at the market, so Mademoiselle settled the bill."

"Mademoiselle Jehane?" the stranger looks up sharply.

"My niece, monsieur; you have perhaps heard of her, for I see by your easel you are an artist. She is supposed to be of a rare beauty; I think it myself." Jean Potin keeps up a running flow of talk as he conducts his visitor down the long bare passages, past blistered yellow doors.

"It is a double room I must give you, vacated, as you heard, but this very morning. They were going to stay longer, Monsieur and Madame Guillaumet, but of a sudden she changed her mind. Oh, she was of a temper!" Potin raises expressive eyes heavenwards. "It is ever so when May weds with December."

"He was much older than his wife, then?" queries the artist, politely feigning an interest he is far from feeling.

"*Mais non, parbleu*! It was she who was the older—by some fifteen years; and not a beauty. But rich—he knew what he was about, giving his smooth cheek for her smooth louis!"

Left alone, Lou Arnaud proceeds to unpack his knapsack; he lingers over it as long as possible; the task awaiting him below is no pleasant one. Finally he descends. The small smoky *salle à manger* is full of people. There is much talk and laughter going on; the clatter of knives and forks. At the desk near the door, a young girl is busy with the accounts. Her very pale gold hair, parted and drawn loosely back over the ears, casts a faint shadow on her pure, white skin. Arnaud, as he chooses a seat, looks at her critically.

"Bah, she is insignificant!" he thinks. "What can have possessed Claude?"

Suddenly she raises her eyes. They meet his in a long, steady gaze. Then once again the lids are lowered.

The artist sets down his glass with a hand that shakes. He is not imaginative, as a rule, but when one sees the soul of a mocking devil look out, dark and compelling, from the face of a Madonna, one is disconcerted.

He wonders no more what had possessed Claude. On his way to the door a few moments later, he pauses at her desk.

"Monsieur wishes to order breakfast for to-morrow morning?"

"Monsieur wishes to speak with you."

She smiles demurely. Many have wished to speak with her. Arnaud divines her thoughts.

"My name is Lou Arnaud!" he adds meaningly.

"Ah!" she ponders on this for an instant; then: "It is a warm night; if you will seat yourself at one of the little tables in the court yard at the back of the house, I will try to join you, when these pigs have finished feeding." She indicates with contempt the noisily eating crowd.

They sit long at that table, for the man has much to tell of his young brother Claude; of the ruin she has made of his life; of the little green devils that lurk in a glass of absinthe, and clutch their victim, and drag him down deeper, ever deeper, into the great, green abyss.

But she only laughs, this Jehane of the wanton eyes.

"But what do you want from me? I have no need of this Claude. He wearies me—now!"

Arnaud springs to his feet, catching her roughly by the wrist. He loves his young brother much. His voice is raised, attracting the notice of two or three groups who take coffee at the iron tables.

"You had need of him once. You never left him in peace till you had sucked him of all that makes life good. If I could—"

Jean Potin appears in the doorway.

"Jehane, what are you doing out here? You know I do not permit it that you speak with the visitors. Pardon her, monsieur, she is but a child."

"A child?" The artist's brow is black as thunder. "She has wrecked a life, this child you speak of!"

He strides past the amazed innkeeper, up the narrow flight of stairs, and down the passage to his room.

Sitting on the edge of the huge curtained four-poster bed, he ponders on the events of the evening.

But his thoughts are not all of Claude. That girl—that girl with her pale face and her pale hair, and eyes the grey of a storm cloud before it breaks, she haunts him! Her soft murmuring voice has stolen into his brain; he hears it in the drip, drip of the ram on the sill outside.

Soon heavy feet are heard trooping up the stairs; doors are heard to bang; cheery voices wish each other good-night. Then gradually the sounds die away. They keep early hours at the "Loup Noir"; it is not yet ten o'clock.

Still Arnaud remains sitting on the edge of the bed; the dark plush canopy overhead repels him, he does not feel inclined for sleep, Jehane! what a picture she would make! He *must* paint her!

Obsessed by this idea, he unpacks a roll of canvas, spreads it on the tripod easel, and prepares crayons and charcoal; he will start the picture as soon as it is day. He will paint her as Circe, mocking at her grovelling herd of swine!

He creeps into bed and falls asleep.

Softly the rain patters against the window-pane.

A distant clock booms out eleven strokes.

Lou Arnaud raises his head. Then noiselessly he slides out of bed on the chill wooden boarding. As in a trance he crosses the room, seizes charcoal, and feverishly works at the blank canvas on the easel.

For twenty minutes his hand never falters, then the charcoal drops from his nerveless fingers! Groping his way with half-closed eyes back to the bed, he falls again into a heavy, dreamless slumber.

The early morning sun chases away the raindrops of the night before. Signs of activity are abroad in the inn; the swish of brooms; the noisy clatter of pails. A warm aroma of coffee floats up the stairs and under the door of number fourteen, awaking Arnaud to pleasant thoughts of breakfast. He is partly dressed before his eye lights on the canvas he had pre pared.

"*Nom de Dieu*!"

He falls back against the wall, staring stupefied at the picture before him. It is the picture of a girl, crouching in a kneeling position, all the agony of death showing clearly in her up turned eyes. At her throat, cruelly, relentlessly doing their murderous work, are a pair of hands—ugly, podgy hands, but with what power behind them!

The face is the face of Jehane—a distorted, terrified Jehane! Arnaud recoils, covering his eyes with his hands. Who could have drawn this unspeakable thing? He looks again closely; the style is his own! There is no mistaking those bold, black lines, that peculiar way of indicating muscle beneath the tightly stretched skin—it *is* his own work! Anywhere would he have known it!

A knock at the door! Jean Potin enters, radiating cheerfulness.

"Breakfast in your room, monsieur? We are busy this morning; I share in the work. Permit me to move the table and the easel—*Sacré-bleu*!"

Suddenly his rosy lips grow stern. "This is Jehane. Did she sit for you and when? You only came last night. What devil's work is this?"

"That is what I would like to find out; I know no more about it than you yourself. When I awoke this morning the picture was there!"

"Did you draw it?" Potin asks suspiciously.

"Yes. At least, no! Yes, I suppose I did. But I—"

Potin clenches his fist: "I will have the truth from the girl herself! There is something here I do not like!" Roughly he pushes past the artist and mounts to Jehane's room.

She is not there, neither is she at her desk. Nor yet down in the village. They search everywhere; there is a hue and cry; people rush to and fro.

Then suddenly a shout; and a silence, a dreadful silence.

Something is carried slowly into the "Loup Noir." Something that was found huddled up in the shadow of the wall that borders the court yard. Something with ugly purple patches on the white throat.

It is Jehane, and she is dead; strangled by a pair of hands that came from behind.

The story of the picture is rapidly passed from mouth to mouth. People look strangely at Lou Arnaud; they remember his loud, strained voice and threatening gestures on the preceding night.

Finally he is arrested on the charge of murder.

I was the judge, gentlemen, on the occasion of the Arnaud trial.

The prisoner is questioned about the picture. He knows nothing; can tell nothing of how it came there. His fellow-artists testify to its being his work. From them also leaks out the tale of his brother Claude, of the latter's infatuation and ruin. No need now to explain the quarrel in the courtyard. The accused has good reason to hate the dead girl.

The Avocat for the defence does his best. The picture is produced in court: it creates a sensation.

If only Lou Arnaud could complete it—could sketch in the owner of those merciless hands. He is handed the charcoal; again and again he tries—in vain.

The hands are not his own; but that is a small point in his favour. Why should he have incriminated himself by drawing his own hands? But again, why should he have drawn the picture at all?

There is nobody else on whom falls a shadow of suspicion. I sum up impartially. The jury convict on circumstantial evidence, and I sentence the prisoner to death.

A short time must elapse between the sentence and carrying it into force. The Avocat for the defence obtains for the prisoner a slight concession; he may have picture and charcoal in his cell. Perhaps he can yet free himself from the web which has inmeshed him!

Arnaud tries to blot out thought by sketching in and erasing again fanciful figures twisted into a peculiar position; he cannot adjust the pose of the unknown murderer. So in despair he gives it up.

One morning, three days before the execution, the innkeeper comes to visit him and finds him lying face downwards on the narrow pallet. Despite his own grief, he is sorry for the young man; nor is he convinced in his shrewd bourgeois mind of the latter's guilt.

"You *must* draw in the second figure," he repeats again and again. "It is your last, your only chance! Think of the faces you saw at the 'Loup Noir.' Do none of them recall anything to you? You quarrelled with Jehane in the garden about your brother. Then you went to your room. Oh, what did you think in your room?"

"I thought of your niece," responds Arnaud wildly. "How very beautiful she was, and what a model she would make. Then I prepared a blank canvas for the morning, and went to bed. When I woke up the picture was there."

"And you remember nothing more—nothing at all?" insists Jean Potin. "You fell asleep at once? You heard no sound?"

Against the barred window of the cell the rain patters softly. A distant clock booms out eleven strokes.

Something in the artist's brain seems to snap. He raises his head. He slides from the bed. As in a trance he crosses the cell, seizes a piece of charcoal, and feverishly works at the picture on the easel!

Not daring to speak, Jean Potin watches him. The figure behind the hands grows and grows beneath Arnaud's fingers.

A woman's figure!

Then the face: a coarse, malignant face, distorted by evil passions.

"Ah!"

It is a cry of recognition from the breathless innkeeper. It breaks the spell. The charcoal drops, and the prisoner, passing his hand across his eyes, gazes bewildered at his own work.

"Who? What?"

"But I know her! It is the woman in whose room you slept! She was staying at the 'Loup Noir' the very night before you arrived, and she left that morning. She and her husband, Monsieur Guillaumet. But it is incredible if *she* should have—"

I will be short with you, gentlemen. Madame Guillaumet was traced to her flat in Paris. Arnaud's Avocat confronted her with the now completed picture. She was confounded—babbled like a mad woman—confessed!

A reprieve for further inquiry was granted by the State. Finally Arnaud was cleared, and allowed to go free.

The motive for the murder? A woman's jealousy. Monsieur and Madame Guillaumet had been married only ten months. Her age was forty-nine; his twenty-seven. Every second of their married life was to her weighted with intolerable suspicions; how soon would this young husband, so dear to her, forsake her for another, now that his debts were paid? It preyed upon her mind, distorting it, unbalancing it; each glance, each movement of his she exaggerated into an intrigue.

On their way to Paris they stayed a few days at the "Loup Noir"; Charles Guillaumet was interested in racing. Also, he became interested in a certain Mdlle. Jehane. Madame, quick to see, insisted on an instant departure.

The evening of the day of their departure she missed her husband, and found he had taken the car. Where should he have gone? Back to the inn, of course, only half-an-hour's run from Paris. She hired another car and followed him, driving it herself. It was not a pleasant journey. The first car she discovered forsaken, about half-a-mile distant from the inn. Her own car she left beside it, and trudged the remaining distance on foot.

The rest was easy.

Finding no sign of Guillaumet in front of the house, she stole round to the back. There she found a door in the wall of the courtyard a door that led into the lane. That door was slightly ajar. She slipped in and crouched down in the shadow.

Yes, there they were, her husband and Jehane; the latter was laughing, luring him on and she was young; oh, so young!

The woman watched, fascinated.

Charles bade Jehane good-bye, promising to come again. He kissed her tenderly, passed through the gate; his steps were heard muffled along the lane.

Jehane blew him a kiss, and then fastened the little door.

A distant clock boomed out eleven strokes, and a pair of hands stole round the girl's throat, burying themselves deep, deep in the white flesh.

"And the husband, was he an accessory after the fact?" inquired the Boy.

"Possibly he guessed at the deed, yes; but, being a weakling, said nothing for fear of implicating himself. It wasn't proved."

The Host moved uneasily in his chair.

"Do you mean to tell me that the mystery of the picture has never been cleared up?" he asked. "Could Arnaud have actually seen the murder from his window, and fixed it on the canvas?"

The little French Judge shook his head.

"Did I not tell you that his window faced front?" he replied. "No, that point has not yet been explained. It is beyond us!"

He made a sweeping gesture, knocking over his liqueur glass; it fell with a crash on the parquet floor.

The Bore woke with a start.

"And did they marry?" he queried,

"Who should marry?"

"That artist-chap and the girl—what was her name?—Jehane."

"Monsieur," quoth the little French Judge very gently and ironically, "I grieve to state that was impossible, Jehane being dead."

The Boy at the corner of the table stood up and threw the stump of his cigar into the fire.

"I think Spiritualism is all rot!" he declared.

The Trial for Murder

Charles Dickens

I have always noticed a prevalent want of courage, even among persons of superior intelligence and culture, as to imparting their own psychological experiences when those have been of a strange sort. Almost all men are afraid that what they could relate in such wise would find no parallel or response in a listener's internal life, and might be suspected or laughed at. A truthful traveller, who should have seen some extraordinary creature in the likeness of a sea-serpent, would have no fear of mentioning it; but the same traveller, having had some singular presentiment, impulse, vagary of thought, vision (so-called), dream, or other remarkable mental impression, would hesitate considerably before he would own to it. To this reticence I attribute much of the obscurity in which such subjects are involved. We do not habitually communicate our experiences of these subjective things as we do our experiences of objective creation. The consequence is, that the general stock of experience in this regard appears exceptional, and really is so, in respect of being miserably imperfect.

In what I am going to relate, I have no intention of setting up, opposing, or supporting, any theory whatever. I know the history of the Bookseller of Berlin, I have studied the case of the wife of a late Astronomer Royal as related by Sir David Brewster, and I have followed the minutest details of a much more remarkable case of Spectral Illusion occurring within my private circle of friends. It may be necessary to state as to this last, that the sufferer (a lady) was in no degree, however distant, related to me. A mistaken assumption on that head might suggest an explanation of a part of my own case,—but only a part,—which would be wholly without foundation. It cannot be referred to my inheritance of any developed peculiarity, nor had I ever before any at all similar experience, nor have I ever had any at all similar experience since.

It does not signify how many years ago, or how few, a certain murder was committed in England, which attracted great attention. We hear more than enough of murderers as they rise in succession to their atrocious eminence, and I would bury the memory of this particular brute, if I could, as his body was buried, in Newgate Jail. I purposely abstain from giving any direct clue to the criminal's individuality.

When the murder was first discovered, no suspicion fell—or I ought rather to say, for I cannot be too precise in my facts, it was nowhere publicly hinted that any suspicion fell—on the man who was afterwards brought to trial. As no reference was at that time made to him in the newspapers, it is obviously impossible that any description of him can at that time have been given in the newspapers. It is essential that this fact be remembered.

Unfolding at breakfast my morning paper, containing the account of that first discovery, I found it to be deeply interesting, and I read it with close attention. I read it twice, if not three times. The discovery had been made in a bedroom, and, when I laid down the paper, I was aware of a flash—rush—flow—I do not know what to call it,—no word I can find is satisfactorily descriptive,—in which I seemed to see that bedroom passing through my room, like a picture impossibly painted on a running river. Though almost instantaneous in its passing, it was perfectly clear; so clear that I distinctly, and with a sense of relief, observed the absence of the dead body from the bed.

It was in no romantic place that I had this curious sensation, but in chambers in Piccadilly, very near to the corner of St. James's Street. It was entirely new to me. I was in my easy-chair at the moment, and the sensation was accompanied with a peculiar shiver which started the chair from its position. (But it is to be noted that the chair ran easily on castors.) I went to one of the windows (there are two in the room, and the room is on the second floor) to refresh my eyes with the moving objects down in Piccadilly. It was a bright autumn morning, and the street was sparkling and cheerful. The wind was high. As I looked out, it brought down from the Park a quantity of fallen leaves, which a gust took, and whirled into a spiral pillar. As the pillar fell and the leaves dispersed, I saw two men on the opposite side of the way, going from West to East. They were one behind the other. The foremost man often looked back over his shoulder. The second man followed him, at a distance of some thirty paces, with his right hand menacingly raised. First, the singularity and steadiness of this threatening gesture in so public a thoroughfare attracted my attention; and next, the more remarkable circumstance that nobody heeded it. Both men threaded their way among the other passengers with a smoothness hardly consistent even with the action of walking on a pavement; and no single creature, that I could see, gave them place, touched them, or looked after them. In passing before my windows, they both stared up at me. I saw their two faces very distinctly, and I knew that I could recognise them anywhere. Not that I had consciously noticed anything very remarkable in either face, except that the man who went first had an unusually lowering appearance, and that the face of the man who followed him was of the colour of impure wax.

I am a bachelor, and my valet and his wife constitute my whole establishment. My occupation is in a certain Branch Bank, and I wish that my duties as head of a Department were as light as they are popularly supposed to be. They kept me in town that autumn, when I stood in need of change. I was not ill, but I was not well. My reader is to make the most that can be reasonably made of my feeling jaded, having a depressing sense upon me of a monotonous life, and being "slightly dyspeptic." I am assured by my renowned doctor that my real state of health at that time justifies no stronger description, and I quote his own from his written answer to my request for it.

As the circumstances of the murder, gradually unravelling, took stronger and stronger possession of the public mind, I kept them away from mine by knowing as little about them as was possible in the midst of the universal excitement. But I knew that a verdict of Wilful Murder had been found against the suspected murderer, and that he had been committed to Newgate for trial. I also knew that his trial had been postponed over one Sessions of the Central Criminal Court, on the ground of general prejudice and want of time for the preparation of the defence. I may further have known, but I believe I did not, when, or about when, the Sessions to which his trial stood postponed would come on.

My sitting-room, bedroom, and dressing-room, are all on one floor. With the last there is no communication but through the bedroom. True, there is a door in it, once communicating with the staircase; but a part of the fitting of my bath has been—and had then been for some years—fixed across it. At the same period, and as a part of the same arrangement,—the door had been nailed up and canvased over.

I was standing in my bedroom late one night, giving some directions to my servant before he went to bed. My face was towards the only available door of communication with the dressing-room, and it was closed. My servant's back was towards that door. While I was speaking to him, I saw it open, and a man look in, who very earnestly and mysteriously beckoned to me. That man was the man who had gone second of the two along Piccadilly, and whose face was of the colour of impure wax.

The figure, having beckoned, drew back, and closed the door. With no longer pause than was made by my crossing the bedroom, I opened the dressing-room door, and looked in. I had a lighted candle already in my hand. I felt no inward expectation of seeing the figure in the dressing-room, and I did not see it there.

Conscious that my servant stood amazed, I turned round to him, and said: "Derrick, could you believe that in my cool senses I fancied I saw a—" As I there laid my hand upon his breast, with a sudden start he trembled violently, and said, "O Lord, yes, sir! A dead man beckoning!"

Now I do not believe that this John Derrick, my trusty and attached servant for more than twenty years, had any impression whatever of having seen any such figure, until I touched him. The change in him was so startling, when I touched him, that I fully believe he derived his impression in some occult manner from me at that instant.

I bade John Derrick bring some brandy, and I gave him a dram, and was glad to take one myself. Of what had preceded that night's phenomenon, I told him not a single word. Reflecting on it, I was absolutely certain that I had never seen that face before, except on the one occasion in Piccadilly. Comparing its expression when beckoning at the door with its expression when it had stared up at me as I stood at my window, I came to the conclusion that on the first occasion it had sought to fasten itself upon my memory, and that on the second occasion it had made sure of being immediately remembered.

I was not very comfortable that night, though I felt a certainty, difficult to explain, that the figure would not return. At daylight I fell into a heavy sleep, from which I was awakened by John Derrick's coming to my bedside with a paper in his hand.

This paper, it appeared, had been the subject of an altercation at the door between its bearer and my servant. It was a summons to me to serve upon a Jury at the forthcoming Sessions of the Central Criminal Court at the Old Bailey. I had never before been summoned on such a Jury, as John Derrick well knew. He believed—I am not certain at this hour whether with reason or otherwise—that that class of Jurors were customarily chosen on a lower qualification than mine, and he had at first refused to accept the summons. The man who served it had taken the matter very coolly. He had said that my attendance or non-attendance was nothing to him; there the summons was; and I should deal with it at my own peril, and not at his.

For a day or two I was undecided whether to respond to this call, or take no notice of it. I was not conscious of the slightest mysterious bias, influence, or attraction, one way or other. Of that I am as strictly sure as of every other statement that I make here. Ultimately I decided, as a break in the monotony of my life, that I would go.

The appointed morning was a raw morning in the month of November. There was a dense brown fog in Piccadilly, and it became positively black and in the last degree oppressive East of Temple Bar. I found the passages and staircases of the

Court-House flaringly lighted with gas, and the Court itself similarly illuminated. I think that, until I was conducted by officers into the Old Court and saw its crowded state, I did not know that the Murderer was to be tried that day. I think that, until I was so helped into the Old Court with considerable difficulty, I did not know into which of the two Courts sitting my summons would take me. But this must not be received as a positive assertion, for I am not completely satisfied in my mind on either point.

I took my seat in the place appropriated to Jurors in waiting, and I looked about the Court as well as I could through the cloud of fog and breath that was heavy in it. I noticed the black vapour hanging like a murky curtain outside the great windows, and I noticed the stifled sound of wheels on the straw or tan that was littered in the street; also, the hum of the people gathered there, which a shrill whistle, or a louder song or hail than the rest, occasionally pierced. Soon afterwards the Judges, two in number, entered, and took their seats. The buzz in the Court was awfully hushed. The direction was given to put the Murderer to the bar. He appeared there. And in that same instant I recognised in him the first of the two men who had gone down Piccadilly.

If my name had been called then, I doubt if I could have answered to it audibly. But it was called about sixth or eighth in the panel, and I was by that time able to say, "Here!" Now, observe. As I stepped into the box, the prisoner, who had been looking on attentively, but with no sign of concern, became violently agitated, and beckoned to his attorney. The prisoner's wish to challenge me was so manifest, that it occasioned a pause, during which the attorney, with his hand upon the dock, whispered with his client, and shook his head. I afterwards had it from that gentleman, that the prisoner's first affrighted words to him were, "At all hazards challenge that man!" But that, as he would give no reason for it, and admitted that he had not even known my name until he heard it called and I appeared, it was not done.

Both on the ground already explained, that I wish to avoid reviving the unwholesome memory of that Murderer, and also because a detailed account of his long trial is by no means indispensable to my narrative, I shall confine myself closely to such incidents in the ten days and nights during which we, the Jury, were kept together, as directly bear on my own curious personal experience. It is in that, and not in the Murderer, that I seek to interest my reader. It is to that, and not to a page of the Newgate Calendar, that I beg attention.

I was chosen Foreman of the Jury. On the second morning of the trial, after evidence had been taken for two hours (I heard the church clocks strike), happening to cast my eyes over my brother jurymen, I found an inexplicable difficulty in counting them. I counted them several times, yet always with the same difficulty. In short, I made them one too many.

I touched the brother jurymen whose place was next me, and I whispered to him, "Oblige me by counting us." He looked surprised by the request, but turned his head and counted. "Why," says he, suddenly, "we are thirt—; but no, it's not possible. No. We are twelve."

According to my counting that day, we were always right in detail, but in the gross we were always one too many. There was no appearance—no figure—to account for it; but I had now an inward foreshadowing of the figure that was surely coming.

The Jury were housed at the London Tavern. We all slept in one large room on separate tables, and we were constantly in the charge and under the eye of the officer sworn to hold us in safe-keeping. I see no reason for suppressing the real name of that officer. He was intelligent, highly polite, and obliging, and (I was glad to hear) much respected in the City. He had an agreeable presence, good eyes, enviable black whiskers, and a fine sonorous voice. His name was Mr. Harker.

When we turned into our twelve beds at night, Mr. Harker's bed was drawn across the door. On the night of the second day, not being disposed to lie down, and seeing Mr. Harker sitting on his bed, I went and sat beside him, and offered him a pinch of snuff. As Mr. Harker's hand touched mine in taking it from my box, a peculiar shiver crossed him, and he said, "Who is this?"

Following Mr. Harker's eyes, and looking along the room, I saw again the figure I expected,—the second of the two men who had gone down Piccadilly. I rose, and advanced a few steps; then stopped, and looked round at Mr. Harker. He was quite unconcerned, laughed, and said in a pleasant way, "I thought for a moment we had a thirteenth juryman, without a bed. But I see it is the moonlight."

Making no revelation to Mr. Harker, but inviting him to take a walk with me to the end of the room, I watched what the figure did. It stood for a few moments by the bedside of each of my eleven brother jurymen, close to the pillow. It always went to the right-hand side of the bed, and always passed out crossing the foot of the next bed. It seemed, from the action of the head, merely to look down pensively at each recumbent figure. It took no notice of me, or of my bed, which was that nearest to Mr. Harker's. It seemed to go out where the moonlight came in, through a high window, as by an aerial flight of stairs.

Next morning at breakfast, it appeared that everybody present had dreamed of the murdered man last night, except myself and Mr. Harker.

I now felt as convinced that the second man who had gone down Piccadilly was the murdered man (so to speak), as if it had been borne into my comprehension by his immediate testimony. But even this took place, and in a manner for which I was not at all prepared.

On the fifth day of the trial, when the case for the prosecution was drawing to a close, a miniature of the murdered man, missing from his bedroom upon the discovery of the deed, and afterwards found in a hiding-place where the Murderer had been seen digging, was put in evidence. Having been identified by the witness under examination, it was handed up to the Bench, and thence handed down to be inspected by the Jury. As an officer in a black gown was making his way with it across to me, the figure of the second man who had gone down Piccadilly impetuously started from the crowd, caught the miniature from the officer, and gave it to me with his own hands, at the same time saying, in a low and hollow tone,—before I saw the miniature, which was in a locket,—"I wasyounger then, and my facewas not then drained of blood." It also came between me and the brother juryman to whom I would have given the miniature, and between him and the brother juryman to whom he would have given it, and so passed it on through the whole of our number, and back into my possession. Not one of them, however, detected this.

At table, and generally when we were shut up together in Mr. Harker's custody, we had from the first naturally discussed the day's proceedings a good deal. On that fifth day, the case for the prosecution being closed, and we having that side of the question in a completed shape before us, our discussion was more animated and serious. Among our number was a vestryman,—the densest idiot I have ever seen at large,—who met the plainest evidence with the most preposterous objections, and who was sided with by two flabby parochial parasites; all the three impanelled from a district so delivered over to Fever that they ought to have been upon their own trial for five hundred Murders. When these mischievous blockheads were at their loudest, which was towards midnight, while some of us were already preparing for bed, I again saw the murdered man. He stood grimly behind them, beckoning to me. On my going towards them, and striking into the conversation, he immediately retired. This was the beginning of a separate series of appearances, confined to that long room in which we were confined. Whenever a knot of my brother jurymen laid their heads together, I saw the head of the murdered man among theirs. Whenever their comparison of notes was going against him, he would solemnly and irresistibly beckon to me.

It will be borne in mind that down to the production of the miniature, on the fifth day of the trial, I had never seen the Appearance in Court. Three changes occurred now that we entered on the case for the defence. Two of them I will mention together, first. The figure was now in Court continually, and it never there addressed itself to me, but always to the person who was speaking at the time. For instance: the throat of the murdered man had been cut straight across. In the opening speech for the defence, it was suggested that the deceased might have cut his own throat. At that very moment, the figure, with its throat in the dreadful condition referred to (this it had concealed before), stood at the speaker's elbow, motioning across and across its windpipe, now with the right hand, now with the left, vigorously suggesting to the speaker himself the impossibility of such a wound having been self-inflicted by either hand. For another instance: a witness to character, a woman, deposed to the prisoner's being the most amiable of mankind. The figure at that instant stood on the floor before her, looking her full in the face, and pointing out the prisoner's evil countenance with an extended arm and an outstretched finger.

The third change now to be added impressed me strongly as the most marked and striking of all. I do not theorise upon it; I accurately state it, and there leave it. Although the Appearance was not itself perceived by those whom it addressed, its coming close to such persons was invariably attended by some trepidation or disturbance on their part. It seemed to me as if it were prevented, by laws to which I was not amenable, from fully revealing itself to others, and yet as if it could invisibly, dumbly, and darkly overshadow their minds. When the leading counsel for the defence suggested that hypothesis of suicide, and the figure stood at the learned gentleman's elbow, frightfully sawing at its severed throat, it is undeniable that the counsel faltered in his speech, lost for a few seconds the thread of his ingenious discourse, wiped his forehead with his handkerchief, and turned extremely pale. When the witness to character was confronted by the Appearance, her eyes most certainly did follow the direction of its pointed finger, and rest in great hesitation and trouble upon the prisoner's face. Two additional illustrations will suffice. On the eighth day of the trial, after the pause which was every day made early in the afternoon for a few minutes' rest and refreshment, I came back into Court with the rest of the Jury some little time before the return of the Judges. Standing up in the box and looking about me, I thought the figure was not there, until, chancing to raise my eyes to the gallery, I saw it bending forward, and leaning over a very decent woman, as if to assure itself whether the Judges had resumed their seats or not. Immediately afterwards that woman screamed, fainted, and was carried out. So with the venerable, sagacious, and patient Judge who conducted the trial. When the case was over, and he settled himself and his papers to sum up, the murdered man, entering by the Judges' door, advanced to his Lordship's desk, and looked eagerly over his shoulder at the pages of his notes which he was turning. A change came over his Lordship's face; his hand stopped; the peculiar shiver, that I knew so well, passed over him; he faltered, "Excuse me, gentlemen, for a few moments. I am somewhat oppressed by the vitiated air;" and did not recover until he had drunk a glass of water.

Through all the monotony of six of those interminable ten days,—the same Judges and others on the bench, the same Murderer in the dock, the same lawyers at the table, the same tones of question and answer rising to the roof of the court, the same scratching of the Judge's pen, the same ushers going in and out, the same lights kindled at the same hour when there had been any natural light of day, the same foggy curtain outside the great windows when it was foggy, the same rain pattering and dripping when it was rainy, the same footmarks of turnkeys and prisoner day after day on the same sawdust, the same keys locking and unlocking the same heavy doors,—through all the wearisome monotony which made me feel as if I had been Foreman of the Jury for a vast cried of time, and Piccadilly had flourished coevally with Babylon, the murdered man never lost one trace of his distinctness in my eyes, nor was he at any moment less distinct than anybody else. I must not omit, as a matter of fact, that I never once saw the Appearance which I call by the name of the murdered man look at the Murderer. Again and again I wondered, "Why does he not?" But he never did.

Nor did he look at me, after the production of the miniature, until the last closing minutes of the trial arrived. We retired to consider, at seven minutes before ten at night. The idiotic vestryman and his two parochial parasites gave us so much trouble that we twice returned into Court to beg to have certain extracts from the Judge's notes re-read. Nine of us had not the smallest doubt about those passages, neither, I believe, had any one in the Court; the dunder-headed triumvirate, having no idea but obstruction, disputed them for that very reason. At length we prevailed, and finally the Jury returned into Court at ten minutes past twelve.

The murdered man at that time stood directly opposite the Jury-box, on the other side of the Court. As I took my place, his eyes rested on me with great attention; he seemed satisfied, and slowly shook a great gray veil, which he carried on his arm for the first time, over his head and whole form. As I gave in our verdict, "Guilty," the veil collapsed, all was gone, and his place was empty.

The Murderer, being asked by the Judge, according to usage, whether he had anything to say before sentence of Death should be passed upon him, indistinctly muttered something which was described in the leading newspapers of the following day as "a few rambling, incoherent, and half-audible words, in which he was understood to complain that he had not had a fair trial, because the Foreman of the Jury was prepossessed against him." The remarkable declaration that he really made was this: "*My Lord, I knew I was a doomed man, when the Foreman of my Jury came into the box. My Lord, I knew he would never let me off, because, before I was taken, he somehow got to my bedside in the night, woke me, and put a rope around my neck.*"

THE VAMPIRE MAID

HUME NISBET

IT WAS THE EXACT KIND OF ABODE THAT I HAD BEEN LOOKING AFTER FOR WEEKS, FOR I was in that condition of mind when absolute renunciation of society was a necessity. I had become diffident of myself, and wearied of my kind. A strange unrest was in my blood; a barren dearth in my brains. Familiar objects and faces had grown distasteful to me. I wanted to be alone.

This is the mood which comes upon every sensitive and artistic mind when the possessor has been overworked or living too long in one groove. It is Nature's hint for him to seek pastures new; the sign that a retreat has become needful.

If he does not yield, he breaks down and becomes whimsical and hypochondriacal, as well as hypercritical. It is always a bad sign when a man becomes over-critical and censorious about his own or other people's work, for it means that he is losing the vital portions of work, freshness and enthusiasm.

Before I arrived at the dismal stage of criticism I hastily packed up my knapsack, and taking the train to Westmorland, I began my tramp in search of solitude, bracing air and romantic surroundings.

Many places I came upon during that early summer wandering that appeared to have almost the required conditions, yet some petty drawback prevented me from deciding. Sometimes it was the scenery that I did not take kindly to. At other places I took sudden antipathies to the landlady or landlord, and felt I would abhor them before a week was spent under their charge. Other places which might have suited me I could not have, as they did not want a lodger. Fate was driving me to this Cottage on the Moor, and no one can resist destiny.

One day I found myself on a wide and pathless moor near the sea. I had slept the night before at a small hamlet, but that was already eight miles in my rear, and since I had turned my back upon it I had not seen any signs of humanity; I was alone with a fair sky above me, a balmy ozone-filled wind blowing over the stony and heather-clad mounds, and nothing to disturb my meditations.

How far the moor stretched I had no knowledge; I only knew that by keeping in a straight line I would come to the ocean cliffs, then perhaps after a time arrive at some fishing village.

I had provisions in my knapsack, and being young did not fear a night under the stars. I was inhaling the delicious summer air and once more getting back the vigour and happiness I had lost; my city-dried brains were again becoming juicy.

Thus hour after hour slid past me, with the paces, until I had covered about fifteen miles since morning, when I saw before me in the distance a solitary stone-built cottage with roughly slated roof. "I'll camp there if possible," I said to myself as I quickened my steps towards it.

To one in search of a quiet, free life, nothing could have possibly been more suitable than this cottage. It stood on the edge of lofty cliffs, with its front door facing the moor and the back-yard wall overlooking the ocean. The sound of the dancing waves struck upon my ears like a lullaby as I drew near; how they would thunder when the autumn gales came on and the seabirds fled shrieking to the shelter of the sedges.

A small garden spread in front, surrounded by a dry-stone wall just high enough for one to lean lazily upon when inclined. This garden was a flame of color, scarlet predominating, with those other soft shades that cultivated poppies take on in their blooming, for this was all that the garden grew.

As I approached, taking notice of this singular assortment of poppies, and the orderly cleanness of the windows, the front door opened and a woman appeared who impressed me at once favourably as she leisurely came along the pathway to the gate, and drew it back as if to welcome me.

She was of middle age, and when young must have been remarkably good-looking. She was tall and still shapely, with smooth clear skin, regular features and a calm expression that at once gave me a sensation of rest.

To my inquiries she said that she could give me both a sitting and bedroom, and invited me inside to see them. As I looked at her smooth black hair, and cool brown eyes, I felt that I would not be too particular about the accommodation. With such a landlady, I was sure to find what I was after here.

The rooms surpassed my expectation, dainty white curtains and bedding with the perfume of lavender about them, a sitting-room homely yet cosy without being crowded. With a sigh of infinite relief I flung down my knapsack and clinched the bargain.

She was a widow with one daughter, whom I did not see the first day, as she was unwell and confined to her own room, but on the next day she was somewhat better, and then we met.

The fare was simple, yet it suited me exactly for the time, delicious milk and butter with home-made scones, fresh eggs and bacon; after a hearty tea I went early to bed in a condition of perfect content with my quarters.

Yet happy and tired out as I was I had by no means a comfortable night. This I put down to the strange bed. I slept certainly, but my sleep was filled with dreams so that I woke late and unrefreshed; a good walk on the moor, however, restored me, and I returned with a fine appetite for breakfast.

Certain conditions of mind, with aggravating circumstances, are required before even a young man can fall in love at first sight, as Shakespeare has shown in his Romeo and Juliet. In the city, where many fair faces passed me every hour, I had remained like a stoic, yet no sooner did I enter the cottage after that morning walk than I succumbed instantly before the weird charms of my landlady's daughter, Ariadne Brunnell.

She was somewhat better this morning and able to meet me at breakfast, for we had our meals together while I was their lodger. Ariadne was not beautiful in the strictly classical sense, her complexion being too lividly white and her expression too set to be quite pleasant at first sight; yet, as her mother had informed me, she had been ill for some time, which accounted for that defect. Her features were not regular, her hair and eyes seemed too black with that strangely white skin, and her lips too red for any except the decadent harmonies of an Aubrey Beardsley.

Yet my fantastic dreams of the preceding night, with my morning walk, had prepared me to be enthralled by this modern poster-like invalid.

The loneliness of the moor, with the singing of the ocean, had gripped my heart with a wistful longing. The incongruity of those flaunting and evanescent poppy flowers, dashing the giddy tints in the face of that sober heath, touched me with a shiver as I approached the cottage, and lastly that weird embodiment of startling contrasts completed my subjugation.

She rose from her chair as her mother introduced her, and smiled while she held out her hand. I clasped that soft snowflake, and as I did so a faint thrill tingled over me and rested on my heart, stopping for the moment its beating.

This contact seemed also to have affected her as it did me; a clear flush, like a white flame, lighted up her face, so that it glowed as if an alabaster lamp had been lit; her black eyes became softer and more humid as our glances crossed, and her scarlet lips grew moist. She was a living woman now, while before she had seemed half a corpse.

She permitted her white slender hand to remain in mine longer than most people do at an introduction, and then she slowly withdrew it, still regarding me with steadfast eyes for a second or two afterwards.

Fathomless velvety eyes these were, yet before they were shifted from mine they appeared to have absorbed all my willpower and made me her abject slave. They looked like deep dark pools of clear water, yet they filled me with fire and deprived me of strength. I sank into my chair almost as languidly as I had risen from my bed that morning.

Yet I made a good breakfast, and although she hardly tasted anything, this strange girl rose much refreshed and with a slight glow of color on her cheeks, which improved her so greatly that she appeared younger and almost beautiful.

I had come here seeking solitude, but since I had seen Ariadne it seemed as if I had come for her only. She was not very lively; indeed, thinking back, I cannot recall any spontaneous remark of hers; she answered my questions by monosyllables and left me to lead in words; yet she was insinuating and appeared to lead my thoughts in her direction and speak to me with her eyes. I cannot describe her minutely, I only know that from the first glance and touch she gave me I was bewitched and could think of nothing else.

It was a rapid, distracting, and devouring infatuation that possessed me; all day long I followed her about like a dog, every night I dreamed of that white glowing face, those steadfast black eyes, those moist scarlet lips, and each morning I rose more languid than I had been the day before. Sometimes I dreamt that she was kissing me with those red lips, while I shivered at the contact of her silky black tresses as they covered my throat; sometimes that we were floating in the air, her arms about me and her long hair enveloping us both like an inky cloud, while I lay supine and helpless.

She went with me after breakfast on that first day to the moor, and before we came back I had spoken my love and received her assent. I held her in my arms and had taken her kisses in answer to mine, nor did I think it strange that all this had happened so quickly. She was mine, or rather I was hers, without a pause. I told her it was fate that had sent me to her, for I had no doubts about my love, and she replied that I had restored her to life.

Acting upon Ariadne's advice, and also from a natural shyness, I did not inform her mother how quickly matters had progressed between us, yet although we both acted as circumspectly as possible, I had no doubt Mrs. Brunnell could see how engrossed we were in each other. Lovers are not unlike ostriches in their modes of concealment. I was not afraid of asking Mrs. Brunnell for her daughter, for she already showed her partiality towards me, and had bestowed upon me some confidences regarding her own position in life, and I therefore knew that, so far as social position was concerned, there could be no real objection to our marriage. They lived in this lonely spot for the sake of their health, and kept no servant because they could not get any to take service so far away from other humanity. My coming had been opportune and welcome to both mother and daughter.

For the sake of decorum, however, I resolved to delay my confession for a week or two and trust to some favourable opportunity of doing it discreetly.

Meantime Ariadne and I passed our time in a thoroughly idle and lotus-eating style. Each night I retired to bed meditating starting work next day, each morning I rose languid from those disturbing dreams with no thought for anything outside my love. She grew stronger every day, while I appeared to be taking her place as the invalid, yet I was more frantically in love than ever, and only happy when with her. She was my lone-star, my only joy—my life.

We did not go great distances, for I liked best to lie on the dry heath and watch her glowing face and intense eyes while I listened to the surging of the distant waves. It was love made me lazy, I thought, for unless a man has all he longs for beside him, he is apt to copy the domestic cat and bask in the sunshine.

I had been enchanted quickly. My disenchantment came as rapidly, although it was long before the poison left my blood.

One night, about a couple of weeks after my coming to the cottage, I had returned after a delicious moonlight walk with Ariadne. The night was warm and the moon at the full, therefore I left my bedroom window open to let in what little air there was.

I was more than usually fagged out, so that I had only strength enough to remove my boots and coat before I flung myself wearily on the coverlet and fell almost instantly asleep without tasting the nightcap draught that was constantly placed on the table, and which I had always drained thirstily.

I had a ghastly dream this night. I thought I saw a monster bat, with the face and tresses of Ariadne, fly into the open window and fasten its white teeth and scarlet lips on my arm. I tried to beat the horror away, but could not, for I seemed chained down and thralled also with drowsy delight as the beast sucked my blood with a gruesome rapture.

I looked out dreamily and saw a line of dead bodies of young men lying on the floor, each with a red mark on their arms, on the same part where the vampire was then sucking me, and I remembered having seen and wondered at such a mark on my own arm for the past fortnight. In a flash I understood the reason for my strange weakness, and at the same moment a sudden prick of pain roused me from my dreamy pleasure.

The vampire in her eagerness had bitten a little too deeply that night, unaware that I had not tasted the drugged draught. As I woke I saw her fully revealed by the midnight moon, with her black tresses flowing loosely, and with her red lips glued to my arm. With a shriek of horror I dashed her backwards, getting one last glimpse of her savage eyes, glowing white face and blood-stained red lips; then I rushed out to the night, moved on by my fear and hatred, nor did I pause in my mad flight until I had left miles between me and that accursed Cottage on the Moor.

The Vengeance of a Tree

Eleanor F. Lewis

Through the windows of Jim Daly's saloon, in the little town of C——, the setting sun streamed in yellow patches, lighting up the glasses scattered on the tables and the faces of several men who were gathered near the bar. Farmers mostly they were, with a sprinkling of shopkeepers, while prominent among them was the village editor, and all were discussing a startling piece of news that had spread through the town and its surroundings. The tidings that Walter Stedman, a laborer on Albert Kelsey's ranch, had assaulted and murdered his employer's daughter, had reached them, and had spread universal horror among the people.

A farmer declared that he had seen the deed committed as he walked through a neighboring lane, and, having always been noted for his cowardice, instead of running to the girl's aid, had hailed a party of miners who were returning from their midday meal through a field near by. When they reached the spot, however, where Stedman (as they supposed) had done his black deed, only the girl lay there, in the stillness of death. Her murderer had taken the opportunity to fly. The party had searched the woods of the Kelsey estate, and just as they were nearing the house itself the appearance of Walter Stedman, walking in a strangely unsteady manner toward it, made them quicken their pace.

He was soon in custody, although he had protested his innocence of the crime. He said that he had just seen the body himself on his way to the station, and that when they had found him he was going to the house for help. But they had laughed at his story and had flung him into the tiny, stifling calaboose of the town.

What were their proofs? Walter Stedman, a young fellow of about twenty-six, had come from the city to their quiet town, just when times were at their hardest, in search of work. The most of the men living in the town were honest fellows, doing their work faithfully, when they could get it, and when they had socially asked Stedman to have a drink with them, he had refused in rather a scornful manner. "That infernal city chap," he was called, and their hate and envy increased in strength when Albert Kelsey had employed him in preference to any of themselves. As time went on, the story of Stedman's admiration for Margaret Kelsey had gone afloat, with the added information that his employer's daughter had repulsed him, saying that she would not marry a common laborer. So Stedman, when this news reached his employer's ears, was discharged, and this, then, was his revenge! For them, these proofs were sufficient to pronounce him guilty.

Yet that afternoon, as Stedman, crouched on the floor of the calaboose, grew hopeless in the knowledge that no one would believe his story, and that his undeserved punishment would be swift and sure, a tramp, boarding a freight car several miles from the town, sped away from the spot where his crime had been committed, and knew that forever its shadow would follow him.

From the tiny window of his prison Walter Stedman could see the red glow of the heavens that betokened the setting of the sun. So the red sun of his life was soon to set, a life that had been innocent of all crime, and that now was to be ended for a deed that he had never committed. Most prominent of all the visions that swept through his mind was that of Margaret Kelsey, lying as he had first found her, fresh from the hands of her murderer. But there was another of a more tender nature. How long he and Margaret had tried to keep their secret, until Walter could be promoted to a higher position, so that he could ask for her hand with no fear of the father's antagonism! Then came the remembrance of an afternoon meeting between the two in the woods of the Kelsey estate—how, just as they were parting, Walter had heard footsteps near them, and, glancing sharply around, saw an evil, scowling, murderous face peering through the brush. He had started toward it, but the owner of the countenance had taken himself hurriedly off.

The gossiping townspeople had misconstrued this romance, and when Albert Kelsey had heard of this clandestine meeting from the man who was later on to appear as a leader of the mob, and that he had discharged Stedman, they had believed that the young man had formally proposed and had been rejected. But justice had gone wrong, as it had done innumerable times before, and will again. An innocent man was to be hanged, even without the comfort of a trial, while the man who was guilty was free to wander where he would.

That autumn night the darkness came quickly, and only the stars did their best to light the scene. A body of men, all masked, and having as a leader one who had ever since Stedman's arrival in town, cherished a secret hatred of the young man, dragged Stedman from the calaboose and tramped through the town, defying all, defying even God himself. Along the highway, and into Farmer Brown's "cross cut," they went, vigilantly guarding their prisoner, who, with the lanterns lighting up his haggard face, walked among them with the lagging step of utter hopelessness.

"That's a good tree," their leader said, presently, stopping and pointing out a spreading oak; when the slipknot was adjusted and Stedman had stepped on the box, he added: "If you've got anything to say, you'd better say it now."

"I am innocent, I swear before God," the doomed man answered; "I never took the life of Margaret Kelsey."

"Give us your proof," jeered the leader, and when Stedman kept a despairing silence, he laughed shortly.

"Ready, men!" he gave the order. The box was kicked aside, and then—only a writhing body swung to and fro in the gloom.

In front of the men stood their leader, watching the contortions of the body with silent glee. "I'll tell you a secret, boys," he said suddenly. "I was after that poor murdered girl myself. A d——little chance I had; but, by ——, he had just as little!"

A pause—then: "He's shunted this earth. Cut him down, you fellows!"

"It's no use, son. I'll give up the blasted thing as a bad job. There's something queer about that there tree. Do you see how its branches balance it? We have cut the trunk nearly in two, but it won't come down. There's plenty of others around; we'll take one of them. If I'd a long rope with me I'd get that tree down, and yet the way the thing stands it would be risking a fellow's life to climb it. It's got the devil in it, sure."

So old Farmer Brown shouldered his axe and made for another tree, his son following. They had sawed and chopped and chopped and sawed, and yet the tall white oak, with its branches jutting out almost as regularly as if done by the work of a machine, stood straight and firm.

Farmer Brown, well known for his weak, cowardly spirit, who in beholding the murder of Albert Kelsey's daughter, had in his fright mistaken the criminal, now in his superstition let the oak stand, because its well-balanced position saved it from falling, when other trees would have been down. And so this tree, the same one to which an innocent man had been hanged, was left—for other work.

It was a bleak, rainy night—such a night as can be found only in central California. The wind howled like a thousand demons, and lashed the trees together in wild embraces. Now and then the weird "hoot, hoot!" of an owl came softly from the distance in the lulls of the storm, while the barking of coyotes woke the echoes of the hills into sounds like fiendish laughter.

In the wind and rain a man fought his path through the bush and into Farmer Brown's "cross cut," as the shortest way home. Suddenly he stopped, trembling, as if held by some unseen impulse. Before him rose the white oak, wavering and swaying in the storm.

"Good God! it's the tree I swung Stedman from!" he cried, and a strange fear thrilled him.

His eyes were fixed on it, held by some undefinable fascination. Yes, there on one of the longest branches a small piece of rope still dangled. And then, to the murderer's excited vision, this rope seemed to lengthen, to form at the end into a slipknot, a knot that encircled a purple neck, while below it writhed and swayed the body of a man!

"Damn him!" he muttered, starting toward the hanging form, as if about to help the rope in its work of strangulation; "will he forever follow me? And yet he deserved it, the black-hearted villain! He took her life—"

He never finished the sentence. The white oak, towering above him in its strength, seemed to grow like a frenzied, living creature. There was a sudden splitting sound, then came a crash, and under the fallen tree lay Stedman's murderer, crushed and mangled.

From between the broken trunk and the stump that was left, a gray, dim shape sprang out, and sped past the man's still form, away into the wild blackness of the night.

Was It a Dream?

Guy de Maupassant

I had loved her madly!

Why does one love? Why does one love? How queer it is to see only one being in the world, to have only one thought in one's mind, only one desire in the heart, and only one name on the lips—a name which comes up continually, rising, like the water in a spring, from the depths of the soul to the lips, a name which one repeats over and over again, which one whispers ceaselessly, everywhere, like a prayer.

I am going to tell you our story, for love only has one, which is always the same. I met her and loved her; that is all. And for a whole year I have lived on her tenderness, on her caresses, in her arms, in her dresses, on her words, so completely wrapped up, bound, and absorbed in everything which came from her, that I no longer cared whether it was day or night, or whether I was dead or alive, on this old earth of ours.

And then she died. How? I do not know; I no longer know anything. But one evening she came home wet, for it was raining heavily, and the next day she coughed, and she coughed for about a week, and took to her bed. What happened I do not remember now, but doctors came, wrote, and went away. Medicines were brought, and some women made her drink them. Her hands were hot, her forehead was burning, and her eyes bright and sad. When I spoke to her, she answered me, but I do not remember what she said. I have forgotten everything, everything, everything! She died, and I very well remember her slight, feeble sigh. The nurse said: "Ah!" and I understood, I understood!

I knew nothing more, nothing. I saw a priest, who said: "Your mistress?" and it seemed to me as if he were insulting her. As she was dead, nobody had the right to say that any longer, and I turned him out. Another came who was very kind and tender, and I shed tears when he spoke to me about her.

They consulted me about the funeral, but I do not remember anything that they said, though I recollect the coffin, and the sound of the hammer when they nailed her down in it. Oh! God, God!

She was buried! Buried! She! In that hole! Some people came—female friends. I made my escape and ran away. I ran, and then walked through the streets, went home, and the next day started on a journey.

* * * * *

Yesterday I returned to Paris, and when I saw my room again—our room, our bed, our furniture, everything that remains of the life of a human being after death—I was seized by such a violent attack of fresh grief, that I felt like opening the window and throwing myself out into the street. I could not remain any longer among these things, between those walls which had inclosed and sheltered her, which retained a thousand atoms of her, of her skin and of her breath in their imperceptible crevices. I took up my hat to make my escape, and just as I reached the door, I passed the large glass in the hall, which she had put there so that she might look at herself every day from head to foot as she went out, to see if her toilette looked well, and was correct and pretty, from her little boots to her bonnet.

I stopped short in front of that looking-glass in which she had so often been reflected—so often, so often, that it must have retained her reflection. I was standing there, trembling, with my eyes fixed on the glass—on that flat, profound, empty glass—which had contained her entirely, and had possessed her as much as I, as my passionate looks had. I felt as if I loved that glass. I touched it; it was cold. Oh! the recollection! sorrowful mirror, burning mirror, horrible mirror, to make men suffer such torments! Happy is the man whose heart forgets everything that it has contained, everything that has passed before it, everything that has looked at itself in it, or has been reflected in its affection, in its love! How I suffer!

I went out without knowing it, without wishing it, and toward the cemetery. I found her simple grave, a white marble cross, with these few words:

She loved, was loved, and died.

She is there, below, decayed! How horrible! I sobbed with my forehead on the ground and I stopped there for a long time, a long time. Then I saw that it was getting dark, and a strange, mad wish, the wish of a despairing lover, seized me. I wished to pass the night, the last night, in weeping on her grave. But I should be seen and driven out. How was I to manage? I was cunning, and got up and began to roam about in that city of the dead. I walked and walked. How small this city is, in comparison with the other, the city in which we live. And yet, how much more numerous the dead are than the living. We want high houses, wide streets and much room for the four generations who see the daylight at the same time, drink water from the spring, and wine from the vines, and eat bread from the plains.

And for all the generations of the dead, for all that ladder of humanity that has descended to us here, there is scarcely anything, scarcely anything! The earth takes them back, and oblivion effaces them. Adieu!

At the end of the cemetery, I suddenly perceived that I was in its oldest part, where those who had been dead a long time are mingling with the soil, where the crosses themselves are decayed, where possibly newcomers will be put to-morrow. It is full of untended roses, of strong and dark cypress-trees, a sad and beautiful garden, nourished on human flesh.

I was alone, perfectly alone. So I crouched in a green tree and hid myself there completely amid the thick and somber branches. I waited, clinging to the stem, as a shipwrecked man clings to a plank.

When it was quite dark, I left my refuge and began to walk softly, slowly, inaudibly, through that ground full of dead people. I wandered about for a long time, but could not find her tomb again. I went on with extended arms, knocking against the tombs with my hands, my feet, my knees, my chest, even with my head, without being able to find her. I groped about like a blind man finding his way; I felt the stones, the crosses, the iron railings, the metal wreaths, and the wreaths of faded flowers! I read the names with my fingers, by passing them over the letters. What a night! What a night! I could not find her again!

There was no moon! What a night! I was frightened, horribly frightened in these narrow paths, between two rows of graves. Graves! graves! graves! nothing but graves! On my right, on my left, in front of me, around me, everywhere there were graves! I sat down on one of them, for I could not walk any longer, my knees were so weak. I could hear by heart beat! And I heard something else as well. What? A confused, nameless noise. Was the noise in my head, in the impenetrable night, or beneath the mysterious earth, the earth sown with human corpses? I looked all around me, but I cannot say how long I remained there; I was paralyzed with terror, cold with fright, ready to shout out, ready to die.

Suddenly, it seemed to me that the slab of marble on which I was sitting was moving. Certainly it was moving, as if it were being raised. With a bound, I sprang upon the neighboring tomb, and I saw, yes, I distinctly saw the stone which I had just quitted rise upright. Then the dead person appeared, a naked skeleton, pushing the stone back with its bent back. I saw it quite clearly, although the night was so dark. On the cross I could read:

> Here lies Jacques Olivant, who died at the age of fifty-one. He loved his family, was kind and honorable, and died in the grace of the Lord.

The dead man also read what was inscribed on his tombstone; then he picked up a stone off the path, a little, pointed stone, and began to scrape the letters carefully. He slowly effaced them, and with the hollows of his eyes he looked at the places where they had been engraved. Then, with the tip of the bone that had been his forefinger, he wrote in luminous letters, like those lines which boys trace on walls with the tip of a lucifer match:

> Here reposes Jacques Olivant, who died at the age of fifty-one. He hastened his father's death by his unkindness, as he wished to inherit his fortune; he tortured his wife, tormented his children, deceived his neighbors, robbed everyone he could, and died wretched.

When he had finished writing, the dead man stood motionless, looking at his work. On turning round I saw that all the graves were open, that all the dead bodies had emerged from them, and that all had effaced the lies inscribed on the gravestones by their relations, substituting the truth instead. And I saw that all had been the tormentors of their neighbors—malicious, dishonest, hypocrites, liars, rogues, calumniators, envious; that they had stolen, deceived, performed every disgraceful, every abominable action, these good fathers, these faithful wives, these devoted sons, these chaste daughters, these honest tradesmen, these men and women who were called irreproachable. They were all writing at the same time, on the threshold of their eternal abode, the truth, the terrible and the holy truth of which everybody was ignorant, or pretended to be ignorant, while they were alive.

I thought that she also must have written something on her tombstone, and now running without any fear among the half-open coffins, among the corpses and skeletons, I went toward her, sure that I should find her immediately. I recognized her at once, without seeing her face, which was covered by the winding-sheet, and on the marble cross, where shortly before I had read:

She loved, was loved, and died.

I now saw:

Having gone out in the rain one day, in order to deceive her lover, she caught cold and died.

It appears that they found me at daybreak, lying on the grave unconscious.

What the Moon Brings

H. P. Lovecraft

I hate the moon—I am afraid of it—for when it shines on certain scenes familiar and loved it sometimes makes them unfamiliar and hideous.

It was in the spectral summer when the moon shone down on the old garden where I wandered; the spectral summer of narcotic flowers and humid seas of foliage that bring wild and many-coloured dreams. And as I walked by the shallow crystal stream I saw unwonted ripples tipped with yellow light, as if those placid waters were drawn on in resistless currents to strange oceans that are not in the world. Silent and sparkling, bright and baleful, those moon-cursed waters hurried I knew not whither; whilst from the embowered banks white lotos blossoms fluttered one by one in the opiate night-wind and dropped despairingly into the stream, swirling away horribly under the arched, carven bridge, and staring back with the sinister resignation of calm, dead faces.

And as I ran along the shore, crushing sleeping flowers with heedless feet and maddened ever by the fear of unknown things and the lure of the dead faces, I saw that the garden had no end under that moon; for where by day the walls were, there stretched now only new vistas of trees and paths, flowers and shrubs, stone idols and pagodas, and bendings of the yellow-litten stream past grassy banks and under grotesque bridges of marble. And the lips of the dead lotos-faces whispered sadly, and bade me follow, nor did I cease my steps till the stream became a river, and joined amidst marshes of swaying reeds and beaches of gleaming sand the shore of a vast and nameless sea.

Upon that sea the hateful moon shone, and over its unvocal waves weird perfumes brooded. And as I saw therein the lotos-faces vanish, I longed for nets that I might capture them and learn from them the secrets which the moon had brought upon the night. But when the moon went over to the west and the still tide ebbed from the sullen shore, I saw in that light old spires that the waves almost uncovered, and white columns gay with festoons of green seaweed. And knowing that to this sunken place all the dead had come, I trembled and did not wish again to speak with the lotos-faces.

Yet when I saw afar out in the sea a black condor descend from the sky to seek rest on a vast reef, I would fain have questioned him, and asked him of those whom I had known when they were alive. This I would have asked him had he not been so far away, but he was very far, and could not be seen at all when he drew nigh that gigantic reef.

So I watched the tide go out under that sinking moon, and saw gleaming the spires, the towers, and the roofs of that dead, dripping city. And as I watched, my nostrils tried to close against the perfume-conquering stench of the world's dead; for truly, in this unplaced and forgotten spot had all the flesh of the churchyards gathered for puffy sea-worms to gnaw and glut upon.

Over those horrors the evil moon now hung very low, but the puffy worms of the sea need no moon to feed by. And as I watched the ripples that told of the writhing of worms beneath, I felt a new chill from afar out whither the condor had flown, as if my flesh had caught a horror before my eyes had seen it.

Nor had my flesh trembled without cause, for when I raised my eyes I saw that the waters had ebbed very low, shewing much of the vast reef whose rim I had seen before. And when I saw that this reef was but the black basalt crown of a shocking eikon whose monstrous forehead now shone in the dim moonlight and whose vile hooves must paw the hellish ooze miles below, I shrieked and shrieked lest the hidden face rise above the waters, and lest the hidden eyes look at me after the slinking away of that leering and treacherous yellow moon.

And to escape this relentless thing I plunged gladly and unhesitatingly into the stinking shallows where amidst weedy walls and sunken streets fat sea-worms feast upon the world's dead.

However, we had promised, so that was an end of it.

The White Villa

Ralph Adams Cram

When we left Naples on the 8:10 train for Paestum, Tom and I, we fully intended returning by the 2:46. Not because two hours time seemed enough wherein to exhaust the interests of those deathless ruins of a dead civilization, but simply for the reason that, as our *Indicatore* informed us, there was but one other train, and that at 6:11, which would land us in Naples too late for the dinner at the Turners and the San Carlo afterwards. Not that I cared in the least for the dinner or the theatre; but then, I was not so obviously in Miss Turner's good graces as Tom Rendel was, which made a difference.

However, we had promised, so that was an end of it.

This was in the spring of '88, and at that time the railroad, which was being pushed onward to Reggio, whereby travellers to Sicily might be spared the agonies of a night on the fickle Mediterranean, reached no farther than Agropoli, some twenty miles beyond Paestum; but although the trains were as yet few and slow, we accepted the half-finished road with gratitude, for it penetrated the very centre of Campanian brigandage, and made it possible for us to see the matchless temples in safety, while a few years before it was necessary for intending visitors to obtain a military escort from the Government; and military escorts are not for young architects.

So we set off contentedly, that white May morning, determined to make the best of our few hours, little thinking that before we saw Naples again we were to witness things that perhaps no American had ever seen before.

For a moment, when we left the train at "Pesto," and started to walk up the flowery lane leading to the temples, we were almost inclined to curse this same railroad. We had thought, in our innocence, that we should be alone, that no one else would think of enduring the long four hours' ride from Naples just to spend two hours in the ruins of these temples; but the event proved our unwisdom. We were *not* alone. It was a compact little party of conventional sight-seers that accompanied us. The inevitable English family with the three daughters, prominent of teeth, flowing of hair, aggressive of scarlet Murrays and Baedekers; the two blond and untidy Germans; a French couple from the pages of *La Vie Parisienne*; and our "old man of the sea," the white-bearded Presbyterian minister from Pennsylvania who had made our life miserable in Rome at the time of the Pope's Jubilee. Fortunately for us, this terrible old man had fastened himself upon a party of American school-teachers travelling *en Cook*, and for the time we were safe; but our vision of two hours of dreamy solitude faded lamentably away.

Yet how beautiful it was! this golden meadow walled with far, violet mountains, breathless under a May sun; and in the midst, rising from tangles of asphodel and acanthus, vast in the vacant plain, three temples, one silver gray, one golden gray, and one flushed with intangible rose. And all around nothing but velvet meadows stretching from the dim mountains behind, away to the sea, that showed only as a thin line of silver just over the edge of the still grass.

The tide of tourists swept noisily through the Basilica and the temple of Poseidon across the meadow to the distant temple of Ceres, and Tom and I were left alone to drink in all the fine wine of dreams that was possible in the time left us. We gave but little space to examining the temples the tourists had left, but in a few moments found ourselves lying in the grass to the east of Poseidon, looking dimly out towards the sea, heard now, but not seen,—a vague and pulsating murmur that blended with the humming of bees all about us.

A small shepherd boy, with a woolly dog, made shy advances of friendship, and in a little time we had set him to gathering flowers for us: asphodels and bee-orchids, anemones, and the little thin green iris so fairylike and frail. The murmur of the tourist crowd had merged itself in the moan of the sea, and it was very still; suddenly I heard the words I had been waiting for,—the suggestion I had refrained from making myself, for I knew Thomas.

"I say, old man, shall we let the 2:46 go to thunder?"

I chuckled to myself. "But the Turners?"

"They be blowed, we can tell them we missed the train."

"That is just exactly what we shall do," I said, pulling out my watch, "unless we start for the station right now."

But Tom drew an acanthus leaf across his face and showed no signs of moving; so I filled my pipe again, and we missed the train.

As the sun dropped lower towards the sea, changing its silver line to gold, we pulled ourselves together, and for an hour or more sketched vigorously; but the mood was not on us. It was "too jolly fine to waste time working," as Tom said; so we started off to explore the single street of the squalid town of Pesto that was lost within the walls of dead Poseidonia. It was not a pretty village,—if you can call a rut-riven lane and a dozen houses a village,—nor were the inhabitants thereof reassuring in appearance. There was no sign of a church,—nothing but dirty huts, and in the midst, one of two stories, rejoicing in the name of *Albergo del Sole,* the first story of which was a black and cavernous smithy, where certain swarthy knaves, looking like banditti out of a job, sat smoking sulkily.

"We might stay here all night," said Tom, grinning askance at this choice company; but his suggestion was not received with enthusiasm.

Down where the lane from the station joined the main road stood the only sign of modern civilization,—a great square structure, half villa, half fortress, with round turrets on its four corners, and a ten-foot wall surrounding it. There were no windows in its first story, so far as we could see, and it had evidently been at one time the fortified villa of some Campanian noble. Now, however, whether because brigandage had been stamped out, or because the villa was empty and deserted, it was no longer formidable; the gates of the great wall hung sagging on their hinges, brambles growing all over them, and many of the windows in the upper story were broken and black. It was a strange place, weird and mysterious, and we looked at it curiously. "There is a story about that place," said Tom, with conviction.

It was growing late: the sun was near the edge of the sea as we walked down the ivy-grown walls of the vanished city for the last time, and as we turned back, a red flush poured from the west, and painted the Doric temples in pallid rose against the evanescent purple of the Apennines. Already a thin mist was rising from the meadows, and the temples hung pink in the misty grayness.

It was a sorrow to leave the beautiful things, but we could run no risk of missing this last train, so we walked slowly back towards the temples.

"What is that Johnny waving his arm at us for?" asked Tom, suddenly.

"How should I know? We are not on his land, and the walls don't matter."

We pulled out our watches simultaneously.

"What time are you?" I said.

"Six minutes before six."

"And I am seven minutes. It can't take us all that time to walk to the station."

"Are you sure the train goes at 6:11?"

"Dead sure," I answered; and showed him the *Indicatore.*

By this time a woman and two children were shrieking at us hysterically; but what they said I had no idea, their Italian being of a strange and awful nature.

"Look here," I said, "let's run; perhaps our watches are both slow."

"Or—perhaps the time-table is changed."

Then we ran, and the populace cheered and shouted with enthusiasm; our dignified run became a panic-stricken rout, for as we turned into the lane, smoke was rising from beyond the bank that hid the railroad; a bell rang; we were so near that we could hear the interrogative *Pronte?* the impatient *Partenza!* and the definitive *Andiamo!* But the train was five hundred yards away, steaming towards Naples, when we plunged into the station as the clock struck six, and yelled for the stationmaster.

He came, and we indulged in crimination and recrimination.

When we could regard the situation calmly, it became apparent that the time-table *had* been changed two days before, the 6:11 now leaving at 5:58. A *facchino* came in, and we four sat down and regarded the situation judicially.

"Was there any other train?"

"No."

"Could we stay at the Albergo del Sole?"

A forefinger drawn across the throat by the Capo Stazione with a significant "cluck" closed that question.

"Then we must stay with you here at the station."

"But, Signori, I am not married. I live here only with the *facchini*. I have only one room to sleep in. It is impossible!"

"But we must sleep somewhere, likewise eat. What can we do?" and we shifted the responsibility deftly on the shoulders of the poor old man, who was growing excited again.

He trotted nervously up and down the station for a minute, then he called the *facchino*. "Giuseppe, go up to the villa and ask if two *forestieri* who have missed the last train can stay there all night!"

Protests were useless. The *facchino* was gone, and we waited anxiously for his return. It seemed as though he would never come. Darkness had fallen, and the moon was rising over the mountains. At last he appeared.

"The Signori may stay all night, and welcome; but they cannot come to dinner, for there is nothing in the house to eat!"

This was not reassuring, and again the old station-master lost himself in meditation. The results were admirable, for in a little time the table in the waiting-room had been transformed into a dining-table, and Tom and I were ravenously devouring a big omelette, and bread and cheese, and drinking a most shocking sour wine as though it were Chateau Yquem. A *facchino* served us, with clumsy good-will; and when we had induced our nervous old host to sit down with us and partake of his own hospitality, we succeeded in forming a passably jolly dinner-party, forgetting over our sour wine and cigarettes the coming hours from ten until sunrise, which lay before us in a dubious mist.

It was with crowding apprehensions which we strove in vain to joke away that we set out at last to retrace our steps to the mysterious villa, the *facchino* Giuseppe leading the way. By this time the moon was well overhead, and just behind us as we tramped up the dewy lane, white in the moonlight between the ink-black hedgerows on either side. How still it was! Not a breath of air, not a sound of life; only the awful silence that had lain almost unbroken for two thousand years over this vast graveyard of a dead world.

As we passed between the shattered gates and wound our way in the moonlight through the maze of gnarled fruit-trees, decaying farm implements and piles of lumber, towards the small door that formed the only opening in the first story of this deserted fortress, the cold silence was shattered by the harsh baying of dogs somewhere in the distance to the right, beyond the barns that formed one side of the court. From the villa came neither light nor sound. Giuseppe knocked at the weather-worn door, and the sound echoed cavernously within; but there was no other reply. He knocked again and again, and at length we heard the rasping jar of sliding bolts, and the door opened a little, showing an old, old man, bent with age and gaunt with malaria. Over his head he held a big Roman lamp, with three wicks, that cast strange shadows on his face,—a face that was harmless in its senility, but intolerably sad. He made no reply to our timid salutations, but motioned tremblingly to us to enter; and with a last "good-night" to Giuseppe we obeyed, and stood half-way up the stone stairs that led directly from the door, while the old man tediously shot every bolt and adjusted the heavy bar.

Then we followed him in the semi-darkness up the steps into what had been the great hall of the villa. A fire was burning in a great fireplace so beautiful in design that Tom and I looked at each other with interest. By its fitful light we could see that we were in a huge circular room covered by a flat, saucer-shaped dome,—a room that must once have been superb and splendid, but that now was a lamentable wreck. The frescoes on the dome were stained and mildewed, and here and there the plaster was gone altogether; the carved doorways that led out on all sides had lost half the gold with which they had once been covered, and the floor was of brick, sunken into treacherous valleys. Rough chests, piles of old newspapers, fragments of harnesses, farm implements, a heap of rusty carbines and cutlasses, nameless litter of every possible kind, made the room into a wilderness which under the firelight seemed even more picturesque than it really was. And on this inexpressible confusion of lumber the pale shapes of the seventeenth-century nymphs, startling in their weather-stained nudity, looked down with vacant smiles.

For a few moments we warmed ourselves before the fire; and then, in the same dejected silence, the old man led the way to one of the many doors, handed us a brass lamp, and with a stiff bow turned his back on us.

Once in our room alone, Tom and I looked at each other with faces that expressed the most complex emotions.

"Well, of all the rum goes," said Tom, "this is the rummiest go I ever experienced!"

"Right, my boy; as you very justly remark, we are in for it. Help me shut this door, and then we will reconnoitre, take account of stock, and size up our chances."

But the door showed no sign of closing; it grated on the brick floor and stuck in the warped casing, and it took our united efforts to jam the two inches of oak into its place, and turn the enormous old key in its rusty lock.

"Better now, much better now," said Tom; "now let us see where we are."

The room was easily twenty-five feet square, and high in proportion; evidently it had been a state apartment, for the walls were covered with carved panelling that had once been white and gold, with mirrors in the panels, the wood now stained every imaginable color, the mirrors cracked and broken, and dull with mildew. A big fire had just been lighted in the fireplace, the shutters were closed, and although the only furniture consisted of two massive bedsteads, and a chair with one leg shorter than the others, the room seemed almost comfortable.

I opened one of the shutters, that closed the great windows that ran from the floor almost to the ceiling, and nearly fell through the cracked glass into the floorless balcony. "Tom, come here, quick," I cried; and for a few minutes neither of us thought about our dubious surroundings, for we were looking at Pæstum by moonlight.

A flat, white mist, like water, lay over the entire meadow; from the midst rose against the blue-black sky the three ghostly temples, black and silver in the vivid moonlight, floating, it seemed, in the fog; and behind them, seen in broken glints between the pallid shafts, stretched the line of the silver sea.

Perfect silence,—the silence of implacable death.

We watched the white tide of mist rise around the temples, until we were chilled through, and so presently went to bed. There was but one door in the room, and that was securely locked; the great windows were twenty feet from the ground, so we felt reasonably safe from all possible attack.

In a few minutes Tom was asleep and breathing audibly; but my constitution is more nervous than his, and I lay awake for some little time, thinking of our curious adventure and of its possible outcome. Finally, I fell asleep,—for how long I do not know: but I woke with the feeling that some one had tried the handle of the door. The fire had fallen into a heap of coals which cast a red glow in the room, whereby I could see dimly the outline of Tom's bed, the broken-legged chair in front of the fireplace, and the door in its deep casing by the chimney, directly in front of my bed. I sat up, nervous from my sudden awakening under these strange circumstances, and stared at the door. The latch rattled, and the door swung smoothly open. I began to shiver coldly. That door was locked; Tom and I had all we could do to jam it together and lock it. But we *did* lock it; and now it was opening silently. In a minute more it as silently closed.

Then I heard a footstep,—I swear I heard a footstep *in the room,* and with it the *frou-frou* of trailing skirts; my breath stopped and my teeth grated against each other as I heard the soft footfalls and the feminine rustle pass along the room towards the fireplace. My eyes saw nothing; yet there was enough light in the room for me to distinguish the pattern on the carved panels of the door. The steps stopped by the fire, and I saw the broken-legged chair lean to the left, with a little jar as its short leg touched the floor.

I sat still, frozen, motionless, staring at the vacancy that was filled with such terror for me; and as I looked, the seat of the chair creaked, and it came back to its upright position again.

And then the footsteps came down the room lightly, towards the window; there was a pause, and then the great shutters swung back, and the white moonlight poured in. Its brilliancy was unbroken by any shadow, by any sign of material substance.

I tried to cry out, to make some sound, to awaken Tom; this sense of utter loneliness in the presence of the Inexplicable was maddening. I don't know whether my lips obeyed my will or no; at all events, Tom lay motionless with his deaf ear up, and gave no signs.

The shutters closed as silently as they had opened; the moonlight was gone, the firelight also, and in utter darkness I waited. If I could only *see!* If something were visible, I should not mind it so much; but this ghastly hearing of every little sound, every rustle of a gown, every breath, yet seeing nothing, was soul-destroying. I think in my abject terror I prayed that I might see, only see; but the darkness was unbroken.

Then the footsteps began to waver fitfully, and I heard the rustle of garments sliding to the floor, the clatter of little shoes flung down, the rattle of buttons, and of metal against wood.

Rigors shot over me, and my whole body shivered with collapse as I sank back on the pillow, waiting with every nerve tense, listening with all my life.

The coverlid was turned back beside me, and in another moment the great bed sank a little as something slipped between the sheets with an audible sigh.

I called to my aid every atom of remaining strength, and, with a cry that shivered between my clattering teeth, I hurled myself headlong from the bed on to the floor.

I must have lain for some time stunned and unconscious, for when I finally came to myself it was cold in the room, there was no last glow of lingering coals in the fireplace, and I was stiff with chill.

It all flashed over me like the haunting of a heavy dream. I laughed a little at the dim memory, with the thought, "I must try to recollect all the details; they will do to tell Tom," and rose stiffly to return to bed, when—there it was again, and my heart stopped,—the hand on the door.

I paused and listened. The door opened with a muffled creak, closed again, and I heard the lock turn rustily. I would have died now before getting into that bed again; but there was terror equally without; so I stood trembling and listened,—listened to heavy, stealthy steps creeping along on the other side of the bed. I clutched the coverlid, staring across into the dark.

There was a rush in the air by my face, the sound of a blow, and simultaneously a shriek, so awful, so despairing, so blood-curdling that I felt my senses leaving me again as I sank crouching on the floor by the bed.

And then began the awful duel, the duel of invisible, audible shapes; of things that shrieked and raved, mingling thin, feminine cries with low, stifled curses and indistinguishable words. Round and round the room, footsteps chasing footsteps in the ghastly night, now away by Tom's bed, now rushing swiftly down the great room until I felt the flash of swirling drapery on my hard lips. Round and round, turning and twisting till my brain whirled with the mad cries.

They were coming nearer. I felt the jar of their feet on the floor beside me. Came one long, gurgling moan close over my head, and then, crushing down upon me, the weight of a collapsing body; there was long hair over my face, and in my staring eyes; and as awful silence succeeded the less awful tumult, life went out, and I fell unfathomable miles into nothingness.

The gray dawn was sifting through the chinks in the shutters when I opened my eyes again. I lay stunned and faint, staring up at the mouldy frescoes on the ceiling, struggling to gather together my wandering senses and knit them into something like consciousness. But now as I pulled myself little by little together there was no thought of dreams before me. One after another the awful incidents of that unspeakable night came back, and I lay incapable of movement, of action, trying to piece together the whirling fragments of memory that circled dizzily around me.

Little by little it grew lighter in the room. I could see the pallid lines struggling through the shutters behind me, grow stronger along the broken and dusty floor. The tarnished mirrors reflected dirtily the growing daylight; a door closed, far away, and I heard the crowing of a cock; then by and by the whistle of a passing train.

Years seemed to have passed since I first came into this terrible room. I had lost the use of my tongue, my voice refused to obey my panic-stricken desire to cry out; once or twice I tried in vain to force an articulate sound through my rigid lips; and when at last a broken whisper rewarded my feverish struggles, I felt a strange sense of great victory. How soundly he slept! Ordinarily, rousing him was no easy task, and now he revolted steadily against being awakened at this untimely hour. It seemed to me that I had called him for ages almost, before I heard him grunt sleepily and turn in bed.

"Tom," I cried weakly, "Tom, come and help me!"

"What do you want? what is the matter with you?"

"Don't ask, come and help me!"

"Fallen out of bed I guess"; and he laughed drowsily.

My abject terror lest he should go to sleep again gave me new strength. Was it the actual physical paralysis born of killing fear that held me down? I could not have raised my head from the floor on my life; I could only cry out in deadly fear for Tom to come and help me.

"Why don't you get up and get into bed?" he answered, when I implored him to come to me. "You have got a bad nightmare; wake up!"

But something in my voice roused him at last, and he came chuckling across the room, stopping to throw open two of the great shutters and let a burst of white light into the room. He climbed up on the bed and peered over jeeringly. With the first glance the laugh died, and he leaped the bed and bent over me.

"My God, man, what is the matter with you? You are hurt!"

"I don't know what is the matter; lift me up, get me away from here, and I'll tell you all I know."

"But, old chap, you must be hurt awfully; the floor is covered with blood!"

He lifted my head and held me in his powerful arms. I looked down: a great red stain blotted the floor beside me.

But, apart from the black bruise on my head, there was no sign of a wound on my body, nor stain of blood on my lips. In as few words as possible I told him the whole story.

"Let's get out of this," he said when I had finished; "this is no place for us. Brigands I can stand, but—"

He helped me to dress, and as soon as possible we forced open the heavy door, the door I had seen turn so softly on its hinges only a few hours before, and came out into the great circular hall, no less strange and mysterious now in the half light of dawn than it had been by firelight. The room was empty, for it must have been very early, although a fire already blazed in the fireplace. We sat by the fire some time, seeing no one. Presently slow footsteps sounded in the stairway, and the old man entered, silent as the night before, nodding to us civilly, but showing by no sign any surprise which he may have felt at our early rising. In absolute silence he moved around, preparing coffee for us; and when at last the frugal breakfast was ready, and we sat around the rough table munching coarse bread and sipping the black coffee, he would reply to our overtures only by monosyllables.

Any attempt at drawing from him some facts as to the history of the villa was received with a grave and frigid repellence that baffled us; and we were forced to say *addio* with our hunger for some explanation of the events of the night still unsatisfied.

But we saw the temples by sunrise, when the mistlike lambent opals bathed the bases of the tall columns salmon in the morning light! It was a rhapsody in the pale and unearthly colors of Puvis de Chavannes vitalized and made glorious with splendid sunlight; the apotheosis of mist; a vision never before seen, never to be forgotten. It was so beautiful that the memory of my ghastly night paled and faded, and it was Tom who assailed the station-master with questions while we waited for the train from Agropoli.

Luckily he was more than loquacious, he was voluble under the ameliorating influence of the money we forced upon him; and this, in few words, was the story he told us while we sat on the platform smoking, marvelling at the mists that rose to the east, now veiling, now revealing the lavender Apennines.

"Is there a story of *La Villa Bianca*?"

"Ah, Signori, certainly; and a story very strange and very terrible. It was much time ago, a hundred,—two hundred years; I do not know. Well, the Duca di San Damiano married a lady so fair, so most beautiful that she was called *La Luna di Pesto;* but she was of the people,—more, she was of the banditti: her father was of Calabria, and a terror of the Campagna. But the Duke was young, and he married her, and for her built the white villa; and it was a wonder throughout Campania,—you have seen? It is splendid now, even if a ruin. Well, it was less than a year after they came to the villa before the Duke grew jealous,—jealous of the new captain of the banditti who took the place of the father of *La Luna,* himself killed in a great battle up there in the mountains. Was there cause? Who shall know? But there were stories among the people of terrible things in the villa, and how *La Luna* was seen almost never outside the walls. Then the Duke would go for many days to Napoli, coming home only now and then to the villa that was become a fortress, so many men guarded its never-opening gates. And once—it was in the spring—the Duke came silently down from Napoli, and there, by the three poplars you see away towards the north, his carriage was set upon by armed men, and he was almost killed; but he had with him many guards, and after a terrible fight the brigands were beaten off; but before him, wounded, lay the captain,—he man whom he feared and hated. He looked at him, lying there under the torchlight, and in his hand saw *his own sword.* Then he became a devil: with the same sword he ran the brigand through, leaped in the carriage, and, entering the villa, crept to the chamber of *La Luna,* and killed her with the sword she had given to her lover.

"This is all the story of the White Villa, except that the Duke came never again to Pesto. He went back to the king at Napoli, and for many years he was the scourge of the banditti of Campania; for the King made him a general, and San Damiano was a name feared by the lawless and loved by the peaceful, until he was killed in a battle down by Mormanno.

"And *La Luna?* Some say she comes back to the villa, once a year, when the moon is full, in the month when she was slain; for the Duke buried her, they say, with his own hands, in the garden that was once under the window of her chamber; and as she died unshriven, so was she buried without the pale of the Church. Therefore she cannot sleep in peace,—*non è vero?* I do not know if the story is true, but this is the story, Signori, and there is the train for Napoli. *Ah, grazie! Signori, grazie tanto! A rivederci! Signori, a rivederci!*"

The White Witch of the River

A Clyde Legend

J. E. Muddock

Many, many years ago, long before Helensburgh, on the River Clyde, had grown into the important place that it is now; when, in fact, it was only a primitive fishing village, whose inhabitants knew little of the world beyond their own doors, there dwelt there an honest fisher-lad, named Robert Rennie. He had been a fisher all his days, as his father and grandfather had before him, and no more fearless boatman existed in that part of the country. He was of an adventurous turn of mind, too, and had explored the lonely Loch Long, Loch Goil, the Gareloch, and the Holy Loch, which, as all travellers by the Clyde know, run north from the river, with the exception of the Holy Loch, which trends west, and back into the mountains. Wild and mysterious were these regions in those days, for the iron horse had not broken the solitudes of mountain and moorland, where the lordly eagle still held sway, and the hill fox reared her cubs in peace. In fact

> So wondrous wild, the whole might seem
> The scenery of a fairy dream.

And many, indeed, were the strange stories that were told of beings, not of mortal mould, who roamed about in these mountain fastnesses. Robert in his wanderings had often seen some of these creatures, and at night, round the turf fire, when the wind whistled shrilly about the cottages with their thatched roofs, he was wont to tell eerie stories to his awe-struck companions, who listened with open eyes and gaping mouths until their hair rose on end, and the blood curdled in their veins. The simple folk, in fact, used to say that there was something uncanny about Robert himself, and it was a common belief that he had made some unholy compact with the evil spirits that haunted the lochs and the gloomy glens. One thing is certain: he would start off alone on the darkest night, and with his boat penetrate up one or other of the lochs, and would return when day broke with his boat laden with fish. Now, is it not certain that to do this he must have had supernatural aid? At least that is what the simple villagers thought and even said. Then again he often journeyed to the wondrous wild Loch Long, and would sometimes be absent two and three days together. When he was asked how he found shelter during his absence in such an inhospitable place, he replied that he lived in the ruins of Carrick Castle. Well, indeed, might his listeners shudder when they heard this, for no man residing in the neighbourhood would have had the hardihood to doubt that Carrick Castle was the haunt of ghouls and spirits.

Loch Long runs for nearly eighteen miles, trending north and east, but halfway it is joined by Loch Goil, which trends to the west, and Carrick Castle frowns on the gloomy loch from a lofty crag, and many a stirring scene of bloodshed has it witnessed. Loch Goil is merely a narrow arm of the sea, at its broadest point not exceeding a mile, while the rocky sides are rent with many a seam, and in places so steep as to be inaccessible, and the peaks that tower above reach at their highest points 2,000 to 2,500 feet. Midway up this rock-bound strip of water stands the Castle, that in some faroff time must have been a place of immense strength, and was so, in fact, down to 1685, when a body of wild hill men, instigated by the personal enemies of the Marquis of Argyll, to whom the stronghold then belonged, swept down from the mountains when the place was undefended, and with fire and rams turned it into a blackened ruin, so that it was said when referring to the Argylls—

Their old Castle Carrick is peeled to its walls,
And fleshless things grin in its once lordly halls.

Time dealt kindly with the ruin, clothing its blackened walls with ivy and lichen; but the raven and the night-owl made it their abode, and strange spirits revelled there. Yet to this place Robert Rennie was in the habit of going and passing two or three days at a time; and it was whispered that it was in this ghostly ruin he had made his fearsome compact, whereby he was enabled to fill his boat with fish when other fishers were afraid to put to sea. What the compact stipulated he should give in return for this privilege was not stated.

Rennie had the reputation of being well off, and he was the sole support of his widowed mother and a crippled brother. He had built a neat cottage that stood facing the river, and was the best cottage in all the village. He was a fine, stalwart young man, and not bad-looking, although he had such a peculiar expression about his steel-grey eyes that some folk shunned him as being possessed of the "evil eye."

Notwithstanding the reputation he had thus acquired, there were plenty of girls in the village who would have jumped at him had he but given them the slightest encouragement; but, strange to say, he seemed to shun all female society, though there were those in the village who were ready to affirm most solemnly that they had seen him occasionally in the gloaming seated in his boat, accompanied by a most beautiful woman, dressed all in white, who was known as "The White Witch of the River."

She was a being of radiant beauty; with hair like a raven's plume, and a form of faultless mould, while her eyes shone like gleaming gold; and with a voice that was low and sweet, she could lure men to her feet, unless they turned their eyes to heaven and uttered a prayer. It was fatal to hear this syren singing, as she often did when the gloaming had enfolded the hills in purple shadows; or the pale moon made a silvery track on the river. Often at such a time the marvellous creature was seen gliding down the river like a mist-wreath from off the hill-side. But those who saw her would instantly avert their gaze and hurry away, lest, with her flutelike voice, she should lure them to destruction.

And yet, although it was known that the White Witch of the River fascinated men to follow her in order to drown them in the blue depths of the lonely lochs, there were those who asserted solemnly that they had seen her with Robert Rennie in his boat. No wonder, therefore, that he came to be shunned by many of the villagers as an uncanny person with an evil eye. In disposition he was somewhat morose, and seemed to prefer solitude. But with these exceptions, no one could say aught against him. He was kind to his mother and crippled brother, and they believed that he was the cleverest youth for many miles round, and that some day he would be a great man. But if the old people and the men looked upon him with suspicion, many of the young women uttered a silent sigh as he passed them. To all except one, however, he was utterly indifferent. But this one did not live in Helensburgh. She was the daughter of a rich merchant in Greenock. Two or three nights a week Robert would sail his boat across the river from Helensburgh to Greenock, and secretly meet this young lady, so that it seemed as if she favoured his suit. Her name was Florence, and she enjoyed the reputation of being the belle of Greenock. It is difficult to say when they first met or how their acquaintance grew; the fact remains she was, all unknown to her father and her brother, in the habit of meeting him and allowing him to talk love to her. Perhaps he had fascinated her with his evil eye, and she bore him no real love. At any rate, one night when he crossed the river and landed at the usual spot, where he had been in the habit of finding her waiting for him, instead of Florence there were two men. They at once announced themselves as the father and brother of Florence. They said she had confessed that she had been in the habit of granting him stolen interviews, thus disgracing her family. They had come now to caution him to return no more. Florence, they said, was not for the likes of him, and they had resolved that if he returned again they would kill him.

Drawing himself up proudly he told them with scorn in his voice, and with the fire of indignation flashing from his eyes, that he should return again and again until he heard from the girl's own lips that she loved him not.

This haughty and defiant answer aroused the father and son to fury, and, each being armed with a stout stick, they suddenly fell upon him and beat him until he fell senseless to the ground. Thinking he was dead, and being frightened now lest the crime should be discovered, they lifted his body and carried it to the very edge of the water, so that when the tide rose and receded again it would bear his corpse out to sea. They next set his boat adrift, knowing that if it was found, as it was almost sure to be, it would create an impression he had fallen out and been drowned. This done, they went away, believing that they had rid themselves for ever of the troublesome lover.

A few minutes later the moon came from behind a dense mass of black cloud and lighted the water up with the sheen of silver, and presently what seemed like a wreath mist, but having a vague resemblance to a woman, floated gracefully along the silvery path of light, and as it came nearer the shore it developed into the perfect shape and form of "The White Witch of the River."

Truly she was a being of the most dazzling beauty—a beauty that was unearthly. Her eyes gleamed like stars on a frosty night; her face, faultless in all its features, was white and cold like the face of a marble statue; and the deathly whiteness of the face was enhanced by her blue-black hair that hung like a great veil down her back to her feet. A robe of spotless white, that seemed to he woven from gossamer or mist, clung to her rounded limbs in the most graceful folds, while round her waist was a girdle of jewels that broke into a thousand points of dazzling fire as the moonlight caught it.

With a wave of her white arm she arrested the drifting boat, and then, with another wave, drew it towards the shore, and, when its keel grated on the shingle, she slightly stooped and raised the insensible Robert as if he had only been a feather. Gently she placed him in his boat, and then, by some invisible power, the sail was raised. This done, the White Witch faded away, but a strange cloud of rosy, luminous mist entirely enveloped the boat, which sped along before a strong wind, though the cloud of mist went with it.

On went the boat with extraordinary speed: down the river first of all until it reached the mouth of the Holy Loch; then the same invisible power that had guided it so far turned its prow almost due north, and, with the luminous cloud still enveloping it, it sped up Loch Long to where Loch Goil joins it and runs towards the west. Up Loch Goil went the boat until it stranded at the head of the loch; then the luminous cloud faded away.

By-and-by the mountains began to stand out clear and distinct in the pearly light of the coming dawn; and gradually the purple that lay on mountain and water warmed to gold, until at last the weird landscape was ablaze with the brilliant fire of the rising sun, whose rays seemed to revive Robert Rennie, so that he sat up in his boat and gazed wonderingly around him.

For some little time he appeared to be dazed, and he passed his hand repeatedly over his eyes as if trying to clear his mental vision.

"Was it a dream?" he muttered, as he began to recall the events of the preceding night.

No, it could not be a dream, for he had an ugly wound in his temple where he had been struck, and almost every bone in his body ached. But how was it he had got to where he then found himself? It was a long way from Greenock, and he had not the slightest recollection of anything after Florence's father and brother attacked him. All after that was shrouded in the deepest mystery to him; but when he remembered how shamefully he had been treated he became furious, and stepping on shore he wandered like one distraught into the gloomy glen that begins at the head of Loch Goil and runs west to Loch Fyne. Down this strange and desolate glen runs the *Styx*, and the wild, rugged mountains, bleak and barren, rise up so high on either side as to involve the glen in almost constant gloom, while the only sound that breaks the silence is the hoarse cry of the ravens. It seemed to be a fitting place for Robert to give vent to his wrath, and,

> While the mists
> Flying, and rainy vapours, call out shapes
> And phantoms from the crags and solid earth,

to utter an oath that he would yet possess Florence and be revenged for the outrage upon him.

For three days he remained in this weird solitude, not wishing to return to his people showing traces of the outrage he had been subjected to. He lived as best he could on herbs and berries, and at night he crept for shelter under some jutting rock. During the dark hours, too, he heard strange sounds and witnessed strange sights, for the glen was the home of "fleshless things." Blue lights flitted about, and every now and again, out of the blackness, were evoked nebulous forms that bore some resemblance to human beings. These forms seemed to be indulging in fantastic dances, forming chains, crossing and recrossing each other's path, bowing and receding, and then suddenly vanishing into the darkness from whence they had come. And there were sighings and moanings, and eldritch screams that woke the echoes with startling sharpness. All night long these uncanny sights and sounds went on, but the fleshless things slunk away when the morning light first beamed, and the only sounds heard then were the hoarse murmuring of the Styx, and the ravens' dismal croaking. At last Robert Rennie had so far recovered that he left this haunted spot, and sailing down the loch returned to his people.

Many were the questions asked of him, and great was the wonderment expressed at his changed appearance; for his face looked careworn and haggard, and he had become more grave and morose. To the questions he made no answer; to the wonderment he was stolidly indifferent.

For weeks he brooded over his wrongs, while the sullen gloom that seemed to have settled on his face repelled people from him, and he was shunned with fear. Scarcely a night passed now, no matter what the weather was, but he went out in his boat, and his neighbours whispered one to another—and shuddered while they avowed—that the White Witch of the River was frequently sitting beside him as he sat at the tiller.

Whatever the mystery was, Robert kept it to himself. The seal of silence was on his lips. But that he still thought of Florence was proved one day as an old woman from the village was crossing to Greenock to transact some business. He took her aside, and, putting a piece of gold in her hand, bade her deliver secretly a message to the girl. The message was in the form of a prayer and a threat. He prayed her to meet him at the old trysting-place for the last time in order that he might bid her farewell for ever, and she was to be informed that if she failed to come a dreadful calamity would befall her and her people. Faithful to her trust, the old woman delivered the message, and Florence was evidently influenced by it, for, after deep reflection, she bade the messenger say she would keep the tryst.

Two nights later Robert crossed the river to Greenock. It was a strange night, weird and gloomy. Great jagged black clouds filled the sky, and between the rents the moonlight sometimes streamed, calling into being gigantic and fantastic shadows that flitted over the river and the landscape. The wind blew coldly in from the sea, and it moaned like a thing in pain. The month was October. The sere leaves were dropping from the trees, and the trees themselves shivered and sobbed in the pitiless gale.

A quarter of an hour after Robert had sprung on shore Florence appeared. She was enveloped in a large cloak, and seemed to be excited and flurried.

"What wish you with me?" she asked in a voice so stern and so unlike the loving tones that he was in the habit of hearing from her, that he started back and exclaimed:

"Surely this is not *my* Florence!"

"No, not yours, though I once thought I was," she answered with a sigh. "But I have seen my error. You fascinated me. I mistook my feeling for love. I must have been mad, but I am mad no longer. We part, and part for ever. But I have come in deference to your wishes, and, for the sake of what we have been to each other, to say farewell. My coming here is not unattended with risk, for I shudder to think what the consequences may be if my father and my brother discover my absence. So what you have to say you must say quickly, and let me go."

He listened to her in gloomy silence. When she finished speaking he asked her in a voice that seemed hollow and broken:

"Is your love for me quite dead?"

"I never had love for you," she answered. "I thought at the time it was love, but I know now I was mistaken."

"You have been false to me, then," he cried with passionate earnestness. "You have lured me into a belief that you loved me, only to fling me off now with heartless cruelty. But it shall not be. We will not part. You shall be mine, even though we are wedded in death."

With a shudder of fear she shrank from him, and at that moment sounds of hurrying and approaching footsteps were heard. Some instinct, perhaps, told her that her father and brother were coming to seek her. She turned as if she intended to run forward and meet them, but at the same instant Robert Rennie caught her in his powerful arms, and as she struggled to free herself she uttered a shrill and piercing scream that went echoing round the hills until it died down on the night wind with a melancholy wail. He carried her over the shingle to his boat, placed her in it, and pushing off sprang in himself, and hoisted the sail just as the father and brother appeared in sight.

Florence made a frantic appeal to them to rescue her, and almost beside themselves they rushed along the shore until they saw a fisherman's boat moored to a stake. Regardless of cold and wet they swam out to it, and, getting in, hoisted the sail and started in pursuit. But Rennie's boat had got a long start, and now that strange luminous cloud seemed to envelope it again. The moonlight fell in broken bars across the dark water that was fretted into foaming wavelets by the salt sea wind. Fear had overcome Florence, and she had fallen in a faint at the bottom of the boat. Grim and silent, with face white as the moonbeam rays, Robert Rennie sat in the stern-sheets holding the tiller and looking always ahead, never back.

On went the pursued and the pursuer, the latter gaining slowly but surely, for the two men propelled with oars as well as the sail. The wind increased as they neared the mouth of the loch, and the boats sped on at fearful speed until they entered Loch Long. The pursuing boat was then within a few yards of the other. Florence still lay insensible, and Robert, with scarcely a sign of life, still sat grasping the tiller. Then from out the luminous cloud two long arms seemed to stretch, and, lifting the inanimate form of Florence, they raised her up, and let her fall into the sea in front of the advancing boat. A cry of horror burst from the lips of father and son, and the hills seemed to echo and re-echo a wild and mocking peal of laughter. The two men stopped their boat, and, seizing the clothes of the poor girl as they were expanded on the dark waters, they dragged her in; but she was cold and white as veined marble, and never would she be otherwise, for she was stone dead.

Robert Rennie, who had never so much as looked round, still sat in the stern, and his boat tore on up the loch. But he was not alone. Another form sat beside him—a form of exquisite and unearthly beauty. It was the form of the White Witch of the River; her arm was round his waist, her head was pillowed on his shoulder, and her night-black hair fell over him like a funeral pall.

As the broken-hearted father and son bore back their dear, dead burden, the boat containing Rennie and his ghostly companion sped away up the loch until it was lost to sight. Then the gathering clouds in the sky grew denser, until the moonlight was blotted out. A sobbing rain fell, and the wind shrieked from the sea and lashed the water into hissing foam, like the wind of death. When the morning broke the coast people declared they had not experienced such a wild night for many and many a day.

For many a long month no tale nor tidings of Robert Rennie were ever heard. But when winter snows were melting before the genial breath of spring, a shepherd, searching for some strayed sheep in the gloomy recesses of the glen, found the skeleton of a man, and he recognised by the clothing that the dead man was Robert Rennie, and this was corroborated when a little later he found Robert Rennie's boat crushed and broken on the Lochgoilhead shore, where it had been flung on that wild, weird night.

The mystery surrounding the strange man's death was never cleared up, but, even at the present day, old wives, sitting over their winter fires, will tell you that he was lured to his destruction by the White Witch of the River.

White Zombie

Vivian Meik

Geoffrey Aylett, acting commissioner of the Nswadzi district, was frightened. During his twenty years in Africa never before had he experienced the feeling of being so definitely baffled. He felt as if something was pressing against him, something that he could neither see nor locate, but, nevertheless, something that seemed to envelop him, and, in some inexplicable way, threatened to stifle him. Lately he had begun to wake suddenly at nights, struggling for breath and almost overcome by a feeling of nausea. After the nausea had disappeared there still remained a strange suggestion of some nameless, horrible odour, an odour that was strongly reminiscent of the earlier battles of the Mesopotamia campaign. Those had been days of foul disease, when cholera dysentery, sunstroke, typhoid and gangrene, had raged unchecked; where hundreds had lain where they had fallen; when, pressed by enemies and forgotten by friends, the survivors were forced to let even the elementary decencies of death go by the board. . . . He remembered the flies and the corruption, and the temperature of a hundred and twenty degrees. . . .

And now, eighteen years later, that same smell of foetid corruption seemed to hover about him like some evil invisible presence when he awoke at nights.

Aylett was, first and foremost, a rational man accustomed to face facts. His knowledge of the mystery of Africa, of its depths and jungles, of its eerie atmosphere, was as complete as that of any white man—he smiled whimsically as he emphasized to himself how little that was—and he looked for some concrete reason that would explain the bridging of the years by this horrible harmonic. Failing a satisfactory solution he would be forced to conclude that it was about time he went go home on a long leave.

Carefully, as befitted of a man of his experience of the ways of the dark gods, he searched his innermost soul, but failed to find the answer he sought.

There was only one connection in the district between him and the Mesopotamia of 1915—a certain John Sinclair, late of the Indian Army, but that connection was already a broken link long before the first appearance of these nauseating nightmares.

Sinclair had been a brother officer in the old days, and, mainly on Aylett's advice, had taken up a few thousand acres of virgin country in the comparatively unknown Nswadzi district immediately after the war. But he had died more than a year previously—and, what was more to the point, had died a natural death. Aylett himself had been present at the passing of his friend.

Being both a mystic as a result of his knowledge of Africa, and a logician as a result of his Western upbringing, Aylett methodically considered the platitudinous truth that there are more things in heaven and earth than are dreamed of in our philosophy, and went over the entire period of his association with Sinclair in every detail.

At the end of it all, he was forced to admit failure, and, indeed, judged either logically or mystically, there was no adequate reason for linking Sinclair with his present troubles. Sinclair had died peacefully. He even remembered the utter content of the last sigh . . . as if some great burden had been lifted.

It was true that before this, Sinclair—and Aylett himself for that matter—during the first two years of the War, had been through a hell that only those who had experienced it could appreciate. It was also true that Sinclair had saved Aylett's life at a great risk to his own, on a certain memorable occasion, when Aylett, left for dead, had been lying badly wounded . . . in the sun. Aylett had, naturally, never forgotten that, but being a typical Englishman, had done very little more than shake his friend's hand, and mumble something to the effect that he hoped one day there would be an opportunity to repay. Sinclair had waved the matter aside, with a laugh, as one of no account—merely a job in the day's work. There the incident had ended, and each went about his own lawful occasions.

As a settler, Sinclair had been a complete success. In due course, he had married a very capable woman, who, it appeared to Aylett, whenever he had broken journey at the homestead, was eminently suited to the hard existence of a planter's wife.

At first Sinclair had seemed very happy, but as the years passed Aylett had not been quite so sure. He had had occasion more than once to notice the subtle change for the worse in his old friend. Staleness, he diagnosed, and recommended a holiday in England. Lonely plantations, far from one's own kind, are apt to get on the nerves. Nothing came of his suggestion, however, and the Sinclairs stayed on. They had grown to love the place too well, they said, though he thought that Sinclair's enthusiasm did not ring true. Anyway, it had not been his business.

That was all he could recall in his contemplation, and he repeated again how it had all finished over a year ago. But old memories cling. He found himself living over again that ghastly day after Ctesiphon, when Sinclair had literally brought him back to life.

He began to wonder—idly, fantastically. The afternoon dimmed to sundown, sundown gave way to the magic of the night. Still Aylett made no move to leave the camp-chair under the awning of his tent and go to bed. After a while, the last of his "boys" came up to ask whether he might retire. Aylett answered him absently, his eyes on the glowing logs of camp-fire.

As the hours wore on he could hear the sound of the night drums more distinctly. From all the points of the compass the sounds came and went, drum answering drum . . . the telegraph of the trackless miles that the world called Africa. Lazily he wondered what they were saying said, and how exactly they transmitted their news. Strange, he thought, that no white man had ever mastered the secret of the drums.

Subconsciously he followed their throbbing monotony. He gradually became aware that the beat had changed. No more were simple news or opinions being transmitted. That much he could understand. There was something else being sent out, something of importance. He suddenly realized that whatever this was, it was apparently regarded as being of vital urgency, and that, at least for an hour, the same short rhythm had been repeated. North, south, east and west, the echoes throbbed and throbbed again.

The drums started began to madden him, but there was no way to stop them. He decided to go to bed, but he had been listening too long, and the rhythm followed him. Eventually he dropped into a listless disturbed sleep, during which the implacable staccato throbbing kept hammering away its unreadable message into his subconscious.

It seemed only a moment later that he awoke a moment later. A malarious mist had rolled up from the swamps below and had pervaded his camp. He found himself gasping for breath. He tried to sit up, but the mist seemed to be pressing him down where he lay. No sound issued from his lips when he endeavoured to call his "boys." He felt himself being steadily submerged—down, down, down and still down. Just before he lost consciousness he realized that he was being suffocated, not by the heavy mist, but by a foul miasma reeking with all the horror of corruption. . . .

Aylett looked about him in a bewildered fashion when he opened his eyes again. A kindly bearded face was bending over him, and heard a voice that seemed to be coming a great distance that encouraged him to drink something. His head was throbbing violently, and his breath came in deep gasps. But the cool water cleared in some measure the foul odour that seemed to cling to his brain.

"Ah, *mon ami, c'est bon*. We thought you were dead when the 'boys' brought you in." The bearded face broke into a grin: "but now you will be well, *hein*? You are—what you say?—a tough, *hein*."

Aylett laughed in spite of himself. Why, of course, this was the mission station of the White Fathers, and his old friend, Father Vaneken, placid and reliable, was looking after him. He closed his eyes happily. Now there was nothing more to fear, everything would soon be well. Then, as suddenly as it had come, that terrible clinging odour of death and decay left him. . . .

"But, padre man," he discussed his horrible experience later, "what could have happened? We are both men of some experience of Africa—"

The missionary shrugged his shoulders. "*Mon ami,* as you imply, this is Africa . . . and I have no evidence that the curse on Ham, the son of Noah, has ever been lifted. The dark forests, they the stronghold of such whose unconscious spirits have rebelled and have not yet come out to serve as was first ordained. Who knows? . . . We—I—do not look too deeply there. When I first came out, in my early idealism I sought but the convert, now I—I am content to do mostly the cures for fevers and wounds, and hope that *le bon Dieu* will understand. It is the same everywhere where the curse of Noah carries. Civilization counts not. Regard Hayti—I spent twelve years there—Sierra Leone, the Congo, and here. What can I say about your attack by the mist? Nothing, *hein?* You—you thank God you live, for here, *mon ami*—here is the cradle of Africa, the oldest stronghold of the sons of Ham. . . ."

Aylett regarded the missionary intently. "Padre," he spoke deliberately, "what exactly are you trying to make me understand?"

The two men, old in the ways of the black jungle, faced each other steadily. "*Mon ami,*" the priest said quietly, "you are my old friend. On the forms of religion we think differently, you and I, but this is not conventional Europe, thank God, and side by side, we have done our best according to our lights. God himself cannot do more. So I will tell you. *I have seen the mist before . . . twice. Once in Hayti and once in this district.*"

"Here?"

The padre nodded. "I was in the camp at the catechumen's school by Mrs. Sinclair's estate—"

"Go on." Aylett's voice was low.

"As you know, Mrs. Sinclair has run the plantation since her husband's death. She refused to go home. At first you, I—all the countryside—thought she was mad to stay there alone, but—" the missionary shrugged his shoulders, "*que voulez-vous?* A woman is a law to herself. Anyway, she has made it a greater success than ever, and we are silent, *hein?*"

"But the mist?"

"I was coming to that. It caught me by the throat that night. I was living at the house, as we do all do who pass that way—Central Africa is not a cathedral close—but beyond not knowing anything of what happened for several hours, nothing happened to me." He touched the emblem of his faith on the rosary that was part of his dress. "Mrs. Sinclair said that I had been overcome by the heat, but to me that explanation would not do. . . ."

"But that doesn't explain anything."

"Perhaps not—*but Mrs. Sinclair said that she had not noticed anything peculiar. . . .*"

"How was that?"

The priest shrugged his shoulders. "I am not Mrs. Sinclair," he said abruptly, and Aylett knew that not another word about her would the missionary say.

"Tell me about Hayti, padre," he asked.

The priest replied quietly. "We understood it there to mean that it was artificially produced by *voodoo* black magic—a very real thing, *mon ami,* which my church readily admits as you probably know—and there they call it 'the breath of the dead.' Why? . . ." He shrugged his shoulders again.

Aylett turned away and looked out steadily into the distance. For a long time he fixed his gaze on the line of distant hills, thinking deeply. He recalled a picture where just such hills appeared in the background—a photograph taken by a man who had almost been almost beyond the border-line to give truth to the world. But he had failed. The picture showed a group of figures. That was all until one studied them, and even then no one would believe that this was a photograph of dead men—*who were not allowed to die*.

For hours the two men sat silently, each busy with his own thoughts. Night mantled the tiny mission station, and from afar the sound of drums came through on the soft breeze. Aylett turned suddenly to the missionary. "Padre man," he said quietly, "It's only twenty miles from here to the Sinclair estate. . . ."

The padre nodded. "I understand, *mon ami,*" he replied. Then after a moment, "Would you think it an impertinence if I asked you to keep this in your pocket—till you come back?" He produced a small silver crucifix.

Aylett held out his hand. "Thank you," he said simply.

The sun had set when Aylett's *machila*[1] was set down on Mrs. Sinclair's verandah. She came forward to welcome him. "I wondered if I should ever see you again." She

1. Machila—a stretcher slung on a pole—the standard means of transport in the "bush."

looked at him quietly. "You haven't been here since—for over a year now." Then she changed her tone. She laughed. "As a district officer," she said, "you've neglected your duties shamefully!"

Aylett smilingly pleaded guilty, excusing himself on the ground that everything had gone so well in this section, that he had hesitated to intrude on perfection.

"Has it fallen from perfection now?" she countered.

"Not at all," he replied, "this visit is merely routine."

"Er—thank you," she said dryly. "Anyway, come in and make yourself comfortable, and to-morrow will show a perfect estate."

Aylett studied his hostess carefully through dinner. He felt uneasy at what he saw whenever he caught her off her guard. He could hardly believe that this was the same woman he had welcomed as a bride a few years ago. The lonely life had hardened her, but he had expected that. There was something more, though—a kind of bitter hardness, he called it, for want of a better term.

After her formal welcome Mrs. Sinclair spoke very little. She seemed preoccupied with the affairs of the plantation. "My very own stake in Africa," she said. "Oh, how I love the country, its magic and mystery and its vast grandeur." She reminded him how she had refused to go home. But to-morrow, she said, when he saw *her* Africa—the plantation—he would understand.

Aylett retired early, distinctly puzzled. He had noticed her looking over the swept and garnished tidiness of the plantation before she had said good-night. She had unconsciously stretched out her hands to it a kind of adoring supplication, and yet in the brilliant moonlight under this sensual adoration, he distinctly noticed the contrast of the hard lines on her face and the bitterness of the mouth. Africa . . .

Exhausted as he was, he slept well. Whether the little cross the padre had given him had anything to do with it or not, he did not know, but in the morning he waked more refreshed than he had been for weeks. He looked forward to the visit over the estate.

Mrs. Sinclair had not exaggerated when she had used the word perfection. Fields had been hoed till not a stray blade of grass grew among the crops; barns stood in serried rows; wood fuel was stacked in the neatest of "cords"; the orchard and the kitchen garden were luxurious, and the pasture in the miniature home farm was the greenest he had seen in the tropics.

"For what?" his subconscious brain kept hammering at him. "Why—and above all, *how?*"

Aylett had noticed something that only an expert would have seen. There was a great shortage of labor, though such as were dotted about seemed to be very busy.

As if she divined his thoughts, Mrs. Sinclair answered them. "My 'boys' *work*," she said, in even tones as she flicked the hippo hide whip she carried.

Aylett raised his eyebrows. "Portuguese methods," he asked quietly and looked at the whip.

Mrs. Sinclair was turned to him. For the first time he noticed her deliberate antagonism. "Not at all," she said evenly, "a knowledge of how to get the most out of a native, a faculty which I notice officialdom has not yet acquired."

The district official took the rapier-like thrust without faltering. "*Touché,*" he answered, but nevertheless he knew he had not been wrong about the labor. "Queer," he thought, "damnably queer. . . ."

Mrs. Sinclair took no notice of his acknowledgment of her point. Her lips were set hard and she spoke coldly. She continued. "It's only a matter of getting to the heart of Africa—the throbbing beating heart below all this—Africa has no use for those who do not join their own souls." Suddenly she realized what she was saying, but before she could change the subject Aylett took up the question. He matched her tone.

"Very interesting . . ." he said, "but we don't encourage Europeans, especially European women, to go 'native.'"

The last word, however, was with the woman.

"All the perspicacity of officialdom!" she murmured. Then she looked Aylett full in the face. "Do I sound *native,*" she said harshly, "or *look* native?"

Aylett was hardly listening. He was staring at her. Her eyes belied her words, for if ever he saw expression of masterful, baleful perversion in any human face, he saw it then. He began to understand. . . .

He was thankful when the inspection was over, and felt relieved that she did not offer the formal suggestion that he should stay a little longer.

Five miles beyond her boundary he had a bivouac tent behind a thorn-bush, and stored two days' rations in the shade. He sent his *safari* on at the double to the mission station, and watched it till it was out of sight. Then he sat down to wait for the night.

"The heart of Africa . . ." he repeated to himself, but his voice was grim, and his eyes flashed with cold anger.

It was not until he heard the news drums throb that Aylett retraced his steps along the ill-defined track to the plantation. At the edge of the estate he merged himself in the shadows of the forest fringe, and gradually worked his way along the eucalyptus wind breaks. He crawled noiselessly as far as the tree that grew in the garden before the homestead.

In a little while he saw Mrs. Sinclair come out on to the verandah. Beside her stood a gigantic native who looked like some obscene devil, a witch doctor, sinister and grotesque, and naked but for a necklace of human bones dangling and rattling on his enormous chest. Daubs white clay and red ochre plastered his face.

Only partly covered by a magnificent leopard skin, the white woman stepped down into the clearing and snapped the whip she had in her hands. It sounded like a revolver shot. As if it were a signal, heard Aylett heard the roll of drums near at hand. From one of the barns began the most grotesque procession he had ever seen. The drums throbbed malevolently—the short staccato throb that had preceded the foetid mist which had almost suffocated him. Louder they grew and louder. The message rolled through the jungles, was caught up and answered again. There was no doubt as to its meaning.

He crouched lower when the drums approached, his eyes fixed on the macabre scene before him. Following the drums, as regularly as a column on the march, moved the men who worked the perfect plantation. In columns of four they moved, heavy footed and automatic—but they moved. Every now and then the crack of that terrible whip sounded like a pistol shot through the roll of drums, and every now and then Aylett could see that cruel thong cut through naked flesh, and a figure drop silently, only to pick itself back up again and rejoin the column.

They marched round the garden. As they came near Aylett held his breath. He had to strain every nerve in his body to prevent himself screaming. Almost as if he were hypnotized he looked on the dull, expressionless faces of the silent, slow-moving automatons—faces on which there was not even despair. They simply moved to the command of that merciless whip, as they would shortly move off to their allotted tasks in the fields. Bowed and crushed, they passed by him without a sound.

The nervous tension nearly broke Aylett. Then the realization came to him—*these pitiful automatons were dead—and they were not allowed to die. . . .*

The figures in the unbelievable photograph came back to him; the padre's words; the magic of the *voodoo* acknowledged as fact by the greatest Christian Church in history. The dead . . . who were not allowed to die . . . Zombies, the natives called them in hushed voices, whenever the curse of Noah was borne . . . and *she* called it knowing Africa.

A cold terror came over Aylett. The long column was nearing its end. Mrs. Sinclair was walking down the line, her whip cracking mercilessly, her face distorted with perverted lust, the foul witch doctor leering over her naked shoulder. She stopped by the tree behind which he crouched. A single bent figure followed the column. With a gasp of horror Aylett recognized Sinclair. Sinclair. Then whip crashed against the poor thing who had once died in his arms.

"My God!" Aylett muttered helplessly. "It's not possible—" but he knew that the witch doctor's voodoo had thrown the impossibility in his face. The whip cracked again, hurling the sole white Zombie to the ground. Slowly, it picked itself up—without a sound, without expression—and automatically followed the column. He heard, as in a nightmare, unbelievably foul obscenities fall from the woman's lips—cruel taunts. . . . And the whip cracked and bit and tore, again and yet again. At the head of the column the drums throbbed on.

Horror gave way at last. Aylett found himself desperately clutching the tiny cross the padre had given him. With the other hand he found his revolver and took aim with icy coolness. . . . Four times he fired at a point above the leopard skin, and twice into the ochred face of the witch doctor. . . . Then he leapt forward, cross in hand, to what had once died as Sinclair.

The figure was standing silently, bent and expressionless. It made no sign as Aylett approached, but as the crucifix touched it a tremor shook the frame. The drooping eyelids lifted and the lips moved. "You have repaid," they whispered gently. The body swayed slightly and toppled over. "Dust to dust. . . ." Aylett prayed. In a few moments all that remained was a grayish powder. A tropical year had passed, Aylett remembered with a shudder. . . . Then he turned, and, crucifix in hand, walked along the column. . . .